THE
HONOR
✪ OF ✪
SPIES

ALSO BY W.E.B. GRIFFIN

THE
HONOR
☆ OF ☆
SPIES

W.E.B. GRIFFIN

AND WILLIAM E. BUTTERWORTH IV

G. P. PUTNAM'S SONS
NEW YORK

PUTNAM

G. P. PUTNAM'S SONS
Publishers Since 1838
Published by the Penguin Group
Penguin Group (USA) Inc., 375 Hudson Street, New York, New York 10014, USA • Penguin
Group (Canada), 90 Eglinton Avenue East, Suite 700, Toronto, Ontario M4P 2Y3, Canada (a division
of Pearson Penguin Canada Inc.) • Penguin Books Ltd, 80 Strand, London WC2R 0RL, England •
Penguin Ireland, 25 St Stephen's Green, Dublin 2, Ireland (a division of Penguin Books Ltd) •
Penguin Group (Australia), 250 Camberwell Road, Camberwell, Victoria 3124, Australia (a division
of Pearson Australia Group Pty Ltd) • Penguin Books India Pvt Ltd, 11 Community Centre,
Panchsheel Park, New Delhi–110 017, India • Penguin Group (NZ), 67 Apollo Drive, Rosedale,
North Shore 0632, New Zealand (a division of Pearson New Zealand Ltd) • Penguin Books
(South Africa) (Pty) Ltd, 24 Sturdee Avenue, Rosebank, Johannesburg 2196, South Africa

Penguin Books Ltd, Registered Offices: 80 Strand, London WC2R 0RL, England

Library of Congress Cataloging-in-Publication Data

Griffin, W. E. B.
The honor of spies / W.E.B. Griffin and William E. Butterworth IV.
p.   cm.
ISBN 978-0-399-15566-6
1. United States. Office of Strategic Services—Fiction.
2. Intelligence officers—United States—Fiction.   3. Prisoners of war—Germany—Fiction.
4. Hitler, Adolf, 1889–1945—Assassination attempts—Fiction.   5. World War, 1939–1945—Secret
service—Fiction.   6. World War, 1939–1945—Argentina—Fiction.   7. Nazis—Argentina—Fiction.
I. Butterworth, William E. (William Edmund).   II. Title.
PS3557.R489137H665   2009   2009042635
813'.54—dc22

Printed in the United States of America
1   3   5   7   9   10   8   6   4   2

IN LOVING MEMORY OF

Colonel José Manuel Menéndez,
Cavalry, Argentine Army, Retired

He spent his life fighting Communism and Juan Domingo Perón.

THE
HONOR
✪ OF ✪
SPIES

PROLOGUE

By August 1943, the United States of America had been in the Second World War for twenty months.

England had been at war for four years, since 1 September 1939, when—a week after German leader Adolf Hitler signed a non-aggression treaty with the Soviet Union—Germany launched its Blitzkrieg ("Lightning War") against Poland.

England and France declared war.

By 6 October 1939, Poland had fallen and was divided between the Soviet Union and Germany. "The Phony War" followed, with the belligerents taking little—virtually no—action against each other.

One significant exception to this occurred two months later, when, on 13 December 1939, Royal Navy cruisers engaged the German pocket battleship Admiral Graf Spee *off the Atlantic coast of South America and forced the damaged ship to seek refuge in Montevideo, Uruguay.*

Diplomatic pressure (largely from the United States, although this was denied at the time) on Uruguay forced that small country to insist on following international law, which required belligerent vessels to leave sanctuary ports within seventy-two hours. On 17 December, Captain Hans Langsdorff, to save further loss of life in a battle he knew he could not win, scuttled the Graf Spee *just outside the mouth of the Montevideo harbor. He then went to Argentina, buried his dead, made arrangements for the internment of his crew—and then shot himself in the temple, arranging that event so his body would fall on the German navy battle flag.*

The Phony War turned real on the night of 9/10 May 1940, when the Germans occupied Luxembourg and launched another Blitzkrieg, this time into the Netherlands and Belgium. The Dutch surrendered 15 May.

On 5 June 1940, the Germans solved the problem of the "impregnable" French Maginot Line of fortresses by going around them. Paris fell on 14 June. Not all French were desolated; substantial numbers of them embraced the motto "Better Hitler Than Blum." André Léon Blum, a socialist, already had twice served as France's prime minister.

The French capitulated on 25 June 1940.

The only good news for the English during this period was their brilliant evacuation of 300,000 British soldiers and some 38,000 French from Dunkirk.

Germany began a massive aerial bombardment of England as the prelude to a cross-Channel invasion. The Royal Air Force's valiant and effective defense of England caused Winston Churchill, its prime minister, to utter the famous line "Never in the field of human conflict was so much owed by so many to so few."

The severe losses suffered by the Luftwaffe are cited by some historians as the reason Adolf Hitler called off the invasion. Other historians feel that it was Hitler's decision to stab the Soviet Union in the back that brought him to that decision. He would deal with the English after he had dealt with the Communists.

The backstabbing—"Operation Barbarossa," named in honor of Frederick I, Holy Roman Emperor—was the largest attack of the Second World War, and initially the most successful. It began on 22 June 1941.

It was brilliantly planned, brilliantly executed, and took the Russians entirely by surprise.

On 15 September, German forces began the siege of Leningrad. They—and almost everyone else—thought it would be over in about a month. With that in mind, the Germans on 2 October 1941 began their march on Moscow and soon the gilded tops of the Soviet capital's churches could be seen through German binoculars.

Before things (including the weather and Soviet tenacity) turned against them, the Germans held 750,000 square miles and had nearly 100 million people under their boot.

On 5 December, the attack on Moscow was called off. Winter had set in, and the Germans were simply unprepared to fight in the terrible cold. The troops were freezing and could not be properly supplied. Moscow could wait until spring.

Two days later—7 December 1941, a date President Franklin D. Roosevelt declared "would live in infamy"—the Japanese attacked the U.S. Navy base at Pearl Harbor, Territory of Hawaii. That, too, was a brilliant operation, one meticulously planned, effectively carried out, and which took the Americans by complete surprise. When it was over, most American battleships in the Pacific were at the bottom of Pearl Harbor.

And things promptly got worse.

On 11 December, Germany and Italy declared war on the United States. On Christmas Day 1941, Japan took Hong Kong, and on 2 January 1942, Manila was declared an open city and fell to the Japanese.

With the fall of all the Philippines to the Japanese only a matter of time, and aware that the morale of the American people was as low as it had ever been—and sinking—President Roosevelt authorized a near-suicidal bombing attack on Japan.

On 18 April 1942, Lieutenant Colonel Jimmy Doolittle led a small flight of

B-25 Mitchell bombers from the deck of an aircraft carrier to Tokyo. The physical damage they caused was minimal, but the damage to Japanese pride was enormous. And the United States could finally claim to be fighting back.

Eighteen days later, on 6 May 1942, Lieutenant General Jonathan M. Wainwright surrendered the Philippines to the Japanese. It was the largest surrender in U.S. history.

Japan was now poised to invade Australia from bases in the Solomon Islands. But on 7 August 1942, the just-formed U.S. First Marine Division, which was not supposed to be ready to fight for a year, was thrust into the breach and landed on Guadalcanal.

Surprising just about everybody, the landing was a success and the Marines took the island, fighting without their heavy artillery and living off captured Japanese rations.

Australia was saved, and some dared to hope the tide of war had changed. Some proof of this hope came on 8 November 1942, when United States Army troops, under Lieutenant General George S. Patton, landed in North Africa. The French valiantly defended their North African colonies against the Americans, and in a thirty-six-hour battle, with negligible damage to themselves, the battleship USS Massachusetts, the cruisers USS Augusta, USS Brooklyn, USS Tuscaloosa, and USS Wichita, and aircraft from the carrier USS Ranger either sank or knocked out of action most of the French fleet, including the battleship Jean Bart and the cruisers Primaguet, Fougueux, Boulonnais, Brestois, and Frondeur.

Two months later, in captured/liberated Casablanca, Roosevelt and Churchill met and decided to invade Sicily as soon as possible. They also decreed that Germany would not be allowed to seek an armistice, but must surrender unconditionally.

And two weeks after that, on 31 January 1943, there came what most historians agree was the beginning of the end for Germany. Newly promoted Field Marshal Friedrich Paulus was forced to surrender his troops—90,000 of them, who were surrounded, out of ammunition, and reduced to eating their horses—at Stalingrad.

But the war was by no means over, and historians now agree that it could easily have gone the other way.

If, for example, Germany had won the race to build the atomic bomb.

If, for example, Germany had managed to get into production the Me-262, a jet fighter capable of causing unacceptable losses to the flights of British and American bombers that were reducing German cities to rubble.

If, for example, the Germans had perfected a means of accurately aiming their rocket-powered missiles.

If, for example, German submarines could have successfully interdicted the shipment of troops and the matériel of war from the United States to Europe.

If, for example, the inevitable Allied invasion of France could have been thrown back into the English Channel.

Hitler devoutly believed all of the above were possible, even probable. But many members of the Führer's inner circle were more pragmatic and had begun to consider the ramifications of a German defeat.

"Operation Phoenix" was born. If there were temporary reverses in the fortunes of the Thousand-Year Reich—if, for example, the Russians took Berlin—all would not necessarily be lost. National Socialism and its leaders could rise phoenixlike from the ashes.

All it would take would be some place of refuge for the leaders to bide their time, and some place to conceal vast amounts of money from the victorious Allies until the time came to spend it to restore the Reich, probably immediately after the West and Russia had both been fatally weakened in the inevitable war between them.

Argentina seemed to be just the place. Argentina, ostensibly neutral, leaned heavily toward the Axis powers. The Argentine army was armed with Mauser rifles, wore German steel helmets and uniforms patterned on those of the Wehrmacht, and had its headquarters in the Edificio Libertador in Buenos Aires, a magnificent structure built with the generous assistance of Germany.

While it was also true that the Argentine navy leaned toward the British (and to some degree, toward the Americans) and that there were large numbers of Jews in the country who hated Nazism and all it stood for, these problems could be dealt with.

Operation Phoenix was put into play even before the Stalingrad surrender.

I

A white two-ton 1940 Ford truck with a refrigerator body followed a white 1938 Ford Fordor sedan down the unnumbered macadam road that branched off National Route Three to Tandil.

The truck body had a representation of a beef cow's head painted on it, together with the legend FRIGORÍFICO MORÓN, and there was a smaller version of the corporate insignia on the doors of the car.

They were a common sight in the area, which bordered on the enormous Estancia San Pedro y San Pablo, the patrón of which did not know within five or six thousand exactly how many head of cattle grazed his fields. Nor did he know who operated the estancia's eight slaughterhouses, of which Frigorífico Morón had been one of the smallest, until recently, when Frigorífico Morón had been shut down to make room for the runways and hangars of South American Airways.

The car and the truck slowed and turned off the macadam road onto a narrower road of crushed stone, then stopped when they came to a sturdy closed gate, above which a sign read CASA CHICA.

A sturdy man in his fifties with a full, immaculately trimmed cavalryman's mustache got out of the car and walked toward the gate, holding in his hand a key to the massive padlock that secured the chains in the gate.

He had just twisted the key in the lock when a man on horseback trotted up, holding a rifle vertically, its butt resting on the saddle. Without speaking to him—which the man on horseback correctly interpreted to be a signal of disapproval; he knew he should have been at the gate before the man with the mustache reached it—the man returned to the Ford. He got in and waited for the peon to get off the horse and finish dealing with the chain and swing open the gate.

When the car and truck had passed through the gate, the peon went to the right post of the gate, pulled a piece of canvas aside, and then knelt beside an Argentine copy of the U.S. Army's EE-8 field telephone. He gave its crank several hard turns, then stood up, holding the headset to his ear as he looked up the steep hill to Casa Chica.

An identical field telephone rang in the comfortable living room of Casa Chica, a bungalow sitting near the crest of the hill.

There were five people in the room. A middle-aged balding man wearing a sweater over his shirt sat across a desk from a younger man wearing a loosely knit white turtleneck sweater. A Thompson submachine gun hung from the back of the younger man's chair.

Another rifle-armed peon—this one leaning back in a chair that rested against a wall—had been on the edge of dozing off when the telephone rang. A large, even massive, dark-skinned woman in her thirties sat on a couch across from a middle-aged woman in an armchair, who was looking bitterly at the middle-aged balding man at the desk. When the telephone rang, the large woman rose with surprising agility from the couch and went to it.

The balding man stopped what he was doing, which was working on an organizational chart, and looked at the massive woman.

"You just keep on working, Herr Frogger," the young man said not very pleasantly in German.

"I don't have all these details in my memory, Major," Frogger said.

"Try harder," the young man said coldly.

He was Sergeant Sigfried Stein, U.S. Army, although Herr Wilhelm Frogger and his wife, Else, had been told—and believed—that he was a major.

Until weeks before, Wilhelm Frogger had been the commercial attaché of the German Embassy in Buenos Aires. On the fourth of July, he had then appeared at the apartment of Milton Leibermann, a "legal attaché" of the U.S. Embassy, and offered to exchange his knowledge of German Embassy secrets for sanctuary in Brazil.

Leibermann was *de facto* the Federal Bureau of Investigation's man in Argentina. He had no place to hide the German defectors from either the Germans or the Argentine authorities—who, he knew, would be told the Froggers had been kidnapped—nor any means to get the defectors out of Argentina. So he had turned them over to someone he thought could do both.

He knew that Don Cletus Frade, patrón of Estancia San Pedro y San Pablo, was in fact a U.S. Marine Corps major and the *de facto* head of the U.S. Office of Strategic Services in Argentina. He also knew that having any dealings at all with anyone connected with the spies of the OSS had been absolutely forbidden by FBI Director J. Edgar Hoover, and for that reason Leibermann had not reported to the FBI that the Froggers had come to him, or what he had done with them.

Frade was interested in the Froggers because he knew more of the secret activities of the German Embassy than Frogger thought he could possibly know, most importantly about something the Germans called "Operation Phoenix."

Frogger steadfastly denied any knowledge of Operation Phoenix, which convinced Frade he was a liar. It had also become almost immediately apparent that Frau Else Frogger was an unrepentant National Socialist who not only had decided that defecting had been a mistake but that if they could only get away from Frade and his *gottverdammt Jude*—"Major" Stein—all would be forgiven at the German Embassy.

Frade, however, knew enough about the SS officers in the German Embassy to know that before or after the Froggers were returned to Germany to enter a concentration camp they would be thoroughly interrogated about Leibermann and about Frade's operation. And the Froggers had seen too much to let that happen.

Letting them go was not an option.

Frade had no immediate means of getting them even to Brazil without taking unjustifiable risks. So while they were, so to speak, in limbo, he was hiding them on a small farm that his father had used for romantic interludes in the country.

There was a chance that Siggie Stein could break down one of them—or both—and get them to reveal what they knew about Operation Phoenix. Not much of a chance, though, for Stein was a demolitions man turned communications/cryptography expert, not a trained interrogator. Still, on the other hand, he was a refugee from Nazi Germany, and had some relatives who'd not been able to escape and had perished in concentration camps.

The massive Argentine woman, who was known as "The Other Dorotea"—Don Cletus Frade's Anglo-Argentine wife was Doña Dorotea Mallín de Frade—listened to the telephone and then reported, "It is Suboficial Mayor Rodríguez."

Stein rose from his chair, picking up the Thompson.

"Watch them," he said to the peon with the rifle, then turned to Herr Frogger and said, "Keep at it," and then walked out of the room and onto the verandah to wait for Rodríguez.

The incline in front of Casa Chica was very steep, and between the house and the road and gate, but not visible from either, a landing strip had been carved out of the hillside. Frade had told Stein his father had used it to fly his lady love into the house in one of Estancia San Pedro y San Pablo's fleet of Piper Cubs.

The car and the truck appeared a moment later, moving slowly in low gear, and turned onto the landing strip. When they stopped, Suboficial Mayor Enrico Rodríguez—who had been Cavalry, Ejército Argentino, and had retired with the late Coronel Jorge Frade from the Húsares de Pueyrredón, Argentina's most prestigious cavalry regiment—got out of the car and started toward the house, going up the stairs carved into the hillside. He carried a Remington Model 11 self-loading twelve-gauge riot shotgun in his hand.

The driver of the refrigerator truck got out from behind the wheel, went to the rear doors, and pulled them open. A dozen peones, all armed with Mauser rifles, began to pile out of the truck and then to unload from it equipment, including ammunition cans, blankets, food containers, and finally a Browning Automatic Rifle.

Rodríguez put his arm around Stein's shoulders and pounded his back affectionately, but did not speak.

"What's going on, Sergeant Major?" Stein asked in Spanish.

Their relationship was delicate. Rodríguez had a long service history and had held the senior enlisted rank for ten years of it. He knew that Stein had just been promoted to staff sergeant yet had been in the army not even two years.

On the other hand, Don Cletus Frade had made it clear to Rodríguez that Stein was in charge of the Froggers and Casa Chica.

"I have had a telephone call from an old friend," Enrico Rodríguez said. "There are two trucks of Mountain Troops on their way here. They have with them a half-dozen Nazi soldiers—the ones who came off the submarine? The ones with the skulls on their caps?"

Stein nodded his understanding.

"What makes you think they're coming here?"

"My friend, he is also of the Húsares, heard the Nazi officer tell his men they were going after traitors to the Führer."

He mispronounced the title, and without thinking about it, Stein corrected him and then asked, "How would they know we have the Froggers here?"

Rodríguez shrugged.

"We will defend them," Rodríguez said seriously.

"That's what those guys are for?" Stein asked, nodding down the stairs toward the peones now milling around on the landing strip.

"There are twelve, all old Húsares," Rodríguez said.

"Sergeant Major, with the twelve we have here, that's two dozen. Against how many soldiers on two trucks?"

"Probably forty, forty-two," Rodríguez said. "What I have been thinking is that they are coming in such strength thinking we have only the dozen men, and they can make us give them the Froggers without a fight. If they see we are so many, they may decide that there will be a fight, and they know that if there is a fight against us, there would be many casualties. How would they explain the deaths of ten or fifteen Mountain Troops so far from their base?"

"Sergeant Major, I think it would be best if there were no confrontation," Stein said carefully.

"You mean just turn the Froggers over to them?"

"No. I mean get the Froggers out of here, back to someplace on Estancia San Pedro y San Pablo."

"Don Cletus said they were to be kept here in Casa Chica," Rodríguez said.

"That was before he knew about this," Stein argued.

After a pause, the old soldier said, "True."

Stein had to suppress a smile, both at the old soldier and at the Christian scripture that had for some inexplicable reason popped into his Jewish head: *Blessed are the peacemakers, for they will be called children of God.*

Ninety seconds ago, he reminded himself, *I was asking myself whether I had the balls to shoot both of those goddamn Nazis rather than see them freed, and decided that I did.*

"You have some place to take them?" Stein pursued.

"I will tell the driver where to take you," Rodríguez said. "And then later meet you there."

"You're not going to take them?"

"I am going to stay here and see what these bastards are up to," Rodríguez said.

"And so will I," Stein said, somewhat astonished to hear himself say it.

Rodríguez was visibly unhappy to hear this.

"Do you have a saying in the U.S. Army that there can only be one commander?"

"Sergeant Major, I recognize that your experience in matters like these is much greater than mine." *Which is practically nonexistent.* "I am at your orders."

"We will send six of the men, plus the driver, with the Froggers," Rodríguez ordered as he assumed command. "You tell The Other Dorotea to prepare the Nazis to be moved. Tell her I said I want them tied and blindfolded."

Stein managed to keep himself from saying, *Yes, sir.*

"Got it," he said.

"And while you're doing that, I will have the Ford car and your vehicles moved over there," he said, pointing to a line of hills that began a quarter of a mile the other side of the road. "There's a dirt road. I want nothing in the house when they get here."

Why? What's that all about?

"Good idea."

"And I will set up my command post there," Rodríguez said, pointing. "Just below the military crest of the hill."

What the hell is "the military crest of the hill"?

Stein nodded.

"And you have the little German camera Don Cletus brought from Brazil?"

"The Leica," Stein said. "It's in the house."

"We will need photos of everything that happens here to show Don Cletus when he returns. You would be useful doing that."

"Okay."

"I'll send two men with you down there," Rodríguez said, pointing to a roof-less, windowless old building on the edge of the road about a hundred meters from the gate. "I think you will be able to see both the house and the approaches, as well as the road, from the upper story." He paused and chuckled. "If there still is a second story. If not, you'll have to do as best you can from the ground floor."

"Understood."

While I am trying to take their pictures from the ground floor of a decrepit old building in the middle of Argentina, I am going to be shot to death by the SS.

Jesus Christ!

Thirty minutes later, on the second floor of the old building, Staff Sergeant Stein sat patiently while one of the two old Húsares with him carefully painted his face, his hands, and whatever shiny parts of the Leica Ic camera with a mixture of dust from the building and axle grease. They took extra care with the camera so as not to render it useless.

When they had finished that, they draped Stein in a sort of shroud made from burlap potato bags, which covered his head and his body to his ankles. Then, very carefully, they stuck a great deal of dead leafy vegetable matter into the burlap shroud.

While he had been undergoing the transformation, the other old Húsar took apart an Argentine copy of a U.S. Army EE-8 field telephone, disconnected the bells that would ring when another EE-8 was cranked, and then carefully put the phone back together.

Then he communicated with four other old Húsares, plus Suboficial Mayor Enrico Rodríguez, who had apparently stationed themselves in places Stein could not see, although he tried very hard.

And finally, they painted each other's faces with the axle grease and dust compound, put on potato sack shrouds, and adorned these with dead leafy vegetation. One of them had a Mauser army rifle with a telescopic sight, and the other a Thompson submachine gun like Stein's. They wrapped them with burlap, looked around, and then wrapped Stein's Thompson in burlap.

Twenty minutes after that, the man who had camouflaged Stein had a conversation over the telephone, which surprised Stein since he had not heard it ring, although he was no more than four feet from it. Then he remembered watching the man disconnect the bell.

"Ten minutes, give or take," the old Húsar said conversationally.

The first vehicle to appear, five or six minutes later, was not the army truck Stein expected from the west but a glistening, if olive-drab, Mercedes-Benz convertible sedan. And it came down the road from the east.

It slowed almost to a stop at the intersection of the road to Casa Chica. Stein saw that Colonel Juan D. Perón was in the front passenger seat, but did not think to record this photographically for posterity until after the Mercedes had suddenly sped down the road and it was too late to do so.

Both of the old Húsares looked askance at Stein.

Ten minutes after that the Mercedes came back down the road, now leading an olive-drab 1940 Chevrolet sedan and two two-ton 1940 Ford trucks, also painted olive drab, and with canvas-covered stake bodies.

Stein was ready with the Leica when Colonel Perón got out of his car and exchanged salutes with two officers in field uniforms who got out of the Chevrolet. While to Stein the sound of the shutter clicking and then the film advancing sounded like the dropping of an anvil into a fifty-five-gallon metal drum, followed by a lengthy burst of machine-gun fire, none of the people on the road apparently heard it.

Troops began getting off the trucks. One of them—probably a sergeant, Stein decided—started shouting orders. Some of the troops began to trot toward the gate, where one of them cut the chain with an enormous bolt-cutter. The gate was pushed open, and the troops spread out facing the Casa Chica hill on both sides of the road.

The sergeant looked at the old house, shouted an order, and two soldiers armed with submachine guns trotted toward it.

Stein's heart began thumping. The old Húsares rolled onto their backs and trained their weapons at the head of the staircase. More accurately, where stairs had once led to the second floor. When Stein and the others had come to the building, they had found that the stairs were just about rotted away. They had climbed onto the second floor from the outside, using one another as human ladders.

Stein could hear movement on the lower floor, and watched the stairwell opening for a head to pop up. None came.

"Nobody's been in here in years," a voice said in German.

A moment later, Stein rolled back onto his stomach and saw that the soldiers were trotting back to the trucks and to the sergeant. He tried and finally got a shot of that.

And then he saw that something else was being off-loaded from the trucks.

I know what that is. That's a Maxim Maschinengewehr. Poppa showed me one in the Krieg museum in Kassel. He told me that he'd been an ammunition bearer for a Maxim in France.

My God, there's two of them! And there's the ammunition bearers!

Four soldiers trotted through the gate carrying a heavy water-cooled machine gun mounted on a sort of sled. The sled had handles like a stretcher. They were followed by two soldiers, each carrying two oblong olive-drab metal cans looking very much like those used by the U.S. Army.

There's probably two hundred rounds in each can.

But they're in a cloth belt, not metal-linked, like ours.

What the hell are they going to do with all that ammo?

And then another Maxim crew ran through the gate with another machine gun on its sled, followed by two more ammo bearers.

Who the hell do they think is in Casa Chica? The 40th Infantry Division?

No. If they knew where to look for us, then they'd know there's no more than a dozen men. What they are going to do with this show of force is make the point that they're irresistible, get us to surrender without a fight.

And aren't they going to be surprised when they go in the house and find there's nobody there at all.

Stein had trouble with the film-advance mechanism and looked at the Leica and saw why. He'd used all of the twenty-four frames in the film cartridge.

I will be damned! I was not paralyzed by fear!

When he had changed film—which required great care so that he did not get any dust-grease inside—and rolled back into place again, he saw something else had happened. The Maxims were set up and ready to fire, but they were now each manned by a two-man crew. The four men who had carried the weapons into place and the two ammo bearers for each were now trotting back to the trucks. As Stein watched—and took their picture—they took rifles from the trucks and formed loosely into ranks.

Ah-ha. The reserve. To be thrown into the breach when the 40th Infantry valiantly refuses to surrender.

Not to worry, guys. There's nobody in that house to surrender, much less shoot back at you.

The sergeant now trotted up to Colonel Perón and the two officers, came to attention, and saluted.

They had a brief conversation, duly recorded on film, and then saluted one another. One of them gave a crisp straight-armed Nazi salute.

Click.

Got you, you Nazi sonofabitch!

The Nazi sonofabitch now trotted through the gate, past the machine guns, and started up the hill.

Click.

Colonel Perón went to his staff car and leaned on the fender. The other officer and the sergeant went to the Chevrolet and leaned against its side.

Click.

The Nazi sonofabitch was no longer in sight as he made his way up the hill.

Shouldn't you be holding up a white flag of truce?

For three minutes, which seemed much longer, Stein tried in vain to see the man moving up the hill.

There came the sound of a shot.

Oh, shit! Rodríguez couldn't resist the temptation!

I should have thought about that, and tried to talk him out of it. Not that it would have done any good.

But that wasn't loud enough for a shotgun; it was a different sound, like a pistol. What the hell? And what happens now?

The answer to that came immediately, as Stein looked at Colonel Perón to see what, if anything, he was going to do.

First one of the Maxims and then the other began to fire.

Colonel Perón screamed something but was drowned out by the sound of the firing weapons. He ran to the officer leaning on the Chevrolet. Almost immediately, the sergeant ran—not trotted—toward the firing machine guns.

Perón walked very quickly—almost ran—back to his Mercedes.

Click.

Perón got in and the car, wheels screeching, started heading east.

Click.

Stein saw—click, click, click—the walls and windows of Casa Chica literally disintegrate as the machine-gun fire struck.

The sergeant was now at the closest Maxim. He was excitedly waving his arms, obviously trying to make them stop firing. They didn't.

Click.

And then, as suddenly as it had started, the firing stopped.

The crews of both machine guns stood up and pulled something from their ears. Then the crew of one shook hands.

Click.

When the crew of the other saw this, they shook hands.

Click.

The officer who had gone up the hill now came down it, apparently unhurt.

Click.

The soldiers who had been fanned out on both sides of the road were now summoned to the guns. Some of them picked up the sleds and ran with them to the trucks. Others began picking up the fired cartridge cases and putting them into the now empty ammunition cans. When the cans were full, the soldiers started stuffing their pockets with the empties that didn't fit in the cans.

Click.

Casa Chica did not seem to be on fire, but what looked like smoke was coming out of where the windows had been and from the holes in the tile roof.

The soldiers who had manned the Maxims came to attention and rendered the Nazi salute when the officer who had come down the hill walked up to them.

Click.

He returned the salute and then offered them cigarettes from a silver case and finally shook hands with each of them.

Click.

The officer who had been at the Chevrolet came up to them and again salutes were exchanged.

Click.

The officer went to one of the soldiers picking up brass and said something to him, whereupon the soldier and another soldier ran to the trucks. They ran back a moment later, this time carrying Schmeisser MP38 machine pistols, which they gave to the soldiers who had manned the Maxims.

Click.

The sergeant and others were now urging all the soldiers to move more quickly back to the road and onto the trucks. This was accomplished in a very short time, and then the trucks and the Chevrolet started to drive away.

Click.

This left the officer, the four men who had manned the Maxims, and another man who had appeared from somewhere standing alone by the side of the road.

Click.

Now what?

They started walking up the hill and soon disappeared from sight.

Stein changed film, just to be sure.

Five minutes later, there came the sound of more gunfire. Not much. A ragged burst of shots, as if weapons had been fired simultaneously on command, and one or two of the shooters had been a little late in complying. And then another shot, and a moment later, another.

"We go now," one of the old Húsares said.

They lowered Stein first out the window to the ground, one on each arm, and then used his shoulders as a ladder to climb down themselves.

They walked toward the gate. They were almost there when the gray Ford with the Frigorífico Morón corporate insignia on its doors appeared.

That's right, I forgot. Rodríguez told them to hide it across the street.

They got in that and rode up the hill.

Four bodies were sprawled close together in just about the center of the landing strip. Two were on their stomachs, one on his back, and the fourth on his side. A fifth body was on its stomach halfway up the stairs leading to the verandah of Casa Chica, and the sixth on his stomach on the runway twenty meters from the others, as if he had been shot in the back trying to run away.

There was a great deal of blood. At least three of the bodies had suffered head wounds.

Stein got out of the Ford.

Suboficial Mayor Enrico Rodríguez was kneeling by one of the bodies. Stein waited for him to get out of the picture.

Rodríguez walked over to him and handed him a stapled-together document.

"Identity document?" he asked. "I just took it off that one."

Stein took it. He flipped through it. He was surprised at the wave of emotion that suddenly came over him. His hand was shaking.

"This is the SS *ausweis*—identity card—of Wilhelm Heitz," he read softly, "who was an obersturmführer—lieutenant—in the headquarters company of the Leibstandarte SS Adolf Hitler of the Schutzstaffeln of the National Socialist German Workers' Party."

"You think we ought to keep it?" Rodríguez asked.

"I think we ought to do more than that with it," Stein said. He walked to the corpse. The eyes were open.

He laid the identity card on the blood-soaked chest.

Click. Click.

He picked up the *ausweis,* now dripping blood, shook as much off it as he could, then held it somewhat delicately with his thumb and index fingers.

Rodríguez took it from him and placed it in a canvas bag.

"And then I think we should do the same with the other bodies. And then, I respectfully suggest, Sergeant Major, that we get the hell out of here."

[TWO]
4730 Avenida Libertador
Buenos Aires, Argentina
1605 5 August 1943 (six days previously)

The black Mercedes-Benz with Corps Diplomatique license plates drove north on Avenida Libertador, passed the Ejército Argentino polo field on the left, then, on the right, started to drive past the Hipódromo until the Mercedes and all the cars behind it were stopped by a traffic policeman.

The passenger, Karl Cranz—a well-dressed, blond, fair-skinned, thirty-five-year-old who was accredited to the Republic of Argentina as "commercial attaché" of the embassy of the German Reich—looked out the window and saw on his left his destination, a four-story mansion behind a tall, cast-iron fence and gate.

"There it is, Günther," he said to the driver. "Make a U-turn."

Making a U-turn across the heavy traffic on the eight-lane Avenida Libertador was illegal. But if one had diplomatic status, and one was being driven in a vehicle with diplomatic license plates, one was immune to traffic regulations.

"Jawohl, Mein Herr," Günther Loche said. He put his arm out the window, signaling that he was about to turn.

Loche was twenty-four years old, tall, muscular, and handsome. Cranz often joked that he was going to send Loche's photograph to Germany, where it could be used on recruiting posters enticing young men to apply for the Schutzstaffel. He was a perfect example of the "Nordic Type."

Loche, however, was not eligible for the SS, as membership in it was understandably limited to German citizens. He was an Argentine citizen, an "ethnic German" born in Argentina to German parents who had immigrated to Argentina after the First World War and prospered in the sausage business. He was a civilian employee of the German Embassy, known as a "local hire." He originally had been taken on as a driver, but now, under Cranz, had been given other, more "responsible" duties.

Like his parents, Loche believed that National Socialism was God's answer to godless Communism, and that Adolf Hitler was God's latter-day prophet— if not quite at the level of Jesus Christ, then not far below it.

"Let me out in front of the house," Cranz ordered. "I'll have someone open the gate for you so that you can park in the basement. Then go upstairs and wait for me in the foyer. I may need you."

"Jawohl, Mein Herr."

El Coronel Juan Domingo Perón, a large, tall man with a full head of shiny black hair, who was the secretary of state for labor and welfare in the government of General Arturo Rawson, received Cranz in the mansion library.

He was in civilian clothing, but Cranz nevertheless greeted him in almost a military manner.

"Mi coronel," Cranz said, and gave Perón a somewhat sloppy version of the Nazi salute; he raised his hand from the elbow, palm out, rather than fully extending his arm.

"It is always good to see you, Herr Obersturmbannführer," Perón said, and then offered his hand.

"Oh, how I miss being called that," Cranz said.

Perón waved Cranz into one of two matching armchairs facing a small, low table.

A maid appeared.

"Coffee?" Perón offered. "Or something a little stronger? Whiskey, perhaps?"

"I think a little whiskey would go down well," Cranz said. "You are most kind."

Perón told the maid to bring ice and soda, then rose from his chair and went to a section of the bookcases that lined the walls of the room. He pulled it open, and a row of bottles and glasses was revealed.

"American or English?" Perón asked.

"As another secret between us, I have come to really like the sour mash whiskey," Cranz said.

Perón took a bottle of Jack Daniel's from the bar, carried it to the table, and set it down.

"Whatever secrets we have to talk about," Perón said, "I think we had best wait until after she brings the ice and then leaves. I don't know who she reports to—el Coronel Martín, Father Welner, or Cletus Frade—but to one of them, I'm sure."

"Or all three," Cranz said jocularly.

El Coronel Alejandro Martín was chief of the Ethical Standards Office of the Bureau of Internal Security at the Ministry of Defense. While he officially reported to the minister, both Cranz and Perón knew that he also reported, officially or unofficially, directly to President Rawson.

At great risk to his own life, and for the good of Argentina, not for personal gain, Martín, then a teniente coronel, had chosen to support the *coup d'état* being planned and to be led by el Coronel Jorge Frade against President Ramón S. Castillo. When Frade had been assassinated in April 1943, before "Operation Blue" could be put into play, Martín had transferred his allegiance to General Rawson, who became president when the coup was successful.

Martín's services had been so valuable that Rawson proposed waiving promotion standards and making Martín chief of military intelligence as a General de Brigada, maybe even a General de División.

Martín had declined promotion beyond coronel, knowing that taking a general's stars would make him hated by officers over whom he had been jumped.

But not taking the stars in no way diminished his power. Both Cranz and Perón regarded Martín as a very dangerous man.

Father Kurt Welner, S.J., had been el Coronel Frade's best friend, and served—if unofficially—as family priest to the late Coronel Frade, to his sister, and to his brother-in-law, el Señor Humberto Duarte, managing director of the Anglo-Argentine Bank, and to la Señora Claudia Carzino-Cormano, who was one of the wealthiest women in Argentina and who for decades had lived—until his death—in a state of carnal sin with the late Coronel Frade.

Both Cranz and Perón regarded Father Welner as a very dangerous man.

But it was the third man, twenty-four-year-old Cletus Frade, whom Cranz and Perón regarded as the most dangerous of all.

Born in Argentina to an American mother, Cletus, el Coronel's only son, had been estranged from his father since infancy. After his mother a year later had died giving birth in the U.S., Frade's American grandfather, a wealthy and powerful oilman, had successfully exerted his power to keep year-old Cletus from leaving America, and to keep Jorge Frade out of the United States.

Frade had been raised in Texas by his mother's brother and his wife. He had grown to manhood accepting his grandfather's often-pronounced opinion that Jorge Guillermo Frade was an unmitigated wife-murdering three-star sonofabitch.

Cletus Frade entered the United States Marine Corps and became a fighter pilot. Flying F4F Wildcats off "Fighter One" on Guadalcanal in the South Pacific, he became, by shooting down four Japanese Zero fighters and three Betty Bombers, an "Ace Plus Two."

That was enough for the Marine Corps to send him home, ultimately to pass on his fighter pilot's skill to fledgling fighter pilots, but first to participate in a War Bond Tour during which real live heroes from the war would be put on a stage to encourage the public to do their part by buying War Bonds Until It Hurt.

The first leg of the tour had found the war hero in California:

Frade was in his room in the Hollywood Roosevelt Hotel taking on a little liquid courage for his first appearance on stage when a well-dressed, neatly mustached man appeared at his door and inquired in Spanish if Frade happened to know an aviator and motion picture producer by the name of Howard Hughes.

"Who wants to know?" Frade said.

"Colonel Alejandro Frederico Graham, USMCR, wants to know, Mr. Frade. And stand to attention when you're talking to him."

There had been something about the civilian's tone of voice that caused Frade to stand to attention.

Colonel Graham pushed past Frade, entered his room, and closed the door.

"The question was, 'Are you acquainted with Howard Hughes?' You may answer 'Yes, sir' or 'No, sir.'"

"Yes, sir."

"Mr. Hughes told me you are the son of Jorge Guillermo Frade. You have the same answer options, Mr. Frade."

"Yes, sir."

"Good."

"Sir, permission to speak, sir?"

"Granted. You may stand at Parade Rest."

"Yes, sir. Sir, did Howard tell you I wouldn't know the sonofabitch if I fell over him?"

"He did mention something along those lines. Tell me, Mr. Frade, are you looking forward to the War Bond Tour? And teaching people how to fly?"

"No, sir."

"If I could get you out of both, would you accept a top-secret overseas assignment involving great risk to your life?"

"What kind of an assignment?"

"What part of 'top secret' didn't you understand, Mr. Frade?" Graham said.

Then he handed Frade a photograph of a man wearing what looked like a German uniform, including the steel helmet, standing and saluting in the backseat of an open Mercedes-Benz.

"That's what your father looks like. I don't want you falling over the sonofabitch without knowing who he is."

"Colonel, what's this all about?"

"I'll answer that, Mr. Frade, but it's the last question you get. What I want you to do is go down to Argentina and persuade your loving daddy to tilt the other way. Right now he's tilted toward Berlin."

He handed Frade a sheet of paper. The letterhead read: OFFICE OF STRATEGIC SERVICES, WASHINGTON, D.C. *Clete had never heard of it.*

"Sign that at the bottom. It's a formality. What it is is your acknowledgment that you fully understand all the awful things your government will do to you if you run off at the mouth."

There was too much small print to read. Frade looked at Graham.

"Or don't sign it, Mr. Frade. Your call. But I'm on a Transcontinental and Western flight to Washington in ninety minutes. With you or without you."

He extended a pen to Frade, who took it and scrawled his signature.

Graham then folded the sheet of paper and put it in his suit coat's inside pocket.

"Welcome to the OSS, Mr. Frade," Graham said. "And I bring greetings from your grandfather. If you're a good boy, I'll try to get you a couple of days with him before we put you on the Panagra flight to Buenos Aires."

"You know my grandfather?"

"He doesn't like your father very much, does he?" He did not wait for a reply, and nodded toward the bedroom. "Now, you'd better pack."

"That will be all, Amelia," el Colonel Perón said. "No calls, no visitors."

"*Sí, señor.*"

Cranz waited until the maid had closed the double doors to the library.

"Juan Domingo," Cranz began, "you were right about Tandil. I'm almost positive Frade has the Froggers there."

Perón nodded just perceptibly.

"Cletus Frade has arrived in Los Angeles," he said. "At the Lockheed airplane factory. There was a Mackay radiogram. De Filippi called me yesterday."

Guillermo de Filippi was chief of maintenance of South American Airways.

Cranz did not regard that as especially good news; a great many of his problems would have been solved if the Lockheed Lodestar that Frade was flying had lost an engine—preferably both—and gone down somewhere—anywhere—during the hazardous six-thousand-mile flight from Buenos Aires, never to be heard from again.

But unfortunately, the airplane was brand new, his copilot was the very experienced chief SAA pilot Gonzalo Delgano, and Frade himself was both a superb pilot and someone who apparently had more lives than the nine of the legendary cat.

Cranz's predecessor as the senior SS-SD officer in Argentina had not only botched a very expensive attempt to remove Cletus Frade from the equation, but had shortly thereafter died when a rifle bullet fired by one of Frade's men—or perhaps by Frade himself—had caused his skull to explode on the beach of Samborombón Bay.

Cranz had taken great care to make sure that his arrangements to eliminate Frade would not fail this time.

"Juan Domingo, something has to be done about the Froggers," Cranz said.

Perón didn't reply.

"And we both know that Cletus Frade has them."

Cranz felt sure he knew (a) why Frogger, the German Embassy's commercial attaché, and his wife had disappeared, and (b) why Frade had them.

Frogger was privy to many details of Operation Phoenix, the plan conceived by Reichsführer-SS Heinrich Himmler; Reichsleiter Martin Bormann, head of the Nazi Party; Admiral Wilhelm Canaris, chief of German Military Intelligence; and other very senior members of the Nazi hierarchy, who understood that the war was lost and had no intention of facing Allied vengeance.

Cranz knew all about Operation Phoenix: Hundreds of millions of dollars were to be spent to purchase South American sanctuary for high-ranking members of the Nazi establishment—probably including Der Führer, Adolf Hitler, himself, although Cranz wasn't sure about this—from which, after some time passed, National Socialism could rise, phoenixlike, from the ashes of the Thousand-Year Reich.

Cranz had been sent to Argentina to make sure nothing went wrong with the plan—after something had gone terribly wrong.

An attempt had been made at Samborombón Bay, on the River Plate, to smuggle ashore a half-dozen crates stuffed with English pounds, American dollars, Swiss francs, gold coins and bars, and thirty-odd leather bags heavy with diamonds. The transfer was made on boats from the *Comerciante del Océano Pacífico,* a Spanish-registered freighter. But someone had been waiting. Cranz suspected Cletus Frade and members of his OSS team, though he wasn't absolutely sure of this; it could have been Argentines.

There had been a brief burst of gunfire from a concealed position near the beach. Two of the three German officers—SS-Oberst Karl-Heinz Grüner, the military attaché of the German Embassy, and his deputy, SS-Standartenführer Josef Luther Goltz, had been dropped in their tracks, their skulls exploded by the rifle fire.

The snipers had missed the third officer, Major Hans-Peter von Wachtstein, the embassy's deputy military attaché for air. Von Wachtstein had managed to get the crates—"the special shipment"—and the bodies of Grüner and Goltz onto the *Comerciante del Océano Pacífico*'s boats and back out to the ship.

The captain of the *Océano Pacífico,* who had been in one of her boats, had been more than effusive in describing von Wachtstein's cool courage under fire. Courage was something to be expected of an officer who had received the Knight's Cross of the Iron Cross from Hitler personally, of course, but Cranz wasn't really sure if von Wachtstein had been extraordinarily lucky or whether the snipers had intentionally spared him.

What Cranz was sure of was that the attack made clear that the embassy housed a traitor. And he was just about certain that that was the reason Frogger had deserted his post, taking his wife with him.

Not that Frogger was the traitor. So far as Cranz knew, the Froggers were—or until their desertion, had been—patriotic Germans. They had lost two of their officer sons in Russia, and the third, the eldest, Frogger's namesake, Oberstleutnant Wilhelm Frogger, had been captured when General von Arnim had surrendered the Afrikakorps.

Furthermore, Cranz knew that Frau Else Frogger secretly had been on the payroll of the Sicherheitsdienst, the Secret Police of the SS, and had been charged with reporting on the other Germans in the embassy to Oberst Grüner.

There was a downside to these faultless patriotic credentials. The Froggers had seen enough of the functioning of the SS-SD to know that with as much at stake as there was, if the actual traitor in the embassy could not be found, one would be created. Himmler and Bormann would want to be told the problem had been dealt with.

The Froggers knew that if Cranz, who had replaced Grüner, and Naval Attaché Kapitän zur See Karl Boltitz, who had come to Argentina with Cranz, and almost certainly was working for Admiral Canaris, could not find the traitor, they would be replaced. In which case, they would be sent—if they were lucky—to the Eastern Front. Or to a concentration camp.

Furthermore, Frogger was aware that while he was privy to the secrets of Operation Phoenix, he was by no means a member of the inner circle. He knew too much.

Worse, he was privy to many of the details of an even more secret operation—which didn't have a code name—run by SS-Brigadeführer Ritter Manfred von Deitzberg, first deputy adjutant to Reichsführer-SS Himmler. Von Deitzberg had charged Cranz with making sure that this operation—in which senior SS officers were enriching themselves by arranging the release of Jews from concentration camps, and their subsequent movement to Argentina, on payment of a substantial ransom—was kept running and kept secret.

Cranz therefore thought it very likely that when the Froggers had been ordered to return on the next Condor flight to Berlin, Frogger had decided—or his wife had decided, or the both of them—that they had been set up as the scapegoats. And knowing what that meant, they had deserted their posts.

Now they were going to have to be killed before they could barter their knowledge of Operation Phoenix and the ransoming operation for their own sanctuary.

Perón said: "While I am fully aware of the problem the Froggers pose, Karl, I don't want anything to happen to Cletus Frade. He is my godson. His father— my dearest friend—died unnecessarily and I don't want the death of Cletus weighing on my soul as well."

"I understand your position, Juan Domingo. But—the reason I asked you to receive me on such short notice—I have come up with a rough plan that, since Cletus Frade is in the United States, poses no threat to him whatever."

"We don't know when he will return," Perón said.

"But not within the next three or four days, wouldn't you agree?"

"No, of course not," Perón said impatiently. "He just got there. He has to do what has to be done to get the SAA pilots the licenses Lloyd's of London in- sists they have to have, however long—three or four days—that will take, and then fly back here."

"De Filippi will know," Cranz said. "More important, will he tell you when Frade will actually be here?"

"Of course."

"And you will tell me?"

"Why would you want to know?"

"As I said, Juan Domingo, I know, and respect, your feeling *vis-à-vis* your godson. If I know when he will return, I can either adjust my plan, or call it off completely, if it would in any way put Frade at risk."

"I'm glad we understand one another," Perón said.

"May I speak bluntly, Juan Domingo?"

"Please do."

"I think you are as aware as I am of the problems the Froggers will cause both of us if we can't return them to German control and get them out of Argentina."

"Let's hear what you have in mind," Perón said tartly.

"The reason I'm sure the Froggers are in Tandil is that one of my men has seen them there."

"You sent someone from the SS to Tandil?" Perón asked on the edge of anger.

"I sent an Argentine, an ethnic German who works for me, down there to see what he could learn. Would you like to hear from him what that is?"

"How could I do that?

"He's here, in the foyer. May I get him?"

Perón considered that for a long moment.

"You did consider, of course, that Martín's men would see you bringing him here? What that would mean?"

"I'm sure they did," Cranz said, smiling. "He was driving my car; he's my chauffeur."

Perón considered that a moment, then smiled.

"You are good at what you do, aren't you, Karl? Yes. Bring him in."

[THREE]
Building T-209
Senior German Officer Prisoner of War Detention Facility
Camp Clinton, Mississippi
1850 6 August 1943

Building T-209 had been erected in four days just over a year before. Sitting on concrete blocks, it was a one-story frame structure containing a living room, a kitchen, and two bedrooms.

In each of the bedrooms, a curtained-off cubicle held a sink, a toilet, and a cement-floored shower. The furniture was what was prescribed in an Army Regulation titled "Colonels Through Major Generals, Temporary Bachelor Accommodations, Furnishings For."

That is to say, the single beds in the bedrooms were marginally larger and had more comfortable mattresses than the "*Cots, Steel w/mattress*" provided for officers of lower rank. And the living room held a simple, if comfortable, cloth-upholstered couch, two matching armchairs, and a coffee table. There was a refrigerator and a stove and a kitchen table with two chairs in the kitchen. Officers of lesser rank had none of these creature comforts.

A very large fan on a pole had been placed in the open kitchen door so that it blew toward the open living room door. It didn't cool the cottage much against the stifling heat of Mississippi in August, but it was much better than nothing.

Colonel J. Stanton Ludlow, Sr., Corps of Military Police—a tall, gray-haired fifty-six-year-old; a "Retread," having served in World War One—entered

Building T-209. He was trailed by a serious-looking lieutenant, a wiry twenty-two-year-old with closely cropped black hair.

They found six men in the living room, three of them in uniform.

The officers in uniform rose and came to attention in respect to the presence of the Camp Clinton commander. Two of them, a lieutenant and a major, wore MP brassards and the other accoutrements of military policemen, including holstered Model 1911A1 .45 ACP pistols, on their khaki shirts-and-trousers uniforms. The third wore short khaki pants and a khaki tunic onto which had been pinned and sewn the insignia of an oberstleutnant—lieutenant colonel—of the Afrikakorps.

The third was of course Oberstleutnant Wilhelm Frogger, who had been captured when General Hans-Jürgen von Arnim had surrendered the Afrikakorps, and who was the sole surviving son of Wilhelm and Else Frogger.

"At ease," Colonel Ludlow ordered, and turned to the eldest of the three civilians, who was sitting in one of the armchairs. He was wearing a sweat-soaked shirt. He had his sleeves rolled up and his tie pulled down. Gaily striped suspenders held up his pants.

"Thank you for coming so quickly, Colonel," Colonel A. F. Graham, USMCR, said.

"What can I do for you, Colonel?" Colonel Ludlow said, and looked at the two other men in the room, both of whom were wearing sort of a uniform of knit polo shirts, khaki slacks, and aviator's sunglasses as they leaned against the wall and held bottles of Coca-Cola.

"I don't mean to offend," Colonel Ludlow said to the taller of the two, "but has anyone ever told you that you look like Howard Hughes?"

"I've heard that before," Hughes said.

"Hughes is much better-looking, Colonel," the man beside him—Major Cletus Frade, USMCR—said. "And isn't going bald."

Colonel Graham flashed Frade an impatient look, then pushed himself out of the armchair.

"With the caveat that the classification is Top Secret, Colonel," Graham said, "would you please take a look at this?"

He handed Ludlow a four-by-five-inch envelope.

"Didn't you show me this when you first came?" Colonel Ludlow asked as he opened the envelope.

"What I showed you when I came was my authorization to see Colonel Frogger," Graham said. "This is somewhat different."

Ludlow read the document:

TOP SECRET

UnNumbered
Not For File
Duplication Forbidden

HEADQUARTERS
War Department
Washington, D.C.

3 August 1943

SUBJECT: Colonel A.F. Graham, USMCR

(One): Subject officer is operating at my direction on a classified mission of great importance.

(Two): Subject officer is to be provided with whatever assistance of whatever kind that he deems necessary to request of any command within the U.S. Armed Forces. The Chief of Naval Operations concurs.

G.C. Marshall
George C. Marshall
General
Chief of Staff

TOP SECRET

Ludlow's face showed his surprise as he looked at Colonel Graham.

"This is a blank check for anything, Colonel," Ludlow said.

"Yes, it is," Graham said. "I have to ask about your lieutenant. Do you want him to participate in what I'm going to need, or would you rather I have Major Frade take him into the kitchen, tell him what certainly will happen to him if he breathes a word of this to anyone for the rest of his life, and send him away?"

Ludlow considered that for a moment.

"Colonel Graham, this is Lieutenant Mark Dalton. I trust him. The question is whether he wants to become further involved with what's going on here." Ludlow looked to the wiry lieutenant. "Dalton?"

"You may show him that note," Graham said.

Ludlow handed the note to Dalton, who read it.

"In or out, Lieutenant?" Graham asked.

"In, sir," Lieutenant Dalton said.

"We don't shoot people who run off at the mouth about things like this, Lieutenant," Graham said. "But what we do, instead, is confine them in Saint Elizabeth's Hospital in Washington, where they stay incommunicado at least for the duration of the war, plus six months. If Colonel Ludlow trusts you, I'd like to have you, but I want you to be sure you know what you're letting yourself in for."

"In, sir," Lieutenant Dalton repeated.

"Incommunicado means your family will be informed you are missing in action."

"In, sir," Dalton said after a just-perceptible hesitation.

Graham nodded, then introduced Frade, Hughes, and Frogger, then said: "All right. What we are going to do is give Colonel Frogger a polo shirt and long-legged khakis. Lieutenant Dalton, you are then going to back Colonel Ludlow's staff car up to the back door and open the trunk. As the rest of us form as good a shield as we can, Colonel Frogger will then get in the trunk.

"Colonel Ludlow and Colonel Frogger will then get in that car. Major Frade and Mr. Hughes and I will get in the other car. We will follow you to the Jackson Army Air Base, where we will drive directly to our airplane, a Constellation. We then will again make as good a quick shield as we can while the trunk is opened and Colonel Frogger gets out, then goes up the ladder and into the aircraft.

"We will take off as soon as possible." He looked between Ludlow and Dalton. "You two will return here, and at 2300 hours, you will—in addition to whatever else you do when there is an escape—notify your superior headquarters and the FBI that Colonel Frogger has escaped."

He let that sink in, then added: "Don't let anyone—especially the FBI—know we were here at all."

"You're asking me to lie to the FBI?" Colonel Ludlow asked.

"I'm ordering you to lie to the FBI. I have the authority from the chief of staff to do so. It is important that the FBI believes that Colonel Frogger has actually escaped. If I didn't send them—and everybody else—on a wild-goose chase looking for Frogger, then someone will smell a rat."

"God, Alex, you are really a master of the mixed metaphor," Howard Hughes said.

Frade chuckled.

"What kind of an airplane did you say?" Lieutenant Dalton asked.

"A Constellation," Frade answered. "A Lockheed 1049, a great big four-engine, triple-tailed beautiful sonofabitch."

"I don't think I've ever seen one," Dalton said.

"Not many people have," Colonel Graham snapped. "Now, if it's not too much trouble, can we get this show on the road?"

[FOUR]
Office of the Deputy Director for Western Hemisphere Operations
Office of Strategic Services
National Institutes of Health Building
Washington, D.C.
1630 8 August 1943

There came a quick knock at the door.

"I said 'nobody,' Alice," Colonel A. F. Graham called. He was sitting behind his desk, his feet resting on an open drawer, holding a short squat glass dark with bourbon whiskey.

"Does that include me?" a stocky, gray-haired, well-tailored man in his sixties asked as he entered the room.

"I told you, Allen," Graham said to the man sitting on his couch in the process of replenishing his martini glass, "that the other shoe was going to drop."

Allen Welsh Dulles chuckled. He was in his fifties, had a not-well-defined mustache on his lip, somewhat unkempt gray hair, and was wearing what members of his class thought of as a "sack suit," a black single-breasted garment with little or no padding on the shoulders. He also wore a white button-down-collar shirt and a bow tie.

"And Deputy Director Dulles," the stocky, well-tailored man said, "my day is now complete. You *were* going to stop by my office and say hello, weren't you, Allen?"

"Not today, if I possibly could have avoided it," Dulles said. "Bill, you have this remarkable ability to cause it to rain on any parade of mine."

"What are you celebrating? What is that, a martini?"

"May I offer you a small libation, Mr. Director?" Graham asked.

"No, thank you," Colonel William J. Donovan said. "I try to set an example for my subordinates."

"Is that why you wear those gaudy neckties?" Graham asked.

"How many of those have you had, Alex?"

"Probably one-third to one-half of what I will ultimately have," Graham said seriously.

"And neither of you is going to tell me what it is that you're celebrating?"

"Actually, Bill," Graham said, "what Allen and I were discussing when you burst uninvited in here was how little we could get away with telling you."

"I don't think you're kidding," Donovan said not very pleasantly.

"He wasn't," Dulles said. "You've heard, I'm sure, that the only way a secret known to three people can remain a secret is if two of the three are dead?"

"But you agreed—in what we lawyers call 'a condition of employment'— that there would be no secrets between us. Remember that?"

"And if it were not for your buddy Franklin," Graham said, "both Allen and I would happily live up to that condition of employment. But you keep telling him things you shouldn't."

"To rain on your parade, Alex," Donovan said, "my buddy Franklin happens to be the President of the United States."

Dulles put in pointedly: "And who has in his immediate circle a number of people—especially the Vice President—who I would be reluctant to trust with any secret, much less this one, as far as I could throw the White House."

"This secret is one we really don't want to get to Uncle Joe Stalin via Mr. Henry A. Wallace's close friends in the Russian Embassy," Graham said.

They had had this argument, or ones very like it, many times before.

In any conventional organization, in ordinary times, subordinates don't challenge the boss; if they do, the boss gets rid of them. The Office of Strategic Services was not a conventional organization, and these were not ordinary times.

William J. Donovan was the director of the Office of Strategic Services, which in theory answered to General George C. Marshall, the Army's chief of staff, but in practice only to President Franklin Delano Roosevelt.

Allen W. Dulles and Alejandro F. Graham were the OSS deputy directors for Europe and the Western Hemisphere, respectively. They were both uniquely qualified for their roles. Both were prepared—in other words, were privy to all of the OSS's secrets—to take over at a moment's notice if anything should happen to Donovan.

The truth was that while all three had great admiration for one another, they often didn't like one another very much, although Dulles and Graham liked each other much better than either did Donovan. For his part, Donovan, realizing how important Dulles and Graham were to the OSS, very often passed over clear insubordination from them that he absolutely would not have tolerated from anyone else.

He was doing so now.

Graham's remark *What Allen and I were discussing when you burst uninvited in here was how little we could get away with telling you* had quietly enraged him. He hadn't actually taken a deep breath and counted to ten to avoid blowing up, but he had told himself that he had to be careful. Blowing up—no matter how justified—would have been counterproductive.

"You are going to tell me, aren't you, Allen, exactly what it is you don't want Vice President Wallace to pass on to our Russian allies?"

Dulles met his eyes.

"Reluctantly, Bill, I will," Dulles said. "Alex and I had just agreed that the President will inevitably ask you what was going on in the Hotel Washington, and that it would be best if we prepared you for the question."

"And what *was* going on at the Hotel Washington? You don't mean with Putzi Hanfstaengl?"

Both Dulles and Graham nodded.

Ernst "Putzi" Hanfstaengl was another Columbia University classmate of President Roosevelt and Director Donovan.

The scion of a wealthy Munich publishing family, he had been attracted to Hitler and National Socialism in its early days. Among other things, Hanfstaengl had loaned Joseph Goebbels, the Nazi party propagandist, the money to start up the *Völkischer Beobachter,* the official newspaper of the National Socialist German Workers' Party.

He became part of Hitler's inner circle, but as he became progressively more disenchanted with Hitler and the Thousand-Year Reich, Hitler became progressively more disenchanted with Hanfstaengl. A friend warned Hanfstaengl that he was about to have an SS-engineered accident, and Hanfstaengl fled Germany.

In the United States, Hanfstaengl looked up Roosevelt and Donovan. Both helped him get settled, and he began working in the family's New York office. When war came, he was automatically an enemy alien. Under the law, and especially because of his known ties to the Nazi regime, he was required to be incarcerated as a threat to national security.

On the other hand, Hanfstaengl's judgment of how senior Nazi officials and top-ranking military officers would react in a given circumstance was obviously of great value to Roosevelt. But equally obviously, Hanfstaengl could not be seen wandering around the White House, and picking his brain would be difficult if he were locked up somewhere in the Arizona desert with the other German threats to American National Security.

The solution proposed by Donovan and ordered executed by the commander in chief saw Hanfstaengl incarcerated under military guard in a suite in the Hotel Washington, a stone's throw from the White House. The guard was U.S. Army Sergeant Egon Hanfstaengl, who called his prisoner "Poppa."

Roosevelt would visit his old pal by having his wheelchair rolled into a laundry truck at the White House. The truck would then drive to the basement service entrance of the Hotel Washington, and Roosevelt would then be wheeled through the kitchen to an elevator operated by a Secret Service agent and taken to Hanfstaengl's suite.

"What were you doing with Hanfstaengl?" Donovan demanded. "And who was there?"

"Originally, myself," Graham said. "And Howard Hughes. And Cletus Frade. And a German lieutenant colonel named Frogger. And then the President came in."

"What the hell is this all about?" Donovan snapped. "And start at the beginning."

His control then suddenly disappeared.

"You took *Cletus Frade* to see Hanfstaengl?" he demanded as spittle flew. "And some *German* officer? You better have a goddamned good reason."

Dulles said softly: "How about a chance—admittedly not a very good one, but a chance—to eliminate Hitler? To remove Der Führer permanently from this vale of tears?"

It was a long moment before Donovan replied.

"I can't believe that either of you, even half in the bag as you are, would joke about something like that."

"We're not," Graham said simply. "And if you can keep your Irish temper under control, Bill, I'll tell you what has happened."

"Have at it," Donovan snapped.

"Hoover's head man in Buenos Aires—a fellow named Milton Leibermann, who learned to speak Spanish when he was an FBI agent in Spanish Harlem—defied J. Edgar's strict orders to have no contact with the OSS down there by bringing to Cletus Frade the commercial counselor of the German Embassy and his wife, who had deserted their posts and come to him asking for asylum."

"Why did he do that?" Donovan asked.

"You mean this guy Frogger?" Graham said. "According to Frade, he thought he was being thrown to the wolves by the SS people in the embassy. When the Froggers were ordered home to Germany, they took off."

"Interesting, but I was asking about the FBI agent."

"He told Frade he had no place to hide them," Graham explained, "and he thought Frade could use them—or we could—to help keep track of all that Operation Phoenix money. So Frade took them. And told Allen about having them when they met at the Canoas Air Base in Brazil."

"You met with Cletus Frade in Brazil?" Donovan asked. He was visibly angry, and now his voice was icy. "Funny, I never heard about that, Allen. Another of those things you decided I didn't have to know?"

Dulles's eyes tightened.

"I seem to recall, Bill, that the 'condition of employment' you mentioned before gave me the authority to run Europe as I see fit. Is that your recollection as well?"

Donovan didn't reply.

"My understanding was that it did," Dulles said. "And operating on that premise, I didn't think I had to have your permission to meet with Cletus Frade, or to tell you that I had until I decided it was appropriate."

Dulles let that sink in for a moment, then went on: "One of the players in Operation Valkyrie is Galahad's father."

Donovan knew that Operation Valkyrie was the code name used by disaffected members of the German High Command to identify their plan to assassinate Adolf Hitler.

Donovan said: "I suppose that since you and Alex have decided that neither I nor the commander in chief can be trusted with Galahad's identity, you're not going to identify his father either."

"Only that he is a generalleutnant on Hitler's inner staff who sees him on a daily basis," Dulles said.

"Bill," Graham said, "we'd be willing to trust you with both names if we knew you wouldn't run to the President with them. It boils down to the same thing. Things leak from the Oval Office, and we simply can't take that risk with this."

"I know you don't think much of the FBI," Donovan said. "But J. Edgar Hoover's more competent than you give him credit for being. The President has ordered him to find out who Galahad is. And sooner or later, he will."

"Possibly," Dulles said. "And if that happens, I'll know that Valkyrie has been compromised and will take the appropriate action."

After a moment, Donovan asked, "Are you going to tell me what you and Frade discussed in Brazil?"

"When Frade told me about the Froggers, I thought we might suddenly have been struck with good fortune. It was the same surname as one of the players in Valkyrie. I couldn't be sure—and I couldn't find out while I was in Brazil—so what I asked Frade to do was have a photograph of himself taken with his Froggers, and to stand by, so to speak, for further orders.

"I did not tell him what I hoped, and he did not learn until yesterday, that Lieutenant Colonel Wilhelm Frogger, the Froggers' sole surviving son, a Valkyrie conspirator, had been captured when General von Arnim surrendered the Afrikakorps and was now in the senior officers' POW camp in Mississippi.

"When I had that information, I brought Frade to the United States."·

"You didn't think," Donovan asked, more than a little sarcastically, "that Frade suddenly coming up here from Argentina might look a little suspicious?"

"What Allen did, Bill, was have Lloyd's of London cancel the insurance of South American Airways," Graham said. "Otherwise known as Franklin Roosevelt's Stick It to Juan Trippe Airline."

"I don't think that's funny, nor do I understand," Donovan said.

"South American Airways—Frade—was informed that inasmuch as SAA's pilots did not hold an internationally recognized Airline Transport Rating, they were forced to cancel SAA's insurance," Dulles explained. "This caused, as I suspected it would, a furious—and always resourceful—Cletus Frade to deal with the situation in his own way. What he did was load a dozen SAA pilots on one of his Lodestars and fly them to the Lockheed plant in Burbank to take the necessary examinations and get their ratings. And incidentally, to take back to Argentina a half-dozen of those 'surplus' Lodestars."

Graham picked up the story: "Howard Hughes and I were waiting for him in his hotel room at the Chateau Marmont in Hollywood. The next morning, the SAA pilots—including Frade—were dropped off one at a time at SAA Lodestars to meet the examination pilots. Frade was dropped off last, at a Constellation, where Howard and I were again waiting for him.

"We flew to the Jackson Army Air Base in Mississippi. En route, we told Frade what was going on. We drove out to Camp Clinton and met with Oberstleutnant Frogger. He's one starchy sonofabitch, incidentally, who would only recite his name, rank, and serial number even after we showed him the pictures of Frade with his parents.

"We told him that we would protect his family from the Germans, even eventually allow them to come to the States, if he could talk them into helping Frade keep track of where the Operation Phoenix money was going. He professed to know nothing of Operation Phoenix, but he agreed to come with us to Washington 'to meet someone who would confirm that Operation Phoenix existed.'

"We took him to see Putzi. Frogger knew who Putzi was, of course, and was impressed, as I thought he would be. And then we threw Galahad's name at Frogger and told him we knew he was involved with Valkyrie. He was still adjusting to the shock that we knew about Valkyrie when the door opened and a Secret Service agent wheeled in the President."

"My God!" Donovan said. "And?"

"We got lucky again," Graham said. "Roosevelt didn't say much beyond 'You must be Major Frade' to Cletus, and then he left. I had the feeling that while he didn't have any idea what was going on, he'd better give me the benefit of the doubt."

"You didn't tell him?" Donovan asked.

Graham shook his head. "And, amazingly, he didn't ask. That's what you're going to have to do, Bill: come up with a story to explain to Roosevelt what we were doing there that does not, repeat not, even hint about Operation Valkyrie."

Donovan, who did not at all like being bluntly told what he was going to have to do, nevertheless did not lose his temper.

"And then?" Donovan asked.

"Frogger came on board, said he'd do whatever we asked."

"And now there is a secret within a secret," Dulles said. "Frogger will go to

Argentina to help Frade with Operation Phoenix. That's a secret. But his primary role will be to help me help the Valkyrie conspirators."

"How are you going to get him to Argentina?" Donovan asked. "And don't you think he'll be missed at Camp Clinton, both by the Army and the Germans?"

"He's now in Las Vegas, Nevada," Graham said. "As soon as the Documents people can come up with what he needs to prove that he's a South African named Fischer—the whole nine yards, passport, driver's license, clothing, even suitcases—and we can get it out there, he'll be flown—probably by Howard, in a Constellation—to Canoas and wait there for Frade to appear and get him into Argentina."

"How's Frade going to do that?"

"Frade is very resourceful," Dulles said. "He'll think of something."

"Frade gives new meaning to the term 'loose cannon,'" Donovan said. "And what about the POW camp? What happens there?"

"At 2300 last night, the camp commander reported to the local authorities, the provost marshal general, and the FBI that Oberstleutnant Frogger cannot be found and must be presumed to have escaped."

"Clever," Donovan said. "But J. Edgar will blow a fuse when he finds out he's been spending what he calls his 'finite resources' trying to find a German POW we have."

Dulles shrugged. "I don't want Hoover to know that. Now. Or ever. I want the FBI looking in every nook and cranny for Colonel Frogger."

"If I didn't know better, that might sound like an order," Donovan said, his voice tense.

"If you're not willing to go along with that, I'll go see the President, right now, and make my case," Dulles said. "This has to be kept secret, Bill."

"Second the motion," Graham said.

After a very perceptible pause, Donovan said, "Okay. I'll go along. I'm not sure if I'm doing so because I think you're right, or because there is a certain appeal to the thought of J. Edgar being increasingly humbled by not being able to find an escaped POW, or because I really don't want the President to have proof that the both of you are half in the bag before five o'clock in the afternoon."

Neither Graham nor Dulles replied.

"This is where I usually say 'keep me posted,'" Donovan said. "But that would be a waste of breath with you two, wouldn't it?"

He pushed himself out of his chair and walked out of the office.

II

When Cletus Frade came down the stairs into the basement garage of the mansion, he looked—and felt—both very tired and upset. He also felt grimy. He was wearing the same clothing—except for underwear that he had changed twice—he had put on forty-odd hours before in Los Angeles: a polo shirt and khaki trousers, and battered Western boots. Once he had arrived in Argentina, where it was winter, he had added a fur-collared leather jacket, the breast of which had sewn to it a leather patch bearing a stamped-in-gold representation of Naval Aviator's wings and the legend C. H. FRADE ILT USMCR.

Except for maybe six hours spent on the ground taking on fuel, buying food (usually sandwiches), visiting some really incredibly foul gentlemen's rest facilities, and changing his linen, he had been either at the controls of a Lockheed Lodestar or catching what sleep he could lying in the aisle between the seats in the passenger compartment.

Finally, the Lodestar had touched down, twice, in Argentina.

The first time had been at Estancia San Pedro y San Pablo, where he had dropped off Mr. Wilhelm Fischer, a South African, and where Frade's wife had told him the bad news:

That she had gone to Casa Chica the previous afternoon with provisions for Sergeant Stein and the others and found only a nearly destroyed Casa Chica, large pools of blood on the airstrip, and nothing and nobody else. Stein was gone, and so were Suboficial Mayor Rodríguez, the Froggers, The Other Dorotea, and the dozen ex-Húsares de Pueyrredón peones who were supposed to be guarding the place.

There hadn't been time then to do anything about that. The SAA Lodestar was due at Aerodromo Jorge Frade in Morón in an hour—he had sent a telegram from Brazil announcing their Estimated Time of Arrival—and if it didn't land more or less on time, el Coronel Martín, who Frade was sure would be there to meet him, would suspect that the Lodestar had landed somewhere else. For example, at Estancia San Pedro y San Pablo.

And taking into account what Dorotea had told him had happened at Casa Chica, it was also quite possible that Martín would be waiting at Jorge Frade with a warrant for his arrest as at least a conspirator in the kidnapping, or whatever it might be called, of the Froggers.

Clete Frade did the best with what he had. And what he had was his own Lodestar and someone who could fly it—SAA's chief pilot, Gonzalo Delgano. Delgano would not be suspected by Martín of having anything to do with the Froggers because Delgano was actually a BIS major charged by Martín with keeping an eye on Frade.

Frade had somewhat turned Delgano. The day before, during a fuel stop at La Paz, Bolivia, he had appealed to Delgano. And Delgano had, if not changed sides, then—after praying for guidance and being swayed by his concept of a Christian Officer's Code of Behavior—decided that he was morally obliged to help Frade smuggle Herr Fischer/Oberstleutnant Frogger into Argentina aboard the Lodestar.

If the whole thing had blown up—and it looked as if it had—and everything came out—as it inevitably would—Delgano was in deep trouble. But neither Frade nor Delgano thought el Coronel Martín would be waiting at Jorge Frade with handcuffs for both of them. With a little bit of luck, Delgano could just go home from the airfield.

Or get in a car and drive to Estancia San Pedro y San Pablo and fly the Frade Lodestar, with Oberstleutnant Frogger and the others of Frade's OSS team, across the River Plate to sanctuary in Uruguay.

Frade had ordered that everything the OSS owned on Estancia San Pedro y San Pablo be prepared for demolition and for all the OSS personnel to be prepared to get on the Lodestar at a moment's notice.

Then he and Delgano had flown the SAA Lodestar to Aerodromo Coronel Jorge Frade in Morón, where neither was surprised to find el Coronel Martín waiting for them.

Not with handcuffs, but with the announcement that el Coronel Perón had some new information regarding the missing Froggers that he wished to discuss with Frade, and he thought that it would be a good idea for Frade to hear what he had to say.

"Not in the next couple of days, Don Cletus. Right now," Martín had said. "I'm afraid I must insist. You can follow me to the house on Libertador and then go home."

"How am I going to follow you?"

Martín pointed toward one of the hangars. Frade looked and saw Subofi-cial Mayor Enrico Rodríguez standing beside one of Estancia San Pedro y San Pablo's Ford station wagons.

On the way to the house on Libertador, Enrico had told Frade what had happened at Casa Chica, told him that the Froggers were safe and well protected in one of Estancia San Pedro y San Pablo's casas, and shown him a thick stack of photographs that Sergeant Stein had taken at Casa Chica.

The meeting was brief. Afterward when Frade came down the stairs into the basement garage of the mansion, both very tired and upset, he was annoyed but not surprised to find Martín still waiting for him.

"Alejandro, what a pleasant surprise," Frade said sarcastically. "We're going to have to stop meeting this way; people will talk."

Enrico was with him, his riot shotgun held vertically against his leg.

Martín was not amused by Frade's wit.

"That didn't take long," Martín said.

"Well, we didn't have much to talk about," Frade said.

"What did he have to say?"

"Very little after I told him I knew he was there when my Casa Chica was machine-gunned."

"Excuse me?"

Frade took the sheaf of pictures from the pocket of his leather jacket and handed them to Martín.

Martín tried very hard and almost succeeded in suppressing his surprise at the photographs.

"I didn't hear about any bodies," Martín blurted. "Where are they now?"

"God only knows," Frade said. "Why did you insist I come here, Alejandro?"

Martín took a moment to consider his reply, then said, "I thought perhaps el Coronel Perón could make the point that either kidnapping—or aiding and abetting the desertion of—German diplomats was a very dangerous thing to do."

"You thought what happened at Casa Chica was in the nature of a warn-ing?" Frade asked.

"I didn't know it was anything like this," he said. "It happened while you were in the United States?"

Frade nodded. "Yesterday. You really didn't know?"

Martín shook his head.

"Did they get the Froggers?" he asked.

"The who? Next question."

Martín looked at him for a long moment, then asked: "Anything else of interest to me happen upstairs?"

"Well, I told him I wanted him out of this house by tomorrow. That was about it."

While many people knew the mansion to be el Coronel Perón's residence, and many even thought he owned it, the fact was that it belonged to Cletus Frade, and Perón had been using it as a sort of tolerated unwelcome guest.

Martín, who knew who owned the house, shook his head in disbelief.

"Actually, what I said was, 'Tío Juan, you degenerate sonofabitch. You're going to have to find someplace else for your little girls. I want you out of here by tomorrow.' That was after he waved his pistol at me."

"He did what?" Martín asked incredulously.

"For a moment I thought he was going to shoot me. But then Enrico chambered a round in the riot gun and he thought better of it. Now that I've had a couple of minutes to think it over, I almost wish he had tried. The tragic death of Juan Domingo in his godson's library because poor old Enrico didn't know his shotgun was loaded would have solved a lot of my problems."

"And now?"

"Now, nothing. I told him that if I even suspect an attempt is made on my life, my wife's life, or the life of anybody close to me, the photographs—and some other material I have—will be made public. The only people who know what happened upstairs just now are Enrico and me. And now you."

Martín considered that for a long moment.

"I'm sure you understand, my friend, that it isn't a question of if this situation will erupt but when. I really don't see Perón trying to kill you—at least personally—but there are a number of others who would like to see you out of the way."

Karl Cranz, for instance, Martín thought.

Cranz would be very unhappy indeed about the failure of the Tandil operation. Cletus Frade was making enemies left and right.

Frade nodded.

"We did not have this conversation," Martín went on. "What happened tonight was that I insisted you come here, as el Coronel Perón asked me to do, and waited here only until I was sure that you had met with him."

Frade nodded again.

The two shook hands.

"Enrico," Martín said, "I'm very glad there was no accident because you didn't know your shotgun was loaded."

Enrico nodded at Martín but said nothing.

Martín walked across the garage to a 1939 Dodge sedan. The driver saw him coming and had the engine started before he reached the car. Martín got in the front seat and the car drove off.

"We go to the estancia now, Don Cletus?" Enrico asked.

"I need a bath first," Frade said. "I haven't had one since I left Los Angeles. Wives—write this down, Enrico—don't like men who smell."

"The apartment in the Hotel Alvear?" Enrico asked when they had gotten into a 1941 Ford Super-Deluxe station wagon.

"The house," Frade answered. "Hotel managers don't like men who need a bath any more than wives do."

[TWO]
1728 Avenida Coronel Díaz
Palermo, Buenos Aires
1620 12 August 1943

"There is a silver lining in every black cloud, Enrico," Frade said as they approached the huge, turn-of-the-century mansion. "Now that my Tío Juan is out of Uncle Willy's house—and after I have it fumigated—we can use that instead of this."

Enrico pulled the station wagon up to the massive cast-iron gates and tapped the horn. When there was no response in sixty seconds, he tapped it again.

"What I think we have here is one more proof that when el patrón is away, the mice will play," Frade said.

When there was no response to the second tooting of the horn, Frade said, "Go open the gate."

Enrico got out and shoved the left gate open. From painful experience— he had scraped the fender of his 1941 Buick—Frade knew that as massive as they were, both of the gates had to be opened for an American car to pass. The house had been built before the arrival of the automobile.

Frade slid across the seat, intending to close the driver's door and drive the car inside himself.

He had just reached for the door when he saw Enrico take his pistol—an

Argentine manufactured-under-license version of the 1911 Colt .45 ACP self-loading pistol—quickly work the action, and assume a crouching two-handed firing stance.

Frade grabbed Enrico's Remington Model 11 riot shotgun from where it was held in a clip against the dash, with the butt riding on the transmission hump, and dove out the open door.

He heard both the .45 firing and the sharper sound of something else firing as he hit the sidewalk. One of the windows in the Ford shattered.

Just to be sure, he worked the action, and a brass-cased shell flew out of the weapon.

I now have five.

He ran around the front of the Ford and stood up with the shotgun at his shoulder. There was a black 1938 Peugeot sedan stopped in front of the house. There were three men in it, one driving and two firing pistols. One had just taken aim at Frade when he staggered backward with a load of double-aught buckshot from the Remington in his chest. Clete had just taken a bead on the driver—the other man with the pistol was nowhere in sight—when the man's head exploded when a 230-grain, soft-nose lead bullet from Enrico's .45 struck him in the mouth.

It was suddenly very quiet. Clete could hear a car shifting gears. Without realizing he was doing it, Clete used the USMC signal for *advance on the left* to Enrico and they ran to opposite ends of the Peugeot. The third man was lying on the street in a growing pool of blood from his head.

Enrico crossed himself, then cursed.

Clete felt a little light-headed, and steadied himself on the Peugeot.

"Don Cletus, you are all right?"

"Hunky-dory," Frade said. "We better call the cops."

The moment he said it, he saw that would be unnecessary. Two policemen were coming down the street at a run on the left, and a third from the right.

After a moment, Clete realized that the cops were calling for him to drop the gun. He made a gesture of surrender and laid Enrico's shotgun on the roof of the Peugeot.

Enrico Rodríguez was not cowed by the police.

"This is Don Cletus Frade," he bellowed. "How dare you point a gun at him?"

This was followed by an order: "Get on the telephone and report to el Coronel Martín of the BIS that an assassination attempt has been made on Don Cletus Frade!"

[THREE]
The Embassy of the German Reich
Avenida Córdoba
Buenos Aires, Argentina
1640 12 August 1943

The commercial counselor of the embassy of the German Reich looked up with annoyance when there was a knock at his office door.

"Whoever that is, get rid of him," he ordered softly. "I am not available."

Fräulein Ingeborg Hässell, a middle-aged woman who wore her graying hair drawn tight against her skull, ending in a bun at the nape of her neck, quickly stood up and went to the door and opened it. A moment later, she closed the door and announced:

"It's Günther Loche, Herr Cranz. He said it's important."

Cranz's eyebrow rose, and he made a *Let him in* gesture with his well-manicured fingers.

Fräulein Hässell opened the door and signaled for Loche to enter.

Cranz smiled warmly at Loche.

"I gather you have something to tell me about our friend, Günther?"

"Yes, sir," Loche said. He was now standing almost at attention. His eyes flicked nervously at Fräulein Hässell.

"Be good enough, please, Fräulein Hässell, to give Günther and me a moment?"

She went through the door and closed it after her.

"So what have you to tell me, Günther?" Cranz asked.

"Herr Cranz, some men attempted to kill Frade as he was opening the gates of his house on Avenida Coronel Díaz."

"And?"

"Frade and his bodyguard killed them. There were three of them. Frade used a shotgun and his bodyguard a pistol."

This was not what Cranz hoped to hear.

"Frade was not injured?"

"No, sir. Neither he nor his bodyguard."

"And the men who did this: You think they all died?"

"Yes, sir. They were all dead."

Well, there's the silver lining in the dark cloud. If they're dead, the police can't tie me or Raschner to this.

"You did very well, Günther," Cranz said. "There's one more thing I want you to do. Go to Herr Raschner's apartment and tell him—and absolutely no one, *no one,* else—what you just told me."

SS-SD-Sturmbannführer Erich Raschner, his "deputy commercial attaché," had organized the hit for Cranz.

"Jawohl, Herr Cranz."

"And send Fräulein Hässell back in here, will you, please, on your way out?"

"Jawohl, Herr Cranz," Loche barked. He gave Cranz the straight-armed Nazi salute, barked "Heil Hitler!" did an about-face, and marched to the door.

Cranz shook his head and waited for Fräulein Hässell to reappear.

When she had, he said, "Please set up a meeting for eight-thirty tomorrow morning between the ambassador, Herr Gradny-Sawz, Kapitän zur See Boltitz, and myself."

Fräulein Hässell nodded.

"Please ask the ambassador if we might use his office. And tell Herr Raschner to make sure that he inspects the ambassador's office for listening devices."

She nodded again.

He smiled warmly at her. "And now where were we, Fräulein Ingeborg, when we were so rudely interrupted?"

[FOUR]
1728 Avenida Coronel Díaz
Palermo, Buenos Aires
1705 12 August 1943

Police of varying ranks had come to the scene, but the interrogation of Frade and Rodríguez had been stopped by a telephone call from the Bureau of Internal Security, which announced it was taking over the investigation and that el Coronel Martín was en route.

When Martín arrived at the mansion ten minutes later, he found two policemen guarding the door of the library, and Frade and Rodríguez inside. Frade was sitting in an armchair with a glass in his hand and a bottle of Johnnie Walker on the low table in front of him.

"Alejandro, what a pleasant surprise," Frade said. "But we're going to have to stop meeting this way; otherwise people will talk."

Martín had not been amused when Frade had said it before, and he was not amused this time either.

"What happened?" Martín asked.

"Enrico was opening the gate when people started to shoot at us," Frade said. "Who the hell are they? *Were* they?"

"All we know so far is that the car was stolen," Martín said. "If I had to guess, I'd say the dead men were members of the criminal element."

"God, you're a veritable Sherlock Holmes!" Frade said. "And I'll bet they followed us here from Libertador, right?"

"If I had to guess, I'd say they followed us from Aerodromo Coronel Jorge Frade to Libertador and then followed you here. I can't ask them, of course, as they are no longer with us."

Clete, after first taking a sip, laid down his glass of scotch whisky, picked up a telephone, and dialed a number from memory.

"Tío Juan, this is your godson, Cletus. Three members of the criminal element just tried to kill Enrico and me. I'm giving you the benefit of the doubt and accepting that you just didn't find the time immediately to call your German friends and call them off. But if I were you, I'd call them right now."

Then he hung up.

He looked at Martín, who shook his head.

"You don't really think el Coronel Perón had something to do with what happened here, do you?" Martín asked.

"I think his German friends had a lot to do with it."

"But you have no proof?"

"As you said, the people who tried this are no longer with us."

"Hypothetically speaking: What if one or more of them were still with us? What if one or more of them said, '*Sí*, señor. We were hired by'—let's say Commercial Attaché Karl Cranz—"

"You mean SS-Obersturmbannführer Cranz?"

Martín ignored the interruption.

He continued: "Or perhaps Sturmbannführer—excuse me, *Deputy Commercial Attaché* Raschner—to carry out this dastardly deed. I'm sure both of them would regard the charges as absurd. But that's moot. Cranz and Raschner have diplomatic immunity; they don't even have to answer any of my questions. The worst that could happen to them would be being declared *persona non grata* and told to leave Argentina. That would cause a diplomatic incident, at the very least, and the Germans would, tit for tat, expel a like number of Argentine diplomats from Berlin. And on the Condor that flew the Argentines home there would be the replacements for Cranz and Raschner."

"Why am I getting the idea that you think the Argentines should stay in Berlin?"

"I have no idea. And I denounce as scurrilous innuendo that the Argentine agricultural attaché in Berlin, who was a classmate of mine at the military academy, has any connection with the Bureau of Internal Security."

"Suggesting that someone has a connection with the BIS is a terrible thing to say about anybody," Frade said.

"I thought you might feel that way," Martín said, and then went on: "Earlier in his career, I just remembered, my classmate was privileged to serve in the Húsares de Pueyrredón under your late father."

Frade picked up his glass, took a deep swallow of his scotch whisky, then said, "How interesting. So tell me, Alejandro, what happened here tonight?"

"My initial investigation tends to suggest that three known members of the criminal element were observed by the police trying to break into these premises. When the police challenged them, the criminals fired at them. The superior marksmanship of the police prevailed, and the malefactors unfortunately went to meet their maker."

Frade considered that a moment, nodded his acceptance, and then asked, "Can you get Rodríguez's weapons back from the cops?"

"The 'cops'? Oh, you mean the police. Why would the police have the sub-oficial's weapons?" Martín said. He nodded, then added, "It's always a pleasure to see you, Don Cletus. But we're going to have to stop meeting like this, lest people start to talk. I can show myself out. I'm sure you're anxious to get to Estancia San Pedro y San Pablo and the charming Doña Dorotea."

"Just as soon as I have a shower," Frade said. "Enrico will show you out."

When Enrico came back into the library a minute or so later, he had the Remington Model 11 in one hand, the .45 pistol stuck in his waistband, and a leather bandolier of brass-cased shotgun cartridges hanging around his neck.

"How are we going to get home?" Frade asked.

"When I put the Ford in the garage, I will see," Rodríguez said. "I think the old Buick is down there."

"And what happens to the Ford?"

"I will have it taken to el Coronel's garage at the estancia. I don't know about the window glass, but we can repair the other damage."

"I don't want Dorotea to see it," Frade said.

Rodríguez made a deprecating shrug and extended the pistol to Frade.

"I don't think I'll need that in the shower, Enrico."

"You are the one who taught me, Don Cletus, that one never needs a weapon until one needs one badly."

"Point taken, my friend," Frade said, and took the pistol.

[FIVE]
Estancia San Pedro y San Pablo
Near Pila
Buenos Aires Province, Argentina
2055 12 August 1943

The "old Buick" Enrico thought he would find in the basement garage of the mansion had been there. It was a black 1940 Buick Limited four-door "touring sedan." In other words, a convertible. It had a second windshield for the rear seat, spare tires mounted in the fenders, and enormous extra headlights on the bumper. It had been el Coronel's pride and joy until he had acquired a Horch—an even larger car—in Germany. Once that had been taken off the ship in Buenos Aires, he had never driven the Buick again. But he hadn't wanted anyone else driving the Buick, so it had been, so to speak, put to pasture in the mansion basement until he could decide what to do with it.

The black Buick was the only vehicle on the two-lane macadam road crossing the pampas. There were 300,000 square miles of the pampas—an area roughly half the size of Alaska, a little larger than Texas, and just about twice as big as California—which ran from the Atlantic Ocean just south of Buenos Aires to the foothills of the Andes Mountains. The name came from the Indian word for "level plain."

The road was straight as an arrow, but as the speedometer hovered between seventy and eighty miles an hour, the headlights illuminated nothing but the road itself and a line of telephone poles marching at hundred-meter intervals beside it.

Enrico Rodríguez was driving. His shotgun was propped between the door and the dashboard. His pistol and the bandolier of shells were on the seat beside him. Cletus Frade sat in the front passenger seat, asleep, his head resting against his window.

Rodríguez took his right hand from the steering wheel, leaned across the front seat, and almost tenderly pushed Frade's shoulder.

It took several more pushes of growing force before Frade wakened. But when he did so, he was instantly wide awake, looking quickly around as if he expected something to be going wrong.

"We are nearly home, Don Cletus," Enrico said.

Frade looked out the windows, then said what he was thinking: "How the hell can you tell?"

All that could be seen out the Buick's windows were the road and the telephone poles. There was nothing whatever to indicate where they were on the more than eight-hundred-square-kilometer Estancia San Pedro y San Pablo, or, for that matter, where they had been or were going.

"I *know*, Don Cletus," Enrico said. "In ten, eleven minutes, we will be home."

"Then why didn't you wake me in ten, eleven minutes?"

"I thought you might wish to use the shaving machine, Don Cletus," Enrico said. "There should be one in the glove box. Your father believed a gentleman should always be shaved."

And yet another comparison I have failed with my father, Frade thought as he felt his chin.

And Enrico's right. I need a shave. I should have shaved when I showered. Maybe I had other things on my mind, like the look on that poor bastard's face when he took the load of double-aught buck in his chest.

Frade was uncomfortable using the Remington electric shaver; it had been his father's. But finally, after a moment's hesitation, he took it out and plugged it into the cigar lighter hole and, as the razor's blades hummed, started rubbing it against his face.

Two minutes after he started, Enrico slowed the Buick to a crawl, crossed himself, and muttered a prayer.

Now Frade knew where they were and why Enrico was praying—they were passing the spot where Frade's father had died. He didn't like to think about that.

Six minutes later, the three-row-thick stand of enormous poplars that surrounded the casa grande—"the big house"—protecting it from the winds of the pampas, appeared on the horizon.

A minute after that, the estancia airfield began to come into focus. A twin-engine Lockheed Lodestar, painted a brilliant red, was sitting in front of the hangar, dwarfing the four Piper Cubs parked beside it. Two peones on horseback sat watching it. When the Buick came closer still, Frade saw that they were cradling rifles in their arms and that a large fire extinguisher on wheels was beside the left engine of the Lodestar.

The plane was, as he had ordered it to be, ready to go at a moment's notice.

One of the gauchos doffed his flat-brimmed cap.

When the Buick passed through the outer line of poplars, the "big house" was visible beyond the inner two rows of trees. The term was somewhat misleading. There was indeed "a casa grande"—a rambling structure surrounded on three sides by wide porches—but the inner rows of poplars also encircled a complex of buildings. These included the small church La Capilla Nuestra Señora de los Milagros, seven smaller houses for the servants and the senior managers of the estancia, a large stable beside a polo field, the main garage, and "el Coronel's garage."

To which the shot-up station wagon will soon be taken—with a little luck, outside the view of Dorotea.

Between the second line of poplars and the line closest to the "Big House" was the English Garden, covering more than a hectare. Today, looking more than a little out of place, three more peones sat on their mounts, rifles cradled in their arms, as the horses helped themselves to whatever carefully cultivated flowers seemed appetizing.

The peones respectfully removed their wide-brimmed hats and sort of bowed when they saw Frade in the Buick. He returned the greeting with a sort of military salute. When he'd first become patrón of Estancia San Pedro y San Pablo, he had returned their gesture with a wave, as a salute was obviously inappropriate between himself, a Marine major, and Argentine civilians.

Waving had made him feel like he was pretending to be the King of LaLa-Land, condescendingly acknowledging the homage of his loyal subjects. Enrico had solved that problem by telling him that not only was there universal military service in Argentina, but el Coronel, and before him, el Coronel's father, Don Cletus's grandfather, also el Coronel Frade, had encouraged the "young men of the estancia" to enlist in the Húsares de Pueyrredón Cavalry Regiment for four years, rather than just doing a year's conscript service.

The result was that just about most of the more than one thousand male peones of Estancia San Pedro y San Pablo had been soldiers at one time. Frade thought, but did not say, that the real result was that he had, if not a private army, then a private battalion at his command. And lately he had cause to think he might have to use it.

So now Frade tossed a salute when el Patrón was saluted or otherwise acknowledged.

They passed through the inner line of poplars and rolled up to the big house. There were three more peones on horseback. And three people sitting bundled up against the winter chill in wicker chairs on the verandah. One was a tall muscular man in white riding britches, glistening boots, and a thick yellow woolen sweater. A beautiful sorrel mare tied to a hitching rail showed how he had come to the big house. Next to him was a large man in full gaucho regalia. A Ford Model A pickup truck parked nose-in against the verandah was his mode of transportation. Beside the gaucho, Doña Dorotea Mallín de Frade sat in a wicker armchair.

Frade did not see, however, whom he expected to see, and the moment he stepped out of the car, he asked, "Where's 'Wilhelm Fischer'?"

"Hello, my darling," the blonde said in British-accented English. "I'm so happy to be home. And how is every little thing with my beloved mother-to-be wife?"

"Hello, my darling," Frade said, "I'm so happy to be home. And how is every little thing with my beloved mother-to-be wife? And where the hell is 'Wilhelm Fischer'?"

She pointed to La Capilla Nuestra Señora de los Milagros, and when Frade looked at it, he saw there were two more peones on horseback, one in front of the chapel, the other to one side.

"He's not going anywhere he shouldn't, Major," the gaucho sitting on the porch said. "He asked if he could go to the church, and I figured, why not?"

The gaucho—despite his calf-high soft black leather boots, with billowing black *bombachas* tucked into them, loose white shirt with billowing sleeves, broad-brimmed black hat, wide silver-studded and buckled leather belt, wicked-looking fourteen-inch knife in a silver scabbard, and faultless command of the Spanish language—was not actually a gaucho.

For one thing, the last time he had been on a horse, it had been a pony at a Coney Island amusement park in Brooklyn. He had been six at the time, had fallen off, had his foot stepped on, and had since kept the vow he had made then to never again get on the back of a horse. He had acquired his Spanish from what he perhaps indelicately referred to as his "sleeping dictionary"—which was to say when he had been serving as a chief radioman at the U.S. Navy's Subic Bay facility in the Philippines. He was Lieutenant Oscar J. Schultz, USNR, and known as "El Jefe," which was Spanish for "The Chief."

"I need to talk to him," Frade said, and started to walk toward the church.

"Why don't you leave him alone?" Dorotea Mallín de Frade asked, on the edge of plaintively.

When her husband ignored her, she shook her head, got out of her wicker chair, and walked off the verandah to follow him.

Oberstleutnant Wilhelm Frogger, wearing a business suit, was on his knees at the communion rail of the chapel when Frade walked in.

In his pocket was a passport identifying him as Wilhelm Fischer, a vineyard owner and vintner, of Durban, South Africa.

Frade had carefully opened and then closed the heavy door behind him when he entered the church. He didn't think Frogger sensed that he was no longer alone.

Dorotea Frade tried to do the same, but a sudden burst of wind was too much for her and the door slammed noisily shut.

Frogger's head snapped to see what was happening, and then he returned to his prayers. Twenty seconds later, he stood up and walked down the aisle between the pews to Frade.

"You have learned what has happened to my parents?" he asked.

"God must have been listening," Frade said. "They're alive and well."

"Cletus! What a terrible thing to say!" Dorotea exclaimed.

"What, that his father and mother are alive?" Frade responded. "And I have something else to say, Colonel, that will probably upset my wife."

Frogger waited for him to go on, but didn't say anything.

"Your mother, sir, apparently believes that Hitler is a great man and that National Socialism is the hope of the world; she would, I am sure, do whatever she can to make her way back to the German Embassy. You'll understand I couldn't permit that to happen before you came here. Now that you are here, I must presume that she will know or learn—or guess—something of your relationship with Colonel von Stauffenberg, Major von Wachtstein, and Kapitän zur See Boltitz. Something, in other words, about Operation Valkyrie. I think your father shares your opinion of Hitler, but I'm not sure of that, and I can't take any chances. I absolutely cannot take the risk that your mother or father ever find themselves talking to any Germans under any circumstances. You take my meaning?"

Frogger met his eyes, then nodded. "I understand, Major."

Dorotea asked, obviously surprised, "He knows Peter? And Karl? And what's Operation Valkyrie?"

"I'll explain later," Frade said.

Her face showed she didn't like the response, but she didn't challenge it.

"I have to be absolutely sure we understand each other, Colonel," Frade said.

"I know the rules of the game we're playing, Major."

"That's a poor choice of words. It isn't a game."

"We understand each other, Major," Frogger said. "When will I be permitted to see my parents?"

"They're about three kilometers from here. But it's late, and I think it would be better if we went there first thing in the morning."

Frogger nodded but did not reply.

"Can you ride?" Frade asked.

"Of course."

"All right, then. I'll have Rodríguez have horses brought here at first light. Too early?"

"First light will be fine with me."

"Rodríguez and I'll go with you. I think that you should know that if it wasn't for Rodríguez, your parents would be dead, at the hands of some SS troops who came ashore from the U-405. He saved your parents' lives at no small risk to his own."

"Then I am, of course, grateful beyond—"

Frade silenced him by raising his hand.

"Rodríguez is a retired Argentine sergeant major who is not very fond of Germans. This is largely—but not entirely—because he was seriously wounded in the successful assassination attempt on my father, with whom he served all of his adult life. The assassination was ordered by either Himmler himself or someone close to him. Argentines carry grudges a long time."

What the hell, I'm going to have to tell her sooner or later—why not now?
Get it over with. . . .

"But while we're on the subject, Colonel, the Germans have twice attempted to assassinate me, most recently a couple of hours ago."

"Cletus, my God!" Dorotea exclaimed.

Frade looked at her and said, "All they managed to do was shoot up the Ford station wagon pretty badly."

He turned back to Oberstleutnant Frogger.

"I've just jumped on you, Colonel, for using the word 'game.' This is why; this isn't a game."

"Where did they try to kill you?" Dorotea asked softly.

"In front of the house on Avenida Coronel Díaz. I went there to take a shower. Three guys in a stolen Peugeot. Now deceased." He paused, looked between them, and went on: "In a massive understatement, I've had a busy day. What I want to do now is get a sandwich or something, then go to bed. We can talk some more in the morning, if you'd like."

"Fine," Frogger said.

"Rude question: How well do you ride? We have gentle mounts and the other kind; mostly the other kind."

"I think one of the gentle mounts, please. I really would prefer to wait for a Valkyrie maiden to carry me to Valhalla than get there—after having come all this way—by breaking my neck falling off a horse here."

He smiled shyly at Frade, and a hint of a smile crossed Frade's lips.

[SIX]
The Embassy of the German Reich
Avenida Córdoba
Buenos Aires, Argentina
0845 13 August 1943

Kapitän zur See Karl Boltitz had been told by Fräulein Hässell that the meeting had been called by Manfred Alois Graf von Lutzenberger. Lutzenberger was a small, very thin, slight, balding—he wore what was left of his hair plastered to his skull—fifty-three-year-old who served as Ambassador Extraordinary and Plenipotentiary of the German Reich to the Republic of Argentina. But the moment Boltitz walked into the ambassador's elegantly furnished office and saw "Commercial Attaché" Karl Cranz, he knew the meeting had been called by Cranz.

Boltitz, a tall, rather good-looking blond man of thirty-two, was the embassy's naval attaché.

"I am so glad that you could find time in your busy schedule for us, Herr Kapitän zur See," Cranz greeted him, smiling.

"Am I the last to arrive?"

"Rather obviously, wouldn't you say?" a man's voice asked just on the edge of nastily.

Boltitz turned toward the voice and saw Anton von Gradny-Sawz. A tall, almost handsome, somewhat overweight forty-five-year-old with a full head of luxuriant reddish-brown hair, von Gradny-Sawz was the embassy's first secretary. Boltitz considered him the typical Austrian: charming to superiors, condescendingly arrogant to those lower on the ladder. Boltitz also privately thought of him as "Die Grosse Wienerwurst."

"Mr. Ambassador," Boltitz said, looking back at Lutzenberger, "I am truly sorry to be late. I didn't know of the meeting until I came in, on time for my nine o'clock appointment with you."

Lutzenberger smiled—barely—but said nothing directly in reply.

"This meeting has been called at the request of our commercial attaché," von Lutzenberger said, and gestured toward Cranz.

"This is going to be one of those meetings that never happened," Cranz said with a smile.

This got the expected and dutiful polite laughter.

"Everyone is, of course, aware that our distinguished co-worker, Foreign Service Officer Grade 15 Wilhelm Frogger, and the charming Frau Frogger are among the missing," Cranz began. "There are a number of theories about this, to which we will turn in a moment, but before that, I'm afraid that I must inform you that we must add Obersturmführer Wilhelm Heitz and five of his fine men to the list of the missing."

"What happened to them?" von Gradny-Sawz asked in great surprise.

"The good news is they were not guarding those things placed into their hands when they went missing, and that those things are, as of—as of when, Raschner?"

"Oh eight fifteen, Mein Herr," Erich Raschner, a short, squat, phlegmatic Hessian, replied.

Boltitz thought that Raschner, at forty-five, was the second-oldest and second-most-dangerous man in the room—second in longevity to Ambassador von Lutzenberger and second in capacity for ruthless cruelty and cold-blooded murder only to Cranz.

And between those two, it's almost a tie.

"The special shipment was safe as of quarter past eight this morning," Cranz continued.

"I don't understand," von Gradny-Sawz said.

"That's the purpose of this meeting, Anton," Cranz said softly. "To, as well as I am able to do so, make you understand. May I continue?"

Von Gradny-Sawz flushed but didn't reply.

"This situation involves our good friend Oberst Juan Domingo Perón," Cranz went on. "To whom I went to see if he could be of some help in locating Herr and Frau Frogger for us.

"You will recall that when they went missing, several theories were floated about. One held that they didn't wish to be returned to Germany, that they suspected there were those who believed they were the traitors here in the embassy. Another was that they were in fact the traitors. I frankly never gave the latter much credence.

"Still another theory was that they had sold out to Herr Milton Leibermann, the 'legal attaché' of the American Embassy. Although we have nothing concrete to support this theory, I haven't completely discounted it. That obscene Hebrew is not nearly as stupid as he appears, and God only knows what he has been able to learn about our Uruguayan operation from the local Jews.

"And, of course, the name of Don Cletus Frade came up. I think we should all be prepared to admit that in judging this enemy of the Third Reich we all erred. That flamboyant cowboy act of his fooled us all. He is a very skilled and dangerous intelligence officer, and worse, very well connected with the president of Argentina and many of its senior army officers. In that regard, I think we must be objective and admit that the elimination of Oberst Frade was ill-advised; all it did was antagonize the Argentine officer corps and permit young Frade to ingratiate himself with them."

He paused to ask rhetorically, "Does Frade have the Froggers?" and then answered his own question:

"I just don't know. When I went to Oberst Perón, the oberst seemed to think this was a possibility. He said it had come to his attention that there was unusual activity at a small house, Casa Chica, Frade owns some distance from his estancia, near a place called Tandil. The late Oberst Frade used it, according to Perón, for romantic interludes with our Hansel's mother-in-law."

"Our Hansel" was Luftwaffe Major Freiherr Hans-Peter von Wachtstein, the embassy's assistant military attaché for air. He was married to Alicia de Carzino-Cormano, the youngest daughter—she was twenty—of la Señora Claudia de Carzino-Cormano, a widow who was one of the most wealthy women in Argentina.

"Perón said Casa Chica is quite charming—a small house on a mountainside, with a stream running past, far from curious eyes. That description was why I thought there might be something to Oberst Perón's notion that Don Cletus Frade might have been behind the disappearance of the Froggers and might in fact have them there.

"I asked Herr Raschner to look into it, and he sent Günther Loche down there to make discreet inquiries.

"And I must say our Günther did a good job," Cranz went on. "The details of what he found are unimportant except that they convinced me that there was a very strong likelihood that the Froggers were enjoying the hospitality of Don Cletus Frade.

"You will recall that shortly before SS-Brigadeführer von Deitzberg returned to the Fatherland, he issued orders that the security of the Reich demanded that the Froggers be eliminated wherever and whenever found. In the absence of orders to the contrary from Berlin, von Deitzberg's order remained in force. And I considered it my duty to carry out that order.

"The question then became, 'Now that we have found the Froggers, how do we eliminate them?'

"Günther reported there were at least ten of Don Cletus Frade's peones tending the two milk cows at Casa Chica, under the supervision of a man named Rodolfo Gómez, who we know is a retired cavalry sergeant who usually spends his time guarding Doña Dorotea Frade. That suggested that some of the peones might have military experience of their own. This theory was buttressed by Günther's report that, except for several of them armed with Thompson submachine guns, they were all armed with Mauser rifles.

"That then raised the question, 'How do we do what we feel has to be done? Where do we get the necessary forces to overcome a dozen or so well-armed men?'

"Raschner, in his usual tactless manner, quickly pointed out to me that the solution was right there in front of my nose. And—I always like to see that credit goes to where it belongs—came up with the solution to our problem.

"You will recall that Oberst Perón arranged with the commander of the Mountain Troops in San Martín de los Andes—a dedicated National Socialist and friend of Germany—to provide the security for the discharge of the special cargo from U-boat 405 at Samborombón Bay.

"So what I proposed to Perón was that he arrange for a suitable force of these men—say, forty men; two truckloads; about what they provided for Samborombón Bay—to be quietly moved to Tandil on a routine road-march maneuver.

"The Mountain Troops, noticing unusual activity at the late el Coronel Frade's little love nest, would investigate. Ten or a dozen gauchos, even those with prior military service—or perhaps *because* of that service—would not attempt to resist forty Mountain Troops, especially if they were armed with two water-cooled Maxim machine guns.

"The Froggers would be released, Oberst Perón could claim the credit for their being found and liberated, and Don Cletus Frade would have a good deal of explaining to do."

"That's absolutely brilliant, Herr Cranz," von Gradny-Sawz said.

"So Oberst Perón thought," Cranz said dryly. "But please let me continue. What *was* brilliant, Herr von Gradny-Sawz, was Raschner's modification to that plan. At Raschner's suggestion, I suggested to Oberst Perón the one flaw in the plan, and the solution for the flaw.

"Actually, if the plan Perón and von Gradny-Sawz thought was so brilliant had played out, it would have left us with the problem of the Froggers being alive. Getting them back to Germany would have been difficult at best, and once there, God only knows what they would have said to save their miserable lives.

"As I was saying, I suggested to Oberst Perón that there was a possible flaw in what he now thought of as his plan: What if, rather than the Froggers, Casa Chica held some dear friends of Don Cletus Frade—or, for that matter, Hansel's mother-in-law, la Señora Carzino-Cormano herself? Oberst Perón and the Mountain Troops would look pretty foolish if they trained machine guns on prominent Argentines having a more or less innocent romantic holi-day in the countryside.

"I also proposed a solution to the problem: that the Mountain Troops bring with them Obersturmführer Heitz and half a dozen of the other SS men enjoying the hospitality of the Mountain Troops.

"They could, I suggested, since they knew—and none of the Argentines knew—what the Froggers looked like—"

"How did they know?" von Gradny-Sawz interrupted. "Heitz and his men have never been to Buenos Aires; they went directly to San Martín de los Andes from Samborombón Bay."

"Bear with me, please, von Gradny-Sawz," Cranz said. His tone was icy.

Boltitz thought: *Cranz doesn't like Die Grosse Wienerwurst any more than I do. I suspect the only reason he hasn't ordered him back to Germany is that he knows he's going to need a scapegoat sooner or later, and Gradny-Sawz will be the man.*

"Before I was interrupted," Cranz went on, "I was saying, I suggested to Oberst Perón that the SS men could identify the Froggers and solve that problem.

"He thought that was a splendid idea. Then, when we had the schedule, Raschner met the little convoy some fifty kilometers from Tandil and had a pri-vate word with Obersturmführer Heitz.

"The plan that agreed with Perón, you will recall, was for the Mountain Troops to surround the house and put the machine guns in place. Obersturmführer Heitz would then reconnoiter the house to determine if it actually held the Froggers. If it did, he would return to the road and call for the occupants of the house to give up the Froggers.

"According to the story I got from Oberst Perón, Heitz had just about reached the house when someone fired at him. He naturally returned the fire—"

"Who shot at him?" von Gradny-Sawz asked.

Cranz gave him a withering look.

"That was a little theater, Gradny-Sawz," Cranz said. "His returning the hostile fire was a cue to his men to open fire. Can you grasp that?"

Von Gradny-Sawz did not reply.

"Which they immediately did," Cranz went on. "At that point, Oberst Perón, apparently having decided discretion was the better part of valor, ordered the Mountain Troops back onto their trucks and called to the men manning the machine guns, the storm troopers, to stop firing. Considering the roar of the guns, it is not surprising that they couldn't hear him. Or didn't understand his Spanish. In any event, they continued to fire.

"By the time that was straightened out, they had pretty well shot up the house. In Oberst Perón's professional military opinion, no one in the house could possibly have lived through the machine-gun fire.

"But Oberst Perón hadn't counted on the Froggers being killed at the hands of the Mountain Troops. It would have been embarrassing for the Mountain Troops and for him, personally, if that came out.

"Obersturmführer Heitz heroically volunteered to stay behind with his men when the Mountain Troops drove off. They would make sure that whoever had been in the house was in fact dead, and then deal with the bodies. Then one of the trucks would come back and pick them up.

"The truck returned for Heitz and his men when planned—that is to say, after nightfall. By then the press of his other duties had forced Oberst Perón to return to Buenos Aires, and the Mountain Troops, now all crammed into the other truck, were on their way back to San Martín de los Andes.

"The truck that went back for Heitz was under the command of a lieutenant. He reported to Oberst Perón that they found the bodies of Obersturmführer Heitz and his men in several places on the approaches to Casa Chica.

"Interestingly, there were no bodies in the house, or any blood to suggest that anyone in it had been wounded. It was the lieutenant's professional opinion that the people in the house had been warned of the coming attack and were prepared for it. In the lieutenant's opinion, Don Cletus Frade's gauchos had watched from a distance as the empty house was machine-gunned and as the trucks drove away.

"And then, when Heitz and his men, satisfied there was no one left alive in the house, approached it to make sure the Froggers were among the dead— Heitz's orders were to bury the Frogger bodies somewhere on the pampas where they would never be found—they were ambushed."

He paused to let them consider that.

Then finished: "And now the bodies of Obersturmführer Heitz and his men are buried where they will never be found on the pampas. The Mountain Troops lieutenant correctly decided that that was the option preferable to his having to explain at a roadblock what he was doing with the bullet-ridden bodies of half a dozen men in his truck. And so we have another example of what the Scottish poet Robert Burns had in mind when he wrote, *'The best laid schemes o' mice an' men Gang aft a-gley.'*"

"Our traitor strikes again," von Gradny-Sawz said solemnly.

"You think so, Gradny-Sawz?" Cranz asked.

Boltitz thought: *Wienerwurst, you are about to have that foot that's in your mouth shoved up your fat ass.*

"Herr Cranz, you yourself said the gauchos had been warned."

"And they probably had," Cranz agreed. "But by whom? Only Sturmbannführer Raschner and I knew the details of the operation. And trust me, Gradny-Sawz, on my SS officer's honor, neither of us betrayed the Fatherland.

"One possibility which must be considered, I suggest, is that, in addition to the gauchos tending the milch cows, there were gauchos elsewhere, and when two army trucks bearing the markings of the Mountain Regiment came down the road, they telephoned to Casa Chica. 'It may be nothing, Pedro,'" Cranz said in a mock Spanish accent, "'but there are two Mountain Regiment trucks headed your way.'"

"I didn't think of that possibility," von Gradny-Sawz admitted.

"Well, perhaps your talents lie in the diplomatic area, rather than the military," Cranz said. "Nor in the field of intelligence."

Cranz gave von Gradny-Sawz a long moment to consider that, then went on: "So where are we now? The black side of the picture is that the Froggers are not only still alive, but by now are far from Casa Chica.

"And since we must presume that if there were gauchos watching the exercise, they saw both the Mountain Troops and Oberst Perón.

"But I would rather doubt that they would bring this matter to the attention of the Argentine government. That would put Don Cletus Frade in the awkward position of explaining what he had at Casa Chica that was of such interest to Oberst Perón and, of course, the SS-SD.

"Now, with regard to Major Frade of the OSS: He landed in one of South American Airways' new Lockheed Lodestars at the Aerodromo Coronel Jorge G. Frade in Morón at five past one yesterday afternoon. His copilot was SAA Chief Pilot Gonzalo Delgano.

"They were met by el Coronel Alejandro Bernardo Martín, the Chief of the Ethical Standards Office of the Bureau of Internal Security, and by Sergeant Major Enrico Rodríguez, Cavalry, Retired. They went directly from the airfield to Don Cletus's house across from the Hipódromo on Libertador, which is currently occupied by Oberst Perón. We can presume that the faithful Sergeant Major Rodríguez told Don Cletus what had transpired at Casa Chica as they drove from the airport.

"I was aware that Oberst Perón had asked el Coronel Martín to bring Frade to him, the idea being that Perón would have a friendly, perhaps even fatherly, word with Frade about the foolishness of attempting to harbor the Froggers.

"Raschner and I, without confiding in Oberst Perón, had come up with an idea to send the Widow Frade an unmistakable message of exactly how dangerous it is to assist traitors to the German Reich. I will get to that shortly."

"The *Widow* Frade?" Boltitz asked.

"I'll get to that shortly, Boltitz. Pray let me continue."

"I beg pardon," Boltitz said.

Cranz nodded his acceptance of the apology, then went on: "Loche reported that Frade went to see Perón only after Martín very strongly insisted that he do so. Loche also reported that there was nothing on the airplane but cargo, presumably spare parts for the Lodestars.

"Since Raschner has so far been unable to get someone into the Frade mansion on Libertador, I didn't know what had transpired during their short meeting until Perón called me last evening and told me.

"I think we may also assume that el Coronel Martín had heard—possibly before Frade returned—at least something of what transpired. We know, of course, that Chief Pilot Delgano is actually Major Delgano of the Bureau of Internal Security, and that his role with SAA is to make sure that SAA does nothing against Argentine neutrality, with the secondary mission of keeping an eye on Frade generally.

"And knowing that Delgano would inevitably hear of what had happened at Casa Chica, I suspect that Doña Dorotea Frade would report to the authorities that there had been an attack for unknown reasons by a roving band of bandits, or whatever, on the house.

"We just don't know. We will have to find out. Raschner's working on that, and we all know how good our Erich is at that sort of thing.

"We do know what Oberst Perón told me on the telephone last night, and I'm afraid it was proof that once again I committed the cardinal sin of underestimating one's enemy.

"Frade lost no time whatever, it seems, in showing Oberst Perón that he had photographic proof that Perón had been at the machine guns with Heitz and his men, as well as photographs of the bullet-riddled bodies of Heitz and his men.

"He also told Perón that he had photographs of the map SS-Brigadeführer von Deitzberg had given him of postwar South America."

"Excuse me?" von Gradny-Sawz asked, visibly confused.

"Oh," Cranz said. "That's right. You weren't made privy to that, were you, Gradny-Sawz?"

Neither was I, Boltitz thought. *I have no idea what he's talking about. But he is intimating that Wienerwurst was the only one who doesn't know.*

"No, I wasn't," von Gradny-Sawz said, somewhat petulantly.

Did someone steal your ice-cream cone, Wienerwurst?

"It was a map prepared by the Army Topographical people showing South America after our Final Victory," Cranz explained. "Briefly, Uruguay and Paraguay will become provinces of Argentina."

I will be damned. Is that a fact, or something created to dazzle Perón?

"Frade told Perón that the first time he suspected an attempt was made on his life or on the lives of anyone close to him, the photographs and the map would be placed in the hands of the president of the Argentine Republic and appear in the world's newspapers."

"He's bluffing," von Gradny-Sawz said firmly.

"Possibly, even probably," Cranz said. "But we don't *know* that, do we, Gradny-Sawz? And do we want to chance he is not?"

Von Gradny-Sawz did not answer.

"Finally," Cranz said, "Frade told Perón he wanted him out of his house by today. And then—after Frade was attacked—he called Perón and said he was going to give Perón the benefit of the doubt, that Perón simply had not had the time to call his German friends off before the attack, but that he suggested that Perón should make that call now."

"What attack on him?" Boltitz asked.

"According to today's *La Nación,*" Cranz said conversationally, "three criminals bent on robbing the Frade mansion—actually, it didn't say 'Frade mansion'; it said 'a residence on Avenida Coronel Díaz'—were interrupted by alert police and died in a gun battle that followed."

And that explains the message you were going to send to the Widow Frade, doesn't it, you murderous bastard?

"To recapitulate, gentlemen: Both operations—eliminating the Froggers in Tandil and eliminating Frade here—failed. The only good thing to come out of it is that we have further leverage with Oberst Perón.

"We must presume that the Froggers are still alive. That situation is unacceptable. I think we can safely presume that Don Cletus Frade has them. Or at least had them. There has been a report that a British cruiser in Rio de Janeiro took aboard a middle-aged couple, but until we know it was the Froggers, we must presume it wasn't them."

He looked around the room.

"Any questions, comments?"

"We have to get rid of Frade," von Gradny-Sawz said solemnly.

"You think so, Gradny-Sawz?" Cranz asked softly.

"To me it is self-evident."

"Let me tell you what is self-evident to me, Gradny-Sawz, and probably to these other gentlemen. We have been sent a message by el Coronel Martín. And that message is that he knows we have failed, for the second time, to remove el Señor Frade from the scene. Otherwise, you see, Gradny-Sawz, el Señor Frade would be facing criminal charges for manslaughter. He could probably successfully plead self-defense, but it would be all over the newspapers.

"If that happened, people would ask, Gradny-Sawz, who could possibly want to assassinate the son of one of Argentina's beloved sons, who was himself assassinated. Give your imagination free rein, Gradny-Sawz, and guess who would come under suspicion. The French, perhaps? The Uruguayans?

"Do you think it's possible people would suspect us? And if that came to pass, do you think that Frade's photographs, sure to be introduced at his trial, would serve to confirm that suspicion?

"Our mission, Gradny-Sawz, is to ensure the Argentines think of Germany as an honorable ally in the battle against the godless Communists. Having it come out that we are even remotely connected with the assassination of el Coronel Frade, the *two* failed assassination attempts on his son, and the incident at Casa Chica would hardly serve to confirm the image we are trying to project, would it?"

Von Gradny-Sawz looked very uncomfortable.

"Well, I'll tell you what, Gradny-Sawz," Cranz went on. "You come up with a plan that absolutely precludes the possibility that photographs of Juan Domingo Perón with a group of SS personnel at a machine gun, the bodies of those SS personnel sometime later, riddled with bullets, and a map showing what looks like the Third Reich's plans for South America appearing in *La Nación* or any other newspaper, and I will give you permission to eliminate Don Cletus Frade yourself.

"And while you're doing that, I will inform SS-Brigadeführer von Deitzberg that it is my professional judgment that this American OSS sonofabitch poses an immediate threat to Operation Phoenix and the other operation and has to be dealt with. I will seek SS-Brigadeführer von Deitzberg's wise advice and direction on how to do that, as I can think of no way to do anything that would not cause an international incident that would pose serious problems to Operation Phoenix.

"Except, of course, to send Boltitz home with von Wachtstein to charm the sonofabitch as best they can, and to learn as much as they can about what he's up to. Understand, Gradny-Sawz? The Yankee OSS sonofabitch has got us cornered. And I'm not going to be the man responsible for the failure of Operation Phoenix."

He let that sink in a moment, then stood up.

His right arm snapped out in front of him.

"Heil Hitler!" he barked, then marched out of the room.

[SEVEN]
Estancia San Pedro y San Pablo
Near Pila
Buenos Aires Province, Argentina
1230 13 August 1943

Don Cletus Frade, wearing khaki trousers and a yellow polo shirt, came out onto the shaded verandah of the big house carrying a bottle of Bodega Don Guillermo Cabernet Sauvignon '39, two long-stemmed wineglasses, a long black cigar, and a corkscrew bottle opener.

Two people hurried after him. One was a plump female in her late forties wearing a severe black dress, Elisa Gómez. The other was Enrico Rodríguez, wearing a business suit and cradling his twelve-gauge Remington Model 11 riot gun in his arms. Around his neck was a leather bandolier of brass-cased double-aught buckshot shells.

"All you had to do was ring, Don Cletus," Elisa Gómez chided him as she took the bottle from him. Her tone suggested that the chief housekeeper of Estancia San Pedro y San Pablo was not in awe of its patrón.

"I humbly beg your pardon," Frade said, deeply insincere.

She shook her head, quickly uncorked the wine, poured a taste in one of his glasses, and waited for his reaction. He swirled the wine, sniffed at the glass, and finally took a sip. And grimaced.

"I think I've been poisoned," he announced.

She shook her head, filled the glass, and marched into the house.

"Enrico, why do I think she doesn't like me?" Frade asked.

"Don Cletus, she loves you," Enrico said, and then added, "And you know it."

Frade lowered himself onto a leather-cushioned wicker armchair, crossed his battered Western boots on the matching footstool, bit the end from the cigar, and then lit it carefully with a wooden match. Then he picked up the wineglass and took a healthy sip.

Five minutes later, a glistening black 1940 Packard 160 convertible coupe drove through the windbreak of trees that surrounded the heart of Estancia San Pedro y San Pablo. Frade had been waiting for the Packard to appear. As soon as the car had left Estancia Santa Catalina on a road that led only to Estancia San Pedro y San Pablo, its presence had been reported to the big house by one of Frade's peones.

Clete thought the Packard was gorgeous. It had been the top of the Packard line, except for limousines, and only a few—no more than two hundred—had been manufactured. Beneath its massive hood was the largest Packard Straight-Eight engine, which provided enough power for it to cruise effortlessly and endlessly at well over eighty miles an hour. It was upholstered in red leather and had white sidewall tires.

Each front fender carried a spare tire and wheel, and sitting on the front edge of the fenders was the latest thing in driving convenience: turn signals. With the flipping of a little lever on the steering wheel, one of the front lights flashed simultaneously with one on the rear, telling others you wished to change direction, and in which direction.

The Reverend Kurt Welner, S.J., stepped out of the Packard, put on his suit jacket—shooting his cuffs, which revealed gold cuff links adorned with some sort of gemstone—then walked up the shallow flight of stairs to the verandah.

Enrico, who was sitting in a folding wooden chair, got respectfully to his feet. Frade didn't move.

"Welcome home," Welner said.

"Thank you," Clete said. "But you could have told me that at Claudia's 'Welcome Home, Cletus' party tonight. What are you up to?"

"I wanted to talk to you."

"You could have done that tonight, too, or on the phone."

"In person."

"About what? Be warned: If I don't like the answer, no wine flows into your glass."

"Is this one of those days when you're determined to be difficult?"

"Probably."

"Well, one of the things on my mind is that you have to go to the Recoleta cemetery within the next couple of days."

"Why would I want to do that?"

"Because the brothers want to see if you approve of their cleaning of the Frade tomb."

"Since I don't think you're trying to be funny, you can have a little wine."

"You are so kind," Welner said as he sat down in the other wicker chair.

Frade poured wine into the priest's glass.

"Being kind gets me in all kinds of trouble," Frade said. "By 'the brothers,' you mean the monks who run the cemetery?"

"No. I meant the brothers. Are you interested in the difference between monks and brothers?"

"Spare me. Why did they clean the tomb?"

"Because the marble was dirty, and I understand there was a little corrosion here and there."

"I think I'm beginning to understand. In addition to my saying 'thank you,' they would not be offended if I slipped them an envelope stuffed with money?"

"That would be very nice of you, if you should feel so inclined."

"Am I supposed to believe that you drove all the way over here from Claudia's just to tell me that?"

"I had a few other things on my mind."

"For example?"

"How did you find the United States?"

"Well, I set the compass on north-northwest, and eventually, there it was, right out in front of the airplane."

The priest shook his head tolerantly.

"Things went well?"

"All the pilots of South American Airways now have their air transport rating, if that's what you're asking."

"The problem of insurance has been resolved?"

"It's a done deal," Frade said.

"That's good to hear."

"Why do I have this feeling that, having beat around the bush long enough, you are about to get to your real reason for coming over here?"

"I happened to be driving past your house on Avenida Libertador—"

"Ah-ha! And was that before or after your spies on the premises—"

"Getting right to the point, Cletus: Why did Juan Domingo Perón suddenly stop accepting your kind hospitality?"

"Now that you mention it, it probably had something to do with what I said to him."

"And what was that?"

"If I remember correctly, and I usually do, what I said was, 'One more thing, Tío Juan, you degenerate sonofabitch. You're going to have to find someplace else for your little girls. I want you out of here by tomorrow.' Or words to that effect."

"You didn't!" Welner blurted.

"Tell him, Enrico."

The priest looked at Enrico, who nodded.

"Are you out of your mind, Cletus?" Welner asked.

"Not so far as I know. I confess to being a little annoyed with my godfather at the time."

"About what?"

"Well, just before I said that, he pointed a pistol at me. I get very annoyed when people point pistols at me. And so does Enrico. For a couple of seconds there, I thought Enrico's shotgun might go off and cause a tragic accident."

Welner again looked at Enrico, who again nodded.

"What set this off?" Welner asked.

"Well—are you sure you want to know?"

"Yes, I'm sure."

"Saved by the belle," Frade then said.

"Excuse me?"

"Belle with an 'e' at the end. As in: 'Belle on horseback.' Drink your wine, Father, before the posse gets here and the sheriff tries to shut us off before dinner."

When Frade had awakened that morning, he'd been alone in bed. It was long after first light, and Dorotea was nowhere around. He found a note stuck with a blob of Vaseline onto the bathroom mirror:

Darling, I didn't have the heart to wake you. Madison and I have taken Mr. Fischer to see his family. Be back for lunch or earlier. Dorotea.

Frade now pointed at the break in the trees, and Welner looked where he pointed.

A line of people on horseback, led by Doña Dorotea and trailed by Wilhelm Fischer, Captain Madison R. Sawyer III, and half a dozen peones, was coming toward them at a walk.

This was lost on Father Welner, but there was more than a passing similarity to a scene in a Western movie where the posse returns from cutting off the bandits at the pass. Everyone but Fischer was holding a long arm either cradled in the arm or upright, with the butt resting on the saddle. Dorotea had a double-barreled shotgun, and Sawyer a Thompson submachine gun with a fifty-round drum magazine. Everything else was there except dead bandits tied across saddles.

Dorotea, Sawyer, and Fischer walked their horses to the verandah, dismounted, tied the horses to a hitching rail, and went onto the verandah.

"Howdy," Frade said. "How about a little something to cut the dust of the trail?"

Dorotea looked at her husband and shook her head. Then she kissed her husband affectionately and the priest formally.

"Father, this is Mr. Wilhelm Fischer," Dorotea said. "He's come all the way from South Africa to see how we grow grapes and make wine. Willi, this is Father Welner, an old and dear friend."

Frade saw the look on Welner's face.

"Hey, Padre," Frade said as Welner and Fischer shook hands, "you ever hear that curiosity killed the cat?"

The priest did not reply directly.

"Welcome to Argentina, Mr. Fischer," he said.

III

Cletus Frade was well turned out in a tweed suit from London's Savile Row for the "supper" la Señora Claudia de Carzino-Cormano was giving to mark the return of Frade from the United States. "Supper" was a code word. "Dinner" would have meant black-tie. Frade had one of those, too, also from Savile Row. He also had a silk dressing gown and two dozen shirts from Sulka's in Paris.

All of the clothing had been his father's. He was comfortable wearing it, because when he had found it in one of the two wardrobes in the master suite of the big house, it all had been in unopened boxes.

A tailor from Buenos Aires had been summoned to adjust the unused clothing to fit Clete—not much had been required—and to adjust the clothing that his father actually had worn to fit Enrico. His father had been, to use a term from Midland, Texas, where Clete had been raised, something of a clotheshorse.

Frade had observed at the time that he now had all the clothing he would need for his lifetime.

He would not have been mistaken for a Londoner, however, or even for an Argentine who patronized the tailors of Savile Row or the linen shops on the Rue de Castiglione in Paris. Because when he climbed down from the driver's seat of the Horch before the verandah of the big house of Estancia Santa Catalina, not only was he wearing a gray Stetson "Cattleman" hat, but when his trouser legs were pulled up, they revealed not silken hose but the dully gleaming leather calf of Western boots, finely tooled, and bearing his initials in contrasting red leather.

There were a dozen large automobiles already parked at Claudia's big house, including two Rolls-Royces, two Cadillacs, half a dozen Mercedeses, and a pair of Packards, one of them Father Welner's. He didn't see the olive-drab

Mercedes that was provided to el Coronel Juan D. Perón as the Argentine secretary of state for labor and welfare.

The Rolls-Royce Wraith Saloon Touring limousine belonged to his uncle, Humberto Valdez Duarte, who was the managing director of the Anglo-Argentine Bank. In Argentina, managing director translated to chairman of the board. Duarte, a tall, slender man of forty-six, was married to Beatriz Frade de Duarte, Clete's father's sister.

The 1939 Rolls-Royce Phantom III James Young–bodied "Drop Head" (convertible) belonged to Clete's father-in-law, Enrico Mallín, managing director of the Sociedad Mercantil de Importación de Productos Petrolíferos (SMIPP). Mallín—a forty-two-year-old Argentine who stood six-foot-two, weighed one hundred ninety-five pounds, and had a full head of dark-brown hair and a massive, immaculately trimmed mustache—didn't like his son-in-law at all. And the feeling was mutual.

As Clete walked onto the verandah with Dorotea, he could see the other guests having a cocktail in the sitting room, the other side of a reception line headed by Doña Claudia de Carzino-Cormano with her daughters, Alicia, Baroness von Wachtstein, and Isabela, a quite beautiful, black-haired, stylishly dressed female whom Clete thought of, and often referred to, as "El Bitcho."

Dorotea led the way down the reception line.

She and Claudia exchanged compliments.

Fischer followed her.

"Claudia, this is Wilhelm Fischer. He's from South Africa, and he's come here to show us how to grow grapes. Willi, this is our hostess, la Señora Carzino-Cormano, known as the Lioness of the Pampas."

"How do you do?" Claudia replied as she flashed Clete an icy look. "Welcome to Estancia Santa Catalina."

"You are very kind to have me, madam," Fischer replied, and—certainly without thinking about it—clicked his heels as he bent over her hand.

"I thought only Germans did that," Cletus said.

"Cletus, my God!" Claudia exclaimed.

"Did I say something wrong again?"

She did not respond directly.

"This is your party, Cletus," Claudia said. "You're supposed to be standing here greeting people. And then you're the last to show up."

Then she kissed his cheek—a real kiss, as opposed to *pro forma*.

"I don't do standing in line very well," he said.

She shook her head, then said, "Juan Domingo called. He can't be here."

"Oh, God, what a shame!" Frade replied with great insincerity, then moved to Alicia.

"Alicia, this is . . ."

"I heard," she said. "Welcome to our home, Mr. Fischer. I'm Alicia von Wachtstein."

"The baroness von Wachtstein," Clete furnished. "You are required to back out of her presence."

"Oh, God, Clete, don't you ever stop?" she said, giggling.

"You are very kind," Fischer said, and bent over her hand, this time not clicking his heels.

"And this, Willi, is la Señorita Isabela Carzino-Cormano."

Isabela neither smiled nor offered Fischer her hand.

"How do you do?" she said rather icily to Fischer.

"Any friend of mine, right, Izzy baby?" Frade said.

Isabela glowered at Frade, then put out her hand to Fischer, who bent over it and remembered again not to click his heels.

Dorotea and Alicia, now arm in arm, walked into the house.

"Now that the ladies have gone to powder their noses, or whatever, Willi, why don't we go to Switzerland?"

"Excuse me?"

"Over there," Clete said, nodding at a corner of the room where Father Welner, Karl Boltitz, Peter von Wachtstein, and Humberto Duarte stood talking.

He took Fischer's arm and propelled him across the room. It was an opportunity he didn't think he would have.

The men, all holding drinks, stopped talking when Frade and Fischer walked up.

"I was just telling Willi, here," Frade said, "that this is Switzerland, a neutral corner of the property where, under the benevolent eye of Father Welner, we're all noncombatants. Willi, you know Father Welner, of course, and my Uncle Humberto."

Humberto Duarte smiled and said, "Of course," although he had never seen Fischer before.

"These gentlemen, Willi, are Major Freiherr Hans-Peter von Wachtstein, whose wife you just met, and Kapitän zur See Karl Boltitz, of the German Embassy. Gentlemen, this is Wilhelm Fischer, whom Humberto prevailed upon to come all the way here from South Africa to teach me how to grow better grapes."

In turn, von Wachtstein and Boltitz clicked their heels as they offered Fischer their hands. And again Fischer remembered not to click his.

A maid walked up with drinks on a tray, interrupting the conversation. When Frade had taken a bourbon and water and Fischer a glass of red wine, and she left, Boltitz asked: "If I may ask, Mr. Fischer, is Afrikaans anything like German?"

"If you're politely asking if Willi speaks German, Karl," Frade said. "Yes, he does."

"Then we can chat in German," Boltitz said.

"He got his the same way Hansel and El Jefe got their Spanish," Frade said.

"How is that?" Boltitz asked a little uneasily.

"He had a sleeping dictionary," Frade said. "And even more interesting, you have a mutual friend. Claus something. What was your friend's last name, Willi?"

Fischer met his eyes for a moment.

"Von Stauffenberg," Fischer said. "Claus, Graf von Stauffenberg."

"I don't place the name," Boltitz said.

"Nor I," von Wachtstein said.

"Sure you do, Hansel," Frade said. "You told me you visited him in the hospital."

Von Wachtstein looked at Frade as if Frade had lost his mind.

"I was with Claus the day before he was . . . injured," Fischer said.

"Cletus, what the hell is going on here?" von Wachtstein snapped.

"Just remember that this is Wilhelm Fischer, of Durban, South Africa, whom Humberto arranged to come here to teach me how to grow better grapes," Frade said. "None of us can afford to have anyone—especially El Bitcho—looking at him suspiciously."

"Cletus," Boltitz said very seriously, "Delgano is paid to be suspicious, he's very good at being suspicious, and it looks as if he's about to walk over here."

"Not a problem. He already knows who Willi really is."

"And who might that be?" von Wachtstein asked more than a little sarcastically.

"Oberstleutnant Wilhelm Frogger, late of the Afrikakorps, Herr Major," Fischer said. "And more recently of the Senior German Officer Prisoner of War Detention Facility at Camp Clinton, Mississippi."

He let that sink in a moment.

"I saw it as my duty as a German officer to give my parole to Major Frade in order to assist him in dealing with my parents. And to assist however I can in that other project you and our friend Claus are involved in."

Neither von Wachtstein nor Boltitz could keep their surprise—even shock—off their faces.

"We'll all have to get together, and soon, to have a little chat," Frade said, then turned to face a short, muscular man of about forty with large dark eyes.

"Ah, Gonzalo!" he said. "Willi, this is Gonzalo Delgano, chief pilot of South American Airways. Gonzo, this is Mr. Wilhelm Fischer, who has come all the way from South Africa to teach me how to grow grapes."

"How do you do, Mr. Fischer?" Delgano asked. "Welcome to Argentina."

[TWO]
Estancia Santa Catalina
Near Pila
Buenos Aires Province, Argentina
2320 13 August 1943

Cletus Frade was already annoyed when Father Welner came up to him in the library, where, over postdinner brandy and cigars, he was talking business with Humberto Duarte, Gonzalo Delgano, and Guillermo de Filippi, SAA's chief of maintenance. Frade, at Delgano's suggestion, had hired de Filippi away from Aeropostal, the Argentine airline, to work for SAA.

Like Delgano, de Filippi was a former officer of the Argentine army air service. According to Delgano, he had gone to Aeropostal after he had failed a flight physical and could medically retire. Frade wasn't sure how true this story was. It was entirely possible that de Filippi, like Delgano, was actually working for the Bureau of Internal Security and that el Coronel Alejandro Bernardo Martín had ordered Delgano to get SAA to hire him as another means of keeping an eye on SAA.

But it wasn't this that bothered Frade, who knew that Martín and BIS were going to watch SAA as a hawk watches a prairie dog. It was de Filippi himself. Behind his back, when talking to Delgano, he called de Filippi "Señor Mañana," which made reference to de Filippi's standard reply when asked when something he had been told to do would be done. *Mañana* was the Spanish word for "tomorrow."

De Filippi had just told Frade that it would not be the day after *mañana*, but the day after the day after *mañana* before the Lodestar that Clete and Delgano had flown from Burbank would be ready to fly to Rosario, Córdoba, and Mendoza.

"May I see you a moment, Don Cletus?" the priest asked.

Frade held up a finger to ask Welner to wait, then turned to de Filippi.

"Tell you what we're going to do, Guillermo," Frade said. "Two things. One: It is now standard company policy that the absolute maximum turn-around time for any of our aircraft not requiring scheduled maintenance—like, for example, a one-hundred-hour overhaul—is twelve hours. Two: The day after *mañana*, since Gonzo and I are trying to get this airline off the ground sometime this year, SAA will rent my Lodestar for our trip. Any problem with that, Guillermo?"

He didn't wait to hear Señor Mañana's reply, if any, instead pushing himself somewhat awkwardly out of his chair—he had a large cigar in one hand and a large brandy snifter in the other—and motioned with his head toward a relatively unoccupied corner of the library.

When the priest had followed him there, Frade said unctuously, "Tell me how I may help you, my son."

Welner, smiling, shook his head in resignation.

"I don't suppose it has occurred to you that the way you jumped all over de Filippi might be counterproductive?"

"On the other hand, it might not. *Mañana* is not a good way to do business."

"This is Argentina, Cletus. Not the U.S. Corps of Marines."

"I've noticed. Your nickel, Padre."

"Excuse me?"

"An Americanism. Since you dropped a nickel in the telephone to talk to me, the presumption is that you had something to say."

"I never heard that before. What I wanted to ask, Cletus, is if I might stay at Estancia San Pedro y San Pablo tonight."

"Why would you want to do that?"

"I presumed I was invited on the bird shoot tomorrow."

Oh, shit. I thought I'd gotten rid of him.

"If you would be so kind as to put me up," Welner went on, "I wouldn't have to get up in the wee hours to drive over there. And if I left here, some other of Claudia's guests could spend the night."

"You're a bird shooter?"

"Does that surprise you?"

"Yeah, it does."

"Did you notice the four Browning over-and-under shotguns in the gun cabinet to the left?"

"Yeah, I did. Two identical Diamond Grade .16s and two .28s. It made me curious."

"One of each, thanks to your father's generosity to a poor priest, are mine."

Frade exhaled audibly.

"You know you're always welcome in my house," he said. "But tomorrow's not such a good idea."

"I thought you might have something in mind for tomorrow in addition to slaughtering innocent perdices, or maybe even instead of slaughtering them."

"Not admitting anything, but would your feelings be hurt if I told you I don't think you'd want to know what that might be?"

"You can't hurt my feelings, Cletus. I would have thought you would know that by now. And you're wrong. I do want to know. I can't help you if I don't know what you're up to."

Frade didn't reply.

After a moment, the priest said, "Maybe I can help in some way to keep Mr. Fischer's parents alive. I would like to try."

Frade met Welner's eyes for a long moment.

"Tell you what, Padre," he said. "Why don't you spend the night at Estancia San Pedro y San Pablo? That way you won't have to get up in the middle of the night to drive over there."

"What an excellent idea," the priest said. "I should have thought of that myself."

"Changing the subject: Are you familiar with that old English saying 'In for a penny, in for a pound'?"

"Oh, yes," Welner said.

Frade raised his brandy snifter.

"Mud in your eye, Padre."

[THREE]
Estancia San Pedro y San Pablo
Near Pila
Buenos Aires Province,
Argentina
0630 14 August 1943

While it was assumed that the peones of Estancia San Pedro y San Pablo were completely trustworthy, Enrico pointed out that money talked, and that it was unlikely but possible that some of the technicians working on the place might be on the payroll of someone else.

They knew, for example, that Carlos Aguirre, the airframe and power plant mechanic el Coronel had hired to maintain his Beechcraft Staggerwing and the Piper Cubs, was an agent of the Bureau of Internal Security. They knew because Gonzalo Delgano told them. Delgano knew because, when he had been on the estancia's payroll as the Beechcraft's pilot and as el Coronel's instructor pilot, he had all the time been an army officer attached to the BIS, charged with reporting on el Coronel Frade's activities.

Against the remote—but nevertheless real—possibility that someone besides Carlos Aguirre was in the employ of BIS, or, for that matter, someone in the employ of the German Embassy, would report that when the group came to Estancia San Pedro y San Pablo before sunrise, von Wachtstein, Boltitz, Father Welner, and Humberto Duarte had not gone bird hunting as announced, Clete Frade decided that they would in fact go bird hunting.

A fairly complicated hunting expedition was organized. A wrangler had horses waiting for all the men when they came out of the big house after a breakfast buffet. So was a horse-drawn wagon carrying shotguns, ammunition, and the makings of a midmorning snack break. A second horse-drawn wagon carried the dogs—eight Llewellyn setters—and three handlers for them.

Everyone mounted up. Then Clete—to the amusement of the dozen mounted peones who would go with them—had his usual difficulty with Julius Caesar. The large, high-spirited black stallion had never been ridden by anyone but el Coronel and manifested its resentment of its new master by trying very hard to throw Clete. When Frade finally got control of his mount, the party walked their horses through the formal gardens and out onto the pampas, with the wagons following.

Four kilometers or so from the big house, they dismounted and collected their weapons from the wagon. Clete's father's hunting equipment included something he had never seen before: a leather shell bag, which looked to him like a woman's purse on an extra-long strap.

And he was again wearing more of his father's clothing, in this instance boots and a Barbour jacket. He had never seen one of these before, and as Father Welner had seen him suspiciously eyeing and feeling the material, the priest said, "Not to worry, my son, the Queen has one just like it."

"It looks greasy," Clete said.

"They wax the thread before they weave the cloth."

All four of the Diamond Grade Brownings had been brought along in a rack that looked as if it had been made for precisely that purpose. Clete saw the priest take the 28-bore rather than the 16.

Ah, we're going to play King of the Mountain!

He took the other 28-bore from its rack.

"The way your father and I shot," the priest said, "was by turns. You shoot until you miss, and then the other chap."

"After you, Padre," Clete said, grandly waving Welner ahead of him onto the grass of the plain.

The Llewellyns were both very good hunters and superbly trained. They picked up a scent within two minutes, found birds not quite a minute after that, and held the point perfectly until the birds took flight and the priest had fired.

Two perdices fell to the ground.

"Good shooting," Clete said politely.

"Lucky," the priest said politely.

He was lucky six times in a row before he missed.

"Tough luck," Clete said politely as he fed two shells to his over-and-under shotgun.

"I think it was badly loaded shells," the priest said. "You might take that into consideration should you have any difficulty."

The eyes of Texas are upon you, Cletus, he thought as he started after the Llewellyns.

As well as those of the smug Jesuit.

And, of course, the eyes of the members of your private army, who are probably praying the Good Father makes a monkey of el patrón.

Don't fuck up!

He dropped nineteen birds—eight of them in doubles—before missing. When he finally missed, he turned to Father Welner and said, "You must be right about the faulty shells. I usually shoot much better than this."

By then it was quarter past ten, and they stopped the hunt for a break.

And to get down to the business of the day. Which was getting Frogger to trust Hans-Peter von Wachtstein and Karl Boltitz and vice versa.

As far as he was concerned regarding Frogger, Allen Dulles apparently knew enough about him to trust him. Clete had had no choice but to go along with that. Moreover, unprofessionally, he had the gut feeling that Frogger was one of the good guys.

And he, of course, knew that Boltitz and von Wachtstein could be trusted.

The problem was that they didn't trust Frogger—they didn't know him, or that he was what he said he was. And the reverse was true. Clete thought that if he were in any of their shoes, he would have felt the same way.

That had to be changed.

If their conversation—mutual interrogation—went sour, as it very possibly would, Clete had a hole card in his chest pocket. It was a letter from General von Wachtstein that Captain Dieter von und zu Aschenburg, at considerable personal risk, had carried to Hans-Peter von Wachtstein shortly after von Wachtstein had arrived in Argentina.

In the letter, General von Wachtstein told his son that he had belatedly realized it was his duty to do whatever he could to rid Germany of Adolf Hitler.

He had begun the letter: *The greatest violation of the code of chivalry by which I, and you, and your brothers, and so many of the von Wachtsteins before us, have tried to live is, of course, regicide. I want you to know that before I decided that honor demands I contribute what I can to such a course of action, I considered all of the ramifications, both spiritual and worldly, and that I am at peace with my decision.*

Clete's father had read the letter. It had caused the tough old cavalryman to weep.

If things did not go the way Frade hoped they would—*the way they had to go*—Frade was going to show the letter to Frogger, even though this would enrage Peter, would make him feel that Frade had not only betrayed him but had sentenced his father to death by hanging from a butcher's hook by piano wire.

Frade raised his arm over his head and, fist balled, made the U.S. Marine Corps hand signal for *Gather on me* by making a pumping motion.

Whether that was also a hand signal of the Húsares de Pueyrredón or not, Enrico Rodríguez, whom Clete was starting to think of as the wagon master leading the pioneers across the prairie, understood it. He and the wagons and horsemen, who had followed the hunters across the pampas, now headed for them.

"Leave the lunch wagon," Clete ordered when Enrico rode up, "and then take everybody far enough away so they won't be able to hear us talking."

"*Sí, señor.*"

Frade turned to Welner and said, "Father, I have no problem with you hearing this, but it's up to them, not me."

Frogger, von Wachtstein, and Boltitz looked at them.

"For what it's worth, I trust Father Welner with my life," Clete said. "And he already knows a hell of a lot; just about everything."

The three Germans looked among themselves.

"Father," Boltitz finally said, "are you sure you want to know about this?"

"I wish I didn't know any of it," the priest said. "What I am sure of is that what I would like to do is keep your parents alive. The more I know, the better chance I will have to do that. If I have to say this, I swear before God that nothing I hear here today will go any further."

The Germans looked at each other again. Finally, von Wachtstein and then Frogger nodded.

"Please stay, Father," Boltitz said. "And getting right to the point of this, what Peter and I have to do, with the lives of many people at stake, is determine that Oberstleutnant Frogger is who he and—no offense intended—Major Frade say he is."

"And the reverse is true, Herr Kapitän zur See," Frogger said stiffly. "The only person vouching for you is Major Frade. How do I know you are who you say you are?"

The irony of three traitors standing around a wagon in the middle of nowhere on the pampas drinking coffee and eating pastry while trying to determine that the others were also *bona fide* traitors was not lost on Frade. It would have been almost funny if so much, and so many lives, were not at stake.

It also made him consider treason and traitors. Until he came to Argentina, it had been simple: *Anyone who is a traitor is a no-good sonofabitch. One beneath contempt.*

But these three honorable men, these decent officers who actually tried to live by a code of chivalry that Frade thought was ridiculous in these times, were putting their lives on the line to be traitors. He admired them all, and doubted that he would have been able to handle being in their shoes.

Peter and I don't belong in this. We should be at the controls of fighter planes. Philosophical introspection is not needed in a cockpit. You shoot the other guy down, or he shoots you down. Very simple.

The mutual investigation lasted for thirty-five minutes. Frade was impressed with Boltitz's skill as an interrogator, and Frogger was nearly as good.

By comparison, Peter and I seem rank amateurs. Which, of course, we are.

"I pray to God that I am not wrong, Herr Kapitän zur See," Frogger said finally. "But I believe that you are who you say are, personally, and further that you are allied with us in what we have undertaken."

Boltitz gave Frogger his hand.

"Hey, what am I?" Peter asked.

"Claus vouched for you, Herr Major," Frogger said. "He said if it was impossible to keep you out of our enterprise, then I could trust you with my life."

And who the hell am I? Frade wondered. *Like it or not, guys, I'm the guy you have to trust with your lives.*

"Our immediate problem is my mother," Frogger said.

"How's that?" Welner asked.

"When I saw her yesterday, Father," Frogger said evenly, "and told her that I had come to see that she and my father cooperated with Major Frade in collecting information about Operation Phoenix and on that ransoming operation, she said I was a despicable traitor to Germany and to my family and my late brothers, and that she hoped I was going to burn in hell for breaking my vow of obedience to 'unser Führer.'"

The priest shook his head.

"Perhaps I can reason with her, perhaps pray with her for God's guidance."

"I don't think that would be a solution to the problem, Father," Frogger said. "Especially if she suspects—and I'm afraid she's paranoid enough to do just that—what we plan to do to 'our leader.'"

[FOUR]
Casa Número Cincuenta y Dos
Estancia San Pedro y San Pablo
Near Pila, Buenos Aires Province
Republic of Argentina
1205 14 August 1943

Frade knew there was something wrong the moment he walked Julius Caesar up to the verandah of the house.

Both Dorotea and El Jefe, who had been sitting on the verandah, stood up the moment they saw him, but neither smiled or waved.

They look like they're waiting for Daddy to give them a whipping, now that he's home from the office.

Or for the Grim Reaper.

The door opened and Staff Sergeant Sigfried Stein came onto the verandah. He didn't look particularly happy either, and when he saw Frade, his look changed to very glum.

What the hell has happened?

There were seventy-odd "casas," each numbered, scattered around the three hundred forty square miles of Estancia San Pedro y San Pablo. The use of the Spanish word for "house" was somewhat misleading. There was always more than just a house. Each so-called casa had stables and barns and all the other facilities required to operate what were in effect the seventy-odd farming subdivisions of the estancia. And on each casa there was always more than one house; often there were four or more.

Some of them were permanently occupied by the *capataz*—supervisor of the surrounding area—and, of course, his family and the peones who worked its land. And some of them were used only where there was a good deal of work to be done in the area, and the workers were too far from their casas or the village near the big house to, so to speak, commute.

House Number 52 was one of the medium-size houses. Built within a double stand of poplars, the casa itself had a verandah on three sides. On either side there were two smaller houses. Inside the larger house there was a great room, a dining room, an office, a kitchen, and two bedrooms. It had a wood-fired parrilla and a dome-shaped oven. One building housed a MAN diesel generator that powered the lights, the water pumps, the freezers, and the refrigerators. El Patrón had taken good care of his workers.

It was reasonably comfortable, secure, and far from prying eyes.

And thus the best place that Enrico and El Jefe could think of to hide the Froggers after the shooting at Casa Chica.

They'd agreed: *When Don Cletus returns from the United States, he will know what to do.*

Frade had been home two days now and didn't have a clue as to what he should do with the Froggers. Although he was painfully aware that keeping them on Estancia San Pedro y San Pablo was not an option. Sooner or later, their presence would be confirmed and someone would come after them, either the Argentine authorities or the Germans.

One of the peones—a boy of about fourteen—ran up to Julius Caesar. Clete tossed him the reins, then slid out of the saddle. He had been carrying his shotgun—adhering to his belief that you never need a gun until you need one badly—but now no longer needed it. Siggy Stein had a Thompson .45 ACP submachine gun hanging from his shoulder.

He walked back to one of the wagons in the column and handed the shotgun to one of the bird-boys. Bird-boys were responsible for taking the birds from the hunters when the pouches were full, and later—now—plucking and gutting the perdices. The bulk of the cleaned birds, save for a few that would be taken by the peones, would be roasted ritually over a fire at lunch.

Frade was surprised to see how many birds there were. A fifty-kilogram burlap potato bag was full, and another nearly so. Several families of peones were about to have a perdiz feast. The hunting had been great, but the afterglow of that had vanished when he saw the faces on Dorotea, El Jefe, and Stein.

As he walked to the verandah, the other hunters dismounted and followed him.

"Okay, what happened?" Clete asked as he walked onto the verandah.

"There's been a small problem," Dorotea said.

"I would never have guessed from your happy faces," Clete said. "What kind of a small problem?"

"Right after we got here, la Señora Frogger asked if she could go for a walk," Dorotea said.

Dorotea and Schultz had carried the makings of lunch from the big house, bringing the food, the wine, the tableware, cooks, and several maids in Schultz's Model A Ford pickup truck. That, too, was in case anyone was watching.

"And you said, 'Okay,' right?"

"I did," Chief Schultz said, more than a little uncomfortably. "I sent Dorotea with her."

He was now speaking of The Other Dorotea, who was euphemistically described as "El Jefe's housekeeper."

"And then what happened?" Clete asked softly.

"Well," Schultz began, and then stopped. He sighed, then went on: "Clete, I sent a couple of guys on horses with them. Told them to stay out of sight but to keep their eyes open. . . ."

"And then what happened?" Clete repeated softly.

"Well, I guess they were half a mile, maybe a kilometer, out in the boonies when Dorotea took a little break. . . ."

"What do you mean, 'a little break'?"

"She went behind a bush, so to speak, is what I mean," Schultz said uncomfortably. "You know?"

That triggered a mental image of the massive "housekeeper" Frade would just as well have not had.

"And then what happened?" Clete asked for a third time.

"Then the Kraut belted her behind the ear with a thing from the fireplace—you know, a poker. She must have had it hidden in her skirt."

Clete looked back to Schultz. "And then?"

"The Kraut took off running," Schultz said. He then remembered that three of the men listening to him were German and might consider that a pejorative term. He tried to justify his lack of tact by saying, "Jesus, she could have killed Dorotea with that goddamn poker."

"Is Dorotea badly injured?" Clete inquired.

"She's got a lump behind her ear the size of a baseball."

"Where did Frau Frogger think she was going?" Frade asked.

Schultz shrugged.

"She didn't get far," Schultz said. "Dorotea went after her."

"And where is she now?" Father Welner asked.

"In the house," Schultz said. "He's taking care of her."

"I presume you mean Herr Frogger?" Clete asked.

Schultz nodded.

"Define 'taking care of her,'" Frade ordered.

Schultz now looked even more uncomfortable.

"When she caught her, Dorotea did a job on her," he said. Then he added: "It took two of the guys to pull her off of her." There was another pause, this one a little longer. "And it took them a little time to get there to pull her off."

"May I see her?" Oberstleutnant Frogger asked softly.

"Perhaps it would be better if I went in to see her first," Father Welner said. When neither Frogger nor Frade replied, the priest added, "You said earlier, Wilhelm, that there was some difficulty between you two when you first saw her."

Frogger nodded. "Thank you, Father."

Welner reached down and unbuttoned several of the buttons on his plaid woolen shirt. Then he reached inside and pulled out a dickey to which was attached a clerical collar. In a few seconds, he had fastened the collar around his neck and rebuttoned the shirt.

He looked at Frade and the others, and asked, "All right?"

They nodded.

Frade said what he was thinking: "In that plaid shirt, she's going to think you're a Presbyterian."

Von Wachtstein chuckled. Everybody else gave him a dirty look.

Welner went back to his horse and retrieved what looked like a small doctor's bag from where he had it tied to the saddle. Then he walked purposely past everyone and onto the verandah. He went in the house without knocking.

"Now that everything's in capable Jesuit hands," Frade said, "I'm going to have a little fermented grape while waiting to see what happens next."

He went onto the verandah, where the luncheon table had been set up, and helped himself to a large glass of red wine. Von Wachtstein joined him almost immediately, and then the others, one by one.

For the next ten minutes, everyone on the verandah could hear the sound of an excited female voice inside the house and the murmurs of male voices. The thick walls of the house and drawn draperies kept them from understanding any of it.

Gradually, the sound of the female voice became less audible, and finally it stopped.

Two minutes after that, the door opened and Father Welner pointed first at Oberstleutnant Frogger and then Cletus Frade and motioned them to come inside.

Frade had the unkind thought that the priest's gesture was not unlike the one the headmaster of his boarding school—also a priest, albeit an Episcopalian—had used to summon miscreants into his office to face the bar of ecclesiastic justice.

And then, knowing that he probably should not, he refilled his wineglass before going through the door.

Frau Frogger was half-lying on the couch. After a moment, Frade saw that she was asleep.

Not asleep, stupid. The way she was howling a couple of minutes ago, there's no way she could have just dozed off.

She's been drugged.

Christ, Welner drugged her!

She was an ordinary-looking middle-aged woman, just an inch the far side of plump. Her black, faintly patterned dress was dirt-smudged and torn in several places.

Her face was battered, and Clete had a mental image of the two gauchos trying to pull the massive Dorotea off her as Dorotea's arms flailed beating her.

"*Mein Gott!*" Oberstleutnant Frogger said softly.

"She'll be sore for a while, and I'm afraid she's going to lose a tooth," the priest said. "But aside from that, she's not seriously injured physically."

"She's sedated?" Oberstleutnant Frogger asked.

The priest nodded. "I gave her something."

"She attacked the Father," Herr Frogger said softly. "She . . . your mother smashed a water pitcher against the table, and then tried to shove what was left of it in the Father's face."

"She's disturbed," Father Welner said, using the calm, considerate tone of a priest.

"That makes trying to shove a broken water pitcher in your face okay?" Frade said sharply.

"We had to wrestle her to the ground," Herr Frogger said. He exhaled. "I had no idea she was that strong."

No one said anything for a moment.

"That's when Father gave her the injection," Herr Frogger said. "If he hadn't done that, I don't know what would have happened."

"How long will she be out?" Clete asked.

"She'll sleep soundly for four or five hours—perhaps longer, because she's physically exhausted as well—and then she will gradually become awake."

Oberstleutnant Frogger asked what Clete was thinking: "And then what?"

"Then we're back to square one," Clete said. "And we can't have that."

"My mother belongs in a hospital. Not for what that woman did to her, but for her . . . that uncontrollable, irrational rage."

"Colonel," Frade said. "You know that's not an option."

"Well, then," Oberstleutnant Frogger replied, "what do we do, put her in chains?"

"That is one option," Clete said.

"Cletus, you can't be serious," Father Welner said.

"I'm perfectly serious," Frade said. "She's made it clear that she will do anything—she could have killed Dorotea—to get away. She has decided that both her husband and her son are the enemy. And, for that matter, that you are. And since putting her in a hospital is out of the question, what other option is there?"

"Actually, I can think of one," the priest said.

"Well, let's have it," Frade said, more sharply than he intended.

"When your Aunt Beatriz became unstable after your cousin Jorge's passing—"

"He didn't *pass,* Father," Frade said. "You know what happened to him."

Oberstleutnant Frogger looked at Frade.

"He was an Argentine army officer, Colonel," Frade said. "A quote unquote neutral observer at Stalingrad. The damned fool went flying around in a Storch and got himself killed when it was shot down."

"That's a bit cruel, don't you think, Cletus?" the priest asked.

"It's the truth. Cruel? Maybe. We're in a cruel business. Let's hear your possible solution. The other options I can think of start with chaining her to the floor."

"At the risk of Major Frade taking offense at my defense of him, Father," Oberstleutnant Frogger said, "there are things in play here involving many lives."

"Are you going to tell me what they are?" the priest asked.

"No," Frade said. "And 'things in play here' was a very bad choice of words. The one thing we're not doing is playing."

The priest gathered his thoughts for a moment, then said, "All right, speaking bluntly: When your Aunt Beatriz lost control, your Uncle Humberto and your father were agreed that she should not be kept in the hospital any longer than necessary. A 'nervous breakdown' was one thing, perhaps even to be expected under the circumstances. An indefinite period of hospitalization in the psychiatric ward of the German Hospital was something else. *'What would people think? She could never raise her head in society again.'*"

"Oh, for Christ's sake!" Frade said disgustedly.

"Unfortunately, may God forgive them, it's true," the priest said. "The solution finally reached was that she would be released from the German Hospital, and as long as she could be controlled by drugs and kept under supervision, she would be allowed to remain at home."

"She doesn't seem to be very controlled to me," Frade said.

"Relatively speaking," the priest said carefully, "she's farther down the road to recovery than any of us thought would be the case. In the beginning, when we took her from the hospital, Cletus, your Aunt Beatriz was much sicker than she is today.

"But, as I was saying, in the event that she would not show improvement, or grew worse, another means to deal with the situation was put in place. There is a hospital operated by the Little Sisters of Santa María del Pilar in Mendoza. It's a nursing order, and the sisters—some of whom, including the Mother Superior, are physicians—have experience in dealing with the mentally ill—"

"Cutting to the chase," Clete interrupted. He saw on everyone's face that no one understood that, but went on anyway. "You're suggesting I put Frau Frogger in a psychiatric hospital in Mendoza? What's the difference between that and putting her in the German Hospital in Buenos Aires? She would either escape—"

"Let me finish, please, Cletus," the priest said, not very patiently.

"Sorry," Clete said, but it was clear he wasn't.

"That wine you're drinking comes from one of your vineyards, Don Guillermo, which is in the foothills of the Andes near Mendoza. On the property is a rather nice house, Casa Montagna, designed by an Italian architect for your Granduncle Guillermo in the Piedmont style. It sits on the side of a mountain overlooking the vineyards and the bodega. No one lives there, not even the Don Guillermo manager, but there is a small staff so that it will be ready on short notice should we need it for Beatriz. I can't remember your father ever going there or even mentioning it. I learned of it—went there—only after he had offered it to Humberto for Beatriz."

"I don't understand," Clete said.

"What Humberto did—actually, what I did for him—was convert one wing into a place where Beatriz could be cared for in comfort. I had the garden walled in, and converted the rooms above her apartment into living quarters suitable for the Little Sisters who would care for her around the clock."

"You arranged for the nuns?" Frade asked.

Welner nodded.

"The Mother Superior came to understand that the greatest good for the greatest number would come from the generous contribution that would be made by Humberto as an expression of his appreciation for the Little Sisters' care of Beatriz. They could use the money to treat the less fortunate."

"How could they have been sure Beatriz would stay there?" Frade asked.

"Well, they were prepared to watch her twenty-four hours a day. Suicide was a potential problem. Thank God that's passed. And as I said, the garden was walled in. There are locks."

"How much is it going to cost me to put Frau Frogger in there?"

"Wouldn't, using your terminology, 'putting Frau Frogger in there' be the decision of her family?"

"No," Frade said simply.

"We are in Major Frade's hands, Father," Oberstleutnant Frogger said.

"I can't be a party to taking her there as a prisoner," the priest said.

"If you can arrange for the nuns to take my wife, Father," Herr Frogger said, "you will be saving her life, mentally and physically."

And Frade had a sudden insight: *Welner wouldn't have brought this up unless he knew it was the best solution possible. But he now has convinced Frogger, father and son, to think it's their idea.*

Goddamn, he's clever!

"Then the problem becomes: How do we get her there?" Welner said.

Frade walked to the wall-mounted telephone intending to call Gonzalo Delgano, but then changed his mind.

He walked instead to the door.

"Enrico, I need a half-dozen reliable men to go to Mendoza with me right now. Don't tell them where we are going, only that they'll be there several weeks at least."

"We are taking the German woman to Casa Montagna, Don Cletus?"

Enrico knows about Casa Montagna?

"That's right."

"You are going to fly?"

"Just as soon as I can get the Lodestar in the air."

"And who will help you fly?"

"Doña Dorotea."

"What will Delgano say?"

"I think he will be distressed that I allowed Doña Dorotea to fly the airplane from here to Jorge Frade, when it appears there first thing tomorrow morning. It's about six hundred miles to Mendoza."

"He will be even more distressed if you kill yourself and everybody else before tomorrow morning, Don Cletus. Call Major Delgano. Either have him come here or, if time is so important, go to Buenos Aires."

"Then he would learn what I'm doing."

"He would learn anyway, Don Cletus. Don Cletus, you would insult him if you did this without him. He is now one of us."

Frade considered that a moment.

Damn it, he's right.

If I were Delgano, after all he's done already, and got the idea I was hiding something from him, I'd be insulted.

"What I think we should do, Don Cletus, is drive into Buenos Aires to his home. . . ."

"I don't know where he lives."

"I do. And you tell him what you need. The worst thing that can happen is that he will tell you he doesn't want to do it. But he would not betray you. I told you. He is now one of us."

"You're right, Enrico. Thank you, my friend."

"Or—I just thought of this—you could telephone him and tell him that there is something he needs to look at on your airplane. And then go to Buenos Aires in one of the Pipers and bring him here. If the clowns are listening, there is nothing suspicious about that."

"You would let me fly into Buenos Aires all by myself?"

The gentle sarcasm was lost on Enrico.

"If you give me your word of honor you will not leave the airfield when you are there and are very careful while you are there."

Frade, knowing he could not trust his voice, clapped the old soldier on both arms. He went back into the house, picked up the telephone, and, when the estancia operator came on the line, told her to get Chief Pilot Gonzalo Delgano in Buenos Aires for him.

IV

"I have been in here before," Gonzalo Delgano's voice came over the earphones.

"Chief Pilot," Frade ordered sternly, "take command of the aircraft."

Frade took his hands off the yoke and raised them much higher than was necessary to signal he was no longer flying the Lodestar.

Delgano smiled at him.

"Sometimes there's a little crosswind coming off the mountains," Delgano said, nodding toward the Andes. "You can tell when the wind-sock pole is bent more than forty-five degrees."

He demonstrated a bent wind-sock pole with his index finger.

Frade smiled at him.

Delgano shoved the yoke forward so that he could make a low-level pass over the field to have a look at the wind sock.

They were not in communication with the El Plumerillo tower. Delgano was not surprised; he told Clete that there was only one Aeropostal flight into Mendoza every day at about noon—and sometimes not that often—and as soon as it took off again, the tower closed down. There was some other use of the field by the military, and even some private aviation traffic, but not enough to justify a dawn-to-dusk tower. The runway was not lighted, which made a tower useless at night.

Delgano had told Frade just after they had taken off that at this time of year they should not be surprised if the field was closed due to weather or—flying dead-reckoning navigation due to no reliable radio navigation aids—they could not even find the field before dark. Winds aloft could knock them as much as fifty or a hundred miles off course.

They were in no danger. There was more than enough fuel to take them back to Buenos Aires, where runway and taxi lights had been installed at Aero-dromo Jorge Frade in Morón while they had been in the United States. Nor would they have trouble finding Jorge Frade, as there was both a radio beacon and an around-the-clock tower operation using a Collins Model 7.2 trans-ceiver, which was just about the latest thing in the States.

And the radio direction finder would be working, awaiting the six Lodestars en route from the United States. No one knew when they would leave or arrive, but Jorge Frade had to be ready to guide them in.

The primitive conditions at El Plumerillo would soon change. While they were in the United States, Guillermo de Filippi—"Señor Mañana," SAA's chief of maintenance—had finally managed to get contracts for the construction of a combined hangar/passenger terminal/tower, as well as landing lights.

Frade had quickly decided that simply installing the landing lights and having SAA give them to the airfield would be cheaper in the long run—and get them installed much quicker—than would entering into lengthy ne-gotiations, with the inevitable greasing of the appropriate palms of the local authorities to have them do it.

The wind sock was full and parallel to the runway, indicating that the wind was blowing along the runway. But the pole was perfectly erect, so no crosswind.

Delgano moved the throttles forward and picked up the nose. He would gain a little altitude, then make a 180-degree turn for a straight-in approach.

"Try very hard not to bend it, Gonzo," Frade said.

Delgano took a hand from the yoke long enough to give Frade the finger.

The passenger compartment was crowded, just about full. The first three rows of seats were occupied by six peones, all of them former members of the Húsares de Pueyrredón, five of whom were having their first experience with ae-rial flight. In the aisle between their seats were bags holding rifles, pistols, and submachine guns that had been stored in the basement of el Coronel's garage since the time he had been planning to stage a *coup d'état* against the then-pres-ident of Argentina.

Sergeant Sigfried Stein—who had come to Argentina as Team Turtle's ex-plosives expert and been converted to a reasonably well-qualified radio techni-cian and, more recently, to "Major" Stein to deal with the Froggers—had been brought along not only to continue dealing with the Froggers but also to set up a Collins Model 7.2 transceiver and the SIGABA encryption device. Not at the airport, though; a Collins for that purpose would be flown in when the tower was finished.

The transceiver and encryption equipment on the Lodestar would be installed in Casa Montagna for use by Captain Madison R. Sawyer III. Sawyer, who was no longer needed to blow up German replenishment ships in the River Plate, now was to be in command of what Frade privately thought of as "the insane asylum." Using the very latest cryptographic technology, Sawyer would be able to communicate with Frade in Buenos Aires and with Second Lieutenant Len Fischer at the Army Security Agency facility at Vint Hill Farms Station, Virginia, and through Vint Hill with Colonel Graham in Washington, D.C.

In the row behind the peones sat Enrico Rodríguez. Doña Dorotea's in-flight luggage filled the seat across the aisle from him.

In the next row, Sawyer was sitting across the aisle from Stein.

Behind him sat Oberstleutnant Frogger, across from his father.

Behind them, Father Welner and Doña Dorotea sat where they could keep a close eye on Frau Frogger, who lay on a mattress in the aisle. An hour before, Welner had woken her long enough to give her a drink laced with sedative.

So far, Cletus Frade thought as the Lodestar slowed on its landing roll, *everything has gone off without a hitch—*

Gonzo had been waiting for him at Jorge Frade. When Frade had explained what he wanted to do—more accurately, more importantly, what he was asking Delgano to do—Delgano had considered it for no more than two seconds, then said, "Let me get my bag. I told my wife I'd probably be gone for a couple of days."

When they landed on the Estancia San Pedro y San Pablo strip, just about everything had been loaded aboard the Lodestar but Frau Frogger, and she appeared minutes later, on a mattress on top of a makeshift stretcher. They were airborne in the Lodestar thirty minutes after Frade landed the Piper.

It had been a little rougher at 5,000 feet than it would have been at a greater altitude, but when flying dead reckoning, it is useful to be able to see things on the ground. The weather had been clear and they had had no trouble finding their way to Mendoza, where Gonzo had set the Lodestar down very smoothly.

They were five minutes ahead of their ETA guesstimate.

—and therefore the other shoe is certainly about to drop.

They were not expected. It was a given that the telephone lines to Estancia San Pedro y San Pablo were being listened to by the Bureau of Internal Security, so telephoning ahead to the airport, or to Estancia Don Guillermo and especially to the Convent of the Little Sisters of Santa María del Pilar, had not been an option if they didn't want el Coronel Martín to know they were going to Mendoza long before they got there.

The result of that would have been representatives of the local BIS office waiting for them to see who got off the airplane and where they went. And the local BIS would have descriptions of the Froggers.

The airplane itself was going to cause a stir, because as far as either Delgano or Frade knew, this was going to be the first time that a Lodestar—and a brilliantly red one, at that—had landed at El Plumerillo airfield.

Their only option seemed to be brazening it out, and that's what they did.

When the on-duty official of El Plumerillo came out to greet the airplane before the engines had died, Enrico and Delgano got off the airplane and professed surprise and anger that there was no one there to meet them, and implied the official greeting them was probably the miscreant responsible. *Don Cletus Frade was going to be very angry that his guests were going to be inconvenienced.*

The official quickly took them to a telephone, where Enrico called Casa Montagna and ordered that whatever cars were there, plus a closed truck, be sent immediately to the airport for Don and Doña Frade and their guests.

A 1938 Ford two-and-a-half-ton stake body, a 1939 Ford Fordor, a 1936 La Salle five-passenger sedan, and a strange-looking 1941 Lincoln Continental—a four-door sedan—arrived forty-five minutes later. Clete had never seen a Lincoln Continental four-door sedan; he didn't even know they made one.

With Father Welner directing, the peones gently installed Frau Frogger in the backseat of the La Salle with her son and husband on either side of her. Her condition was explained as airsickness, and Father Welner assured the airfield official there was nothing to worry about. Enrico got in the front seat and the La Salle started off for the estancia.

Sergeant Stein supervised the loading of the Collins transceiver and SIGABA into the truck, then the bagged weapons, which he identified as Don Cletus Frade's golf clubs. He then got into the 1939 Fordor, into which also squeezed as many of the peones—four—as would fit. The other two rode in the back of the truck with the luggage.

And finally, Doña Dorotea and Don Cletus descended regally from the Lodestar and allowed themselves to be installed in the backseat of the Lincoln Continental sedan beside Father Welner.

"Take us to the convent of the Little Sisters of Santa María del Pilar, please," the priest ordered the driver of the car, who was the resident manager of Estancia Don Guillermo.

"*Sí, Padre,*" the driver said, then added: "Don Cletus, if I had only known you were coming, we would have been waiting for you."

"Not to worry," Frade said grandly. "That sort of thing happens."

On the way to the convent, Welner explained the Lincoln. It was Beatriz Frade de Duarte's car and had been sent to Mendoza when it was thought she would be going there.

"I didn't know they made a four-door sedan," Frade said.

"They don't. When it came down here, it was a drop-top coupe, and Beatriz said that mussed her hair, so she had it rebodied in Rosario."

Cletus had, and was immediately ashamed of, the unkind thought that his Aunt Beatriz had apparently always been some kind of a nut.

[TWO]
The Convent of Santa María del Pilar
Mendoza, Mendoza Province, Argentina
1820 14 August 1943

The Mother Superior of the Mendoza chapter of the Order of the Little Sisters of Santa María del Pilar, who received them in a dark office crowded with books, was a leathery-skinned, tiny woman of indeterminate age.

"Thank you for receiving us, Reverend Mother, on such short notice," Welner greeted her.

There's just a touch of sarcasm in that, Clete thought.

The nun who'd answered the convent door had told them the Mother Superior's schedule was full for the day and they would have to make an appointment to see her when she was free, possibly tomorrow. After Welner told her his business with the Mother Superior was quite important, the nun had reluctantly disappeared through a door and left them standing for fifteen minutes in the cold and chairless foyer before finally returning to announce, "Follow me, please."

"You're always welcome in this house of God, Father," Mother Superior said.

And there was sarcasm in that, too. What the hell is going on here?

"This is Don Cletus Frade, Reverend Mother," Welner said. "And la Señora Dorotea Mallín de Frade."

That got Mother Superior's attention. She stared intently at Clete for thirty seconds, then said, "Yes."

"How do you do?" Clete said politely.

"So this is how you turned out," Mother Superior said. "Your mother would be pleased."

"Excuse me?"

"I can see your father in you," she said. "But there is fortunately much more of your mother."

This seemed to please her.

"Are you a Christian?" she asked.

"You knew my mother?"

"We were dear friends," she said. "I asked if you were a Christian."

"I didn't know you knew Cletus's mother," Welner said.

"Respectfully, Father, there's probably a good deal you don't know," Mother Superior said. "Well, did whoever raised you bring you to our Lord and Savior?"

"How did you know my mother?"

"I asked whether you are Christian or not."

"If you're asking if I'm Roman Catholic, no."

"I was afraid that would happen. I have never been able, and I have prayed, to forgive your father for abandoning you."

"My father did not abandon me," Clete said softly.

Dorotea's eyes showed alarm. She knew that when her husband was really angry, he spoke so softly it was hard sometimes to hear what he said.

"What would you call it?" Mother Superior asked. "When your mother died, he returned from the United States without you. He never came here again. When I finally saw him in Buenos Aires and asked about you, he said you were none of my business. Actually, his words were 'It's none of your goddamn business.' Then he walked out of the room. I never saw him or heard from him again."

"Why did you think he might feel that way?" Clete asked very softly.

"I told you, your mother and I were dear friends."

"How did that happen?"

"When your father and mother were first married, they spent a good deal of their time here. Your mother loved Casa Montagna. She came to a retreat here at the convent, and we met. She knew that she was ill, so we prayed together for the safe delivery of her first child—you—and rejoiced together when that happened."

Clete looked at Welner.

"Obviously, you didn't know about this?"

The priest shook his head.

"Let me tell you about my father," Clete said, still speaking very softly. "He didn't abandon me. There were two factors involved. One was my grandfather, my mother's father. He could not find it in his heart—and still doesn't—to forgive the Catholic Church for convincing my mother that contraception was a sin, even when another pregnancy would probably kill her. As it did.

"When my mother died, and my father tried to bring me to Argentina, my grandfather stopped him and had him deported. When my father reentered the United States from Mexico with the intent to take me, my grandfather had him arrested, and my father spent ninety days in chains on a Texas road gang for illegal entry. My grandfather had my father's visa revoked so that he could never again legally enter the United States. It was implied that my mother's father would have my father killed if he again returned and tried to take me.

"My father could have, of course, made an effort to kidnap me, and he told me that he had considered this seriously. But finally he realized that he couldn't, even shouldn't, try to raise an infant by himself. There were two female relatives who could. One was my Aunt Martha, my mother's brother's wife, a good solid woman, and the other was his sister, and my father knew Beatriz was a fruitcake."

"Cletus!" Dorotea exclaimed.

Clete looked at her, then back at the Mother Superior, and despite not trusting his voice as his anger rose, went on: "My father decided that what was best for me was my Aunt Martha. And he was right. You have nothing to forgive him for. And as far as abandoning me is concerned, not only did he not marry the woman he loved for the rest of his life, because your country's absurd rules of inheritance would have kept him from leaving me everything he owned, but he hired people to keep an eye on me. He knew every time I fell off my horse. The shelves in his study at Estancia San Pedro y San Pablo are lined with scrapbooks about me, and the walls covered with pictures of me."

Clete felt his throat constrict, cleared it, then finished: "And as far as forgiving people is concerned, my father told me he long ago had forgiven my grandfather for what the man had done to him. He said in his shoes he would have done the same thing."

Mother Superior looked at him for a long moment.

"Your mother, may she rest in peace, would be pleased to know you were reunited with your father," she said finally.

"Are we through here?" Frade said sharply, and stood.

"I thought you came here seeking my help," Mother Superior said.

"Sit down, darling," Dorotea ordered softly.

Father Welner made a *Sit down* gesture. After a moment, Frade made a face, then slowly sank back in his seat.

"We have a woman with us who is mentally ill," Welner began. "She needs not only care but . . . it's rather delicate, Mother."

"Who is she?" Mother Superior asked.

"I'll tell you who she is," Frade said. "And if you let your mouth run, her death will be on your conscience—"

"Cletus!" Dorotea said warningly.

"She's a German, a Nazi, and if the Germans find out where she is, they will do their best to kill her and her husband—and maybe anyone else who gets in their way."

"What's your connection with her?" Mother Superior asked after a very long moment.

"Aside from telling you I'm an American intelligence officer, that's none of your goddamn business."

"I find it hard to believe the Germans would kill a woman," Mother Superior said.

"Why not? They murdered my father, and they sort of liked him."

"Your father was murdered by the Germans? I heard he was killed in a robbery attempt."

"He was murdered in cold blood at the order of the same bastards who have tried hard to kill me twice, the last time yesterday."

He saw the looks on Welner's and Dorotea's faces.

"No, I haven't lost my mind. Since the Germans know who I am, and Colonel Martín knows what I do for a living, who are we trying to keep it a secret from?"

"There was another attempt on your life yesterday?" Father Welner said.

"Three guys in front of the house on Avenida Coronel Díaz," Clete confirmed. "Rodríguez put two of them down, and I got the third one." He looked at Mother Superior. "The story in *La Nación* said the police killed them during a robbery attempt."

"You didn't say anything," Welner said.

"Rodríguez?" Mother Superior asked. "*Enrico* Rodríguez? Is that who you're talking about? Your father's—what's that term?—*batman?*"

"I don't know if he was my father's batman or not," Frade said. "But he was one of my father's two true friends."

"Father Welner being the other?" she asked.

Frade nodded.

"Are you aware, Cletus," Mother Superior said, "that Enrico's sister Marianna took care of you from the day you were born until your mother went to the United States?"

Frade nodded. "Yes, I am. La Señora Rodríguez de Pellano was my housekeeper in the house across from the Hipódromo on Libertador. She had her throat cut in my kitchen the night the assassins came after me the first time."

"I hadn't heard that," Mother Superior said as she crossed herself. Then she added, "Where is Enrico now?"

"At the estancia with the German woman," Clete replied.

"And what precisely is the nature of the German woman's illness?"

"She's crazy," Frade said.

"Damn it, Cletus!" Dorotea said in exasperation.

Clete, unbowed, explained: "Yesterday, she told her sole surviving son that he's a traitor who will burn in hell for all eternity. Doesn't that sound a little crazy to you?"

"Her son is with her?" Mother Superior asked.

"And her husband," Welner said.

"And six of my men, in case the Germans learn where they are and come to kill all three."

A moment later, the door to the office opened and a nun—this time a huge one, reminding Clete of The Other Dorotea—stepped inside.

She had to be waiting outside, and somehow Mother Superior summoned her.

"Yes, Reverend Mother?"

"Please ask Sister Mónica to select three very reliable sisters to deal with a woman suffering from mental illness. Ask them to pack enough clothing for three or four days. Bring a van around. Put my medical bag in it. I will drive."

"Yes, Reverend Mother."

The huge nun left, carefully closing the door behind her.

"That will take a few minutes," Mother Superior said. "There's no reason for everyone to wait for me. I know my way out there. And if you would be so good, Father, to hear my confession while we wait?"

[THREE]
Casa Montagna
Estancia Don Guillermo
Km 40.4, Provincial Route 60
Mendoza Province, Argentina
1915 14 August 1943

Darkness had fallen, but there was enough light from the headlights for Clete to be able to see the white stone kilometer markers along the road as the resident manager of Estancia Don Guillermo—whose name, if he had ever known it, Clete had forgotten—drove the Lincoln down the macadam road.

They were now at Km 39.8.

That means we're point-six kilometer from where we'll turn onto Estancia Don Guillermo, and thirty-nine-point-eight kilometers from where they started counting, probably at a marker in the Mendoza town square.

That's not saying we're thirty-nine-point-eight kilometers from the center of town, but that we're thirty-nine-point-eight kilometers down the road from the marker.

The way this road weaves, we're a lot closer as the bird flies than that.

Why the hell do people say that?

"As the bird flies" means in a straight line? I've never seen a bird fly more than twenty-five yards in a straight line.

Jesus Christ, it's odd thoughts time! And that means C. Frade's tail is really dragging.

I have every right in the world to have my tail dragging. Not only did I just fly from the States across Central and South America, and then fly down here, I also just threw Tío Juan out of Uncle Willy's house, had people try to kill me, and—and what else?

Doesn't matter what else.

I have every right to be tired, and I damn sure am.

What does matter, however, is that when my tail is really dragging, I tend to do really stupid things. Like, for example, being a little less than charming to Mother Superior at the convent and then actually getting ready to walk out of her office.

If Dorotea and Welner hadn't stopped me, I think I would have, and that would have really screwed up things.

Watch it, Little Cletus. You just can't afford to screw something up.

Ten seconds later, the Lincoln slowed and turned off the highway. Fifty meters off the road, there was a gate in a wire fence. Beyond the fence, the headlights lit up rows of grapevines as far as he could see.

There was a Ford Model A pickup truck inside the fence. A man got out of it, walked to the gate, and swung it open. The Lincoln's lights flashed over the pickup as they drove through the gate, and Frade saw there was a second man standing by the side of the truck, a Mauser rifle cradled in his arms. This one he recognized. He was one of the peones he'd brought from Estancia San Pedro y San Pablo.

When they drove past, the man saluted. Clete returned it.

They drove for a kilometer, perhaps a little more, through endless rows of grapevines. The road suddenly became quite steep—the resident manager had to shift into second gear—and made a winding ascent of a mountainside.

And then there was a massive wooden gate blocking the road.

But there's no fence or anything to the right of the gate.

Why have a gate if people can just drive around it?

He looked out his side window and saw why people could not just drive around this gate. Three feet from the side of the car a stone curb marked the side of the road. Beyond the curb there was a precipitous drop-off; he could not see the bottom.

Well, since there's a granite mountain on the left and nothing but air on the right.

I guess that if they don't open the gate, you either blow it up or you don't get in.

The gate swung inward as they approached it.

There was another Model A pickup with another man holding a rifle just inside the gate, and again Clete recognized him as one of his men from Estancia San Pedro y San Pablo. This one didn't salute as the Lincoln inched carefully past the Ford.

The road now was so steep that the estancia manager did not shift out of low.

They turned a curve and suddenly were on a level plateau perhaps three hundred meters wide and two hundred meters long. A low stone wall on three sides suggested—it was too dark to see—a drop-off like the one beside the gate.

At the far end of the plateau, with what looked like a light in every window—and there were a lot of windows—was the house and its outbuildings.

The main house was three stories and red-tile-roofed. The third floor had dormer windows, and the roof extended over a verandah whose pillars seemed vine-covered. The Andes Mountains were on the horizon behind it, bathed in moonlight.

And now we know why they call it Casa Montagna.

That is indeed a mountain house.

"It's beautiful!" Dorotea said from the backseat.

Enrico Rodríguez, Madison Sawyer, and Gonzalo Delgano were standing on the verandah.

If they're waiting for us, they knew we were coming, and that means there's a telephone at either or both gates.

Nobody's going to get in here by surprise.

"No nuns?" Sawyer greeted them as he waved them into the house.

Inside the door was a foyer. In the center was a fountain in a circular pool.

"Classy," Frade said.

"This whole place is classy," Sawyer said. "And that fountain has no pumps. Enrico showed me. It's fed by a mountain stream. There's a tank, and that provides the pressure. And after the water goes through the fountain, it's fed back into the stream and goes down the mountain."

"Fascinating," Frade said.

Enrico showed him how the fountain works? That means that Enrico knows this place pretty well.

And never told me about it.

What the hell else can I own?

"I don't suppose that at a vineyard there's a pump spitting out wine?" Frade said.

"No, but there's a very nice bar in there," Sawyer said, pointing.

"Why don't we have a look at that?" Frade said.

"The nuns should be here any minute," Dorotea said.

Translation: Now is not wine time.

"Where's Frau Frogger?" Frade asked.

Sawyer pointed to the left.

"There's an apartment there with barred windows and lockable doors. Enrico put her in there. Her husband and son are with her, and one of our guys is sitting in the foyer outside. Stein's setting up the SIGABA and the Collins."

"Well, as soon as I have a glass of wine, I'll have a look at both," Frade said.

Dorotea shook her head in resignation.

Clete walked through the door that Sawyer had indicated and found himself in a comfortable room, two walls of which were lined with books, one half of a third wall with oil paintings and framed photographs and half with a bar, complete with stools. The fourth wall held French doors that opened onto a rear patio and provided a panoramic view of the Andes.

Clete went behind the bar and looked through the bottles of wine in a rack on the wall, finally pulling out a Don Guillermo Cabernet Sauvignon. He took a quick look at the label and then a longer look.

"My God!" he said. "This says one of 2,505, 1917. *Nineteen seventeen?*"

"I think it gets better with age, like Kentucky bourbon," Sawyer said.

"Either that or we have a bottle of twenty-six-year-old vinegar," Clete said, and fed the bottle to a huge and ornate cork-pulling device mounted on the wall. He poured some in a glass and sipped.

"Mother Superior and the nuns will be here any minute," Dorotea said.

"So you keep saying," Clete replied. "Well, don't worry. I won't give her any of this twenty-six-year-old vinegar."

He poured his glass half full and took a healthy swallow.

"Terrible, absolutely terrible," he said. "I don't think you'd like this at all, Polo."

"Why don't you let me decide for myself?"

"Because anyone who has volunteered to jump out of a perfectly functioning airplane is obviously incapable of making wise decisions."

Sawyer snatched the bottle from him and poured wine into a glass.

"Nectar of the gods," Sawyer pronounced a moment later.

Frade found more glasses under the bar and poured wine for Delgano and Rodríguez.

"And there's a whole wall of it," Frade said, pointing at the wine rack. "I'm starting to like this place."

And then his eyes fell on a silver-framed photograph on a table.

He walked quickly to the table and picked it up.

"What, honey?" Dorotea asked.

"My parents' wedding picture," he said softly.

He extended it to her.

"Saint Louis Cathedral, Jackson Square, New Orleans," Frade said.

Dorotea examined it and then handed it to Sawyer. It showed the bride, in a long-trained gown, and the groom and the other males in the rather large wedding party in formal morning clothes, standing in front of an altar.

"Is that Perón?" Sawyer asked.

"That's Ol' Juan Domingo," Frade said. "The fat Irishman is the cardinal archbishop. Also present are my grandfather, whose uncontrollable joy is evident on his face. And my Uncle Jim and my Aunt Martha, who raised me." He turned to Enrico. "You were there, too, right?"

"*Sí*, Don Cletus."

"How come you're not in the picture?"

Enrico's face showed he didn't like the question; he ignored it.

"Since they didn't expect us, Don Cletus," Enrico said, "there was no food, or not enough, but I have sent to Señor Alvarez's home for a cook and food for tonight and the morning."

Whose home?

Ah, the resident manager, the guy who was driving the Lincoln.

Where the hell does he fit in here?

"I hope that wasn't an imposition, Señor Alvarez," Dorotea said politely.

"How could it be an imposition, señora?" Alvarez asked. "The cook will stay here for as long as necessary. . . ."

He paused, making the statement a question.

"We'll be here—in and out of here—indefinitely," Clete said. "Chief Pilot Delgano and I will be in and out on a regular basis in connection with South American Airways business, and Mr. Stein and Mr. Sawyer with the wine business. And I brought six men from Estancia San Pedro y San Pablo with me, who will also be here indefinitely."

"There is plenty of room, Don Cletus," Alvarez said. "There are seventeen rooms in Casa Montagna, in addition to the . . . special suite. And, depending how you wish them set up, more than a dozen bedrooms in the out-buildings."

"The men I brought with me can stay in the outbuildings," Frade said. "And I will probably bring another half-dozen."

"Don Cletus," Enrico said. "There are already a half-dozen men here. All from the Húsares. I have spoken to them. . . ."

Alvarez saw the questioning look on Frade's face, but he mistook it to mean Frade was wondering why there were a half-dozen old soldiers in a house rarely occupied.

Alvarez explained: "There are a number of works of art in Casa Montagna, Don Cletus, that el Coronel wanted to make sure were protected, as the house was so rarely used."

That, however, wasn't the question in Clete's mind. He asked, of Enrico, the one that was: "You knew all about this place, didn't you?"

Rodríguez nodded.

"But you never mentioned it to me. Why?"

"I knew you would come here eventually. That would be the time to tell you."

The telephone rang.

Enrico went to a small table. There were two telephones on it; one was an ordinary—if, to Clete, old-fashioned—device and the other apparently the Argentine version of the U.S. Army Signal Corps EE-8 field telephone. Enrico picked up the latter, listened, then pushed the butterfly switch and snarled, sergeantlike, something into it, then put the handset back in its leather case.

"Mother Superior and the nuns are at the lower gate," he announced.

Clete asked the question that had popped into his mind when he saw the military field telephone.

"What's that military telephone doing in here?"

"It is connected to the lower and upper gates right now, but there is a field switchboard."

"That's not what I asked."

Enrico looked uncomfortable.

"When el Coronel was leading Operation Blue," he said finally, making reference to the *coup d'état* that would have, had he not been assassinated, made el Coronel Frade the president of Argentina, "we needed Casa Montagna."

"And is there anything else you'd like to tell me about that?"

"El Coronel knew this was the logical place for it, but as he did not wish to come here, he sent me to set it up."

"A logical place for what?"

"There is a cache of weapons in the basement, Don Cletus."

"What kind of weapons?"

"Enough to equip four troops of the Húsares de Pueyrredón, Don Cletus. El Coronel was concerned that they would not be available if they were needed; that someone might seize the regimental and troop armories. So he cached enough here . . ."

"You're talking about rifles, pistols, that sort of thing?"

"And some machine guns, Don Cletus. Even some mortars and hand grenades. And, of course, the ammunition for the weapons. That is really why the old Húsares are here. To keep an eye on the cache, so that it wouldn't fall into the wrong hands, until I could tell you about it and you could decide what you want to do about it."

"Enrico, if you weren't so ugly, I think I would kiss you," Frade said.

"You should not say things like that, Don Cletus."

Frade turned to Alvarez. "Did you know about this?"

"I am proud to say, Don Cletus, that your father took me into his confidence."

"It is so, Don Cletus," Enrico confirmed. "El Señor Alvarez may be trusted."

"I'm very glad to hear that," Clete said, meaning it, and then went on: "Señor Alvarez, it is very important that no one learns that la Señora Fischer is here. Her life would be in danger otherwise."

Alvarez nodded. "No one, Don Cletus, will know anything beyond that the sisters of Santa María del Pilar are caring for an ill woman."

"I keep waiting for the other shoe to drop," Cletus said. "As I'm sure it will. But what I think I'm going to do now is have another glass of this twenty-six-year-old nectar of the gods to give me the courage to face Mother Superior."

"Cletus, for God's sake!" Dorotea said. "What is el Señor Alvarez going to think of you?"

"I have already made up my mind, Doña Dorotea," Alvarez said. "He is his father's son."

The Mother Superior of the Mendoza chapter of the Little Sisters of Santa María del Pilar marched into the library four minutes later, trailed by the enormous nun who had been in her office and three others. Father Welner brought up the rear.

I know who the big nun is, Clete decided. *She's the convent version of Enrico.*

"Enrico," Reverend Mother ordered, "you will please make yourself available to me when we finish the business immediately at hand."

"Yes, Reverend Mother."

"I will introduce myself to these other gentlemen at that time. For now you have met Sister Carolina." She pointed to the huge nun. "These sisters are Sister Mónica, Sister Theresa, and Sister Dolores. Sisters, this is Don Cletus Frade and la Señora Frade. Enrico, you know."

The nuns wordlessly bobbed their heads.

"You will get to meet the others later," she went on. "For now get yourselves settled. You know where to go. Sister Mónica, you will decide who goes on duty now. When you have done so, and your selection is settled, send her to the apartment. If Father and I are inside, wait for us to come out." She turned to Father Welner. "Are you ready, Father?"

"Yes, Reverend Mother."

With that they all marched out of the library.

Clete smiled.

"I'm almost afraid to ask, darling," Dorotea said. "But what are you thinking?"

He grunted. "When I was in Los Angeles just now, I heard that since February there have been women in the Marine Corps. I was thinking that Mother Superior would make a fine gunnery sergeant."

"What the hell, Clete," Sawyer said. "Why not? They've had women in the Army and the Navy for a long time."

Frade began, very cheerfully, to sing to the melody of "Mademoiselle from Armentières": "'The WACs and WAVEs will win the war, *parlez-vous.* The WACs and WAVEs will win the war, *parlez-vous.* The WACs and WAVEs will win the war, so what the hell are we fighting for? Inky dinky *parlez-vous.*'"

Sawyer laughed. Dorotea glared at him and asked, "How much of that wine have you had?"

"Not as much as I'm going to," he said, and reached for another bottle of Don Guillermo Cabernet Sauvignon 1917.

Mother Superior returned much sooner than Frade thought she would, this time trailed by Father Welner, Oberstleutnant Frogger, and Herr Wilhelm Frogger. But no nuns.

"Enrico," she said, "I didn't know about Marianna until Cletus told me. I am so very sorry."

"Marianna and El Coronel are now at peace with all the angels, Mother," Enrico said. "I have avenged their murder."

"'Vengeance is mine, saith the Lord,'" Welner quoted.

"I have avenged them," Enrico repeated.

Mother Superior changed the subject: "Frau Frogger—"

"Frau *Fischer*," Cletus interrupted her. "*Fischer*. There's nobody named Frogger here."

Mother Superior looked at him very coldly.

He met her eyes. "The name is Fischer. And make sure your nuns don't forget that."

"Cletus!" Dorotea started to protest.

Mother Superior stopped her with an upraised hand, then went on: "La Señora *Fischer*, in addition to what else might be troubling her, is not only exhausted but has apparently been beaten."

"That was after she tried to kill a woman with a fireplace poker," Clete said. "The woman she tried to kill didn't like it much."

"So Father Welner told me," Mother Superior said calmly. "She's lost a tooth and may require dental attention. We can deal with that if it becomes a problem. What she needs now is rest. Sister Mónica will be with her overnight. If she awakens, I have prescribed—given Sister Mónica—a sedative to give her. I'll try to talk to her tomorrow afternoon."

Staff Sergeant Sigfried Stein came into the library. When no one said anything to him, he announced cheerfully, "I bring greetings from Vint Hill Farms. We're up. And to the estancia."

"Good man," Frade said.

"You must be Major Stein," Mother Superior said.

Stein looked at Frade, who nodded.

"Yes, ma'am," Stein said.

"Both la Señora Fischer's husband and her son have told me that the very sight of you triggers feelings—uncontrollable feelings, irrational feelings—of rage in la Señora Fischer."

"I don't think she likes Jews very much," Stein said.

"And you are a Jew?"

"Guilty," Stein said.

"What is your first—I almost said 'Christian'—name?"

Stein looked at Frade again, and Frade nodded again.

"Sigfried," he said, not very pleasantly. "Jewish first name Sigfried."

"May I call you 'Sigfried'? Or would you prefer 'Major Stein'?"

"Siggie is what people call me," he said finally.

"Forgive me, Siggie," Mother Superior said. "I have to ask you this: Have you even done anything to her—said something cruel, or struck her, restrained her, anything like that?"

"No, ma'am," Stein said. "Never. Not that I haven't been tempted." He heard what he had blurted and quickly added: "Sorry, I shouldn't have said that."

Mother Superior made an *It doesn't matter* gesture with both hands.

She said: "I thought I knew that when I looked into your eyes. You have very kind eyes. Siggie, if you're willing, you can be very important in bringing la Señora Fischer back to good health."

"Excuse me?"

"We don't have to get into the details now. I just need to know if you'd be willing to help."

Stein looked at Frade, whose face showed nothing.

"If it's all right with the major," Stein said finally, "then okay. I'll do what I can."

"It would help, Siggie," Frade said. "Having her craz . . . like she is now isn't doing us any good."

"Okay. Just tell me what you want me to do."

"I'll have to give it some thought," Mother Superior said. "Knowing that you're willing to help will be useful."

She turned to Delgano and Sawyer.

"And you are?"

They introduced themselves.

"What is that you're drinking, Cletus?" Mother Superior asked.

"Wine," Frade said. "They make it from grapes."

"You've obviously had more of it than you should," she said.

"You're right, Clete," Sawyer said. "Mother Superior would make a fine gunnery sergeant."

"May I offer you a glass?" Clete said.

"What is it?" she asked, and went to the bar, picked up the bottle, and examined the label.

"This has to be vinegar," she said.

Clete shook his head. He poured wine an inch deep in a glass and offered it to her.

Surprising him, she took it, smelled it, took a small sip, swirled it around in her mouth, then swallowed. She pushed the glass to him.

He poured three inches of wine into the glass.

"'Take a little wine for thy stomach's sake,'" he said. "That's from Saint Timothy."

"Yes, I know," she said. "You took that from there?"

She indicated the wine rack.

He nodded.

"It's hard to believe, but that wine must have been there the last time I was in this room. The last time you and I were in this room."

"I've never been in this room before in my life," Clete said.

"Yes, you have. Your mother put you on that couch"—she pointed—"and then put two of those chairs"—she pointed again—"up against it so you wouldn't roll over and fall on the floor. You were a very active baby."

Frade didn't say anything.

"It was the night your mother and father took the train to Buenos Aires to take the Panagra flight to Miami. The train left at eight, so we had an early supper in here. That was the last time I saw you until you came to the convent today."

Clete didn't reply.

Mother Superior didn't quite gulp the wine, but the glass was nearly empty much sooner than Clete expected it to be. Clete picked up the bottle, but she put her hand over the glass.

"I have to drive," she said.

"Why don't you take a couple of bottles—hell, a dozen bottles—with you?"

She didn't reply to that. Instead, she said, "I was just thinking that despite what you think, rather than coming here for the first time, you are really coming home. And that Casa Montagna, after waiting so long for that to happen, has really been expecting you, is prepared for you."

What the hell is she talking about?

Mother Superior turned to Dorotea.

"How far are you along?"

"Six months," Dorotea said.

"I'll have a look at you tomorrow. Everything, so far as you know, is going well?"

Dorotea nodded.

Mother Superior went behind the bar, took two bottles of the Cabernet Sauvignon from the rack, and put them into her medical bag.

"Sister Caroline is not impressed with the wisdom of Saint Timothy," Mother Superior said. "And I don't like to upset her."

Clete chuckled.

"Enrico," Mother Superior said, "if you were to somehow wrap or box or whatever a half-dozen bottles of the wine so that it doesn't look like half a dozen bottles of wine, and put them in the van when I come here tomorrow, I would be grateful to you."

"*Sí*, Reverend Mother. I will do it."

There was half an inch of wine left in Mother Superior's glass. She drained it and walked out of the room.

"That is a very nice woman," Dorotea said.

"That is a very tough woman," Frade said admiringly.

He turned to Sawyer.

"Do they teach Army officers how to lay in a machine gun? Fields of fire, that sort of thing?"

"Only the brighter ones," Sawyer said. "Parachute officers, for example."

"First thing in the morning, get with Enrico, see what's available, reconnoiter the area, and let me know what you think should be done."

"Yes, sir," Sawyer said.

"I have already done that, Don Cletus," Enrico said.

"Okay, then show Captain Sawyer how things are done by the Húsares de Pueyrredón."

Enrico nodded.

"When do we eat?" Frade asked.

"Half an hour, Don Cletus."

"Which I will spend writing the after-action report for Colonel Graham."

"Do you have to do that tonight?" Dorotea asked.

"Yeah, baby, I do."

Sending the report was a three-stage process. First, Clete wrote it on a typewriter. Then he edited what he had written, using a pencil. Dorotea then took this and retyped it on the keyboard of the SIGABA device. This caused a strip of perforated paper, which now held the encrypted report, to stream out of the SIGABA. Siggie Stein, after making sure that the SIGABA device at Vint Hill Farms Station was ready to receive, fed the strip of paper to the Collins transceiver.

Not quite a minute later, Stein reported that the message had been received in Virginia.

Frade nodded. "Good. Now, let's eat."

Clete had the same uncomfortable feeling—one of intrusion—as he entered the master suite—now his—of Casa Montagna that he had felt the first time he had moved into his father's bedroom in the big house on Estancia San Pedro y San Pablo.

But now it was worse.

There had been nothing of his mother's in the master suite at the estancia.

Here, before a mirrored dressing table, were vials of perfume, jars of cosmetics, a comb, and a hairbrush with blond hair still on it.

And that got worse.

He pulled open a drawer in a chest of drawers and found himself looking at underwear that had to be his mother's.

He slammed the drawer closed.

Dorotea came out of the bathroom in a negligee.

"There's a set of straight razors in there, and a mug of shaving soap," she announced. "All dried out, of course, but I put water in it. That might make it usable. Who knows?"

Clete didn't reply.

"It looks as if they expected to come back," Dorotea said.

"Yeah."

"I wonder what's in here?" Dorotea said, pulled open a door, and gasped. "Oh, God! Clete, look at this!"

He went to the door and looked in.

There was a crib, and infant's toys, and a table—he had no idea what they called it—where an infant could be washed and dried and have diapers changed. And shelves, with stacks of folded cotton diapers and a large can of Johnson's baby powder.

"Jesus Christ!" he said, almost under his breath.

"I wondered what she was talking about," Dorotea said.

"What who was talking about?"

"Mother Superior, when she said you were really coming home. That this house has really been expecting you, is prepared for you."

He looked at her but said nothing.

"She should have said for us," Dorotea said. "For us and our baby."

She saw the look on his face.

"I want to have our baby here, darling. I want to wash him in there, where your mother washed you, and change his nappy with your nappies."

He tried to ask, "How can you be sure the baby's a him?"

But only three words came out before he lost his voice, and his chest heaved, and he realized he was crying.

Dorotea went to him, held him against her breast, and stroked his hair.

[FOUR]
Office of the Deputy Director for Western
Hemisphere Operations
Office of Strategic Services
National Institutes of Health Building
Washington, D.C.
0720 15 August 1943

A second lieutenant of the U.S. Army Signal Corps was sitting in one of the chairs in the outer office when Colonel A. F. Graham, uncommonly in uniform, came to work—as usual, before his secretary had gotten there.

Lieutenant Leonard Fischer stood and more or less came to attention. He was holding a sturdy leather briefcase. Graham saw that he was attached to the briefcase with a handcuff and chain, and that one of the lower pockets of his uniform blouse sagged—as if, for example, it held a Colt Model 1911A1 .45 ACP pistol.

"Good morning, Fischer," Graham said as he waved the young officer ahead of him into his office. "Dare I hope we have heard from Gaucholand?"

"Yes, sir," Fischer said, and held up the briefcase.

"And?"

"That Marine has landed, sir, and the situation is well in hand."

Graham smiled at him, waved him into a chair, and waited for him to detach the briefcase and unlock it. He took from it a manila envelope, stamped TOP SECRET in several places in large red letters, then got up and walked to Graham's desk and handed it to him.

"I would offer you a cup of coffee, Len, but I don't think there is any."

"Not a problem, sir."

Graham tore open the envelope, took two sheets of paper from it, and started to read from them.

```
PRIORITY

TOP SECRET LINDBERGH

DUPLICATION FORBIDDEN

FROM TEX

MSG NO 213 2305 GREENWICH 14 AUGUST 1943

TO AGGIE

AFTER ACTION REPORT

MAKE USE OF PREVIOUSLY ESTABLISHED CODE NAMES.

WITH ABSOLUTELY ESSENTIAL ASSISTANCE OF BIS, THE GUY
FROM BUILDING T-209, HEREAFTER GRAPES, SUCCESSFULLY
INFILTRATED AND PUT IN CONTACT WITH GALAHAD JOHNPAUL
AND TIO HANK WHO WILL NOW CONFIRM GRAPE HISTORY TO
ANYBODY INTERESTED.
```

From previous messages, Graham knew that BIS was Gonzalo Delgano, the Bureau of Interior Security man assigned to watch Frade and South American Airways; that Galahad (the courageous knight on the white horse) was Major von Wachtstein; that JohnPaul was Kapitän zur See Boltitz (after naval hero John Paul Jones); and that Tío Hank was Frade's Uncle Humberto Duarte, managing director of the Banco de Inglaterra y Argentina.

If Tío Hank's going to confirm Grape history—that Frogger is a South African winegrower—that means Frade probably told him what's going on. I don't know if that was smart or not.

But it's his call. I am sitting behind a desk in Washington.

Why do I think Cletus had more than a little grape when he wrote this? Because that's the code name he gave Colonel Frogger?

The question was answered in the next several paragraphs.

> THERE HAVE BEEN SEVERAL MINOR PROBLEMS, TO WIT:
>
> WHILE I WAS IN THE STATES THERE WAS AN ASSAULT ON MY
> FATHER'S COUNTRY PLACE IN TANDIL, WHERE I HAD
> STASHED THE TOURISTS. I SUSPECT TIO JUAN—WHO WAS
> THERE WITH AN ARGENTINE ARMY DELEGATION WHEN THE
> STORM TROOPERS WHO CAME OFF U405 JUST ABOUT TOOK
> THE PLACE DOWN WITH MACHINE-GUN FIRE—MIGHT HAVE HAD
> SOMETHING TO DO WITH THAT.
>
> SOME OLD CAVALRY BUDDIES OF SIDEKICK TIPPED HIM OFF
> AND THE SS SHOT UP AN EMPTY HOUSE, THE TOURISTS HAVING
> BEEN TAKEN TO CIRCLED WAGONS ON MY LITTLE SPREAD.
> AFTER FIRING NOT A SHOT, THE ARGENTINE ARMY AND TIO
> JUAN LEFT, AND SHORTLY THEREAFTER THE SS, SIX OF THEM,
> RODE OFF TO VALHALLA. THE NEXT TIME WE GET TOGETHER, I
> WILL SHOW YOU THE PHOTOS BEERMUG TOOK OF THE DEPARTED
> WITH THE ID CARDS ON THEIR CHESTS.

Graham knew the Tourists were the Froggers, Tío Juan was Juan Domingo Perón, Sidekick was Suboficial Mayor Rodríguez, and Beermug was Staff Sergeant Stein.

How in hell will he keep what must have been a hell of a firefight and six dead Germans from coming out?

> JEDGAR MET BIS AND ME WHEN WE LANDED—GRAPES HAVING
> PREVIOUSLY BEEN DROPPED OFF AT MY SPREAD—AND
> INSISTED ON MY GOING TO SEE TIO JUAN. I DID SO AND
> SAID SOME UNKIND THINGS TO HIM AND LEFT. I THEN
> WENT TO TAKE A SHOWER AT WHAT MY FATHER CALLED HIS
> MONEY SEWER ON AVENIDA DIAZ. AS SIDEKICK WAS
> OPENING THE GATE, THREE MEMBERS OF THE LOCAL MAFIA
> DRIVING A STOLEN PEUGEOT TRIED TO SHOOT US. VIRTUE

TRIUMPHED AGAIN, AND ALL THREE RODE OFF TO WHEREVER
FAILED MAFIOSO HIT MEN GO.

JEDGAR APPEARED SHORTLY THEREAFTER AND TOLD ME HE
DIDN'T THINK WE SHOULD REPORT OUR SUSPICIONS THAT
THE GERMANS HAD HIRED THE HIT MEN AS THIS WOULD
CAUSE A DIPLOMATIC FLAP WHICH WOULD CAUSE THE
EXPULSION FROM BERLIN OF AN ARG DIPLOMAT, THE
AGRICULTURAL ATTACHE, KNOWN TO HIM—HE JUST ABOUT
ADMITTED THE GUY IS BIS—AND WHO ONCE SERVED UNDER
MY FATHER. I COULDN'T GET A NAME, BUT RESPECTFULLY
SUGGEST, COLONEL, SIR, THAT MR. DULLES WOULD BE
INTERESTED IN THAT.

Jedgar, from J. Edgar Hoover, was el Coronel Martín of the BIS.

Christ, they tried to kill him again!

And he's right. Allen will be interested in the Argentine agricultural attaché in Berlin.

Unless he already knows him. Which is likely.

AT ABOUT THIS TIME, OL' TEX DECIDED IT WAS TIME TO GET
THE HELL OUT OF DODGE, WHICH I PROMPTLY DID. TAKING
THE TOURISTS, BEERMUG, GRAPES, POLO, SIDEKICK, COWGIRL,
AND A POSSE OF SIX COWPOKES FROM THE SPREAD WITH US,
BIS AND I FLEW TO YET ANOTHER PLACE MY FATHER OWNED
AND I DIDN'T KNOW ABOUT IN THE FOOTHILLS OF THE ANDES.

WE ARE NOW COMFORTABLY, VERY COMFORTABLY, SET UP IN
CASA MONTAGNA NEAR MENDOZA. IS IT SAFE? YOU KNOW HOW I
FEEL ABOUT THE MARINE RAIDERS. THE ENTIRE FIRST RAIDER
BATTALION COULDN'T GET UP THE HILL TO TAKE THIS PLACE.

THIS IS WHERE WE'RE GOING TO WORK FROM. BIS AND I
HAVE THE CREDIBLE EXCUSE OF FLYING IN AND OUT OF

> HERE FREQUENTLY IN CONNECTION WITH AROUND-AND-
> THROUGH-THE-ANDES AIRLINES, AND BEERMUG HAS
> ESTABLISHED CONTACT WITH THE CHIEF AND OBVIOUSLY
> WITH THE OTHER FISCHER IN VIRGINIA.
>
> PASS TO MR. DULLES PLEASE
>
> RESPECTFULLY SUBMITTED
>
> TEX
>
> PS: WHO GETS THE BILL FOR REPAIRS TO CASA CHICA?

Not only was he half in the bag when he started to write this, he obviously had a couple of belts while he was writing it.

And the one thing I can't do is let Donovan see it.

"It strays a little from the form and substance one expects from an official after-action report, wouldn't you say, Lieutenant Fischer?"

"Just a little, sir."

"Things like that tend to upset Director Donovan. So, what I'm going to do, just as soon as my secretary gets here, is dictate a synopsis . . ."

As if on cue, the office door opened and his secretary, a gray-haired middle-aged woman, walked in.

"Good morning, Colonel," she said.

". . . and send that to him," Graham finished. "Good morning, Grace. Would you get your pad and pencil, please?"

"Before or after I get you your wake-up cup of coffee?"

"Coffee won't be necessary. Lieutenant Fischer and I are going to have breakfast at the Army-Navy Club and put to rest those nasty rumors that the Army and Marine Corps don't talk to each other."

She backed out of the office and returned a moment later with a stenographic notepad in hand.

"Interoffice memorandum, Secret, dictated but not signed, to the director," Graham dictated. "Subject: Major Cletus Frade, After-Action Report of. The Marine has landed, situation well in hand. Respectfully submitted."

"Do I get to see it?" Grace asked.

"Not only do you get to see it, but after you have it microfilmed and send that over to State for inclusion in today's diplomatic pouch to Mr. Dulles in Berne, you get to file it someplace where it can't possibly come to the attention of the director."

She shook her head, and said, "Yes, sir."

"Give the nice lady your briefcase, Len. And the pistol. We don't want to scare people at the Army-Navy Club."

[ONE]
Führerhauptquartier Wolfsschanze
Near Rastenburg, Ostpreussen, Germany
0655 19 August 1943

Generalleutnant Graf Karl-Friedrich von Wachtstein—a short, slight, nearly bald, fifty-four-year-old—walked briskly down a cinder path from the Führerhauptquartier bunker to the bunker in which Generalfeldmarschall Wilhelm Keitel, Germany's senior military officer—he was chief of the Oberkommando der Wehrmacht—had his quarters.

Wolfsschanze held fifty bunkers—ugly buildings with eight- and ten-foot-thick concrete walls and roofs. Wehrmacht engineers had begun—in great secrecy and on a cost-be-damned basis—the construction of "Wolf's Lair" in 1940. A 3.5-square-kilometer area in the forest east of Rastenburg in East Prussia had been encircled with an electrified barbed-wire fence and minefields.

Next came the erection of another barbed-wire enclosure inside the outer barrier. Only then, within this interior barrier, had construction begun of the artillery-proof and aerial-bomb-proof bunkers. The compound had its own power-generating system, a railway station with a bomb-proof siding for the

Führer's private train, an airstrip (between the inner and outer fences), several mess halls, a movie theater, and a teahouse.

An SS-hauptsturmführer and two enlisted men, all armed with Schmeisser machine pistols, stood outside the heavy steel door to Keitel's bunker.

"Generalleutnant von Wachtstein to see the generalfeldmarschall. I am expected."

The hauptsturmführer clicked his heels and nodded to one of the enlisted men, who walked quickly to the steel door and pulled it open, standing to attention as von Wachtstein walked into the bunker.

Von Wachtstein found himself in a small room. An oberstleutnant, a stabsfeldwebel, and a feldwebel, who had been sitting behind a simple wooden table, jumped to their feet.

The oberstleutnant gave the straight-armed Nazi salute.

"Good morning, Herr General," he said. "You are expected. If you would be so good as to accompany the stabsfeldwebel?"

Von Wachtstein followed the warrant officer farther into the bunker to another steel door, which he pulled open just enough to admit his head. He announced, "Generalleutnant von Wachtstein, Herr Generalfeldmarschall."

"Admit him."

The door was opened wider. Von Wachtstein marched in, came to attention, and gave the Nazi salute.

Keitel, a tall erect man who was not wearing his tunic, had obviously just finished shaving; there was a blob of shaving cream next to his ear and another under his nose.

"Well?" he demanded.

"Reichsmarschall Göring, Herr Generalfeldmarschall, reports there is some mechanical difficulty with his aircraft, and there is no way he can get from Budapest here before three this afternoon, or later."

Keitel considered that a moment.

"In this regrettable circumstance, von Wachtstein, I see no alternative to you informing the Führer. He will, of course, want to know of this incident as soon as possible."

"Jawohl, Herr Generalfeldmarschall."

The "incident" was the suicide of Generaloberst Hans Jeschonnek, chief of the general staff of the Luftwaffe, who had shot himself just after midnight.

Among his other duties, Jeschonnek, Göring's deputy, had been charged—personally, by the Führer—with the protection of the rocket establishment at

Peenemunde. Hitler believed that once rocket scientist Wernher von Braun "worked the bugs out" of the V2 missile, it would cow the English into suing for peace.

The V2, which had a speed of about a mile a second, carried 1,620 pounds of high explosive in its warhead. It had a range of two hundred miles, enough to reach large parts of England. The bugs that Hitler expected von Braun to soon work out concerned navigation. The best accuracy obtained so far was that half of all missiles launched could be reasonably expected to land within an eleven-mile circle.

The rockets considerably annoyed the British, but they didn't by any means cow them. Their solution to the problem was to ask the Americans to destroy Peenemunde with B-17 bombers, as Peenemunde was too small a target to be seen by their Lancaster bombers at night.

Jeschonnek was not only unable to stop the Americans, whose bombs just about destroyed the Peenemunde installation, but made things far worse for himself by deciding that a large formation of fighter aircraft near Berlin were American and ordering the Berlin antiaircraft to shoot them down. The attack had knocked nearly one hundred of them from the sky.

Unfortunately for the Reich, they turned out to be German fighter planes.

When Jeschonnek learned of this, he put his pistol in his mouth and blew his brains all over the concrete walls of his bunker quarters.

The only question in von Wachtstein's mind about Jeschonnek's suicide was whether he had killed himself out of shame for failing to protect Peenemunde, or because nearly one hundred of his fighter pilots were dead because of his orders, or whether he did so rather than face Adolf Hitler's legendary wrath.

On his way back to the Führerhauptquartier bunker, von Wachtstein wondered if Keitel had any inkling at all of the contempt von Wachtstein felt for him. And he felt that not only because the man—referred to by his colleagues as *Lakaitel* ("Little Lackey") and as the "Nodding Donkey"—was sending him to face Hitler's wrath.

Von Wachtstein considered Keitel a disgrace to the German officer corps. While Hitler had appointed himself *Oberster Befehlshaber der Wehrmacht*— Supreme Commander of the Armed Forces—it was still clearly the duty of his officers to advise him when they thought his judgment was wrong. Keitel never disagreed with anything Hitler decided.

Stalingrad was an example. Keitel never said a word when von Paulus, nearly out of ammunition and reduced to eating his horses, had requested permission to fight his way out of his encirclement, but Hitler instead ordered him to fight to the last man. Hitler had then promoted von Paulus to field marshal and pointedly told him that no German field marshal had ever surrendered, a clear suggestion that von Paulus was honor bound to commit suicide.

The result of that had been 150,000 German soldiers dead and 91,000 captured—von Paulus among them—when the Red Army ultimately and inevitably triumphed.

Von Wachtstein knew that not only had Keitel tacitly approved the horrors that Himmler's death squads had visited on Russian soldiers and civilians, but that he had personally ordered that French pilots flying in the Normandie-Niemen fighter regiment of the Soviet air force not be treated as prisoners of war when captured. He ordered them summarily executed.

Von Wachtstein thought again that Keitel—not Adolf Hitler himself—was the real reason he had joined Operation Valkyrie. Hitler was in power solely because Keitel and the clique that surrounded him kept him in power. If Keitel survived the attempt on Hitler's life, von Wachtstein would happily shoot him himself, or preside over the court of honor to strip him of his field marshal's baton before standing him against a wall. Or, better yet, hanging him.

SS-Obersturmführer Otto Günsche, a very handsome blond man in his early twenties, who was Hitler's personal adjutant, was sitting on a Louis XIV chair outside Hitler's living quarters, obviously waiting for the Führer to appear.

"Günsche, would you please ask the Führer to receive me? It's quite important."

"Jeschonnek?"

"Has he heard?"

Günsche shook his head.

"One moment, Herr General, I will ask."

A moment later, Günsche waved von Wachtstein through the door to Hitler's living quarters.

Hitler was sitting on a Louis XIV couch, holding a Meissen teacup in his hands.

Von Wachtstein gave the Nazi salute as SS-Obersturmführer Otto Günsche stepped to a corner.

"Good morning, my Führer," von Wachtstein said.

Hitler returned the salute with a casual wave of the hand.

"Günsche said it was important."

"My Führer, I regret to inform you that Peenemunde suffered severe damage yesterday afternoon."

"So I have heard."

"And a great many of our fighters were shot down yesterday near Berlin."

"How many is 'a great many,' von Wachtstein?"

"Approximately one hundred, my Führer."

"How did that happen?"

"They were mistaken for American fighters, my Führer."

"Who made that mistake?"

"General Jeschonnek ordered the attack, my Führer."

"Günsche, get General Jeschonnek in here."

"My Führer, General Jeschonnek took his own life just after midnight," von Wachtstein said. "By pistol shot."

Hitler looked at him.

"I presume Reichsmarschall Göring has been informed?"

"Yes, my Führer," von Wachtstein said.

"And where is the reichsmarschall?"

"In Budapest, my Führer," von Wachtstein said. "He is experiencing some technical difficulty with his aircraft. He expects to be able to get here sometime after three this afternoon."

"How is it that the reichsmarschall learned of this before I have?"

"My Führer, Generalfeldmarschall Keitel has directed me to contact the reichsmarschall, inform him of General Jeschonnek's death, and to relay the generalfeldmarschall's suggestion that Reichsmarschall Göring come here as soon as possible."

"I see," Hitler said. "Oh, how well I see."

And here is where I get to feel the wrath.

"Is there anything else you have to tell me, General von Wachtstein?"

"No, my Führer."

"Then that will be all, von Wachtstein."

"Yes, my Führer."

Am I somehow going to escape the wrath?

Von Wachtstein saluted and walked toward the door.

"Günsche, find Parteileiter Bormann and ask him to come see me immediately."

"*Jawohl,* my Führer."

"Von Wachtstein!" Hitler barked.

Von Wachtstein, who was almost at the door, stopped and turned.

"Yes, my Führer?"

Now I get the wrath.

"It is not true, General von Wachtstein, that I always lose my temper with the bearer of bad news. Sometimes I understand why the bearer is the bearer."

He made an impatient gesture of dismissal.

Von Wachtstein did an about-face and left.

[TWO]
Aboard Führerhauptquartier Flug Staffel No. 12
Near Rastenburg, Germany
0655 19 August 1943

Although there was room for ten in the passenger compartment of the twin-engine aircraft, there were only three men in it.

One of them, Rear Admiral Wilhelm Canaris, a short fifty-five-year-old whose face was just starting to jowl, and who was chief of the Abwehr—Intelligence Division—of the German Armed Forces High Command, was privately—very privately—amused at the situation.

Among the most senior officers of the Nazi hierarchy, the competition was fierce for any seat on a "Hitler Squadron" Heinkel 111 flying from Berlin to "Wolf's Lair."

Almost as intense, Canaris thought, *as the competition to get a seat beside—or even near—Der Führer in his car or at dinner.*

And since the last thing I want is to go to Wolfsschanze or have dinner with the Bavarian Corporal, here I am on my way to Wolfsschanze almost certainly to have to eat at least lunch with him, and leaving behind me at Tempelhof Field ten furious very senior officers who thought they had successfully competed in the race for a seat on the eight o'clock flight.

And they can't be angry with me, either. For when they make inquiries, they will be told that SS-Obersturmführer Otto Günsche had called, announcing that I was on my way to Tempelhof, and the moment I got there, I was to be put aboard the Heinkel, which would then immediately depart for Wolfsschanze.

When the young and junior officer spoke, as a number of senior officers had learned to their pain, he spoke with the authority of the Führer.

Günsche had called Canaris earlier:

"Heil Hitler! Obersturmführer Günsche, Herr Admiral. The Führer requests your presence at your earliest convenience, Herr Admiral. An aircraft will be waiting for you at Tempelhof. May I tell the Führer that you are hastening to comply with his request, Herr Admiral?"

With Canaris in the plane—a converted bomber, or more accurately one of Germany's first (1934) commercial transport aircraft, which had been converted into a bomber and then, to move senior officials around, converted back to an airliner—were two officers. One was Canaris's deputy, Fregattenkapitän Otto von und zu Waching, a small, trim, intense Swabian. The other was Oberstleutnant Reinhard Gehlen, also trim and intense, but larger in stature than von und zu Waching. Gehlen, the senior intelligence officer of the German General Staff on the Russian front, had been in Canaris's office when Günsche had called.

There were several reasons Canaris had brought Gehlen along on the trip to Wolfsschanze. It was entirely likely Hitler would like to talk to him, for one. For another, he hadn't had enough time to talk to him before Günsche had called; Gehlen had returned to Berlin only late the night before. But the most important reason was that the opportunity to show Gehlen the inside of Wolfsschanze seemed to have been dumped in his lap.

Gehlen was an Operation Valkyrie conspirator. More than that, he had volunteered to give his own life if that was what it would take to remove Hitler. The only way Canaris could see to kill Der Führer was to do so at Wolfsschanze, and obviously, having access to the Führerhauptquartier would be necessary to accomplish that.

The compound was protected by the Leibstandarte Adolf Hitler Regiment of the SS. They made sure that no one who could possibly put Hitler, or any of the other members at the top of the Nazi power structure, in any danger could get near any of them.

Canaris motioned for Gehlen to come to his seat.

When Gehlen was squatting in the aisle beside him, Canaris said, "I didn't have time to ask, Gehlen, but are you acquainted with Oberstleutnant Wilhelm Frogger, late of the Afrikakorps?"

"I know who he is, Herr Admiral."

"There was an interesting message from Mexico City overnight," Canaris said. "The guards at border crossings from the United States have been alerted to look for him. He has apparently escaped from the prisoner-of-war camp in Mississippi and may be trying to get into Mexico."

It is equally possible, Canaris thought, *since there have been virtually no other escapes from POW camps in the United States, that Frogger said something he should not have—or approached, tried to recruit—the wrong person in the POW camp, and, following an ad hoc, secret, middle-of-the-night court-martial, was convicted of being a traitor, executed, and buried.*

Gehlen did not reply.

"I didn't know him well," Canaris went on, "but he never struck me as the sort of chap who would succeed in something like escaping from a POW cage."

"I don't know what to think, or say, Herr Admiral," Gehlen said.

"It has been my experience, Gehlen, that if you don't know what to think, it is best to think some more, and if you don't know what to say, it is best to say nothing."

Canaris turned his attention to his briefcase, and Gehlen knew he had been dismissed.

Among senior intelligence officers, there was a saying: *"One should not listen to what Canaris says; one should pay attention to what he does not say."*

There were four Heinkel 111s parked at the airfield. One was always kept there against the unlikely possibility that the Führer might suddenly decide to go to Berlin or Berchtesgaden or Vienna. The other three aircraft suggested to Canaris that the three most powerful men in the Nazi hierarchy—Hermann Göring, Heinrich Himmler, and Martin Bormann—also had been summoned to Wolfsschanze. They were the only officers important enough to have their own aircraft kept waiting for them.

Göring had the grandest title. He was Reichsmarschall des Grossdeutschen Reiches. He was the most popular—after Hitler, of course—with the people. But he had failed to bomb England into submission, and later to protect Germany from American and British bombers. Moreover, he had become the next thing to a drug addict, and tales circulated of homosexual orgies at Carinhall, his hunting estate in the Schorfheide Forest north of Berlin, and his influence had suffered.

Canaris knew that many of the rumors about Göring's sexual proclivities and drug addiction had been, if not invented, then circulated by the man everyone agreed was the most dangerous senior Nazi, Heinrich Himmler. He had two titles: He was Reichsprotektor Himmler and Reichsführer-SS Himmler. And, playing on Hitler's distrust of his generals, Himmler had managed to create his own army—thirty divisions strong—called the Waffen-SS.

The third man likely to have traveled to Wolfsschanze in his own Heinkel, Martin Bormann, also had two titles. Originally, he had been the Parteileiter of the Nazi party, running it as Hitler's deputy, and answering only to him. Recently, without objection from the Führer, he had started referring to himself as Reichsleiter Bormann, suggesting he was leading the Reich, not only the political party, and again subordinate only to Hitler.

And if those three—or only two of them—were there, Canaris reasoned, then chances were good that so was the clubfooted minister of public enlightenment and propaganda, Paul Joseph Goebbels, Ph.D.

He probably caught a ride with Bormann. Or Günsche commandeered a Heinkel for him as he did for me.

Four vehicles—a large Mercedes open sedan and three Kübelwagens, militarized, canvas-topped versions of the Volkswagen—came to meet the Heinkel as ground handlers showed the pilot where to park. An SS-hauptsturmführer was standing in the front seat of the Mercedes. Nine storm troopers under an SS-oberscharführer, all armed with Schmeisser machine pistols, got quickly out of the Kübelwagens and surrounded the airplane.

When the hauptsturmführer saw that his men were in place, he gestured rather imperiously to the sergeant to go to the airplane. He then got out of the Mercedes and walked to the Heinkel.

The door in the fuselage opened and Canaris came out.

The hauptsturmführer and the oberscharführer gave the Nazi salute. Canaris returned it with an almost casual wave of his arm and walked to the Mercedes, followed by von und zu Waching and Gehlen. They all got in.

The oberscharführer went into the Heinkel as the hauptsturmführer walked quickly to the Mercedes, which started off as soon as he got in.

They drove off the airfield to the collection of buildings and yellow-and-black-striped barrier pole guarding access to the inner compound.

A half-dozen SS officers and enlisted men gave the Nazi salute, and one of the latter trotted to the Mercedes and opened the car's passenger doors. Canaris and the others got out. The barrier pole was raised, and they walked past it and got into another open Mercedes.

Changing cars saved the time it would take to thoroughly search a car entering the interior compound.

The car, a Mercedes reserved for senior officers, carried them a kilometer and a half past stark concrete bunkers and finally stopped before one of them, where another half-dozen SS officers and enlisted men, all armed with Schmeisser machine pistols, gave the Nazi salute.

They had reached the Führerbunker itself.

Canaris, von und zu Waching, and Gehlen got out of the Mercedes and walked to a sturdy steel door, which an enlisted man pulled open just as they reached it and closed after they had passed through.

They were now in a barren room, presided over by an SS-obersturmbann-führer. There was a table, and a row of steel cabinets each large enough for a suitcase. A double shelf above a coatrack held perhaps twenty uniform caps.

The obersturmbannführer gave a crisp Nazi salute and barked, "Heil Hitler!"

Canaris again made a causal wave of his arm.

"These officers are, Herr Admiral?"

"They are with me," Canaris replied.

"Regulations require I have their names and organizations, Herr Admiral, and see their identity documents."

"Fregattenkapitän Otto von und zu Waching, my deputy," Canaris replied, "and Oberstleutnant Reinhard Gehlen, of Abwehr Ost."

As the two handed over their identity documents, which the obersturm-bannführer scrutinized carefully before handing them to a clerk, who wrote the names and the date and time on a form, Canaris took his pistol, a 9mm Luger Parabellum, from its holster and laid it on the table.

"The Führer's security, Herr Oberstleutnant," Canaris said evenly, "requires that you surrender your sidearm, and any knives you might have, to these officers."

"*Jawohl, Herr Admiral,*" Gehlen said, and laid his pistol on the table. "No knives, Herr Admiral."

Canaris gave his uniform cap to one of the enlisted men, who put it on the rack. Canaris then raised his arms to the sides at shoulder height.

"With your permission, Herr Admiral," the obersturmbannführer said, and patted him down.

Gehlen and von und zu Waching went through the same routine.

The obersturmbannführer nodded at a hauptsturmführer, who clicked his heels and said, "If you will be good enough to come with me, gentlemen?"

He led them through a steel door, down concrete corridors and stairwells, and finally stopped before another steel door.

Canaris had been here often enough to know this was not the door to where Hitler could usually be found poring over a stack of maps.

"What's this, Herr Hauptsturmführer?"

"Reichsleiter Bormann wished to have a word with you, Herr Admiral, before you are received by the Führer."

"Very well."

"A word alone with you, Herr Admiral," the hauptsturmführer said.

Canaris nodded and went through the door. Bormann was not there; the room was empty and unfurnished.

Is this a trick to get me in here?

What happens next?

The Bavarian corporal and half a dozen of Himmler's thugs rush in to knock me to the floor?

Then Hitler looks down at me and says, "We know all about Valkyrie. I wanted to spit in your traitorous eyes before I turn you over to the SS"?

The door opened and Martin Bormann entered and closed the door.

"I'll have to make this quick, Canaris. He knows you're here."

"What's this all about, Bormann?"

"Early this morning, he sent for me. I found out later that he'd just heard Jeschonnek blew his brains out."

"What did he want?"

"He said he was worried about Operation Phoenix."

"Himmler told him how they blundered again over there?"

"No. He doesn't know about that, and I'm not going to tell him. What he said—he was quite emotional—was that 'if things go badly' he and his senior officers will of course fight to the death in Berlin. But that it was important that National Socialism survive, and that meant some of its 'relatively senior officers'—he mentioned von Wachtstein, which surprised me, until I learned that Keitel had sent von Wachtstein to tell him about yesterday's disaster.

"Anyway, he said that we have to make sure relatively senior officers, military and especially in the party, find refuge in South America, and that they have the funds to keep National Socialism alive and bring it back. That I should consider it a high priority."

"My God!"

"I told him things were going along according to plan, and he gave me a look that made me think he knew about the Froggers, et cetera. But then he said, 'I'm going to send for Canaris. He's reliable, he knows Argentina, and I don't think he's playing an active enough role in Operation Phoenix.'"

Canaris did not respond.

"And then he left. I thought I should tell you before you go in there. We're going to have to be very careful, Canaris."

"I understand. Thank you."

"You better get in there. I know he's waiting for you."

Canaris nodded, then walked to the door and pulled it open.

"Shall I announce you, Herr Admiral?" the hauptsturmführer at the door of what Canaris thought of as "the map room" asked.

"That won't be necessary. The Führer sent for me."

The hauptsturmführer pulled open the door. Canaris, with von und zu Waching and Gehlen on his heels, walked in.

Adolf Hitler—surprising Canaris not at all—was bent over a large, map-covered table. He was wearing rather ugly eyeglasses. His military staff, headed by Generalfeldmarschall Wilhelm Keitel, plus all the people Canaris expected to be there, including Himmler and Goebbels, were standing in a rough half-circle at the table. Behind them, against the wall, were lesser lights, among them Generalleutnant von Wachtstein and Luftwaffe General Kurt Student.

Canaris had expected to see von Wachtstein, but he wondered what Student was doing here; an advocate of "vertical envelopment," Student had lost favor with Hitler after his Fallschirmjäger troops not only hadn't easily captured Crete when they had parachuted onto it, but had suffered severe casualties.

The only ones who acknowledged Canaris, and that with a just-perceptible nod, were Keitel and Grand Admiral Karl Dönitz, the commander in chief of the navy. The others looked at him as if they had never seen him before.

After perhaps thirty seconds, Hitler looked up at Canaris, who rendered another sloppy salute and said, "My Führer."

Von und zu Waching and Gehlen stood to attention.

Hitler pointed at Gehlen.

"Who is this officer?"

"Oberstleutnant Gehlen, Reinhard, my Führer," Canaris said. "The senior intelligence officer of the OKH."

"And the oberstleutnant is here why?"

"I thought you might wish to receive him, my Führer. He returned from Russia only last night."

Hitler started to walk around the table.

"Very thoughtful of you, Admiral," he said. "But unnecessary. Bad news travels very fast. I have already learned of the daily disaster there. And the daily disaster here in Germany."

He was now standing in front of Gehlen.

"Colonel, how good of you to come," he said, putting out his hand and oozing charm. "I am always delighted to meet a fighting soldier; one doesn't see many of them around here."

He patted Gehlen's arm, then turned to Canaris.

"What I hoped the admiral could tell me is the present location of Benito Mussolini. But before we get into that, I want to hear the admiral's sage evaluation of the death of General Jeschonnek."

"My Führer, I was very saddened to hear of General Jeschonnek's death."

"I asked, Admiral, for your evaluation of the effect of his death on Germany, not its effect on you."

Canaris suddenly realized that Hermann Göring, head of the Luftwaffe, was not in the room.

I should have seen that sooner.

"My Führer, as I understand the situation—and I don't know much; it only happened last midnight—General Jeschonnek took his life because he was in a state of depression and temporarily bereft of his senses. Apparently he felt that he had failed—the Luftwaffe had failed—to adequately protect Germany from Allied air raids."

"As it has," Hitler said. "But this 'failure,' as you so delicately put it, has not caused Reichsmarschall Göring to become depressed—to blow *his* brains out—and I would say, Admiral, wouldn't you, that the reichsmarschall is at least as responsible for the Luftwaffe's failure as was General Jeschonnek?"

"My Führer, I don't pretend to understand suicide. My feeling is that men have different breaking points. I can suggest only that General Jeschonnek reached his when he realized what had happened."

"Germany cannot afford to have its generals blowing their brains out every time they suffer a temporary setback," Hitler said bitterly.

Hitler glared at him for a long moment, during which Canaris had decided it was his time to be on the receiving end of one of Hitler's tyrannical rages.

"Dr. Goebbels suggests that we report that General Jeschonnek met his end, quote, test-flying a new fighter plane, end quote," Hitler said, "and that he be buried, with all the attendant publicity, with full military honors. I have mixed feelings. I wonder if Jeschonnek didn't take the coward's way out."

He looked at Canaris, waiting for him to reply.

"My Führer, I am wholly unqualified to offer an opinion about anything Dr. Goebbels says *vis-à-vis* a delicate situation like this one."

Hitler stared at him with icy eyes.

Here it comes. I am about to be dressed down by the Austrian corporal in front of the leadership—less Göring, of course—of the Thousand-Year Reich.

It didn't.

"Where, in your opinion, Admiral, is Benito Mussolini?" Hitler asked.

My God, where did that question come from?

On 25 July, Italian king Victor Emmanuel had stripped Italian fascist dictator Benito Mussolini of his power and arrested him. Nine days later, a representative of Marshal Badoglio, who had replaced Mussolini, secretly surrendered Italy unconditionally to a representative of General Dwight D. Eisenhower, the Supreme Allied Commander. The surrender would not be made public for weeks, on 8 September 1943.

"On the island of Ponza, my Führer."

"Where?"

"On the island of Ponza, my Führer," Canaris repeated. He pointed at the map-strewn table. "May I?"

"Please do," Hitler said.

Canaris went to the table, found the map he needed, and pointed his index finger at a cluster of islands in the Tyrrhenian Sea off the west coast of Italy.

"On Ponza, the larger island, my Führer," Canaris said.

"Himmler, would you take a look at this, please?" Hitler asked.

Heinrich Himmler walked quickly to the table.

"That is where Admiral Canaris tells me Mussolini is," Hitler said. "It is not where you told me he is. I wonder which of you is right."

Himmler said firmly: "Captain Skorzeny reported within the last forty-eight hours, my Führer, that Il Duce is being held in the Campo Imperatore Hotel in Abruzzi, in the Apennine Mountains."

"Admiral?" Hitler asked very softly.

"I have a man in the Italian marines who are guarding Il Duce, my Führer," Canaris said. "In his daily report—as of four this morning, Mussolini is on Ponza."

"Your man sends you a daily report on Il Duce's whereabouts?" Hitler asked.

"Yes, my Führer. He has previously reported that Mussolini will be taken—as soon as safe travel can be arranged—to the Campo Imperatore Hotel."

"Tell the admiral, Himmler, who Hauptmann Skorzeny is," Hitler said softly.

"SS-Hauptmann Otto Skorzeny is something of a legend within the Waffen-SS, Canaris. I assigned him—as the best man for the job available to me—to track Il Duce when the Italians betrayed us and Mussolini was arrested. I can't believe he made a mistake like this."

"I can," Hitler said. "Which leaves us with something of an administrative problem." He fixed his eyes on Canaris. "You will learn, Admiral, if you already haven't, that the reward for someone who doesn't make mistakes is that other onerous chores are soon added to what chores he is already bearing by those who do make mistakes."

Canaris thought: *Someone like yourself, you mean? Who is incapable of making a mistake, and is thus doomed to correct the errors of others?*

Hitler looked around at the other senior officers who were still standing in a rough semicircle behind him. He didn't see what he was looking for, and he turned his attention to the officers lined up against the wall.

"General von Wachtstein, would you be good enough to join us?"

Von Wachtstein walked over to Hitler, who went on:

"General, Reichsprotektor Himmler and Admiral Canaris are about to return to Berlin, where, together with General Student, they will replan and execute the liberation of Il Duce from his captors. Replanning is necessary because if the original plan—General Student's Fallschirmjägers taking the Campo Imperatore Hotel in Abruzzi with irresistible force—had been executed, Il Duce would not have been there.

"A little mistake on the part of one of the Reichsprotektor's men. Or perhaps on the part of the Reichsprotektor himself; he didn't consider it necessary to consult with the chief of Abwehr intelligence *vis-à-vis* the actual location of Il Duce. Why should he? The SS is perfect and knows everything.

"Your role in this, General von Wachtstein, is to witness the discussions between these gentlemen and, when they have made any decision at all, to relay that decision to me so that I will have the chance to stop any blunders before they occur. Telephone each decision these gentlemen reach to Obersturmführer Günsche, who will pass it to me. Any questions?"

"No, my Führer," von Wachtstein said.

"That will be all, gentlemen," Hitler said.

And then he walked to Gehlen.

"I very much appreciate the good work Abwehr Ost has been doing, Herr Oberstleutnant. Please convey my compliments to your associates when you return to the east."

"*Jawohl,* my Führer. Thank you, my Führer."

Hitler walked back to the map-covered table and leaned over it.

One by one, Himmler, von Wachtstein, Student, Canaris, von und zu Waching, and Gehlen walked to the door, gave the Nazi salute, and left. Nobody seemed to notice.

[THREE]
Tempelhof Airfield
Berlin, Germany
1605 19 August 1943

Himmler said virtually nothing to anyone on the flight to Berlin.

Canaris wondered if Himmler really was fascinated with the contents of his briefcase, or whether he was angry with him for making him look like a fool with Hitler.

Canaris went over what had happened at Wolfsschanze several times in his mind. With the exception of that very long three or four seconds during which he felt sure he was about to feel Hitler's often irrational rage, everything had gone well.

And Hitler hadn't mentioned Operation Phoenix at all. Canaris wondered if Bormann had told Himmler about that encounter with the Bavarian corporal.

On reflection, Canaris didn't think he was going to get into any difficulty about the operation to rescue Mussolini; his only contribution to that was going to be providing the intelligence regarding the deposed Italian dictator's location. And he was sure he knew. His man with Il Duce was solid as a rock.

As the Heinkel taxied up to the curved Tempelhof terminal building, Canaris saw that a small convoy of cars was waiting for them.

Himmler's first deputy adjutant—SS-Brigadeführer Ritter Manfred von Deitzberg, a tall, slim, blond, forty-two-year-old Westphalian—was standing beside the lead car, an enormous Mercedes-Benz convertible sedan that carried on its right front fender the metal flag of the Reichsführer-SS.

Canaris's own car, a much smaller Mercedes that carried no indication of whom it would carry, was immediately behind that, and then came slightly larger cars for Generals Student and von Wachtstein, each equipped with the metal flag appropriate to their rank.

Himmler exercised his right to be the first off the airplane. A moment later, Canaris followed him. He was surprised to see that Himmler was waiting for him.

"I have been thinking, Canaris," he said. "Not only do I have a full plate, as I'm sure you understand, but I'm a policeman, not a military man."

He waited for Canaris to respond. He didn't.

After a moment, Himmler went on: "Von Deitzberg, on the other hand, was a soldier. What I'm thinking is that I will take von Deitzberg with me now, tell him what happened at Wolfsschanze, then send him to you and Student and von Wachtstein so that you can work out what has to be done between you. Where will you be, at your office?"

The Reichsführer-SS has apparently decided that if something else goes wrong with this absurd mission to rescue Il Duce, it won't be his fault. If he can blame whatever goes wrong on me, fine.

That will teach me it is not wise to have more accurate intelligence than he does. And if he can't blame me, he'll blame von Deitzberg.

"I thought I would take General Student and General von Wachtstein to my house for an early dinner with Gehlen. We missed lunch at Wolfsschanze."

"Well, there is a silver lining in every black cloud, isn't there?" Himmler said, smiling as he made a little joke. The meals served at Wolfsschanze were standard army field rations, invariably bland and unappetizing. It was the Führer's idea, intended to remind all the senior officers of the troops in the field.

Himmler rarely made little jokes, and when he smiled he reminded Canaris of a funeral director who had just sold an impoverished widow the most expensive coffin he had for sale.

"I think I should take Student with me," Himmler went on. "He can tell von Deitzberg what he has planned. And then all of you can get together first thing in the morning?"

That wasn't a question. That's what he wants done.

"Would half past seven at my office be too early for General Student, do you think, Herr Reichsführer? I like to get to the office early."

"I'll have him there," Himmler said. "And if von Deitzberg can find him for me, I'll have Hauptsturmführer Skorzeny there, too."

"Fine," Canaris said.

Skorzeny, you are about to find out that Himmler's rages, while not quite as loud and long-lasting as those of the Führer, are nearly as devastating.

Himmler did not like being humiliated before the Führer because you provided him with inaccurate intelligence.

Himmler gave a Nazi salute about as sloppy as Canaris usually gave. It was returned as sloppily by Canaris, and very crisply by everyone else.

Then Himmler got into the enormous Mercedes. Von Deitzberg got in beside him. General Student walked to the Luftwaffe Mercedes sedan, got in, and it pulled out of line and followed Himmler's car.

"General von Wachtstein," Canaris said, "I was just thinking, since we will have to be at my office early in the morning, that what we should do is let your car go, and you can come spend the night at my house."

"I would hate to be an imposition, Herr Admiral."

"Not at all. My wife is visiting her family in Bremen."

Actually, she's in Westertede, which I devoutly hope is far enough from Bremen so that it won't be bombed even by mistake by the B-17s of the Eighth Air Force.

"In that case, Herr Admiral, I think accepting your kind invitation would be a good idea."

[FOUR]
357 Roonstrasse, Zehlendorf
Berlin, Germany
1605 19 August 1943

En route from the airfield, there was a good deal of evidence of the efficacy of the daily—by the U.S. Eighth Air Force—and nightly—by the Royal Air Force—bombing of Berlin. But once the suburb of Zehlendorf was reached there was virtually no sign of the war except the absence of streetlights and lights in windows.

There were two civilian policemen on the street in front of Canaris's house, and Canaris knew there was another patrolling the alley and gardens behind it.

One of the policemen checked the identity cards of everyone in Canaris's Mercedes, then signaled to the other policeman to open the gate.

The driver stopped the car under a portico on the left side of the house, then hurried to open the rear passenger door on the other side before Canaris could do so himself. He failed.

Admiral Canaris walked to a door, which opened just before he got there. General von Wachtstein, Oberstleutnant Gehlen, and Fregattenkapitän von und zu Waching followed him into the house.

The door was closed, and the lights in the foyer came on.

They now saw who had opened and closed the door: a burly man in his sixties. He had closely cropped gray hair and wore a white cotton jacket—and he suddenly said, "Shit! I forgot Max."

The lights went off. The door was opened, and the driver of the car came into the room. The door was closed, and the lights went on again.

"Gentlemen, this is Egon, who was chief of the boat when I commanded U-201 in the first war," Canaris said, motioning toward the burly one. "And this is Max, who was my chief bosun when I commanded the *Schlesien*. They take care of me."

He pointed at the officers with him and identified them.

"Egon, see that no one can hear what's said in the living room," Canaris said.

"I did that when they called and said send the car," Egon said.

"And then, since we have all earned it, bring us something—something hard—to drink in there. And when you've done that, get us something to eat. We missed lunch at Wolfsschanze."

"I can have sauerbraten, potatoes, and carrots in thirty minutes."

"That sounds fine," Canaris said, then waved the men with him ahead of him into the living room.

Everybody took seats in an assortment of armchairs. Max, now wearing a white cotton steward's jacket, came in carrying a large tray heavy with glasses, an ice bucket, a siphon bottle, and two bottles of Johnnie Walker Black Label scotch whisky. He set it on a table.

"I regret I am out of schnapps," Canaris said. "This decadent English swill will have to do."

A faint smile flickered across von Wachtstein's lips.

"We can make our own drinks, Max," Canaris said. "Go help Egon burn the sauerbraten."

Max nodded his acceptance of the order.

Canaris waited until he had left the living room and had closed the door behind him, then said: "So far as Max and Egon are concerned: They hear more than they should about things that should be of no concern to them. That's not a problem, as I trust them with my life. But I generally make an effort to ensure they don't hear anything more than they have to.

"The scenario now is that tomorrow, while General von Wachtstein watches us, General Student will tell us what he has planned for the rescue of Mussolini when we learn Il Duce has been moved from Ponza to Abruzzi, if indeed that's where they take him.

"I will agree with whatever plan Student has, as I suspect whatever that is will have the approval of the Reichsführer. And I will agree to the participation in the rescue by Hauptmann Skorzeny, as I suspect the Reichsführer, for reasons he has not seen fit to share with me, wants him to participate.

"Von Wachtstein will relay our agreement to the Führer via Obersturmführer Günsche. We will then wait until there is word from Ponza—I get a daily report, usually first thing in the morning—that Il Duce has been moved.

"Von Wachtstein will report that Il Duce is being moved, that it has been confirmed that he has safely arrived wherever that is, and then I will ask the Reichsführer's permission to ask the Führer for permission to proceed with the operation. The Reichsführer may, of course, elect to ask the Führer himself."

He looked around the table to see that everyone had understood the nuances of what he had said.

"I was pleased when the Führer was so gracious to Oberstleutnant Gehlen. I thought it was important that Gehlen see where it is that the Führer and his staff conduct the war."

He checked to see that they had all understood the nuances of that, too.

"I have had a communication from Kapitän zur See Boltitz in Buenos Aires. Lamentably, he reports that he has as yet been unable to detect the traitor many feel we have in our embassy there. In this endeavor, he has enlisted the aid of Major von Wachtstein.

"He did report that an attempt to rescue the Froggers from where they were being held not only failed but resulted in the deaths of half a dozen SS men.

"He further reported that another attempt by unknown persons on the life of Cletus Frade, who many believe is the OSS man in Argentina, failed, resulting in the death of three Argentines.

"And finally, I learned from my man in Mexico City that U.S. Border Patrol posts have been alerted to look for Oberstleutnant Wilhelm Frogger, who has apparently escaped from his POW enclosure and may be trying to get into Mexico."

He paused and looked around the table again.

"Otto, it has just occurred to me that, inexcusably—the fact that I was summoned to Wolfsschanze is not a valid excuse—I failed to notify either

Parteileiter Bormann or the Reichsführer of what I learned from Argentina. Will you please remember to remind me to do so first thing in the morning?"

"*Jawohl, Herr Admiral,*" von und zu Waching said.

"A toast, gentlemen," Canaris said as he rose from the table.

"Our Führer and the Final Victory," Canaris said.

The others raised their glasses and there was a chorus repeating the toast.

And if you have been listening to this, Herr Reichsführer, despite Egon's skilled sweep of the place for listening devices—never underestimate one's enemy—then I hope you are satisfied that I am not only one of the faithful, but always willing to defer to your superior judgment.

And after we have our supper and von und zu Waching goes home and the rest of us "go to bed," we'll have another chat in my bomb shelter.

Getting a listening device through the eight-inch concrete walls of that is simply impossible.

That was not to happen.

They had just sat down to their sauerbraten and carrots when Egon came into the dining room. He took a telephone from a sideboard, set it on the table in front of Canaris, and announced, "Von Deitzberg."

Canaris nodded and picked up the telephone.

"What can I do for you, Herr Brigadeführer?"

"Won't it wait until the morning?"

"In fifteen minutes, we'll be having dinner. Can you give us thirty minutes for that?"

"I understand."

He put the handset in its cradle and stood up.

"Von Deitzberg wants to see me before the morning meeting," he said. "He will be here in thirty minutes, probably less than that."

He pointed at the floor, then turned to Egon.

"In twenty minutes, Egon, I want this table to look as if you've just served."

Egon nodded.

The bomb shelter was illuminated with American Coleman gas lanterns hanging from the low ceiling. It was furnished with three steel cots, a desk with a typewriter, four small armchairs, and a portable toilet.

"It is always best for people involved in something like we are to know nothing they don't absolutely have to know," Canaris began. He was sitting far back in one of the armchairs, tapping the balls of his spread fingers together. "In this case, however, I think we have to ignore that wisdom."

Admiral Canaris glanced at General von Wachtstein, Oberstleutnant Gehlen, and Fregattenkapitän von und zu Waching. Gehlen and von und zu Waching nodded. Von Wachtstein grunted.

Carnaris went on: "In light of the recent events in Argentina, both the Führer's sudden interest in Operation Phoenix and because what I think von Deitzberg wants is my assistance, or at least my acquiescence, in his going to Argentina.

"He will most likely tell me that he is concerned with dangers posed to Operation Phoenix by the defection of the Froggers. What he is really concerned about is the possibility that the Americans, now that they have learned about it from Herr Frogger, will make the ransoming operation public.

"If they should do so, von Deitzberg reasons, it would come to the attention of Himmler. So far as I have been able to determine, Himmler is unaware of the ransoming operation. If it came out, the best scenario *vis-à-vis* von Deitzberg would be Himmler's displeasure with him for failing to discover the operation; the worst scenario for him, of course, being that Himmler would learn that von Deitzberg was the brains behind it.

"These factors apply. The Americans knew all about the ransoming operation long before the Froggers deserted. President Roosevelt has decided that exposing the operation would serve only to ensure that no other Jews escaped the ovens. Aside from collecting data—evidence—to be introduced at the trials of these scum after the war, the Americans will do nothing to interfere with the ransoming operation.

"Insofar as Operation Phoenix is concerned, the Americans know all about that, too, and did before the Froggers deserted. The decision there has been to interfere if possible—in other words, if they could learn of other shipments, where they would be landed, they would inform the Argentines, so that Germany would be embarrassed and the funds lost—but not to take action themselves.

"Again, their intention is to collect evidence not only that the Phoenix funds were sent to Argentina, but about how they were expended. When the war is lost, they can then claim both any unexpended funds and what property, et cetera was acquired with the funds, as enemy property.

"I have decided it would be counterproductive to inform the Americans—

if indeed I could find out, and I am not going to ask any questions, and no one else should—of the dispatch of special funds by submarine, and their arrival sites and dates.

"Von Deitzberg knows nothing of all this, and I am reasonably sure he thinks I don't know about the ransoming operation. But he will proceed on the assumption that I do—in his shoes, so would I.

"What von Deitzberg wants to do is make sure there is absolutely nothing in Argentina—or Uruguay, which is usually the destination of the Jews extracted from the concentration camps—that could possibly tie him to the ransoming operation.

"So let us consider what we have in Buenos Aires: The man Bormann sent there over my objections, Kapitän zur See Boltitz, has proven to be a better counterintelligence officer than I thought he would be—"

"Over your objections, Admiral?" Gehlen interrupted. "I thought—"

"That he was one of us? The sure way to get him there was to convince Bormann I didn't want him to go. May I go on?"

"I beg your pardon, Herr Admiral," Gehlen said.

"As I said, Boltitz proved to be a far better counterintelligence officer than I thought he would be. And since his orders from me were to find the traitor, or traitors, in the embassy, he did just that: It didn't take him long at all to find out that Major von Wachtstein had passed—to Major Frade of the OSS—the details of when and where the *Océano Pacífico* was going to attempt to land the special cargo.

"That resulted—I think everybody but you knows this, Gehlen—in the *Océano Pacífico* being met by either Argentine army snipers—or representatives of the OSS—who shot Oberst Grüner, the military attaché, and his assistant, Standartenführer Josef Goltz, to death and forced the landing of the special cargo to be aborted.

"Boltitz confronted Major von Wachtstein and they reached a between-honorable-officers agreement: Major von Wachtstein would have a fatal accident in his Storch and Kapitän zur See Boltitz would not only not reveal his treason, but destroy what evidence he had collected.

"While Major von Wachtstein was perfectly willing to carry out his end of the agreement—doing so would keep General von Wachtstein from being hung from one of Himmler's butcher's hooks—he saw it as his duty to tell Ambassador von Lutzenberger, whom he knew to be a Valkyrie conspirator, what had happened.

"That forced the ambassador to make Boltitz privy to what was going on long before I wanted that to happen.

"While I was delighted, of course, that Major von Wachtstein did not have a fatal accident, I confess that I had—that I have—certain concerns *vis-à-vis* the ability of either of these young officers, neither of whom has any experience to speak of in matters of this sort, to handle their new situation.

"The SS man in Buenos Aires, Obersturmbannführer Karl Cranz, and his deputy, Sturmbannführer Erich Raschner, are both very good at what they do. For reasons he did not choose to share with me, Bormann arranged for Cranz to be sent there, replacing von Deitzberg, while leaving Raschner, who has been von Deitzberg's deputy there.

"Having said that, I am at a loss to understand why Cranz sent Obersturmführer Heitz and his men—whose mission in Argentina was to guard the special shipment until it could be used for Operation Phoenix—to try to rescue—more likely eliminate—the Froggers at Frade's farm.

"Nor do I understand why that mission was a complete failure. One possible scenario is that the chief of Argentina's BIS, a Colonel Martín, who is very competent, could have learned about the plan and warned Frade—that is, warned Frade's men, as Frade was in the U.S. at the time of the attack.

"This is not to suggest that Frade has turned Colonel Martín, or even that Martín is more sympathetic to the Allied cause than previously suspected. It is more likely that he is acting solely in what he perceives to be Argentina's best interests.

"Supporting this scenario, but not confirming it, are these facts: Nothing appeared in the Argentine press, nor was anything mentioned discreetly by Argentine authorities to the ambassador about either the attack on Frade's farm or the attempted assassination of Frade shortly after he returned to Argentina from the United States.

"It could be—purely conjecture—that whether or not Martín was actively involved in seeing that both attacks failed, his failure to take official notice of either gave the German Embassy—not only Cranz, but the ambassador as well—the message that any future efforts along these lines would not only similarly fail but would also greatly annoy the Argentine officer corps, which is to say the government.

"Much of the Argentine officer corps was greatly annoyed when Oberst Frade was assassinated. The assassination was arranged for—over the objections of Oberst Grüner, who knew how popular Frade was within the officer corps—by Standartenführer Goltz acting at the orders of Himmler or, more likely, von Deitzberg.

"The idea, apparently, was to strike terror into the hearts of the Argentine officer corps: Anyone who posed a threat to the ambitions of the German Reich, even someone about to become president of Argentina, as Frade was, could be eliminated.

"To their surprise, the reaction of the officer corps to Oberst Frade's murder was not fear but outrage. The *coup d'état*, which followed shortly, put into power a man who is anything but convinced of our Final Victory. Moreover, Frade's son participated, apparently showing great personal courage, in the *coup d'état*, which made him, in the eyes of many officers, a son of Argentina come home, rather than the OSS man in Argentina.

"After the disaster at Samborombón Bay, von Deitzberg put on a major general's uniform and went to Argentina, where he assured Oberst Juan Domingo Perón that the German officer corps was as outraged over Frade's assassination as he was. He told Perón the assassination had been the late Oberst Grüner's idea.

"Von Deitzberg also carried with him a map of how South America will look after our Final Victory. Uruguay, Paraguay, and parts of Brazil will become part of Argentina. He also made it clear that Germany would help in any way it could to see that Perón became president. And showed him how profitable it would be for him to assist in the investment of Operation Phoenix funds.

"How much of this Oberst Perón swallowed whole is unknown.

"Another unknown here is what role the first secretary of our embassy, Anton Gradny-Sawz, has played, if any, in any or all of this. The ambassador feels he has played no role at all. On the other hand, Gradny-Sawz has demonstrated his willingness to change sides whenever he feels his side is going to lose. He's a Viennese, one who was very helpful to the Third Reich before the Anschluss returned Austria to the Grossdeutsches Reich.

"It is possible, I suggest, that Gradny-Sawz, who is privy to Operation Phoenix, has decided to ingratiate himself with the Argentines in case the Final Victory doesn't take place. That, in other words, he approached the Argentines or, more likely, Martín approached him and found him receptive. I just don't know.

"I think we are all agreed that our priority must be the removal of the Austrian corporal before he destroys what's left of Germany.

"So what I must decide, with your counsel but right now, as we don't have the time to gather further intelligence, or to consider the matter at leisure, is how to deal with SS-Brigadeführer von Deitzberg when he comes here in twenty minutes to discuss Operation Phoenix with me. I really think he's going to solicit my assistance in having him returned to Argentina.

"Another factor that has to be considered is the quote unquote escape of Oberstleutnant Frogger from his POW camp. There are, I suggest, two possibilities. One is that somehow his connection with Valkyrie came to light, and that after interrogation—during which he revealed we have no idea what—he was, at General von Arnim's orders, ordered before a secret *pro forma* court-martial, convicted of treason, executed, and buried in a Mississippi cotton field.

"The second possibility is that Frogger was taken from the camp by the OSS, who made the connection between him and his parents. The questions here are whether he went willingly or unwillingly, and what he decided to tell the Americans, if anything, about Valkyrie.

"If they have turned Frogger—unlikely, but one dares hope; they are not nearly as inept in matters like this as they would have us believe—that would be of enormous value to Valkyrie. He and von Stauffenberg were close; he knows as much as—possibly more than—I do about whom we can trust in not only carrying out Hitler's removal, but immediately afterward, when senior people are still making up their minds which way to jump.

"I feel confident that I will have an explanation of his escape—an honest one—from my American contact. But when I will have the opportunity to communicate with him is an unknown, except certainly not before Brigadeführer von Deitzberg comes here tonight.

"Inasmuch, again, as our priority is Valkyrie, the question then becomes: Is von Deitzberg more dangerous to Valkyrie here—or running around Argentina desperately trying to cover his connection with the ransoming operation?"

He paused, let that be considered a moment, then went on:

"Now, these factors enter into that question. If von Deitzberg is returned to Argentina, he will have been charged by Himmler and Bormann with discovering the traitor. Two scenarios occur: One—and bear in mind that von Deitzberg is far more experienced than Boltitz—that he uncovers Major von Wachtstein. Or, two, that he doesn't. But von Deitzberg is going to find the traitor, even if he has to invent one. Two candidates for that role: Von Wachtstein and Gradny-Sawz. I tend to think he will choose Gradny-Sawz, but that, of course, isn't at all certain."

Canaris looked at each man for a moment.

"Gehlen? You look as if you want to say something."

"What would happen to the ransoming operation if von Deitzberg were eliminated?"

"It would continue under Cranz."

"And if Cranz were eliminated?"

"Then I suspect the underlings would just stop, praying that they wouldn't be exposed to Himmler."

"You don't know who these underlings are?" Gehlen asked.

Canaris shook his head, then said, "I've made a point of not looking into that. If it blows up in their faces, I want to be as surprised as Himmler; I don't want the Führer wondering why, if I even suspected something, I didn't say anything to Himmler or Bormann. And if I did look into it, that would come out."

"Herr Admiral," Gehlen said carefully, "I suspect if something happened to von Deitzberg and Cranz, the others involved in the ransoming operation would do more than pray. They would be frantically trying to cover their tracks. And if they were doing that . . ."

"They would have less time to look into things like Valkyrie?" Canaris finished the sentence, making it a question.

"Yes, sir," Gehlen said.

"That's an interesting thought, but I don't think either Boltitz or von Wachtstein would be very effective assassins."

"For moral or practical reasons?"

"Both."

"What about the Americans? You said they killed Grüner and Goltz at Samborombón Bay."

"I said *either* the Argentines or the Americans," Canaris said.

There was a tone in Canaris's voice that Otto von und zu Waching knew said: *Pay me the courtesy of listening carefully to what I say.*

"Are you suggesting that I try to have him sent to Argentina?" Canaris then asked.

"Admiral, if von Deitzberg is busy in Argentina, he can't be looking for Valkyrie here," Gehlen said.

"General von Wachtstein?" Canaris asked, looking toward him.

"Better that von Deitzberg is there than here, Herr Admiral, would be my judgment."

"Otto?"

"And better still, Herr Admiral, if he could be—if Cranz and he—could be eliminated over there," von und zu Waching said.

Canaris looked at him thoughtfully for a moment before asking, "By the Americans, you mean?"

"Yes, sir."

"That would presume the Americans would be amenable to such a suggestion. Even relaying the suggestion to them would be difficult. And once that had been done, they might decline, for a number of reasons. For one, it might interfere with the status quo agreement they seem to have with the Argentines. And, for another, they would have to somehow get close enough to him to do it."

He let that sink in a moment, then went on.

"I suggest we go upstairs and have as much of our supper as possible before von Deitzberg shows up and ruins our appetites."

Von und zu Waching, who had long ago learned to listen to what Canaris was not saying, rather than what he was saying, realized that Canaris had accepted Gehlen's suggestion that the best way to deal with the problems von Deitzberg and Cranz were posing was to have the Americans eliminate them in Argentina.

And I don't think either General von Wachtstein or Oberstleutnant Gehlen understands that.

Gehlen possibly—he's bright and an intelligence officer—but von Wachtstein has no idea what Canaris has just decided.

[FIVE]

Ten minutes later, as they were sitting over their supper listening to the news from the BBC in London over an ornate Siemens radio on a sideboard, Egon appeared at the door. This time he was far more formal than he had previously been. Standing at rigid attention, he barked:

"Heil Hitler! Herr Admiral, I regret the intrusion. SS-Brigadeführer von Deitzberg's compliments, Herr Admiral. The brigadeführer asks that you receive him."

"Show him in," Canaris said.

"Jawohl, Herr Admiral!"

A moment later, Egon returned and again popped to attention and barked, "Herr Admiral, SS-Brigadeführer Ritter von Deitzberg!"

Von Deitzberg marched in, gave a straight-armed Nazi salute, and barked, "Heil Hitler!"

Von Wachtstein, Gehlen, and von und zu Waching returned it snappily. Canaris made a sloppy wave of his arm.

"I didn't expect to see you, von Deitzberg, until tomorrow morning," Canaris said, not too pleasantly. "I hope it's important. As soon as I finish my supper, I want to go to bed."

"I thought it would be best to have a word with you, Herr Admiral, before tomorrow morning."

"You want something to eat?"

The invitation was not warm.

"Very kind of you, Herr Admiral. But no, thank you."

"Well, then fix yourself a drink, have a seat, and as soon as I'm finished and the news is over, we can talk."

About ten minutes later, torn between listening to cricket scores of teams he had never heard of, which he had no interest in whatever, and watching von Deitzberg squirm impatiently in his chair, which he did find amusing, Canaris opted for seeing what the squirmer wanted.

"Well, that's another onerous chore done," he announced. "If we are to believe the BBC, the war is lost. What's on your mind, von Deitzberg?"

"No offense to these gentlemen, of course, but I would like to speak with you in private, if that would be possible, Herr Admiral."

"Of course. We can go into the living room."

Canaris stood up.

"Excuse us, gentlemen," he said. "Feel free to retire, which is what I'm going to do as soon as the brigadeführer is through with the fregattenkapitän and me."

He led von Deitzberg into the living room, with von und zu Waching following, waved them into chairs, and sat down.

"I had hoped to see you earlier today, Admiral, and I really think it might be best if we were alone."

"Earlier today, the Führer sent for me," Canaris replied. "As so far as the fregattenkapitän is concerned, I like him to be present at meetings where no one is making written notes. What's on your mind, von Deitzberg?"

Canaris's curtness with von Deitzberg was intentional on several levels, starting with the psychological. He knew von Deitzberg would interpret ordinary cour-

tesy, and certainly amiability, as recognition on Canaris's part that he was dealing with an equally powerful man. The pecking order had to be maintained.

The curtness came easily; Canaris despised the handsome SS officer. He
knew more about him than von Deitzberg suspected, and the more he learned,
the more he despised him.

The SS was—and always had been, from the beginning—laced with common criminals and social misfits. Not only in the ranks—the SS had been
formed to provide bodyguards for Hitler, and thugs were naturally going to be
part of something like that—but also at the very top of the SS hierarchy.

SS-Obergruppenführer Reinhard Heydrich was a case in point. Until he had
been assassinated by Czech agents in Prague the year before, he had been the
number-two man under Himmler, the Reichsprotektor of Bohemia and
Moravia. Before Heydrich had joined the SS he had been cashiered from the
navy for moral turpitude.

SS-Brigadeführer Ritter von Deitzberg, who was working hard to be
named Heydrich's replacement, had been forced to resign from the army for "the
good of the service," which Canaris had taken the trouble to find out meant
that he had been caught with his hand in the regimental officers' mess cash box
and having an affair with a sergeant's wife.

And now he was getting rich ransoming Jews from the concentration
camps.

Heinrich Himmler was something of a prude, and among other things that
made him dangerous was that he really believed in the honor of the SS. Learning of the ransoming operation would really enrage him.

But as much as it would have pleased Canaris to see von Deitzberg and
his cronies exposed to Himmler's wrath, he knew it was a card he had to keep
hidden until it could be played for something more important—probably
something to do with Operation Valkyrie—than the satisfaction of having
von Deitzberg and his slimy cronies hung from a butcher's hook by Himmler
himself.

"I'm very concerned about Operation Phoenix, Herr Admiral," von Deitzberg
said.

"Why?"

"Well, you know what's happened over there."

"Why don't you say what you mean?"

"It doesn't look as if Cranz is up to handling his responsibilities, does it?"

"What specifically are you talking about?"

"Not only has he not been able to neutralize the traitorous Froggers, but he has been incredibly inept in his efforts to do so. I presume you've heard that Obersturmführer Heitz and his men have been killed."

Canaris nodded.

"I personally selected Heitz to guard the special shipment funds. He was no Skorzeny, but he was a fine SS officer," von Deitzberg went on. "And considering his mission, guarding the special shipment funds, I would have thought twice before sending him to attempt to get the Froggers back from Frade."

"Where are you going with this?" Canaris asked.

"I think I should go to Argentina and straighten things out."

"What's that got to do with me? Shouldn't you make that recommendation to Reichsleiter Himmler?"

"I have. The Reichsleiter sent me here to discuss this with you; to ask for your cooperation."

That's interesting. Himmler can just order him onto the Condor.

Does this mean Bormann did tell Himmler of Hitler's sudden interest in Operation Phoenix?

Why do I think he didn't?

"I don't think I understand."

"I think the Reichsleiter would prefer that the idea of my going to Argentina come from someone other than himself."

What in the world is that all about?

Okay. Himmler is covering his backside again. He's very good at that.

"What I could do, I suppose, to assist the Reichsleiter is have a word with Bormann."

Which I will do tomorrow, when he returns to Berlin.

I will broach the subject of sending someone to Argentina to, as von Deitzberg puts it, "straighten things out." If he mentions von Deitzberg, I will oppose the idea. That will guarantee his being sent there.

If he doesn't mention this slime, I will, saying that I wish he could be spared, but Himmler certainly wouldn't agree.

Same result. Von Deitzberg will go to Argentina.

Where he and Cranz and possibly even Raschner will be eliminated by the Americans, ridding the world of three scum it can well do without.

And very possibly do something to keep Operation Valkyrie from being uncovered.

And, as the icing on the cake, humiliate Himmler. Three of his best men eliminated by those incompetent Americans.

"I think that might well deal with the situation, Herr Admiral," von Deitzberg said.

VI

[ONE]
Hauptquartier Abwehr
Bendlerblock, 76 Tirpitzufer
Berlin, Germany
0655 20 August 1943

Canaris's Mercedes, which was smaller and far less ostentatious than any of the other official cars of the senior members of the Nazi or OKW hierarchy, was crowded.

Max—now wearing a somewhat shabby dark blue business suit and a light gray snap-brim felt hat, both of which looked too small on the muscular old sailor—was driving. Canaris rode beside him.

General von Wachtstein, Oberstleutnant Gehlen, and Fregattenkapitän von und zu Waching were in the backseat, each holding a briefcase on his lap.

When Max drove into the Bendlerblock—a large, drab collection of connected four-story masonry buildings south of the Tiergarten—there were three larger official Mercedeses backed into the four-place parking area reserved for the cars of senior officers. Two of them had mounted on the right front fender a metal flag appropriate to the rank of the passenger it would carry. One flag was that of a General der Fallschirmtruppe and the other that of an SS-Brigadeführer.

That meant that von Deitzberg and Student were already here waiting for him. Canaris wondered who was in the third car.

Canaris thought that while there were at least a half-dozen brigadeführers in the SS—maybe more—there was only one General der Fallschirmtruppe in the Luftwaffe: Kurt Student.

A pilot in World War I, Student had stayed in the service, and had been involved with German military aviation from the beginning, before there had been a Luftwaffe and while Germany was at least paying lip service to the Versailles Convention, which forbade Germany to have an air force.

Student had taught fledgling German pilots to fly gliders, hiding the program as a sport. He had become, in the process, an expert in engineless aircraft, and had drawn plans for the construction of enormous gliders. These would be towed by transport aircraft once the Germans had stopped following the proscriptions of the Versailles Convention.

While they were waiting for the right moment to do that, Germany struck a secret deal with the Soviet Union. It made available airfields deep in Russia on which German pilots were secretly taught to fly powered aircraft and German engineers secretly built and tested a whole new generation of fighter and bomber aircraft. All far from prying French and English eyes.

Student had been in charge of this program, reporting to Hermann Göring and Hitler directly. In those days, not all senior officers could be trusted to keep their mouths shut about Germany's blatant violation of the Versailles Convention, and what was secretly going on in Russia was very much a secret in Germany as well.

Until the Crete disaster provoked Hitler's wrath, Student had what looked like a promising career before him in the upper echelons of the German armed forces. He had had the backing of Göring, not only because he was a fellow World War I pilot and had made such substantial contributions to the Luftwaffe, but also because the Fallschirmtruppe were, in effect, the infantry of the Luftwaffe—much like the U.S. Marine Corps is the Navy's infantry—and Göring liked the idea of having his own army, especially now that Heinrich Himmler had formed the Waffen-SS as the private army of the Schutzstaffel, which had begun as Hitler's bodyguard.

And Hitler's displeasure had been tempered. He had ordered that henceforth the Fallschirmjäger would fight as ordinary infantry, but he had not stripped Student of his rank. Hitler even permitted Student to remain on the periphery of those gathered around his Wolfsschanze map tables.

But until the rescue of the deposed Italian dictator had come along—General von Wachtstein had told Canaris that it had been named Unternehmen Eiche (Operation Oak)—Student had not been given, by Hitler or by the OKW staff, any meaningful duties or missions.

That told Canaris that Student was fully aware that the success or failure of Operation Oak was a second chance for him. If he were able to carry it off, he could again bask in the Führer's approval. However, if he failed, he could count on being sent to the Eastern Front—if he was lucky. Hitler had stripped other general officers he thought had failed him of their ranks, their medals, and even their pensions.

Max stopped the car before the entrance. Canaris was out of it before the guard could trot up to open the door for him.

The officers in Canaris's far-from-opulent outer office rose as Canaris walked in. Including General Kurt Student, which Canaris found interesting, as he was junior to the parachute troops general.

I think he knows he needs me.

As indeed he does.

Canaris acknowledged only Student. He said, "Heil Hitler," gave a somewhat sloppy Nazi salute, then offered his hand.

"Good morning, General," he said. "I hope I haven't kept you waiting."

Student smiled and made an *It doesn't matter* gesture. Canaris motioned Student toward the door to his office and gestured for the others to follow. He waved Student into the chair at one end of a long, somewhat battered conference table. He took the seat at the opposite end.

Without being invited, SS-Brigadeführer von Deitzberg sat down beside Student. The other men in the room—a major and a lieutenant, both Fallschirmtruppe officers, and an enormous Waffen-SS captain—came to attention.

"Please be seated," Canaris said, pointing to the chairs around as General von Wachtstein, Fregattenkapitän von und zu Waching, and Oberstleutnant Gehlen entered the office. Von Wachtstein took a seat beside Canaris and von und zu Waching took one across from him.

"In a moment, Frau Dichter will bring us what is supposed to be coffee and then we can start talking about Operation Oak," Canaris said. He paused. "General Student, I don't know these gentlemen."

The Waffen-SS captain leapt to his feet and barked, "SS-Hauptsturmführer Skorzeny, Herr Admiral, of SS Special Unit Friedenthal."

Canaris nodded at Skorzeny, then made a somewhat impatient wave of his hand telling him to sit down. The parachute officers were now standing at attention. Canaris waved at them to sit down.

"Admiral," Student said, pointing as he spoke, "these gentlemen are Major Harald Moors and Leutnant Otto von Berlepsch."

"Actually, the leutnant is Leutnant *Count* Otto von Berlepsch," von Deitzberg said.

"Is he really?" Canaris asked, dryly sarcastic.

Tell you what, Baron von Deitzberg: You and Count von Berlepsch put on your suits of armor, and General Student and I will help you get on your horses. Feel free to stand on our backs as you do so.

The anger came quickly and unexpectedly and was immediately regretted for two reasons: Coming close to losing his temper with von Deitzberg approached stupidity, for one. For another, the looks of contempt on both von Berlepsch's and Generalmajor Count von Wachtstein's faces showed they were as contemptuous of von Deitzberg's evoking of the Almanach de Gotha as he was.

"As of one o'clock this morning," Canaris announced, "the Carabinieri were completing their plans to move Mussolini from the Isle of Ponza to the Campo Imperatore Hotel in the Apennine mountain range, some eighty miles northeast of Rome. The Carabinieri have arranged for patrol torpedo boats to move him and his guard to the mainland. I don't know where on the mainland, and I don't know when the move will take place—probably not tomorrow, but early in the morning of the day after tomorrow."

"Admiral, you're sure of your intelligence?" General Student asked.

That wasn't a challenge. He is just making sure.

Canaris nodded.

"If we could find out where they are going to land him on the mainland, we could free Il Duce en route to the Campo Imperatore," von Deitzberg said.

"How would you do that?" Canaris asked evenly.

"I don't think that Hauptsturmführer Skorzeny, Herr Admiral, and his SS Special Unit Friedenthal would have any difficulty in freeing Il Duce from any Italian unit," von Deitzberg said.

"How much do you know about the Carabinieri, von Deitzberg?" Student asked softly.

"They're Italian, aren't they? And haven't we all learned that whatever else our former Italian allies might be good at—making wine, for example—they are not very good at making war?"

"Forgive me, von Deitzberg, but I have to disagree," Student said. "You've heard, I'm sure, that one should never underestimate one's enemy."

"Are you suggesting, Herr General," von Deitzberg challenged, "that a unit—a special unit, such as the Special Unit Friedenthal of the Waffen-SS— is not superior to any Italian unit?"

Student did not answer directly. Instead, looking at Canaris and von

Wachtstein, he said, "Forgive me, gentlemen, if I'm telling you something you probably know as well as I do.

"The Carabinieri Reali—Royal Carabinieri—has been around since 1814," Student began, as if lecturing a class at the Kriegsschule. "The term 'Carabinieri' refers to the unit being armed with shortened, bayonetless rifles, carbines. These were—and remain—special troops not intended to march in formation across the battlefield toward the enemy. Forerunners, one might say, of latter-day special troops, such as the Waffen-SS and, of course, the Fallschirmjäger.

"They began to acquire their legendary reputation as warriors right from the beginning, when, the year after they were formed, they engaged and soundly defeated Napoleon's best at Grenoble in 1815. Subsequently they served— with equal distinction—in the Crimean War and performed admirably in the wars of Italian Independence, Eritrea, and Libya.

"In this war, the Carabinieri have fought with valor in Greece and East Africa under impossible odds."

General von Wachtstein nodded his agreement. Von Deitzberg saw this and his lips tightened even more.

Canaris thought: *Student is certainly aware that it's unwise to challenge Himmler's right-hand man.*

But he's also aware that rescuing Il Duce is his last chance. And that Himmler wants this rescue operation for the SS. And he can't let that happen.

So—with the old principle that the best defense is a good offense—he's going to take on von Deitzberg.

Good for him.

"So, von Deitzberg," Student went on, "while I am second to no one in my admiration for the SS, I submit that your Special Unit Friedenthal—it is approximately of company strength, as I understand it?"

"A reenforced company, Herr General. A little over three hundred men—"

"All of whom, I am sure, are a credit to the SS and Germany. I doubt, however, that even such a splendid body of men can take on a battalion—six or seven hundred strong—of the Carabinieri who have been personally charged by their king with guarding Il Duce."

Von Deitzberg glared at him. His face showed that he was preparing a sarcastic, perhaps caustic, reply.

He ran out of time.

"Then, may I tell the Führer, Admiral Canaris," General von Wachtstein asked, surprising Canaris, who hadn't expected him to open his mouth, "that you and General Student are agreed that the attempt to liberate Mussolini should take place after he is moved to the Campo Imperatore Hotel rather than on the Isle of Ponza, or when he is being moved from one to the other?"

That wasn't a question.

Von Wachtstein was telling von Deitzberg that he agreed with Student.

"Yes," Canaris said.

"Concur," Student said.

That makes three of us who have crossed von Deitzberg. Not only Student and me, but also von Wachtstein, for asking the question.

Why did he do that?

One general supporting another against the SS?

Or maybe to show von Deitzberg that there are only three senior players in this little game, and von Deitzberg is not one of them?

Well, he had his reasons and he's no fool.

And that means he knew I wouldn't support von Deitzberg.

"Can we now get to the details of the operation itself?" von Wachtstein asked. "I hate to rush any of you, but the Führer is waiting to hear what you have decided."

Well, that I understand: He's making the point to von Deitzberg that he represents the Führer.

Von Deitzberg said: "I believe Hauptsturmführer Skorzeny has a very good plan—"

"I'm sure he does," Student interrupted him.

"If I have to say this," von Deitzberg said, "Reichsführer-SS Himmler feels the SS Special Unit Friedenthal should play a significant role in this operation."

"The Führer has honored me with the responsibility for carrying it out," Student said.

"Let's hear what the SS has to say, General Student," von Wachtstein said.

"Certainly," Student said.

"Skorzeny," von Deitzberg said.

Skorzeny popped to attention, then opened his briefcase and took a large map and a number of large photographs from it. He unfolded the map and then laid it on the table.

In front of von Wachtstein, which means he acknowledges that von Wachtstein is really in charge.

"I have personally reconnoitered the Campo Imperatore Hotel by air," Skorzeny said. "In a Fieseler Storch. If you will notice, gentlemen, the map has keys to the photographs."

Canaris examined the map and the photos with interest. All he had previously seen was a prewar advertising brochure for the hotel. It wasn't that he was disinterested but rather because, before Hitler had involved him in the rescue of Il Duce, he couldn't imagine being involved himself.

As both Gehlen and von und zu Waching had heard him often say, "Effective intelligence is far less the gathering of information than being able to find the two or three tiny useful bits in the mountains of useless data."

Canaris simply hadn't the time to try to learn anything but the two or three useful bits: where Mussolini was being held, and when and where he was going to be moved.

Looking at the map and the photographs now, Canaris understood why the Carabinieri had chosen the Campo Imperatore Hotel as the place to confine Il Duce. It sat atop the Gran Sasso, the highest mountain in the Italian Apennines, accessible only by cable car from the valley. Mussolini would not only have to escape his captors but also somehow use the cable car to get down the mountain. And cable cars were not like automobiles; one could not operate them by oneself.

More important, no one trying to free him could do so without using the cable car. All the Carabinieri would have to do to thwart a rescue attempt was disable the cable car and call for help, which could get there—even from Rome—long before the rescuers could scale the Gran Sasso.

"Simply," Skorzeny said, "my plan is that 108 members of the SS Special Unit Friedenthal, under my command, will land in a dozen of General Student's DFS 230 assault gliders. Once the Carabinieri have been dealt with, and Il Duce freed, a Fieseler Storch will land, and Il Duce and I will get in it and fly to Rome."

"I find a few little things in your plan that concern me," Student said sarcastically. "For example, the Storch is a two-seat aircraft. Or are you planning on flying it yourself, Herr Hauptmann?"

The door opened and Frau Dichter, Canaris's anemic-looking secretary said, "Forgive the intrusion, Herr Admiral, but . . ."

Reichsführer-SS Heinrich Himmler pushed past her into the room.

". . . Reichsführer Himmler."

Everyone rose quickly to their feet.

Himmler's right arm shot out in the Nazi salute.

"Heil Hitler," he announced softly. "Take your seats, gentlemen. I hope I'm not interrupting anything."

"Would you like to sit here, Herr Reichsführer?" von Deitzberg asked.

"This will be fine," Himmler said as he took one of the chairs lining the conference table.

When he had seated himself, the others sat back down.

"Actually," Himmler announced, "I came to have a word with Admiral Canaris. But since I am here, and we all know how important Operation Oak is to our Führer, perhaps this is one of those fortuitous circumstances one hears so much about. Please go on."

Von Deitzberg shot to his feet.

"Herr Reichsführer, General Student was about to tell us what he finds wrong with Skorzeny's plan."

"Which is? Skorzeny's plan, I mean."

"Admiral Canaris has learned that Mussolini will shortly be taken to the ski resort—the Campo Imperatore Hotel—on the crest of the Gran Sasso," von Wachtstein said. "It was just agreed that that is where the rescue will take place. Skorzeny proposes that 108 men of the SS Special Unit Friedenthal under his command land by glider and free Il Duce, who will be then flown to Rome in a Storch."

"And General Student finds weaknesses in that plan?" Himmler said. "I'll be interested to hear what they are."

"Several things concern me, Herr Reichsführer," Student began, only to be interrupted by Himmler raising a hand to cut him off.

"Actually, Student, I learned something from you soldiers," Himmler said, then paused, smiled his undertaker's smile, and made his little joke: "As hard as that may be to believe."

There was dutiful laughter.

"What I learned, and it has really proven useful, is that if the junior officer is asked for his opinion first, then one may be reasonably sure that his answers are what he believes, rather than what he believes his superiors wish to hear. Why don't we try that here? Who is the junior officer?"

"I believe I am," von Berlepsch said as he stood. He quickly added, "Herr Reichsführer."

But the delay was noticeable.

"And you are?" Himmler asked.

"Leutnant von Berlepsch, Herr Reichsführer."

"And what do you think of Brigadeführer von Deitzberg's . . . excuse me, *Hauptmann Skorzeny's* plan, Herr Leutnant?"

Canaris thought: *So von Deitzberg has been playing soldier and planning op-*

erations? I wonder why he decided to say it was Skorzeny's plan. Perhaps because, so far, von Deitzberg has yet to hear a shot fired in anger and doesn't want to give anyone the opportunity to mention that?

Or is there something Machiavellian in play here?

Himmler wants Skorzeny to be a hero, because he has plans for him?

"As I am sure the Reichsführer is aware," von Berlepsch began, "any type of vertical envelopment operation is very difficult in mountainous terrain."

"Vertical envelopment means parachutists, gliders?" Himmler asked.

"Precisely, Herr Reichsführer. In the case of the Gran Sasso, the wind conditions are such that parachute envelopment is impossible. The only way to envelop the hotel is by glider, and they will, for lack of a better term, have to be crash-landed."

"Von Berlepsch, aren't all glider landings, for lack of a better term, 'crash landings'?" von Deitzberg asked.

"Yes, Herr Brigadeführer, they are. My point here is that Fallschirmjäger troops are trained in glider crash landings—necessary because, under optimum conditions, one glider landing in four is a crash landing—and I don't think this is true of the Waffen-SS troops you envision employing."

"I don't think I'm following this, von Berlepsch," Himmler said. "Let me put a question to you: Suppose it was absolutely necessary that a number—say, twenty-five—of the Friedenthal unit participate in Operation Oak. How could that be done?"

Von Berlepsch looked first at Major Moors and then at General Student for guidance.

"I asked you, von Berlepsch," Himmler said curtly.

"If such a requirement were absolutely necessary, Herr Reichsführer—and I would hope that it would not be—I would put the SS men in the last three gliders."

"Why the last three?" von Deitzberg asked almost angrily.

Himmler pointed an impatient finger at him to shut him up, then made a *Let's have it* gesture with the same finger to von Berlepsch.

"Herr Reichsführer," von Berlepsch said, "I of course have no idea what Hauptmann Skorzeny has planned, but in our plan—"

"The author of which is who?" Himmler asked.

"Major Moors and I drew it up for General Student's approval, Herr Reichsführer."

"Go on."

"There will be a dozen gliders towed by Junkers Ju-52 aircraft, Herr Reichsführer. The aircraft will be in line, one minute's flying distance apart. Each will be cut loose from the towing aircraft as it passes over a predetermined spot on the mountain. I can show you that point on Hauptmann Skorzeny's maps, Herr Reichsführer . . ."

Himmler made a gesture meaning that wouldn't be necessary.

". . . which will cause the gliders to land at one-minute intervals on a small flat area—not much more than a lawn, actually—near the hotel."

"That will take twelve minutes," von Deitzberg protested. "Why can't they land at thirty-second intervals? For that matter, fifteen-second intervals? Fifteen seconds can be a long time." Then he began to count: "One thousand one. One thousand two. One thousand three. One thous—"

"Because a sixty-second interval is what these officers recommended to General Student," von Wachtstein interrupted, "and what General Student approved. I think we can all defer to his judgment and experience."

"And your reason for putting Skorzeny and his men in the last three of the gliders to land?" Himmler asked von Berlepsch.

"Because by then the Fallschirmjäger in the first gliders to land will be in a position to help the Waffen-SS troops get out of their crashed gliders," von Berlepsch said.

"Unless they themselves have crashed, of course," von Deitzberg said sarcastically.

"Some of them will have crashed, von Deitzberg," Student said icily. "We expect that. What von Berlepsch has been trying to tell you is that Fallschirmtruppe are trained to deal with that inevitable contingency."

"Well," Himmler said, "that would seem to solve the problem, wouldn't you agree, von Wachtstein?"

"If what you are saying is that General Student, Admiral Canaris, and you are agreed . . ."

"I'm just a visitor here, General," Himmler said. "The agreement must be between Student and Canaris."

Canaris thought: *And the translation of that is that if this absurd operation fails—as it well may—Student and I will take the blame.*

If it succeeds, Himmler and the SS will get the credit because Skorzeny was involved.

"Admiral Canaris?" von Wachtstein asked.

"If General Student is happy with this, I will defer to his expertise and judgment."

"I will so inform the Führer," von Wachtstein said.

"And now, if I may delicately suggest to you, Admiral, that your knowledge of the fine points of an operation like this is on a par with my own, and that neither of us is really of any value here, I wonder if we could have a few minutes alone?"

"There's a battered desk and several chairs in my cryptographic room," Canaris said. "Would that be all right with you, Herr Reichsführer?"

"That would be fine," Himmler said. "Von Deitzberg, when you're finished here, come to my office and bring me up to date."

Von Deitzberg popped to attention and clicked his heels.

"*Jawohl, Herr Reichsführer.*"

Himmler gave the Nazi salute wordlessly and waited for Canaris to show him where to go.

[TWO]

"Be so good as to give the Reichsführer and me a few minutes alone in your luxurious accommodation," Canaris said after one of his cryptographic officers had unlocked the door to a small room crowded with equipment.

"*Jawohl, Herr Admiral.*"

"Is there coffee?"

"A fresh pot, Herr Admiral."

Himmler waited until the cryptographic officer had left.

"In the nature of a state secret of the highest category—in other words, not to go further than this room—I really don't like von Deitzberg," Himmler volunteered. "He's very useful, but there is something about him I just don't like."

What's that all about?

Whatever it is, I'm not going to react to it.

"In the nature of a state secret," Canaris said, "the coffee I just asked about is not only full of caffeine, but was smuggled into Germany. I think you'll like it."

"How smuggled?"

"Usually, in one of two ways. Several of the stewards on the Lufthansa Condor flights to Buenos Aires are mine. In addition to keeping an eye on the passengers and crew for me, they bring me Brazilian coffee beans. And then, from time to time, I have to send someone to Lisbon—or go there myself—and in Lisbon, one can go into any grocery store and buy as much coffee as one can afford."

"The Führer would be very disappointed in you if I told him that," Himmler said. "I gave up on our Victory Coffee a year ago and went to tea. And now the tea is going the same way as the coffee did."

"I'm coffee rich at the moment. May I offer you a half-kilo?"

"A *cup* I will gratefully accept. But thank you, no, about the half-kilo. If I took it, I would again become addicted, and withdrawal is just too painful." Himmler smiled his undertaker's smile. "Actually, what I wanted to talk to you about is a conversation I had over a cup of tea with our Führer yesterday at Wolfsschanze—after you left."

"How was the tea?"

"Excellent. It was a gift of the Japanese ambassador."

"And did the Führer offer you a half-kilo?"

"You know better than that, Canaris. What he did want to talk about was South America."

"Really?"

"He said that he was just letting his imagination run, but what did I think about sending Il Duce, once he has been freed, to South America."

"To seek asylum from the King? Victor Emmanuel?"

"He had in mind Operation Phoenix," Himmler said evenly.

"That would be difficult without a good deal of preparation."

"So I told the Führer. Then he said something to the effect that he was sure the mechanism of movement was in place. The statement was, of course, in fact a question."

"'The mechanism of movement'? He was asking about the submarine? Submarines, plural?"

Himmler nodded.

"I told the Führer that I had turned over control of U-405 to you some weeks ago and that I knew you were either planning, or had already put into play, a test run of U-405 to see if there were any flaws in your scheme for transporting and secretly inserting senior officials into Argentina."

Himmler looked at Canaris to see what his reaction to this would be.

Canaris hoped his face did not show the fury he felt.

You sonofabitch!

You never turned over control of U-405 to me.

What the hell are you up to?

He waited for Himmler to explain. Himmler waited for Canaris to say something.

Canaris reached into his inside jacket pocket and took from it a small, leather-bound notebook. He flipped through it until he found what he wanted.

"So, that's what Kapitänleutnant von Dattenberg's submarine was doing yesterday afternoon at South Longitude 39.91, West Latitude 43.76."

"Is that where it is? And where is that?" Himmler asked, smiling.

"That's where it is, Herr Reichsführer. In the South Atlantic, about eight hundred miles from the mouth of the River Plate—far enough out to avoid aerial detection by the B-24s that the Americans are flying out of Brazil."

"I had no choice, Canaris. You know as well as I how it is with the Führer. When he asks a question, he expects an answer, and becomes . . . what shall I say? . . . *excitedly disappointed* when there is none."

Canaris smiled and nodded his understanding.

And you knew, you slimy bastard, that there was virtually no chance of me going to the Bavarian corporal and saying, "Reichsführer Himmler never turned U-405 over to me; he's lying."

Having someone say anything against anyone in the inner circle really "excites" the Führer. He reserves that privilege to himself.

"Let us say, Admiral, that U-405 leaves its current position the day after tomorrow, to meet with a submarine which would depart the pens at Saint-Nazaire at about the same time. How much time would it take it to make the rendezvous, take on the senior person to be smuggled into Argentina, and then sail to wherever it is in Argentina where that would happen?"

"If you're looking for an answer to give the Führer, Herr Reichsführer, I can give you a rough one off the top of my head, and in ten minutes I can have von und zu Waching come up with estimates accurate within an hour or so."

"Off the top of your head?"

"Saint-Nazaire is—off the top of my head—about 6,000 nautical miles from Buenos Aires. Von Dattenberg and the U-405 are about 500 nautical miles from Buenos Aires. So we're talking about splitting 5,500 nautical miles. Presuming fuel consumption is not a problem, and it can sail on the surface, a U-405-class U-boat can make fifteen knots in ordinary seas.

"Fifty-five hundred miles divided by fifteen is right at 370 hours. Say, two weeks, and a day or two to make the rendezvous. And that much, plus the extra 500 miles, back. Say thirty-two, thirty-three days from the order to go to put your imaginary very important officer on the beach."

"Buenos Aires is that far?" Himmler asked incredulously.

"That far, Herr Reichsführer. As I said, von und zu Waching in ten minutes or so could come up with a more precise estimate."

"I wonder if von Deitzberg will like his ocean voyage," Himmler said, smiling.

This time Canaris did not—perhaps could not—suppress the look of surprise that crossed his face.

"Yes, von Deitzberg will make this voyage," Himmler said. "For several reasons: One, I can report that to the Führer. I had hoped to be able to tell him 'SS-Brigadeführer von Deitzberg has tested the transport mechanism,' but now I suppose it will be, 'My Führer, as we speak SS-Brigadeführer von Deitzberg is personally testing the transport mechanism.'

"The second reason is that once von Deitzberg has been smuggled into Argentina, he can straighten out the mess we both know exists there. We have to eliminate both the Froggers and that American OSS agent who's causing us all the trouble. What's his name?"

"Frade, Herr Reichsführer. Cletus Frade."

"Yes, I'd forgotten. Frade has to be eliminated, and von Deitzberg is the man to do it, since no one else seems to be capable of doing it."

"You're absolutely right, Herr Reichsführer," Canaris said. "More coffee?"

"I shouldn't. What is it they say, Canaris? 'The greatest pleasure is indulging one's nasty habits'?"

"I've heard that, Herr Reichsführer. When do you plan to put this into action?"

"I'll tell von Deitzberg when he comes to the office. Give him a day to pack, settle things, and another day to get to Saint-Nazaire. You can deal with the navy, can't you, Canaris? I'd really hate to involve Grand Admiral Karl Dönitz in this unless I have to."

"I can deal with the navy, Herr Reichsführer."

Himmler nodded.

"And now, before you corrupt me completely with your smuggled coffee, I'd better get back to work. Don't say anything to von Deitzberg, please. I want to see the look on his face when I tell him."

[THREE]
The Embassy of the German Reich
Avenida Córdoba
Buenos Aires, Argentina
0910 25 August 1943

"Herr Cranz is here, Excellency," Fräulein Ingeborg Hässell announced from the door.

"Ask him to come in, please," Manfred Alois Graf von Lutzenberger said, not quite finishing the sentence before Karl Cranz shouldered past Fräulein Hässell into the room.

"Heil Hitler!" he announced conversationally. "You wanted to see me, Herr Ambassador?"

Von Lutzenberger barely acknowledged Cranz's presence.

"No visitors, no calls, please, Ingeborg," he said, and then he rummaged in a desk drawer as his secretary left the room and closed the door. Finally, he found what he was looking for—a box of matches—and lit one of them, and then a cigarette.

As he extinguished the match by waving it rapidly, he pointed to a sheet of paper on his desk with his other hand.

"The only person who's seen that is Schneider," von Lutzenberger said. "He had it waiting for me when I came in this morning."

Consular Officer Johann Schneider, a twenty-three-year-old Bavarian, was actually an SS-untersturmführer, the equivalent of second lieutenant. He was the first of his lineage ever to achieve officer status, and the first to receive education beyond that offered by the parochial school in his village.

He gave full credit for his success to Adolf Hitler, Heinrich Himmler, and the tenets of National Socialism. He believed he had been selected for his assignment to Buenos Aires—instead of being posted to one of the SS-regiments on his graduation from officer candidate school at Bad Tölz—because his superiors recognized in him a dedicated officer of great potential.

He was never disabused of this notion by any of his superiors in Germany or Buenos Aires. But the truth was that he had been sent to Argentina because he was a splendid typist. The then-senior SS officer in Buenos Aires, Karl-Heinz Grüner—ostensibly the military attaché, who wore the uniform of a Wehrmacht oberst but was actually an SS-standartenführer—had confessed to Reichsführer-SS Heinrich Himmler that he had had quite enough of menopausal females and needed a classified files clerk who could type as well as any woman and could be told to work all night, every night, without breaking into tears.

A sympathetic Himmler had ordered an underling to see what was available for Oberst Grüner at Bad Tölz, and four days later newly commissioned SS-Untersturmführer Schneider had boarded a Lufthansa Condor in Berlin. Thirty-eight hours later, he reported to Grüner in Buenos Aires.

To keep his new typist/classified file clerk happy—Schneider had immediately made it clear that he believed his Argentine assignment was to assist Grüner in high-level intelligence activities—Grüner had permitted Schneider to think of himself as an unofficial member—or perhaps a probationary member—of the SS-Sicherheitsdienst, or Secret Service.

Whenever he saw Schneider chafing at the bit over his clerical functions, Grüner ordered him to secretly surveille certain members of the embassy staff, most of them unimportant except for First Secretary Anton von Gradny-Sawz.

This was because Grüner neither liked von Gradny-Sawz nor fully trusted him. He didn't think men who had changed sides could ever be fully trusted.

Von Gradny-Sawz's primary—if not official—function around the embassy was what Grüner and Ambassador von Lutzenberger thought of as "handling the canapés"; neither was willing to trust von Gradny-Sawz with anything important, but he *was* good with the canapés.

As von Gradny-Sawz was fond of saying, his family had been serving the diplomatic needs of "the state" for hundreds of years. The implication was the German state. The actuality was that von Gradny-Sawz had been in the diplomatic service of the German state only since 1938.

Before then—before the Anschluss had incorporated Austria into the German Reich as Ostmark—von Gradny-Sawz had been in the Austrian Foreign Service. The ancestors he so proudly spoke of had served the Austro-Hungarian Empire for hundreds of years.

Having seen the handwriting on the wall before 1938, von Gradny-Sawz had become a devout Nazi, made some contribution to the Anschluss itself, and been taken into the Foreign Service of the German Reich.

Ambassador von Lutzenberger, who understood how sacred the canapé-and-cocktails circuit was to the diplomatic corps, had arranged for von Gradny-Sawz's assignment as his first secretary. Von Gradny-Sawz could charm the diplomatic corps while he attended to business.

The secret reports on von Gradny-Sawz that Schneider gave to Grüner showed that the first secretary divided his off-duty time about equally between two different sets of friends. The largest group was of deposed titled Eastern European blue bloods, a surprising number of whom had made it to Argentina with not only their lives but most of their crown jewels. The second, smaller group consisted of young, long-legged Argentine beauties whom von Gradny-Sawz squired around town, either unaware or not caring that he looked more than a little ridiculous.

SS-Oberst Grüner was now gone, lying in what Schneider thought of as a hero's grave in Germany beside his deputy, SS-Standartenführer Josef Luther Goltz. They had been laid to eternal rest with all the panoply the SS could muster, after they had given their lives for the Führer and the Fatherland on the beach of Samborombón Bay while trying to secretly bring ashore a "special shipment" from a Spanish-registered ship in the service of the Reich.

Specifically, both had been shot in the head by parties unknown, although there was little doubt in anyone's mind that Cletus Frade of the American OSS had at least ordered the killings, and more than likely had pulled the trigger himself.

Schneider had gone first to Ambassador von Lutzenberger and then, when SS-Obersturmbannführer Karl Cranz had arrived in Buenos Aires to replace Grüner, to Cranz offering to personally eliminate Frade, even if this meant giving his own life to do so.

Both told him, in effect, that while his zeal to seek vengeance for the murders of Grüner and Goltz was commendable and in keeping with the highest traditions of SS honor, the situation unfortunately required that everyone wait until the time was right to eliminate Frade.

They told him the greatest contribution he could make to the Final Victory of the Fatherland was to continue what he was doing with regard to handling the classified files, the dispatch and receipt of the diplomatic pouches, and the decryption of the coded messages the embassy received from the Ministry of Communications after they had received them from the Mackay Cable Corporation.

Neither told him that was sort of a game everyone played. The Mackay Corporation was an American-owned enterprise. They pretended that they did not—either in Lisbon, Portugal, or Berne, Switzerland—make copies of all German traffic and pass them to either the OSS or the U.S. Embassy. And the Germans pretended not to suspect this was going on.

Important messages from or to Berlin were transmitted by "officer courier," which most often meant the pilot, copilot, or flight engineer on the Lufthansa Condor flights between the German and Argentine capitals.

And when these messages reached the Buenos Aires embassy, they were decoded personally by Ambassador von Lutzenberger or Commercial Attaché Cranz, not Schneider. Schneider had no good reason—any reason at all—to know the content of the messages.

Cranz picked up the message and read it:

```
CLASSIFICATION: MOST URGENT

CONFIDENTIALITY: MOST SECRET

DATE: 22 AUGUST 1943

FROM: CHIEF ABWEHR

TO: IMMEDIATE AND PERSONAL ATTENTION OF THE REICH
AMBASSADOR TO ARGENTINA BUENOS AIRES

HEIL HITLER!

PRELIMINARY ADVISORY

ON OR ABOUT 25 SEPTEMBER A SENIOR OFFICER TO BE
LATER IDENTIFIED TO YOU AND A DETAIL OF ONE SS
OBERSTURMFÜHRER AND EIGHT OR TEN OTHER SS RANKS
WILL BE DELIVERED AS A SPECIAL SHIPMENT.

IN ANTICIPATION OF THE FOREGOING YOU WILL TAKE THE
FOLLOWING ACTION.
```

1-WITH REGARD TO THE SENIOR OFFICER:

A. YOU WILL ARRANGE FOR HIM THE NECESSARY BONA FIDE
CREDENTIALS, INCLUDING A NATIONAL CARD OF IDENTITY,
A DRIVER'S LICENSE, AND OTHER DOCUMENTS AN ORDINARY
PRIVATE CITIZEN WOULD HAVE IN HIS POSSESSION. THE
DOCUMENTS SHOULD STATE THAT HE IS OF GERMAN ORIGIN,
AND THE NAME CHOSEN FOR THIS IDENTITY SHOULD REFLECT
THAT. SEE B. BELOW FOR ADDRESS PARTICULARS.

HIS PHYSICAL CHARACTERISTICS FOLLOW:

HEIGHT 1.85 METERS. WEIGHT 82 KILOS. HAIR BROWN.
EYES GRAY. CLEAN SHAVEN. NO FACIAL SCARS OR
EYEGLASSES.

IF POSSIBLE A PHOTOGRAPH AND ITS NEGATIVE WILL BE
FURNISHED TO YOU FOR USE IN THIS CONNECTION. IF THIS
PROVES TO BE IMPOSSIBLE, HAVE THE CREDENTIALS
PREPARED WITH A PHOTOGRAPH OF SOMEONE MEETING THE
ABOVE DESCRIPTION, SUCH PHOTO TO BE EASILY REPLACED
WHEN AN ACTUAL PHOTO BECOMES AVAILABLE.

B. WITH THE UTMOST DISCRETION, MAKING SURE THAT NO
CONNECTION CAN BE MADE WITH THE GERMAN EMBASSY OR
ANY OF ITS OFFICERS, PROCURE BOTH A SUITABLE
APARTMENT WITH TELEPHONE AND AN AUTOMOBILE FOR HIS
USE. THE IMAGE THIS OFFICER WISHES TO PROJECT IS
THAT OF A MIDDLE-LEVEL MANAGER. YOUR SUGGESTIONS IN
THIS AREA ARE SOLICITED.

2-WITH REGARD TO THE SS PERSONNEL: THEY ARE TO
BE MOVED IN SECRECY TO THE LOCATION OF THE
SPECIAL SHIPMENT. THEY ARE NOT TO LEAVE THAT
AREA WITHOUT THE SPECIFIC APPROVAL OF EITHER MYSELF OR
REICHSFÜHRER HIMMLER. THEIR SOLE DUTY IS TO GUARD THE

```
SPECIAL SHIPMENT PRESENTLY IN ARGENTINA AND ANY FUTURE
SPECIAL SHIPMENTS THAT MAY BE MADE.

3-YOU ARE AUTHORIZED TO MAKE THIS ORDER KNOWN TO SUCH
EMBASSY PERSONNEL AS YOU FEEL ARE ABSOLUTELY NECESSARY
TO ACCOMPLISH THE FOREGOING. THE FEWER PERSONNEL SO
CHOSEN, THE BETTER. YOU WILL FURNISH THE NAMES OF
THOSE CHOSEN, AND INDIVIDUAL REPORTS AS NECESSARY.

4-NO INQUIRIES REGARDING THE IDENTITY OF THE SENIOR
OFFICER OR THE PURPOSE OF THIS MISSION ARE DESIRED.

AT THE DIRECTION OF THE FÜHRER:

CANARIS, VIZEADMIRAL, CHIEF, ABWEHR

CONCUR: HIMMLER, REICHSFÜHRER-SS
```

Cranz looked at von Lutzenberger.

"You said Schneider had this waiting for you when you came in this morning?"

Von Lutzenberger nodded.

"A Condor arrived in the wee hours," he said. "Our Johann met it, and the courier gave him that."

"When did you start letting 'Our Johann' decode messages like this?"

"It came that way," von Lutzenberger said, and handed Cranz two envelopes. "The outer one is addressed to 'The Ambassador'; the inner one said 'Sole and Personal Attention of Ambassador von Lutzenberger.'"

"Interesting," Cranz said as he very carefully examined both envelopes.

"It could be that they were preparing to send it as a cable, and then for some reason decided to send it on the Condor," von Lutzenberger suggested.

Cranz considered that for a long moment.

"If a Condor was coming, that would keep it out of the hands of Mackay," Cranz said, and then wondered aloud, "Not encrypted?"

Von Lutzenberger shrugged.

"Maybe there wasn't time; the Condor may have been leaving right then. And that brings us to the question: 'What the hell is this all about?'"

"Questions," von Lutzenberger corrected him. "'Who is this senior officer?' 'What is he going to do once he gets here?' And most important: 'What are we going to do about this?'"

Cranz nodded, signifying he agreed there was more than one question.

"Was there anybody interesting on the Condor?"

"Businessmen, two doctors for the German Hospital. No one interesting."

"Which means the Condor could have been held at Tempelhof."

"Unless that might have delayed the Condor a day, and they wanted to get this to us as soon as possible."

"Which brings us back to: 'What are we going to do about it?'" Cranz said.

"Unless you have some objection, or better suggestion, what I'm going to do is tell Schneider that he is to tell no one anything about the message for me. Then I'm going to call Gradny-Sawz in here as soon as he comes to work, show him this, and tell him that he is to tell no one about it, and that he is responsible for getting the identity card, the driver's license, et cetera, and the apartment."

"And not bring Boltitz and von Wachtstein in on this?"

"And not bring anyone else in on this, *anyone* else. Then, if it gets out, we will know from whom it came."

Cranz considered that for a long moment, then nodded.

"Raschner?" he asked.

"That's up to you, of course. But I can see no reason why he has to be told about this now."

After a moment, Cranz nodded again.

[FOUR]
Aeropuerto Coronel Jorge G. Frade
Morón, Buenos Aires Province, Argentina
1545 30 August 1943

First Lieutenant Anthony J. Pelosi, Corps of Engineers, AUS, who was an assistant military attaché of the United States Embassy, stood outside the door of Base Operations and watched as a South American Airways Lodestar turned on final, dropped its landing gear, and touched smoothly down on the runway.

Pelosi was in uniform and could have posed for a U.S. Army recruiting poster. He wore "pinks and greens," as the Class "A" uniform of green tunic and pink trousers was known. The thick silver cord aiguillette of an attaché hung from one of his epaulettes. His sharply creased trousers were "bloused" around his gleaming paratrooper boots.

Silver parachutist's wings were pinned to the tunic. Below the wings were his medals—not the striped ribbons ordinarily worn in lieu thereof. There were just three medals: the Silver Star, the National Defense Service Medal, and the medal signifying service in the American Theatre of Operations.

Pelosi was one of the very few officers—perhaps the only one—to have been awarded the nation's third-highest medal for valor in combat in the American Theatre of Operations. There was virtually no combat action in the American Theatre of Operations. The citation for the medal was rather vague. It said he had performed with valor above and beyond the call of duty at great risk to his life in a classified combat action against enemies of the United States, thereby reflecting great credit upon himself, the United States Army, the United States of America, and the State of Illinois.

He could not discuss—especially in Argentina—what he had done to earn the Silver Star.

Pelosi had earned the medal while flying in a Beechcraft Staggerwing aircraft piloted by then–First Lieutenant Cletus H. Frade, USMCR. What they had done—getting shot down in the process—was illuminate with flares a Spanish-registered merchant vessel then at anchor in Samborombón Bay.

Illuminating the ship, which was then in the process of replenishing the fuel and food supplies of a German submarine, had permitted the U.S. submarine *Devil Fish* to cause both the submarine and the ship to disappear in a spectacular series of explosions.

All of this naval activity—German, Spanish, and American—was in gross violation of the neutrality of the Republic of Argentina. Samborombón Bay, on the River Plate, was well within Argentine waters. After some lengthy consideration, the government of Argentina decided the wisest course of action was to pretend the engagement had never happened.

But of course the story had gotten out. The officers with whom Lieutenant Pelosi had shared an official lunch for military and naval attachés of the various embassies at the Officers' Casino at Campo de Mayo—the reason he was wearing his uniform—knew not only the story but also of Pelosi's role in it.

No one had mentioned it, of course, but it sort of hung in the air. Pelosi had been understandably invisible to the German naval attaché, Kapitän zur See Boltitz; the German assistant military attaché for air, Major Hans-Peter Baron von Wachtstein; and to their Japanese counterparts.

Peter von Wachtstein had managed to discreetly acknowledge Tony Pelosi while they were standing at adjacent urinals, and some Argentine officers—all naval officers but one—had been quite cordial, as had the Italian naval and military attachés. That, Tony reasoned, was probably because King Victor Emmanuel had bounced Il Duce and had the bastard locked up someplace.

South American Airways Lodestar tail number 007 was wanded into a parking spot beside almost a dozen of its identical brothers.

The rear door opened and Sergeant Major Enrico Rodríguez (Ret'd) came down the stairs, carrying his shotgun. When he saw Pelosi, he smiled.

"Don Cletus will be out in a minute," he announced. "I have to find a truck."

Pelosi asked with hand gestures if he could go into the aircraft. Enrico replied with a thumbs-up gesture, and as he walked away, Pelosi marched toward the aircraft and went inside.

The chief pilot of South American Airways, Gonzalo Delgano, and the managing director of the airline, Cletus Frade, were in the passenger compartment. Pelosi saw that all but two of the seats had been removed. There were two enormous aluminum boxes strapped in place.

Delgano was in uniform: The uniform prescribed for SAA captains was a woolen powder blue tunic with four gold stripes on the sleeves, darker blue trousers with a golden stripe down the seam, a white shirt with powder blue necktie, and a leather brimmed cap with a huge crown. On the tunic's breast were outsized golden wings, in the center of which, superimposed on the Argentine sunburst, were the letters *SAA*.

Chief Pilot Delgano, as was probably to be expected, had five golden stripes on his tunic sleeves and the band around his brimmed cap was of gold cloth.

The managing director of SAA, who was bent over one of the aluminum crates, was wearing khaki trousers, battered Western boots, and a fur-collared leather jacket that had once been the property of the United States Marine Corps.

Cletus Frade came out of the box holding a lobster by its tail. Pelosi decided the lobster had to weigh five pounds, maybe more.

"You're still alive, you great big ugly sonofabitch!" Frade proclaimed happily. "God rewards the virtuous. Remember that, Gonzo."

Delgano shook his head.

Frade spotted Pelosi.

"And, by God, we're safe! The 82nd Airborne is here!"

"Where'd you get the lobster?" Pelosi inquired.

"Santiago, Chile, from which Delgano and I have flown in three hours and thirteen minutes. At an average speed of approximately 228 miles per hour, while attaining an altitude of nearly 24,000 feet in the process. We had to go on oxygen over most of the Andes, and it was as cold as a witch's teat up there. But neither seems to have affected my friend here, despite the dire predictions of my chief pilot."

"I thought the cold and/or lack of oxygen would kill them," Delgano said.

"What are you going to do with it?" Pelosi asked.

"Well, at first I thought I'd organize a lobster race, but now I think I'll eat him. And at least some of his buddies in the tank. If you promise to behave, Tony, you are invited to a clambake this very evening at the museum. You may even bring your abused wife."

Tony knew that the museum was the Frade mansion—which indeed resembled, both internally and externally, a museum—on Avenida Coronel Díaz in Palermo.

"You've got *clams?*"

"Clams, oysters, and lobster. Santiago is a virtual paradise of seafood."

"Don Cletus thinks we can make money flying it in," Delgano explained.

"Trust me, Gonzo," Frade said. "And now curiosity is about to overwhelm me: What are you doing here, dressed up like some general's dog-robber?"

"Curiosity just overwhelmed me," Delgano said. "'Dog-robber'?"

"Aides-de-camp, who must be shameless enough to snatch food from the mouths of starving dogs to feed their general, are known as dog-robbers," Frade explained.

Delgano shook his head.

Pelosi said: "I was at a reception for foreign attachés at Campo de Mayo. You had to go in uniform with medals."

"And was Major Baron von Wachtstein there, dazzling everybody with his Knight's Cross of the Iron Cross?"

Pelosi nodded.

"Good. That means he's in town and can come."

"So was el Coronel Perón."

"He can't."

"And there's a package for you."

"Yeah?"

"From Room 1012, National Institutes of Health Building, Washington, D.C. It was in the pouch. My boss said to get it to you, and to get a receipt."

The headquarters of the Office of Strategic Services was in the National Institutes of Health Building.

Pelosi's boss, the military attaché of the U.S. Embassy, was not fond of either Pelosi or Frade. He had received a teletype message from the vice chief of staff of the U.S. Army directing him not to assign Lieutenant Pelosi any duties that could possibly interfere in any way with his other duties. The other duties were unspecified. The military attaché knew that Pelosi was the OSS man in the embassy and worked for Cletus Frade.

"He didn't happen to open it before he gave it to you to give to me, did he?"

Pelosi shook his head.

"Where is it?"

"In my car."

"You left the report of my Wasserman test in your car where anybody can get at it? Go get it! My God, what if Dorotea should see it?"

Pelosi got quickly off the Lodestar.

"What test is that?" Delgano asked.

"They draw blood. And test it. If you flunk your Wasserman test, you have syphilis. And it has to be that. I can't think of anything else the National Institutes of Health could possibly be sending me. Can you?"

Delgano knew where OSS headquarters was.

"Not really," he said, shaking his head. "Cletus, you are impossible."

Pelosi had to wait to get back on the airplane until half a dozen workmen had unstrapped the aluminum crates and manhandled them into the back of a 1940 Chevrolet pickup truck.

Then he came aboard and handed Frade a large padded envelope.

Frade tore it open.

It contained an inch-thick book. Clete flipped through it, then handed it to Delgano, who read the title aloud: "'Pilot's Operating Manual, Lockheed L-049 Constellation Aircraft.'"

Delgano then looked at Frade, who handed him a small note that had been paper-clipped to the book.

"Constellation? Is that that great big new airplane? The one with three tails?" Pelosi asked.

"It has three *vertical stabilizers*, Tony," Frade said as he read the note.

Howard Hughes

```
Keeping in mind that a little knowledge is a
dangerous thing, Little Cletus, see if you can find
a real pilot to explain the hard parts to you.

You never know when you might find yourself flying
one of these again,

Howard
```

When he had finished reading the note, Delgano looked at Frade. "Again?" he asked.

"I have no idea what this is all about," Frade confessed. "If I figure it out, you'll be the first to know."

[FIVE]
Sidi Slimane U.S. Army Air Force Base
Morocco
1250 4 September 1943

Captain Archer C. Dooley Jr., USAAF, commanding officer of the 94th Fighter Squadron, studied the runway behind him in the rearview mirror of his P-38, saw what he wanted to see, then looked to his left, saw that he had the attention of First Lieutenant William Cole, smiled at him, raised his right hand, and gestured with his index finger extended, first pointing down the runway and then in a circling motion upward.

When Cole had given him a smile and a thumbs-up gesture, Dooley put his hand on the throttle quadrant and pushed both levers forward to take-off power.

This caused the twin Allison V-1710 1,475-horsepower engines of his P-38 "Lightning" to roar impressively and the aircraft to move at first slowly, and then with rapidly increasing velocity, down the runway.

He lifted off—with Cole's Lightning perhaps two seconds behind him—retracted the gear, and retarded the throttles to give him the most efficient burning of fuel as he climbed to altitude and to the rendezvous point over the Atlantic Ocean.

Sixty seconds later, two more P-38s roared down the runway, and sixty seconds after they had become airborne, two more, and sixty seconds after that, two more, for a total of eight.

"Mother Hen, check in," Captain Dooley ordered.

One by one, the seven other P-38s in the flight reported in, starting with "Chick One, sir. All okay."

When Chick Seven had been heard from, Dooley went on: "Pay attention to Mother Hen. We're going out over the drink on this heading, our speed and rate of climb governed by our concern for fuel consumption. Think fuel conservation. Better yet, think of what a long swim you are going to have if you don't think fuel conservation. We are going to eleven thousand feet, which should put us above Grandma. Everyone, repeat everyone, will monitor the frequencies you have been given for Grandma's squawk. Everyone will acknowledge by saying, 'Yes, Mother.'"

The responses began immediately: "Chick One. Yes, Mother."

Two of the Chicks were unable to keep the chuckles out of their voices. They tried. The Old Man could be a real hard-ass if he was crossed.

Captain Dooley had been the valedictorian of the 1942 Class at Saint Ignatius High School in Kansas City, Kansas. He still was not old enough to purchase intoxicating spirits—or, for that matter, even beer—in his hometown.

He had become an aviation cadet, been commissioned, been selected for fighter pilot training and graduated from that, in time to be assigned to the aerial combat involved in the American invasion of North Africa, flying P-51s for the 403rd Fighter Squadron of the 23rd Fighter Group.

Four weeks and six days after Second Lieutenant Dooley had reported to the 403rd and flew his first mission, the Squadron First Sergeant had handed him a sheet of paper to sign:

```
Headquarters
403rd Fighter Squadron
23rd Fighter Group
In The Field
```

```
2 March 1943

The undersigned herewith assumes command.

                              Archer Dooley, Jr.
                              Archer Dooley, Jr.
                              Capt., USAAF


File
201 Dooley, Archer, Jr. 0378654
Copy to CO, 23rd Fighter Group
```

Officer promotion policies within the 23rd Fighter Group were quite simple:

16. In the case of a combat-caused vacancy, the next-senior officer will temporarily move into the vacant position. If no replacement officer of suitable rank becomes available within seven (7) days of such temporary assignment, the temporary assignment will become permanent, and the incumbent will be promoted to the rank called for by the Table of Organization & Equipment without regard to any other promotional criteria.

When Dooley assumed command of the 403rd, eleven of the pilots who had been senior to him when he had reported for duty as a second lieutenant with the 403rd had been killed or otherwise been rendered *hors de combat.*

At just about the time Archie became the Old Man, the United States achieved aerial superiority over the battlefield, and the 403rd didn't have very many—almost no—aerial battles to wage. The mission became ground support and logistics interdiction. The latter translated to mean they swept low over the desert and shot at anything that moved. Locomotives were ideal targets, but single German staff cars, or Kübelwagens—for that matter, individual German soldiers caught in the open—were fair targets.

Captain Dooley had dutifully repeated to his pilots the orders from above that even one dead German soldier meant one fewer German who could shoot at the guys in the infantry. But he confessed to his pilots that he himself had very bad memories of a Kraut Mercedes staff car he'd taken out when he'd come across it as it moved alone across the desert.

"Orders are orders," Captain Dooley told his pilots.

When things had calmed down a little, the brass had had time to consider officer assignments, putting officers where they could do the most good. Some of the replacement officers sent to the 403rd after Captain Dooley's assumption of command were senior to him. On the other hand, back at Sidi Slimane in Morocco, there was a newly arrived squadron none of whose officers had yet flown in combat. The problem was that the 94th Fighter Squadron was flying Lockheed P-38 Lightnings, not P-51s. Captain Dooley was not qualified to fly P-38s.

A command decision was made.

"Fuck it. Dooley's one hell of a pilot. Give him a quick transition into P-38s and send him to command the 94th. All they're doing back there is running escort for transports flying in from the States. He's a quick learner. He's proven that. And he can teach the others how to fly combat when they're not escorting transports. They'll pay attention to a guy with two DFCs even if he looks like a high school cheerleader."

Aerial resupply of the North African Theatre of Operations was performed by Douglas C-54 four-engine transports. Carrying high-priority cargo ranging from fresh human blood through spare parts to critically needed personnel, they flew from East Coast airfields to Gander, Newfoundland, and after refueling, from Gander to airfields in England.

Fighter aircraft from fields in Scotland flew out over the ocean to escort them safely past German fighters flying out of France. To keep a German fighter formation from happening upon a fleet of transports, the transports flew separately.

The same protection system was put in place as the transports flew from England to North Africa. They were escorted out over the Atlantic by fighters, then flew alone far enough out to sea to avoid German interception as they flew south, until they were met by North Africa–based American fighters over the Atlantic a hundred miles at sea, then escorted to North African air bases, most often Sidi Slimane.

"Aircraft squawking on One One Seven, this is Mother Hen. How do you read?" Captain Dooley inquired. They were approximately 130 miles out over the Atlantic.

"Mother Hen, Five Oh Nine reads you loud and clear."

"Grandma, read you five by five. I should be able to see you. Are you on the deck?"

"Actually, Mother Hen, I'm at twenty thousand. From up here, I can see what looks like a bunch of little airplanes at what's probably ten thousand. Is that you?"

Dooley looked up, searching the sky. He saw the sun glinting off the unpainted skin of an aircraft that looked vaguely familiar, and for a moment he had a sick feeling in his stomach.

Jesus Christ, is that a Condor?

The Germans were running their long-range transport, the Condor, from fields in Spain to South America. The 94th had been ordered to "engage and destroy" any such aircraft they encountered.

Archie Dooley did not want to shoot down an unarmed transport.

Orders are orders.

Fuck it!

"Mother Hen to all Chicks. Follow me. Do not—repeat, do not—engage until I give the order."

He pushed his throttles forward and began his climb.

Getting to twenty thousand feet didn't take much time, but catching up with the sonofabitch took a hell of a long time.

He has to be making three hundred miles an hour! I didn't think the Condor was anywhere near this fast.

Jesus, that's not a Condor!

What the fuck is it?

Dooley finally pulled close enough to see that the airplane, whatever the hell it was, was American. There was a star-and-bar recognition sign on the fuselage, and when he picked up a few more feet of altitude, he saw that U.S. ARMY was painted on the wing.

He looked back at the tail to see if there was a tail number.

Tail, hell. It's got three of them!

"Five Oh Nine, this is Mother Hen."

"Oh, hello there, Mother Hen. I wondered how long it was going to take you to get up here."

Dooley pulled closer and parallel to the cockpit of the huge—*And beautiful! Jesus, that's good-looking!*—airplane.

The pilot waved cheerfully at him.

Dooley saw that he was not wearing an oxygen mask.

Don't tell me it's pressurized! It has to be. He's at twenty thousand with no mask!

Jesus, I know what it is. It's a Constellation! I've seen pictures.

What the hell is it doing here?

Dooley saw that his airspeed indicator needle was flickering at 320.

"Five Oh Nine, Mother Hen. We are going to form a protective shield above and ahead and behind you and lead you in."

"Thank you very much."

I will be goddamned if I will ask him if that's really a Constellation.

Dooley went almost to the deck with the Constellation, watched it touch smoothly down, then shoved his throttles forward and picked up the nose so that he—and the rest of the flight—could go around and get in the landing stack.

When Dooley's P-38 was at the end of its landing roll, he was surprised to see that instead of at Base Ops, where he expected it to be, the Constellation was at a remote corner of the field, where maybe fifty people were hurriedly erecting camouflage netting over it.

"Mother Hen to all Chicks. Refuel, check your planes, but don't get far from them. I was told to expect another mission when we got back."

He switched radio frequencies from Air–to–Air Three to Air–to–Ground Two.

"Sidi Tower, Mother Hen is going to taxi to the Constellation."

"Negative, Mother Hen. You are denied—"

Dooley turned his radios off and taxied to the Constellation.

By the time he got there, the camouflage netting was in place and the staff car of the base commander was parked at the foot of a long ladder that reached up to the fuselage of the Constellation.

The base commander glowered at Dooley.

Fuck it! What's he going to do, send me to North Africa?

He started to shut down the Lightning.

He had to wait until someone brought a ladder so that he could climb down from the P-38 cockpit.

By the time he got close to the Constellation, two civilians were climbing down the ladder.

That guy looks just like Howard Hughes.

The guy who looked just like Howard Hughes said, "Why do I think you're Mother Hen?" Then, without waiting for a reply, he said to the other civilian, "This is the guy who shepherded us in here, Colonel."

"I was very happy to see you out there, Captain," the other civilian said, offering Dooley his hand. "Thank you. And are you going to take care of us on the way to Lisbon?"

The base commander put in: "I thought I'd wait, Colonel Graham, until you got here before I told the captain where he was going next."

"But he is prepared to leave shortly?" Colonel Graham asked.

"Just as soon as his aircraft is refueled," the base commander said, then looked at Dooley. "Right, Captain?"

"Yes, sir."

The base commander looked back at Graham and added, "And he picks up the flight plan at Base Ops, of course, and confers with the C-47 crew."

"Good," Colonel Graham said. "We have a very narrow window of time."

"Any questions, Captain Dooley?" the base commander asked.

"Actually, I have two, sir. Three, if I can ask this gentleman if he's the pilot I saw when we made rendezvous."

The tall civilian nodded.

"How long did it take you to come from England in that beautiful airplane?"

"Actually, we came by way of Belém, Brazil. It took us a little over eleven hours from Belém. That's two questions."

"Did anyone ever tell you you look like Howard Hughes?"

"I hear that all the time," Howard Hughes said.

VII

[ONE]
Hotel Britania
Rua Rodrígues Sampaio 17
Lisbon, Portugal
1745 4 September 1943

The deputy director of the Office of Strategic Services for Europe cracked open the door of his suite, saw the deputy director of the Office of Strategic Services for the Western Hemisphere standing in the corridor, pulled the door fully open, and gestured for him to enter.

"Nice flight, Alex?" Allen Dulles asked as the two shook hands.

"Coming in here from Morocco on that old-fashioned Douglas DC-3 was a little crowded and bumpy. But the rest of the trip, on the Constellation, was quite comfortable," Colonel A. F. Graham said.

Dulles chuckled.

"Howard knows how to take care of himself," Graham added. "There's a galley, and a couple of stewards, and bunks with sheets and pillows. And we flew so high, we were above the bad weather. What's up?"

"Wild Bill know you're here?" Dulles asked.

"You said don't tell him, so I didn't." Graham met Dulles's eyes, smiled, and asked, "What are we hiding from our leader?"

He took a long, thin, black cigar from a case, then remembered his manners and offered the case to Dulles, who shook his head.

"There's been a very interesting development," Dulles said. "What would you say, Alex, if I told you that the Germans know a great deal about the Manhattan Project?"

"You sound surprised," Graham said.

"A very great deal, Alex," Dulles said.

There was a battered leather briefcase on a desk. Dulles went to it, unlocked it, matter-of-factly took a yellow-bodied thermite grenade from it, set it carefully on the desk, then went back into the briefcase and came out with a stack of eight-by-ten-inch photographs, which he handed to Graham.

TOP SECRET

COPY 2 of 3, Page 1 of 64

DUPLICATION FORBIDDEN

Weekly Progress Report, Site X, For Period 2 July—9 July 1943

Part 1 X-10 Graphite Reactor Research Pilot Plant

Part 2 Y-12: Electromagnetic Separation Uranium Enrichment Plant

```
Part 3 K-25: Gaseous Diffusion Uranium Enrichment
Plant

Part 4 S-50: Thermal Diffusion Uranium Enrichment
Plant
```

TOP SECRET

Graham read the photograph of the cover sheet carefully, then looked through the stack of photographs of the rest of the document.

"I have no idea what I'm looking at," he confessed.

"You know about the Manhattan Project's facility in Tennessee?"

"Oak Ridge?"

"Oak Ridge is Site X," Dulles said. "What this is—these are—are photographs of the weekly progress report on the four projects they're setting up there to separate enough weapons-grade uranium from uranium ore to make a weapon. Or weapons. Atomic bombs."

"Where'd you get this report?"

"From the Germans. Specifically, from Fregattenkapitän Otto von und zu Waching, who is Admiral Canaris's deputy."

"Meaning the Germans have a spy—spies—in Oak Ridge?" Graham asked incredulously. "That's bad news. You haven't told Donovan?"

"No, I haven't told Donovan."

"Why not?"

"The Germans don't have spies in Oak Ridge. The Russians do. The Germans apparently have people in the Kremlin. According to von und zu Waching, that's where those photos came from."

"How long have you known about this?" Graham asked.

"Since two o'clock this afternoon. Canaris got word to me that he thought it would be to our mutual interest if we got together with von und zu Waching—"

" 'We'?" Graham interrupted.

"You and me. He asked for you by name. So I sent you the 'come to Portugal very quietly' message. Canaris doesn't play games, for one thing, and for another, I really didn't want to deal with whatever this was by myself."

"What the hell is it all about?"

"What comes immediately to mind, obviously, is that it is not in the best interests of the German Reich for the Soviets to have an atomic bomb. Stealing the knowledge of how to make one from us is a quick way for them to get one."

Graham nodded his agreement.

"This is all you got from this guy? What's his name?"

"Fregattenkapitän Otto von und zu Waching. That's all. He asked if you were coming, and when I told him you were, he 'suggested' we wait until you got here before we got into anything else."

"Where is he now?"

"In his room, waiting for me to call him."

"Call him," Graham said.

[TWO]

"Good evening," Fregattenkapitän Otto von und zu Waching said five minutes later, with a bob of his head.

He was in civilian clothing, a gray-striped woolen suit that looked a little too large for him, a once-white shirt—which instantly brought to Graham's mind the advertising campaign that tried to convince American housewives that the use of a certain soap powder would absolutely protect their husbands' white shirts from turning "tattletale gray" and thus suggesting they were failing to properly care for the family breadwinner—and worn-out shoes.

The Germans are running short of soap. And material for suits. And shoes.

It's as simple as that.

"My name is Graham," Graham said, offering his hand.

"Your reputation precedes you, Colonel," von und zu Waching said. "I am, as I'm sure Mr. Dulles has told you, Otto von und zu Waching, and I have the honor of being Vizeadmiral Canaris's deputy. Thank you for coming. I am sure you will feel the effort was worthwhile."

His English was fluent, with a strong upper-class British accent.

"Let's hope so," Graham said.

"Would either of you be offended if I outlined my position here? Our positions here? I suggest that would be useful."

"By all means," Dulles said.

"I am a serving officer. Our nations are at war. I have, as has Admiral Canaris, come to the conclusion that Adolf Hitler, and most of the senior officials and military officers around him, must, in the interests of Germany, be removed from power.

"This is an internal matter. While on its face it is treason, that treason is limited to removing the National Socialist government—the Nazis—from power. Neither Admiral Canaris, nor myself, nor any of those associated with us are willing to betray our soldiers, airmen, or seamen by taking any action, or providing to you or anyone else any intelligence which could affect their combat efficiency and therefore place their lives in danger.

"Is that your understanding of the situation?"

"Frankly, Captain . . ." Graham replied, so quickly that Dulles looked at him with what could have been surprise or alarm or both. ". . . is that what I call you, 'Captain'?"

"If it pleases you," von und zu Waching said.

Graham went on: "You're aware, I'm sure, Captain, that we are both serving officers in the naval service of our respective nations; that the U.S. Marine Corps is part of the U.S. Navy?"

"So I understand."

"Well, in the United States Navy, we have a saying, and I would be surprised if there isn't a similar saying in the Kriegsmarine."

"And that saying is?" von und zu Waching asked with a smile.

Graham switched to German and said, rather unpleasantly, "Why don't we cut the bullshit and get down to business?"

"I beg your pardon?"

"There are two cold facts coloring this conversation," Graham said pointedly. "One is that you've lost the war, and you know it, and the second is that you want something from us. So why don't we stop splitting hairs about what constitutes treason and get down to what you want from us?"

Von und zu Waching's face turned white.

"Captain," Graham said, "I came a very long way at considerable inconvenience because I thought that Admiral Canaris had something important to say, not to listen to crap like you just mouthed."

Von und zu Waching looked at Dulles.

Graham snapped: "Don't look to Dulles to bring me up short, Captain. I don't work for him, and he can't order me to give you whatever it is you want from me. And you wouldn't have asked him to get me here if you could get what you want from him."

Von und zu Waching said nothing.

Neither did Dulles.

"Okay, getting to the bottom line, Captain," Graham said, coldly reasonable, "why don't you tell me what it is you want from me, and what you're willing to offer in exchange?"

"Has Mr. Dulles shown you the material from Oak Ridge?"

"He showed me what *you purport* to be material from Oak Ridge," Graham said.

"The Russians have spies in Oak Ridge and elsewhere within your Manhattan Project. I am prepared to identify them to you."

"Come on, Captain. If you work for Canaris, you didn't get into the intelligence business last week."

"I don't know what you mean," von und zu Waching said.

"Okay, a couple of givens in here. Germany doesn't want the Russians to get their hands on the atomic bomb, or the details of how one makes an atom bomb."

"I would suggest, Colonel, that keeping the Russians from getting the atomic bomb is also in the interests of the United States."

"Well, we've found something to agree on," Graham said sarcastically. "Let's see if we can build on that. So you know there are Russian spies at Oak Ridge. Why didn't you just give their names to the FBI?"

Von und zu Waching did not reply.

Graham went off on a tangent: "As Admiral Canaris's Number Two, I presume that you are privy to most of his communications with others?"

The question surprised both Dulles and von und zu Waching.

"I would say that I am privy to just about all," von und zu Waching said, more than a little arrogantly.

"If I wasn't clear about this, Colonel Graham," Allen Dulles said, "I have it on good authority—from the admiral himself—that the fregattenkapitän is indeed Vice Admiral Canaris's deputy."

I don't really know, Graham thought, *if that remark was intended for von und zu Waching or me.*

Is he trying to convince von und zu Waching that he has a friend?

No!

What he's doing is more or less politely suggesting that he doesn't approve of the way I'm dealing with von und zu Waching.

Allen, you're wrong!

Von und zu Waching is a sailor, a navy officer, and I know how to deal with navy officers.

You think like a diplomat, Allen, and a diplomat is the last thing I need right now!

"I'm going to show you one of those communications, Captain," Graham said, "and ask you to explain what it means. If I like your answers, that means you have told me the truth. That will be another step in our blossoming relationship. Fair enough?"

Von und zu Waching nodded.

Graham went into his briefcase, pulled out a manila envelope, and took from it two photographs of a message—obviously pages one and two of the message—which he handed to von und zu Waching.

"May I ask what that is?" Dulles asked.

"You may, but I'm frankly shocked that you would ask. Have you forgotten what Secretary of State Stimson said?"

Dulles shook his head in disbelief.

"'Gentlemen do not read each other's mail,'" von und zu Waching said, smiling after he quoted Henry Stimson's 1931 justification for shutting down the government's small—and only—cryptographic office.

"Listen to the Captain, Allen," Graham said.

"Would that we were all still living in such an age of innocence," von und zu Waching said.

"Amen, brother!" Graham said.

"Actually, I wrote this," von und zu Waching said, holding up the message. "And frankly, I'm amazed . . ."

He stopped in midsentence.

"That it was compromised so quickly?" Graham finished for him.

Von und zu Waching nodded.

"Show it to Mr. Dulles, Captain. Curiosity is about to consume him." He gave him just enough time to do so before asking, "So who's the senior officer?"

Von und zu Waching looked into Graham's eyes for a long moment.

"SS-Brigadeführer Ritter Manfred von Deitzberg," von und zu Waching said. "He is *de facto*, if not *de jure*, Himmler's deputy."

"But he was just in Argentina—wearing the uniform of a Wehrmacht general."

Von und zu Waching knew it was more of a question than a statement. He began: "There are three reasons why he's going to Argentina—"

"On U-405?"

"You even know the number?"

"And the name of her skipper," Graham said. "Kapitänleutnant Wilhelm von Dattenberg."

"Yes, on the U-405. For three reasons. The Bavarian corporal inquired of

Himmler if the 'mechanism for the transport of senior officers' to South America was in place. The admiral told me Hitler had a half-formed idea that Il Duce, once he's freed, might be the first senior officer to seek asylum under Operation Phoenix."

"My God! Really?" Dulles asked incredulously.

"According to the admiral, Himmler said he had disabused the Führer of that notion. But Hitler wanted to know, as I said, if the mechanism is in place."

"I want to hear about freeing Mussolini," Graham said. "But first, let's get to the other two reasons von Deitzberg is being sent to Argentina."

Von und zu Waching looked at him, nodded, and went on: "Himmler told Hitler that he had turned over control of U-405 to Admiral Canaris—this was not true—and that Canaris was in the process of seeing if 'the mechanism was in place'; that von Deitzberg was en route to Argentina is the test of the mechanism."

"So von Deitzberg had to go," Graham said. "Reason Two?"

"Himmler wants your man there, Frade, eliminated. Apparently, Cranz has been unable to accomplish this. Von Deitzberg is very good at that sort of thing. And he's close to Colonel Perón."

"And Three?"

"That—his connection with Perón—may be Three. But it could be something else. I just know, and the admiral agrees, that there's more to Himmler's sending von Deitzberg to Argentina than checking to see if the 'transport mechanism' works and eliminating Frade."

"You said when Il Duce has been freed?" Dulles asked.

"By now the Carabinieri, in whose hands the king placed him, should have moved him to a ski resort—the Campo Imperatore Hotel on the Gran Sasso—" He paused and looked between Dulles and Graham to make sure they understood him, and after they nodded he went on: "From which, in the next few days, a task force of paratroops augmented by some special SS troops will try to rescue him."

"You're suggesting that you're not sure the operation will work?" Graham asked.

"The admiral isn't sure, either. On one hand, the paratroops are very good, and the SS are special troops. On the other, there's a battalion of Carabinieri who are also very good."

"Why is rescuing Mussolini so important?" Dulles wondered aloud. "There is no way he could resume power."

"Because the Bavarian corporal thinks it is," von und zu Waching said. "Case closed."

Dulles nodded a sad agreement.

"Okay," Graham said. "What is it you want from me in Argentina? And what do you offer in return?"

"Money is the primary thing I want from you," von und zu Waching said.

"Money is usually the last thing mentioned," Graham said. "After you convince the other fellow that he really wants what you're selling, *then* you tell him how much it costs. What are you going to give me for my money?"

"Abwehr Ost," von und zu Waching said. "Files, dossiers, analyses, even agents in place. How much would you like to have that?"

"We have a saying, Captain, that when something sounds too good to be true, it usually is," Graham said. "The first thing that comes to mind is: 'How could he possibly deliver on that?' And the second is: 'Why would he want to?'"

"Oberstleutnant Gehlen . . . you know of whom I speak?"

Graham nodded. "He runs Abwehr Ost for Admiral Canaris. I've always wondered why he's only a lieutenant colonel."

"To keep him from Hitler's attention," von und zu Waching said. "He met the Führer for the first time a week or so ago."

"Okay," Graham said. "I can understand that."

"Oberstleutnant Gehlen wants three things," von und zu Waching went on carefully. "In the following order: To protect the families of his officers and men. To protect, insofar as this may be possible, the lives of his officers and men and agents and assets in place in the Soviet Union."

Graham nodded, grunted, and said, "That's two things."

"You very possibly won't like his third."

"We won't know until you tell me, will we?"

"Gehlen feels it would be a shame—worse, criminal, even sinful—if all the knowledge of Abwehr Ost, acquired at such great effort and the cost of so many lives, should be flushed down the toilet when Soviet tanks roll down the Unter den Linden."

"What would he like to see happen to it?" Dulles asked softly.

"He believes that his intelligence would be useful, even the determining factor, in defeating the Soviet Union when, inevitably, there is war between the United States and the Soviet Union."

"And do you believe that war is inevitable between the United States and our Soviet allies?" Dulles pursued.

Von und zu Waching took a moment before replying: "I would say that it is inevitable unless the United States develops and produces atomic weapons before the Soviet Union does and demonstrates its willingness to use them."

"Even against Germany?" Graham asked.

Von und zu Waching didn't reply to the question. Graham decided not to push him.

"The Russians are, of course, aware of Gehlen," von und zu Waching said, "and almost certainly have the names of his important people on their Order of Battle charts. Probably, they have the names of everyone connected with Abwehr Ost down to the last obergefreiter and female civilian typist. It follows that if we have penetrated them, they have penetrated us."

"Yeah," Graham thought aloud.

"But they don't—self-evidently—know the identities of Gehlen's people in the Kremlin. They will want those names. We would, and I suggest you would, under the same circumstances. The difference being that we would not torture the wives and children of their officers to get that information."

"You think the Russians would torture women and children?" Dulles asked softly.

"Probably with about as much enthusiasm as the SS does when they have a Russian woman or child in their hands," von und zu Waching said.

"What do you want from me?" Graham asked. "I don't seem to be getting an answer."

"Gehlen wants to set up an operation something like Phoenix for his people," von und zu Waching said. "What he wants to do immediately is send one of his officers to Argentina to see what has to be done. That's why I said he needs—I suppose I mean we need—money. Abwehr doesn't have warehouses full of no-longer-needed gold wedding rings, dental prostheses, and eyeglass frames that can be turned into cash."

"You don't think that anyone would notice that one of Gehlen's officers— and he would have to be one of his senior officers—was suddenly no longer around?" Graham asked.

"The officer Gehlen has in mind—a major—will ostensibly give his life for the Fatherland on the Eastern Front. We can get him as far as here, or Madrid, one or the other, with identity credentials that should get him past the border guards."

"And from here, or Madrid, to Buenos Aires?"

"That you'd have to arrange," von und zu Waching said.

"And what do we get?" Graham asked.

"Eventually everything, and that includes Oberstleutnant Gehlen and myself. And possibly even the admiral. Immediately, we will give you the names of the people the Soviets have at Oak Ridge, Los Alamos, the University of California at Berkeley, and elsewhere. There are eleven names in all. More will be furnished when they turn up, as I'm sure they will. Stalin wants your bomb and is working hard to get it."

"And how much money are you asking?" Dulles asked.

"It will probably turn out to be several millions of dollars. Not all at once, of course. In the immediate future, probably not more than a hundred thousand dollars."

Neither Dulles nor Graham said anything.

After a long silence, von und zu Waching said: "And we will, of course, furnish you with whatever we learn about Operation Phoenix and what von Deitzberg is really doing."

"The idea, if I understand this correctly," Graham said, "is that once this officer gets himself established in Argentina, he will then arrange for other officers . . ."

"The admiral has told him he can have no more than two more officers. More than that would attract unwanted attention. The next people to be sent will be the families of those officers and soldiers in which we feel the Russians have the greatest interest. In other words, the selection will be on the basis of who the Russians think has the greatest knowledge, rather than on rank."

Dulles said, "But by those criteria, Captain, the first officer who would go to Argentina would be the admiral. And then Gehlen. And then you."

"I'm sure Colonel Graham will understand, Mr. Dulles. It's naval tradition. The admiral and Gehlen will stay on the bridges of their respective sinking ships until all the women and children are safely off and into lifeboats. And then the men. And, finally, the other officers."

There was a long moment of silence, which Allen Dulles finally broke: "Obviously, Captain, neither Colonel Graham nor I have the authority to accept or reject a proposal like this—"

"Or even to have been having this conversation," Graham interrupted. "There are those who would consider it trafficking with the enemy . . ."

"Even giving aid and comfort to the enemy," Dulles chimed in.

"But you have been honest and forthcoming with us," Graham said. "And we'll try to be the same with you. What I think Mr. Dulles and I are going to have to do is decide, first, if we should—if we dare—bring Admiral Canaris's offer to the attention of our respective superiors . . ."

"Which might well carry the risk of seeing one or both of us relieved of our posts," Dulles chimed in again.

"So, if you will be so good, Captain, to give Mr. Dulles and myself a little time—say, thirty minutes—to decide between us whether we can take the next step, bringing this to the attention of our respective superiors or not. And if not, what other—"

"I understand," von und zu Waching said. "I will await your call, your decision."

Von und zu Waching walked to the door, unlocked it, opened it, turned to look at Graham and Dulles, bobbed his head, and then went through the door.

Dulles waited a full thirty seconds—which seemed longer—before breaking the silence: "The basic question, of course, is whether or not he's telling us the truth, the whole truth, and nothing but."

"I think that we have to presume he is not, Allen. And further, that he has an agenda we can't even guess at."

"And insofar as telling Colonel Donovan about this, can you imagine his reaction if he knew about this meeting?"

"Or that I flew over here to participate?"

"Or what the President would do if he heard about this?"

"Well, he would certainly tell the Vice President, and Uncle Joe Stalin would know within twenty-fours that we know he has spies all over the Manhattan Project. Do you know General Graves, Allen? Know him well?"

Dulles nodded.

"He told me that he thinks at least six of Dr. Oppenheimer's geniuses are—how did he put it? 'Far to the left of Vice President Wallace.'"

"Graves told me that when he went to J. Edgar Hoover, Hoover told him that when he tried to bring up the subject of Soviet spies in the Manhattan Project to the President, Roosevelt flashed his famous smile at him and said since the Russians knew nothing of the Manhattan Project, how could they have spies trying to penetrate it?"

They lapsed into silence for another long moment.

Finally, Dulles again broke it.

"I would say then that we are agreed we don't mention this to Donovan?"

Graham nodded.

"What about Hoover?" Graham asked.

"Hoover already knows about the Russian spies. I suspect J. Edgar has some of his best people keeping their eyes on them."

"Nevertheless, when von und zu gives us the names of his spies, I think we should pass them on to J. Edgar; his spies may not be the same as Canaris's spies." Dulles nodded, and Graham went on: "Slip them under J. Edgar's door in the dead of night; I don't think he should know they came from us."

"That leaves only two minor problems to be resolved," Dulles said. "Where do we get the one hundred thousand dollars immediately, and the million we will need later? Probably more than a million dollars. Estimates for this sort of thing are invariably far short of what is actually required."

"I don't see that as a problem. What's the other thing?"

"How do we get this officer of Gehlen's from here to South America? And the families von und zu is talking about? And subquestion a: What do we do with him—with, ultimately, all of Gehlen's women and children—once they are there? And why isn't a million dollars a problem?"

"I've been giving that some thought. If you and I suddenly spent even the hundred thousand from our nonvouchered funds, Donovan would be all over us wanting to know what we spent it on."

"Leaving us where?"

"With Cletus Marcus Howell."

"Who?" Dulles said.

"Cletus Frade's grandfather, a.k.a. Howell Petroleum. He's got that kind of money—more important, he's got it in Venezuela, out of sight of the Internal Revenue Service—and I'm sure that all I'll have to tell him is that his grandson needs to borrow it for the duration plus six months."

"And moving all these people to Argentina?"

Graham nodded and said, "Donovan told me the President is really happy that Juan Trippe is really unhappy that South American Airways has established—or is in the process of establishing—regularly scheduled service between Buenos Aires, Rio de Janeiro, Santiago, Montevideo, and other places in South America. All I have to do is figure a way to make the President think of how utterly miserable Juan Trippe would be to learn that this upstart airline is offering . . . oh, say, twice-weekly service between Buenos Aires and Madrid? Or Lisbon? Or Casablanca? Or all three?"

"Which they could do if they had a 'surplus' Constellation?"

"I was thinking more on the lines of three Constellations," Graham said.

"Why am I getting the feeling that this Constellation idea didn't suddenly pop into your head in the last fifteen minutes or so?"

"Because you know how devious—some might say Machiavellian—I am beneath this polished veneer of refined Texas gentleman."

Dulles chuckled. "I have to say this, Alex: You realize that we are giving aid and comfort to the enemy, betraying our Russian ally, and agreeing to deceive not only our boss but the President?"

Graham's face was sober as he nodded his understanding.

But then he smiled.

"It's in a good cause, Allen. Now get on the phone and get von und zu back in here so we can tell him he's got a deal."

[THREE]
Aboard MV _Ciudad de Cádiz_
South Latitude 26.318
West Longitude 22.092
0625 11 September 1943

Kapitänleutnant Wilhelm von Dattenberg paused at the interior door to the bridge, waited to be noticed, and when that didn't happen, asked, "Permission to come onto the bridge, Kapitän?"

Von Dattenberg, a slim, somewhat hawk-faced thirty-two-year-old, was wearing navy blue trousers, a black knit sweater, and a battered, greasy Kriegsmarine officer's cap, which was sort of the proud symbol of a submarine officer.

Capitán José Francisco de Banderano, master of the _Ciudad de Cádiz,_ who had been standing on the port flying bridge holding binoculars to his eyes, turned to look at von Dattenberg. José de Banderano looked very much like Wilhelm von Dattenberg—in other words, more Teutonic than Latin—but was a few years older. He was wearing blue trousers and a stiffly starched white shirt with four-stripe shoulder boards.

"You have the freedom of this bridge, Capitán," de Banderano said. "I thought I told you that. Four or five times."

"I must have forgotten."

Von Dattenberg walked onto the flying bridge and looked over the side. His vessel—U-405, a type VIIC submarine—lay alongside, the German naval battle flag hanging limply from a staff on her conning tower.

Her diesels were idling; if necessary, she could be under way in a minute or two and submerged a few minutes after that. It was unlikely that she would have to do that. They were just about equidistant from Africa and South America, in the middle of the Atlantic, and off the usual shipping lanes.

The chief of the boat was in the conning tower, resting on his elbows. Two seamen were manning a machine gun.

"Morgen!" von Dattenberg called. He had "the voice of command"; it carried.

The seamen popped to attention. The chief of the boat looked up and waved his right arm in a gesture that was far more a friendly wave than a salute.

A white-jacketed steward touched von Dattenberg's arm and, when he looked, handed him a steaming china mug.

"The capitán asks that you join him for breakfast, Capitán."

"Thank you," von Dattenberg said, and walked off the flying bridge into the wheelhouse, then through it to the chart room, and from there to the door to the master's cabin.

De Banderano waved him in. A table had been set with a crisp white table-cloth and silver. A steward—not the one who had given von Dattenberg the coffee—immediately began to deliver breakfast.

It was an impressive display of food. They were served a basket of breads and rolls, thin slices of ham rolled into tubes, a plate of curled butter, and another of jams and marmalades.

De Banderano poked at the ham tubes with his fork, then announced: "A ham steak, please, Ricardo. Two eggs, up."

"Yes, sir," the steward said, and looked at von Dattenberg. "Capitán?"

"Not for me, thank you," von Dattenberg said, then immediately changed his mind. "Yes, please. Same thing." He met de Banderano's eyes. "God only knows when I'll eat this well again."

"Yes, sir."

The steward had just poured von Dattenberg another cup of coffee—this time into a delicate Meissen cup sitting on a saucer—when the third mate, serving as officer of the deck, appeared at the door.

"Excuse me, Capitán. There is a submarine dead ahead at maybe three kilometers."

"Can you read her flag?"

"No, sir. The submarine could be anything."

"Perhaps it's Swiss," de Banderano said. "Have the Oerlikons manned just in case. I have never trusted the Swiss navy."

Von Dattenberg chuckled.

The odds against any submarine but a U-boat not immediately submerging when spotting a ship were enormous. And there was no Swiss navy.

The *Ciudad de Cádiz* had a half-dozen Oerlikon 20mm machine guns mounted in various places in her superstructure, all but two of them behind false bulkheads that could be swung quickly out of the way.

"Yes, sir."

The third mate returned before von Dattenberg and de Banderano had finished their coffee.

"The Oerlikons are manned, sir, and we have notified the U-405."

"Very well," de Banderano said. "Capitán von Dattenberg and I will be on the bridge shortly."

"Send, *Lie along our port side*," Capitán de Banderano ordered the seaman standing beside him with a signaling lamp.

"*Lie alongside our port side*. Aye, aye, sir," the signalman said, and began tapping his key.

"That's the U-409," von Dattenberg said.

"You know her? Her master?"

"I don't know if I do or not," von Dattenberg said.

"Submarine sends, *Will lie along your port*," the signalman reported.

"Very well," de Banderano said. "Make all preparations to take passengers and cargo aboard, with refueling and replenishment of food supplies to follow. Have the galley prepared to feed her crew. Have the table set in the wardroom to feed officers. Alert the laundry."

"Aye, aye, sir," the third mate responded.

"Take the helm, Señor Sanchez."

"I have the helm, sir," Third Mate Sanchez said.

"Why don't we go below, Capitán, and greet our visitors?" Capitán de Banderano suggested.

By the time de Banderano and von Dattenberg had made their way from the bridge to the just-above-the-waterline Seventh Deck, enormous watertight doors in the *Ciudad de Cádiz's* hull had been slid upward and a huge cushion— lashed-together truck tires—was being lowered into place.

Lines were tossed aboard by sailors on the submarine, and hawsers then fed to the submarine from the ship. The U-409 was pulled carefully against the cushion.

A gangway was slid from the deck of the ship onto the submarine. Two men walked toward it as it was lashed into place. One was dressed, as was von Dattenberg, in a sweater and trousers topped off by an equally battered hat. Despite his neatly trimmed full beard, the captain of the U-409 looked very young.

The man with him was in a black SS uniform, its insignia identifying him as an SS-brigadeführer. He was pale-faced, and the uniform was mussed.

And probably dirty, von Dattenberg thought.

The captain of the U-409 walked up the gangway, stopped, raised his arm in a salute, and said, "Permission to board, Kapitän?"

The SS-brigadeführer pushed past him onto the ship.

De Banderano returned the salute. "Granted. Welcome."

The SS-brigadeführer threw his arm straight out in the Nazi salute and barked, "Heil, Hitler!"

Von Dattenberg returned the salute more than a little sloppily.

De Banderano just looked at him.

"Take me to the kapitän, please."

"I'm the master of the *Ciudad de Cádiz.*"

"Kapitän, I am SS-Brigadeführer von Deitzberg. I have your orders."

"You have *my* orders?" de Banderano said as if surprised.

Von Deitzberg handed him an envelope. As de Banderano tore it open, the submarine captain walked to them, gave a military salute—as opposed to the Nazi salute—and said, "Kapitänleutnant Wertz, Kapitän. I have the honor to command U-409."

De Banderano returned that salute and offered his hand.

"Von Dattenberg, U-405," von Dattenberg said.

"Aside from this gentleman," de Banderano said, nodding at von Deitzberg, "what have you got for us?"

"One more SS officer, an obersturmführer; ten SS of other ranks; and one wooden crate."

"I was thinking more of mail," de Banderano said.

"And a packet of mail."

"Why don't you send for that?" de Banderano said. "And then we'll see about feeding you and getting you a bath and some clean clothing."

"The crate, the special shipment, and my men are more important than the mail," von Deitzberg said. "Get them on here first."

"After you've gotten the mail, Capitán, you can bring aboard everything else that comes aboard," de Banderano said calmly.

He handed the orders von Deitzberg had given him to von Dattenberg.

"I didn't give you permission to show him those orders!" von Deitzberg flared.

"There's one thing you should understand, Señor von Deitzberg. I am the master of this vessel. I don't need anyone's permission to do anything, and no one tells me what to do."

Von Deitzberg colored, but he didn't say anything.

"Capitán von Dattenberg," de Banderano said. "Why don't you take Capitán Wertz to your cabin, get him a bath and some clean clothing, and order him breakfast."

"Aye, aye, sir."

"And then, when the crate and the SS personnel who are so important to him are safely aboard, we'll see about getting this fellow a bath and something to eat."

"Aye, aye, sir," von Dattenberg said, and turned to Wertz. "If you'll come with me, Kapitän?"

Kapitänleutnant Wertz waited until von Dattenberg had closed his cabin door before he announced, "I think I like this Spanish kapitän."

"He's a good man."

"And he's not impressed with SS-Brigadeführer von Deitzberg."

"He doesn't seem to be."

"Everybody at Saint-Nazaire was. I wanted to throw up."

"Why am I getting the idea you don't like the brigadeführer?"

"The only nice thing I can say about that SS bastard is that he got seasick the moment we hit the deep water outside Saint-Nazaire, and stayed that way whenever we were on the surface—and we were on the surface most of the way."

Von Dattenberg smiled but said nothing.

Wertz warmed to his subject as he began pulling off his clothing.

"He showed up at the pens like royalty. And all of our never-leave-the-port superiors fell all over each other trying to kiss his ass. He has *four* fucking suitcases, big ones."

"Where did you stow them?"

"We took off *four* torpedoes to make room for them. And the crap those storm troopers had with them."

"Well, there are torpedoes aboard the *Cádiz*. This is a floating warehouse."

Von Dattenberg, as Wertz went on, realized that the cork was out of the bottle: "When I showed the SS sonofabitch my cabin, and graciously, in the tradition of the naval service, showed him the fold-down bunk and told him I would sleep there, and that he could use my bunk, he said, 'I really think you should find some other accommodation.'"

"Jesus!"

"So I moved in with my Number One, and we played hot sheets all across the Atlantic."

"Well, he is an SS-brigadeführer."

"Who showered at least twice a day, usually throwing up in the stall—which *was* sort of funny—and then complained about how long it took my men to clean up after him. He used up more fresh water taking showers than my crew got to drink."

Kapitänleutnant Wertz was now down to his shorts, which were once white but now gray and oil-stained.

"If he hadn't been seasick all the time, I'd have thrown the sonofabitch over the side—or shot him out of a tube and reported he had died gloriously for the Führer."

"Take it easy, Wertz," von Dattenberg said seriously. "You don't want anyone hearing you talk like that."

Now there was concern on Wertz's face.

"Except another U-boat skipper, of course," von Dattenberg added to ease his mind. "And now that you've told me the brigadeführer suffers terribly from *mal de mer*, I'll do my best to stay on the surface until we're nearly where we're going with him."

"Where are you going?"

"They didn't tell you?"

"No, and sorry, I shouldn't have asked."

"I'd love to tell you, just to piss him off, but that would be dangerous for both of us."

Wertz nodded his understanding.

"Go have your shower," von Dattenberg said. "There's fresh clothing on the bunk, and while you're doing that, I'll order your breakfast. Ham and eggs?"

[FOUR]
Wardroom
MV *Ciudad de Cádiz*
0915 11 September 1943

SS-Brigadeführer Manfred von Deitzberg, now attired in an ordinary seaman's blue shirt and trousers, was eating—wolfing down—his breakfast of ham steak and eggs and fried potatoes at the master's table in the wardroom.

"You were hungry, weren't you?" Capitán de Banderano asked, smiling.

Von Deitzberg, obviously making an attempt to pour some oil on what he recognized as troubled waters, smiled at both von Dattenberg—who was sitting across from him at the table—and de Banderano, who was tilted back in his chair at the head of the table.

"Obviously, I am not cut out to be a mariner," he said. "I haven't had much to eat but crackers and tea for days."

"So Capitán Wertz said," de Banderano said. "Well, you can make up for that now."

"You have a dry cleaning facility on here? The steward said something . . ."

"There is a dry cleaning machine *aboard,*" de Banderano said. "And a laundry. And stocks of uniforms for the men from the Unterseebooten. Unfortunately, no SS uniforms. We don't see many SS men."

"And the food! This is marvelous ham! And fresh eggs! Where do you get all this?"

"Either in Montevideo or Buenos Aires. We enter those ports, usually alternately, every two weeks or so. We top off our fuel tanks and take on stocks of fresh food."

"With which you replenish the Unterseebooten," von Deitzberg said.

"We do."

"And you have no trouble getting into and out of those ports?"

De Banderano shook his head.

"Let me ask you this, Kapitän. Could I leave your ship in either port without being noticed?"

"My orders—you gave them to me, didn't you read them?—say that I am to land you and your men and that crate at Samborombón Bay in the River Plate estuary."

"I'm not talking about the SS men. I meant just me."

"I'm not saying it would be impossible, but I don't think I want to take that risk. The authorities watch me pretty close in both places. They suspect—know—what we're doing. But so long as I don't violate their neutrality, they leave me alone. If I was caught smuggling something ashore—you, for example—they wouldn't let me into their ports again. That would mean there would be no fresh food, and, more importantly, no diesel fuel for the Unterseebooten."

When von Deitzberg didn't reply, de Banderano went on: "And then we have our orders. You and your men are to be put ashore on Samborombón Bay."

"Orders are subject to change," von Deitzberg said. "Presumably you are in radio contact with Berlin?"

"Let me explain how that works," de Banderano said, a touch of impatience in his voice. "With rare exceptions, we do not communicate with the station. It's in Spain, by the way. It used to be in North Africa, but now the Americans are there. There was such a transmission today. One word. The code word for 'shipment received; proceeding.'

"We don't want anyone finding us out by triangulation, which they would most likely do if we sent long messages. We receive our orders, which are encrypted by an Enigma machine, from the station in Spain. The enemy cannot locate a radio receiver by triangulation.

"Tomorrow, when you and your men are aboard U-405, and she has sailed for Samborombón Bay, and U-409 resumes patrol, I will transmit a two-word message. One will be the code word for U-405 proceeding according to orders, and the second the code word for U-409 resuming patrol.

"En route to Argentina, the station will transmit specific orders to Capitán von Dattenberg giving him the details regarding where you and your men are to be put ashore in the rubber boats.

"I don't intend to jeopardize this system by transmitting a long message in which you will attempt to justify to Admiral Canaris putting you ashore in Montevideo or Buenos Aires despite the risks that would pose to not only your mission, but also mine. Do you understand, Señor von Deitzberg?"

After a long moment, von Deitzberg smiled. "Of course. I simply didn't understand. As I said before, I am not a mariner."

[FIVE]
ABC Restaurant
Lavalle 545
Buenos Aires, Argentina
1320 18 September 1943

"There it is, on the left," Anton von Gradny-Sawz said, pointing as he leaned forward in the rear seat of the embassy's Mercedes.

"Jawohl, Herr von Gradny-Sawz," Günther Loche said crisply.

"Pick me up in an hour and a half, Günther," von Gradny-Sawz ordered as Loche pulled into the curb. "At ten minutes before three."

"Jawohl, Herr von Gradny-Sawz."

"Get yourself some lunch during that time, but before, *before* you eat, find a public telephone—there's a booth at the intersection of Lavalle and Carlos Pellegrini—and call the embassy and tell Ambassador von Lutzenberger or Fräulein Hässell—no one else; keep trying until you get one or the other—that I am taking lunch with el Coronel Martín and possibly someone on his staff at the ABC; that I expect to be finished before three and will then go to the embassy."

"Jawohl, Herr von Gradny-Sawz."

"Now, Günther, who are you going to call, and when, and what are you going to say?"

"Before I eat, Herr von Gradny-Sawz, I am to find a public telephone, and call the ambassador or Fräulein Hässell and tell them you're having lunch with el Coronel Martín at the ABC restaurant, and expect to be finished before three, and after that will go to the embassy."

"And, Günther, and?"

"Excuse me, Herr von Gradny-Sawz?"

"And who are you going to give that message to if neither Ambassador von Lutzenberger nor Fräulein Hässell is available?"

Günther was visibly confused for a moment, but then said, "Herr von Gradny-Sawz, you said I was to keep trying until I got one of them; not give the message to someone else."

"Correct," von Gradny-Sawz said, and got out of the car.

As he crossed the sidewalk and pushed open the door to the restaurant, von Gradny-Sawz thought, somewhat smugly: *What that zealous but none-too-bright would-be Sicherheitsdienst agent is going to do is go to the pay phone, call*

Commercial Counselor Karl Cranz or, failing to get him on the phone, Deputy Commercial Counselor Erich Raschner—

"Deputy Commercial Counselor" Raschner, my left foot's big toe!

Does SS-Obersturmbannführer Cranz really think people don't know SS-Sturmbannführer Raschner's not a diplomat? Raschner is crude, ignorant, and a peasant!

—and tell one or the other of them that I'm having lunch in the ABC with Martin.

Only then—or perhaps even after he has his lunch—will he try to call Ambassador von Lutzenberger and tell him what I'm doing.

Which is exactly what I want him to do.

Cranz and Raschner will think both that (a) Günther is keeping a close eye on me and (b) that I don't even suspect that he is.

Von Gradny-Sawz felt a little light-headed.

He was, he realized, about to cross the Rubicon.

There was something surreal about it, even though this would not be the first time he had realized that he had had to, so to speak, cross the Rubicon.

From the moment Ambassador von Lutzenberger had shown him the message from Canaris about the "senior officer to be later identified" and told him to set up the identity card, driver's license, and the rest of it, von Gradny-Sawz had known he was going to have to do whatever was necessary to keep himself from being identified as the traitor everyone—certainly including the "senior officer to be later identified"—knew was in the embassy.

That *he* wasn't the traitor was irrelevant.

They were going to find a traitor, he well knew, even if they had to invent one.

Actually, von Gradny-Sawz wasn't sure who "they" were, only that the senior officers of the embassy—Ambassador von Lutzenberger, "Commercial Attaché" Cranz, and Naval Attaché Boltitz—who were all, of course, under suspicion themselves, were understandably not going to find themselves and their families in Sachsenhausen or Dachau as long as they could throw someone else to the Sicherheitsdienst.

But von Gradny-Sawz recognized that First Secretary Anton von Gradny-Sawz could easily be that sacrificial lamb.

When Wilhelm Frogger, the commercial attaché of the embassy, had gone missing with his wife, there had been a brief moment's hope that they had been the traitors. Yet that hope had been shattered when "they" had decided the Froggers had been kidnapped by the American OSS.

Von Gradny-Sawz thought what had happened was that Frogger—or, for that matter, his wife, who was *sub rosa* working for the Sicherheitsdienst—had decided that he was going to be the sacrificial lamb and had gone to the Americans to save his life.

That scenario had not sat well with Cranz—and with his superiors in Berlin—because it would have meant that one of their own, Frau Frogger, had been a traitor. That would have damaged the image of the Sicherheitsdienst, and that couldn't be tolerated.

The arrow was again pointing at Anton von Gradny-Sawz, and, having come to that conclusion, he had understood he really had no choice in the matter; he had to do what he was about to do.

El Coronel Alejandro Martín, chief of the Ethical Standards Office of the Bureau of Internal Security, was sitting in a booth halfway down the right side of the ABC, buttering a chunk of rye bread.

He was wearing a tweed suit that von Gradny-Sawz thought was "cut on the English style" and didn't look much like what came to mind when thinking of someone who was Argentina's senior intelligence—and, for that matter, counterintelligence—officer.

"I hope I haven't kept you waiting, el Coronel?"

Martín rose and offered von Gradny-Sawz his hand.

"Actually, I came a bit early. How are you, Mister Secretary?"

"I thought we'd agreed you weren't to call me that?"

"At the time, we agreed you wouldn't call me 'Coronel.'"

"Touché, Alejandro," von Gradny-Sawz said. "Shall I go out and come back in and do it right?"

"Sit down, Anton, and as soon as we decide which of our governments is paying for our lunch, we'll have a look at the wine list."

Von Gradny-Sawz managed to slide onto the opposing bench, and he reached for the red-leather-bound wine list.

"Before we allow the subject to get in the way of our lunch, Anton," Martín said, "I regret that I have been unable to turn up any trace of Señor Frogger. Or Señora Frogger."

"They seem to have simply fallen off the edge of the earth, haven't they?" von Gradny-Sawz said. "But now that we have talked business, diplomatic protocol gives me no choice in the matter. Our luncheon is on the Foreign Ministry of the German Reich."

"I will not argue with diplomatic protocol," Martín said. "And since I know nothing of German wines, I'm happy to bow to your expertise."

"Have you thought of what you would like to eat?"

"They do a marvelous sauerbraten here."

"Yes, they do," von Gradny-Sawz agreed cheerfully. "And that would call for a red." He looked up from the wine list, smiled happily at Martín, and announced, "And here it is!"

He pointed. Martín looked.

"That's Argentine," Martín said.

"Yes, I know," von Gradny-Sawz said. "And since, with all modesty, I am something of an expert on German wines—which range from the tolerable to the undrinkable—I will confess—trusting in your discretion—that I never drink them unless it is my diplomatic duty to do so."

Martín smiled at him but didn't reply.

"Hungarian wines are marvelous," von Gradny-Sawz began, interrupting himself when a waiter appeared. Then, switching to German, he ordered: "Be so good, Herr Ober, as to bring us a bottle of the Don Guillermo Cabernet Sauvignon 1939 if you have it. If not, 1941."

"Jawohl, Exzellenz."

"And then make sure there is another; I suspect it may be necessary."

"Jawohl, Exzellenz."

The waiter bowed and backed away from the table.

"An ethnic German, I would suppose," von Gradny-Sawz said, switching back to Spanish. "What is it they say about converts to Roman Catholicism? 'They become more Papist than the Pope.' I suspect we are being served by a devout follower of the Führer."

Martín chuckled.

"Where was I? Oh. Hungarian wines. They really are wonderful. Something else the Bolsheviks are going to wind up with. Including a vineyard that's been in my family since the Romans."

"That sounds as if you think the Allies are going to win the war," Martín said carefully.

"As a loyal German, I of course have absolute faith in the ultimate Final Victory."

Martín smiled and shook his head. Von Gradny-Sawz smiled back.

"Changing the subject," Martín said, "I know something about that Don Guillermo Cabernet I suspect you don't."

"The initial pressing is by the bare feet of nubile virgins?"

"The 'Don Guillermo' makes reference to Don Guillermo Frade, grand-uncle of the present owner, Don Cletus Frade. He established the vineyard in Mendoza."

"And now it's in the hands of an American! War is really hell, isn't it, Alejandro?"

"Yes, I think it is," Martín said seriously. "But speaking of the war, may I ask you a question, friend to friend?"

"Certainly."

"What's going on with Mussolini? What was that all about?"

"You saw the story in *La Nación*?"

"And we heard from our embassy in Berlin that the newspapers there reported that after his brilliant rescue he's on his way to see Hitler."

"King Victor Emmanuel had him confined in a ski resort not far from Rome in the Gran Sasso. Lovely place; I often skied there. The Campo Imperatore Hotel. He was in the hands of the Carabinieri. The only way to get to the hotel is by cable car. It was therefore believed his rescue was impossible. Even if his rescuers parachuted onto the mountaintop, or landed there in gliders, which is what they ultimately did, Mussolini could be shot by the Carabinieri rather than waiting for the trial the king planned for him after the Americans take Italy. The king was determined that Il Duce should not be freed to attempt to resume control of the government."

"I saw that the Allies have landed . . ."

"At Anzio," von Gradny-Sawz confirmed. "And Italy has surrendered unconditionally to the Allies. The Wehrmacht is in the process of disarming the Italian army."

The waiter appeared with two bottles of Don Guillermo Cabernet Sauvignon, apologized for not having the 1939, but reported that he had a bottle of both 1938 and 1937, and hoped His Excellency would approve.

They went through the opening, tasting, and pouring ritual.

They ordered *sauerbraten mit Kartoffelknödel und sauerkraut.*

They raised their glasses.

"To good friends, good food, and good wine," Martín offered.

"In the best of all possible worlds, a Hungarian Bikavér, as red as the blood of a bull, but failing that, this magnificent Don Guillermo," von Gradny-Sawz responded.

They sipped, swallowed, and smiled.

"So what was the purpose of rescuing Il Duce?" Martín asked.

"I'm sure the Führer had his reasons. Our Führer doesn't always explain his decisions, but we are all agreed that he is virtually incapable of making a mistake."

Martín did not reply.

"According to the story our commercial counselor, Señor Cranz, got from some friends of his in Germany," von Gradny-Sawz went on, "what the SS did—and I think this *was* brilliant—was kidnap a senior Carabinieri officer, a colonel or a general, I didn't get his name. They loaded him on one of the gliders and took him to the hotel. Under a flag of truce, the senior SS officer present—most of the attackers were parachutists, but this was an SS captain named Skorzeny—went to the senior Carabinieri officer and told him he had a choice. Either release Mussolini and no one would be hurt, or shoot Mussolini, whereupon the SS would shoot the Carabinieri colonel and then all the Carabinieri.

"Il Duce was released. Not a shot was fired. A Storch and a pilot were waiting nearby . . ." He waited to see on Martín's face that he knew what a Storch was, then went on: "Then Captain Skorzeny squeezed Il Duce and himself into the plane and flew to Rome."

Martín said: "I thought the Storch—you have one at the embassy, right?"

Von Gradny-Sawz nodded.

"—was a two-place airplane?"

"I wondered about that, too," von Gradny-Sawz said. "But I have found it wise never to question Herr Cranz about any detail of an SS operation."

"I understand," Martín said.

"Herr Cranz was inspired by the kidnapping," von Gradny-Sawz said.

"Excuse me?"

The waiter appeared with their *sauerbraten mit Kartoffelknödel und sauerkraut.*

"In Germany, you understand, Alejandro, where they don't have your magnificent Argentine beef, the meat sometimes has the consistency of shoe leather. I don't find that a problem. I love the sauce. If I were facing execution, I think I would request for my last meal the Kartoffelknödel and the sauce, hold the sauerbraten. And, of course, a bottle of Bikavér and some hard-crusted bread."

Martín chuckled.

"You were saying something about Señor Cranz being inspired by the kidnapping?"

By the time he asked the question, von Gradny-Sawz had a mouthful of the sauerbraten. When he finally had it all chewed and swallowed, he said:

"If I was guaranteed Argentine beef like this, I *would* add sauerbraten to my last meal." And then, without a perceptible pause, he continued, "What SS-Obersturmbannführer Cranz plans to do is kidnap Señora Pamela Holworth-Talley de Mallín, Doña Dorotea Mallín de Frade's mother. He also plans to kidnap Doña Dorotea's fifteen-year-old brother Enrique—and possibly Señor Mallín himself. And then he plans to exchange them all for the Froggers."

He then sawed off a piece of the *Kartoffelknödel*, moved it around his plate to coat it with the sauce, and put it into his mouth.

Martín laid down his knife and fork, then took a swallow of his wine before asking, "Anton, why are you telling me this?"

Von Gradny-Sawz finished chewing the *Kartoffelknödel*, dabbed at his mouth with a napkin, and took a swallow of his wine. He refilled his glass before continuing.

"Two reasons, Alejandro, one of them being that I like to think of myself as a Christian gentleman, and as such am morally offended at the involvement of an innocent woman and her fifteen-year-old son in this sordid business, let alone Señor Mallín."

Martín considered that for a moment before asking, "And the other?"

"The other reason is quite selfish," von Gradny-Sawz said. "The possibility exists that I might find it necessary at some time in the future to . . . how do I say this? . . . *seek asylum* in this beautiful country of yours, and I would like a highly placed friend should that become necessary."

Martín looked at him intently. Von Gradny-Sawz met his eyes for a very long moment, then picked up his wineglass again.

"Anton," Martín said carefully, "if you are serious about seeking asylum, it will take me a couple of days to . . ."

"I don't think—operative word *think*—that such action will be immediately necessary. I would like to think of myself as a loyal German, a loyal diplomat, who would not take such action unless it was absolutely necessary. I am not a traitor. What I would like to do is have the asylum ready should I need it. In the meantime, I will carry out my duties at the embassy and, while doing so, make what might be considered deposits in my account with you."

"For example?" Martín asked.

"What I just gave you, for example. A violation of the generally accepted standards of decency, which I don't consider are covered by questions of loyalty."

Martín nodded his understanding or agreement, or maybe both.

I've got him, von Gradny-Sawz decided. *El Coronel Martín not only took the bait but swallowed it whole.*

Kidnapping Don Cletus Frade's mother-in-law and brother-in-law to ex-change them for the Froggers would be a clever thing to do, the sort of thing Cranz—if he were considerably more intelligent than he believes himself to be—would dream up.

"Do you have any idea when this kidnapping is supposed to take place?"

Since it exists only in my imagination, Alejandro, I know it will never be attempted.

Von Gradny-Sawz shook his head.

"If I am able to learn more, Alejandro, I'll let you know."

I have just given him several problems.

What is he to do?

Put guards on Señora de Mallín and the boy, which would carry with it the risk that questions would be asked that he wouldn't want to answer? Such as who told him?

Tell Don Cletus Frade, which could pose all sorts of problems?

Tell his superiors, who might decide to have a quiet word with von Lutzenberger, pointing out the risks of kidnapping a very prominent Argentine woman?

Would von Lutzenberger decide that Cranz, who was capable of such a scheme, was again acting behind his back?

Would any of these scenarios raise questions about Anton von Gradny-Sawz in von Lutzenberger's mind? Or in Cranz's or Boltitz's?

I think not.

This is the second time I have crossed the Rubicon. It becomes easier if one has done it before.

Von Gradny-Sawz raised his hand over his shoulder, snapped his fingers, and called, "Herr Ober!"

The waiter appeared and von Gradny-Sawz mimed for him to open the second bottle of Don Guillermo Cabernet Sauvignon.

VIII

[ONE]
Office of the Managing Director
Banco de Inglaterra y Argentina
Bartolomé Mitre 300
Buenos Aires, Argentina
1430 19 September 1943

"You have an international call, Señor Duarte," Humberto Duarte's secretary announced at his office door. "It is Señor Frade calling from Brazil."

"Put it through, put it through," Duarte said impatiently.

He had the handset of his ornate, French-style telephone to his ear before his secretary had moved from the door.

It took ninety seconds before Frade came on the line.

"What did I do, Humberto? Interrupt your lunch?"

"Where the hell are you?" Humberto began, and then before Frade could possibly reply, went on, "No one knew where you were."

"And you thought I had crashed? I'm touched by your concern."

"I didn't know what to think. El Coronel Martín has been looking all over for you."

"He does like to keep an eye on me, doesn't he?"

"Cletus, for God's sake, can't you ever be serious? Martín said he has to see you as quickly as possible. He said it was very likely a matter of life or death."

The tone of Frade's voice changed. He now was serious.

"That's interesting. He say whose life?"

"Does it matter, for God's sake? Martín is a serious man. What in the world have you done now?"

"This is what I need you to do, Humberto. And it's not open for debate . . ."

"My God!"

"I want you to call President Rawson . . ."

"The president?"

"Are there two of them?"

"Have you been drinking?"

"I haven't so much as sniffed a cork," Frade said. "Tell el General that I would be very pleased if he, and such members of his staff as he sees fit, would have a glass of champagne with me at five o'clock this afternoon at Aeropuerto Coronel Jorge G. Frade."

"What?"

"I think you heard me, Humberto. If he shows reluctance, insist. If he's really reluctant, go so far as to remind him that he told me if there was anything I ever wanted from him, all I had to do was ask. Just get him there, Humberto."

"What the hell are you up to? You really haven't been drinking?"

"Boy Scout's Honor, I haven't had a drop in four days."

"I asked what this is all about, Cletus," Duarte said as sternly as he could manage.

"Take him up in the control tower. Have him there at five," Frade said, ignoring the question. "And once he's agreed to be there, get on the horn, call Claudia and tell her to be there, too—with both daughters, if possible, and von Wachtstein. And Father Welner. I suppose I'd better ask my beloved Tío Juan. I'd hate to hurt his feelings for not getting invited. And call my beloved father-in-law, speaking of people who don't like me. Get him out there, too. The more the merrier, in other words. Oh, hell! And call el Coronel Martín, too. And you better call *La Nación, La Prensa,* and the *Herald,* too. And tell them where el Presidente is going to be at five."

"Cletus, you listen to me," Duarte said sternly. "I'm not going to do any of this until you tell me what's going on."

"Just goddamn do it, Humberto. It's really important."

"I said no."

"And I said have everybody at the field at five o'clock. Just do it, goddamn it!"

There was a click, and Duarte realized that Cletus had hung up.

He took the handset from his ear and looked at it for a moment. Then he slowly replaced it in the base. He stared at that for a very long moment, exhaled audibly, then reached for the handset.

When his secretary came on the line, he said, "Call the Casa Rosada, please, and tell whoever answers the phone in the president's office that I am calling on behalf of Don Cletus Frade."

[TWO]
The Control Tower
Aeropuerto Coronel Jorge G. Frade
Morón, Buenos Aires Province, Argentina
1700 19 September 1943

General Arturo Rawson, president of the Republic of Argentina, and his aide-de-camp were both in uniform as they stood with Señora Claudia de Carzino-Cormano, Señor Humberto Duarte, and Reverend Kurt Welner, S.J., in the control tower. They all held stems and sipped champagne. The windows of the tower provided them an excellent view of the airfield's runways, tarmac, and the surrounding buildings and area.

There were six Lockheed Lodestars visible. President Rawson had commented what beautiful aircraft they were, and had watched intently as one had landed and two others had taken off.

Behind the hangar, the parking lot was crowded with large automobiles. Their passengers—those not in the control tower; there was regrettably only so much room—were standing on the tarmac in front of Base Operations, where a table had been set up so that white-jacketed waiters could serve champagne and canapés.

As the sweep second hand of the large clock approached the numeral twelve, indicating the time to be precisely 17:00:00, a familiar voice came over the tower's loudspeakers.

"Jorge Frade, this is South American Three Zero One."

"That's Cletus," Señora Carzino-Cormano declared unnecessarily.

"Señor Duarte, we don't have an aircraft with that tail number," the controller announced.

"Answer him," Duarte snapped.

"South American Three Zero One, Jorge Frade, go ahead."

"Three Zero One is at fifteen hundred meters, indicating four hundred kilometers per hour, fifty kilometers north of your station. Request approach and landing."

"How fast did he say he was going?" General Rawson asked.

"He said four hundred kilometers, *mi general,* but that can't be right," the general's aide-de-camp said.

"Three Zero One, Jorge Frade. Descend to one thousand, report when the field is in sight."

"Three Zero One, leaving fifteen hundred for one thousand," Frade's voice came over the loudspeaker.

Two minutes later, Frade's voice announced, "Three Zero One at one thousand meters, indicating three hundred kilometers. Request straight-in approach to runway Three Three."

"He said three hundred kilometers this time," General Rawson announced. "I could hear him clearly."

"Three Zero One, Jorge Frade clears you for a straight-in approach and landing as Number One on runway Three Three. Report when the runway is in sight."

"Three Zero One has the airfield in sight. Understand cleared as Number One on Three Three," the loudspeaker announced, and then: "Put the wheels down, Gonzo. It's smoother if you do that."

"My God," Claudia Carzino-Cormano said. "What is that? It's absolutely enormous."

The Lockheed Constellation, landing gear and flaps down, touched down at the far end of the runway.

Then it taxied to the terminal. As it got closer, everyone in the tower could now see that it had SOUTH AMERICAN AIRWAYS lettered in red on the fuselage, the flag of Argentina painted on all three of its vertical stabilizers, and the legend CIUDAD DE BUENOS AIRES lettered beneath the cockpit windows.

As it got really close to the terminal, small side windows in the cockpit opened, hands came out, and a moment later Argentine flags on holders were fluttering in the wind.

Frade's voice came over the speakers again.

"How about somebody getting a ladder out here so we can get out of this thing?"

"Oh, Claudia," the president of Argentina said emotionally, thickly, dabbing at his eyes with a handkerchief. "If only our Jorge were here to see this!"

"Arturo, I know in my heart he's watching," Claudia said.

The two embraced.

Humberto Duarte thought: *I have no goddamn idea what Cletus is up to. But whatever it is, he just got away with it.*

[THREE]
Aeropuerto Coronel Jorge G. Frade
Morón, Buenos Aires Province, Argentina
1710 19 September 1943

It is entirely likely, Cletus Frade thought as he looked out the cockpit window, *that there's not a ladder within miles of here that's long enough to reach up to the door, which will tend to put a damper on the triumphal arrival of the Big Bird.*

He looked down at the people standing on the tarmac, most of them holding up champagne stems in salute as they looked with what approached awe at the Lockheed Corporation's latest contribution to long-distance commercial aviation.

Claudia probably set that up; Humberto wouldn't think of it.

Whoever did it, it was a good idea.

Frade saw that Major Freiherr Hans-Peter von Wachtstein, who was not in uniform, was almost feverishly taking photographs of the airplane with a Leica camera.

Just like the one we used to take pictures of the Froggers.

And, of course, of Tío Juan's map of South America after the Final Victory.

He spotted el Coronel Juan Domingo Perón standing beside el Coronel Martín.

And you're here, aren't you, you sonofabitch?

And what the hell were you talking about, Martín, when you said you had to see me as soon as possible on a matter of "life and death"?

Well, at least it doesn't concern Dorotea or anyone at Casa Montagna. I talked to her just before we took off from Canoas. I told her I was about to fly here. I didn't tell her in what I was about to fly here, just that I was, and that I would see her there just as soon as I could deal with what I had to do in Buenos Aires.

There was a Collins Model 7.2 transceiver installed in the Connie; it had connected easily from Canoas with the Collins transceiver at Casa Montagna and with the one at Estancia San Pedro y San Pablo. As a result of the latter call, there would be at least three of the estancia's station wagons, three sedans, and a stake-bodied truck waiting at the airfield to transport the Connie's passengers and their luggage. Frade's Horch was, he presumed, parked where he had left it in the hangar.

Among the passengers aboard were three ASA people from Vint Hill Farms Station: Second Lieutenant Len Fischer and two young enlisted men who were both T-3s. T-3 was an Army rank Fischer had to explain to Frade, as there was no such rank in the Marine Corps. Their staff sergeants' chevrons had a "T," meaning "Technician." And staff sergeant was Pay Grade Three, hence T-3.

The ASA people, however, were not in uniform. They all wore civilian clothing and carried passports, draft cards, and other identification saying they were employees of the Collins Radio Corporation, Cedar Rapids, Iowa.

There were other civilian technicians aboard, some of them actually civilians. One of the *bona fide* civilians was an employee of the Curtiss-Wright Aircraft Engine Company. He would stay in Argentina only long enough to ensure that two other "employees of Curtiss-Wright"—actually, two U.S. Army Air Force technical sergeants—both were qualified to care for Curtiss-Wright R-3350-DA3 18-cylinder supercharged 3,250-horsepower radial engines and were prepared to teach their art to employees of South American Airways. Four of the Curtiss-Wright radials powered the Constellation.

Additionally, there was a *bona fide* civilian employee of the Lockheed Aircraft Corporation and two more Army Air Force noncoms in mufti, who would both care for the airframe and see to the necessary instruction of South American Airways personnel to function as flight engineers.

At Howard Hughes's suggestion, Chief Pilot Gonzalo Delgano had decreed that the flight engineers would have to be fully qualified pilots.

Six of these pilots were also aboard, getting their training hands-on.

Which meant that three of SAA's Lodestars, which the pilots had flown to Canoas, would have to sit there on the tarmac until Frade and Delgano could figure out how to get them back to Argentina.

That problem being compounded by the delivery to Canoas of the second Constellation and, within the week, the expected arrival of the third Connie.

They would have to be stripped of their U.S. Army Air Force markings, then repainted in the South American Airways scheme—one as the *Ciudad de Mendoza* and the other as the *Ciudad de Córdoba*—and then flown to Buenos Aires, that problem compounded by the fact that only two SAA pilots—Frade and Delgano—had as many as fifteen takeoffs and landings, and neither Frade nor Delgano was willing to turn one of the Constellations over to less experienced pilots no matter how high their enthusiasm.

There were also aboard two slightly older *bona fide* civilians. Both were accountants, and looked like it, but for obvious reasons their identification did not indicate that they in fact practiced their profession as employees of the Federal Bureau of Investigation.

The accountants would stay in Argentina—Frade had not decided whether in Buenos Aires or in Mendoza—to keep track of and make sense of whatever the Froggers, father and son, would tell them and what could otherwise be learned from other sources on how the German Operation Phoenix money was being invested—hidden—in the Argentine economy.

The voice of an SAA pilot who had been taking on-the-job training as a flight engineer came over Frade's earphones: "Captain, they're bringing a ladder."

"Thank you," Frade said. "Keep me posted."

He turned to Delgano. "You get off first, Gonzo, that guy next, and you give the impression you're the pilot and he's the number two. I'll get off later."

Delgano made a thumbs-up gesture, unfastened his harness, got out of the copilot's seat, and walked into the passenger compartment.

Where the hell is Humberto? Frade wondered as he carefully looked out a side window.

More important, where the hell is General Rawson?

If Humberto couldn't get him to come out here, this whole thing is going to blow up in my face!

Frade, ten minutes later, looked out the side window again.

The last time he had looked, Peter von Wachtstein had been one of six or eight photographers taking pictures of the Constellation. Now he was alone.

Where the hell are the others?

What's going on?

Then he saw that the photographers were backing toward the airplane, taking pictures of General Rawson, Humberto Duarte, Father Welner, and Claudia de Carzino-Cormano. Their party had just come out of the building and was walking toward the Constellation.

The president of the Argentine nation was smiling broadly.

And with the exception of my beloved father-in-law, so is everybody else out there.

———

"Captain," Delgano's voice came over the headset. "The ladder they brought is a meter too short."

"Shit! Now what?"

"They sent for a truck. They're going to put the ladder in the bed of the truck."

Frade tried to take a look from the cockpit window. The only thing he could see was a Chevrolet pickup truck approaching the aircraft. He couldn't see the door to the passenger compartment.

He quickly unstrapped himself, went into the passenger compartment, and looked out a window there. The pickup truck was backing up toward the airplane. In it, supported by four men, was a stepladder—a very long one. Then he no longer could see the truck.

He looked down the aisle. Delgano was standing in the door, facing inward, one leg gingerly extended downward out the door.

Then, very slowly, he disappeared.

Clete could see nothing out the window.

Then the SAA pilot/flight-engineer-in-training backed into the door and warily reached for the ladder with his leg.

"Change of plans!" Clete announced. "All SAA pilots go down the ladder!"

The five remaining SAA pilots formed a line by the door.

Out the window, Clete could see that Delgano had made it safely to the bed of the pickup, from which he jumped to the ground. Then the first SAA pilot came into view.

God, don't let any of them take a dive off that damn ladder with all those cameras trained on them!

Finally, everybody had gone down the ladder, jumped off the truck, and had lined up behind Gonzo and Pilot Number One. They all adjusted their uniforms.

Delgano issued a command. Everybody marched six steps forward. Delgano issued another command and everyone halted.

They were now facing General Rawson, his entourage, Claudia de Carzino-Cormano, Father Welner, and Humberto Duarte.

Delgano saluted.

"*Señor Presidente, mi general,*" he barked. "I have the honor to present Argentina's first international passenger aircraft!"

Frade couldn't actually hear what Delgano was saying, but he had spent thirty minutes rehearsing him on what he was to say before they left Canoas.

General Rawson saluted, then took three steps forward, kissed—more or less—Delgano on both cheeks, then each of the other pilots. Colonel Juan D. Perón appeared and joined Rawson's entourage as they walked after the president, each of them shaking each pilot's hand.

By then, Frade was at the door.

Enrico Rodríguez came to him, carrying his shotgun.

"Leave that on the airplane," Clete commanded. Then he raised his voice and ordered: "Everybody sit tight. I'll come for you as soon as I can."

He backed out the door, found the top step of the ladder with his left leg, then the step below it with his right, and went down the ladder into the bed of the pickup.

As he jumped to the tarmac, he saw that General Rawson had seen him and was smiling happily. When Rawson had finished kissing—more or less—the last SAA pilot, he headed right for Clete.

The president embraced Frade and kissed him—fully and wetly—on both cheeks, then again embraced him, then finally, holding on to both of Frade's arms, backed away and looked into his eyes.

"Cletus, your father would be so proud of you!"

Rawson was so sincere that the cynicism with which Frade had been viewing the entire performance instantly vanished. He felt his eyes water, and his voice was not firm when he replied, *"Muchas gracias, mi general."*

"Cletus, as much as I want to see inside the airplane, the Papal Nuncio is at this moment waiting for me at Casa Rosada. But I will be back."

"By then, *mi general,* there will be proper aircraft steps for you when you can find time in your schedule for us."

Rawson squeezed both of Frade's arms, then turned and marched off.

El Coronel Juan D. Perón marched up to Frade. He kissed—*pro forma*—Frade's cheeks. "I am presuming, Cletus, that there is some good reason why I didn't hear about this—"

He gestured at the airplane, at Claudia de Carzino-Cormano, at Humberto Duarte, and at General Rawson.

"—until an hour ago."

"There certainly is, Tío Juan," Frade said enthusiastically. Then he kissed Perón wetly on the cheek and said, "You're going to have to excuse me."

Frade walked quickly to Claudia, kissing her fondly but not wetly.

Perón's face tightened and for a moment it looked as if he might follow Frade. At the end, he marched toward his car.

"How's my favorite stockholder?" Clete asked Claudia.

She shook her head in resignation.

"Frankly, wondering what the hell is going on around here."

"I saw an opportunity and took it. We gringos call that 'striking while the iron is hot.' I have no idea what that really means, but that's what we say."

"How much did that cost?" Claudia asked, gesturing toward the Constellation.

"A lot," Clete admitted. "And we have three of them."

"And where's the money going to come from?"

"So far it's come from my grandfather, which brings us to that, Humberto."

"Excuse me?" Duarte said.

"There are two accountants aboard the *Ciudad de Buenos Aires,*" Clete said, "dispatched by my grandfather to make sure I don't squander his money on whiskey and wild women. Tonight, I'm going to put them up in the house on Coronel Díaz. But we're going to have to find them someplace to live—someplace nice; they're high-priced CPAs—maybe the Alvear or the Plaza. Can you deal with that?"

Duarte nodded.

"The immediate problem is to get them off the airplane, by which I mean we need the service of Immigration and Customs."

Humberto pointed. Clete saw a half-dozen uniformed Immigration and Customs officers.

"But first we need a better way to get things off the Connie than that stepladder," Frade said. "I wonder where Señor Mañana is." He looked around and spotted him.

"Señor de Filippi?" he called.

Guillermo de Filippi, SAA's chief of maintenance, walked to him.

"Our immediate problem, Guillermo," Frade said, "is to unload our new aircraft. That stepladder won't do. Any suggestions?"

"Señor Frade, we don't have a ladder that tall."

"We have wood, right?" Frade said. He pointed to two railroad flatcars, both bearing enormous stacks of lumber intended for the construction of a third hangar. "And carpenters? Does that suggest anything to you?"

"Señor Frade, the carpenters stop work at five o'clock, and it's after that. There would be problems with the union."

"I will deal with the workmen, Don Cletus," Enrico Rodríguez said.

Frade turned and saw him standing behind him. Holding his shotgun.

How the hell did he get down the ladder with the shotgun?

I don't think that being forced to build a stairway with a shotgun aimed at you would be good labor-management practice.

"Enrico, tell them it's two days' pay if they can build a stairway up to the plane in half an hour."

Father Welner chuckled. Señor de Filippi looked confused.

"And I'll throw in a case of beer," Frade added, then turned to de Filippi. "And there's a couple of other things that have to be done. On the airplane are airframe and engine engineers . . ."

He stopped in midsentence when a line of cars started to stream from behind the hangar onto the tarmac.

"What are we going to do, have a parade?" Frade quipped.

"We are having a cocktail and small buffet at your house on Coronel Díaz," Claudia said. "To celebrate whatever is going on here."

"You set that up, did you?"

"I was with your father for many years, Cletus. I didn't think you would mind my using the house."

"I was just about to say, 'Thank you very much, that's a great idea.'"

"And while that's going on," Claudia said, "we're going to have a quick board of directors meeting in the upstairs sitting room."

"We are?" he asked, smiling at her.

"We are," Claudia said flatly. "And I mean right now."

"There's a lot that has to be done here," Frade said.

"Aside from getting your passengers off that airplane and into the cars—and that can be dealt with by Señor de Filippi—there's nothing you have to do here that won't wait until tomorrow morning. Humberto and I have a right to know what's going on here, and I insist you tell us. And right now."

Actually, there is one thing I have to do here that won't wait until morning. My back teeth are floating.

"Claudia, I'm going to go directly into the hangar, get in the Horch, and when you get to the house I'll greet you at the door."

He pointed to the automobile, which was sitting just inside the door, and then at Rodríguez.

"Enrico, have someone throw my bags off the Connie and put them in the Horch. We're going to Coronel Díaz. Señor de Filippi can get the ladder built. Right, Guillermo?"

"Of course, Señor Frade."

"And then bring everybody to my house on Coronel Díaz. You know where it is?"

De Filippi nodded.

Claudia eyed Frade suspiciously.

"I trust that that will be satisfactory, Claudia?" Frade asked with a smile.

She examined his face carefully and finally said, "All right." Then she added, "Be there, Cletus."

He grabbed her, kissed her wetly on both cheeks, and then walked quickly toward the hangar.

He walked past the Horch until he found the men's room.

A moment after he had reached one of the urinals, someone walked to the adjacent fixture. Frade looked to see who it was.

"Please don't say it, Cletus," el Coronel Alejandro Martín said.

"But people *will* talk, Alejandro, if you keep following me into men's rooms."

He sighed. "I should have known better than to ask."

"Humberto said you were looking for me," Frade said.

"We have to talk."

"Okay."

"Not in here."

"I presume you've been invited to Señora Carzino-Cormano's cocktail and small buffet?"

Martín shook his head.

"Not to worry. It's her party, but my house. You're invited. So we can talk there. Or better yet, ride into town with me. We can sit in the back of the Horch and wave at our loyal subjects."

He turned slightly away from the urinal and well mimicked the regal flat-handed slow wave of British Royalty.

Martín smiled and chuckled.

"I think I should warn you, Cletus, that I have learned you are at your most dangerous when you're playing the clown."

"I have no idea what you're talking about, *mi coronel.*"

"Okay, I'll ride in with you. What we need to talk about has nothing to do with what happened here today. But I want to talk about that, too."

[FOUR]
Ruta Nacional No. 7
Near Morón
Buenos Aires Province, Argentina
1750 19 September 1943

"I hope this doesn't make you think I'm paranoid, *mi coronel*," Frade said, "but I think we are being followed."

Frade was at the wheel of the Horch. Martín sat beside him. Enrico was in the back. The canvas top of the Horch had been lowered.

"We are," Martín said. "Please tell Enrico not to shoot them; they belong to me."

"Enrico," Frade called, raising his voice. "Don't shoot at the people in the car behind us. They belong to el Coronel Martín."

"There's two cars of them, Don Cletus," Enrico called. "They've been with us since we left the airfield."

Frade looked at Martín, held up two fingers, and wordlessly asked with a raised eyebrow, *What the hell is that all about?*

Martín explained: "About a month ago—on August 12, to be precise—there was an incident near your home on Coronel Díaz. You may have read about it in the press. It was necessary for the police to kill three criminals they came across in the middle of a robbery."

"I do seem to recall something about that," Frade said.

"I didn't want something like that to mar Doña Claudia's little party today. Better safe than sorry, as they say."

"You really think that's likely?"

"I'd say it's far more likely that unknown malefactors who don't like you would have another go at you while you're—while *we're*—riding along here like targets in a carnival shooting gallery."

"How would they know I'm here?"

"How many cars like this Horch would you say there are in Argentina?"

"Good point," Frade said.

"Cletus, can we have one of our off-the-record conversations?"

"Same rules?"

"Same rules. We don't have to answer a question, but if we do, it has to be the truth."

"Ask away."

"Let's start with what happened today: What's going on with that enormous airplane?"

"Airplanes. There's three of them."

"*Three* of them?"

"There's another at the Canoas airfield, being painted, and another on the way there."

"And what are you going to do with them? More to the point, what are you going to do with them for the OSS?"

"The what?" Frade replied. "The OSS? What's that?"

They smiled at each other.

Frade went on: "But to answer the question generally: South American Airways is about to begin one-stop—at Belém, Brazil—service between Buenos Aires and Lisbon, Portugal. Or maybe Madrid. I won't know that until I make a test run. Could be to both places. And maybe to Switzerland, too. Anyway, at least one flight each way a week, maybe two."

"What's that all about?"

"What I was told was there is a problem moving civilians between Europe and the States by air . . ."

"Civilians? Or spies from that organization you never heard of?"

"Civilians. Diplomats. Not only Americans, but neutrals—French, Spanish, Swiss, et cetera. Businessmen, too. Right now, if we have to send a diplomat to Spain, for example, he has to either wait for a Spanish ship—or other neutral ship, and there aren't many of either—or travel by air on one of our transport airplanes, which means some military officer gets bumped . . ."

"'Bumped'?"

"Doesn't get to go. Anyway, he goes by military air to England—sometimes by bomber, riding in the back, where the bombs go—and then they get him to Spain either by a neutral-country civilian airplane, and there aren't many of those, or by a neutral ship. Getting the picture?"

Martín nodded.

"The Swiss—I didn't even know they had an airline until last week—have been asking for Douglas transports and, specifically, for Constellations. Which is what I flew in here today."

"Beautiful airplane. Enormous airplane. Where did you learn how to fly one?"

"I thought you knew I used to be a Marine fighter pilot. If it's got wings, a Marine fighter pilot can fly it."

Martín shook his head resignedly. "And Delgano?"

"I taught Delgano at Canoas. Then we partially trained another half-dozen SAA pilots—"

"Partially trained?"

"They've made a half-dozen takeoffs and landings, but they're not ready to fly the Connies anywhere."

"Getting back to how you came to get the airplanes?"

"Okay. They offered the Connies to me. I jumped at it, borrowed the money . . ."

"What I was asking was why did they—and who's 'they'?—offer them to you?"

"They were offered to me by Howard Hughes . . . the aviator, the movie guy?"

"I know who he is."

"We're old friends. More important, he's close to my grandfather. He's also in tight with Lockheed. I think he probably owns it, but that's just a guess. Anyway, Howard told me what I just told you, and said that the government doesn't want to sell airplanes of any kind to the Swiss—or just about anyone else in Europe, or to the Brazilians, but SAA is sort of special."

"Because the managing director works for the OSS?"

"The what?" Frade replied.

They smiled at each other, and then Frade went on: "The only thing the Constellation is good for, Alejandro, is hauling people long distances. It is not a submarine hunter; it can't drop bombs and there are no machine-gun turrets. And the Americans already have submarine-hunting aircraft—modified B-24s—at Canoas and other places in Brazil. As you well know."

"So why does your friend Howard Hughes think SAA is special?"

"Because Argentina is neutral—"

"Some of us actually are," Martín interrupted.

"Let me finish. When SAA establishes probably a twice-a-week service back and forth to Portugal or Spain, the problem of moving civilians back and forth from the States by air is solved. The airplanes take off from a neutral country, Argentina, and fly with only one stop, Canoas, to another neutral country. If you want to go to Europe, you get on one of the Pan American Grace Clippers, the flying boats, and go to Canoas. SAA will then fly you to Lisbon."

"Why is the United States being so nice to Argentina?"

"The Connies will give the finger"—he demonstrated the gesture—"to the only other airline, Lufthansa, offering commercial service to Europe. Everybody knows the Constellation is an American airplane. They call that 'public relations.'"

"You believe all this, Cletus?"

"All I know for sure is that I am about to own three Constellations with which I hope to make a lot of money."

"That presumes the Argentine Civil Aviation Dirección gives you—gives SAA—permission."

"Come on, Alejandro. The airplanes are owned by an Argentine company—"

"There is a nasty rumor going around that the major stockholder in that company is in the OSS," Martín interjected.

"—and will be flown by Argentine pilots, many of whom"—Frade turned to look Martín in the eyes—"a nasty rumor has it, are actually military officers assigned to the Bureau of Internal Security." Frade looked back to the road and went on: "As will be, I suspect, the Immigration and Customs officers who will carefully check each plane before it takes off, and when each one lands. This has nothing to do with the OSS, Alejandro."

"So you say, Major Frade. Or did a promotion come with your added responsibilities to the OSS?"

"And then there's that other thing," Frade said, ignoring the comment. "I somehow got the impression just now that General Rawson thinks this is a lovely idea, that offering intercontinental air service will add to the prestige of the Argentine Republic."

"Since we are still off the record, Cletus, I will admit that was brilliant, what you did at the airfield."

"You are too kind, Alejandro."

And it was.

Colonel Graham actually orchestrated that entire arrival business like a symphony conductor.

But, Alejandro, if you want to think I'm that clever, help yourself!

"What did you say about borrowing money?"

"My grandfather, who always knows a bargain when he sees one, has elected to make a substantial investment in South American Airways."

"Wouldn't that make it a mostly North American–owned company?"

"Not at all. As you know, I am an Argentine by birth. And many years ago, when he first started looking for oil in Venezuela, my grandfather became a citizen of that splendid South American country. Something to do with excessive taxes laid on foreigners. You know, dual citizenship. Like me. SAA is entirely owned by South Americans."

Martín shook his head.

"You're good, Cletus. This round goes to you."

"That suggests there will be other rounds."

"You and I both know there will be," Martín said.

"All I can do is hope that your careful scrutiny of every little detail of our operations, which I fully expect will finally convince you that my motive in this is solely to make a lot of money. And, of course, to add a little prestige to the country of my birth."

"You already have a lot of money."

"Money is like sex, Alejandro," Frade said solemnly. "You can never get too much of it."

Martín laughed, but then said: "I already warned you that I've learned you are most dangerous when you're playing the clown."

"Can we turn to this 'you have to see me on a matter of life-and-death importance'?" Frade said. "I never clown about things like life and death."

"Neither do I," Martín replied. "Okay. Here it is: The Germans may be planning to kidnap your father-in-law, your mother-in-law, and your brother-in-law, and exchange them for the Froggers."

Frade didn't say a word.

After a long moment, Martín said, "For God's sake, Cletus, don't pretend you don't have the Froggers."

"What I was thinking was: How good is your source?"

"It came from someone in a position to know," Martín said.

"That's not the same thing as saying 'reliable' or 'very reliable,' is it? Where'd you get that, Alejandro?"

"Next question?"

"You've got somebody in the German Embassy?" Frade said, but before Martín could respond, he went on: "I don't understand why they would tell you that. Or, if this *is* true, why they haven't already done it. It's probably bullshit, which brings me back to: Why did they tell you?"

"It may very well be, to use your word, bullshit. But, on the other hand, they just might be getting ready to kidnap your in-laws."

"You've said 'may be planning' and 'just might be getting ready.' Which suggests to me that you don't have much faith in your source."

Martín didn't reply for a long moment, then asked: "You're hearing this for the first time?"

Frade nodded. "I never even thought of something like this as a possibility."

"I'm surprised. You generally think of just about everything. Unless, of course, you have a reason for believing the Germans won't do anything to get the Froggers back."

"Short of causing harm to me or anyone close to me, they're capable and probably willing to do anything to get the Froggers back." He stopped and smiled at Martín. "'The Froggers.' There's that name again. Who are the Froggers, incidentally? I never heard of them."

Martín shook his head in resignation. "Tell me," he said, "why won't they cause harm to you or people close to you?"

"I thought I told you that."

"Tell me again."

"I told my beloved Tío Juan—and you were there, Alejandro, when I called him from my house on Coronel Díaz, right after they tried to kill Enrico and me—that I was giving him the benefit of the doubt that he didn't have time to call off his German friends, but that he'd better get right on the phone."

"I remember that. But I don't remember hearing what it was that el Coronel Perón was supposed to tell the Germans that would make them reluctant to harm you."

"Well, for one thing, there's photographs of my Tío Juan with the SS just before they shot up my house in Tandil. I don't think the Germans would like to see them plastered all over the front pages of *La Nación, La Prensa,* et cetera."

Martín's eyebrows rose.

"Uh-huh," Frade said, nodding. "And then there are photographs of boats trying to smuggle crates from the Spanish-registered merchantman *Comerciante del Océano Pacífico* onto the beach at Samborombón Bay. Taken from up close with one of those marvelous German Leica cameras. Some of those pictures show the German assistant military attaché for air . . . What's his name?"

"Galahad, maybe?"

Frade, looking forward and showing no reaction, said, "*'Galahad'*? Never heard that name, either. Now I remember: *von Wachtstein.* The photos— remarkably clear photographs, as I said—show *von Wachtstein* loading the bodies of the German military attaché, Oberst Grüner, and his assistant, Standartenführer Goltz, onto the *Océano Pacífico's* boats. Very graphic photographs. Both men had been shot in the head. Blood and brain tissue all over them. And von Wachtstein."

Martín exhaled audibly. He said, "Well, I suppose keeping those photographs out of the newspapers would tend to make the Germans reluctant to really make you angry."

"And there are more."

"If you have these photographs . . ."

"I have them, and there's more."

Martín raised his hand to interrupt him.

"I can't help but wonder why you just don't give them to the press."

"Next question?"

Martín shrugged his acceptance of the rules.

"I've changed my mind," Frade said thoughtfully a moment later. "But this is really off the record, Alejandro."

Martín nodded.

"President Roosevelt made the decision that as outrageous as Operation Phoenix is, and as despicable and disgusting as the SS-run Buy-the-Jews-Out-of-Extermination-Camps Operation is, as much as he would like to expose both operations to the world, the bottom line is that some Jews are being saved from the ovens. If it came out, no more Jews could be saved, and the Germans would probably kill the rest of the Jews as quickly as possible so there would be no proof, no witnesses."

Martín exhaled audibly again. This time it sounded like a groan.

"My orders are to keep track of where that money is going," Frade said. "So that when the war is over—"

"That's an admission, you realize . . ."

"Yeah. I realized that when I decided you had a right to know what's going on."

"And the Froggers are giving you information, or at least names—that sort of thing—regarding the money from both Operation Phoenix and the other one? Does the other one have a name?"

"The who? Never heard of them. And, no, the other filthy operation doesn't have a name."

"Do the Germans know you know about the unnamed operation?"

"They don't know how much we know about it."

"How much do you know?"

"A good deal. And when the war is over, when faced with the alternative of either telling us what we don't know or a hangman's noose, I suspect the slimy SS bastard running the operation in Montevideo will sing like a canary."

"Montevideo?"

Frade nodded.

"Your sergeant was killed in Montevideo," Martín said.

"Technical Sergeant David Ettinger," Frade said. "They stuck an ice pick in his ear in the garage of the Hotel Casino de Carrasco. More precisely, the SS bastard hired a local assassin—probably assassins—to do it. Ettinger was getting too close to that unnamed operation."

"Has the 'SS bastard' a name?"

"Why do you want his name?"

"For my general fund of knowledge, Cletus."

"There is a man in Montevideo who was offended by what happened to David Ettinger . . ."

"An American, perhaps?"

Frade nodded.

"Maybe in the OSS?"

"Next question?" Frade said, and then went on: "This man believes in the Old Testament adage about an eye for an eye. But he was refused permission to take out the SS bastard. That's when they told us FDR had decided that he wanted the unnamed operation to continue, to save as many Jews as possible. To keep an eye on this SS bastard, but keep him in place. If you had his name, Alejandro, I don't know what you'd do with it."

"I understand," Martín said. "If I were you, I wouldn't trust me with it either. Even if I gave you my word that I would keep it to myself, and pass on to you anything that came my way about him. And the unnamed operation."

They locked eyes for a long moment.

"Sturmbannführer Werner von Tresmarck," Frade said. "He has diplomatic cover, of course. He's a homosexual. His wife is involved in it up to her eyeballs . . ."

"I thought you just said he was homosexual."

Frade nodded. "He is. That's how they keep him in line. He either does what they tell him, with absolute honesty, and keeps his mouth shut, or he winds up in a concentration camp with a pink triangle pinned to his suit."

"And the wife?"

"Inge. She is not homosexual. That's what they call an understatement. She was sort of a high-class hooker in Berlin after her first husband was killed in Russia. She was given the choice between marrying this guy and keeping an eye on him, or going to work in a factory. Inge is feathering her own nest with what she can skim from the unnamed operation money."

"If I didn't know better, I'd think someone—Galahad probably—also knows Señora von Tresmarck and has been gossiping about her to you."

"I don't know anybody named Galahad. I thought I told you that."

Martín smiled. He was silent for a long moment. Then, quietly, he said, "If

I understand you, Cletus, until I told you about this kidnapping of the Mallíns, you thought you had sort of an arrangement, an armistice, with the Germans."

"An uneasy armistice, but yeah. They would be very unpopular in Berlin if they got themselves declared *persona non grata* and got kicked out of Argentina. So—I thought—they'd be willing to just let things stand as they are while they're waiting for their ultimate victory."

"Then what's this kidnapping about?"

"Now you sound as if you believe it's serious."

"I'm not prepared to ignore it. Are you?"

"So if you're not prepared to ignore it, what are you doing about it?"

Martín, obviously considering his answer, took a long moment before replying.

"I've got people on them," he said finally. "All of them. Including your father-in-law."

"Which might tip our German friends that you know of the plan, and wonder where you got your information," Frade said.

Martín did not reply, but after a moment shrugged his agreement.

"How about this?" Frade suggested. "Tomorrow morning, I take my mother-in-law and the boy to Mendoza . . ."

"I heard you had Doña Dorotea at Casa Montagna," Martín said. "What's that all about?"

"Next question? And how come you know about Casa Montagna?"

"Next question?"

"As I was saying, I'll put some people from the estancia on my father-in-law," Frade said. "Conspicuously. Four guys—all ex-Húsares—in a station wagon with 'Estancia San Pedro y San Pablo' painted on the doors. He won't like it, but I don't think he wants to go to Mendoza, and I'm sure he doesn't want to be kidnapped."

"Is he going to be at Doña Claudia's little party?"

"Reluctantly, I think."

"This is none of my business, but why doesn't he like you?"

"You mean, what prompted him to tell his wife—he didn't know I was in the house, of course—'I curse the day that depraved gringo sonofabitch walked through our door!'?"

"He actually said that?"

"It may have something to do with me going to be the father of his first grandchild."

"But why 'depraved'?"

"That probably has something to do with me marrying his daughter."

"His opinion of you doesn't seem to bother you much."

"It bothers me a lot, even when I think that a married man—married to a really great woman like Dorotea's mother—who had a mistress doesn't have a hell of a lot of right to ride up on the high horse of righteousness."

"You know the mistress? *Ex-mistress?*"

"Why does that make me think you know her?"

"I wouldn't know her, Cletus, if she walked into Doña Claudia's party on the arm of a diplomat."

Frade nodded at Martín. Somehow, the nod expressed thanks.

[FIVE]
Office of the Ambassador
The Embassy of the German Reich
Avenida Córdoba
Buenos Aires, Argentina
0930 20 September 1943

Major Hans-Peter von Wachtstein walked into the office carrying a thick sheaf of eight-by-ten-inch photographs. He was in civilian clothing. Günther Loche, carrying a nearly identical stack of photographs, followed him.

Von Wachtstein laid the photographs on Ambassador von Lutzenberger's desk and motioned for Loche to do the same thing. Then von Wachtstein came to attention, clicked his heels, gave the Nazi salute, and said, "Heil Hitler!"

Loche tried and almost succeeded in doing the same simultaneously.

Ambassador von Lutzenberger returned the salute.

Commercial Attaché Karl Cranz glowered at von Wachtstein.

Anton von Gradny-Sawz demanded, "Where in the world have you been?"

There was no expression on the face of the naval attaché, Kapitän zur See Karl Boltitz.

Von Wachtstein pointed to the two stacks on von Lutzenberger's desk.

"Since six this morning, Herr von Gradny-Sawz, I have been up to my ears in chemicals in the photo lab. As you can see, there are a great many photographs."

"There were a great many photographs in the press, von Wachtstein," Cranz said. "Presumably you've seen them?"

"No, sir."

"Have a look, von Wachtstein," Cranz said, and pointed to the conference table. There were at least a dozen newspapers spread out on it. On the front pages of all of them were photographs—sometimes just one, more often two and even three or four—of what had happened at Aeropuerto Coronel Jorge G. Frade the previous afternoon.

Just about all of them had a photo of the SAA Constellation coming in for a landing. And there were shots of the Constellation as it taxied up to the hangar with Argentine flags flying from holders at the cockpit windows. Others showed Gonzalo Delgano saluting General Rawson, of Rawson embracing Delgano, of Rawson, hands on hips, looking up with admiration—maybe even awe—at the enormous airplane.

"Take a look at that one, von Wachtstein," Cranz said, pointing to a photo of a beaming General Rawson embracing Cletus Frade. He then read aloud the cutline under one of the photos:

"'The President of the Republic embraces Don Cletus Frade, Managing Director of South American Airways. Frade is the son of the late and beloved Coronel Jorge G. Frade, whose monument is now the airport named in his memory, from which the new aircraft will soon begin to fly to Europe.'"

He paused, looked at von Wachtstein, and challenged, "Well?"

"Excuse me, Herr Cranz?"

"Wouldn't you say you've been wasting your time, '*up to your ears in chemicals*,' printing photographs that were already spread across the front page of every goddamn newspaper in Argentina?"

Von Wachtstein's face tightened, but his voice was under control when he said, "With respect, Herr Cranz, I don't think our engineers could do much with newspaper photographs of the Constellation."

"What did you say?" asked von Gradny-Sawz.

"I'm sure our engineers will be very interested in the photographs I took of the Constellation."

"Why?"

"Because it is the fastest, largest long-range transport aircraft in the world," von Wachtstein said.

"You're not suggesting that it is a better aircraft than our Condor?" von Gradny-Sawz pursued.

Help came from an unexpected source:

"Obviously, von Gradny-Sawz, it is," Cranz said. "Von Wachtstein is suggesting our engineers will want to know as much about it as they can learn."

"I didn't think about that," von Gradny-Sawz said.

"Obviously," Cranz said dryly. "And he's right. It is going to be a problem for us in several areas. Propaganda Minister Goebbels is going to be very unhappy when this story—these pictures—appears in newspapers all over the world. And the Americans will make sure that it does."

"But it's not a new airplane," von Gradny-Sawz argued.

"Yes, it is, you *Trottel*!" Cranz snapped. "And it has never before (a) been in the hands of anyone but the Americans or (b) used to transport people across the Atlantic from a third-rate country—"

"More people and faster," von Wachtstein interjected.

Cranz nodded and went on: "Suggesting that the Americans have so many of them they can spare some for Argentina."

If von Gradny-Sawz took offense at being called a *Trottel*—which translated variously as "moron," "clown," but most often as "blithering idiot"—there was no sign of it on his face.

Cranz continued: "If this comes to the attention of the Führer—they try to spare him distractions, but I suspect *this* distraction will come to his attention—I suggest that it is entirely likely that the Führer will order that it be shot out of the sky . . ."

"It's an *Argentine* aircraft," Ambassador von Lutzenberger said.

Cranz glared at him for a moment. Then he admitted, "Good point. Which means he's likely to order its destruction without the services of the Luftwaffe. In other words: here, by us."

"Well, then, I guess that's what we're going to have to do," von Gradny-Sawz said solemnly. "Destroy it here, on the ground."

Cranz glowered at him for a long moment but in the end did not reply directly. Instead, he turned to von Wachtstein.

"What I'm having trouble understanding, Major von Wachtstein, is why the arrival of this airplane, this whole business of Argentina getting an aircraft capable of flying across the Atlantic Ocean, came as such a surprise to you."

"I'm not sure I understand the question, Herr Cranz," von Wachtstein replied.

"Your mother-in-law is a member of the board of directors of South American Airways, is she not?"

"Yes, sir, she is, but—"

Cranz shut him off with a raised hand.

"And Herr Duarte, whose son died a hero at Stalingrad, and who is reliably reported—by Ambassador von Lutzenberger, now that I think about it—to have said he has come to look upon you as a son, is also a member of that board, is he not?"

"Yes, sir."

"And you heard nothing of this at all from either of them? Is that what you're saying?"

"The first I heard anything at all about what happened yesterday was when Señor Duarte telephoned me to say that something was going on at the airport—SAA's private airport, Aeropuerto Jorge Frade—at five o'clock. Duarte had no idea what, but said that Señor Frade had suggested I be invited."

"Señor Frade suggested to Señor Duarte that you be invited?"

"That's what I was told, sir."

"That was very courteous of him," Cranz said sarcastically.

"I think he wanted to rub my nose in it, Herr Cranz."

"Excuse me?"

"When Frade returned from California, after getting the SAA pilots their certificates, or licenses, or whatever they had to have to get insurance, Señora de Carzino-Cormano gave a dinner—a supper, to be precise—at Estancia Santa Catalina. Frade made a point of telling me that he had seen the Constellation aircraft at the Lockheed factory."

"Why would he want to do that?" von Gradny-Sawz asked.

"I think it was to annoy my sister-in-law."

"I was there," Boltitz said, smiling. "Señorita Isabela de Carzino-Cormano is—how do I say this?—a *great admirer* of Lufthansa Kapitän Dieter von und zu Aschenburg. As soon as Frade began extolling the merits of the Constellation, Señorita Isabela leapt to defend the Condor. She called upon von Wachtstein for support, and, ever the gentleman, von Wachtstein did so."

"I don't think I understand," Cranz said.

"When Frade said the Constellation flew at so many kph, von Wachtstein assured everyone that the Condor was fifty kph faster; when Frade said the Constellation could fly at ten thousand meters, von Wachtstein said the Condor routinely flew at twelve thousand meters . . ."

"Everyone at the table had seen the Condor, Herr Cranz," von Wachtstein said. "No one had seen even a picture of the Constellation."

"Von Wachtstein made Frade look the fool," Boltitz said. "No one believed him."

"As well they shouldn't have. Americans are notorious for their boasting," von Gradny-Sawz offered.

"Unfortunately, Gradny-Sawz," Boltitz said, "the Constellation is everything Frade said it was. And when Frade saw the chance to get his revenge on von Wachtstein, he took it."

"Which, of course, he may now have, on reflection, regretted," von Wachtstein said. "Once I was invited out there, he could hardly tell me not to take photographs."

Cranz, who had not looked at von Wachtstein's photographs before, now went to von Lutzenberger's desk and picked up one of the stacks. He went through it carefully, then picked up the second stack and examined each of them.

"I now see what you mean, von Wachtstein," he said. "I thought I was going to see—how shall I put this?—*postcard views* of that airplane, like those in the press. Your photographs are of technical features, parts of the airplane. I can see where they would be of great value to an aeronautical engineer."

"That's what I intended to do, Herr Cranz."

"If what I just said sounded something like an apology, von Wachtstein . . ."

"No apology is necessary, Herr Cranz, and none was expected, sir."

"An apology is called for, and you may consider that one has been offered."

"I can only repeat, sir, that no apology is necessary."

"Indulge me, von Wachtstein. Accept my apology."

"Yes, sir."

"When is the next Condor flight due here?" Cranz asked.

"Either tomorrow or the day after," Boltitz said.

"And will return to Germany when?"

"If weather permits, they usually leave as soon as they can after forty-eight hours."

"Between now and then," Cranz said to von Wachtstein, "you—and Loche—will be up to your ears in those chemicals you spoke of. I want four copies of each photograph—in addition to the sets you have already made."

"Yes, sir."

"Three sets of these will go to Berlin on the Condor," Cranz announced. "One for General Galland and the second for Reichsmarschall Göring and the third for Reichsführer-SS Himmler."

"May I suggest a fourth set, Herr Cranz, for Canaris?" Boltitz said.

"Why not?" Cranz replied. "Make five sets, von Wachtstein."

"Yes, sir."

"Let me confess that I am being political," Cranz said. "I think we would all agree that the only officer who will do something useful with them is

General Galland. Well, perhaps Canaris can find something useful in them. The Reichsmarschall gets a set because he would be uncomfortable if the Führer asks him about this airplane and he knew little or nothing about it. And the Reichsführer gets a set because I think when the Führer orders the destruction of this aircraft, he is going to turn again to the SS. If the SS could so successfully liberate Il Duce . . .

"If that is the case, the Reichsführer will lay that responsibility on me. When that happens—and I confidently predict it will—I am, *we are,* going to be ready. We will have plans prepared to destroy all three of this aircraft, on the ground or in the air.

"Our assistant attaché for air is obviously the best-qualified person to do this. The task is herewith assigned to him. Sturmbannführer . . . excuse me, *Deputy Commercial Counselor* Raschner will lend his talents to the operation, which I of course will supervise.

"Has anyone any comments?"

No one had.

IX

[ONE]
Office of the Assistant Military Attaché for Air
The Embassy of the German Reich
Avenida Córdoba
Buenos Aires, Argentina
1130 24 September 1943

Commercial Attaché Karl Cranz pushed open the door to Assistant Military Attaché for Air Major Hans-Peter von Wachtstein's office without knocking.

He found Kapitän Dieter von und zu Aschenburg sitting on a small couch and holding a cup of coffee. Von Wachtstein was sitting at his desk, his feet resting on an open lower desk drawer.

"Aschenburg, Untersturmführer Schneider tells me you have one of the diplomatic pouches," he accused without any preliminaries.

"I did have one of them," von und zu Aschenburg said evenly. "Actually, I had all of them. I gave all but one to your untersturmführer."

"You can give it to me," Cranz said. "Right now."

"I can't do that. Ambassador von Lutzenberger has it."

"The ambassador has it?" Cranz asked dubiously.

"Would you like to see the acknowledgment of receipt he signed?"

Cranz nodded.

Von und zu Aschenburg produced a small printed form and showed it to him.

Cranz examined it carefully. He then said, "The standard procedure here is that SS-Untersturmführer Schneider takes possession of all diplomatic pouches at the airport."

"I'm just a simple servant of the state, Herr Cranz," von und zu Aschenburg said on the edge of sarcasm. "When an obersturmbannführer wearing the cuff band of the Leibstandarte Adolf Hitler comes into my cockpit at Tempelhof, takes one of the pouches—there were a half-dozen—and tells me that *this* one is from Reichsführer-SS Himmler and that I am to give it personally to Ambassador von Lutzenberger—and to no one else—I try very hard to do just that. I didn't think I needed give your untersturmführer an explanation. I just told him not to worry, I had it."

As if a switch had been thrown, Cranz's arrogant annoyance was suddenly replaced with smiling charm.

He handed the receipt back to von und zu Aschenburg with a smile.

"I'm glad you didn't give an explanation invoking the Reichsführer to Schneider. He probably would have pissed his pants." He smiled again, then went on, "I didn't mean to jump on you, Aschenburg. But we have been expecting that pouch from Reichsführer-SS Himmler, and when it wasn't among the others . . . Well, you understand."

"Not a problem," von und zu Aschenburg said. "I understand."

"Nevertheless, I apologize."

Von und zu Aschenburg made an *It's unnecessary* gesture.

"We expected you yesterday," Cranz said. "Something went wrong?"

"Headwinds," von und zu Aschenburg said.

"Pardon me?"

"When we shot our position just before the fuel gauges indicated half remaining, we weren't nearly as far across the Atlantic as we should have been. I turned back. And tried again last night."

"Would you explain what you just said? 'Shot our position'? What does that mean?"

"Did you ever notice, on the Condor, that there is a sort of plastic bubble on the fuselage? Just over the rear of the flight deck?"

"No," Cranz said with a chuckle. "I confess I haven't."

"Are you really interested in all this, Herr Cranz? Any of it?"

"Fascinated."

"Okay. In exactly the same way as the master of a ship shoots the stars with a sextant . . ."

The door opened again. This time it was Fräulein Ingeborg Hässell, von Lutzenberger's secretary.

"The ambassador would like to see you, Herr Cranz."

Cranz smiled at von und zu Aschenburg.

"Well, we'll have to get back to this. And soon. I'm really fascinated."

"Any time."

Cranz walked quickly out of the room. He did not close the door behind him.

Von und zu Aschenburg got to his feet and closed the door.

"What the hell was that all about?" he asked.

Von Wachtstein shrugged.

"I have no idea, but whenever Cranz smiles at me the hair on the back of my neck stands up."

"If you can rely on that, Hansel, you just might live through this war."

"I wonder what the chances of that really are?" von Wachtstein asked seriously.

Von und zu Aschenburg met his eyes, then shrugged, holding up his hands in a gesture of helplessness.

"Changing the subject, I really would like to have a look at that airplane."

"That might just be possible," von Wachtstein said. "I think I know how that can be arranged. It'll cost you, though."

Von und zu Aschenburg asked, with his eyebrows, what he meant.

"I'm not sure you're up to it," von Wachtstein said. "You're probably very tired from flying that far."

"Come on, Hansel!"

"If my sister-in-law, Señorita Isabela, were—how do I phrase this delicately?—*satisfied* with her relationship with you . . ."

"Screw you, Hansel."

"Precisely. Congratulations, you picked up on that right away. If El Bitcho, for reasons I won't—being an officer and a gentleman—discuss was really pleased with you—more precisely, satisfied after you . . ."

"Enough, Hansel!" von und zu Aschenburg said, but he was smiling.

". . . and wanted to show her appreciation, you, being the silver-tongued devil you are, you could probably talk her into convincing her mother, who is on the board of South American Airways, that it would be the courteous thing to show a Lufthansa pilot the newest addition to their fleet."

"Why do I think you're serious?"

"I am."

"What about Frade?"

"He's not here. He's got one of them in Chile . . ."

"They've got more than one?"

Von Wachtstein nodded, held up three fingers, and continued: ". . . teaching his pilots how to land in Santiago. He won't be back for a couple of days. Not that I think he'd really mind you getting a good look. He loves to show off that airplane. The other two are here. SAA pilots and flight engineers are getting checked out on them, usually by flying them back and forth to Montevideo. I think if El Bitcho talks nice to her mommy, Claudia can arrange a tour of one of them for you."

"That woman is a shark. The last time I had teeth marks on my neck for a week!"

"My mother-in-law did that to you?" von Wachtstein said, feigning shock.

"Your sister-in-law, Hansel."

"I don't know about a shark, but Isabela does remind me of a piranha."

"A what?"

"A small fish," von Wachtstein said, and held his hands about ten inches apart to show the size. "Native to this part of the world. Razor teeth, powerful jaws. They swim in . . . What do you say for fish when you mean packs, herds?"

Von und zu Aschenburg shrugged to show he had no idea.

"Anyway," von Wachtstein went on, "they have a show for tourists on the River Piranha. They kill a small pig and throw it in the water. The piranhas appear in less than a minute. Lots of them. When they pull the pig out a couple of minutes later, there's nothing but the skeleton."

"You actually saw this, or it is a quaint folk legend?"

"I saw it on my honeymoon. Alicia wanted me to see it. She said that would happen to me if I ever even thought of hiding my sausage in the wrong—anyone's but hers, in other words—hard roll."

"And are you a faithful husband, Hansel?"

Von Wachtstein nodded.

"Because of this carnivorous fish?"

"Because I'm in love, believe it or not. That's why I want to live through this war."

Von und zu Aschenburg met his eyes, then fell silent for a long moment. Finally, he said, "Well, let's go pay my respects to Señorita Piranha. I really want to take a look at that Constellation. You sure it won't get you in trouble here? Sucking up to the American enemy?"

"Not at all. It will be in the line of duty. Cranz will be pleased."

"Why?"

"It will be what is known as reconnoitering the enemy. I'm supposed to come up with a plan to make sure that SAA does not establish a one-stop service to Lisbon."

"How are you supposed to do that?"

"I don't know. Right now we're in the planning stage."

"What are you going to do, Hansel? Aside from warning Frade?"

"I don't know, Dieter," von Wachtstein admitted.

He kicked his desk drawer shut, stood, and made an exaggerated gesture bowing von und zu Aschenburg out of the room.

[TWO]
Office of the Ambassador
The Embassy of the German Reich
Avenida Córdoba
Buenos Aires, Argentina
1150 24 September 1943

"Baron von Wachtstein would like to see you for a moment, Exzellenz," Fräulein Ingeborg Hässell announced.

"Give me a few seconds, please," von Lutzenberger said, and quickly swept into his desk drawer a large manila envelope and a letter, and then—as an afterthought—took the yellow diplomatic pouch from which he had taken the manila envelope and also put it in the well of his desk.

Then he signaled for Fräulein Hässell to show in von Wachtstein. When von Wachstein entered, Kapitän Dieter von und zu Aschenburg was on his heels.

"We're sorry to disturb you, Exzellenz," von Wachtstein said politely, and then, looking around the room, added, "Gentlemen."

Cranz and von Gradny-Sawz were sitting at von Lutzenberger's conference table.

Von Wachtstein went on: "But I have an idea to get Kapitän von und zu Aschenburg onto one of the Constellations. I'd like to ask permission to try."

"How are you going to do that?" the ambassador asked.

"Señorita de Carzino-Cormano is a friend of the kapitän. I think she can suggest to her mother that it would be a courtesy to give von und zu Aschenburg a tour."

"And you think Frade would allow that?" von Gradny-Sawz challenged sarcastically.

"He's in Santiago, Herr Gradny-Sawz."

"And why would Señorita de Carzino-Cormano want to do this?" von Gradny-Sawz challenged.

"Open your eyes, for God's sake, Gradny-Sawz," Cranz said. "She looks at von und zu Aschenburg like he gives milk." He smiled at von und zu Aschenburg. "I was about to commend you for being willing to make any sacrifice for the cause, Aschenburg, but then I thought that your . . . *charming* . . . the lady isn't really going to be that much of a sacrifice, is it?"

"May I suggest I know the lady better than you do?" von und zu Aschenburg said. "But I really would like to get a look at one of those airplanes."

"I wish she were as interested in me as she is in you," Cranz said. "I would happily make the sacrifice you're implying."

There was dutiful laughter.

"Go ahead," Cranz said. "What have you got to lose?"

"As a gentleman, I obviously must decline to answer that question," von und zu Aschenburg said.

"With your permission, Exzellenz?" von Wachtstein asked.

"Let me know how it comes out," von Lutzenberger said.

Von und zu Aschenburg and von Wachtstein left, closing the door after them.

Cranz got up, walked to the door, locked it, and then went back to the conference table.

"May I have another look at that, please?" Cranz asked.

Von Lutzenberger handed him the letter that had been inside the manila envelope, the only thing that the diplomatic pouch had held.

MOST SECRET

Hauptquartier Der Reichsführer-SS
Berlin

24 September 1943

By Hand of Senior Officer Courier
Manfred Alois Graf von Lutzenberger
Ambassador of the German Reich
Buenos Aires

Exzellenz:
Heil Hitler!

Word has been received from the transfer point that U-405 has departed for Point 6.01. She has aboard SS-Brigadeführer Ritter Manfred von Deitzberg; one SS-Obersturmführer; ten SS other ranks; and one "special shipment" wooden crate weighing approximately 65 kilograms.

It is anticipated that U-405 will be prepared to discharge her cargo at first light 28 September, but, taking into consideration that unforeseen events may occur, you should be prepared to receive the shipment at first light every day commencing 27 September.

It is presumed that you have complied with previous orders regarding the establishment of a covert identity for von Deitzberg, and in this connection, forwarded herewith are photographic negatives and prints of the brigadeführer.

It is emphasized that the brigadeführer's presence in Argentina is Most Secret. The brigadeführer will explain his mission personally on arrival.

SS-Obersturmbannführer Cranz is to be made aware of these orders, and to place himself at the brigadeführer's orders.

In the service of the Führer:

H.Himmler
Reichsführer
Concur:

Canaris
Vizeadmiral Canaris

MOST SECRET

"Von Wachtstein knows nothing of this, right?" Cranz asked. "You didn't let anything slip, Gradny-Sawz?"

"Of course not."

"And Boltitz?" Cranz pursued.

"No, he doesn't know anything about this. The only people who do are in this room, plus of course Raschner."

"I want it kept that way," Cranz said. "And your covert identity arrangements . . . Everything is in place?"

"Including, as of yesterday, a nice flat—two servants included—in a petit-hotel at O'Higgins 1950 in Belgrano."

Cranz nodded and said: "So all that remains is to see Oberst Perón, to get those Mountain Troops to provide security on the beach, and to move the special shipment and the SS guard detail to San Martín de los Andes. The latter may pose a problem."

"How so?"

"The incident at Frade's house upset Oberst Perón," Cranz said. "But I think I can deal with him."

[THREE]
Apartamento 5B
Arenales 1623
Buenos Aires, Argentina
1750 24 September 1943

El Coronel Juan Domingo Perón was in uniform, but his tunic was unbuttoned and his tie pulled down, when he came out of his apartment onto the elevator landing. He was not smiling.

"Commercial Counselor" Karl Cranz was not surprised. The *portero* in the lobby of the building had told Cranz—as he obviously had been instructed to do—that Perón was not at home, and it had been necessary to slip him ten pesos—and, when that didn't work, ultimately fifty—before he was willing to forget his instructions and telephone Perón's apartment only when Cranz was on the elevator and it was too late to stop him.

"*Mi coronel,*" Cranz said as charmingly as he could, "please believe me when I say I would not intrude on your privacy were it not very important."

Perón did not reply to that directly. Instead, he said, "I didn't know you knew where I lived, Cranz."

"I went to the Frade house on Libertador, *mi coronel.* The housekeeper told me."

That was not true. The housekeeper in the Frade mansion across from the racetrack on Avenida Libertador had—and only reluctantly—told him only that el Coronel Perón no longer lived in the mansion and that she had no idea where he had moved.

It had cost Raschner two days of effort and several hundred pesos to get the address, which came with the information that he was sharing his new quarters with his fourteen-year-old "niece."

"That woman has a big mouth," Perón said unpleasantly.

"*Mi coronel,* I have to have a few minutes of your time," Cranz said.

"Why?"

"Another special shipment is about to arrive. We need your help."

The news did not seem to please Perón.

"Wait," he ordered curtly. He turned and went back into his apartment and closed the door.

Cranz instantly decided he was going to give Perón three minutes—180 seconds—to reopen the door before he pushed the doorbell. He looked at his wristwatch to start the timing.

One hundred and seventy seconds later, Perón pulled the door open and motioned for Cranz to come into the apartment.

Cranz found himself in a small foyer. Three doors—all closed—led from it. The only furnishing was a small table with a lamp sitting on it, and a squat jar holding two umbrellas.

"Well?" Perón asked.

"We had word from Berlin today—there was a Condor flight—giving the details of a new special shipment," Cranz said. "We need your help again; el Coronel Schmidt and his Mountain Troops."

"The last time I had the Mountain Troops 'help' you, Cranz, at Tandil, it was nearly a disaster. It *was* a disaster, and it could have been much, much worse."

"You're a soldier, *mi coronel*. You know as well as I do that things sometimes get out of hand. The SS officer who let things get out of hand at Tandil paid for it with his life."

"*I* almost paid for *his* letting 'things get out of hand' with *my* life," Perón said.

"It was a very bad situation, *mi coronel*. We cannot ever let something like that happen again."

"No, we can't. If you came here to suggest that I be anywhere near where the special shipment will be landed, or have anything to do with it, I must disappoint you."

"*Mi coronel*, it was not my intention—everyone recognizes how important you are to all those things we are trying to do, and that we would be lost without you—to suggest that you go to Samborombón Bay, or that the Mountain Troops go to the beach. We are prepared to handle the landing operation ourselves.

"But what I was hoping is that you would see the wisdom of authorizing another 'road march exercise' for Schmidt's Mountain Troops. In addition to the special shipment, there will be another SS security detachment. An officer and ten other ranks—"

"To be taken to San Martín de los Andes, you mean?"

"And we realize that both you and el Coronel Schmidt have expenses"— Cranz took a business-size envelope from his pocket and extended it to Perón—"which we of course are happy to take care of."

After a moment, Perón took the envelope and glanced inside. It was stuffed with U.S. one-hundred-dollar bills.

There were 250 of them, none of them new. They had come from the currency in the special shipments. The $25,000 in American currency was equivalent to almost 100,000 Argentine pesos, a very substantial amount of money. And American dollars were in demand. German Realm Marks had virtually no value in the international market.

For a moment, Perón appeared to be on the verge of handing the dollar-stuffed envelope back to Cranz.

"You will handle the landing operation itself?" Perón asked. "You can do that?"

"I believe we can, *mi coronel.* But looking at the worst-case scenario: Even if something went terribly wrong on the beach, this would not involve the Mountain Troops at all. They wouldn't be anywhere near the beach."

Perón considered that for a moment.

Then he slipped the envelope into his right lower tunic pocket. The deal had been struck. The Mountain Troops would take the special shipment and the SS men to San Martín de los Andes.

Cranz wondered how much—if any—of the $25,000 Perón would share with Oberst Schmidt.

Probably none.

"Tell me about the kidnapping planned for Señor Mallín," Perón said. "I should have heard about that; I should not find myself in the position of having to ask."

"Excuse me, *mi coronel*?"

"I think you heard me, Cranz."

"I don't know a Señor Mallín."

"He is Cletus Frade's father-in-law," Perón said. "And Don Cletus apparently believes that someone is planning to kidnap him."

"Mi coronel," Cranz said after a just-perceptible hesitation, "I know nothing of an attempt to kidnap anyone."

Perón's eyes tightened; it was obvious to Cranz that Perón didn't believe him.

"I give you my word of honor as a German officer, *mi coronel.*"

Perón looked into his eyes for a long moment.

"For lunch today, I went to the Yacht Club," Perón said. "As we drove up, I saw Señor Mallín's car. He drives a Rolls-Royce drop-head coupe—"

"Excuse me, a what?"

"Canvas roof," Perón explained impatiently. "It was parked on the curving drive leading up to the main entrance of the Yacht Club. Behind it was a Ford station wagon, of the Estancia San Pedro y San Pablo. In it were three men whom I recognized as former soldiers of the Húsares de Pueyrredón. Inside the foyer, at the door to the main dining room, there was another. He recognized me from our service together. I asked him what he and the others were up to. He said, 'Don Cletus believes the goddamn Nazis are going to try to kidnap Don Enrico Mallín. If they try it, we will kill them.'"

"'The goddamn Nazis'?" Cranz blurted.

"They believe 'the goddamn Nazis' assassinated el Coronel Frade," Perón said pointedly. He paused, then added, "As you well know, Cranz."

"*Mi coronel*, all I can do is repeat, again on my officer's honor: I know nothing of a planned kidnapping."

"Has it occurred to you, Cranz, has it occurred to anyone, that if something like that happened, Cletus Frade would certainly make good on his threat to ensure that the photographs taken of me at Tandil would be published?"

"Of course it has, *mi coronel.* And we will do nothing that would cause that to happen."

"If those photographs came out—and/or the photograph Cletus Frade has of the map of the South American continent after the Final Victory, which Brigadeführer von Deitzberg was kind enough to give me—not only would my usefulness to the cause end, but General Rawson would be inclined—almost be forced—to seriously consider declaring war on the Axis."

"*Mi coronel*, again, on my word of honor . . ."

"I don't think this kidnapping is a product of my godson's feverish imagination, Cranz. As we have learned, he is a very capable intelligence officer. He didn't move his wife to Mendoza so she could take in the mountain air."

"Well, I'll get to the bottom of this. You have—"

"I know, your word," Perón interrupted. "And tell Ambassador von Lutzenberger this, Cranz. I have taken certain actions to protect myself in the event something like this happens. The result of that would be more than a little embarrassing to everyone in the German Embassy. Understand this: Juan Domingo Perón is not expendable."

"I will get to the bottom of this."

"Once you tell me the date of the arrival of the special shipment, I will get word to you when and where the Mountain Troop convoy will be."

Perón pushed open the door to the elevator foyer and gestured for Cranz to go through it.

"*Buenas noches,* Señor Cranz. I will expect to hear from you shortly."

[FOUR]
Aeropuerto Coronel Jorge G. Frade
Morón, Buenos Aires Province, Argentina
1205 27 September 1943

Cletus Frade was pleased but not really surprised to see SAA's Lodestar *Ciudad de Mar del Plata* taxi up to the terminal. Flight 107, daily nonstop service from Mendoza, was right on schedule; it was due at noon.

Five minutes one way or the other really cuts the mustard.

Neither, three minutes later, was he really surprised to see a visibly pregnant, truly beautiful blond young woman carefully exit the aircraft as the first deplaning passenger.

Now that he had time to think about it, when he had spoken with Dorotea on the Collins late the night before, she hadn't protested at all when he said there was really no reason for her to come to Buenos Aires to see him off. That should have told him she intended to come to Buenos Aires to see him off and was not interested in his opinion on the subject.

He stepped out of the passenger terminal as she walked to it.

"My God, you're beautiful!" his wife greeted him. "Now I'm really glad I came!"

Frade was wearing the uniform of an SAA captain.

"Humberto's idea," Clete said, kissing Dorotea. "They're going to take pictures. I feel like the driver of one of those sightseeing whatchacallums. . . ."

"What?"

"At the New York World's Fair, 1939–40, they had little sightseeing trains that ran all over. The drivers had uniforms just like these. Powder blue with gold buttons and stripes. They'd announce things like, 'And to your left, ladies and gentlemen, is the General Motors Pavilion.'"

"You're right," Dorotea said, and giggled. "They did. God, don't tell anyone."

"You were there?" he asked, surprised.

"Daddy took us," she said. "We could have met."

"In 1939, you were fourteen years old."

"We went in 1940, I was fifteen."

"In 1940, I was a Naval Aviation cadet en route to Pensacola. I wasn't interested in fifteen-year-old girls."

"Only because you hadn't met this one."

"Possibly," he agreed.

"When do you go?" she asked.

He looked at his wristwatch.

"Seventeen minutes," he said. "Time and SAA wait for no man. Even General Rawson."

"He's coming?"

"He's supposed to be coming. And so, if we're really lucky, is my Tío Juan."

"If he does, behave."

"I will, if you promise to be on the three-thirty flight back to Mendoza."

"I'll be all right, don't worry about me." Dorotea looked past Clete and nodded toward a convoy of cars driving onto the tarmac. "Here's the president."

"And there's God's representative," Clete said, pointing to the terminal, from which the Reverend Kurt Welner, S.J., had just emerged. "If he tries to sprinkle my airplane with holy water, I'll have Enrico shoot him."

"Don Cletus, you should not say things like that," Enrico said, genuinely shocked.

"He's coming over here," Dorotea said.

"He's seen my uniform."

"Good afternoon, Father," Dorotea and Enrico said almost in unison.

"I need to talk to you, Cletus," Welner said with no other preliminaries.

"About what?" Clete asked.

"It's a good thing he loves you," Dorotea said. "Otherwise, your tone of voice would make him angry."

"I need a favor," the priest said.

"Oh?"

"More than that, to use your phrase, I'm calling in all my favors."

"What do you want?" Frade asked.

"Have you got room for one more?"

"You want to go to Portugal?" Frade asked incredulously.

"And if you don't have room, start deciding who really doesn't need to be aboard," the priest said.

"What the hell is going on?"

"I'd rather tell you privately."

"I have no secrets from these two, as you damned well know. What's going on?"

"I have heard from Rome . . . ," Welner said.

"By telegraph, or a voice from a burning bush?"

"Cletus!" Dorotea snapped. "For God's sake!"

Welner put up a hand to silence her.

"The Vatican . . . perhaps the Holy Father himself . . . has a message for the cardinal-archbishop they both don't wish to entrust to the usual means of communication, and also wish to get to the cardinal-archbishop as soon as possible."

"And you just happened to mention in passing to the cardinal-archbishop that you just happen to have a friend who just happens to be going to Portugal and then coming right back?"

Welner nodded.

"What's the message, I wonder?" Clete said more than a little unpleasantly. "'Hey, Archbishop, you got a spare room?'"

"Clete, what are you talking about?" Dorotea snapped, both in confusion and in anger.

"Maybe the Holy Father has decided it's time to get out of Dodge," Clete said. "The Germans are occupying Rome, except for Vatican City, and the only thing keeping them out of Vatican City are maybe one hundred— maybe a few more—Swiss Guards wearing medieval uniforms and armed with pikes."

"I can't imagine any circumstance under which the Holy Father would leave the Vatican at this time," Welner said. "And what's keeping the Nazis out of the Holy City is world opinion."

"'World opinion'?" Clete parroted. "Wow! Now, *that* should really scare Hitler."

"I won't beg you, Cletus," Welner said.

Frade met the priest's eyes for a long moment.

"Enrico, take his bag and put it, and him, on the airplane," Frade said. "And then you stay on it."

"Thank you," Father Welner said.

"De nada," Clete said sarcastically, the Spanish expression for "It is nothing."

Capitán Roberto Lauffer, the heavy golden aiguillettes of a presidential aide-de-camp hanging from each shoulder, quickly walked up to them. He kissed Dorotea, and quickly shook hands with Father Welner and Cletus, and then announced, "Cletus, the president wants to wish you luck."

Dorotea went to the stairway—now draped in bunting—with him.

"Behave yourself," Clete said. "I'll be back in a week."

"What was all that about with Father Welner?"

This may be the last thing I'll ever say to my wife; I'm not going to lie to her.

"He was lying to me, sweetheart. I don't know why, or what about, but he was lying to me."

"Then why are you taking him?"

"I owed him, and he called the debt."

She laid her hand on his cheek.

"When you get to the top of the stairs, remember to turn, smile, and wave at the people."

"Take care of our baby."

"Take care of our baby's father."

He kissed her very gently on the forehead. She squeezed his hand, and then he quickly went up the stairs.

At the top, he turned and waved at the crowd on the tarmac.

There was applause and cheers.

Undeserved.

I am really not qualified to fly this thing across the Atlantic Ocean.

What's probably going to happen is that I'm going to dump this thing somewhere in the ocean and take all these people with me.

On the way to the cockpit, he stopped by Father Welner's chair.

"Start praying. We're going to need it."

The copilot—*What the hell is his name?*—was already strapped into his seat and wearing headphones.

"Add 150 kilos to our gross weight," Clete ordered as he sat down. "We have an unexpected extra passenger."

"*Sí, Señor.*"

Gonzalo Delgano had naturally—he was, after all, SAA's chief pilot—wanted to sit in the left seat. Or failing that, if SAA's managing director pulled rank and wanted to be pilot-in-command, to at least be copilot on the first transatlantic flight.

Clete had told him that it just didn't make sense for both of them to be on the same flight, which stood a fairly good chance of winding up in the drink. Clete promised Delgano he would be pilot-in-command on the first paying-passenger flight.

There was a seed of truth in Clete's position. It was also true that Clete believed a commanding officer should not order anyone to do anything he was not willing to do himself.

But the real reason was that there were some things about the flight Clete did not want Delgano to know. Not that Delgano was going to run off at the mouth. But he probably would have told el Coronel Martín that Clete expected to be met off the coast of North Africa by U.S. Army Air Force P-38 fighters flying off the Sidi Slimane U.S. Army Air Force Base in Morocco.

Word of the Connie's departure from Buenos Aires would reach Spain long before the airplane did. Colonel Graham—and Allen Dulles, which made it twice as credible—thought that there would be a genuine risk of the Germans sending fighters to shoot down the Constellation—possibly, maybe even probably, from Spanish airfields that they secretly were using.

"The Argentine brave, but foolhardy, attempt to emulate German Trans-Oceanic commercial air service, sadly, but predictably, ended in tragedy. Their airplane simply vanished somewhere in the Atlantic."

The American fighters would be guided to the rendezvous point by the Collins radio. They would home in on the airplane much as an airplane would home in on a landing field.

Once the rendezvous had been made, SAA Flight 1002 would home in on a radio-direction-finding signal from another Collins radio secretly installed in the U.S. Embassy building in Lisbon, which was conveniently located less than a mile from Lisbon's Portela Airport.

The P-38s would linger over the Portuguese coast long enough to ensure that the Constellation had landed safely. If Allen Dulles suspected that all was not as it should be at the Portela Airport, the radio in the embassy would order the Constellation to divert to Sidi Slimane, to which it would be escorted by the American fighter planes.

Clete stuck his head out the window and saw that the bunting-draped stairway had been pulled back.

He fastened his shoulder harness, put his headset over his ears, and pushed the switch activating the public address system.

"Ladies and gentlemen," he announced, "this is your captain. Welcome aboard SAA Flight 1002, one-stop service to Lisbon, Portugal. We are about to take off. Please fasten your seat belts."

He paused, then smiled and went on. "Then place your head between your knees and kiss your ass good-bye."

The copilot looked at him in shock.

Clete repeated the message in Spanish.

The copilot first smiled, then giggled, then laughed almost hysterically.

"Get on the horn and get us taxi and takeoff," Clete ordered.

Still laughing, the copilot reached for his microphone.

"Flight engineer, you awake?" Clete asked over his microphone.

"Yes, sir."

"Well, let's wind up the rubber bands and see if we can get this big sonof-abitch off the ground."

"Starting Number Three, sir."

There was the whine of the starters and then the sound of an engine—somewhat reluctantly—coming to life. The aircraft trembled with the vibration of a 3,250-horsepower Wright R-3350-DA3 engine running a little rough.

In a moment, it smoothed out.

"Starting Number Four."

The second engine started more easily.

"I have Three and Four running and moving into the green," Clete said.

"Confirmed, Captain."

"We are cleared to taxi, Captain," the copilot reported. "We are Number One for taxi-off."

"Thank you. Disconnect auxiliary power."

"Disconnecting auxiliary power."

"I have auxiliary power disconnected," Clete said after a moment. "Three and Four in the green. Engineer, start Number Two."

"Starting Number Two."

"See if you can get us to the threshold without running over anything big."

"Jorge Frade, SAA 1002 taxiing to the threshold of Runway Three Zero."

"Engineer, start Number One."

"Starting Number One."

"Jorge Frade clears 1002 to take off as Number One."

Two minutes after that, Frade said, "I have everything in the green."

"Confirm all green," the flight engineer said.

Clete then ordered: "Copilot, pay close attention. I am now going to try *real* hard not to bend our bird."

"Yes, sir," the copilot said, smiling.

"Take-off power, please," Clete ordered.

Five seconds later, the copilot reported, "Ten Zero Two rolling."

The pilot-in-command tried very hard to spot the mother of his unborn child on the tarmac, but could not.

[FIVE]
Office of the Ambassador
The Embassy of the German Reich
Avenida Córdoba
Buenos Aires, Argentina
1620 27 September 1943

First Secretary Anton von Gradny-Sawz was already in Ambassador von Lutzenberger's office when Commercial Attaché Cranz appeared at the door.

Von Gradny-Sawz was drinking coffee and eating pastry.

Cranz felt his temper flare.

Gottverdammt Wienerwurst!

"You should have waited for me," Cranz snapped. "I had to ride all the way back in the cab of that goddamned truck. And then take a taxi here."

"Herr Cranz, Herr Raschner came to me, told me you could see no point in waiting any longer for U-405, so we left," von Gradny-Sawz said on the edge of self-righteousness.

"Aside from the inconvenience von Gradny-Sawz caused you—I'm sure inadvertently—were there any problems?" von Lutzenberger asked somewhat coldly.

He's reminding me that he's the ambassador, the ultimate authority.

What we really should have is a rule—a simple order from the Führer would do it—saying that ambassadors are in charge of everything but the missions and activities of the SS.

Himmler's title, after all, is Reichsprotektor.

If that isn't the most important responsibility any German official but the Führer has, I'd like to know what is.

And here is this canapé-pusher sitting with the Wienerwurst, stuffing his face with pastry and asking me what I've been up to.

What I have been doing, Exzellenz, is standing in the rain in the dark on the goddamned beach in the middle of nowhere for four hours waiting to see a flash from a signal lamp I knew goddamned well wasn't coming.

While I am doing this, the gottverdammt *Wienerwurst is sitting in his car a kilometer from the beach, stuffing his fat fucking face with something—when he's not sleeping—while I am getting soaked to my skin and catching pneumonia.*

And then the sonofabitch leaves me there, and I have to spend four hours in the cab of a goddamn truck getting back to Buenos Aires.

Cranz—as he had trained himself to do—smiled as he tried to rein in what he realized was a dangerous tantrum.

And then suddenly the flaming rage was gone, as if it had been washed away with a sudden torrent of ice water. He knew he was now in full control of himself.

My God, why didn't I think of this before?

Von Lutzenberger is behind this kidnapping operation!

He's been here forever. He knows his way around Buenos Aires.

He's the goddamned ambassador, the senior German officer. He doesn't have to tell me he's hired some of the local thugs to kidnap Mallín, much less ask my permission.

If he succeeds, Berlin will think he's a genius, the man who got the Froggers back when I failed to do that.

And he will tell everyone the reason he took it upon himself to deal with the situation was because neither I nor Raschner could.

And because we also failed to eliminate that goddamned American, Frade.

If we've proven we're not smart enough to eliminate Frade, why should he have turned to us to carry out an operation requiring the skill and finesse of an experienced diplomat?

And he doesn't care whether or not Frade makes good on his threat to give the photographs of Perón with the SS in Tandil to the press. Or that map von Deitzberg gave Perón.

God, that was stupid of von Deitzberg!

Actually, von Lutzenberger probably hopes that happens. Then not only does SS-Obersturmbannführer Cranz look like an incompetent moron, but so does SS-Brigadeführer Ritter Manfred von Deitzberg.

And it won't matter that we can explain what happened to Himmler. Even if Himmler believes us, we still will have committed the worst sin of all—making the SS look stupid in the eyes of the Führer. And that the Reichsführer will not forgive.

And if von Lutzenberger's kidnapping operation fails—that goddamned Frade has his private army guarding Mallín; and they have proved they know what they're doing—all he has to do is back off and pretend he knows nothing about it.

Hinting, of course, that SS-Obersturmbannführer Cranz may know something about it.

"Cranz and Raschner were more than a little embarrassed that they had no idea the Froggers were going to desert."

Is anybody in this with him?

Certainly not von Gradny-Sawz. Von Lutzenberger doesn't think the Wiener-wurst can be trusted any further than I do.

Von Wachtstein?

Probably not. Although he could be useful in knowing where and when Mallín would be someplace.

Boltitz?

Now, that makes a little sense. He's close to Canaris, and I have never trusted that sonofabitch. Or sailors in general.

So what do I do now?

"Were there any other problems, Cranz?" von Lutzenberger asked again.

"Excuse me, Exzellenz, I was lost in thought," Cranz confessed, smiling. "No, Exzellenz, there were not. I have communicated with Oberst Schmidt and set up the rendezvous points for tomorrow. All that remains to be done is for Raschner and me to be on the beach of Samborombón Bay at half past four tomorrow morning. And, of course, for von Gradny-Sawz to be prepared to drive Brigadeführer von Deitzberg here once he is safely ashore."

He turned to von Gradny-Sawz and smiled. "Gradny-Sawz, could I impose on you again to drive me down there? Let Raschner ride in the truck with our Günther tomorrow."

"Of course," von Gradny-Sawz said. "Pick you up at midnight?"

"I would really appreciate it," Cranz said.

"My pleasure," von Gradny-Sawz said.

[SIX]
Aboard U-405
South Latitude 36.05, West Longitude 57.17
Samborombón Bay, River Plate Estuary
0430 28 September 1943

Kapitänleutnant Wilhelm von Dattenberg had just spotted the first light from the shore when SS-Brigadeführer Manfred von Deitzberg climbed awkwardly up through the hatch to the conning tower.

It was dark, there was wind from the direction of the beach, and there was a cold drizzle. Von Dattenberg and the signalman standing beside him were wearing oilcloth hooded jackets. Von Deitzberg was in civilian clothing, including a top coat and a homburg hat.

"Send, *Zero Seven,*" von Dattenberg ordered his signalman.

"*Zero Seven,* aye aye, sir," the signalman replied, tapping the key of the signal lamp.

"Well?" von Deitzberg asked.

Von Dattenberg ignored the question.

"Shore sends, *Nine Nine* sir," the signalman reported.

"Send, *One Five,*" von Dattenberg ordered.

"*One Five,* aye, sir."

"We have established contact with the beach," von Dattenberg said to von Deitzberg. "I have just sent them code for '*Commencing disembarkment.*'"

He picked up a telephone handset.

"Open two and five. Put boats on deck and inflate. I want a line on every man on deck."

"What happens now?" von Deitzberg asked, his tone implying that whatever that was, he reserved the right to correct anything of which he did not approve.

"I have ordered the rubber boats to be brought onto the deck," von Dattenberg said. "There are, in all, four of them. They will be inflated and put over the side. Two trips to the beach will be necessary, presuming nothing goes wrong.

"How the boats will be loaded is up to you, Herr Brigadeführer, by which I mean it is your decision whether you want to be put ashore first, or whether you would rather wait until some of your men are ashore. Each boat will carry six men, two of whom will be my sailors.

"We are approximately a thousand meters offshore. I estimate it will take fifteen minutes to row ashore, and probably ten for the boats to return here."

"Why the difference?"

"Coming back to the ship, the rubber boats will be lighter and the wind will be behind them."

"Why can't you go closer to the beach?"

"We would run aground, Herr Brigadeführer," von Dattenberg said simply.

Von Deitzberg was quiet for a moment, then he said, "I think it would be best to put the SS men ashore first. I will go with the special shipment when we know all is well on the beach."

"Whatever you wish, Herr Brigadeführer," von Dattenberg said, then picked up the telephone again.

"Send the SS men to the deck, put a line on each of them, and load them into the rubber boats as soon as possible."

"What is that? 'Put a line on each of them'?" von Deitzberg asked. "You've said that before."

"That's a safety measure, Herr Brigadeführer. In case they fall into the water."

"There's a risk of that?"

"Yes, there is. The hull is curved and slippery."

And if God is in his heaven, you arrogant SS sonofabitch, you will take a bath.

[SEVEN]
Café Dolores
Dolores Railway Station
Dolores, Buenos Aires Province, Argentina
0845 28 September 1943

When the dark green—almost black—1941 Buick Roadmaster sedan pulled into the parking area and stopped, a clean-cut young man in a business suit suddenly appeared and walked quickly to the car.

"Señor . . . ," the driver of the Buick said, not in alarm, but warily.

"That's Sargento Lascano, Pedro, relax," the middle-aged, muscular, balding man in the passenger seat said as he opened the door and got out.

"Buenos días, señor," Sargento Manuel Lascano said.

"Nice suit, Lascano," the muscular man said. He was Inspector General Santiago Nervo, chief of the Special Investigations Division of the Gendarmería Nacional. He was *de facto,* if not actually *de jure,* Argentina's most powerful policeman.

Sargento Lascano had spent five of his twenty-three years in the army, and almost all of that in the infantry, and almost all of that in remote provinces. Just before the *coup d'état* that had made General Arturo Rawson the president of Argentina, Lascano had been transferred to the Edificio Libertador headquarters of the Ejército Argentino for "special duty."

Having been selected as the most promising among ten candidates for training as an intelligence agent, it was intended that he receive a final vetting for suitability by the then–el Teniente Coronel Alejandro Martín—the chief of the Ethical Standards Office of the Argentine Bureau of Internal Security—by "working with him" for a week or two.

The *coup d'état* had changed all that. Sargento Lascano had been given responsibilities during the chaos of the coup far beyond his expected capabilities and handled them remarkably well. Martín had been promoted to coronel, and Lascano had been given the credentials and authority of a BIS agent—and, although this was not made public, the promotion to warrant officer that went with them—and became officially what he had been during the coup, assistant to Martín.

"Thank you, señor," Lascano said. "Señor, el coronel suggests you park your car in the garage over there." He pointed. "They are expecting you."

"Who are we hiding from, Lascano?" Nervo asked.

"Just about everybody, señor."

"Where's your jefe?"

"There is a room in the café."

"Go park the car, Pedro," Nervo said, and then asked, "Is he welcome in the café?"

"You are Subinspector General Nolasco, señor?" Lascano asked.

"You didn't recognize him, right?" Nervo said sarcastically.

"Guilty," the driver said.

"El coronel said Subinspector General Nolasco is welcome, sir."

"Congratulations, Pedro," Nervo said. "Martín trusts you. Go park the car and then join us."

The room in the back of Café Dolores was small and crowded. The tables had been pushed together and held a number of telephones.

To take advantage, Nervo decided, *of the railway telephone network.*

Large maps were pinned to the walls.

There were now ten people in the room. El Coronel Alejandro Martín and "Suboficial Mayor" José Cortina—Nervo knew the stocky, middle-aged man to be both a longtime BIS agent and actually a teniente coronel—were seated at the end of the pushed-together tables. Both were in civilian clothing. Lascano had followed Nervo into the room.

A half-dozen other men in civilian clothing were at the table manning the telephones and two typewriters.

And there was someone else whose presence surprised Nervo: a tall, good-looking man in his late twenties who was wearing the uniform of a capitán of cavalry, the *de rigueur* cavalry officer's mustache, and the heavy golden aiguillettes of an aide-de-camp.

Nervo knew Capitán Roberto Lauffer to be the president's aide-de-camp and more: As with Lascano, the chaos of the *coup d'état* had seen Lauffer given responsibilities far beyond those ordinarily given to young captains.

The successful coup had moved General Rawson into the president's office in the Casa Rosada and put Lauffer in the adjacent office, where he had become, again *de facto* if not *de jure,* chief of staff to the president.

"People will talk, Alejandro, if it comes out we're meeting like this," Nervo said.

Martín smiled, then chuckled, then, shaking his head, laughed heartily out loud.

"Was it that funny?" Nervo asked.

"Whenever I run into Don Cletus Frade, he offers that same tired joke," Martín said. "Is Nolasco with you?"

"He's parking the car. What the hell is going on here?"

"Why don't you all go have a coffee?" Martín said to the men manning the telephones and the typewriters. They quickly got to their feet and left the room.

Deciding that Martín was going to wait for Nolasco before explaining what was going on, Nervo walked to the wall of maps and studied them. One of them—actually three, patched together—showed the national routes between where they were and San Martín de los Andes. Pins—*Probably indicating some sort of checkpoints,* Nervo decided—were stuck along the route.

There were maps, of different scales, of the highways leading to Buenos Aires, of the neighborhood of Belgrano in Buenos Aires, and of the area around Samborombón Bay, all stuck with pins.

Nervo turned to look at Martín, his eyebrows raised questioningly. At that moment, Nolasco entered the room. His face registered surprise when he saw Lauffer.

"Subinspector," Lauffer said.

"Capitán."

"I have been rehearsing my little speech about what you are about to hear," Martín said. "And about asking you to give me your word it doesn't leave this room. But I've decided not to ask that of you. You are all going to have to make that decision yourselves. What I've decided to do—as my friend Frade would say—is roll the dice and see what happens. Go ahead, Cortina."

Cortina stood and walked toward the wall. Then he stopped. Lauffer had put his high-crowned uniform cap on the table. He held his riding crop—a standard accoutrement for a cavalry officer.

"May I?" Cortina asked.

Lauffer nodded.

Cortina walked to the map and pointed the riding crop at the map of Samborombón Bay.

"At approximately oh four-thirty today," Cortina began, "the German submarine U-405 began to land, using rubber boats, two German SS officers and ten other ranks of the SS and a large wooden crate onto the beach at this point on Samborombón Bay.

"One of the SS officers we believe to be SS-Brigadeführer Manfred von Deitzberg, first deputy adjutant to the Reichsführer-SS Himmler. The identity of the other—junior—SS officer we do not know. We believe he is the officer in charge of the detail guarding the wooden crate."

"Is that the same Von Whatsisname who was here before?" Nervo asked. "The German general?"

"Yes," Martín replied, then added: "Santiago, this will go more quickly if you hold your questions until Cortina finishes."

"Okay."

"Waiting for them on the beach were Karl Cranz, ostensibly the commercial attaché of the German Embassy, who is an SS-obersturmbannführer; the deputy commercial counselor, Erich Raschner, who is an SS-SD-sturmbannführer; half a dozen Argentinos of German extraction; and a closed Chevrolet two-ton truck that is registered to Señor Gustav Loche, of Buenos Aires, who is the father of Günther Loche, who is employed by the German Embassy. Father and son were on the beach.

"Everyone was loaded onto the truck, which then drove to this point, near Dolores—about two kilometers from here—where von Deitzberg detrucked and got into a Mercedes sedan—diplomatic license tags—driven by the first secretary of the German Embassy, Anton von Gradny-Sawz. That car took off in the direction of Buenos Aires.

"Twenty minutes ago, the car passed this checkpoint"—Cortina pointed with the riding crop—"which leads us to suspect that it is headed for the petit-hotel at O'Higgins and José Hernández in Belgrano, which von Gradny-Sawz recently leased. We should know that for sure in an hour or two.

"The truck then proceeded to this point"—Cortina pointed again—"on the road to Tres Arroyos. There is a field there in which Company B of the 10th Mountain Regiment had bivouacked overnight while on a road march exercise. The SS officer and his men left Señor Loche's truck and got into two trucks belonging to Company B.

"Cranz and Raschner conferred briefly with el Coronel Schmidt, commander of the 10th Mountain Regiment, and then everybody left. Herr Loche's truck, carrying the Argentinos who had been on the beach, plus Cranz and Raschner, headed up National Route Two toward Buenos Aires—"

He paused and pointed at another map.

"—and twenty minutes ago passed this point. Thirty minutes ago, the Mountain Troop convoy passed this point—" He pointed at another map. "It seems logical to presume they are on their way home to San Martín de los Andes."

Cortina turned his back to the map.

"Does el Coronel wish to add anything?"

Martín said, "No. You covered everything very nicely. But the Inspector General might have a question."

"'*Might have a question*'?" Nervo asked. "Jesus Christ! I don't know where to start!"

"Maybe at the beginning?" Martín asked.

"How the hell did you know where and when the submarine was going to be in Samborombón Bay?"

"An American friend told me."

"Your friend Frade?"

"No. I understand Don Cletus is on his way to Lisbon."

"Another American friend, then. You are going to tell me who?"

"He speaks Spanish like a Porteño, and wears—convincingly—the garb of a gaucho. There is a rumor that he is a U.S. Navy officer working for something called the OSS."

"And he's a friend of yours?" Subinspector General Nolasco asked incredulously.

Martín nodded.

"How did your gaucho friend know about the submarine?" Nervo asked.

"They had a radio device, called a radar, which allows them to see things on the River Plate almost to Uruguay. At night. Even through fog."

"And this machine is where, did you say?"

"There's a rumor it's on Estancia San Pedro y San Pablo."

"You seem to have become very friendly with our American friends," Nervo said.

"I didn't plan it, but that seems to be the way it's turned out," Martín admitted.

"That's what it looks like."

"You're sure it was el Coronel Schmidt?"

"Yeah. This is the second time he's used his trucks to get Germans from Samborombón Bay to San Martín de los Andes. This time I think we have photographs of him."

"Think?"

"The film should be at the Edificio Libertador by now, being processed."

"What's in the wooden crate?" Nolasco asked.

"Money or gold. Or diamonds, other precious metals. Probably some of each."

"A crate full?" Nolasco asked incredulously.

"You didn't tell him about Operation Phoenix, Santiago?"

"He told me. I didn't believe it," Nolasco admitted.

"Didn't, or don't?"

"I'm starting to believe it."

"Then maybe you'd also believe that machine guns from el Coronel Schmidt's Mountain Regiment are what just about took down Don Cletus's house in Tandil." He paused, then added: "And that there are photographs of el Coronel Juan Domingo Perón standing beside those machine guns."

"You asked me to back off from that, and I did," Nervo said. "Perón was there, and you have pictures of him?"

"Perón was there, and Don Cletus has pictures."

"You believe that?" Nervo said. "Not that I wouldn't believe *anything* I heard about that degenerate sonofabitch."

"I believe it," Martín said. "The question now becomes: Do you believe what Cortina just told you?"

"Yeah, I believe it," Nervo said. "You're not smart enough to come up with this yourself."

"Thank you."

"The question I have is: What are you going to do with it?" Nervo said.

"I know what I'm supposed to do with it."

"If you took this to Obregón, you and everybody connected with you would be dumped in the River Plate halfway to Montevideo," Nervo said.

El General de División Manuel Frederico Obregón was director of the Bureau of Internal Security.

"He's another asshole who thinks Hitler and the Nazis are saving the world from the Antichrist," Nolasco said bitterly.

"That thought, both of those thoughts, have run through my mind," Martín said.

"What about taking it to Rawson?" Nervo said. "Lauffer?"

It was obvious that Lauffer was choosing his words before speaking them.

"I really like General Rawson," he said. "He's a good man, but . . ."

"Not very strong, right?" Nervo said sarcastically.

Lauffer did not respond directly.

"Just now, I was thinking that if I went to him with this, the first thing he'd do would be to ask General Obregón what he thought."

"In that case, you and Martín both would be swimming with your hands tied behind you in the River Plate," Nervo said.

"What does your American OSS friend, Don Cletus, suggest should be done about this?" Nolasco said. "Obviously, he knows about it. And—I just thought of this—since he does know, why doesn't he just take it to the newspapers? Here and everyplace else in the world?"

"What the Americans have decided to do is wait until the war is over and then grab all the money the Germans have sent here, and the things the Germans have bought with it."

"How are they going to know about all that?" Nolasco said.

"I would suspect, Pedro, that the Froggers are telling them," Nervo said sarcastically. He looked at Martín. "Frade does have the Froggers, right?"

Martín nodded.

"You know where?"

Martín nodded again.

"Where's where?"

"In for a penny, in for a pound, to quote the beloved headmaster of our beloved Saint George's School, Santiago," Martín said. "They're at Frade's Casa Montagna in Mendoza."

"And, presumably, the weapons el Coronel Frade cached there for the *coup d'état* are still there?"

Martín nodded.

"You two are Saint George's Old Boys?" Lauffer asked.

They nodded.

"Me, too."

"I know what," Nervo said, deeply sarcastic. "Let's call Father Kingsley-Howard and tell him what we're all up to these days."

They all laughed.

"So what are we going to do?" Martín asked.

Nervo said: "I shall probably regret this as long as I live—which under the circumstances may not be long—but I vote to go along with Don Cletus. Do nothing, but keep an eye on the miserable bastards. Especially on our own miserable—and sometimes degenerate—bastards."

No one said anything.

"The reason I say that is that I can't think of anything else we can do," Nervo added.

"Neither can I," Martín admitted. Then he looked at Lauffer. "Lauffer?"

"I think we should pool our intelligence," Lauffer said. "I'm sure that each of us knows something the others should."

Martín considered that a moment.

"You'd be the one to do that. If Santiago and I started getting chummy, people would talk."

"Perhaps, Comisario General," Lauffer said, "you'd be able to find time in your busy schedule to take lunch with me one day at the Círculo Militar? El Presidente eats there three or four times a week, and of course while I have to accompany him, I am rarely invited to share his table."

"That's very kind of you, Capitán. Call me anytime you're free."

[ONE]
The North Atlantic Ocean
North Latitude 35.42, West Longitude 11.84
1300 28 September 1943

On the night of 28 September 1943, 678 bombers of the Royal Air Force—312 Lancasters, 231 Stirlings, and 24 Wellingtons—plus five B-17s of the 8th U.S. Air Force, filled the skies over the German city of Hannover and dropped their mixed loads of high-explosive and incendiary bombs.

Halfway across the world, the Wewak area of New Guinea was attacked by forty U.S. Army Air Force B-24s. Twenty-nine P-38 Lockheed Lightning fighters accompanied the B-24s and shot down eight Japanese fighter aircraft without loss to themselves or the bombers they were protecting.

And, since just after noon on 28 September, Captain Archer C. Dooley Jr., commanding officer of the 94th Fighter Squadron, USAAF, had been flying his P-38, at an altitude of 22,000 feet, in lazy circles over the North Atlantic Ocean. He was about 100 miles south of the southern tip of Portugal and 200 miles west of the Straits of Gibraltar.

During that time, he had seen no other aircraft except the six other P-38s in the flight. Nor had he seen any ships of any kind on the ocean beneath him. Nor had he heard over his earphones what he had been told to expect: a Morse code transmission of three characters, *dit dit dit, dit dah, dit dah.* The code stood for S, A, A, and Captain Dooley had no idea what that meant either.

The silence in his earphones probably explained why the needle of a newly installed dial, labeled SIGNAL STRENGTH, on his instrument panel hadn't moved off its peg. The signal-strength indicator was connected to something else newly installed on the nose of his P-38, above the 20mm cannon and four .50-caliber machine guns. It was an antenna, in the form of a twelve-inch-diameter circle.

The antenna reminded Archie Dooley of the chrome bull's-eye mounted on the hoods of 1941 and 1942 Buick automobiles. And it caused him to think that he was now flying a Lockheed Roadmaster. Two years earlier, Archie's idea of heaven was to get Anne-Marie Doherty, wearing her Saint Ignatius High School cheerleader outfit, into the backseat of a 1942 Buick Roadmaster convertible. Neither was available to him in this life.

A Marine full bull colonel had impressed upon Captain Dooley—as they watched a guy who looked just like Howard Hughes install the antenna on Dooley's P-38—that the antenna was classified Top Secret, as was his mission, and that he was to take those secrets to his grave.

Further, the full bull colonel said, Dooley was forbidden to tell any of the pilots who would fly the mission with him anything more than he absolutely had to—which had not proved difficult, as he had only a very little knowledge to share:

He was to lead his flight to a position off the tip of Portugal, where he was to fly slow circles at 21,000 feet until the radio-direction-finding system detected the Morse code transmission of the letters S, A, A. He was then to fly to the source of the transmission, using the signal-strength meter as a sort of compass. The closer he got to the source of the transmission, the higher the needle on the signal-strength meter would rise.

On arrival at the source of the transmission, he would receive further orders.

While flying in slow circles waiting for the SAA signal, he would use new techniques—primarily low airspeed and fuel leaning—to increase the Lockheed Lightning's "dwell time." These techniques had been developed, the full bull colonel had told him, by Charles A. Lindbergh.

Captain Dooley was to "dwell" until he heard the transmission or until, in his judgment, he had only enough fuel, plus twenty minutes, to return to Sidi Slimane. In the latter eventuality, he would head for Sidi Slimane, and as he got closer, he was to listen for another Morse code signal—*dit dit dit, dit dit dit, dit dah dit dit,* which stood for S, S, L—and would use this signal to find his way home.

And then, all of sudden, there it was: *dit dit dit, dit dah, dit dah.*

The needle on the signal-strength meter quivered, as if it was trying to get off the peg.

Archie turned the Lightning's nose a shade to the right.

The needle—*No question about it,* he thought—came off the peg. Not far off, but off.

Then it fell back toward the peg.

Archie turned the nose a shade farther to the right.

The needle moved up again.

Archie held that heading.

The needle didn't move.

And then, a moment later, it edged upward again.

And this time it didn't fall back.

"Mother Hen to all Chicks. Form a V, below and behind me. Check in."

"Chick Three, I have you in sight."

"Chick Six on the tail of Three."

One by one, the others all checked in.

When Archie looked at the signal-strength meter, it was holding still.

Or maybe moving a little toward the center?

The compass showed they were headed toward the North African coast.

What the hell?

"Mother, where the hell are we going?"

"Maintain radio silence, goddamn it!"

Sixty seconds later, the needle was unmistakably headed back toward the peg.

Goddamn it! Now what?

Archie edged the nose to the right.

The needle dropped farther.

He edged the nose to the left.

The needle started to rise.

He held that course.

The needle continued to rise.

And then the needle began to drop.

What the hell! Is that goddamned transmitter moving, or what?

He moved the nose and the needle stopped dropping, then began to slowly rise.

"Mother, there's an—"

"Radio silence, goddamn it!"

"—airplane, a great big sonofabitch, at eleven o'clock, maybe two thousand above you."

Archie looked up and found it.

"Chicks, follow me, above and behind."

The needle was now almost at the maximum peg.

Archie edged back on the stick and advanced his throttles.

It's a Constellation, that's what it is.

Another one. The Marine full bull colonel and the guy who looked like Howard Hughes had flown into Sidi Slimane in one.

But this one isn't one of ours! There's no bar-and-star on the fuselage!

"Mother, what the hell is that? No American insignia."

"Above me and behind. And for the last fucking time: radio silence!"

Archie caught up with the Constellation and drew parallel to it.

He saw that painted on the three vertical stabilizers were identical flags, the design of which Archie could not remember ever having seen.

The fuselage was boldly lettered SOUTH AMERICAN AIRWAYS.

Archie pulled next to the cockpit, and a voice—an unquestionably American voice—came over his earphones: "Hello there, Little Lockheed. Where the hell have you been? I was getting a little worried you were lost."

"What the hell is going on here?" Archie blurted.

"The general idea," the voice said calmly, "is that you are to escort us into Portuguese airspace and keep the bad guys from shooting us down."

"Are you American, or what?"

"The bad guys can be recognized by the Maltese crosses on their wings and fuselages," the voice said. "You seen anything like that flying around up here?"

"Negative."

"Okay. Get above and behind me. You might want to put one or two of your little airplanes below and ahead of me on this course. I'll let you know when you can go home. Probably in twenty minutes or so."

[TWO]
Room 323, Hotel Britania
Rua Rodrigues Sampaio 17
Lisbon, Portugal
1845 28 September 1943

The reception of South American Airways Flight 1002 at Lisbon's Portela Airport had been strange.

Clete Frade had turned the P-38 Lightnings loose as soon as he was sure he was inside Portuguese airspace, then tuned one of the radio-direction-finding sets to the signal he was told would be transmitted from the Collins in the American Embassy.

He found that signal without trouble and homed in on it. When he tuned the second RDF to the frequency of the transmitter on Portela Airport, he didn't get a signal for a long time, and when it finally came on it was weak.

He was by then close enough to try contacting the Portela tower by radio, and that worked immediately. A crisp, British-accented voice quickly gave him the weather and the approach and landing instructions.

The landing was uneventful, and on the landing roll, the fuel gauges showed that he had enough fuel—more than two hours—remaining with which he could fly to Madrid or, for that matter, to Sidi Slimane.

That means we had a substantial tailwind.

And that means we will probably have a substantial headwind on the way home.

An ancient pickup truck with a FOLLOW ME sign in Portuguese, Spanish, and English had met them at the end of the landing roll and led them to the terminal. There, a farm tractor had pulled a wooden stairway—obviously brand new, painted in SAA red, and with the SAA legend on it—up to the airplane.

Two buses pulled up. A Portuguese immigration officer then came on board the Constellation and told the passengers to deplane and board the buses. When that had happened, more Portuguese came aboard and thoroughly, if courteously, examined the Constellation.

Then the crew—which included the extra SAA pilots and flight engineers, for a total of twelve people—went down the stairs, boarded the buses, and were taken to an office at the rear of a terminal building.

The aircraft's documents, plus the passports and flying certificates, were not only carefully examined but also photographed. And then finally the crew members themselves were photographed, as prisoners are photographed, in frontal and side views while holding chalkboards with their names handwritten on them.

Then their luggage was searched rather thoroughly.

And then they were released.

"Welcome to Portugal, gentlemen," a smiling immigration officer had said, and pointed to a door.

They went through it and found themselves in the passenger terminal.

There was no one in it except for two policemen sitting together, their legs crossed and extended, in a row of passenger waiting chairs.

There was a currency-exchange booth, closed, and even a new South American Airways ticket counter—the paint was fresh—but it, too, was closed. There was a brass bell on the counter—beneath a sign in Portuguese, Spanish, and English reading RING FOR SERVICE—yet banging on it proved fruitless.

Outside, there were three taxis, a Citroën and two Fiats, all small. Fitting twelve men—ten of them large—and their luggage into and on top of them was time-consuming. And then there was the problem of paying for the cabs when they arrived at the hotel.

Frade was reasonably certain that either Dulles or someone working for Dulles would be waiting at the hotel. He didn't think Dulles would have wanted to be seen in public with the "Argentines."

The hotel expected them. An assistant manager was summoned and he paid the cabdrivers. Then he bowed them into the hotel, where they went through the registry process. The desk clerk kept their passports, explaining that they would be returned when they checked out.

Frade didn't like that much, but there was nothing he could do about it.

Finally, he was handed a room key and two bellboys—and they were actually boys; they looked to be no older than twelve—bowed him onto an open elevator and took him to the third floor and down a corridor.

They bowed him into the room. He gestured for them to go first, then followed them.

"May I offer my most profound congratulations, Capitán," Colonel A. F. Graham, USMCR, called in Spanish, "on your transatlantic flight, and also comment on how handsome you are in that splendiferous uniform?"

"Hear, hear," Allen W. Dulles said.

Graham, in civilian clothing, was sitting with Dulles at a dining table.

There were two bottles of wine on the table and a cooler held a bottle of champagne.

Frade was surprised to find the both of them. He wondered idly how Graham had traveled to Portugal.

"Handsome doesn't have any money to tip the bellboys," Frade said in Spanish, then walked to the table.

Dulles took a wad of currency from behind the handkerchief in the breast pocket of his somewhat baggy gray suit, peeled off several bills, and handed them to one of the bellboys. Then he extended about half of the money he had left to Frade.

"That should hold you for a little while," Dulles said.

"Thank you," Frade said, and picked up one of the wine bottles.

"That's Monte do Maio," Dulles offered. "Something like a Merlot. Very nice. Baron de Rothschild owns the vineyard."

Frade poured wine into a glass, took a healthy sip, and then another.

Dulles asked, "How was the flight?"

"We made it," Frade said.

Graham stood up and began to unwind the wire-bound cork of the champagne bottle.

"Did you actually, just before you took off, tell your passengers to put their heads between their knees and kiss their asses good-bye?" Graham asked.

"Who told you about that?"

"A Jesuit priest," Dulles said. "And, as you should know, Cletus, while they have mastered the art of obfuscation, Jesuit priests never lie."

"How the hell do you know Welner?" Clete blurted.

"That's one of the things we need to talk about," Dulles said. "But let's wait until the colonel opens the champagne."

"We have a lot to talk about," Frade said.

At that moment, the cork came loudly out of the bottle and sailed across the room. Graham filled three glasses and passed two of them around.

"What are we celebrating?" Clete asked as they clinked glasses.

"You've been selected for the Naval Command and General Staff College," Graham said. "How about that?"

"With respect, Colonel, I'm not in the mood."

"To Cletus," Dulles said.

"Cletus," Graham said, and raised his glass.

"And to us," Dulles said, looking at Graham.

Graham touched Dulles's glass with his.

"Oh, how sweet it is to be proven right," he said.

"Amen," Dulles said.

They took a sip of the champagne.

"Do you think he'll apologize?" Graham asked.

"I am not going to hold my breath," Dulles replied.

Clete thought: *What the hell?*

Who's not going to apologize?

And for what?

Dulles turned to Frade and said, "For your general fund of knowledge, Major Frade, in the opinion of our beloved chief, Wild Bill Donovan, the chances of your being able to pull off this trip ranged from negligible to zero."

"Don't let this go to your head, Major Frade," Graham added, "but Allen and I are ever so grateful to you for proving Donovan wrong. That rarely happens."

Graham and Dulles took another sip of the champagne.

"*Semper Fidelis,* Major," Graham said. "Which reminds me: I have something from our beloved Corps for you."

He handed Frade an envelope. Frade opened it and found a U.S. government check and a complicated form.

"Your back pay, Major. If you'll endorse it, I'll take it back to Washington and deposit it for you. It is suggested that you purchase War Bonds with twenty percent of the total as your personal contribution to the war effort."

Clete shook his head and took a closer look at the form.

"Surprising me not at all, this is fucked up," he said.

"How so?"

"No flight pay."

"But you weren't flying, were you? Not Marine aircraft . . ."

"Jesus! You're kidding!"

"Not at all. But I checked that form. You did receive that munificent two-dollars-a-month payment that comes with your Distinguished Service Cross. Don't be greedy, Major."

Frade shook his head.

"And you are being paid six dollars *per diem* in lieu of rations and quarters from the day you volunteered for the OSS. That's a nice chunk of change."

"From which the sonsofbitches deducted the price of my watch," Frade said, holding up his wrist, to which was strapped what the U.S. Navy described as *Watch, Hamilton, Chronometer, Naval Aviators, w/strap, leather.*

"The Corps didn't *give* you that watch, Major," Graham said. "They *issued* it to you for use while flying their airplanes. When you stopped doing that, the Corps naturally wanted it back, and when that didn't happen, they presumed you had 'lost' it and deducted the price from your pay."

Frade tossed the check and the accompanying forms on the table and then picked up one of the wine bottles. He grunted derisively as he expertly pulled the cork.

"And as I mentioned, Major Frade," Graham said, "just as soon as you can be spared from your present duties, you have been selected to attend the Naval Command and General Staff College."

Frade looked at him warily. "What is this? 'Remind Frade he's a serving officer'?"

"That's part of it. It started out when the Marine Corps liaison officer—from Eighth and Eye; he keeps track of Marines in the OSS—came to me and asked when you could be expected to return from Brisbane."

"From where?"

"Brisbane. It's in Australia. Some people say 'Down Under.' This chap somehow got the idea that you are in Brisbane evaluating Marine fighter pilots' after-action debriefings so that we may learn more about Japanese capabilities."

"'Oh what a tangled web we weave, when first we practice to deceive,'" Dulles quoted cheerily. "Sir Walter Scott, 1771 to 1832."

"What the hell is that Brisbane nonsense all about?" Clete asked.

Graham ignored the question and went on:

"He told me about your selection for C&GSC, and that he was concerned that you hadn't been paid since September 1942. So I told him to have a paycheck cut and I would get it to you. And then, frankly, it did occur to me, Major Frade, that it was about time to remind you again that you are indeed a serving officer of the Marine Corps."

"That wasn't likely to slip my mind," Frade said.

"Really? I've noticed that you haven't used the word 'sir' very much—as a matter of fact, not once."

"You're giving the orders and I'm obeying them, but if you're waiting for me to stand at attention and salute, don't hold your breath." He paused, chuckled, then added, "Sir."

Dulles laughed.

Graham, after a pregnant pause, said, "Under the circumstances, I'm going to pretend I didn't hear that."

"Okay, now that I'm here, now what?" Frade asked. "I think it's time you finally tell me what the hell this is all about."

"You haven't guessed?" Dulles asked.

"I spent eight or nine hours just now watching the needles on the fuel gauges drop and guessing. The only answer I came up with is that it's about time somebody told me."

"That's all?" Graham asked.

"When I saw the both of you, I *guessed* it was important. How did you get here, anyway?"

"Howard flew me to Sidi Slimane—an Air Force base in Morocco—in a Constellation."

"Howard's here?"

"He's in Sidi Slimane. We brought some Lockheed people with us. Howard's passing on some techniques to extend the range of the P-38 he got from Colonel Lindbergh. And we brought some Collins people with us to maintain the radio-direction-finding equipment."

"Why is the U.S. government being so helpful to South American Airways? I seem to remember you telling me SAA wasn't going to be connected with the OSS."

"Maybe I should have said 'directly connected,'" Graham said.

"I want to know what's going on, Colonel," Frade said. "That's a statement, not a question."

"Two things, Major Frade," Graham said. "One, you're not in a position to make statements; and, two, you don't have the Need to Know."

"Oh, hell," Allen Dulles said. "Tell him, Alex."

"Excuse me?" Graham asked icily.

"He does have the Need to Know, and you know it," Dulles said.

"I don't think so," Graham said. "He already knows far more than he should."

"That's why, in my judgment, he has the Need to Know about what's going on here."

"I disagree," Graham said.

"If you don't tell him, I will," Dulles said softly.

"The hell you will!" Graham exploded. "I forbid it!"

"It would be better if you told him," Dulles said. "But if you don't, I will. If I have to say this, I'm not subject to your orders."

"Leave us alone for a moment, please, Major Frade," Graham said.

"It would save time, Major Frade, if you stayed where you are," Dulles said. "Because there is nothing Colonel Graham can say to me in private that would keep me from telling you what's happening—and your role in it—when you came back."

Graham's face went white.

"Goddamn you, Allen!" he said.

"Your call, Colonel," Frade said. "Do I leave or not?"

After a long moment, Graham said, "Put the cork back in that wine bottle and sit down."

Frade did so.

"This is your call, Allen," Graham said. "So tell him."

"I would rather you did, Alex. But if you insist . . ."

"What specifically do you want to know, Major Frade?" Graham asked.

"Tell me what's going on with SAA. Start there, please."

Graham began: "Power corrupts; absolute power corrupts absolutely—"

"John Edward Dalberg-Acton, First Baron Acton, 1834 to 1902," Dulles offered.

Graham glowered at him for a moment, then chuckled.

"Princetonians, Major Frade," Graham said, "among other obnoxious habits, never lose an opportunity to show off their erudition. You may want to write that down."

Dulles chuckled.

Graham went on: "The case at hand being that of Franklin Delano Roosevelt. Not only does he believe himself incapable of making a mistake in judgment, but considers anyone who dares challenge him to be disloyal and therefore to be punished.

"You've heard this before, I'm sure, but let me quickly recap it. Colonel Charles A. Lindbergh made the mistake of challenging FDR in several ways. First, he was active in the America First movement, which organization—headed by Senator Robert A. Taft—held that our involvement in a war in Europe would be disastrous.

"Next, while in Europe, prewar, he made the mistake of accepting an award for his contributions to aviation from fellow aviator—the former commander of the Richthofen Squadron, now commander of the Luftwaffe—Hermann Göring. Lindbergh compounded this grievous error by saying that in his judgment—and he was, after all, an Air Corps reserve colonel—the Luftwaffe was the best air force in the world, and not only because it was the largest.

"Such behavior, such disloyalty, could not be tolerated, of course. The first thing FDR did was tell the Air Corps they were not to call Colonel Lindbergh to active duty under any circumstances. Lindbergh then continued to work for Juan Trippe at Pan American Airways.

"This directed Roosevelt's anger to Trippe. *'How dare someone give employ-*

ment to a scoundrel like Lucky Lindy?' Trippe was told to fire him. He objected, and I understand there was a nasty scene before Trippe finally gave in to FDR's wrath.

"Lindbergh then went to work for Lockheed.

"But Roosevelt was not finished with Trippe. How to punish the owner of an airline? By starting up another airline to compete with him. Where? What about Argentina? We have—that's the regal 'we,' of course—the OSS down there, right? So FDR summons Wild Bill Donovan and tells him to have the OSS start up an airline; he will see the aircraft are provided.

"Donovan thought the idea was insane. And so did I when I heard about it. But Donovan knew better than to make an issue of it. Both of us are aware of the dangers of arguing with Roosevelt—which, incidentally, since we are making you privy to things you shouldn't know, have grown more dangerous since FDR's health is failing—so we arranged to have airplanes sent to Argentina and told you to set up an airline.

"At that time—as I didn't want what I considered to be the airline nonsense to interfere with the other things you are doing down there—I told you there would be no OSS connection to your airline. But then . . ."

Graham paused and gestured for Dulles to pick up the narrative.

Dulles nodded and said, "Alex and I had rather urgent matters to discuss; we arranged to meet at an airfield in Newfoundland. Alex showed up in a Constellation flown by our mutual friend Howard. I had never seen one, nor knew anything of its capabilities. Once they had been explained to me, we decided that Constellations could be very useful to us."

Graham picked up the narrative again: "If I had gone to General Arnold and asked for Constellations for the OSS, he probably would have laughed at me. But Donovan could see their potential value. So he went to FDR and very skillfully suggested that the way to really stick it to Juan Trippe was to provide the airline we already had in Argentina with aircraft with which they could fly all over South America—Constellations—and possibly even establish service across the Atlantic.

"Roosevelt was enchanted with the idea. So you got your Constellations."

"And what am I supposed to do with them?" Frade asked.

"So far as Donovan and Roosevelt are concerned, all you are doing, so to speak, is rubbing Juan Trippe's nose in the mud. SAA is flying scheduled service between South America and Europe; Pan American is not. When the war is over, SAA will have a tremendous advantage over Pan American."

"And as far as you two are concerned?" Frade asked.

"That's what Colonel Graham has wisely changed his mind about telling you," Dulles said. "Recognizing not only that you do, in fact, have the Need to Know, but that it would not be wise to keep you in the dark."

"About what? You're implying that Donovan doesn't know."

"Unfortunately," Dulles said, "we simply can't take the risk of having what you're going to do get out. And it would get out if Donovan were privy to it."

"Which is?" Frade asked.

"Immediately, what we're going to do . . . ," Graham said, then stopped. "This is the business to which I didn't think you should be privy. It was my intention that you would know nothing about this. But Mr. Dulles disagreed . . ."

Dulles nodded.

". . . and," Graham went on, "I have deferred to what I really hope is his superior wisdom; we are 'agreed' to tell you. The German officer in charge of Abwehr Ost—Russian—intelligence is a lieutenant colonel by the name of Reinhard Gehlen. He is far more powerful than his rank suggests. He is vouched for by Admiral Canaris, and, like Canaris, is involved in Operation Valkyrie."

Frade considered that, then nodded.

"A delegate of Canaris," Dulles carried on, "came to us—right here in this hotel, as a matter of fact—with an interesting offer. Gehlen recognizes the war is lost; that it's just a matter of time. And a relatively short one, if Valkyrie succeeds and Hitler is removed. God only knows how long if Valkyrie fails and Hitler fights to the last member of the Hitler Youth, which he is entirely capable of doing.

"Anyway, Gehlen is willing to turn over to us all his assets, data, and—very important—agents-in-place. He has two reasons. He personally doesn't want to fall into Russian hands. More important, he doesn't want his family to fall into Russian hands."

"In other words," Frade said, "he's covering his ass and wants to set up his own private Operation Phoenix?"

"You could put it that way, I suppose," Dulles said. "But it's not black and white. In our way of life, things are seldom simple."

"His second reason," Graham went on, "is that he believes the United States will ultimately, inevitably, go to war with the Soviet Union—"

"So does my grandfather," Clete said.

"—in which case his information and especially the agents-in-place would be of great value," Graham finished.

"Do you think we're going to have a war with the Russians?" Clete asked softly.

"I don't think the possibility can be dismissed out of hand," Dulles said. "There are a number of knowledgeable people—General George Patton among them—who think we will."

"Among other things that Canaris's delegate offered to give us—in fact, did give us—are the names of Soviet spies in the Manhattan Project," Graham said.

"The Russians know about that atomic bomb?" Frade asked, his surprise showing.

Dulles nodded. "And are trying very hard to steal it for Mother Russia."

"Jesus Christ!"

"What Gehlen and Canaris want is for us to provide sanctuary for their men—and the families of their men—in South America."

"To which they will be flown, via Lisbon, by South American Airways?" Frade asked.

Dulles said, "There are two problems here with which I think you should be made familiar. Colonel Graham is—understandably—uncomfortable with you being aware of them."

"Which are?"

"Colonel Donovan and, of course, the President," Dulles said. "Perhaps I should have said, 'The President and, of course, Colonel Donovan.'"

Graham said, "What we should have done when Canaris made us this offer was refer it to Colonel Donovan. If we had done that, the chances are that Donovan would have gone to Roosevelt, strongly recommending that we make the deal. And the chances are that Roosevelt would have gone along with it."

"But you didn't go to Donovan with it?" Frade asked incredulously. "Is that what you're saying?"

Both Graham and Dulles nodded.

"Donovan, we decided, would have gone to Roosevelt," Dulles said, "which meant that others would learn of it. For example, Vice President Henry Wallace. Wallace is a great admirer of Joseph Stalin and the Soviet Union. He would have insisted that Russia, as our ally, has a right to any and all intelligence Gehlen would provide. And the President would have gone along with him; FDR really believes that Stalin can be trusted; more important, that he can control him.

"Mrs. Roosevelt believes both things, that the Soviet Union is a trustworthy ally and that her husband can control Joseph Stalin."

"Then how is it that the Russians 'don't know' about the Manhattan Project, the atomic bomb?" Frade said.

"There's a difference between not having been told about it and not know-ing about it," Dulles said. "Of course they know about it. The question then becomes who told them about it, and how much they have been told. Or how successful their espionage has been . . .

"Since the Soviets don't *officially* know about it, and inasmuch as they are our trustworthy ally, and allies are not supposed to spy on one another, J. Edgar Hoover is having a hell of a time dealing with Russian spies. He's not even supposed to be looking for them. Counterintelligence is intended to keep the Germans and the Japanese from learning about it."

"But the Germans know about it?"

"In two ways," Dulles said. "Generally, because it's no secret in scientific cir-cles that everyone is working to develop a nuclear bomb; and also, with some specificity, because Gehlen's agents in the Kremlin have access to the material the Soviet spies are sending. And I think we have to presume that the Germans are sharing at least some of their knowledge about the Manhattan Project with the Japanese."

"My God!"

"So after a good deal of thought, Colonel Graham and I decided we could not refuse what Gehlen and Canaris were offering, and also that we could not take the proposition to Colonel Donovan. That we would have to conceal the operation from him."

"Which is on its face disloyalty and more than likely constitutes dealing with the enemy," Graham said. "Which is one of the reasons I thought it would be best to keep you in the dark.

"And there is one other problem we avoid by not bringing Donovan and the President into this: Treasury Secretary Morgenthau. I would judge that he hates the Nazis and Hitler more than anyone else in the Cabinet. He's Jewish and he knows what the Germans have been doing to the Jews. Neither Mr. Dulles nor I can envision any circumstance in which Morgenthau would countenance our providing sanctuary in Argentina to any Nazis, no matter what benefits might accrue to the United States by so doing. We are both agreed that if this arrange-ment came to Morgenthau's attention and Roosevelt didn't immediately bring it to a halt, Morgenthau would go to the press with it."

There was a moment's silence.

"What are you thinking, Clete?" Colonel Graham asked.

That's the first time he called me anything but "Frade" or "Major Frade."
What the hell!

Clete shrugged, then said, "You asked, Colonel. What was running through my mind was that this operation gives a whole new meaning to the term 'insubordination.'"

"What I told myself when I considered this dilemma," Graham responded, "was that I have sworn an oath to defend the United States against all enemies foreign and domestic. Vice President Wallace, Morgenthau, and, for that matter, Eleanor Roosevelt, whose good intentions I don't question for a second, are in a position to cause the United States great harm. I am duty bound to keep them from doing it while I am engaged in something I really believe will help my country—and probably save a hell of a lot of lives in the process."

"When I took that oath," Frade said, "there was a phrase about obeying the orders of the officers appointed over me."

"Which is what you're doing," Graham said. "If this thing blows up in our face—as it very well may—Mr. Dulles and I are prepared to say that you knew nothing of what you just heard. I don't think it will do any good, but we'll do it."

Frade grunted, and there was another silence. Then he asked: "Are you going to tell me how I'm supposed to get these Nazis off the plane in Buenos Aires?"

"Let's start with the first two," Graham said. "Alois Strübel is an obersturmbannführer—a major—in the SS. The Waffen-SS, but the SS. He and his sergeant major, Hauptscharführer Otto Niedermeyer, fell for the Fatherland on the Eastern Front about two weeks ago. They were buried with military honors."

Frade's eyebrows rose, but he said nothing.

"Frau Strübel and their two children were apparently killed—their bodies were never found—in a bombing raid on Dresden on September 11. Frau Niedermeyer and their son were killed in a raid on Frankfurt an der Oder two days later, and buried in a mass grave the next day.

"When all these people arrive in Lisbon, which probably will be the day after tomorrow, the women will be wearing the regalia prescribed for the Little Sisters of the Poor—"

"They'll be dressed as nuns?" Clete said.

Graham smiled and nodded, and went on: "—which noble sisterhood roams the streets of Germany picking up children orphaned by the bombing. Through the largesse of chapter houses in Brazil, Paraguay, and Argentina, these children are taken from the war zone to those countries, where, it is to be hoped, they will be adopted by good Catholic families, but failing that, cared for in orphanages maintained by the Little Sisters of the Poor.

"There are already large numbers of these orphans in Lisbon awaiting transport, which until now, of course, had to be by ship."

"And that problem of moving people between South America and Europe," Dulles offered, "also affected the Vatican. As I'm sure you know, Cletus, the Vatican is sovereign; in other words, it is a nation according to international law. In every country there is a Papal Nuncio, a high-ranking clergyman who speaks for the Pope.

"He is in fact the ambassador, and the residence of the Papal Nuncio for all practical purposes is the embassy of the Vatican. And it is, of course, staffed as an embassy is staffed. And the Vatican has to move people—not only their 'diplomats' but also members of their various religious congregations—back and forth between Rome and South America.

"Somehow, the Vatican heard that South American Airways was going to establish scheduled service between Lisbon and Buenos Aires, with a stop in Belém . . ."

"I wonder who told them that?" Clete asked innocently.

". . . and they approached the SAA representative here . . ."

"I didn't know SAA had a representative here," Clete said.

"Oh, yes," Graham said. "A chap named Fernando Aragão."

"Where did he come from?"

"Connecticut, actually. He went to Brown, but we don't talk much about his time in the United States. He was born here and has Portuguese citizenship. Before this, he was in the business of exporting cork and sherry and other things to the States. You're going to have to work out the details of his employment with SAA when you're here, but for the moment I suggest you let Mr. Dulles finish what he was saying."

"What does this guy know about me?"

"Nothing he doesn't have to," Dulles said. "He does know that you both have files in the National Institutes of Health. Good chap; I'm sure you'll get along well. But, as I was saying, the Papal Nuncio here approached Señor Aragão, saying he was prepared to negotiate for a block of ten seats on every SAA flight between here and South America, said seats to be used for the transport of Roman Catholic religious. The Papal Nuncio further said that should there not be ten religious moving to South America on any one flight, he would like to use their empty seats to transport the orphans of the Little Sisters of the Poor, ones he wanted to move to South America but really hated to send on such a long ocean voyage."

"Jesus Christ!" Clete said.

"Payment is to be made in advance, in gold, pounds sterling, or dollars, in either Switzerland or Buenos Aires."

"Curiosity overwhelms me," Clete said. "How did the Papal Nuncio know to go to Señor Whatsisname?"

"Fernando has been here since early 1942," Dulles said. "During that time, he made a point to cultivate the fellow. They've become rather close friends. But let me continue: Fernando also told the Papal Nuncio that, whenever this is possible, SAA will carry such additional passengers as the Papal Nuncio may send—for whom there is space; unsold seats, in other words—at a special, lower price. As a gesture of respect for the Holy Father and the good works of the Church of Rome."

"I'll be a sonofabitch," Clete said. "Tell me, do you think the Papal Nuncio happens to know Father Welner?"

"I believe they're old friends," Dulles said. "I know that Father Welner is staying with the archbishop at his palace while he's here in Lisbon."

"So you two are really in bed with the Vatican," Clete said.

"Strategic services, like politics, makes for strange bedfellows," Dulles pronounced solemnly, then added, "Allen W. Dulles, April 7, 1893, to God Only Knows."

"Oh, God," Graham said, chuckling.

"On your return flight, Cletus," Dulles said, "you will be transporting eight Portuguese and Spanish diplomats, several Portuguese businessmen going to Brazil, some diplomatic couriers, a half-dozen or more Jesuit priests going to new assignments in South America under the supervision of Father Welner, eight Franciscan priests going to new assignments in South America, and four nuns of the Little Sisters of the Poor and a number of orphans in their care. Among the priests will be Obersturmbannführer Strübel and Hauptscharführer Niedermeyer, suitably attired. All the priests will be traveling on *bona fide* passports issued by the Vatican.

"Colonel Graham and I are agreed—with Fernando Aragão—that it would be best if you don't know which of your passengers are actually the Strübels and the Niedermeyers. They will make themselves known to you in Argentina. Your call, Clete."

"Makes sense," Frade said. "When do I get to meet Aragão?"

"He's going to meet you in the lobby and take you to dinner at nine," Graham said.

"How's he going to know me?"

"That splendiferous uniform should do it."

"One more thing, Cletus," Dulles said. "You will be carrying other passengers from time to time. Would you prefer not to know who they are?"

"Well, since I won't be on every flight or, for that matter, on most or even many of them—"

"I'm glad you brought that up," Graham interrupted. "Will it be any trouble for you to schedule yourself as a pilot at least once a month—better yet, once every three weeks?"

Frade thought about that, then nodded. "I can do that."

"And Aragão will make a monthly trip to Buenos Aires. Between those two things, he should be able to keep you up to speed."

"Okay. What kind of other passengers will SAA be carrying?"

"All kinds," Dulles said. "What comes immediately to mind are scientists we hope to get out, nuclear physicists and aeronautical engineers. The Germans have developed flying bombs—rockets, right out of *Buck Rogers in the Twenty-fifth Century*—and are working on others powered by jet engines. The 8th Air Force just about destroyed their base in Peenemunde in the middle of August, but they're frantically rebuilding it. We're going to try—Canaris is going to try—to get some of their people out. These weapons pose a hell of a threat to England, and the Russians are trying to steal rocket data, too."

"And I'm to find these people some place safe in Argentina, too?"

"That's the idea," Dulles said simply.

"Why not? Some days I just sit around watching the grass grow and wishing I had something to do to pass the time. I don't suppose I can get any help to do all this?"

"That would pose problems," Dulles said.

"What kind of problems?"

"Primarily that Donovan would like nothing more than to send someone down to Argentina, some calm, rational, experienced colonel who could really lash down the loose cannon. And who would sooner or later—probably almost immediately—find out what's going on and feel duty bound to report it."

"I didn't think about that."

Graham grunted. "You better remember to think, Clete." He looked at his watch and announced, "Allen, it's getting pretty close to eight."

"What happens at eight?" Frade asked.

"I catch the train to Madrid," Dulles said. "I have to get back to Bern."

He stood and put his hand out to Frade.

"We'll be in touch, Cletus," he said, nodded at Graham, and walked out of the room.

"I guess you're not coming to dinner with me?" Frade said to Graham.

"I don't think that would be a good idea," Graham said. "The Sicherheits-dienst is all over Lisbon. I don't want them wondering what I have to do with SAA. And then I'm on the seven a.m. British Overseas Airways flight to Casablanca. I've got to get back to Caracas."

"Caracas?"

Graham nodded. "Two reasons. I've got to borrow some more money from your grandfather. And that's where Donovan thinks I am."

"Jesus Christ!"

Graham stood up and put out his hand.

"I suppose it would be a waste of breath to tell you to leave the cork in that wine bottle?"

"Yes, sir, Colonel Graham, sir, it would."

"Good luck, Clete. Keep up the good work. Now, endorse that check so I can get out of here."

[THREE]

The meeting with Fernando Aragão didn't go very much at all as Dulles and Graham had suggested it would.

When Clete, freshly showered and shaved and wearing his just-pressed SAA uniform, got off the elevator at five minutes to nine, there were four SAA captains in uniform already in the hotel lobby, two sitting together and two sit-ting alone.

Clete took a seat in an armchair. He picked up a copy of the *Correio da Manhã* newspaper and pretended to be fascinated with it; he didn't want any of the other SAA pilots to courteously ask him to join them.

Although the Portuguese and Spanish languages are similar enough for Clete to be able to make sense of what he was reading, there was nothing of any interest to him whatever on pages two and three. Then he came upon a small, one-column advertisement at the bottom of page three. It announced that South American Airways was about to offer service to Belém and Buenos Aires and gave a telephone number to call for further information.

At ten past nine, a somewhat chubby fiftyish man with slicked-back hair and a finely trimmed pencil mustache came in through the revolving door that was the hotel's front entrance. He was carrying both an umbrella and a heavy leather briefcase. Clete instantly disliked him.

The man looked around and saw all the men in SAA uniforms. His face showed annoyance. Finally, he made his choice—the oldest SAA pilot, whose name Clete couldn't remember—and spoke to him. The captain shook his head and pointed toward Clete. The man came over.

"Capitán Frade?" he asked in Portuguese-accented Spanish.

Clete lowered the newspaper.

"Sí. Señor Aragão?"

There was surprise on Aragão's face, quickly replaced by a smile and the announcement that his car was at the curb.

It was a gray 1940 Ford. It came with a cap-wearing chauffeur. They got in the backseat.

"Take us to the Hotel Aviz," Aragão ordered regally, then turned to Frade. "The restaurant at the Aviz is better, I think, than at the Britania, and, frankly, there's a better class of people."

Clete said nothing.

He thought: *What a pompous asshole.*

At the Aviz's restaurant, they were shown to an elaborately set table in a corner, and the moment they sat down, busboys put a screen of wooden panels around them.

"I don't suppose you know much about Portuguese wine," Aragão declared. "But if you like Merlot, there's a very nice Merlot type, Monte do Maio. I sent some over to Graham."

"I had some. Very nice," Frade said.

"Well, let's have some of that, and then we'll decide on what to eat."

"Thank you," Clete said politely.

I'm going to have to work with this guy, so the last thing I want to do is antagonize the sonofabitch.

Aragão ordered the headwaiter, the waiter, and the wine steward around so arrogantly that Clete thought they would probably bow and back away from the table and then spit in the soup they would serve them.

As soon as the wine was delivered—and Aragão had gone through the ritual of sniffing cork, then swirling wine around the glass and his mouth before nodding his reluctant approval—Aragão turned to Frade and announced, "Frankly, I expected a somewhat older man; I have a son your age."

Frade's anger flared. His mouth almost ran away with him. At the last instant, he stopped himself.

"Do you?" he asked politely.

"He's a Marine. He was on Guadalcanal. Now he's in the Naval Hospital in San Diego."

Oh, shit!

"I flew with VMF-225 on Guadalcanal," Clete said. "How badly was he hurt?"

"Rather badly, I'm afraid. But he's alive. Colonel Graham didn't mention your Marine service."

"No reason he should have," Clete said.

"I served with Graham in France in the First World War. We stayed in touch. And then, when the Corps said I was too old to put on a uniform, I'd heard rumors that Alex was up to something. I went to him and asked if there was anything I could do. And here I am."

He looked at Frade. Smiling shyly, he said, *"Semper Fi!"*

"Semper Fi, Señor Aragão," Clete replied with a grin.

Thank you, God, for putting that cork in my mouth!

In the next hour and a half, Clete learned a good deal more about the pudgy man with the pencil-line mustache and the slicked-back hair.

The briefcase contained all the paperwork for what the newly appointed Lisbon station chief of South American Airways had done, which included renting hangar space—"That may have been premature," Aragão had said, "as the nose of that airplane you flew in obviously won't fit in the hangar, much less the rest of it. Not to worry; I'll deal with it"—office space, arranging for office personnel, the ticket counter at the airport, and personnel to staff that, too.

The list went on and on.

It was only when he finally had finished all that that Aragão, almost idly, said, "While it can wait, one of these days we'll have to figure out how I'm to be repaid. This really came to a tidy amount."

"You used your own money to pay for all this?" Clete asked.

"I wasn't given much of a choice."

"May I ask what you did before you . . ."

"I'm Portuguese. I'm a fisherman. Someone once calculated that we provide twenty percent of the fresh seafood served in the better restaurants between Boston and Washington. And then, too, we import foodstuffs—anchovies, for example, and olive oil, that sort of thing—into the United States. My grandfather founded that business. I was born here and spent a good deal of time here before the war; no eyebrows rose when I showed up and stayed."

"Give me the account numbers and routing information, and as soon as I get to Buenos Aires, I'll have the money cabled."

Aragão smiled at him.

"Graham said he thought I'd like you."

[FOUR]
Portela Airport
Lisbon, Portugal
2245 30 September 1943

Capitán Cletus Frade of South American Airways, trailed by a flight engineer and one of the backup pilots, took a little longer to perform his "walk-around" of the *Ciudad de Rosario* than he usually did, and he habitually performed a very thorough walk-around.

He had an ulterior motive: He wanted to have a good look at the passengers as they filed down a red carpet to the boarding ladder, and the best place from which he could do so was standing under the wing, ostensibly fascinated with Engine Number Four.

The passengers had just been served their dinner, but in the airport restaurant. That would keep the weight of their dinner and the Marmite containers and the rest of it off the *Ciudad de Rosario*. Once on board, they would be served hors d'oeuvres, champagne, and cocktails. Capitán Frade had made it very clear to the chief steward that every empty bottle, soiled napkin, and champagne stem was to be taken off the aircraft before the door was closed.

The headwind he expected over the Atlantic Ocean worried him. Depending on how strong it was, every ounce of weight might well count if they were to have enough fuel to make it back across. And if not, at least he could see nothing wrong with erring on the side of caution.

Frade paid particular attention to the clergy and religious as they mounted the ladder. There were four nuns escorting half a dozen children. He didn't even try to guess which of them were the children of the two SS officers he was going to fly to Argentina. And any of the nuns could have been the children's mothers, except for one, who looked as if she was well into her eighties.

All but one of the Jesuits were in business suits, looking like Welner; the exception was wearing a black ankle-length garment. The Franciscans were all wearing brown robes held together with what looked like rope. They all wore sandals, and most of them did not wear socks. Clete had no idea which of them usually wore a black uniform with a skull on the cap.

When the last passenger had gone up the stairway, Clete motioned for the people with him to get on board, and then he followed.

As Frade walked down the aisle to the cockpit, Father Welner caught his hand.

"No kiss-anything-good-bye jokes, all right?"

Ten minutes later, Clete eased back on the yoke.

"Retract the gear," Clete ordered.

"Gear coming up," the copilot responded.

"Set flaps at Zero."

"Setting flaps at Zero," the copilot responded. A moment later, he announced: "Gear up and locked. Flaps at Zero."

"You've got it," Capitán Frade said, lifting his hands from the yoke. "Take us to 7,500 meters. Engineer, set power for a long, slow, fuel-conserving ascent to 7,500."

"*Sí, Capitán.*"

Ten minutes after that, there was nothing that could be seen out the windscreen.

"Passing through four thousand meters," the copilot reported.

"Give the passengers the oxygen speech," Clete said.

"Are we going to come across somebody up here, Capitán?"

"I decided I didn't want to waste any fuel trying to meet up with the Americans," Clete said. "And I'm hoping that if there are Germans up here, they won't be able to find us—you'll notice I have turned off our navigation lights—or if they do, we'll be able to outrun them."

"I agree, Capitán," the copilot said.

Clete looked at him.

He was crossing himself and mumbling a prayer.

XI

SS-Brigadeführer Ritter Manfred von Deitzberg, first deputy adjutant to Reichsführer-SS Heinrich Himmler, awoke sweat-soaked in the bedroom of his apartment in the petit-hotel at O'Higgins and José Hernández in the up-scale Belgrano neighborhood.

Worse, he knew that he was going to be sick to his stomach again. He padded quickly across the bedroom to the bathroom and just made it to the water closet before he threw up.

First, an amazing volume of foul-smelling green vomitus splashed into the water. This was followed moments later by a somewhat lesser volume of the green vomitus.

Von Deitzberg now desperately wished to flush the toilet but knew from painful past experience that this was not going to be immediately possible. For reasons known only to the *gottverdammt* Argentines, the water reservoir was mounted so high on the wall, with a flushing chain so short, it was damned near impossible to pull it when sitting on the toilet, and absolutely impossible to do so when one was on one's knees hugging the toilet.

It would be out of reach until he managed to recover sufficiently to be able to get off his knees and stand up with a reasonable chance of not falling over; that, too, had happened.

The entire sequence had happened so often—this was the fourth day—that von Deitzberg knew exactly what to expect, and that happened now. There were two more eruptions—this varied; sometimes there were three or more—after which von Deitzberg somehow knew that was all there was going to be. Then he could very carefully get to his feet, stand for a moment to reach the *gottverdammt* flushing chain handle, and then quickly hoist the hem of his nightgown and even more quickly sit on the toilet seat in anticipation of the burst of vile-smelling, foul-looking contents of his bowels that most often followed the nausea.

Baron von Deitzberg was suffering from what August Müller, M.D., described as "a pretty bad cold, plus maybe a little something else."

Doctor Müller was on the staff of the German Hospital. A Bavarian, he had been in Argentina for ten years. More important, he was a dedicated National Socialist, two of whose sons had returned to the Fatherland and were now serving in the SS.

For these reasons, Dr. Müller could be trusted to understand that there were reasons why SS-Brigadeführer von Deitzberg was secretly in Argentina under the name of Jorge Schenck and, of course, why von Deitzberg could not go to the German Hospital, where questions would certainly be asked.

Dr. Müller would treat the brigadeführer in his apartment and would tell no one he was doing so.

Von Deitzberg was not surprised he was ill. He was surprised that it took so long—until he was in his new apartment—for it to show up. He believed he had contracted some illness—probably more than one; Dr. Müller's "a little something else"—on U-405 during that nightmare voyage.

And he knew where he had caught Dr. Müller's "pretty bad cold." Fifty meters from the shore of Samborombón Bay, the rubber boat in which von Deitzberg was being taken ashore had struck something on the bottom. Something sharp. There had been a whooshing sound as the rubber boat collapsed and sank into the water.

The water was not much more than a meter deep. There was no danger of anyone drowning, and—giving credit where credit was due—the U-405's sailors quickly got von Deitzberg and his luggage ashore. By then, however, von Deitzberg was absolutely waterlogged and so were the two leather suitcases he'd bought on his last trip to Argentina, and of course their contents.

The result had been that von Deitzberg had been soaking wet during the four-hour trip in First Secretary Anton von Gradny-Sawz's embassy car from the beach to his new apartment. There was simply nothing that could be done about it.

By the time they reached the apartment, von Deitzberg had been chilled and was sneezing. Von Gradny-Sawz obligingly arranged for an Old Hungarian Solution to the problem—a hot bath, then to bed after drinking a stiff hooker of brandy with three tablespoons of honey—and said when he returned in the morning he would have with him Dr. Müller. "To be sure things were under control," he'd said.

Von Deitzberg almost refused the physician's services—the more people who knew about him being in Buenos Aires, the greater the chances the secret would get out—but after von Gradny-Sawz had explained who Dr. Müller was, he agreed to have him come.

Dr. Müller was there at nine the next morning, oozing Bavarian *gemuetlichkeit* and medical assuredness. By then von Deitzberg's eyes were running, his sinuses clogged, he was sneezing with astonishing frequency and strength, and he was running a fever. He was delighted to have the services of a German physician, even one who proudly proclaimed himself to be a "herbalist," a term with which von Deitzberg was not familiar.

He soon found out what it meant.

As soon as von Gradny-Sawz had returned from the nearest pharmacy and greengrocer with the necessary ingredients, Dr. Müller showed one of the petit-hotel's maids—actually, she was the daughter of one of the maids; he later learned she was fifteen and that her name was Maria—how to prepare a number of herbal remedies.

He started with showing Maria how to peel and chop four cloves of garlic and then put them in a cup of warm water, making a remedy that von Deitzberg was to take three times a day.

Dr. Müller then showed Maria how to chop ten grams of ginger into small pieces, which were then to be boiled in water and strained. Von Deitzberg was to drink the hot, strained mixture two times a day.

Maria and von Deitzberg were then introduced to the medicinal properties of okra. She was shown how to cut one hundred grams of the vegetable into small pieces, which were then to be boiled down in half a liter of water to make a thin paste. During the boiling process, von Deitzberg was to inhale the fumes from the pot. The boiled-down okra, when swallowed, Dr. Müller said, was certain to relieve von Deitzberg's throat irritation and to help his dry cough.

And finally came turmeric: Half a teaspoon of fresh turmeric powder was to be mixed in a third of a liter of warm milk, and the mixture drunk twice daily.

This was von Deitzberg's fourth day of following the herbal routine.

Dr. Müller further counseled von Deitzberg that, in order to keep his strength up, he was to eat heartily, even if he had to force himself to do so.

Von Deitzberg had little appetite from his first meal, and that hadn't changed much either. The meals were delivered from a nearby restaurant. Breakfast was rolls and coffee. Lunch was a cup of soup and a *postre*, which was Spanish for "dessert." Dinner was the only real meal he could force down, and he had trouble with that.

The appetizer was invariably an *empanada,* a meat-filled pastry. One bite of one of them was invariably quite enough. The first entrée had been a pink-in-the-middle filet of beef accompanied by what the Argentines called *papas fritas.* The second day had been baked chicken accompanied by mashed potatoes; and the third, a pork chop that came with *papas fritas.*

None of them seemed, in von Deitzberg's judgment, to be the sort of thing someone in his delicate condition should be eating. But Dr. Müller's orders were orders, and von Deitzberg tried hard to obey. He had to get well, and as quickly as possible. He had a great deal of work to do, and the sooner he got at that, the better.

The *postres,* however, were something else. They immediately reminded von Deitzberg of Demel, the world-famous pastry shop in Vienna to which his grandfather had taken him when he was a boy.

If anything, the pastry chef here in Argentina had used more fresh eggs and more butter and more confectioners' sugar than even Demel would have used. There of course were very few confectioners' fresh eggs, hardly any butter, and no confectioners' sugar at all these days in Berlin, even in the mess of Reichsführer-SS Himmler.

On the first day, von Deitzberg had sent Maria back to the restaurant for an additional *postre,* and then, on second thought, told her to fetch two. Dr. Müller had told him he had to eat to keep up his strength. Maria had since routinely brought two *postres* with his lunch, and three for his dinner.

Many were new to him, and they were invariably really delicious. One became his favorite: pineapple slices with vanilla ice cream, the whole covered with chocolate syrup. He sometimes had this for both lunch and dinner.

On two of the four nights he had been in the apartment—the first night, he had simply collapsed and slept until von Gradny-Sawz showed up with Dr. Müller the next morning—something occurred that hadn't happened to him in years: On both nights, following an incredibly realistic erotic dream, he awakened to find he had had an involuntary ejaculation.

His first reaction—annoyance and chagrin—was quickly replaced by what he perceived to be the reason. It was clearly a combination of his condition—whatever *gottverdammt* bug he had caught on the *gottverdammt* U-405—and Dr. Müller's herbal medications to treat it.

And then his mind filled with both the details of the erotic dreams and the facts and memories on which the dreams were obviously based, and he allowed himself to wallow in them.

His carnal partner in the dreams had been Frau Ingeborg von Tresmarck, a tall slim blonde who was perhaps fifteen years younger than her husband—Sturmbannführer Werner von Tresmarck—who was the security officer of the Embassy of the German Reich in Montevideo, Uruguay.

One of the things von Deitzberg thought he would probably have to do while in South America was eliminate Werner von Tresmarck, and possibly Inge as well, as painful as that might be for him in her case.

When the lucrative business of allowing Jews—primarily American Jews, but also some Canadian, English, and even some South American—to secure the release of their relatives by buying them out of the *Konzentrationslagern* to which they had been sent en route to the ovens—one of the problems had been to find someone to handle things in South America.

In August 1941, shortly after Adolf Hitler had personally promoted Reinhardt Heydrich—Himmler's Number Two and the Reich Protector of Bohemia-Moravia, as the former Czechoslovakia was now known—to SS-obergruppenführer and von Deitzberg—newly appointed first deputy adjutant to Reichsführer-SS Himmler—to obersturmbannführer, von Deitzberg had confided to Heydrich that, although the promotion was satisfying for a number of reasons, it was most satisfying because he really needed the money.

Two days later, Heydrich handed him an envelope containing a great deal of cash.

"You told me a while ago you were having a little trouble keeping your financial head above water," Heydrich said. "A lot of us have that problem. We work hard, right? We should play hard, right? And to do that, you need the wherewithal, right?"

"Yes, sir," von Deitzberg said.

"Consider this a confidential allowance," Heydrich said. "Spend it as you need to. It doesn't have to be accounted for. It comes from a confidential special fund."

And a week after that, Heydrich told him the source of the money in the confidential special fund.

"Has the real purpose of the concentration camps ever occurred to you, Manfred?" Heydrich asked.

"You're talking about the Final Solution?"

"In a sense. The Führer correctly believes that the Jews are a cancer on Germany, and that we have to remove that cancer. You understand that, of course?"

"Of course."

"The important thing is to take them out of German society. In some instances, we can make them contribute to Germany with their labor. You remember what it says over the gate at Dachau?"

"'Work will make you free'?"

"Yes. But if the parasites can't work, can't be forced to make some repayment for all they have stolen from Germany over the years, then something else has to be done with them. Right?"

"I understand."

"Elimination is one option," Heydrich said. "But if you realize the basic objective is to get these parasites out of Germany, elimination is not the only option."

"I don't think I quite understand," von Deitzberg had confessed.

"There are Jews outside of Germany who are willing to pay generously to have their relatives and friends taken from the concentration camps."

"Really?"

"For one thing, it accomplishes the Führer's primary purpose—removing these parasitic vermin from the Fatherland. It does National Socialism no harm if vermin that cost us good money to feed and house leave Germany and never return."

"I can see your point."

"And at the same time, it takes money from Jews outside Germany and transfers it to Germany. So there is also an element of justice. They are not getting away free after sucking our blood all these years."

"I understand."

"In other words, if we can further the Führer's intention to get Jews out of Germany and at the same time bring Jewish money into Germany while we make a little money for ourselves, what's wrong with that?"

"Nothing that I can see."

"This has to be done in absolute secrecy, of course. A number of people would not understand; and an even larger number would feel they have a right to share in the confidential special fund. You can understand that."

"Yes, of course."

"Raschner will get into the details with you," Heydrich went on. "You know him, of course?"

"I know who he is, Herr Gruppenführer."

Von Deitzberg knew that Sturmbannführer Erich Raschner was one of the half-dozen SS officers—many of them Sicherheitsdienst—who could be found around Heydrich, but he didn't know him personally, or what his specific duties were.

"He's not of our class—he used to be a policeman, before he joined the Totenkopfverbände—but he's very useful. I'm going to assign him to you. But to get back to what I was saying, this is the way this works, essentially:

"As you know, the Jews are routinely transferred between concentration camps. While they are en route from one camp to another, members of the Totenkopfverbände working for Raschner remove two, three, or four of them from the transport. Ostensibly for purposes of further interrogation and the like. You understand."

Von Deitzberg nodded.

Heydrich went on: "Having been told the inmates have been removed by the Totenkopfverbände, the receiving camp has no further interest in them. The inmates who have been removed from the transport are then provided with Spanish passports and taken by Raschner's men to the Spanish border. Once in Spain, the Jews make their way to Cadiz or some other port, where they board neutral ships. A month later, they're in Uruguay."

"Uruguay?" von Deitzberg blurted in surprise. It had taken him a moment to place Uruguay; and even then, all he could come up with was that it was close to Argentina, somewhere in the south of the South American continent.

"Some stay there," Heydrich said matter-of-factly, "but many go on to Argentina."

"I see," von Deitzberg said.

"Documents issued by my office are of course never questioned," Heydrich went on. "Now, what I want you to do, Manfred, is take over the administration of the confidential special fund—I should say 'supervise the administration' of it. The actual work will continue to be done by Raschner and his men. Raschner will explain the details to you. You will also administer dispersals; Raschner will tell you how much, to whom, and when. Or I will."

"Jawohl, Herr Gruppenführer."

"Raschner has suggested that we need one more absolutely reliable SS officer, someone of our kind, as sort of a backup for you. Any suggestions?"

Von Deitzberg had hardly hesitated: "Goltz," he said, "Standartenführer Josef Goltz. He's the SS-SD liaison officer to the Office of the Party Chancellery."

Heydrich laughed.

"Great minds run in similar channels," he said. "That's the answer I got when I asked Raschner for his suggestion. Why don't the two of you talk to him together?"

On their third meeting Raschner had another suggestion to offer. They needed an absolutely trustworthy man—someone with sufficient rank to keep people from asking questions about what he was doing—to handle things in Uruguay. And someone who could be sent there without too many questions being asked.

"Does the Herr Obersturmbannführer know Sturmbannführer Werner von Tresmarck?"

Von Deitzberg did know von Tresmarck, didn't think highly of him, and told Raschner so.

"He does follow orders, and he would be absolutely trustworthy," Raschner argued.

"Absolutely trustworthy? What do you know about him that I don't, Raschner?"

Raschner had laid an envelope filled with photographs on the desk. They showed Werner von Tresmarck in the buff entwined with at least ten similarly unclad young men.

"Because the alternative would be going to Sachsenhausen wearing a pink triangle on his new striped uniform," Raschner explained unnecessarily.

When von Deitzberg went to Heydrich with the idea, he thought the probable outcome would be von Tresmarck's immediate arrest and transport to the Sachsenhausen concentration camp. Homosexuality was one of the worst violations of the SS officer's code of honor, topped only by treason.

Heydrich surprised him.

"I can see a certain logic to this, Manfred," Heydrich had said. "Von Tresmarck would certainly be motivated to do what he was told and to keep his mouth shut about it, don't you think?"

"That's true, Herr Gruppenführer."

"Tell you what, Manfred. See if Raschner can come up with a female in similar circumstances we can marry him to. Make the point to her that if she can't make sure that von Tresmarck keeps his indiscretions in Uruguay behind closed doors, both of them will wind up in Sachsenhausen."

"Jawohl, Herr Gruppenführer."

Raschner was prepared to deal with Heydrich's order. Von Deitzberg realized Raschner had expected Heydrich's reaction.

Raschner showed von Deitzberg the Sicherheitsdienst dossier of a woman believed to pose a threat to the sterling reputation of the SS officer corps.

She was the widow of Waffen-SS Obersturmbannführer Erich Kolbermann, who had given his life for his Führer and the Fatherland at Stalingrad. Officers' ladies in these circumstances were expected to devote their lives to volunteer work for the war effort by working in hospitals, that sort of thing.

If they didn't do what was expected of them, a friendly word from the local SS commander reminded them that their exemption from labor service had ended with the demise of their husband. In other words, either behave or report to the Labor Office, which will find some factory work for you to do.

When Inge—who had been raising eyebrows in Hamburg with her hospitality to young SS officers on leave, not infrequently with two or more at once—was given the friendly word from the local SS man, she disappeared.

She turned up in Berlin, one of the thirty or more attractive young women who congregated in the bars of the Hotel Am Zoo and the Hotel Adlon, where they struck up conversations with senior officers—or Luftwaffe fighter pilots— who were passing through the capital and were able to deal with the prices of the Am Zoo and the Adlon.

The attractive young women were not prostitutes, but they did take presents and accept loans.

Raschner brought Frau Kolbermann to von Deitzberg's office for a friendly chat. Von Deitzberg was drawn to her from their first meeting. Not only was she very attractive, but he thought her eyes were fascinating; naughty, even wicked, *à la* Marlene Dietrich. He restrained himself, knowing that Reichsführer-SS Heinrich Himmler was not only something of a prude but expected the highest moral standards to be practiced by his officers.

Frau Kolbermann readily accepted the proposition Raschner offered. She said she knew where Uruguay was, had even visited it, and spoke passable Spanish, which confirmed what the dossier suggested: a well-bred woman who'd fallen on hard times.

She was formally introduced to von Tresmarck the next day, became Baroness von Tresmarck two days after that, and was on a Condor flight to Buenos Aires ten days after that.

From then on, things had run smoothly for almost a year. But then they began to fall apart.

On May 31, 1942, Gruppenführer Reinhard Heydrich, "Protector of Bohemia and Moravia," had been fatally wounded in Prague when Czech agents of the British threw a bomb into his car.

Before leaving Berlin to personally supervise the retribution to be visited upon the Czechs for Heydrich's murder, Himmler called von Deitzberg into his office to tell him how much he would have to rely on him until a suitable replacement for the martyred Heydrich could be found.

Von Deitzberg was now faced with a serious problem. On Heydrich's death, he had become the senior officer involved with the confidential special fund and the source of its money—yet never had learned from Heydrich how much Himmler knew about it.

He quickly and carefully checked the fund's records of the dispersal of its money before he had taken over. He found no record that Himmler had ever received anything.

It was of course possible that the enormous disbursements to Heydrich had included money that Heydrich had quietly slipped to Himmler; that way there would be no record of Himmler's involvement.

Three months later, however, after Himmler had neither requested money—not even mentioned it—nor asked about the status of the confidential special fund, von Deitzberg was forced to conclude that Himmler not only knew nothing about it, but that Heydrich had gone to great lengths to conceal it from the Reichsprotektor.

It was entirely possible, therefore, that Himmler would be furious if he learned now about the confidential special fund. If the puritanical Reichsprotektor learned that Heydrich had been stealing from the Reich, he would quickly conclude that von Deitzberg had been involved in the theft up to his neck.

When von Deitzberg brought up the subject to Raschner, Raschner said that as far as he himself knew, Himmler either didn't know about the fund or didn't want to know about it. Thus, an approach to him now might see everyone connected with it stood before a wall and shot. Or hung from a butcher's hook with piano wire.

They had no choice, Raschner reasoned, but to go on as they had . . . but taking even greater care to make sure the ransoming operation remained secret.

No one was ever selected to replace Heydrich as Himmler's adjutant. But Himmler gave von Deitzberg the title of "first deputy adjutant" and a week later took him to the Reichschancellery, where a beaming, cordial Adolf Hitler personally promoted him to SS-brigadeführer and warmly thanked him for his services to the SS and himself personally.

Von Deitzberg immediately arranged for Goltz to be promoted to sturmbannführer, and Raschner to hauptsturmführer. And he arranged for both to be sent to Buenos Aires. The risk of someone new coming into the Office of the Reichsprotektor and learning about the confidential special fund seemed to be over.

All of this had been going on simultaneously with Operation Phoenix.

Phoenix was of course the plan concocted by Bormann, Himmler, Ribbentrop, and others at the pinnacle of the Nazi hierarchy to establish a sanctuary for senior Nazis in South America, from which they could rise phoenixlike from the ashes of the Thousand-Year Reich when the war was lost.

It had been no trouble for von Deitzberg to arrange for Standartenführer Goltz to be sent to Buenos Aires as the man in charge of Operation Phoenix. That posting conveniently placed him in a position to be the confidential special fund's man in South America.

By then, curiously, there actually was a problem with the financial success of the fund. There was far more cash floating around than could be spent—or even invested—without questions being raised. It followed that the confidential special fund's leadership—von Deitzberg, Goltz, and Raschner—decided that setting up their own private version of Operation Phoenix was the natural solution. After all, von Tresmarck was already in place in Montevideo; it would pose no great problem for him to make investments for the confidential special fund. He was already doing that for Operation Phoenix.

And then there were the blunders. Von Deitzberg took little pride in being able to recognize a blunder when one occurred. Or an appalling number of them.

The first had been the failed assassination attempt on the American son of el Coronel Jorge G. Frade. When it became known that Cletus Frade—who had ostensibly "come home" to Argentina—was in fact an agent of the Office of Strategic Services and whose purpose in Argentina was to turn his father against Germany, the decision had been made to kill him. His murder would send the message to the man who almost certainly was going to be the next president of Argentina that even his son could not stand up to the power and anger of the Thousand-Year Reich.

But that hadn't worked. Young Frade, clearly not the foolish young man everyone seemed to have decided he was, killed the men sent to kill him. His outraged father then had loaned his pilot son an airplane with which young Frade located the Spanish-flagged—and thus "neutral"—merchant ship that had been replenishing German submarines in Samborombón Bay. Soon thereafter, a U.S. Navy submarine had torpedoed the vessel and the German U-boat tied alongside.

Von Deitzberg never learned who among the most senior of the Nazi hierarchy had ordered young Frade's assassination. And because that attempt had failed, no one was going to claim that responsibility.

They were, however, obviously the same people who had ordered the second blunder, the assassination of el Coronel Jorge G. Frade himself. The intention there was to send the message to the Argentine officer corps that just as Germany was prepared to reward its friends, it was equally prepared to punish its enemies no matter their position in the Argentine hierarchy.

That assassination had been successful. El Coronel Frade died of a double load of double-ought buckshot to his face while riding in his car on his estancia. The results of that assassination, however, were even more disastrous for Germany than the failed assassination of Frade's son.

The Argentine officer corps was enraged by Frade's murder. And during the attempted smuggling ashore of the first "special shipment"—crates literally stuffed with currency and precious jewels to be used to purchase sanctuary— from the *Océano Pacífico* at Samborombón Bay, both Standartenführer Goltz and Oberst Karl-Heinz Grüner—the military attaché and his assistant who were there to receive it—died of high-power rifle bullets fired into their skulls. Only good luck saw that the special shipment made it safely back to the *Océano Pacífico*.

Who actually did the shooting never came to light. It could have been the OSS, perhaps even Frade himself. Or it could have been Argentine army snipers sending the message to the Germans that the assassination of a beloved Argentine officer was unacceptable behavior.

It didn't matter who did the shooting. So far as Bormann, Himmler, and the other senior Nazis behind Operation Phoenix were concerned, Operation Phoenix was in jeopardy. And *that* was absolutely unacceptable.

And there was more: On the death of el Coronel Frade, his only child inherited everything his father had owned, which included his enormous estancia, countless business enterprises, and, perhaps most dangerous of all, what amounted to his own private army. Young Frade now had several hundred former soldiers of the Húsares de Pueyrredón who had returned to their homes on Estancia San Pedro y San Pablo with their devotion to their murdered commander, el Coronel Frade, intact and now transferred to his son. Including, of course, their considerable military skills.

The fury of the Argentine officer corps over Frade's assassination had finally gotten through to the inner circle at Wolfsschanze. Von Deitzberg was sent to Buenos Aires, ostensibly as a Wehrmacht generalmajor, to apologize privately to el Coronel Juan D. Perón for the absolutely inexcusable stupidity of Oberst Karl-Heinz Grüner, who had ordered el Coronel Frade's assassination. Perón had been told that Grüner had already been returned to Germany, where he would be dealt with. Von Deitzberg didn't mention that it was the bodies of both Grüner and Standartenführer Goltz that had been returned to the Fatherland, and that they had made the trip in the freezer of the *Océano Pacífico.*

Von Deitzberg installed SS-Obersturmbannführer Karl Cranz at the embassy to replace Goltz—officially as a diplomat, the commercial attaché—in running both Operation Phoenix and the confidential special fund, and then he went to Montevideo to check up on Sturmbannführer Werner von Tresmarck and his wife.

The von Tresmarcks met the Fieseler Storch in which Major Hans-Peter von Wachtstein had flown von Deitzberg across the River Plate. Frau von Tresmarck was at the wheel of a convertible automobile, an American Chevrolet. She was just as interesting as he remembered. He realized immediately that he wanted to get her alone, which would not be difficult as he had planned to interview them separately.

He then sent von Wachtstein back to Argentina, von Tresmarck to his home to prepare a report of what he was doing, and he took Inge von Tresmarck to the Hotel Casino de Carrasco. They went first to the bar and then to his room.

When von Deitzberg made his first advance to her, she laughed at him. Enraged, he slapped her face. He had never before in his life struck a woman. Yet he suddenly realized that he had never before in his life been so excited as he was now, looking down at her where she had fallen, and her looking at him with terror in her eyes.

He ordered her to strip. When she hesitated, he slapped her again. The clothing came quickly off. He humiliated her both verbally—he told her that her breasts sagged and that her ugly buttocks—he used the word "ass"—were unpleasant to look at—and then physically. Ten minutes after entering his room, Inge von Tresmarck was naked, on her knees, tears running down her face, crawling across the room to him under a command to take his penis into her mouth.

The incident was the most satisfying sexual experience von Deitzberg could ever remember experiencing.

Von Deitzberg had not quite finished shaving when Maria showed up in his room with his breakfast and Dr. Müller's herbal medications. First Secretary Anton von Gradny-Sawz came in a moment later as von Deitzberg was gathering his courage to take the first of his three daily doses of chopped garlic in warm water.

"You're a little early, Gradny-Sawz," von Deitzberg accused.

"I came as quickly as I could," von Gradny-Sawz said. "There was a Condor flight at two this morning."

This somewhat mystifying statement was explained when von Gradny-Sawz ceremoniously opened his briefcase, took an envelope from it, and handed the envelope to von Deitzberg.

He's treating that like a message from God!

When he took the envelope and glanced at it, von Deitzberg saw why von Gradny-Sawz was impressed. On the front of the envelope it simply read DER REICHSFÜHRER-SS BERLIN. On the back, where the envelope was sealed, was Himmler's handwritten signature, his method of ensuring that the envelope could not be opened undetected.

"This has been opened," von Deitzberg accused.

"The ambassador opened it," von Gradny-Sawz said, "and then sent me to deliver it to you."

Von Deitzberg took the two sheets of paper on which the message had been typed and read them:

MOST SECRET

Hauptquartier Der Reichsführer-SS

Berlin

29 September 1943

By Hand of Senior Officer Courier
Manfred Alois Graf von Lutzenberger
Ambassador of the German Reich
Buenos Aires

Exzellenz:
Heil Hitler!

Please make this correspondence known to
Brigadeführer von Deitzberg immediately on receipt.

As the Führer had expressed frequent interest
in von Deitzberg's voyage, I went to Wolfsschanze
immediately on receipt of your "All Packages
Received" message of 28 September 1943. The Führer
expressed his appreciation to Admirals Dönitz and
Canaris and to me, and asked that I pass his warm
regards to von Deitzberg.

There was another development at that meeting
with which I felt you should be made aware:

Propaganda Minister Dr. Goebbels had brought to
the Führer's attention the play paid in the world
press to the newly started twice-weekly transatlantic service being offered by South American
Airways, and in particular to the Portuguese and
Spanish press coverage of the arrival of the first
flight in Lisbon 28 September.

There followed a lengthy discussion of the
situation between the Führer, Reichsmarschall
Göring, Dr. Goebbels, Admiral Canaris, the
undersigned, and others.

The Führer agreed with Dr. Goebbels that the
institution of such service, using Constellation
aircraft apparently superior to Lufthansa's Condor
aircraft in terms of capacity, speed, and range, by

Argentina—which is not, to use Dr. Goebbels's description, "a world-class power by any criteria"—damages Germany's prestige, and is not acceptable.

Admiral Canaris informed the Führer that Abwehr agents had determined that South American Airways is actually controlled by the American Office of Strategic Services, and the proof thereof was Abwehr agents in Lisbon having learned from SAA pilots and flight engineers that their flight had been met off the African coast by USAF P-38 fighter aircraft, which escorted the Constellation aircraft until it was within Portuguese airspace, and that the pilot of the SAA aircraft was Cletus Frade, the son of the late Oberst Jorge Frade and managing director of South American Airways. Frade is known to be an agent of the OSS.

Admiral Canaris further stated that, in coordination with the undersigned, plans are presently under way to cripple the Constellation aircraft in Argentina.

The Führer then suggested a simpler solution to the problem would be to have the Luftwaffe shoot down the SAA aircraft in such circumstances that it or they would appear to have been lost at sea.

Reichsmarschall Göring then explained to the Führer how difficult this would be in terms of locating the aircraft at sea and then shooting it down before it could report by radio that it was under attack by German aircraft.

Admiral Canaris then suggested to the Führer that inasmuch as his agents had learned that all the flights will be carrying a number of Roman Catholic priests and nuns, as well as orphans under their care, there might be public relations problems if it came out the aircraft had been shot down by the Luftwaffe. Dr. Goebbels agreed.

The discussion ended somewhat abruptly at that point when the Führer turned to me and said, in effect, "Von Deitzberg is over there; have him take care of this."

In the service of the Führer:

H. Himmler
Reichsführer

MOST   SECRET

It had been von Deitzberg's intention to return to bed when he had finished shaving. Now, without really thinking about it, he went to the chest of drawers where his linen was now stored, freshly washed after its bath in Samborombón Bay.

When he'd selected underwear, a shirt, and stockings, and started for the bathroom, von Gradny-Sawz asked, "Feeling a little better, are you? Good news from Berlin, I gather?"

Maria said, "Señor Schenck, you are supposed to do the garlic water before breakfast."

"Get that goddamned garlic water out of here," von Deitzberg snapped. "Get *all* of those lunatic remedies out of here."

"Is something wrong?" von Gradny-Sawz asked.

"Go find a public telephone," von Deitzberg ordered. "Call Cranz. Tell him to come here immediately. In a taxi, not an embassy car."

"Something *is* wrong," von Gradny-Sawz proclaimed.

Von Deitzberg thought: *I am surrounded by idiots!*

He ordered: "And when you've done that, station yourself at the door downstairs. If that lunatic Müller gets past you and up here, I'll throw both of you out of the window!"

He turned to the maid. "Maria, after you throw all of that herbal junk away, go to the restaurant and get me some scrambled eggs—*four* scrambled eggs—toast, ham, and a pot of coffee."

She looked at him as if he had lost his mind.

"My God, didn't you hear me?"

Maria began to cry.

Von Gradny-Sawz gave von Deitzberg a dirty look, put his arm around Maria's shoulders, and led her out of the room, speaking softly to her. Von Deitzberg went into the bathroom, took a cold shower, and then dressed.

When Maria returned with his scrambled eggs, von Deitzberg apologized to her for raising his voice and whatever else he had done to cause her to be uncomfortable.

While doing so, for the first time since they'd met, he looked at her as a female. He'd heard somewhere that Latin women—*or was it Italian, Spanish, and Portuguese?*—matured earlier than Aryans. It was apparently true so far as Maria was concerned. She had an entirely mature and quite attractive bosom.

He did not permit his thoughts to wander down that path.

My God, she's fifteen!

Any mature man taking carnal advantage of a fifteen-year-old female child should be lashed at the stake first, and then castrated.

And Perón likes them even younger! That's obscene!

Unfortunately, I don't think I will ever be able to watch el Coronel Perón as he is lashed or castrated.

I have other plans for that degenerate sonofabitch!

Von Deitzberg, to ensure he hadn't missed anything, read Himmler's letter a third time as he ate his scrambled eggs.

He knew that while everything Himmler had written was true, it was not a complete report of what had happened at Wolfsschanze. Himmler was too smart to write that down, and he knew that von Deitzberg—who not only was privy to the backstabbing of the senior Nazis but personally had witnessed at least a dozen of the Führer's legendary tirades—would be easily able to fill in the blanks.

Himmler had not considered it necessary to suggest that Goebbels, the clubfooted propaganda minister, had brought South American Airways' accomplishment to Hitler's attention, not in order to keep the Führer up-to-date, but rather it would direct the Führer's rage at Reichsmarschall Hermann Göring, of whose power he was jealous and whom he loathed.

It wasn't at all hard for von Deitzberg to picture the scene around the map table at Wolfsschanze with Hitler ranting at a cowering Göring. The Führer was wont to stamp his foot. His tirade was often accompanied by a shower of spittle. And a supply of spectacles was kept available to replace those he threw at the floor or at whoever was the target of his rage.

And von Deitzberg could clearly see the concern in Goebbels's eyes when Hitler was on the edge of ordering that the Constellations be shot down, then that concern replaced with relief when Canaris, with his usual skill, kept that from happening.

My God! I'm thinking clearly!

Twenty minutes ago, all I was thinking of was what those gottverdammt *concoctions that that moron Müller has been feeding me are doing to my stomach and bowels. Or daydreaming like a sixteen-year-old with raging hormones about Inge von Tresmarck.*

It's as if I've been asleep, or drugged, and suddenly woken up.

Why? What happened? What woke me up?

After a moment's thought, he knew what had happened.

He was terrified because of the last paragraph of Himmler's letter: "The discussion ended somewhat abruptly at that point when the Führer turned to me and said, in effect, 'Von Deitzberg is over there; have him take care of this.'"

I have been personally given the task of destroying SAA's aircraft, and in such a manner that the finger of suspicion cannot be pointed at Germany.

Every one of those Sohns der einer Hündin at Wolfsschanze must have been delighted.

Canaris, because Hitler hadn't ordered him to do it.

Goebbels, because there would not be an uproar in the world's press over Germans shooting down a civilian airline of a neutral power carrying a load of priests and nuns.

Göring, because Hitler hadn't ordered the Luftwaffe to do the shooting down.

And Heinrich Himmler, because he hadn't been ordered to put the Sicherheitsdienst to work destroying the airplanes.

Not one of them—but me, personally!

"Have von Deitzberg take care of this."

All Himmler was doing was relaying the Führer's orders.

Yet if I somehow succeed in destroying the airplanes, Himmler will of course take all the credit.

And if I fail, I will have Hitler personally furious with me. And I am a lowly SS-brigadeführer, not a senior general. Hitler doesn't scream at unimportant people like me; he just has the Leibstandarte Adolf Hitler stand them in front of a wall.

Unless he's really angry, and orders the Leibstandarte to hang me from a butcher's hook with Goebbels's movie cameras filming so the Führer can watch my agony at his leisure and over and over again.

And it's not as if I don't already have my hands full.

I still have no idea how I'm going to do what else I have to do here—eliminate that gottverdammt *American Frade of the OSS, locate and eliminate the Froggers, find out how much damage the Froggers have done to Operation Phoenix, and check on both how the confidential special fund is being handled in Uruguay and whether that miserable deviate von Tresmarck has been able to keep his mouth shut.*

And now this!

And I am absolutely alone!

Cranz and Raschner are incompetent—not only did they fail to eliminate Frade but they managed to lose an SS officer and half a dozen of his men while shooting up an empty house. Only a fool would not consider that they will shortly receive a letter from Himmler—now that I think about it, it probably came in the same pouch as Himmler's letter to von Lutzenberger and me—ordering them to secretly report on how I am carrying out my assignments.

And Cranz will do a good job on that. That Sohn der einer Hündin would like nothing better than to get me out of the way so he could become first deputy adjutant to the Reichsführer-SS.

Well, as I always say about facing a difficult task: "You need good men and a lot of money."

And I have all the money I could possibly need—or will just as soon as I can get to Uruguay.

But men? Where am I going to find good men?

There's no one at all, except that fat slob—Anton von Gradny-Sawz, the grosse Weinerwurst—and he's stupid and as useless as teats on a boar hog.

Or . . .

Wait a minute! I don't think he's really stupid. He was certainly smart enough to know when to change sides just before the Anschluss. And he's done a remarkable job of covering his Gesäss since he joined the German diplomatic service.

And he's afraid of me!

And what other choice do I have?

Anton von Gradny-Sawz and August Müller, M.D., were standing in the foyer of the petit-hotel when von Deitzberg came quickly down the stairway.

Dr. Müller looked at von Deitzberg curiously. Von Gradny-Sawz had a look of concern, as if he were afraid that von Deitzberg would attack the physician.

"Ah, the Bavarian medical genius!" von Deitzberg then cried happily. "What are you doing here in the foyer? Come up to the room and we'll send Maria out for a little schnapps. We can find schnapps here, right, Anton?"

"I'm not sure if we can," von Gradny-Sawz said uneasily.

"Nothing to drink for me at this hour," Dr. Müller said. "Thank you just the same. I have to go to the hospital."

"Of course, of course," von Deitzberg said. "I understand. But I really wanted to celebrate."

"You're feeling better, I gather?" Müller asked.

"I woke up this morning feeling better than I've felt in years," von Deitzberg said. "Doctor, you are a genius!"

"Oh, I'm just a simple physician trying to do my best."

"You're too modest," von Deitzberg said. "Much too modest. I am deeply in your debt. And at the risk of immodesty, the SS is grateful to you, as well. You have returned this officer to full duty."

"If that is so, I am honored to have been of service," Müller said.

"I wish I could proclaim your genius to the world," von Deitzberg said. "But under the circumstances, you understand, that is not possible."

"I understand," Dr. Müller agreed solemnly.

"But as soon as I can get through to Reichsführer-SS Himmler," von Deitzberg went on, "I'll see that your son's commanding officers are made aware of your contribution to the SS."

"That's very kind of you," Müller said emotionally.

"But now our duty calls," von Deitzberg said solemnly. His right arm shot out in the Nazi salute.

"Heil Hitler!" he barked.

Dr. Müller returned the salute.

"After you, *mein lieber* Gradny-Sawz," von Deitzberg said, and grandly bowed him ahead of him up the stairway.

[TWO]

Von Deitzberg's judgment that von Gradny-Sawz was afraid of him was something of an understatement. Terrified would have been more accurate.

Von Gradny-Sawz had known von Deitzberg's reputation within the SS before "Generalmajor" von Deitzberg had come to Argentina the first time. And that reputation was that he was at least as ruthless and cold-blooded as Reichsführer-SS Himmler himself.

Part of von Deitzberg's mission then—aside from apologizing to the Argentine officer corps for el Coronel Frade's murder, and von Gradny-Sawz would not have been surprised if that order had actually come from SS-Brigadeführer von Deitzberg in the first place—was the detection of the spy, or spies, everyone knew operated in the embassy.

Von Deitzberg had brought three people with him to help him find the spy or spies or traitors, and three people—Major von Wachtstein, Sturmbannführer von Tresmarck, and First Secretary von Gradny-Sawz—were rushed onto the next Condor flight to Berlin "to assist in the investigation."

From the moment the SS-Obersturmbannführer had picked him up at his apartment to take him to the airfield, von Gradny-Sawz had been convinced they were all en route to Sachsenhausen or Dachau.

But it hadn't turned out that way. After four days of thorough questioning, he and von Tresmarck had been returned to Buenos Aires. Von Wachtstein had stayed in Germany, not because he was suspected of treason but because he had gone to Augsburg to learn how to fly the new Me-262 jet-propelled fighter.

In the end, he, too, was returned to Argentina. It came out that the young fighter pilot had caused Alicia, the youngest daughter of Señora Claudia de Carzino-Cormano, to be with child. It had been decided that young von Wachtstein would be of greater value to National Socialism married to the daughter of the richest woman in Argentina than he would be flying, and he was sent back to Argentina under orders to "do the right thing."

Von Gradny-Sawz had not forgotten his terror on being ordered to Berlin, and had vowed then that it would never happen again. He had established—in addition to what he'd talked about with el Coronel Martín—three different places to which he could disappear with reasonable safety should his presence again be demanded in Berlin.

As he walked ahead of von Deitzberg up the stairway to the apartment he had rented for Señor Jorge Schenck, von Gradny-Sawz seriously considered the possibility that the tall, slim, blond Westphalian had gone out of his mind. Rapid mood changes were almost a sure sign of schizophrenia.

And there seemed to be more indications that the war was going to be lost. The newspapers that day carried the story of the bombing on Hamburg of the night of 27 July—it had taken that long to get the story out. According to the correspondent of the Stockholm *Dagens Nyheter,* who had no reason to lie, the bombing had created so much heat that a "firestorm" had been created, a monstrous inferno with winds of more than 240 kilometers per hour and temperatures so high that asphalt streets began to burn. More than twenty-one square kilometers of the city had been incinerated and more than 35,000 people had been burned to death. The *Dagens Nyheter* report said the British had named the raids "Operation Gomorrah."

The Italians had surrendered, although most of northern Italy—including Rome—was under German control. Von Gradny-Sawz thought that Mussolini's declaration of a new Fascist state that was going to drive the English and the Americans from the Italian peninsula was what sailors called "pissing into the wind."

Since the war was almost surely lost, the question to von Gradny-Sawz then became: What would he have to do to protect himself from what was going to happen when that actually happened?

He had no intention of going back to Europe, which would be not much more than a pile of rubble. Going "home" was absolutely out of the question. The Russians were going to seize Hungary, and the first thing they were going to do was confiscate all the property of the nobility. And then, presuming they didn't hang them first, the nobility would be shipped off to a Siberian labor camp.

He was going to have to find refuge in Argentina, just as Bormann, Himmler, and the others intended to. The difference there was that they had access to money—mind-boggling amounts of money—and he didn't. He had managed to get some money out of Hungary, and there were some family jewels. But if he had to buy refuge in Argentina—which seemed likely—that wasn't going to be cheap, and he wasn't going to have much to live on until he could, so to speak, come out of hiding and get a job.

He thought that after a while he could get a job as a professor at the University of Buenos Aires—or perhaps at the Catholic University—teaching history or political science. He had a degree in history from the University of Vienna. He had already begun to cultivate academics from both institutions.

But right now the problem was SS-Brigadeführer Ritter Manfred von Deitzberg, and von Gradny-Sawz really had no idea how he was going to deal with that.

The moment they were in the apartment, von Deitzberg went to his chest of drawers, picked up the bottle of brandy that von Gradny-Sawz had brought him as his home remedy for von Deitzberg's "cold," poured some into two water glasses, and handed one to von Gradny-Sawz.

"It's absolutely true, Anton," von Deitzberg said, smiling charmingly, "that Winston Churchill begins his day with a glass of cognac. 'Know thy enemy,' right? Maybe he's onto something."

Von Gradny-Sawz thought: *Good God, he's insane and now he's going to get drunk?*

"Final Victory," von Deitzberg said as he tapped their glasses.

"Our Führer," von Gradny-Sawz responded, and took a small sip of the cognac.

"You don't really believe in the Final Victory, do you, Anton?" von Deitzberg asked. "Or, for that matter, in the Führer?"

Von Gradny-Sawz felt a chill. He had no idea how to respond.

"The Führer is, as Churchill would say, 'as mad as a March hare,'" von Deitzberg said. "And the war is lost. And we both know it."

Von Gradny-Sawz felt faint.

"Let's clear the air between us, Anton," von Deitzberg said, looking into von Gradny-Sawz's eyes. "I have studied your dossier carefully and made certain inquiries." He let that sink in for a long moment, and then went on. "I know, for example, that your own deviation from the sexual norm is that you like to take two—or three—women into your bed."

Jesus Christ!

"Which frankly sounds rather interesting," von Deitzberg continued. "And I also know that you have violated the law by illegally exporting from the Fatherland some $106,000 plus some gold and diamond jewelry—family jewelry. How much is $106,000 worth in pesos, Anton?"

After a moment, von Gradny-Sawz said, "With the peso at about four to the dollar, a bit more than 400,000 pesos."

I have just confessed my guilt!

What the hell is going on here?

"And how far do you think that will take you when you try to find a new life here? You'll have to buy an apartment or a house, and buy groceries, in addition to what it's going to cost you to grease the necessary Argentine palms."

Von Gradny-Sawz did not reply.

"I'm sure you read Reichsführer-SS Himmler's letter to Ambassador von Lutzenberger; the envelope was not sealed," von Deitzberg went on. "The last paragraph of which is significant: The Führer has told the Reichsführer-SS to have me deal with destroying the aircraft of the OSS airline. You saw that?"

Von Gradny-Sawz nodded but did not speak.

"In the last several weeks, for example, the Soviet army has recaptured both Smolensk and Kharkov. Not to mention what's happened in Italy. The Führer doesn't like to think about those defeats. He turns his attention to something like these airplanes in Argentina. If he issues an order—'Have von Deitzberg deal with this'—he really believes it will be obeyed. His orders to his generals to not yield a meter to the Red Army or the English and Americans don't seem to get obeyed.

"My problem, Anton, is that I don't have any idea how to destroy those airplanes. I don't think Herr Frade is going to leave them sitting unprotected on a field somewhere where my SS people here can sneak up to them in the dead of night and attach a bomb. I don't even have a bomb, and my SS people here—I'm speaking of Cranz and Raschner—are bungling incompetents. They can't find the spies in the embassy. They can't even carry out the assassination of Herr Frade.

"Now, I will of course do my best to carry out the Führer's orders. But I'm a realist, Anton. I don't think I'll be successful. I will get rid of Herr Frade, and I will ensure that Operation Phoenix is running smoothly and I may even be able to find the spies or traitors in the embassy.

"But the Führer will not be impressed with this. All he will know is that the OSS airline is still flying back and forth across the Atlantic. And he will think that SS-Brigadeführer Ritter Manfred von Deitzberg is no better than the other *gottverdammt* aristocrats with which he is surrounded. He refuses to obey his Führer's orders."

Von Gradny-Sawz found his voice: "I can see the problem, Herr Brigadeführer."

"Call me Manfred, Anton. We are of the same class, after all. And let's talk about that, about our noble background that the Führer finds so offensive. Your lands will disappear as down a flushing toilet when the Russians get to Hungary. The von Deitzberg estates disappeared in the depression following the Versailles Convention. I could not follow my noble ancestors in a military career because there was simply no money. I quite literally went hungry when I was a junior officer in the army. I transferred to the SS because I believed—and I was proven right—that I could rapidly advance in rank because my competition would be inept fools like Cranz and Raschner.

"And now even that seems at the edge of being lost," von Deitzberg said almost sadly. "I've given this a great deal of thought, Anton. One thing I asked myself is why, despite all the upheavals of history, there is still nobility, people such as ourselves. Have you ever considered that, Anton?"

"I can't truthfully say I have, Herr . . . Manfred."

"Because we have, over the centuries, adapted to changing circumstances. You've done that yourself, Anton. You were wise enough to see the Anschluss coming, and to make sure you weren't tossed into the gutter when that happened. Wouldn't you agree?"

"That's true," von Gradny-Sawz said.

"As far as I am concerned, Anton, loyalty does not mean one has to commit suicide."

"I think that's true," von Gradny-Sawz said solemnly. "There is a point at which—"

"Precisely!" von Deitzberg interrupted. "And we—you and I—have reached that point."

"I'm not sure I understand."

"We will, as our code of honor requires, do our duty to Germany to the best of our ability just as long as we possibly can. But then . . ."

"Then what?"

"How could we continue to serve Germany if we were returned to the Fatherland as prisoners, Anton?" von Deitzberg asked reasonably. "In chains? Destined for a Russian slave labor camp?"

"I take your point, Manfred."

"If . . . if everything goes wrong, and at the last possible moment we started to look out for ourselves, how would that violate our code of honor?"

"I can't see where it would."

"And what would be wrong with you and me doing what our leaders are doing with Operation Phoenix: setting up a place where we can live in safety until things settle down?"

"Nothing," von Gradny-Sawz said firmly.

"We might even be able to—almost certainly we *would be able to*—provide sanctuary for others who were not able to plan ahead. Widows, for example."

"I can see where that would be entirely possible."

"Now, Anton, if we were to do this, we would have to do it in absolute secrecy."

"Yes, of course."

"Cranz and Raschner must never even suspect."

"I understand."

"It happens that I have access to some funds in Uruguay. Enough funds to finance this."

"Really?"

"If I were to get these funds to you, would you know how to set this up?"

"Oh, yes. Frankly, I've been thinking along these lines myself. I have even taken some preliminary steps. There is a delightful area here, in the footsteps of the Andes, around a charming little town, San Carlos de Bariloche, where I am sure we could, with absolute discretion, acquire just the property we would need. It's very much like Bavaria. Should it come to this, of course."

"Well, I think we have to consider that possibility as being very real."

"Yes, I think we do."

"Then the thing for me to do is get to Uruguay as soon as possible. I presume that von Wachtstein still has that Fieseler Storch?"

"May I make a suggestion, Manfred?"

"Certainly."

"Why don't you fly to Montevideo?"

"I was thinking of having von Wachtstein fly me there in the Storch."

"I meant take South American Airways. They have two flights in each direction every day."

"That would mean passing through both Argentine and Uruguayan customs and immigration, would it not? Are these documents you arranged for . . ."

Von Gradny-Sawz nodded and said more than a little smugly, "Jorge Schenck and his wife—they were childless—were killed in an auto crash in 1938. The people I dealt with have removed the reports of their demise from the appropriate registers. That way, the original number of his Document of National Identity became available. Your documents, Señor Schenck, can stand up under any kind of scrutiny."

"You are an amazing man, Anton."

"What I was going to suggest, Manfred, was that you take the SAA flight this afternoon—it leaves at four and takes less than an hour—then spend the night. And when Cranz comes here—and he should be here any minute—you have him order von Wachtstein to fly to Montevideo tomorrow."

"Why should I do that?"

"Because he enjoys diplomatic privilege," von Gradny-Sawz said. "No authority—Argentine or Uruguayan—can ask to see what's inside a package he might be carrying. As either authority might—probably would—demand of Señor Schenck."

"Allow me to repeat, you are an amazing man, Anton," von Deitzberg said, and put out his hand. "I think our collaboration is going to be a success. Not to mention, mutually profitable."

XII

"Ladies and gentlemen," Capitán Frade announced over the passenger-cabin speakers, "this is your captain. Welcome to Buenos Aires. The local time is five p.m. and, as you can see, it's raining."

"*Ciudad de Rosario,*" the tower operator's voice came over his headset. "Follow the Follow-Me to the terminal. Be advised there is a band on horseback on the tarmac."

"There's a *what*?" Frade asked.

There was no reply from the tower. But when he turned *Ciudad de Rosario* onto the taxiway, there it was—a forty-trooper-strong, horse-mounted military band in dress uniforms getting soaked in the rain.

Frade turned to Capitán Manuel Ramos beside him and said, "Don't let those horses get in the prop wash. It'll be a Chinese fire drill."

Capitán Frade's copilot had no idea what a Chinese fire drill was, but he, too, had been thinking about the effect that the blast of air from the Constellation's four engines was going to have on the band's horses.

"Engineer, shut down Three and Four," Frade ordered.

"Shutting down Three and Four," the engineer replied. "What's going on?"

The *Ciudad de Rosario* taxied toward the tarmac. The horses didn't like the airplane, the noise it made, or the prop wash that had made its way around the Constellation from its left engines and was blowing the water from the rain-soaked tarmac at them. The tuba player and one of the kettle drummers lost their instruments when their mounts became unruly.

"Ah, ha!" Clete said. "Mystery explained. El Presidente is under one of those umbrellas."

Twenty or more people were under a sea of umbrellas in front of the passenger terminal.

"And so is the Papal Nuncio," Ramos replied.

"I'm going to stop it right here, Manuel," Clete said. "We don't want to drown the president."

"Especially not now," Ramos said.

"Why 'especially not now'?"

"Cletus, El Presidente didn't come out here with the band of the Second Cavalry to welcome us home. He came out to rub Brazil's nose in SAA's mud. We now have a transoceanic airline, and the Brazilians don't."

"If I knew you were so smart, Manuel, I would have let you land."

"If you had let me land, it would've been because you know I am a Número Uno pilot," Ramos said. He demonstrated Número Uno by holding up his left fist, balled, with the index finger extended.

Frade laughed.

"How about getting some ground power out here?" he said into his microphone.

A moment later, Clete saw the ground power generator being pushed toward them. And he could see something else in the sea of umbrellas that made his heart jump. Retired Sargento Rodolfo Gómez of the Húsares de Pueyrredón was holding an umbrella over the mother of Clete's unborn child. Over only her. Rodolfo was getting soaked.

There is nothing in this world that I would rather do this instant than run down the aisle, open the door, and—the moment the stairway appears—run down it to Dorotea and wrap my arms around her.

But I can't do that.

"Tell you what, Manuel: While I shut it down, you go back in the cabin and pick some unlucky soul to get off first and deal with El Presidente."

"Cletus, that's your honor," Ramos said. "This would not have happened without you."

"That wasn't a suggestion. That's what they call an order," Frade said.

"I will be embarrassed. I was not the pilot in command."

That embarrassment will last until El Presidente pumps your hand.

"Well, I won't tell anyone if you don't," Frade said. "Do it, Manuel, please, as a favor to me."

"If you insist."

And when your picture appears on the front page of La Nación, *I will have one more good guy in my corner.*

And if your picture is in the newspapers, the picture of Don Cletus Frade, master aviator and OSS agent, won't be.

"We have auxiliary power," the engineer reported.

"Shut down One and Two," Clete ordered. "Go, Manuel! Don't keep El Presidente waiting."

When Clete finally came out of the cockpit, he saw that someone else already had decided who was going to deplane first. The nuns and orphans were standing at the door.

Why did the steward do that?

He then saw the Jesuit priest bringing up the rear of that line, after the nuns, orphans, members of the Order of Saint Francis, and the other Jesuits.

Why? Because Father Welner "suggested" that to him.

What is that wily Jesuit up to?

Clete looked out a window.

Manuel Ramos and the older pilot whose name Clete could not remember were shaking hands with El Presidente and party, everybody under umbrellas.

Where the hell did all those umbrellas come from?

And the people holding them?

The band was playing. Trumpets and flutes only, plus a xylophone.

I guess the rain fucked up the drums.

El Presidente and one other man—a short, pudgy, middle-aged fellow wearing clerical vestments, a wide-brimmed hat, a huge gold cross, and a purple waistband—*Christ, that must be the Papal Nuncio! What the hell is he up to?*—plus umbrella holders—*God, there must be twenty of them. Where the hell did they all come from?*—walked toward the stairway.

Two of the nuns started down the stairway, followed by two orphans. Then two more nuns, followed by four older orphans.

When they got to the tarmac, now shielded by umbrellas, the nuns curtsied before the Papal Nuncio and kissed his ring. The Papal Nuncio made what Clete thought was a gesture of blessing, then patted the orphans on the head.

Then El Presidente patted the orphans on the head.

Flashbulbs from at least fifteen photographers lit the scene.

The umbrella holders then led the nuns and the orphans toward two buses that Clete hadn't noticed before. The buses were parked beside a Mercedes limousine bearing diplomatic license plates.

The number on the plate—0001—caught Clete's eye.

Who the hell gets plate Number One? God?

Close, Cletus.

The Papal Nuncio gets diplomatic license plate Number One, that's who!

Now members of the Order of Saint Francis went through the ritual. They all kissed the Papal Nuncio's ring, but he did not pat their heads, and El Presidente gave them nothing but a smile and a quick handshake.

And then finally the Jesuits. When they had gone through the line, the Papal Nuncio and Father Welner, each with his own umbrella holder, walked to the Mercedes limousine and got in.

Clete turned and went into the galley, which was between the cockpit and the passenger compartment. He quickly found a bottle of brandy and a snifter. He half filled the glass, then took it and the bottle to one of the first seats, sat down, and took a healthy swallow.

A sudden memory filled his mind.

"This is a long goddamn way from our puddle jumper, isn't it, Uncle Jim?" he said softly but aloud, his eyes filling with tears and his voice on the edge of breaking. "Here I am having a little snort after flying this great big beautiful sonofabitch across the Atlantic!" He raised the glass, said, "Mud in your eye!" and drained it.

James Fitzhugh Howell, Clete's uncle, who had raised him and was really the only father he had known as a child and young man, had taught Clete to fly in a Piper Cub when he was thirteen.

He poured more cognac and estimated it would be another three or four minutes before he could leave the *Ciudad de Rosario* and go down the stairway and put his arms around Dorotea and feel her warmth and smell her hair.

Three minutes later, a familiar voice pleaded: "Please don't say it, Cletus."

"But they *will*," Clete said. "If we keep meeting this way on my airplane, people *will* talk."

El Coronel Alejandro Bernardo Martín of the Bureau of Internal Security slipped into the seat beside him.

Clete raised his glass in salute.

"How much of that have you had?" Martín asked.

"A lot. I try never to fly sober."

"We have to talk," Martín said, shaking his head.

"Not now, please, Alejandro. You may not believe this, but I have just flown this great big airplane back and forth across the Atlantic. I have earned this." He raised the glass again. "Care to join me?"

Martín said: "SS-Brigadeführer Manfred von Deitzberg has just flown across the River Plate to Montevideo. In one of your airplanes."

Clete looked at him, both eyebrows raised in surprise.

Martín went on: "Carrying the passport of an ethnic German Argentine—Jorge Schenck—who died in a car crash in 1938."

"I wondered why that sonofabitch came back," Clete said, "and what he wants."

"Well," Martín said, "Adolf Hitler himself has ordered the destruction of your airplanes—the big ones—as well as your elimination. And the elimination of the Froggers. And while von Deitzberg is here, to make sure Operation Phoenix is running smoothly. There's almost certainly more."

"Where are you getting all this?" Clete asked, adding incredulously, *"Adolf Hitler?"*

Martín nodded. Then he asked: "Where are you going from here?"

"First, to Estancia San Pedro y San Pablo, and then, first thing in the morning, to Mendoza. My Lodestar's at the estancia."

"You couldn't spend the night here? Either at your place on Libertador or the big house on Coronel Díaz? There's some people I want you to talk to."

"So far as the house on Coronel Díaz is concerned, the last time that Enrico and I went there"—he nodded toward Rodríguez, who was sitting across the aisle feeding brass-cased shells into his Remington Model 11 riot shotgun—"you might recall that 'members of the criminal element' tried to kill us. Dorotea's here . . ."

"I saw her. With Sargento Gómez and what looks like four of his friends standing with her."

". . . and I don't want some bastard taking a shot at her. And, so far as the house on Libertador is concerned, I'm not sure they've had time to finish fumigating."

"Fumigating? Rats?"

"In a manner of speaking. After my Tío Juan moved out, I had the whole house painted and fumigated."

"That was necessary?"

"I thought so."

The house on Libertador had been built by Clete's late granduncle, Guillermo Jorge Frade, who had the reputation of being very fond of both women and horse racing, not necessarily in that order. The master bedroom, which took up most of the third floor of his mansion, offered a place in which he could entertain his lady guests and watch the races in the Hipódromo across the street, either separately or simultaneously.

When Clete had first come to Argentina and made his peace with his father, his father had turned the mansion over to him. Clete had been in Guillermo Jorge Frade's enormous bed when the first assassination attempt had been made. The assassins came there after slitting the throat of the housekeeper, la Señora Mariana Maria Dolores Rodríguez de Pellano, Enrico's sister, in the kitchen.

And three days later, having learned of the attempted assassination, la Señorita Dorotea Mallín, whom Clete had thought of as "The Virgin Princess," had stormed into the bedroom, angrily berating Cletus for not having called her. In the discussion that followed, la Señorita Mallín had not only lost her virginity but become with child.

The memory of that had caused Clete's stomach to almost literally turn when his mind filled with images of Juan Domingo Perón and his thirteen-year-old paramour in the same bed. He wasn't sure that a coat of paint and a thorough fumigation would correct the situation, but it couldn't hurt.

"Your Tío Juan is one of the things we have to talk about," Martín said. "This is important, Cletus."

"You're asking," Clete said thoughtfully. "Usually, it's 'come with me or get tossed into the back of a BIS car in handcuffs.'"

"I'm asking," Martín said.

After a moment, Clete said, "Okay. I'll send Enrico to put Dorotea in the Horch. It's in the hangar. Then, just as soon as that crowd thins out, we'll drive to the house on Libertador. Under the capable protection of the stalwart men of the Bureau of Internal Security."

"Thank you," Martín said sincerely. And then he chuckled. "I was just thinking, honestly, that 'with Don Cletus's private army out there, it should be completely safe.' How many of your men are out there, anyway?"

"*Mi coronel,* I told Gómez to bring at least thirty," Enrico Rodríguez answered for him. "And I told him that if anything happened to Doña Dorotea or Don Cletus, I would kill him."

He pushed the bolt-release button on the side of the Remington Model 11. With a loud metallic chunk, it fed a brass-cased round of double-ought buckshot into the chamber.

Then Enrico stood up and walked down the aisle of the passenger compartment to the door.

[TWO]
Suite 308
Hotel Casino de Carrasco
Montevideo, Uruguay
1745 1 October 1943

SS-Brigadeführer Manfred von Deitzberg was a little surprised that everything so far had gone as smoothly as von Gradny-Sawz had said it would. Neither the immigration officers in Buenos Aires nor those here had questioned his Jorge Schenck passport.

Halfway across the River Plate, it occurred to von Deitzberg that the South American Airways Lockheed Lodestar was far more comfortable than the last transport aircraft he had flown in—the Heinkel, which had taken him from Berlin to the submarine pens at Saint-Nazaire.

That had triggered several thoughts, the first that he didn't care what he had to do to avoid it, he was not going to return to Germany aboard a *gottverdammt* U-boat. That had been immediately followed by the realization that he probably would not be returning to Germany by any means.

The conversation he had had with von Gradny-Sawz had brought that out in the open. Von Deitzberg had known it all along, of course, but even privately thinking that the war was lost had, until now, seemed treasonous.

How can the truth be treasonous?

Von Paulus had lost 100,000 men defending Stalingrad and had taken the 70,000 still alive into Russian captivity when he finally had to surrender.

Doenitz has had to call off the submarine interdiction of the supply convoys from the United States and South America because of his losses.

Africa has been lost. And Sicily has been lost.

The English and the Americans are in half of Italy, and when they have captured the rest of it, they would start planning the cross-Channel invasion of France, from England. Which would succeed.

How is facing facts with a military professional's eye treasonous?

I will, of course, continue to honorably perform my duty as a German officer as long as that is possible.

But my duty is not to throw my life away by throwing myself under the tracks of a Russian tank rolling down the Unter der Linden—as they will sooner or later.

Rather, my duty is to carry out my orders to establish a sanctuary here in South America from which the leaders of National Socialism can rise, indeed, phoenix-like from the ashes.

I am not *being treasonous; I am being* professionally realistic.

A taxi took von Deitzberg from the airport to the Hotel Casino de Carrasco on the shore of the River Plate. He was shown to a comfortable small suite on the third floor, from which he could see the beach.

On the SAA Lodestar, he had planned his first move. He would call von Tresmarck's home. If he was home, he would tell him first that no one was to know he was in Uruguay, and then to come to the casino hotel and to his suite. If he wasn't home, he would tell Inge—calling her "Frau von Tresmarck"; he was here on duty—to call her husband at the embassy, and tell him the same thing.

She will learn I'm here, and certainly hasn't forgotten what happened the last time I was. She will wonder if it's going to happen again. But since I didn't greet her charmingly, she will wonder if "Frau von Tresmarck" is in some kind of trouble. There is a certain appeal in making Inge a bit uneasy.

That plan fell apart from the start. There was no listing in the telephone book for the von Tresmarck residence. He knew it was in the neighborhood of Carrasco. He'd been there, but he wasn't sure exactly where it was, and he didn't want to get in a taxi and ride up and down streets looking for it.

There was nothing to do but call the German Embassy. The possibility existed that either the Uruguayan authorities or the *gottverdammt* OSS—or both—had tapped the embassy lines. But after thinking it over, von Deitzberg realized he had no choice.

A female answered the telephone.

"Señor von Tresmarck, please," von Deitzberg asked in Spanish.

"I'm sorry. El Señor von Tresmarck is not available."

"Perhaps he's at home. Could you give me that number, please?"

"I'm sorry, sir. I couldn't do that."

He switched to German: "Herr von Tresmarck is an old friend."

So did she: "I'm sorry, Mein Herr, I can't give out home numbers of embassy officers."

"Connect me with Herr Forster, please."

Von Deitzberg didn't want to talk to Forster either, but again realized he had no choice.

Konrad Forster, who was diplomatically accredited to the Republic of

Uruguay as the commercial attaché of the embassy, was actually Hauptsturm-führer Forster of the Geheime Staatspolizei of the Sicherheitsdienst. His mission was to report on the activities of Ambassador Joachim Schulker and of course on Sturmbannführer Werner von Tresmarck, who was officially the embassy security officer. Reports on the latter went directly to the office of the Reichsführer-SS, which normally meant to the desk of First Deputy Adjutant von Deitzberg.

But I'm not there. And if Forster reports that I'm in Montevideo and it comes to the attention of Himmler—as it almost certainly will—the Reichsführer will wonder what I'm doing here when I'm supposed to be blowing up airplanes in Buenos Aires at the specific order of Der Führer.

"Forster speaking."

"Konrad, this is Manfred," von Deitzberg said in German.

"Who?"

"The last time we saw one another was when you were being interviewed for your present assignment."

"Excuse me?"

"Listen to what I just said, and think, you *Trottel*!" von Deitzberg snapped. After a long moment, Forster said, "Herr Brig—"

"Do not use my name!" von Deitzberg interrupted.

"Yes, sir."

"I'm in town unexpectedly, and I don't want anyone to know. Understood?"

"Yes, sir."

"Get in your car and drive to the Carrasco casino—"

"Right now?"

"No, a week from Thursday! You are trying my patience, Forster."

"Yes, sir."

"Drive your car—drive yourself in your personal car—into the basement garage. Come up to the lobby. I will be there reading a newspaper. Do not recognize me. Once you have seen that I have seen you, go back to the garage. Understood?"

"Yes, sir."

Von Deitzberg hung up.

Forster came into the lobby of the casino twenty-five minutes later.

He was a slight man in his early thirties who wore his black hair slicked down and just long enough to part. He wore wire-framed glasses, the lenses of which were round. The result was that he looked very much like Heinrich Himmler.

Forster did as he was ordered. He looked around the lobby, saw von Deitzberg, and then when he was sure von Deitzberg had seen him, turned and walked back to the elevator.

Von Deitzberg waited several minutes, then took the stairway to the basement garage. Forster was nowhere in sight, but a minute later the headlights of a small Opel sedan flashed. Von Deitzberg walked to the car and got in.

"You took long enough to get here, Forster," von Deitzberg greeted him.

"Herr Brigadeführer—"

"Do not use my name or rank," von Deitzberg interrupted him.

"—I had to go to my home to get my personal car, sir."

"I am here on a confidential mission for Reichsführer-SS Himmler," von Deitzberg said. "I am using the name and identity credentials of an ethnic Argentine named Jorge Schenck. I will use that name if I ever have to contact you again. You will tell no one I am here."

"Yes, sir."

"Now, where is von Tresmarck?"

"In Paraguay, sir."

Von Deitzberg thought: *What the hell is that degenerate sonofabitch up to?*

Then he said: "What's he doing in Paraguay?"

"It was in my report to the Reichsführer-SS, sir. Von Tresmarck said he was on a mission for you."

"I didn't see your report," von Deitzberg said. "I was on another mission for the Reichsführer-SS."

Actually, I was on a gottverdammt *submarine.*

"Actually, Konrad"—*This should impress you, you jackass*—"this mission is of such importance and the necessity for secrecy is such that I was transported to Argentina by U-boat. Obviously, I was unable to get your reports while aboard the submarine."

"I understand, Herr Br . . . *Schenck,* you said?"

"Schenck, Jorge Schenck," von Deitzberg furnished. "Don't forget that again!"

He let that sink in, then asked, "Von Tresmarck told you nothing more specific than he was on a mission for me?"

"That was all he told me, sir."

"Good," von Deitzberg said. "Sometimes he talks too much. The question then becomes: 'Which Paraguayan mission is he working on?' Did he travel alone?"

No, of course he didn't. And he and that goddamned whore I had marry him aren't anywhere near Paraguay. They, and God alone knows how much of the confidential special fund's assets, are in Brazil or Bolivia.

"Yes, sir."

"Then Frau von Tresmarck is here?"

"Yes, sir, as far as I know."

"As far as you know? She either is or she is not. Which is it?"

"I saw Frau von Tresmarck yesterday, sir. Sturmbannführer von Tresmarck went to Paraguay twelve days ago, sir."

Inge didn't go?

Then what's he up to in Paraguay?

A little vacation with a homosexual lover?

"I'm sure she will be able to shed some light on the situation," von Deitzberg said. "What I want you to do now, Forster, is go to her home. Tell her I am here, impress upon her the need for secrecy, and then tell her to drive here to the casino garage, park her car, and then go to suite 308."

"May I suggest, Herr Schenck, that perhaps there would be more security if I drove you to the von Tresmarck home?"

"I considered that, of course. One of the problems is that I would have to return here eventually. That would mean either you or Frau von Tresmarck would have to drive me, and we might be seen together. This way . . ."

"Of course. I should have considered that."

"Yes, Forster, you should have. Now get going."

"Jawohl, Herr Schenck."

[THREE]

The knock came at the door of suite 308 forty-five minutes later.

"Finally!" von Deitzberg snapped.

He had spent the last fifteen minutes—he had estimated that it should take Inge no longer than thirty minutes from the time Forster had left the casino to get there from her home; wherever it was, it wasn't far—considering the very real possibility that she wasn't going to come at all. That as soon as she got her orders from Forster and he left, she had departed for parts unknown with whatever confidential special fund cash von Tresmarck had left behind when he went to Paraguay—if he actually had gone to Paraguay. And considering his options if that indeed proved to be the case.

He was obviously going to have to find the both of them, recover as much—if anything—as he could of the money they had stolen, and then eliminate the both of them.

And he had no idea how to do either. And no one to help him to do it.

That had caused him to first think that Anton von Gradny-Sawz would be absolutely useless in tracking them down, and then that the money he had promised Der Grosse Weinerwurst to buy them refuge wasn't going to be available.

And he had of course thought of Inge.

Put those thoughts from your mind.

What you have to do now is think about staying alive.

He walked quickly to the door and pulled it open.

"Guten abend," Inge von Tresmarck said.

She was wearing a skirt and a simple white cotton blouse through which he could see her brassiere.

She's better-looking than I remembered.

He took a step backward and coldly motioned her into the room. Then he pointed to a small couch.

She walked to it, sat down, crossed her legs, and looked at him.

"What is your husband doing in Paraguay?" he demanded.

"I didn't have any idea you were here, or were even coming," she said.

"Answer the question, Frau von Tresmarck."

She didn't immediately reply.

She's making up her mind what to say.

He walked to her and slapped her face.

"Answer my question!"

She put her hand on her cheek and looked at him with terror in her eyes and took a deep breath.

"I have no choice but to put my life in your hands," she said softly and more than a little dramatically.

She rehearsed that line! Gottverdammt *Hure thinks she can play me the way she played those fools in the Hotel Am Zoo!*

He slapped her again, this time in genuine anger.

"Your life has been in my hands since I sent you over here," he said. "What is he doing in Paraguay?"

"May I try to explain?" she said. "Please."

He glowered at her, then nodded.

"Make it quick," he said coldly.

"Herr Brigadeführer," she said, looking up at him, "I know about the confidential special fund."

What the hell does she mean by that? Of course she knows about that.

But, my God, she's not supposed to know anything about it! I made it very clear to that degenerate husband of hers that he was to tell her nothing about it; that if I ever learned she knew anything about it, he wouldn't live long enough to be transported to Sachsenhausen.

"You know about what?" he asked icily.

"The confidential special fund."

"Your husband told you something about—what did you say?—a 'confidential fund'?"

"He didn't tell me. I found out."

"You found out what?"

Why is she looking at my stomach?

My God, I have an erection! That's what she's looking at!

"Everything," she said. "I knew he was doing more than his work for Operation Phoenix, and I wanted to know what."

"And?"

"And I found out. Everything."

He didn't reply immediately.

"That happens to me, too," she said softly.

"What?"

"When you slap me, it excites me, too."

She raised her hand and ran the tips of her fingers along his penis.

"Tell me," she said in an excited whisper.

"Tell you what?"

"Order me," Inge said huskily. *"Order me* to take it in my mouth."

When he had recovered his breath, von Deitzberg turned his head and looked at Inge. Her blouse was open and her brassiere had been pushed off her breasts. Her skirt had been raised over her hips.

God alone knows what happened to her underpants!

And then he remembered tearing them off.

He looked down and saw that his underpants and his trousers were around his ankles. He was still wearing his shoes.

He felt an urge to giggle.

"I have an idea," he said. "Why don't we take our clothes off the next time?"

She chuckled and smiled at him, and raised her hand to touch his cheek.

"Fine with me," she said.

"I heard Werner talking with Ramón—"

"Ramón being his lover?" von Deitzberg interrupted.

She nodded.

They were still in the bed. But the bedcovers had been taken off and von Deitzberg was naked under the sheet. Inge was sitting on the bed with her back propped against the headboard.

When Inge had gone to the bathroom, he had stripped, then hung his trousers and shirt neatly over a chair. Inge was wearing the terry-cloth robe she had found in the bathroom. It hung loosely on her and he could see her breasts.

"Who is this man?" von Deitzberg asked.

"A Uruguayan, of course. He's thirty-something. Not bad-looking. Doesn't look like a poufter."

"A what?"

"That's what they call queers here. It's English, I think. They use a lot of English words here."

"What does he do?"

"He owns a restaurant. Actually, several restaurants and a poufter bar."

" 'A poufter bar'?" he parroted, and chuckled.

"A *poufter bar*," she repeated, smiling. "That's where Werner met him."

"Would you say that Werner has told his *poufter* friend about the confidential special fund?"

She smiled and nodded.

"I'm sure he has."

Then both poufters have to be eliminated.

"How did you get to eavesdrop on their conversation?"

"Conversations, plural. A lot of them. I had to protect myself; Werner would throw me to the wolves and take pleasure watching them eat me."

"And how did you do this?"

"The first time, it was by accident. I'd told Werner I was going to Punta del Este—"

"Where?"

"It's a beachside resort about a hundred kilometers from here. I go there sometimes to lie on the beach."

And possibly to find someone who can give you what you're not getting from your poufter?

"Go on."

"And I had trouble with my car and couldn't go. I had to put the car in the garage. I was in my bedroom when I saw Werner drive up with Ramón. I suspected they came here when they thought I was gone."

"Not to Ramón's house? Apartment?"

"Ramón is married," she said.

"A married poufter?"

"He and Werner have that in common," Inge said. "Anyway, I was curious. I hid in my closet. Werner didn't see my car, but he looked into my bedroom. . . ."

"You have separate bedrooms?"

She nodded. "And when I wasn't there, they went to his. I could hear everything that went on in his bedroom. That was interesting. Werner is the woman. I thought it would be the other way. And when Ramón went home to his loving wife, I walked over here to the Casino and took a room. He didn't suspect a thing.

"Sometimes they didn't even—you know, do it. But they talked about what they should do with Werner's money—the money the Jews gave him; the confidential fund—and I found that fascinating. And then I started looking in his safe. I knew where he kept the combination; he could never remember it. All the details and property deeds—and of course the money waiting to be invested—were in there."

"So what are the poufters doing in Paraguay?"

"Werner is worried about you. He thinks you have concluded he knows too much and are going to order him back to Germany and send him to Sachsenhausen."

"I couldn't risk him running off at the mouth, either on his way to Sachsenhausen or once he was in there," von Deitzberg said.

"I thought about that too," she said matter-of-factly. "And I thought about you, that you should know, but how was I going to get in touch with you?"

"That raises several questions in my mind," von Deitzberg said. "What did you think I should know?"

"That Werner, especially after he decided the war is lost . . . Is the war lost, my darling?"

What does she think, that after we have rolled around like two dachshunden *in heat, that we are now lovers, that she can call me "my darling"?*

"Things do not look good," von Deitzberg said.

She nodded thoughtfully, then said: "Where was I? Oh, yes. Werner decided that even if you didn't order him back to Germany, the war was lost and he had to protect himself. That he had decided to take all the cash and go to Paraguay. With Ramón, of course."

Can I believe her?

Of course I can't believe her. She's a Hotel Am Zoo whore.

A very good one, to be sure, but a Hotel Am Zoo whore.

"Inge, why did you want to tell me all about this?"

"To whom else could I turn?"

"Why would you think I would help you?"

"That's what I meant when I said I have no choice but to put my life in your hands."

"Why, Inge, did you think I would give a damn?"

She exhaled audibly.

"Here goes. You knew all about me before you set me up with Werner . . ."

True. I knew everything about you except your ability to sexually arouse me as no other woman ever has. Arouse and then satsify me.

". . . so you know that not only are we from the same background . . ."

Partially true. You are upper bourgeoisie. Your family had money. My family is noble but had no money. Where is she going with this?

". . . but also are survivors. When we're knocked down, we get up again."

That's at least partially true. I didn't quit when I was nearly on the dole in the army. I put up with it, starved, until I saw an opportunity to better myself.

"Is there a point to this, Inge?"

"And then there is the other thing."

"What other thing?"

"What happened to us the first time we were alone. And again just now."

Okay, now I understand. I wonder why I didn't see it coming?

She wants to buy my protection with her body.
Well, what the hell, let her think that. What have I got to lose?
When the time comes, I can eliminate her.

"Yes," he said, and gave in to the temptation to put his hand into the opening of the terry-cloth robe.

God, she's got a great body!
Control yourself, for Christ's sake!

He withdrew his hand as she put her hand on the sheet covering him.

"You said something about money in the poufter's safe?"

"About two hundred thousand American dollars and fifty thousand English pounds."

A pound is worth four point one U.S. dollars. She's talking about another $200,000. My God!

"Why so much?"

"Well, after they decided to go to Paraguay, Werner just about stopped sending money to Germany. They're going to take it with them when they go."

Well, if he left all that money here, he's going to come back for it.

"When do you think he'll be coming back?"

"I don't really know. Probably not tonight. Maybe tomorrow. Or the next day. They're driving, and the road from the Brazilian border isn't really safe at night.

God, am I glad I asked that question!

"As much as I hate to say this, Inge, you're going to have to put your clothing back on. . . ."

"Oh, really?" she said, and made a sad face.

"And go to your house and bring everything in the safe back here. Everything."

He saw the look in her eyes.

"You're going to have to trust me, Inge," he said, and took her hand. "Before this situation gets out of control and we're both in trouble."

She considered that a moment.

"How do you know you can trust me?" she asked. "I mean, I might just drive to the house, get the money, get back in the car, and go to Brazil myself."

She met his eyes when he didn't immediately reply.

Then he said: "But, as you said a moment ago, we're survivors, and then there's that other thing."

"Manfred, you're naughty!" Inge said. And then she asked, "You are going to take care of me, aren't you?"

"Of course."

"Say it. I'm a woman. I can usually tell when a man is lying."

"I'm going to take care of you, Inge."

Just as long as you don't cause me problems.

She kept looking into his eyes.

After a long moment, she said, "I hope I'm not making a fool of myself, but I believe you."

Inge slid off the bed and started collecting her clothing. She put on her brassiere and then picked up her torn underpants.

She held them out for von Deitzberg to see.

"You're *naughty*, Manfred. Look at what you did!"

He felt a stirring at his groin as he looked at her standing there wearing nothing but the brassiere.

"Well, I'll just have to get another pair at the house," Inge said, and dropped the underpants into a wastebasket.

"Don't do it on my account," he said. "I like you better without them."

"You're naughty, naughty, naughty!"

She walked to him and kissed him rather lasciviously.

"I like it," she said.

"In the morning, Major von Wachtstein— You remember him?"

"The Luftwaffe officer who flies that little airplane?"

"The Fieseler Storch. That's him. You know him?"

"Slightly."

"In the morning, he's going to fly to the airfield here. He should arrive shortly before ten. You will meet him and give him the money. That means it will have to be made into some kind of a package. I don't want von Wachtstein to know what it is."

"He doesn't know about the confidential special fund?"

"No, and I don't want him to. But there is another man, Anton von Gradny-Sawz, in the embassy, who does."

"And what's he going to do with the money, this other man?"

"He is going to buy some property for us in Mendoza, in case the Führer is wrong about the Final Victory and we need someplace to go."

"'We' as in you and this other man, or 'we' meaning you and me?"

"We meaning you and me," von Deitzberg said.

Now that I think about it, Inge might be very useful.

She buttoned her blouse before pulling on the skirt.

She did that on purpose.

And succeeded in making my hormones rage.

I wonder how long that will last.

[FOUR]
4730 Avenida Libertador
Buenos Aires, Argentina
2015 1 October 1943

Don Cletus Frade ran his fingers across the hair of Doña Dorotea Mallín de Frade, marveling at its color and softness.

"And you said there wasn't time," he announced.

"What?" she asked somewhat sleepily, raising her head from his chest to look up at him.

"Write this down," he said. "You are fortunate to have a husband who can *always* find time for a 'Wham, Bam, Thank You, Ma'am!'"

"My God!" she said.

"Yes, my child?" he asked sonorously.

She bit his nipple.

"Jesus Christ!"

"Get up and get dressed. Your guests are downstairs."

"Let 'em wait," he said.

Dorotea rolled away from him, put her feet against his hips, and pushed him out of the bed. He barely managed to avoid being dumped on the floor, but he succeeded in landing on his feet. He looked down at her.

"Don't let this go to your head, but you're the most beautiful thing I've seen—"

"Flattery will get you everywhere."

"—in the last few hours."

She grabbed one of the pillows and threw it at him. He caught it and threw it back at her like a basketball.

Then he raised his arms and crawled across the bed on his knees.

"I never realized before how erotic a pillow fight can be," he said. "How about another quickie?"

She rolled out the other side of the bed.

"Get dressed, Cletus! I'm serious."

"How can you be serious? You're naked."

"Get dressed!"

"Party pooper," he said, and walked toward the bathroom.

When he came out several minutes later, she was back in the bed, covered by the sheet.

"You changed your mind?" he asked.

"Go, Cletus!"

"You're not coming?" he asked.

"He asked, hopefully," Dorotea said. "Relax, my darling. No, I'm not coming. This is Argentina. Women are not welcome in serious meetings between men. What I'm going to do is give you a few minutes and then go down the back stairs and eavesdrop from the pantry."

"With or without your clothes?"

"Go!"

There were nine men in the library when Clete walked in trailed by Enrico Rodríguez. One of them was Antonio LaVallé, who had been el Coronel Jorge Frade's butler and whom Clete had not expected to see; he normally reigned over the staff of the big house on Coronel Díaz.

LaVallé—following the English custom, he was called by his surname—was tending bar. Everyone in the library held a drink in his hand.

"Sorry to keep you waiting," Clete announced.

He recognized only Coronel Alejandro Martín and Capitán Roberto Lauffer, who was aide-de-camp to El Presidente, General Arturo Rawson. But one of the younger men and a tall, ruddy-faced man wearing the uniform of an infantry colonel looked familiar. He couldn't come up with names, but he remembered now that the younger man was Martín's driver.

I really don't know how to handle this.

I can hug Lauffer. We became close during the Operation Blue coup d'état.

But what about Martín? Does he want these other people—and who the hell are they?—to think we're pals?

To hell with it!

He went to Lauffer, said "Roberto," and hugged him and made kissing gestures. Then he went to Martín, said "Alejandro, we're going to have to stop meeting like this," and hugged him but did not make a kissing gesture. Then he turned to Martín's driver.

"I'm Cletus Frade," he said, offering his hand. "I know your face, but I can't come up with a name."

"Sargento Lascano, Don Cletus."

"Actually, Major Frade," Martín said, "he is Suboficial Mayor Lascano. Manuel does for me what Enrico did for your father."

"You mean he carries you home when you've been at the bottle?" Clete asked innocently.

The infantry colonel laughed.

"Major Frade has your number, old boy," he said in a crisp British accent.

Martín shook his head and went on: "It is more practical for our purposes to have him known as 'Sargento,' as it is for you to have people think you are simply Don Cletus."

Clete nodded but didn't say anything.

"Similarly, it is more convenient for el Teniente Coronel José Cortina, who is my deputy"—a stocky, middle-aged man walked up to Frade and shook his hand—"to be thought of as Suboficial Mayor Cortina."

Then the other stocky, middle-aged man in the library walked up to Frade and offered his hand.

"My name is Nervo, Major. I am a policeman."

"Actually," Martín said, "my good friend Inspector General Santiago Nervo is the chief of the Gendarmería Nacional."

Another man put out his hand. "I am Subinspector General Pedro Nolasco, Major. General Nervo's deputy."

The infantry colonel brought up the rear of the line.

"Edmundo Wattersly," he said, crushing Clete's hand. "We've met, but I rather doubt you'll remember."

"I'm sorry, sir, but I don't."

"At your wedding. And of course during your father's funeral. Your dad and I were at the academy together, and then again at the Kreigschule. He used to call me his 'conduit to Berchtesgaden.'"

What the hell does that mean?

Clete nodded, then announced, "We have about half an hour until dinner—"

"We didn't invite ourselves to dinner . . ." Martín interrupted.

"—so may I suggest we get started with whatever this is?" Clete went on.

Martín finished, ". . . but I'm sure we all appreciate your hospitality."

"Dinner will be at nine, Don Cletus," Antonio LaVallé said. "I'm afraid it will be simple."

"I'm sure it will be fine, LaVallé," Clete said. "And that will be all, thank you. We can make our own drinks."

"Cletus," Wattersly said. "You don't mind me calling you that, do you?"

"Not at all."

"If you don't mind, Cletus, may Antonio stay? I've always found that useful."

"Excuse me?" Frade said.

"Your dad and I formed the habit, when we were planning Operation Blue, of having LaVallé and Enrico around. They were our human stenographers, so to speak. Between them, they remember everything, and that way, there's no stenographer's pad left lying about, don't you know, to fall into the wrong hands."

Clete glanced at LaVallé and then at Enrico, who nodded.

"Please stay, LaVallé," Clete said, then added, "I would very much like a drink."

A moment later, LaVallé extended one to him on a small silver tray.

"Gentlemen, if I may?" Martín asked, looked around, and then turned to Frade and began: "The night el Señor von Deitzberg came ashore from U-405—on September twenty-eighth, three days ago—Nervo, Nolasco, Lauffer, and I met to discuss our options. Among the things decided—since we are agreed on what has to be done—was that we should meet regularly to share information. That first meeting was held yesterday at lunch between Lauffer and Nervo at the Círculo Militar. Lauffer and Nervo concluded that there were two additional people who should be involved, el Coronel Wattersly and yourself.

"I concurred. I got in contact with Edmundo, then I met you when you landed at Jorge Frade today. Let me be frank, Cletus. While el Coronel Wattersly fully agrees that you should be part of this, Inspector General Nervo is more than a little nervous. . . ."

"The question in my mind, Don Cletus," General Nervo said, "is where do your loyalties lie? Are you an Argentine or a Norteamericano?"

Clete met Nervo's eyes for a long moment.

What the hell. When in doubt, tell the truth!

"To tell you the truth, which you probably won't like, General, I'm both. I'm a serving officer of the United States Marine Corps—"

"And the Office of Strategic Services," Nervo interjected.

"—attached to the Office of Strategic Services. I am also legally an Argentine and the son—"

"Of an Argentine hero who was murdered by the Nazis," Wattersly said. "And someone who risked his life—for Argentina—during Operation Blue. That should satisfy you, Santiago."

Nervo grunted, gave Wattersly a dirty look, grunted again, and then said: "Don Cletus warned I probably wouldn't like his answer. I don't. But I like it a hell of a lot more than if he had said—as I expected him to—'Not to worry, I'm an Argentine. Trust me.'" He paused. "Okay. Let's get on with this."

"Let me ask you, Santiago," Martín said. "Do you—and you, Nolasco—believe what I told you of the disgusting operation in which Jews are permitted to buy their relatives freedom from German concentration camps—from German poison gas?"

Both men nodded.

"Cletus, is this man von Deitzberg in charge of that?" Martín asked. "Is that what he's doing here?"

"That's two questions. So far as I know, he's the highest-ranking SS officer involved—and it's an SS operation. I don't know if Himmler is involved. I wouldn't be surprised, but I don't know. As to what von Deitzberg's doing here, I'm sure both Operation Phoenix and the ransoming operation are involved, but there's more, I'm sure. I just don't know what."

"That brings us to Herr von Gradny-Sawz, the first secretary of the German Embassy," Martín said. "He is their liaison man with BIS in regard to the missing Froggers."

"And to the Gendarmería Nacional," Nervo said. "You have them, Major Frade, right?"

Clete didn't reply.

"More than likely in one of two places," Nervo went on. "Either on Estancia San Pedro y San Pablo or—this is my gut feeling—at Estancia Don Guillermo in Mendoza. Specifically at your house—what's it called?—Casa Montagna—in the mountains."

That wasn't a question. Not only does he know, but he was giving me the opportunity to lie about it.

"They're at Casa Montagna," Frade said.

"Good God! Another bloody complication!" Wattersly exclaimed.

"Excuse me?"

"Carry on with this, Alejandro," Wattersly said. "I'll pick this up later."

"Well, as I was saying, von Gradny-Sawz invited me to lunch a couple of weeks ago at the ABC on Lavalle. During lunch, he just about asked for asylum, and told me that they—specifically el Señor Cranz, who is the commercial attaché at their embassy and, until von Deitzberg got off the U-boat, was the senior SS man in Argentina—intended to kidnap Señora Pamela de Mallín, Cletus's mother-in-law, her son, and possibly Señor Mallín, and exchange

them for the Froggers. He said something to the effect that he was 'morally offended at the involvement of an innocent woman and her fifteen-year-old son
in this sordid business.'"

"Alejandro, I put Pedro on that," General Nervo said. "He had a talk with
one of our more prominent kidnappers who said—and Pedro believes him—
that neither he nor any of his friends had been approached, nor had he or they
heard anything about kidnapping any of the Mallín family."

"And you believe that, Comandante?" Wattersly asked.

Nolasco nodded. "The man I talked to, Coronel, depending on what the
general tells the court, is facing either five years or twenty-five behind bars.
He is motivated to be as cooperative as he possibly can. And while we're on the
subject, he volunteered the information that he's reliably heard that the assassination community is reluctant to work for our German friends, especially
when that is connected with Don Cletus. They prefer to deal with people who
don't shoot back . . . or at least don't shoot back as well as Don Cletus and
Rodríguez do."

"Carrying that further," General Nervo said. "The people I have in the
German Embassy have heard nothing about this kidnapping plot either. So
what's it all about?"

Frade thought: *So he has people in the German Embassy? Why don't I believe that?*

*Someone in his position would almost be expected to have "people" in the
German Embassy.*

*But for some gut reason, I don't believe him. For one thing, it would be the last
thing someone like him would volunteer without reason.*

Martín shrugged and held both hands up.

"You're saying there never was a plan to kidnap my mother-in-law?"
Clete asked.

"We're saying we don't know," General Nervo said. "If I were you, I
wouldn't take your people off any of them. It's always easier to keep people than
to get them back."

"Returning to Señor von Gradny-Sawz," Martín said. "Yesterday, he called to
tell me that he had just spent several days with von Deitzberg, who was in Argentina covertly and using the identity of a deceased ethnic German-Argentine
named Jorge Schenck; that von Deitzberg had told him that Hitler has personally ordered him to destroy South American Airways' new aircraft—"

"I want to hear about that," General Nervo said. "What the hell that whole
thing is all about, as well as the plans to destroy the airplanes."

"—I misspoke a moment ago. Von Gradny-Sawz said that Hitler had personally ordered *Himmler* to have von Deitzberg 'deal with the airplanes.'"

"If you take that as being true," Wattersly said. "And I find it difficult to believe that Herr Hitler even knows about South American Airways. He has a pretty full plate before him at the moment. But if that *is* the case, one must then assume that Hitler knows von Whatsisname is here. And if *that* is true, one must assume that von Whatsisname is up to something important."

"Von Deitzberg," Martín said somewhat impatiently. "SS-Brigadeführer Ritter Manfred von Deitzberg."

"Thank you," Wattersly said politely.

"Von Gradny-Sawz also said that von Deitzberg told him he is to 'eliminate' the Froggers wherever and whenever found, and do the same to Don Cletus," Martín went on. "And then he told me that von Deitzberg was going to be on this afternoon's SAA flight to Montevideo."

"He's really being helpful, isn't he?" Nervo said. "What do you make of that?"

"Generally, I have the feeling that he's trying to ingratiate himself with me so that he can find asylum here. So far as von Deitzberg flying to Montevideo is concerned, I had the feeling—feeling only, nothing to back it up—that he would not have been distressed had von Deitzberg been arrested at the border."

"Why didn't you have him arrested?" Nervo asked.

"I want to arrest him—if it comes to that—for something more than having illegally entered Argentina. Blowing up airplanes, for example. Or hiring members of our criminal community to have another go at my friend Cletus."

Nervo grunted.

Martín went on: "The thought occurred to me that once I had arrested him, what would I do with him? The president would have to be informed immediately, of course. And he would have questions. 'How did he get into Argentina?' I would then have the choice between pretending I had no idea—in other words, lie—or telling the president about U-405."

"Which would make the president then wonder both how you knew about U-405," Capitán Lauffer said, "and why you didn't arrest him on the beach at Samborombón Bay."

"And that would involve el Coronel Schmidt and his Mountain Troops," Nervo said. "And the German SS men who also came ashore, whom Schmidt took with him to San Martín de los Andes. And why didn't you arrest the lot?" He turned to Lauffer. "Tell me, Roberto, what would El Presidente do if this was laid before him? Seek the wise counsel of el General de División Manuel

Frederico Obregón, the director of the Bureau of Internal Security, to see what he made of it?"

"I'm afraid, sir, that's just what he would do," Lauffer said.

"I don't swim well with my hands tied," Nervo said. "So confiding in El Presidente doesn't seem to be an option."

"If SS-Brigadeführer Ritter Manfred von Deitzberg . . ." Wattersly began, and then stopped. "Was that right, Martín?"

"That was correct, Coronel."

". . . is the major problem, the solution seems obvious. Any suggestions, Rodríguez?"

Frade thought: *What's he talking about? What obvious solution?*

Certainly, he's not suggesting . . .

Enrico popped to his feet, came to attention, and barked, "If Don Cletus approves, *mi coronel,* the Nazi bastard will be dead before the sun sets tomorrow."

"Good chap!" Wattersly said.

"Let's see what the Nazi bastard is up to before we do that," Clete said evenly.

"But, my dear fellow, you heard what Alejandro said. What he's up to is blowing up your airplanes and then killing you and the Froggers, not necessarily in that order. I say nip the whole bloody thing in the bud."

"I'd like to see who he contacts here, people we don't know about," Frade said. Nervo grunted.

"So would I," Nervo said. "We can always kill him later."

"Well, now that that's come up," Wattersly said, "I am a bit curious to see if he tries to contact Coronel Schmidt."

"The Mountain Troops guy?" Clete said. "I thought he was Juan Domingo Perón's good buddy."

"Not exactly, Old Boy," Wattersly said. "You're really not aware of the dichotomous feelings Erich has toward your Tío Juan?"

"That's Schmidt's name, 'Erich'?"

"Erich Franz Schmidt. His mother and mine are cousins," Wattersly said. He paused and looked between Martín and Nervo. "We're getting off the track a bit here, but I think he should hear this. Agreed?"

Martín nodded. Nervo said, "I agree."

"Erich believes—he's from Bavarian Roman Catholic stock; they tend to be devout and nonquestioning—that Stalin, Communism, embodies the Antichrist, and that Hitler and the Nazis are fighting on the side of God.

"He is not a fool. Foolish, sometimes, but not a fool. He fully understands that Juan Domingo Perón's fascination with Fascism and National Socialism is based not so much on religious conviction but on what's good for Juan Domingo Perón.

"Erich is offended by Perón's morality, as manifested in his sexual tastes. He was one of the colonels who went to discuss them with him. You've heard about that, of course?"

"No," Frade said simply.

"A number of his fellow coronels went to Juan Domingo and asked him, in essence, 'Juan Domingo, what about this thirteen-year-old girl?' To which he replied, 'What's wrong with that? I'm not superstitious.'"

"Jesus Christ!" Clete said. "Is that true?"

"Unfortunately," Wattersly said. "I know because I was a member of the delegation."

"That degenerate sonofabitch!" Inspector General Nervo said bitterly.

"Now," Wattersly went on, "when furthering the interests of the Germans—protecting the landing site at Samborombón Bay, for example, or shooting up your Casa Chica in Tandil—coincides with what Perón wants, Erich will do it. He is sure God wants him to.

"But, and this is the point of this, he does not want Perón to become president—and will do whatever he thinks is necessary to see that Perón doesn't."

"That's not in the cards, is it?" Frade asked.

"Edmundo hasn't touched on this, Cletus, so I will," Inspector General Nervo said.

That's the first time he's called me by my first name.

Does that mean he's starting to like me?

Or just a slip of the tongue?

"What all of us in this room are doing is trying to prevent a civil war," Nervo said. "None of us wants what happened in Spain to happen here. Brother killed brother. A half-million people died. Her cities lie in ruins. The Communists took the national treasury to Russia to protect it—then kept it. Priests were shot in the street. Nuns raped. Need I go on?"

"No, sir. I'm aware of the horrors of the Spanish Civil War."

Nervo nodded, then went on: "The reason I looked away when your father—and of course Edmundo—were setting up Operation Blue was that I knew your father would not permit that to happen here. With him in the Casa

Rosada and Ramírez as minister of war, there would be no civil war. Nor would Argentina become involved in the war itself. At the time, I thought the war was not Argentina's business.

"Things changed, of course, when your father was assassinated. I assumed that General Ramírez would step into your father's shoes and become president. That didn't happen. Ramírez decided that as minister of war he could keep a tighter grip on things—I'm talking about the armed forces, of course—than he could from the Casa Rosada. He put General Rawson into the Casa Rosada. I now believe that was the right decision.

"What I should have seen and didn't—Martín did; Wattersly did; others did; I didn't—was that as it becomes apparent to the German leadership that they have lost the war, they are becoming increasingly desperate. Desperate is the wrong word. Irrational? Insane? *Insane.* That's the word.

"I should have seen that when they tried to assassinate you. The first time. Trying to assassinate the son of the man who was about to become president of the nation was insanity! And I certainly should have seen it when they assassinated your father. But I didn't.

"It was only when el Coronel Martín brought to me proof of Operation Phoenix and then this other unbelievable operation of ransoming Jews out of concentration camps that my eyes were really opened.

"Do they really believe the Americans are going to stand idly by while Hitler and Himmler and the rest of the Nazis—thousands of them—thumb their noses at them from their refuge in neutral Argentina?

"What the Americans would do is sail a half-dozen battleships up the River Plate and tell us to hand over the bastards. At which point proud and patriotic Argentines would set out to do battle with our pathetic little fleet of old destroyers! I don't want the Edificio Libertador taken down by sixteen-inch naval cannon.

"Unfortunately, this is life, not a movie. A bugle is not going to sound and the cavalry will not charge across the pampas to set everything right overnight.

"I would estimate that from sixty to seventy percent of the officer corps of the army think all those stories about concentration camps and the murder of hundreds of thousands of people in them are propaganda in the newspapers, which are all controlled by Jews. They believe it is only a matter of time before the godless Communists are driven back into Russia, and the American and British are driven out of Italy and North Africa by the Germans, who have secret weapons they will unleash on the forces of the Antichrist, if not tomorrow, then next week."

He stopped.

"Sorry, I got a little carried away." He passed his whisky glass to LaVallé. "May I have some more of Don Cletus's scotch, please, LaVallé?"

"You're doing fine, General," Clete said.

"Hear, hear," Wattersly said.

Nervo didn't reply. He just looked between Frade, Martín, and Wattersly as he took several deep swallows from a whisky glass that LaVallé had handed him so quickly that Clete decided LaVallé must have had it waiting.

Finally, Nervo took a last sip, signaled LaVallé for another, and went on, his voice now very calm.

"Within the officer corps of the Armada Argentina, I would estimate twenty- or twenty-five percent are German sympathizers. What that translates to mean, come the civil war, is that the navy—after the Nazis are hung, or forced to walk the plank, or simply shot—will be firmly in the hands of the pro-British forces, which means they will be able to bring the Casa Rosada, the Retiro train station, and Plaza San Martín under naval gunfire.

"At those locations, proud and patriotic soldiers—after standing the anti-Germans in the officer corps against a wall and shooting them for treason—will engage the Armada Argentina with field artillery.

"I'm not sure if you know this, Cletus, but everybody else in your library knows that this has happened before in the history of the Argentine Republic. I don't intend to let it happen again," Nervo said softly, then took another sip of his fresh drink.

"None of us do," Martín said.

"I'd say the general has summed up the situation rather well," Wattersly said.

Lauffer nodded.

"All right, Cletus," Nervo said. "Your turn. Tell us—the truth—about your airline."

Frade looked at him.

And now I'm going to have to lie.

Frade then bought a moment of thought by passing his empty glass to LaVallé.

I really don't want to lie to Nervo—to any of these people—but I certainly can't tell them that SAA has already begun to infiltrate Gehlen's men into the country.

So what to do?

"When in doubt, tell the truth" isn't going to work here.

What about "The truth, part of the truth, but nothing about Gehlen"?

LaVallé delivered a fresh drink to Clete, who took a sip, then began: "You're going to find this hard to believe, General, but here's what I know. President Roosevelt wanted to punish Juan Trippe of Pan American Airways because of Colonel Charles A. Lindbergh."

"The first man to fly across the Atlantic?" Nervo asked.

"Yes, sir. What happened is . . ."

It took five minutes—which seemed longer—for Clete to relate the story. Nervo never for a second took his eyes off Clete's while he listened.

"That's what I know, General," Clete finished.

"And you believe this story?"

"Sir, the proof is at Aeropuerto Jorge Frade: three Lockheed Constellation aircraft."

"Edmundo?" Nervo asked.

"That story is so incredible, I'm tempted to believe it," Wattersly said.

"Why was Father Welner on the first flight to Portugal?" Martín asked Frade.

"Yes," Nervo added. "Why?"

"He came to me just before we took off," Frade immediately answered. "He said that the Vatican wanted him to carry a message to the cardinal archbishop here that they didn't want to trust to their usual communications channel."

"And I'm sure that's true," Nervo said. "Jesuits don't lie. The message probably said, 'Bless you, my son, go and sin no more.' But I'd like to know why else Welner wanted to go to Portugal."

"We brought back a flock of nuns and priests and orphans," Clete said. "And the Papal Nuncio in Lisbon arranged for a block of seats on every flight and paid in advance."

"When was the last time, Alejandro, that Customs officers strip-searched a nun entering the country?" Nervo said. "Or even a Jesuit priest?"

Martín shook his head and chuckled.

"The Germans are occupying Rome," Nervo said. "Do you think the Holy Father has decided it's time to move the treasury? Or at least the larger diamonds in the vaults?"

"You're only saying that," Martín said, "because you're a Saint George's Old Boy and you've been corrupted by all those terrible things Father Kingsley-Howard told you about Holy Mother Church."

Nervo and Lauffler chuckled.

"Well, I'll tell you this, Alejandro," Nervo said. "We'll never find out why the Vatican is flying all these nuns and priests. Holy Mother Church—and especially Jesuits like Welner—has been in our business much longer than we have and is much better at it than we are."

"I daresay you're right," Wattersly said.

"You said something before, Coronel," Clete said. "Said you'd get back to it. Something involving Casa Montagna?"

"Oh, yes! I'm glad you remembered. About a week ago, my first cousin once removed Erich Franz Schmidt happened to bump into me at the Círculo Militar and told me that he had been thinking about the weapons cached at Estancia Don Guillermo. He told me he had been running some road movement exercises with his regiment and he had been thinking of sending one of them over there to see if the weapons were still there and, if so, to take possession of them. So they wouldn't fall into the wrong hands."

"Why would he tell you this?" Clete asked.

"I'm the deputy chief for operations on the General Staff," Wattersly replied. "And I might have heard one of his road movement exercises coincided with the attack on Casa Chica in Tandil."

"What did you tell him?" Nervo asked.

"I told him I was sure the weapons cache had been removed when General Rawson became president, but that I would look into it for him."

"Are they still there?" Nervo asked.

"Yes, they are," Clete said.

"And you left it at that, Edmundo?" Nervo asked.

"Except for telling him not to send troops to Estancia Don Guillermo until I got back to him. It might offend Don Cletus, and Cousin Erich knew how close Don Cletus was to El Presidente."

"Maybe you should get them out of there," Martín suggested. "God might tell Schmidt to go get them."

"They're not going anywhere," Clete said evenly. "I need them. My wife lives there."

"And the Froggers, right?" Martín asked.

"And the Froggers," Clete admitted.

"If Schmidt goes there, it would be with at least one company of Mountain Troops."

"I can hold that mountain against his entire regiment," Clete said, unimpressed.

"Which would start that civil war we've been talking about," Nervo said. "That can't be allowed to happen."

"Then you had better figure out a way to keep this guy away from Casa Montagna," Clete said.

"I can stall him for several weeks," Wattersly said. "I mean insofar as 'getting back to him' is concerned. I can't guarantee he won't act on his own."

"You better see that he doesn't, Edmundo," Nervo said.

The library door opened and Dorotea Mallín de Frade stepped into the room.

"I realize I'm interrupting all the naughty stories, but dinner is ready, gentlemen," she said.

"You could not have appeared at a better time, señora," General Nervo said. "I think we have said all that needed to be said. Right, Martín?"

Martín nodded, then looked at Wattersly, who nodded and then looked at Clete, who nodded.

"General Nervo, darling, was telling this story about the two nuns and the Gendarme—"

"I don't want to hear it," Dorotea said.

General Nervo laid his hand on Cletus's arm and motioned for him to follow Dorotea out of the library.

I don't know what the hell it is, but the touch of his hand makes me think I have just passed inspection.

XIII

[ONE]
Estancia San Pedro y San Pablo
Near Pila
Buenos Aires Province, Argentina
0945 2 October 1943

The Reverend Kurt Welner's 1940 Packard 160 convertible coupe, roof down, was parked in front of the big house when the convoy—a 1941 Ford station wagon, the Horch, and a second Ford station wagon bringing up the rear—arrived carrying Don Cletus Frade and his wife to their home.

"Oh, good!" Clete said, thickly sarcastic. "Now I can go to confession. I was getting a little worried. I haven't been to Mass in a week!"

"Cletus!" Doña Dorotea exclaimed.

"And maybe we can get Father Kurt to say Grace before I have my breakfast," Clete, unrepentant, went on.

"If you hadn't insisted on getting up in the middle of the night to come out here," Dorotea said, "you could have had your breakfast in Buenos Aires."

"It was in the hope that I would find peace in my humble home. Peace and breakfast."

"When we go inside, you behave!" Dorotea ordered.

Kurt Welner, S.J., and two other priests—both of whom Clete pegged as some kind of clerical bureaucrats—were in the sitting room when Clete and Dorotea, trailed by Enrico, walked in.

The two priests with Welner rose to their feet. Welner did not.

"Bless you, my children," Clete intoned sonorously as he raised his hand to shoulder level in a blessing gesture.

"Cletus!" Dorotea snapped furiously.

"Father," Enrico said, "Don Cletus is very, very tired. . . ."

Welner made a gesture that said *I understand*—or perhaps *I understand he's crazy.*

Dorotea went to Father Welner and kissed him, then shook the hands of the other two.

"I'm Dorotea Mallín de Frade. Welcome to Estancia San Pedro y San Pablo."

"I absolutely have to have my breakfast," Clete said. "Anyone else hungry?"

"Actually, all we've had is coffee and a biscuit," Welner said, and stood. He pointed his finger at one of the other priests and, switching to German, added, "Cletus, this is Otto Niedermeyer."

Clete now remembered seeing SS-Hauptscharführer Niedermeyer in Lisbon as he boarded the *Ciudad de Rosario.*

Niedermeyer snapped to attention and barked, *"Herr Major!"*

Clete had a sudden chilling series of thoughts:

Jesus Christ! When I so cleverly decided that I could get away with not telling Martín and Nervo about bringing these people to Argentina, I didn't think about them actually being here, and that Martín and Nervo will, as sure as Christ made little apples, find out that they are!

What the hell was I thinking?

Or not thinking?

When they find out I lied to them, there goes that "We're all in this together!"

What the hell am I going to do?

"Don't ever use my rank again!" Clete said unpleasantly in German, then asked, "And the other fellow?"

"If you don't know his name," Welner said, "then you could truthfully say you've never heard of him." He let that sink in. "He's going to arrange for National Identity booklets, et cetera."

And that's just one of the ways they'll find out they're here!

If somebody in the Interior Ministry is passing out National Identity booklets to people who shouldn't have them, Martín knows about it.

And so does Nervo.

And by now Martín's people on Estancia San Pedro y San Pablo—Good Ol' Carlos Aguirre, "my" airframe and power plant mechanic, who I know works for Martín, pops quickly to mind—are already wondering what Welner and the other two Jesuits are doing here. And does Nervo have his own people on Estancia San Pedro y San Pablo, keeping an eye on Don Cletus Frade?

You bet your ass he does!

And are they wondering the same thing?

You bet your ass they are!

"If I don't know his name, how am I going to get in touch with him if I need him?" Clete asked.

"Through me."

"I don't like that," Clete said flatly.

They locked eyes for a moment.

"Cletus," Welner said finally, "this is Father Francisco Silva. Also of the Society of Jesus."

Clete went to Silva and shook his hand.

"Make sure I have your phone number before you leave, Father," he said. "But right now let's get some breakfast."

He walked to the door to the dining room, but before he reached the door, it opened.

Elisa Gómez—Estancia San Pedro y San Pablo's chief housekeeper, a plump female in her late forties who was wearing a severe black dress and had a large wooden cross hanging around her neck—stood there.

"Don Cletus?" she said.

But Clete saw that Elisa was looking at the priests, and with great curiosity.

"We're going to need breakfast," Clete said. "A lot of it." He looked at Welner and asked, "Where are the others?"

"They should be here soon," Welner said. "They're coming in a Little Sisters of the Poor bus."

And when Aguirre and whoever Nervo has watching me see a busload of priests, nuns, and orphan children showing up here in a Little Sisters of the Poor bus, then me flying everybody off in the Lodestar, they're going to say, "How nice! Don Cletus has found religion!"

In a pig's ass they are!

On a scale of one to ten, Major Frade, you have fucked up to at least twelve!

"For a dozen people, Elisa," Clete went on.

"*Sí*, Don Cletus."

"And bring coffee and sweet rolls while we're waiting, please."

The first people to arrive—unexpectedly—were Lieutenant Oscar J. Schultz, USNR, in his gaucho clothing, and Staff Sergeant Jerry O'Sullivan of the United States Army, who was in uniform except that he was wearing neither a necktie nor any headgear. He had a Thompson submachine gun hanging from his shoulder.

Schultz took one look around the room and said, "Oops! Sorry."

Clete waved them into the dining room.

"*Padre,*" Schultz said to Welner.

"Father," O'Sullivan said.

"*Jefe,*" Welner replied. "Jerry."

Clete saw Niedermeyer looking at Schultz with interest bordering on incredulity.

"Say hello to Otto Niedermeyer," Clete said, pointing to him. "When he's not dressed up like a Jesuit priest, he's an SS sergeant major."

Schultz crossed to Niedermeyer and offered his hand.

"I never know when he's kidding," Schultz said in German.

"I kid you not," Frade said.

"And sometimes he even explains things to me," Schultz added, then glanced at Clete. "Is this one of those times?"

"In a minute," Clete said. "Had your breakfast?"

"Cup of coffee is all," Schultz said. "The Other Dorotea spent the night with her mother. The perimeter gauchos said you'd just driven onto the estancia. We thought we'd welcome you home." He looked at Niedermeyer. "Not one of those from the U-boat?"

"There was SS on the U-boat?" Frade asked.

"About a dozen of them, the best I could see," O'Sullivan said.

"Anybody see you while you were looking?" Clete asked.

O'Sullivan shook his head.

"No, sir," he said, and with a smile added, "And there was some kind of big shot. All dressed up. Complete to homburg hat and briefcase. His rubber boat struck something and sank like a rock. He got soaked."

Looking at Niedermeyer, Frade said, "That was probably SS-Brigadeführer Ritter Manfred von Deitzberg. You know who he is?"

Niedermeyer nodded, then blurted, "He's here? He came here by U-boat?"

Clete nodded.

"Which makes me wonder how he came here," Schultz said, nodding toward Niedermeyer.

"On my airplane," Clete said.

"You are going to tell us what's going on, right?" Schultz said.

Clete looked at Schultz.

Maybe, after I figure out how I'm going to explain everything to everybody.

Right now, I don't have a clue how to do that.

"I'm going to wait until everybody is here," Frade said, stalling. "I don't want to do it twice."

Someone else almost immediately appeared at the dining room door, but it wasn't whom Clete expected. It was a svelte, formidable woman in her midfifties who had gray-flecked, luxuriant black hair and wore a simple black dress with a triple strand of pearls.

Shit!

I should have realized that Claudia was likely to show up!

But why the hell couldn't she have invited herself for a late lunch? By then, I'd be out of here.

And how am I going to explain any of this to her?

He said: "Señora Claudia Carzino-Cormano! What an unexpected pleasure."

Claudia went to Dorotea and embraced her affectionately. Then she looked at Cletus: "I've got a message for you, Señor Sarcastic. Can I give it to you now?"

"Whisper it in my ear," Clete said.

"You're serious, aren't you?" she asked.

He nodded.

She went to him.

"I probably shouldn't kiss you," she said, "but I will. I missed you at the airport."

Then she kissed him and, covering her mouth with her hand, whispered in his ear.

He immediately parroted it out loud.

"'Von Wachtstein's on his way in his Storch to meet von Deitzberg at the airport in Carrasco,'" he said, then added rhetorically: "I wonder what the hell that's about? Von Deitzberg went over there on the SAA flight yesterday afternoon. You'd think he would come back that way."

"Unless," Dorotea offered, "he wanted to take advantage of Peter's diplomatic immunity and have him fly something back here he didn't want to risk carrying through customs."

"Yeah," Clete said, accepting that immediately. He gave Dorotea a thumbs-up.

She smiled and shrugged as if to say, *Well, what did you expect?*

"That's all Peter said to tell you," Claudia said, then went to the priests, kissing Welner first.

"I passed a Little Sisters of the Poor bus on the way over here," Claudia said. "That yours, Father Kurt?"

He nodded.

"It's nice to see you again, Father," she said, offering her hand to the *bona fide* Jesuit. Then she turned to Niedermeyer. "I'm afraid I don't know your name, Father."

"His name is Niedermeyer," Clete said. "He's not a priest."

"What did you say?" Claudia asked, but before Clete could respond, she looked at Welner.

"What is going on here, Father Kurt?" she demanded.

"Claudia, I think Cletus would much prefer to answer that."

She looked at Cletus.

"What I would much prefer is not to answer at all," Clete said. "But pull up a chair, Claudia, and I'll think of something."

Why the hell didn't you think of a story to tell all these people, Señor Superspy? You didn't think anybody would be curious?

Claudia sat at the table, looked at him, waited all of thirty seconds, and then asked, "Well?"

"I'm waiting for the others to arrive."

"What others?"

"They should be here any minute," Clete said.

"Why can't you tell me now?" she demanded.

Because I don't know what to say.

"They should be here any minute," Clete repeated.

"I think I just heard somebody drive up," Schultz said.

A minute later, one of the maids opened the door from the foyer.

"Sister María Isabel of the Little Sisters of the Poor asks to see you, Father," the maid announced to Welner.

Welner looked at Clete, who nodded.

"Ask the sister to come in, please," Welner said.

"There are nuns and a priest and children with her, Father," the maid said.

"The more the merrier," Clete said. "Bring them all in."

When the nun came into the room, she had with her a priest wearing a brown cassock with a rope belt, his bare feet in sandals—*That has to be SS-Obersturmbannführer Alois Strübel; I remember him from the plane*—two boys Clete decided were about ten, a girl he thought was probably a year or two younger, and three other nuns.

Two of those nuns clearly are the mothers of the children—and the wives of Strübel and Niedermeyer. But I don't have a clue as to who's who.

Sister María Isabel looks like the economy-size version of Mother Superior of the Little Sisters of Santa María del Pilar. She's a foot taller, probably sixty pounds heavier, but is also old, leathery-skinned, and has the same intelligent eyes and the same fuck with me at your peril *aura of self-confidence.*

For an important intelligence officer—especially an SS officer—Strübel is not very imposing in that monk's costume.

And what do the bona fide *nuns think is going on?*

Those kids are frightened.

Who wouldn't be?

They look like they need a bath, some new clothes, and something to eat. They look like they're starved.

"Elisa," he called loudly in Spanish. "Where the hell is breakfast?"

Clete saw the children flinch.

Nice work, Cletus—if they were scared before, now they're terrorized!

He stood up and walked to the children.

Is this smart, or am I making things even worse?

"Good morning," he said in German. "My name is Clete. I'm the head-waiter. In just a minute, we'll get you some breakfast."

They looked at him with sad eyes. No one responded.

The door to the kitchen opened. The odors of frying bacon and freshly baked sweet rolls came into the dining room. A line of maids came through the door carrying silver-dome-covered trays of food.

Thank God!

"See?" Clete said.

Now there was some interest in their eyes.

Another maid appeared, a large glass pitcher of milk in each hand.

"*Milch?*" the young girl asked softly.

"Enough for you to swim in, sweetheart," Clete said.

The young girl giggled.

Thank God again.

He put his hand on her shoulder and gently pushed her toward the table. After a moment's hesitation, the girl allowed Clete to lead her to the table. The boys started to follow.

Thank God yet again.

No. I mean it. That's not just a figure of speech.

There's no reason for these kids to have to go through what they have and still be hungry, not quite able to believe they can have all the milk they want.

Thank you, God.

He saw Welner get up from where he was sitting and walk toward them.

Jesus H. Christ . . . I've got it!

I know how to explain everything to everybody!

Where the hell did that come from?

Doesn't matter. It'll work!

The maids began uncovering the trays of food. There were fried and scrambled and soft-boiled eggs, bacon, ham, toast, rolls, two bowls jammed with butter curls, and half a dozen bowls of marmalade.

"My God," one of the nuns said softly, wonderingly. "So much food!"

That's somebody's mother.

Welner, now back at his place at the table, tapped his glass with his fork and, when he had everyone's attention, began, "Our Father: We offer our thanks for the safe conclusion of our hazardous journey, and for the bounty we are about to receive. In the name of the Father, the Son, and the Holy Ghost."

Dorotea said, "Amen."

She then looked at her husband, who finally got the message and said, "Amen."

He saw tears rolling down the cheeks of one of the nuns-who-had-to-be-somebody's-mother as she generously buttered a roll and handed it to the girl.

———

Clete had thought it over very carefully as everyone ate. He concluded that not only did he have no choice but to go with the explanation that had suddenly popped into his mind, but also that they very likely just might believe it.

"I suppose everyone is wondering what's going on," he said.

Everyone but the children looked at him.

"What I'm going to do is ask Father Welner if he will please interrupt me whenever I go wrong."

Welner's eyes were wary. But he said, "Of course."

"Do you want to burden Sister María Isabel with this, Father?" Clete asked politely.

In other words, am I supposed to trust her to keep her mouth shut?

"Well, I think Sister María Isabel should hear what you have to say," Welner said. "But if I might make a suggestion, Sister?"

She looked at him suspiciously, but nodded.

"I was thinking that it might save a good deal of time, Sister, if we sent Sister María Encarnación into Dolores to get our guests some regular clothing."

Sister María Isabel nodded.

"And perhaps Enrico could go with her, to see about clothing for the boys and men?" Welner went on.

Rodríguez looked at Clete, who nodded.

"Enough for several days, Sister," Welner said. "Just ordinary clothing, until we can get our guests settled."

"You have money, Enrico?" Clete asked.

"I'll get him some from your desk," Dorotea said. "Don't start your explanation until I get back."

Father Welner looked at Clete and explained, "This way, the sisters can return with the bus to Buenos Aires more quickly. I'm sure it's needed there."

Frade turned to Sister María Isabel. "Why don't you give Rodríguez everyone's shoe and other sizes," he said.

Dorotea was back with a thick wad of currency before Enrico had finished writing down the sizes. She handed it to him, then turned to Welner.

"Do you think we should send the children down to the stables, Father? Have the grooms put them on a horse?"

"Dorotea, I think that's a very good idea," Welner said. "Sister?"

Sister María Isabel gave him a dirty look but motioned to one of the nuns.

"Be careful with them, Sister," she ordered.

"I'll send one of the girls to go with them," Dorotea said.

"That probably would be useful, Señora," Sister María Isabel said.

Dorotea went to the kitchen door, pushed it open, and said, "Elisa, I need someone to show Sister and the children the way to the stable."

One of the maids instantly appeared.

The nun said in German, "Come with me, children," and they immediately pushed themselves away from the table and walked to where she was waiting at the door.

Not with reluctance.

But not with excitement at the prospect of getting a ride on a horse.

Rather, just because somebody is telling them to; has issued an order.

And neither mother—I still can't tell which nun/wife belongs to which priest/SS man—has raised any questions, much less objections.

All of these people—and that includes Sister María Isabel and her nuns—are used to obeying, without question, any orders they get.

[TWO]

Clete waited until Enrico had followed Sister María Encarnación out of the dining room and closed the door after them.

Well, let's see if I can get away with this.

"Actually, this is very simple," Clete began. "But for reasons you will understand, secrecy is of the utmost importance."

Sister María Isabel's face showed she was prepared to disbelieve everything Don Cletus had to say.

"The Germans have lost the war," Cletus announced. "They know it but won't admit it. We know it and have taken certain steps to make sure things go more easily for the German people when their leaders finally surrender."

"For the German people, Don Cletus, or the English and the Americans?" Sister María Isabel challenged.

So I'm wrong. This nun asks questions and expects an answer.

Clete met her eyes.

"For the German people," he said. "I think you would have to agree, Sister, without me getting into the details, that the Germans—the German leadership—are behaving quite badly."

"And the Soviets are not?" Sister María Isabel challenged.

"I am not about to defend the godless Communists, Sister," Clete said.

She looked at him and nodded.

She did not swallow that whole.

Well, I never thought I had it in me to become a really good used-car salesman.

"What Germany is going to need after the war is leaders," Clete went on. "What we are afraid of is that the Nazis realize that those we feel are the ones who should lead Germany after the war are the same people who oppose Hitler. Or whom they *suspect* oppose him. And we fear that they will be punished—executed—in the last days of the war. The very *suspicion* that someone does not fully support Hitler or Nazism—"

"Sister," Welner interrupted. "I know you've been to Rome. Did you perhaps have the chance to see the Ardeatine Caves, near Via Ardeatina?"

What the hell is this? Frade thought.

"Yes, I did," the nun said.

"To support what Don Cletus is saying, Sister, let me repeat what the Papal Nuncio to Portugal told me privately when I was in Lisbon," Welner said. "On March twenty-third, Italian partisans attacked a German formation on the Via Rasella, in the center of Rome. Thirty-three German soldiers were killed.

"When Hitler heard about this—and mind you, Sister, this is what the Papal Nuncio told me, not English or American propaganda—Hitler lost his temper and ordered that Rome—including Vatican City—be razed to the ground and that the entire population of the city be arrested and taken to Germany."

Sister María Isabel inhaled audibly.

Clete thought, *Is Welner making this up?*

Is Hitler actually that nuts?

He saw on Schultz's and O'Sullivan's faces that they were asking themselves the same thing.

No. Jesuits don't lie. They bend the truth a little, but they don't lie.

He looked at Strübel and Niedermeyer and the wives. Their faces were absolutely inscrutable.

As if they—all of them, wives, too—have trained themselves not to let their faces show anything.

"The order was actually issued," Welner went on. "The German commander in Rome—General Albert Kesselring, a Luftwaffe officer who fortunately is a devout Catholic—defied it as well as he could."

How the hell do you defy an order from Hitler "as well as you can"?

"I don't think I understand, Father," Sister María Isabel said. "'As well as he could'?"

Neither do I. Thank you, Sister María Isabel.

"What General Kesselring did was order the execution of ten Romans for each German soldier killed."

Sister María Isabel inhaled audibly again, and this time crossed herself.

"As unspeakable as that sounds, Sister, it was the lesser of two evils. Rome—the Vatican City—was not razed. The Holy Father was not arrested and taken to Germany . . ."

Would they actually have been crazy enough to do that?

Well, yeah. If Hitler was crazy enough to order Rome destroyed, why not arrest the Pope?

". . . but three hundred thirty-five innocent people, Sister," Welner went on, "were taken to the Ardeatine Cave, each shot in the back of the head, and then the mouth of the cave was dynamited."

Sister María Isabel again crossed herself and sucked in her breath.

After a moment, Welner went on: "I'm sorry to have interrupted you, Don Cletus, but I thought it was important that Sister María Isabel really understand what kind of evil people you're dealing with, and why secrecy is so important."

She nodded.

"As I was saying, Sister," Clete continued, "we decided to get these future leaders out of Germany while they're still alive. And their families. The Germans find nothing wrong with punishing—executing—entire families for what they consider the treason of a father, a brother, or a son."

I know that to be true.

And the sonsofbitches murdered my father and tried twice to kill me.

So why does it sound like a lie? Almost as unbelievable as Hitler ordering them to blow up Saint Peter's?

"And the Church is involved in helping these people, Father?" Sister María Isabel asked.

"Our guests have Vatican passports, Sister," Welner said.

She nodded.

I'm not the only liar here, you slick sonofabitch!

Sister María Isabel thinks you just told her the Vatican—maybe even the Pope—knows all about this.

Of course, you didn't lie. You just told her they have Vatican passports. That's not a lie.

But you and I know the only reason they have Vatican passports is that you— or maybe some cardinal—made some kind of a deal I haven't been told about with Allen Dulles or Colonel Graham or both to do I don't know what.

What was it General Nervo said about the Pope moving the larger diamonds from the Vatican's safe to here? "Nuns and Jesuit priests aren't often strip-searched by Customs"?

"Well," Claudia Carzino-Cormano said, "that explains those airplanes, doesn't it? I wondered what the real story was about them."

"Well, you'll understand why Cletus couldn't tell you before, Claudia," Welner said.

God, you are good!

That wasn't a lie either. It was just making a wholly decent woman believe something that's not true.

"Of course," Claudia said.

"And why this can't go any further than this room," Welner pursued.

"I understand," Claudia said. "Would you and Cletus like me to leave, Father?"

"As far as I'm concerned, Claudia, you're welcome to stay. But that decision is really Cletus's to make; he has the responsibility on his shoulders."

And again: You really are good!

What did Nervo say? "Holy Mother Church—and especially Jesuits like Welner—has been in our business much longer than we have and is much better at it than we are."

What Welner's saying indirectly is: "Since Cletus has the responsibility on his shoulders, that makes me nothing more than a simple priest trying to do God's work.

"Smuggling people out of Europe and into Argentina is handled by people with dirty hands, like Cletus.

"Who, although pretty stupid by comparison, is smart enough to know he can't ask you to leave. That would hurt you, piss you off, and he knows he can't do that."

Well, Clete, it's back to "When in doubt, tell the truth."

Frade said: "Claudia, I would have preferred not to involve you in this. But the cow seems to have gotten out of the barn. However, if you leave now, everyone in this room will forget you were ever here."

"Are you telling me to leave?" Claudia challenged, then before he had a chance to reply, went on: "Like your father, you can at times be truly stupid. Of course I'm staying. I want to help."

"Thank you, Claudia," Father Welner said.

"You didn't really think I was going to leave, did you?" Claudia asked. "You know me better than that, Father!"

Frade said: "The fewer people who know about this, Claudia, the better."

"You didn't have to tell me that," she snapped. "My God!"

"Sorry," Clete said.

"So, what happens now?" Claudia asked. "How can I help?"

"Well, as soon as Sister Whatshername and Enrico get back with the clothes, we're going to fly to Casa Montagna."

"Sister María Encarnación," Sister María Isabel corrected him icily.

Welner began: "Cletus, I'm certainly not trying to tell you what to do, or how to do it . . ."

"But?"

"Wouldn't it be better to wait until after we get your guests' papers in order?" He turned to Claudia and explained, "Father Pedro has an understanding and discreet friend in the Interior Ministry who's going to provide National Identity booklets for Cletus's guests."

"You better wait until that's done," Claudia agreed, "before you go to Mendoza."

Was that an order, Claudia? It sure sounded like one.

Claudia looked at Father Silva. "How long is that going to take, Father Pedro?"

"About twelve hours after I give my friend the photographs," the priest said. "I have a camera, but I think we should wait until we have the proper clothing."

"Clete?" Schultz asked.

He might as well have popped to attention and said, "Sir, permission to speak?"

Frade motioned for him to go on.

"What kind of photos do we need, Father?"

The priest answered by taking a National Identity booklet from his pocket and showed it to him.

"For women," the priest said, "there is the Libreta Cívica. A little smaller, but you get the idea. My friend will provide both."

"In other words, all that's holding us up is the regular clothes?" Schultz asked.

"That and the names to go on the documents," Father Welner said.

"Dorotea," Schultz said, "we can come up with clothes—good enough for ID pictures—for the men. Can you get some clothing for the women and the kids?"

"Not a problem," Dorotea said.

"You have any preference for your new names, Strübel?" Frade asked.

"I think it would be best if we used the Spanish translation of the Christian names," Strübel replied immediately. "And Strübel, if you have no objection, could become Möller, and Niedermeyer, Körtig. Similarly, I would suggest retaining the dates of birth. I am presuming we will all have been born here in Argentina."

He just didn't pull that out of thin air. He's given it some thought.

Why not? He's a professional.

One who probably is looking down his professional nose at this American amateur.

I'm going to have to stay one step ahead of this guy.

And why didn't I think of that before?

"That's fine with me," Clete said.

"And we'll need a sheet for a background, Dorotea," Schultz said.

"And when the pictures have been taken," Clete said, "I'll fly Father Pedro to Buenos Aires in one of the Piper Cubs."

"Is that necessary?" Welner asked.

"The sooner we get the identifications, the sooner I can get everybody out of here," Frade replied.

"Yes, of course," Welner agreed. "Father, if Don Cletus flies you to Buenos Aires, when do you think you could have the identity cards ready?"

"Either late tonight, Father, or first thing in the morning."

"If you can bring the identity cards and meet me at Jorge Frade at, say, nine o'clock, I'll make a, quote, fuel stop, unquote, in the Lodestar on our way to Mendoza."

The priest nodded.

"I'll be there."

It took less time than Clete thought it would—about forty-five minutes—to complete the photography. Rodríguez and the nun had not returned from their clothes-buying expedition.

When the last picture had been taken, Clete motioned for O'Sullivan and Schultz to follow him from the temporary studio in the library out into the foyer.

He closed the door, then asked, "You know how to get in touch with Colonel Martín, right?"

"I know how to get in touch with his sergeant major, a guy named José Cortina."

"Good enough. Cortina's really a lieutenant colonel," Clete said. "And he's Martín's deputy. Call him and tell him I'm on my way to Jorge Frade and need to see Martín, really need to see him. Ask him to meet me at the airport. And if at all possible, have General Nervo there, too."

"Cortina's a light colonel?" Schultz asked rhetorically. "Who's General Nervo?"

"He runs the Gendarmería Nacional."

"One of these days you are going to tell me what the hell's going on, right?"

"Just as soon as I get back from Buenos Aires."

The door from the library opened and Strübel—now Möller—came out. He was wearing a shirt and trousers Schultz had liberated from Rodríguez's wardrobe. They were much too large for him. Clothespins still in place at the back of the collar and on the rear of the suit jacket made them fit well enough for the camera.

"May I have a private word with you, Major Frade?" he asked politely.

"I already told Herr Körtig, Herr Möller, never to use my rank. Please don't do so again. And anything you have to say to me can be said before my men."

Möller considered that and nodded.

"Presumably, you have a means to communicate with either Colonel Graham or Herr Dulles?"

Clete nodded.

"I have a message that I would like to send to either, for transmission to Colonel Gehlen."

"We can arrange that," Clete said. "But Gehlen's another name I don't want used here. Any suggestions, Herr Möller?"

"I never gave that any thought," Möller confessed after a moment.

"Who's Colonel Gehlen?" Schultz asked.

"He runs Russian intelligence for the German General Staff; he's Herr Möller's boss. I'll tell you all about that, too, when I get back from Buenos Aires."

"The first Russian thing that comes to my mind is 'Samovar,'" O'Sullivan offered. "You know, that big tea kettle?"

"Too close," Clete said. "But there's nothing wrong with 'Teapot.' Make it 'Big Teapot' for Gehlen, 'Teapot' for Herr Möller."

"And the other one?" O'Sullivan asked.

"Teacup," Schultz said, smiling.

"Done," Clete said.

"Let's have your message, Herr Teapot," Clete said, smiling. "Just as soon as I get back from Buenos Aires, I'll be in touch with Washington; I'll include your message."

Möller was not amused.

He handed Clete a sheet of paper on which was written a series of charac-

ters in five-character blocks. It looked like gibberish, but Clete immediately recognized it for what it was: an encoded message.

"Three things, Herr Möller," Frade said coldly. "One, you are not going to
send any messages in code to anybody. I don't want you reporting to Big
Teapot anything that you or Teacup might hear or see here unless I know what
it is. Two, you will give El Jefe your codebook just as soon as you can. Don't
even think of trying to either hide or destroy it . . ."

"This was not my understanding of how things were to be done,"
Möller said.

"Three, if I learn that you or anyone else has tried to send a message to anyone without my knowledge, I'll have you shot."

Möller looked at him with cold eyes but didn't reply.

"Do we understand each other?" Clete asked.

Möller nodded. "But there is one thing I think you should understand, Herr
Frade: Despite the circumstances, I consider myself and Körtig to be soldiers
obeying the orders we have been given. Not traitors."

"Consider yourself anything you want to," Clete said. "Just as long as you
don't endanger in any way anything I'm doing here."

Again Möller didn't reply.

"But now you've made me curious," Clete went on. "I don't know what
Colonel Gehlen has told you about my . . . *friends* . . . in the German Embassy,
but in any event, you'll soon figure out by yourself that I have people in there.
What about them? Are they traitors, in your opinion?"

"If they swore the same oath of personal allegiance to Adolf Hitler that I
did, the answer is self-evident."

"Then we seem to be agreed to disagree; I consider them to be the opposite: patriots. The bottom line is—"

"Excuse me? 'The bottom line'?"

"*What matters,*" said Clete, "is that when you and I have a disagreement, I
win. And if you're unwilling to go along with my winning, I'll have you shot.
Now, go get the codebook for El Jefe. We'll talk some more later." He motioned
to O'Sullivan with his finger. "Go with him, Jerry. Don't let him out of your
sight. And don't hesitate to shoot him if you think that's called for."

"Yes, sir," O'Sullivan said, and motioned for Möller to go back into the
library.

When the door was closed, Schultz said thoughtfully, "You meant that
about shooting him. It wasn't a bullshit threat."

"I don't know how much . . . what name did we give him? . . . *Körtig* picked up from what was said when Claudia arrived, or how much he'll tell Möller, but we have to assume the worst. And if the choice is between Peter's life and this Nazi sonofabitch's . . ."

"There is no choice," Schultz agreed. "Well, there's one good thing."

"What?"

"That guy is smart, Clete. But he doesn't have any balls. He's not going to call your bluff."

"You don't think so?"

"It doesn't come out often like it did just now, but when it does, it's really impressive."

"What doesn't come out often?"

"With all possible respect, Major, sir, the major is a stainless-steel hard-ass. And that really got through to Möller. Hell, it even got to me; I was already wondering: *What happens to the wives and kids when Clete blows this sonofabitch away?*"

"Let's see if we can keep that from happening," Clete said. "Okay, go get Father Pedro. And then call Cortina and tell him about having Martín and Nervo at the airport."

[THREE]
Aeropuerto Coronel Jorge G. Frade
Morón, Buenos Aires Province, Argentina
1325 2 October 1943

As he landed in the Piper Cub, Cletus Frade saw that there were four Lodestars and two Constellations on the field.

He also saw that the extra security he had ordered after learning that Hitler had ordered von Deitzberg to destroy the Constellations was in place.

He was still having trouble really accepting that Adolf Hitler himself even knew about the Connies, much less had ordered their destruction, but all the clichés from "Be Prepared" to "Better Safe Than Sorry" seemed to apply.

He was not surprised that the extra protection was in place. He'd told Enrico to set it up, and that the old soldier knew all about what the military called "perimeter defense."

There were more peones than he could easily count—at least twenty—on horseback, every one of them a former trooper of the Húsares de Pueyrredón, moving slowly and warily around the field, with either a Mauser rifle or a Thompson submachine gun resting vertically on his saddle.

As he taxied past the Constellations, it seemed as unreal to consider that he had just flown the *Ciudad de Rosario* back and forth across the Atlantic as it was to consider that they personally annoyed Adolf Hitler.

He looked at his passenger to see how he had survived the flight. Father Francisco Silva's smile was nowhere near as strained as it had been when Clete had strapped him into the Piper Cub at Estancia San Pedro y San Pablo.

Then the priest had confessed a bit shyly that their flight to Buenos Aires was going to be his first flight in an airplane.

Hearing this, Clete had made a decision. Instead of flying to Aeropuerto Coronel Jorge G. Frade as he usually did—that is, direct cross-country to Morón at about three hundred feet off the ground, which afforded him the opportunity to look at his own fields and cattle and those of his neighbors—he had climbed to fifteen hundred, flown to Dolores, picked up Ruta Nacional No. 2 there, and flown up it to Buenos Aires, where he flew over the Casa Rosada and the National Cathedral, and from there to the airport outside Morón.

For some reason, he liked the young Jesuit and suspected that, whatever other satisfactions the priest found in his vocation, he didn't have much personal fun or any little luxuries. Fun and luxuries, for example, like Father Kurt Welner S.J.'s Packard convertible, bejeweled gold cuff links, luxury apartment in Recoleta, and box for the season at the Colón Opera House.

And Frade had thought that they had plenty of time for the aerial tour. While there was no question in his mind that Martín would eventually show up at Jorge Frade in response to Schultz's call, he was equally convinced that Martín would not be there when the Cub landed, if for no other reason than to impress on Cletus that the head of the Bureau of Internal Security did not dance to Don Cletus Frade's whistle.

This assumption proved to be wrong.

As he got closer to the passenger terminal building, he saw that el Coronel Martín indeed was waiting for him, and in uniform. Martín was standing beside another uniformed officer, whom Clete recognized after a moment as General Nervo. His military-style uniform was brown. They were standing beside a black 1941 Buick Roadmaster.

"That's General Nervo, Don Cletus," Father Pedro said.

"We've met," Clete replied. "Well, what we'll do now is get you a ride into town."

"I'm sorry to have kept you waiting," Clete said at the passenger terminal building.

Martín and then Nervo embraced Clete cordially.

For the moment, I am a good guy. That may change in the next two or three minutes.

"Not a problem," Martín said. "The general and I were here anyway. Your friend had a reservation on the eleven-thirty flight from Montevideo. Santiago had never seen him, and I thought this would give him the chance."

"What did you think?" Clete asked.

"He missed the flight," Martín said. "And changed his reservation until tomorrow."

"This is Father Silva, General," Clete said.

"I know the Father," Nervo said. "And aren't you lucky to have Don Cletus fly you to Buenos Aires, Father? And spare you the return trip with Father Kurt at the wheel?"

Okay. As if I needed proof, Nervo, as well as Martín, knows just about everything that happens on Estancia San Pedro y San Pablo.

"Yes, it was very kind of Don Cletus," Father Silva said.

"Cletus, in the Gendarmería," Nervo said, "they say that if Father Kurt wasn't the president's confessor, he would have lost his driving license years ago. Have you ever ridden with him?"

Frade shook his head.

"Don't! He thinks that Packard of his has two speeds, fast and faster. And they know that the more he's had to drink, the faster he drives. The Gendarmes along Route Two call him 'Padre Loco.'"

"Oh, I can't believe that's true!" Father Silva said loyally.

"Would I lie to a priest?" Nervo asked righteously.

Martín took pity on the priest.

"He's pulling your leg, Father," he said. "Can we give you a lift into town? We're headed for Plaza San Martín."

"That would be very kind," Silva said. "I'm going to the cathedral."

"Right on our way," Martín said.

"I need ten, fifteen minutes of your time, maybe a little more," Clete said. "Father, would you mind waiting?"

"No, of course not."

"Then why don't you go in the passenger terminal and have a cup of coffee while the general, the colonel, and I take a little walk?"

They walked across the tarmac toward one of the Constellations, the *Ciudad de Buenos Aires*. It was being prepared for its flight to Lisbon the next day; mechanics and technicians swarmed all over it.

About halfway, Cletus touched Martín's arm, a signal for him to stop.

Martín looked at him with a raised eyebrow.

"Are you going to tell us why you're flying a Jesuit priest around?" Nervo asked.

"Well, he's getting me National Identity booklets for two SS men and their wives and children, and the sooner he can do that, the better."

"Somehow, I don't think that's your odd sense of humor at work," Martín said.

"So that's who was in that Little Sisters of the Poor bus," Nervo said. "What's this all about? Who are these people? Where did they come from?"

I can't—I don't want to, and I can't—play any more games with these two. It is now truth, the whole truth, and nothing but the truth time.

"They were on the plane from Lisbon," Clete said.

"And you knew about that?" Martín said.

"I knew they were probably going to be on the plane. I didn't know for sure, and I didn't know who they were, until Father Welner brought them to Estancia San Pedro y San Pablo."

"Who are they?" Nervo asked.

"One of them is an SS major, the other an SS sergeant major. . . ."

"Traveling as priests, nuns, and orphans on Vatican passports," Nervo said bitterly. "Sonofabitch! I knew something smelled when I saw the Papal Nuncio at the airport!"

"What's this all about, Cletus?" Martín asked.

Clete had a clear mental image of himself and Colonel A. F. Graham in the Hollywood Roosevelt Hotel the day he met Graham and heard for the first time of the United States Office of Strategic Services.

Graham, whom he had never seen before, came to Clete's room in civilian clothing, showed him his Marine Corps identification, and came right to the point: "Are you willing to undertake a mission involving great personal risk outside the continental limits of the United States?"

When, after thinking it all over for perhaps twenty seconds, Clete—who was literally willing to do anything to get off what he was doing, which was a Heroes on Display War Bond Tour to be followed by a tour as a basic flying instructor— said that he would, Graham handed him a sheet of paper and said, "Read it and then sign it."

SECRET

The United States of America
Office of Strategic Services
Washington, D.C.

Acknowledgment of Penalties Provided by the United
States Code for the Unauthorized Disclosure of
National Security Information.

    The undersigned acknowledges that the unauthorized disclosure of any information made available to him by any officer of the Office of Strategic Services will result in his prosecution under applicable provisions of the United States Code (including, where applicable, The Rules for the Governance of the Naval Services and/or The Manual for Courts-Martial, 1917) and that the penalties provided by law provide on conviction for the death penalty, or such other punishment as the court may decide.

                                      Cletus Howell Frade

Executed at Los Angeles, California,
this 12th day of October 1942
Witness:
A.F. Graham
Colonel, USMCR

SECRET

He had signed it, and only then asked, "What's the 'Office of Strategic Services?"

Clete looked between Martín and Nervo, and began: "The OSS has made a deal with a German intelligence officer named Gehlen . . ."

"And the goddamn Vatican is involved in this up to the Pope's eyeballs," Nervo said when Clete had finished.

"What are you supposed to do with these people, Cletus?" Martín asked.

"Nobody told me this," Clete replied, "but I have the feeling that this is step one."

"What is 'this'?" Martín asked.

"Getting the officers out of Russia and their families out of Germany, then into Italy, then to Portugal, and finally established here. . . ."

"Established here?" Nervo repeated.

"I am supposed to set them up to disappear in Argentina."

"How are you going to do that?"

"I don't know. We have agreed to provide money. I suppose Welner will help. . . ."

"Let me give you a little friendly advice, my OSS friend," Nervo said. "Never put yourself in debt to Holy Mother Church, especially when it's being represented by a Jesuit, and especially, *especially* when that Jesuit is the beloved Father Kurt Welner, S.J."

"Finish what you were saying, Cletus, about this being step one," Martín said.

"Well—and I'm just guessing—when Gehlen hears that these two made it here and that I've set them up—"

"They have names?" Nervo interrupted.

"The major is Alois Strübel. The sergeant major is Otto Niedermeyer. I went along with Strübel's idea for new names. He's now Möller and Niedermeyer's Körtig. The Möllers have two children, a boy and a girl, ten or eleven, and the Körtigs have a boy about the same age. I've been told the women and children were killed in air raids; that German records show that they were. The men were supposedly killed on the Eastern Front."

"Well," Nervo said, "this Gehlen fellow could have arranged for the men to die that way. But the women and children . . . no one would question a Catholic hospital reporting the death of a mother and her child any more than

Alejandro here would suspect that a nun had a kilo of flawless diamonds in her underwear. Holy Mother Church was involved in that, and in getting the women and children out of Germany."

"Let Cletus finish what he was saying, Santiago," Martín said.

Nervo gestured for Clete to go on.

"What I'm guessing is that when Gehlen learns everything went as promised—"

"How's he going to learn that?" Nervo said.

"Möller had a coded message all prepared to do that."

"And you sent this coded message?"

"No, I didn't. I told him to give me his codebook, and that if I heard he'd sent any messages to anybody, I'd have him shot."

Nervo glanced at Martín and said, "Our OSS friend really is a lot smarter than he looks, isn't he, Alejandro? And I'll bet he doesn't get any friend of his involved in something that'll probably get him shot."

Martín looked at Frade. "Go on, Cletus."

"Well, after we prove we did what we promised to do, it's Gehlen's turn to give us something of value. Presuming he does that, we get some more wives and children of Gehlen's people out of Germany and over here."

"Just the wives and children?"

"For now. The officers will come later."

"What's that all about?" Nervo asked.

"Again, I don't know what I'm talking about here. Just guessing."

"So guess," General Nervo said.

"Most of these people are dedicated Nazis. I know for sure that Möller is. They are going to keep on fighting godless Communism and keeping their oath of personal loyalty to the Führer until the Russians are in Berlin."

"Gehlen, too?" Martín asked.

"No. Not Gehlen. But please don't ask me any more about that, Alejandro."

"If I did, would you tell me?" Martín asked.

Nervo said: "Apropos of nothing whatever, Cletus, what comes to your mind when you hear the term 'Valkyrie'?"

Jesus Christ, they know about that?

Well, Martín did tell me he had a BIS guy in the Argentine Embassy in Berlin he really wanted to keep there.

Sure they know.

"Blond, large-breasted Aryan women who fool around with the braver soldiers? Carry them off for carnal adventures on their horses?"

"Yeah, right," Nervo said, chuckling. "The SS guy at Estancia San Pedro y San Pablo doesn't like Valkyries?"

"I know he thinks that anyone who is not going to keep his vow of personal loyalty to Hitler is a traitor."

"Like Galahad, for example?" Martín said.

"Like who?" Frade said.

"You did hear that he flew his little airplane to Montevideo this morning, and came back about an hour ago?"

"Who did what?"

"He brought back with him a package for Señor Gradny-Sawz," Martín said.

He demonstrated with his hands the size of the package; about that of a shoe box.

"Cletus," Nervo said. "Would you be shocked to hear that I don't think fighting godless Communism is such a bad idea?"

"I'd say you sound like my boss and my grandfather," Clete said.

Nervo chuckled. He patted Clete on the arm and then turned to Martín.

"Alejandro, decision time. You have thirty seconds to decide what we're going to do about all these people violating the sacred neutrality of Argentina."

Martín shook his head.

"Twenty-five seconds," Nervo said, looking at his wristwatch. "Do you want to report to General Obregón that we have reason to believe that the American OSS with the connivance of the Papal Nuncio has just smuggled into Argentina two SS people and their wives and children? And plans to smuggle in more?"

Martín stared icily at him.

"Or that you watched, but did not arrest, an SS general as he was smuggled into Argentina from a German submarine?"

"Christ, Santiago!" Martín protested.

"Or that we have reason to believe that Don Cletus Frade has been concealing two Germans who either ran from their embassy—or who he might have kidnapped—at his Estancia Don Guillermo in Mendoza?"

"I didn't kidnap the Froggers," Clete said.

"Does Father Kurt know about you and the Froggers?" Nervo asked.

Clete nodded.

"Or, Alejandro, do you wish to join with Don Cletus and me in this noble—and I might add, endorsed by Holy Mother Church—battle against godless Communism?"

Nervo glanced at his wristwatch. "Fifteen seconds."

"Goddamn you, Santiago!"

"I would ask if you want to join with Don Cletus and me in the equally—as far as I am concerned—noble battle against more-or-less godless Nazism, but I'm not sure how you and Holy Mother Church really feel about the Nazis."

"You sonofabitch!" Martín said, but he could not restrain a chuckle.

"May I interpret that to mean you're with us?"

"What other choice do I have?"

"Suicide would be an option, but I seem to recall that's a mortal sin."

"What are we going to do?" Martín asked.

"What I'm going to do is get in Don Cletus's airplane . . . the little one . . . and fly to Estancia San Pedro y San Pablo with him to have a word with el Señor . . . what's his name, Cletus?"

"Möller. Alois Möller. We kept their real Christian names."

". . . with Señor *Alois Möller*."

"About what?"

"I'll decide that after I talk with him," Nervo said. "But right now I'm thinking along the lines of suggesting to him that his only option—presuming he wants to stay alive—is to do nothing that might in any way annoy Don Cletus or myself."

"What about Edmundo Wattersly?" Martín asked.

"Tell him we need a daily report on el Coronel Schmidt's activities. We can't have that Nazi sonofabitch going to Casa Montagna looking for the weapons cache. . . . Or, now that I think of it, for the Froggers."

"Okay. But what I meant is: Do we tell him about this?"

Nervo didn't reply for a long moment, before finally asking, "We don't have to make that decision right now, do we?"

"No," Martín said. "But sooner or later. Him and Lauffer."

"Not now," Nervo said.

Martín nodded.

Nervo asked: "Do you want me to send Pedro out to the estancia with your car?"

"How about this?" Clete interrupted. "Father Silva is going to bring the National Identity booklets out here at nine tomorrow morning. I'm going to make a fuel stop at the same time on my way to Mendoza. Santiago, if you want to spend the night at Estancia San Pedro y San Pablo . . ."

"I accept your gracious offer," Nervo said. "Alejandro, have Pedro bring the car here in the morning. Wait . . ." He turned to Cletus. "I'd like Subinspector General Nolasco to see Casa Montagna for himself. Would there be room for him on your airplane?"

Clete nodded. "Plenty of room. You want to send somebody else?"

"Tell Nolasco to pick two other people, who will stay there for a few days, a week. Don't tell them where they are going. Got that?"

"*Sí, mi general,*" Martín said sarcastically.

"Good man," Nervo said.

[FOUR]
Calle Martín 404
Carrasco, Uruguay
1615 2 October 1943

Sturmbannführer Werner von Tresmarck—a somewhat portly man in his forties who wore a full, neatly manicured mustache, *à la* Adolf Hitler—rang the doorbell of his home a second time.

It was literally a door bell, a five-inch brass bell hanging on a chain from the roof of the house. A woven leather cord was attached to the clapper.

When there was again no answer, he turned to the person standing with him, a tall, trim, olive-skinned man in his thirties.

"Dare I hope not only that my beloved wife is still in Punta del Este, but that the maid has taken advantage of this and given herself the day off?"

"Your wife's car is not here," the man with him said.

"Cross your fingers," von Tresmarck said as he took the door key from his pocket.

He pushed the door open and called, "María?"

There was no answer.

Von Tresmarck waved the man with him into the house, then closed the door.

He held up his hand, fingers crossed, and then called, "Inge!"

When there was no answer, he called again.

And when there was still no answer, he called loudly, "Inge, you blond slut! Answer me!"

When there was again no answer, he turned to the man with him and kissed him on each cheek and then on the mouth.

"Now, let us have a drink," he said. "And then a bath."

"I'm up here, Werner," Inge von Tresmarck said.

He looked up and saw her standing in her bathrobe on the landing beside the stairwell.

"*Scheisse!*" von Tresmarck muttered.

"Wait for me in the sitting," Inge said.

"What?" von Tresmarck asked incredulously. He looked at the man with him.

"Your wife said to wait for us in the sitting," a male voice then said unpleasantly.

She's got a man up there? She's never done that before!

"It would seem your wife has a guest," the man said. He obviously found this amusing.

Von Tresmarck looked up at the second floor. There was a man—also wearing a bathrobe—standing beside his wife.

Is that my bathrobe?

He recognized the man, who was indeed wearing his bathrobe.

"Oh, my God!"

"And don't let your friend get away until I have a word with him," the man said. ·

"Wernie, who *is* that man?" the man asked.

Von Tresmarck grabbed the man's elbow and propelled him into the sitting room.

"What's going on here, Wernie?" the man quickly asked, his tone now one of concern.

"Just sit there and be quiet," von Tresmarck ordered. He went to the bookcase, removed four books, put his hand in the space where they had been, and rummaged around.

"What are you doing?" the man asked.

"For the love of God, be quiet!"

When his now frantic search in the space behind the books proved fruitless, von Tresmarck went to the desk and started pulling open drawers.

"Is this what you're looking for?" SS-Brigadeführer Manfred von Deitzberg asked.

Von Tresmarck looked up. Von Deitzberg was lowering himself onto a small couch. He held von Tresmarck's 9mm Luger P08 pistol in his left hand. Not threateningly; he wasn't holding it by the grip, ready to fire, but in his palm, as if it were a pocket watch or a handful of coins he wished to examine.

Von Tresmarck did not reply.

Von Deitzberg turned to the man who was now standing beside von Tresmarck, visibly uncomfortable with the introduction of the pistol.

"You must be Ramón," von Deitzberg said. "Did you two have a pleasant time in Paraguay, Ramón?"

"Who are you?" Ramón asked.

"You may call me señor," von Deitzberg said. "Both of you may call me señor. Answer my question, Ramón!"

"Tell him," von Tresmarck said softly.

"We had quite a nice time, thank you," Ramón said.

"Did Sturmbannführer von Tresmarck tell you that he was under orders not to leave Uruguay—not even to go to Argentina, much less to Paraguay—without specific permission?"

Inge von Tresmarck came into the sitting room. It was evident to her husband that she was wearing nothing under her bathrobe. She walked to von Deitzberg and sat beside him on the couch.

She's obviously fucking von Deitzberg.

Well, why not? She was one of the whores in the Hotel Am Zoo and the Adlon. She'd fuck an elephant to save her skin!

"No, he didn't."

Von Tresmarck began: "Herr Brigadeführer, I went to Paraguay—"

With a sudden swift motion, von Deitzberg tossed the pistol from his left hand to his right, grabbed the grip, and fired a round into the bookcase beside von Tresmarck and Ramón.

The noise in the confined area was deafening, as von Deitzberg knew it would be. He had also fired enough pistols to know that a 9mm bullet would not go far through a line of books on a shelf. And he knew that when most people hear a gunshot, they decide it is the sound of an automobile engine backfiring.

This time, Inge said, *"Scheisse!"*

"I would really prefer not to shoot you, Werner," von Deitzberg said. "But the next time you use my rank or my name, or try to lie to me, I will."

Everyone—Inge included—was now looking at von Deitzberg with terror in their eyes.

"And if I have to shoot you, it will be necessary for me to shoot Ramón, too. Many times, especially in the face, so that it will look like a lovers' quarrel, something both the German Embassy and the Uruguayan government will want to quickly cover up."

He let that sink in.

"You were about to tell me what you were doing in Paraguay, Werner," he went on finally.

Von Tresmarck, visibly nervous, launched into an elaborate explanation of the trip, saying that he had grown afraid that questions would be asked about all the property he'd already bought in Uruguay, and that Ramón, a businessman, had suggested that they begin making investments in Paraguay.

Von Deitzberg let him finish.

"Ramón," von Deitzberg then said, "I'm afraid that Werner also forgot that he was under orders not to share any detail of the confidential special fund with anyone. You understand, of course, how your acquiring that knowledge has reduced your chances of staying alive?"

"I have to go to the toilet," Ramón stammered.

"Certainly," von Deitzberg said. "But hurry back. And don't think of running away. Hauptsturmführer Forster is sitting in his car outside. Werner, tell Ramón who Hauptsturmführer Forster is."

"He's with the Geheime Staatspolizei," von Tresmarck said.

"Do you know what the Geheime Staatspolizei is, Ramón?" von Deitzberg asked.

"Please, I have to go to the toilet right now," Ramón said.

"The Secret State Police. He is under orders to shoot anyone he sees leaving this house without my permission."

"I understand," Ramón said. "May I go?"

"Hurry back," von Deitzberg said.

Ramón hurriedly—and walking unnaturally—left the sitting room.

"I wonder if he's going to make it?" von Deitzberg asked rhetorically. "I tend to think not."

"May I sit down?" von Tresmarck asked.

"I think that would be a very good idea," von Deitzberg said. "What I think I'm going to do, Werner, is tell you what's going to happen and have you explain it to Ramón."

Von Tresmarck nodded.

"The operation is shut down," von Deitzberg began. "There have been reverses in the war, as I'm sure you know, which have resulted in the unexpected transfers of some of the people involved. Others have fallen for the Fatherland. It doesn't really matter why. Intelligent people, Werner, know when to quit.

"I have been sent here under an assumed identity—by U-boat, incidentally, to give you an idea of how important this is considered—to make sure the shutdown is conducted as efficiently and as quickly as possible. And, of course, to make sure that our investments are secure and will be available if—perhaps I should in honesty say 'when'—they are needed.

"You are going to have to disappear from Uruguay. There are a number of reasons for this, including the very real possibility that some of the Jews are liable to make trouble when it becomes apparent to them that their relatives are not going to be coming.

"It would be best for you to disappear, rather than return to the Fatherland. One of the ways for you to disappear would be to die in tragic if sordid circumstances. As I'm sure you are aware, Werner, it is not uncommon for homosexuals to have a falling-out, resulting in the death of both. And this was before I knew about Ramón.

"Frankly, that seemed at first to be the simplest solution to the problem. And even more so when I got here and learned that you had confided all the details of the operation not only to Frau von Tresmarck but—"

"I never told her a thing!" von Tresmarck blurted. "She's a lying whore. . . ."

Von Deitzberg fired another round from the Luger into the bookcase.

"Inge, that may have frightened Ramón," von Deitzberg said. "Make sure he doesn't try to do anything foolish."

Inge jumped quickly to her feet and almost ran out of the sitting room.

"As I was saying, Werner, removing you permanently from the scene seemed a quite logical and simple solution to the problem, especially after I learned you had told both Frau von Tresmarck and Ramón about the confidential special fund and its assets. That was not only very disloyal of you—after all, I'm the fellow who kept you out of Sachsenhausen by sending you here—but stupid.

"But another idea had occurred to me when I learned that—like rats leaving a sinking ship—the Froggers had deserted their post in Buenos Aires.

"I asked myself, *What if Werner disappeared? What if he disappeared as soon as he learned I was back in South America?* If you hadn't been off with Ramón in Paraguay, I'm sure that someone in Buenos Aires would have told you I was here. And I wondered, *What if Werner disappeared, taking all the confidential special fund assets with him?*

"The downside to that would be that when I made that report, there are those who would say—in the presence of the Reichsführer-SS if they could arrange that—that they knew something like that would happen. 'You simply cannot trust a homosexual; they think like women.'

"The upside to that would be—since you had absconded with them—no confidential special fund assets for me to account for."

Von Tresmarck looked at von Deitzberg in utter confusion.

"You take my point, Werner?" von Deitzberg asked.

"I . . . uh . . . don't think I quite understand, Herr Brig . . . Mein Herr."

"It took Hauptsturmführer Forster about five seconds to appreciate the benefits of your disappearance in these circumstances: We not only need no longer to transfer large amounts of cash to Germany, but since you and the assets have disappeared, no one will be clamoring for their share of the real estate, et cetera, here. And that's presuming any of them actually manage to get out of Germany and to South America. Are you beginning to understand, Werner?"

Von Tresmarck nodded.

"The plan hinges on your disappearance," von Deitzberg said. "And the problem with that . . ."

"I can be out of here in a matter of hours," von Tresmarck said.

". . . is that I no longer trust you. And I should tell you that Forster suggests I am a fool for even considering letting you live. But I find myself doing just that. With the caveat that if I even suspect you are not doing exactly what I tell you to do, or that you again have, so to speak, decided to make decisions for yourself, I will have you and, of course, Ramón killed—then there is a way for you to stay alive."

"Ramón had a little accident," Inge announced sarcastically from the doorway.

"Been incontinent, have you, Ramón?" von Deitzberg asked sympathetically. "That sometimes happens to people when they realize they're close to death. Come in and sit down. On the floor. We wouldn't want to soil Frau von Tresmarck's furniture, would we?"

He waited until Ramón had done so before going on.

"Now, let me explain what's going to happen: Frau von Tresmarck has been good enough to turn over to me the material in your safe. Including, of course, the unspent funds. The money is already in Buenos Aires, where I will invest it. Now, where are the deeds to whatever you have purchased in Paraguay? If you lie to me, I will shoot Ramón right now to show you how serious I am about this."

"Ramón has them in his safe," von Tresmarck said. "In his home."

"And they are in whose name?"

Von Tresmarck hesitated before replying, "In Ramón's name. We thought of that as an extra precaution . . ."

"Yes, I'm sure you did," von Deitzberg said. "And how much did you invest in Ramón's name as an extra precaution? How much is it worth in dollars, or pounds?"

Von Tresmarck exhaled audibly.

"A little under a million pounds sterling," he said finally. "They use the British pound."

"How much is a little under a million pounds sterling?"

"Perhaps it was a little over a million pounds sterling," von Tresmarck said.

"That's four million American dollars," von Deitzberg said. "Tell me, Werner, do you think you and Ramón could disappear and find happiness together on, say, one million American dollars?"

"What does he mean, 'disappear'?" Ramón asked.

"Werner will explain that to you later, Ramón," von Deitzberg said. "What's going to happen now is that you're going to go home—Hauptsturm-führer Forster will drive you—and after you change your trousers, you're going to bring all the deeds here.

"We will then select between us which properties you will sign over to Señor Jorge Schenck—all but, say, two hundred fifty thousand pounds' worth. I will then give you ten thousand American dollars for your immediate expenses as you and Werner set forth on your new lives."

"Who's Señor Jorge Schenck?" von Tresmarck blurted.

"He's the man who will hunt you down and kill you as slowly and painfully as possible if I ever hear of either of you again," von Deitzberg said. "Get going, Ramón. Not only does the sight of you make me ill, but you're starting to smell badly."

XIV

[ONE]
Estancia San Pedro y San Pablo
Near Pila
Buenos Aires Province, Argentina
1930 2 October 1943

Inspector General Santiago Nervo and Don Cletus Frade were sitting in wicker chairs on the verandah of the big house. A wicker table between them held bottles of scotch and bourbon.

Frade was wearing khaki trousers, a polo shirt, and battered Western boots. Nervo was in uniform, save for his tunic, which he had shed before they had gone riding.

Nervo had expressed interest in the radar, and Clete had really had no choice but to offer to show it to him.

"It's not far," Frade had said. "I usually ride out there . . ."

It was a question, and Nervo had picked up on it.

"Whatever happened to that magnificent stallion of your father's? What was his name?"

"Julius Caesar. Would you like to ride him out to the radar?"

"No," Nervo had replied immediately. "I watched him throw your father before God and five thousand spectators at the Rural."

The Rural Exposition was the Argentine version of an American county or state fair—but a national affair. The bull, sow, stallion, hen, or whatever that earned a blue ribbon became the best of its breed in Argentina.

"I never heard that story."

"It was considered impolite—even dangerous—to remind el Coronel that he had landed on his ass in dress uniform before everybody he knew," Nervo said.

"Every time I get on that big beautiful bastard, he tries to throw me," Clete said. "After, of course, he tries very hard to bite me as I get on him."

Clete saw in Nervo's eyes that he was going to have to ride Julius Caesar to wipe out the disbelief in the policeman's eyes.

And he had done so. And had kept his seat without getting bitten.

They had ridden out to Casa Número Cincuenta y Dos, where Lieutenant Oscar Schultz, USNR—who of course had driven, not ridden, out there—had proudly shown Nervo how the radar functioned, and introduced the gendarme to the rest of the team.

And now Nervo and Frade were back at the big house, enjoying what Clete had described to Nervo as the sacred Texas tradition of "having a little sip to cut the dust of the trail."

After a short time, there was the sound of a vehicle approaching, and they watched Schultz drive up at the wheel of a Ford Model A pickup truck.

Nervo gestured toward Schultz, who wore full gaucho regalia.

"I'm having trouble believing that," Nervo said. "He *never* rides?"

"Never," Frade confirmed. "When he was a kid, he went on a pony ride, and when he got off, the pony stepped on his foot. He swore he would never get on anything with four legs again, and he hasn't."

"*Hola, Jefe,*" Nervo called cheerfully, and waved.

Then he said: "That isn't the only thing I'm having trouble believing."

"Excuse me?"

"Wait until el Jefe 'dismounts,'" Nervo said, and reached for the bottle of scotch. "I want him to hear this."

Schultz climbed down from the pickup and came onto the verandah. He pulled up a wicker chair, reached for the bourbon, poured himself a steep drink, announced, "In my professional opinion as an officer of the Naval Service, the sun is over the yardarm," took a healthy sip, and then added, "Even down here in Gaucholand."

Clete chuckled and said, "You better tell General Nervo what you mean."

"Cletus, please, 'Santiago,'" Nervo said.

"Me too?" Schultz asked.

"Of course you too," Nervo said.

Why do I not think he's not just schmoozing us?

Why was I not surprised that Nervo and Schultz had immediately taken to each other?

We're the same kind of people?

I think deciding to come clean with Nervo and Martín was probably the smartest thing I've done in the last six months.

"Well, Santiago," Schultz began, "in the old days in the North Atlantic, on sailing ships, at about eleven o'clock in the morning, the sun would rise above the yardarm. That's that horizontal spar"—he demonstrated with his hands—"that's mounted on the mast."

Nervo nodded his understanding.

"Which meant," Schultz went on, "that the officers could go to the wardroom and have a little sip to give them the courage to face the rest of the day."

"Fascinating," Nervo said, chuckling. "May I say something about the way you're dressed, Jefe?"

"Of course," Schultz said, just a little warily.

"As one professional officer to another," Nervo said, "your gaucho costume is complete except for one small detail."

"What's that?"

"I was raised on an estancia in Patagonia," Nervo said. "And never can I remember a gaucho who did not have, very close by—"

"She's visiting her mother," Schultz interrupted, smiling knowingly. "She should be back sometime today."

Nervo literally convulsed; he stood up, spilled his drink, and then, laughing heartily, wrapped his arm around Schultz.

They're buddies, delighted with themselves!

When Nervo finally sat down and was pouring himself another drink, Frade said, "Santiago, tell Casanova what it is that you are also having a hard time believing."

Nervo pointed with his glass at one of the manager's houses, into which the Möllers and the Körtigs and their families had been taken. Clete knew that both Dorotea and Claudia were there "to help with the children" and also that there were enough peones discreetly watching the house to make sure everything remained under control.

"Something smells with those two," Nervo said.

Schultz met his eyes. "Yeah," he said softly.

That's interesting. What have I missed that these two see?

"Look, Cletus," Nervo said, as if he'd read his mind. "I'm a policeman. I'm not like you and Martín, into politics and espionage and all that. Just a simple policeman."

Like hell you're just a simple policeman. You didn't get to be Inspector General of the Gendarmería by being simple.

What is he doing now? Schmoozing me?

"But . . . ?" Frade said.

"Like most old policemen, I have learned to know when people are lying. And those two are."

"About what?"

Nervo shrugged. "You tell me. What have they got to lie about?"

Clete shrugged.

"They're either not who they say they are," Schultz said, "or they're not telling you something, or both."

"What do you mean, they're not who they say they are?"

Now Schultz shrugged.

"Tell me about this Gehlen guy," Nervo said. "He must be pretty smart, would you say?"

Smart enough to run the Russian Intelligence branch of the Abwehr, and smart enough to deal with Allen Dulles.

Yeah, I'd say he has to be pretty smart.

"He'd have to be," Frade said, "wouldn't he?"

"And he knows about Valkyrie, right?"

Frade sipped his drink, then nodded. "Yeah. Knows about—and is involved in—Valkyrie."

"Which makes a simple policeman like me think Gehlen doesn't think

Adolf Hitler is God's sword against the Antichrist, and believes the best thing for Germany is to kill the bastard. Or am I wrong?"

"I think you're absolutely right," Clete said.

"So why did he send Möller?"

"I don't know where you're going," Clete admitted.

"Möller was not lying when he told me I should understand that he considers himself a serving officer who has taken a personal oath of allegiance to Hitler," Nervo said.

"And he made a point of telling you that. And he made a point of telling me that earlier today when we first met," Clete thought aloud. "So what?"

"And this guy comes as a trusted assistant to Gehlen?" Nervo said. "That smells, Cletus."

"What are you suggesting?" Clete asked.

"Well, I'm just a simple policeman, Cletus. But that phone call I made when we first came here, right after we landed?"

"What about it?"

"I told Subinspector General Nolasco to send two of my people to Santa Rosa—that's just about in the middle of the pampas—with orders not to come back until they have the cattle robbers—"

"Rustlers," Clete corrected him without thinking.

Nervo gave him a dirty look, then went on: "—operating down there in handcuffs. They're good people, Cletus, but they like Nazis and don't like Americans, and I didn't want them around to be curious about you and Alejandro and me suddenly becoming good friends. And talking about it."

"You think Gehlen sent Möller here to get rid of him?"

"Maybe to do both things," Nervo said. "To set things up to bring the rest of the Abwehr Ost people here, and to get him out of the way while he works on Valkyrie. But you're the intelligence officer. What do I know?"

What do you know? You knew about Valkyrie, didn't you?

And you didn't have to search your memory very hard to come up with Abwehr Ost, did you?

"You said before that both Möller and Körtig were lying. What's Körtig lying about?"

Schultz now spoke up. "Well, for one thing, I don't think he's really a sergeant major."

Frade looked at him without replying.

Schultz went on: "Clete, I'm certainly no intelligence officer. I spent all my life, from the time I was sixteen until a couple of months ago, as an enlisted sailor. But a lot—most—of that time I was a chief petty officer, and I know another senior noncommissioned officer when I see one, and Körtig ain't one. I have the gut feeling he's the OIC."

"You'll recall, el Jefe," Frade challenged, "that I had to tell you that José Cortina, Martín's sergeant major, is really a lieutenant colonel."

Schultz didn't back down.

"I've never seen Cortina, Clete. All I did was talk to him on the telephone—and only a couple of times. If I'd have seen him, he wouldn't be able to pull that sergeant major bullshit on me."

" 'OIC'?" Nervo asked.

" 'Officer-in-Charge.' Or maybe 'Officer-in-Command,' " Clete furnished.

Nervo nodded his agreement and said: "That would make some sense."

"So you think Möller knows?" Clete asked.

"Sure he does," Nervo said.

Schultz nodded his agreement.

"What would all that be about?" Clete asked. "And spare me that I'm Just an Old Chief and Simple Policeman crap."

"If you're watching Möller, you're probably not going to be watching Körtig. Or at least as closely," Schultz said. "If Körtig has another mission, one you don't know about . . ."

"Do you think either one of them knows about Valkyrie?" Clete asked.

"I don't know about Möller," Nervo said. "But I'll bet Körtig does. Gehlen may have sent him here to make sure Möller—if he doesn't already know about Valkyrie—doesn't find out; or if he does, that he doesn't blow the whistle on Valkyrie to the German Embassy or von Deitzberg. You told me Körtig didn't seem all that surprised to hear that von Deitzberg is here."

Schultz was nodding. "Clete, I think you have to find out what the fuck these two Krauts are really up to."

"Yeah," Frade said. He pushed himself out of his chair. "And the sooner the better."

Nervo stood. Clete waited until he had drained his glass, then said, "Tell me, Simple Policeman. In the Gendarmería, how would you do this? By pulling fingernails?"

Nervo looked at him stonefaced.

"Actually," the inspector general then said, "I've found the best method is to drag people across the pampas behind a horse for fifteen minutes before beginning the interrogation."

[TWO]
Approaching El Plumerillo Airfield
Mendoza, Mendoza Province, Argentina
1410 3 October 1943

Doña Dorotea Frade, in the copilot seat of the Lodestar, pushed the intercom button on her microphone and said, "Let me land it, Cletus, please."

Frade glanced at her, then returned his attention to outside the aircraft as he said, "No. You shouldn't even be sitting there."

"Nonsense. There's nothing an eight-months-and-some-days pregnant woman can't do except lead anything that comes close to a normal life."

"You all right, baby?"

"No woman eight months pregnant is all right, Clete. But I can land this, and I want to. This will be my last flight for a while."

He glanced at her again. "You just decide that?"

"No, I decided it on the plane on the way to Buenos Aires. Once I got back to Mendoza, that was it."

He saw the airfield ahead and started to make a shallow descent to the right.

"I gather that means you are not going to grant the humble request of the mother of your unborn child?"

"No, it means I want to make a low pass over Casa Montagna."

"Why?"

"It's known as terrifying the natives. Puts a little excitement into their lives."

"They know we're coming, Cletus."

"Let's make sure," he said as he headed for Estancia Don Guillermo.

He made two low-level passes over the house on the mountain side, one to the south and one to the north, and then raised the nose.

I could get a Piper Cub in there easily. I wonder if my father had that in mind?

It couldn't have been cheap to dynamite all that rock out of the way and then make everything level.

He climbed to twelve hundred feet, leveled off, then picked up his microphone and pressed the intercom button.

"First Officer, you have the aircraft." He pointed out the windscreen. "The airfield's over thataway."

She put her hands on the yoke and he took his off.

"Thank you, my darling," the first officer said.

———

"That was a good landing," Clete said.

"Well, thank you, darling."

"Any landing you can walk away from is a good landing."

"You bah-stud!"

He saw she was smiling.

If anything had gone wrong, I could have taken it away from her.

I think.

Looking out the windscreen, Clete Frade saw that a considerable number of vehicles were on hand to meet them. He was not surprised to see the four-door Lincoln Continental his Aunt Beatriz had rebodied or even the two dark green army-style trucks and two 1941 Ford sedans painted the same color that obviously went with the maybe a dozen members of the Gendarmería Nacional standing near them. And he had expected the small bus parked beside the gendarmes. There were in all seven Möllers and Körtigs, plus the suitcases now holding the clothing Rodríguez and the nun had bought for everybody.

But he was surprised to see that the Little Sisters of Santa María del Pilar were also on hand, represented by their Mother Superior. She was standing by a small bus, much like the one the Little Sisters of the Poor had had at Estancia San Pedro y San Pablo.

I wonder what that's all about?

"Don Cletus?" a male voice behind him at the cockpit door said.

Clete turned and saw Inspector Peralta, one of the two Gendarmería Nacional officers who had been waiting for him at Jorge Frade when he'd "refueled." The other officer was Subinspector Navarro. The best that Clete could figure was that Peralta was roughly the equivalent of a lieutenant colonel and Navarro a major. Inspector General Nervo's orders to them had been simple: "Place yourself at Don Cletus's orders and keep me posted—twice a day—on what's going on."

Frade made the introduction between Doña Dorotea and Inspector Peralta.

Then Peralta said: "With your permission, Don Cletus, rather than go directly to Estancia Don Guillermo, I will go to the Mendoza headquarters of the Gendarmería and have a talk with Subinspector Nowicki—he came to meet us;

I see his car—and join you later. May I bring Subinspector Nowicki with me when I do?"

He's being polite as hell, but he's sure running the show.

"Of course."

"Subinspector Navarro will escort you now with the trucks and men you see. If you would be good enough to show him the weapons cache, that would be helpful."

Does that mean the weapons will then get loaded on the trucks, and bye-bye weapons cache?

Oh, stop it, for Christ's sake! The next thing, you'll be eyeing Mother Superior suspiciously.

What other choice do I have?

"I'll have Rodríguez show him the cache as soon as we arrive."

"Do you think four of my men will be sufficient to guard the aircraft, Don Cletus? Or shall I arrange for more?"

I never even thought about that. The Constellations in Buenos Aires, yeah. But not the Lodestar here.

You're really on top of things, Señor Superspy!

"I'm sure that will be enough."

"Then I'll see you shortly," Peralta said, saluted, and backed out of the cockpit door.

Clete looked at Dorotea.

"Good man," he began before being interrupted by the voice of Mother Superior at the cockpit door.

"What in the world are you doing up here and in there?" she asked of Doña Dorotea, then turned to Don Cletus. "You really can be, can't you, quite as stupid as your father?" She looked at Dorotea. "Well, come on!"

"Where am I going?" Dorotea said.

"To the convent. The original idea was to examine the German women and children. Now I'll have to see what damage this husband of yours has caused to you."

Dorotea nodded. "I told him that I didn't think I should be sitting up here in my delicate condition."

She waited until Mother Superior was glaring at Cletus and couldn't see her face. Then, looking very pleased with herself, she smiled warmly at him and stuck out her tongue.

And then, with great difficulty, she started to hoist herself out of the co-pilot's seat.

[THREE]
Casa Montagna
Estancia Don Guillermo
Km 40.4, Provincial Route 60
Mendoza Province, Argentina
1525 3 October 1943

Captain Madison R. Sawyer III had been playing polo—sort of—to pass the time when "Frade's Lodestar," as Sawyer thought of it, had buzzed the polo field.

He had found eight mallets—one of them broken, all of them old—hanging at various places on the walls of Casa Montagna, which had of course cut the number of players to three on each team, leaving one spare mallet.

Finding players and horses had posed no problem. When he had asked—at the morning formation of the former cavalry troopers of the Húsares de Pueyrredón now guarding Casa Montagna—if anyone happened to know how to play polo, every hand had shot up. The horses were not, of course, the fine polo ponies he had grown used to at Estancia San Pedro y San Pablo. But even the worst of them seemed to have some idea what was expected of a polo pony.

The problem of no polo balls had been solved by purchasing at a very generous price three soccer balls—what the Argentines called footballs—from the children of peones who lived in the compound. He also promised to see that they would have replacement footballs just as soon as he could send someone into town to buy them.

The air-filled soccer balls of course behaved quite differently than a regulation solid-wood polo ball would have, but that just made the play more interesting.

One of the soccer balls had lasted about ten minutes in play and a second just a few minutes more. The third soccer ball—and the mallets, which surprised him—had endured the stress of play for two chukkers when the flaming red Lodestar had flashed over the field.

Sawyer had decided there was time for one—possibly two—more chukkers before Frade arrived from the aircraft, and they had played two more.

He had just had time to dismount and reclaim his Thompson submachine gun and his web belt holding his .45 Colt when the nose of the Lincoln Continental appeared at the end of the field.

He had not expected the brown vehicles of the Gendarmería Nacional, and was a little worried until he saw Frade climb out from behind the wheel of the Lincoln.

"Subinspector Navarro, this is my deputy, Capitán Sawyer," Frade began the introductions.

Sensing that he was expected to do so, Sawyer saluted.

"I'll explain this all later," Frade then said to Sawyer. "But right now, I want you to show Subinspector Navarro the weapons cache and explain the perimeter defense to him—"

"You make it sound as if we're going to be attacked," Sawyer interrupted.

"That's a strong possibility," Frade said, then went on: "These gentlemen are Señor Körtig and Señor Möller. They will be joined shortly by their wives and children. In the meantime, Enrico's going to—where's Stein?"

Sawyer looked around and then pointed. Stein was walking toward them from the house.

Clete waited until he had joined them, then, after introducing Körtig, Möller, and Subinspector Navarro to "Major" Stein, he asked where Señor Fischer was.

"With his father. You need him?"

"No. What I want you to do is ask him to stay with his father until I send for him."

Stein's raised eyebrows showed his surprise, but he didn't say anything.

"Then," Frade continued, "find the housekeeper and tell her (a) to prepare some of the rooms in one of the outbuildings for the Körtigs and the Möllers. That's two wives and three children—adolescents. They'll be staying here awhile. And (b) to prepare something to eat for everybody; we haven't had anything since breakfast."

"Where are the wives and children?" Stein said.

"With Mother Superior getting a physical; they should be here in forty-five minutes or an hour."

"Doña Dorotea didn't come with you?"

"She's with them. Captain Sawyer is going to show Subinspector Navarro the arms cache and the perimeter defense. He and another Gendarmería officer will need rooms in the big house, and we'll need rooms for eight gendarmes in whatever outbuilding she wants to put the Möllers and the Körtigs. Enrico is going to take Señor Möller and Señor Körtig to the bar. As soon as you can, bring any messages from Mount Sinai to me there."

"No messages from Mount Sinai, Major," Stein said. "You expecting one?"

A very long one. When you don't know what the hell you are doing, ask somebody who presumably does.

And Graham has certainly had enough time to send me my orders.

Clete said: "The SIGABA's up at Vint Hill Farms?"

Stein nodded. "With a net check every hour."

"Well, in that case, there's nothing for Señor Möller and Señor Körtig and me to do but have a glass of wine while we wait for the ladies," Clete said. "Or hear from Mount Sinai. Or for the sky to fall. Whichever comes first."

[FOUR]
Office of the Deputy Director for Western Hemisphere Operations
Office of Strategic Services
National Institutes of Health Building
Washington, D.C.
1715 3 October 1943

Allen W. Dulles entered Graham's office carrying a well-stuffed briefcase and a small, nearly square package wrapped in cheap gray paper and tied with frazzled string.

Whatever that is, he brought it from London. Among other things they don't have in Merry Old England these days is decent wrapping paper and string.

Dulles set the package on Graham's desk and then reached across the desk to shake his hand.

"How was the flight?" Graham asked.

"Long and uncomfortable. The daily courier left without me. I came on a standard Douglas C-54. Via Shannon, Ireland; Gander, Newfoundland; and Westover, in Massachusetts. That's a long way to ride sitting on unupholstered seats or trying to sleep on a pile of mail bags on the floor."

"That's the price of having to respond to the call of your master's voice," Graham said. "How did that go?"

"First, let me open this," Dulles said, nodding at the package and fishing in his pocket.

After a moment, Graham reached into a desk drawer, came up with a pair of scissors, and handed them to Dulles.

"What's in there that's so important?" Graham said.

"My original thought was to give it to you, but I now realize I need it more than you do. I wish that I was unwelcome at the White House."

He finally got the paper off the box, then pulled from it an odd-looking bottle—there were dimples in the glass.

The label read HAIG & HAIG FIFTEEN-YEAR-OLD SCOTCH WHISKY.

"Where the hell did you get that? I thought it had all disappeared, like dinosaurs," Graham said, and then he pushed the lever on his intercom. "Alice, ice and glasses. You won't believe what Mr. Dulles has brought us!"

Alice Dulaney walked in a minute or so later—Dulles was still struggling to remove the champagne-bottle-like wire netting from the neck of the bottle—with three glasses, a bucket of ice, and a water pitcher on a tray.

Although she had resisted—for reasons Graham did not pretend to understand—a more impressive title than "secretary," she was far more important to Graham—and thus to the OSS—than her title suggested.

In Graham's absences—and he spent more time away from his office than in it—she spoke with his authority. This meant she had to be privy to all secrets, official and otherwise.

In certain circumstances, however—like this one, with only Allen Dulles in Graham's office—she dropped her "I'm nothing more than a simple secretary" masquerade and said, "Yes, thank you. Don't mind if I do. Where the *hell* did you get that? I haven't seen any of that for years."

She then took the bottle from Dulles and expertly got rid of the wire and pulled the cork. As if they had rehearsed the routine, Dulles put ice cubes in a glass, which Graham then held up so Alice could splash whisky into it. This was repeated three times. Finally, they tapped glasses.

After his first sip, Dulles said, "Nice. David Bruce told me he would tell me where I could buy two bottles *if* I promised he could have one of them. *I naturally agreed.*"

Colonel David Bruce was the OSS station chief in London.

"And?" Graham said.

"I went to the store in the embassy, where they have cases of it stacked to the ceiling. They are willing to part with two bottles—only—per month for 'special friends of the embassy.' David had already had his ration."

"You should have pulled rank on Bruce," Alice said. "You're the deputy director for Europe; he works for you."

"That thought ran through my mind, but I decided in the end that if I did, the next time I was in London he wouldn't share his knowledge of important things with me."

"You know, I'll bet Frade has cases of this stacked up somewhere," Alice said.

"Remind me to ask him," Graham said. "And speaking of Señor Loose Cannon?"

"I called Vint Hill Farms Station a couple of minutes ago," she said. "All I got was a runaround. I was going to raise hell, but I realized that maybe the reason we don't have his after-action report is because he hasn't gotten around to sending his after-action report."

"Do we know if he made it back to Buenos Aires?" Dulles asked.

"Just that. And we got that from the Associated Press wire that said the first SAA flight from Lisbon had arrived."

Graham shook his head, took a sip from his glass, and said, "God, this is good whisky!"

"The President knew he'd made it to Lisbon," Dulles said. "He was pleased."

"Pleased because Frade managed to get there or because he knew Juan Trippe would be greatly annoyed?" Graham asked.

"Either or both," Dulles said.

"Who else was there?" Graham asked.

"You would know if you had been there. Weren't you invited?"

"I told the director he was at Vint Hill Farms," Alice said. "He didn't seem terribly disappointed."

"Wallace, Hoover, and Morgenthau," Dulles said. "Plus the First Lady."

"That explains why the director wasn't disappointed," Graham said. "Wouldn't you say?"

"You would have enjoyed it," Dulles said. "Hoover and Wallace got into it. J. Robert Oppenheimer had complained to Wallace that Hoover was 'harassing' his atomic scientists. Hoover said that it was his responsibility to root out spies wherever they might be found. Morgenthau chimed in and said he was worried the Germans were going to spy on the Manhattan Project, and then Hoover blurted he was more worried about the Russians than the Germans, which annoyed Wallace and Eleanor. Eleanor pointedly reminded Hoover that the Russians were our allies and wouldn't do anything like that."

"What was the alleged purpose of this meeting of minds?" Graham asked.

"I really think Roosevelt wanted to know how South American Airlines was doing. He really knows how to hold a grudge."

"God save us if Wallace or Morgenthau finds out we're using it to move Nazis to South America," Alice said. "And why."

"Good God!" Graham exclaimed. "Don't say that aloud, even in here!"

"I didn't hear Alice say anything," Dulles said evenly, eyeing his drink. "Did you say anything, Alice?"

"Not that I can remember," she said.

"You're telling me Roosevelt ordered you from Bern just to ask about SAA?" Graham asked.

"That's all I can come up with. The only other question I was asked was about the ransoming of the Jews. Morgenthau asked me."

"And what did you say?"

"I told him that all I knew was that it was still operating, but that I didn't have any details. I suggested you might."

"Thanks a lot," Graham said.

One of the telephones on Graham's desk rang. Alice walked to the desk and answered it.

"Colonel Graham's office. Mrs. Dulaney speaking." There was a brief pause, and then she added, "Send him up, please."

She put the phone down.

"Vint Hill Farms has been heard from," she said.

Then she quickly picked up her glass from the coffee table and walked out of the office.

"There is a Colonel Raymond from Vint Hill Farms for you, Colonel," Mrs. Alice Dulaney, now back in her secretary role, formally announced from the office door.

"Show him in," Graham said as he set down the glass he was holding and lowered his feet from where they had been resting on the open lower right-hand drawer of his desk.

Allen W. Dulles was now sitting on a couch facing a small coffee table, from which he lowered his feet. He set his glass down on the table.

This has to be Frade's after-action report, Graham thought. *I guess it took him this long to get everything sorted out.*

Lieutenant Colonel James Raymond, Signal Corps—a tall, ascetic-looking man in his late thirties—marched into Graham's office, stopped two feet from Graham's desk, and saluted. He wore a web belt from which dangled a holstered

Colt Model 1911A1 pistol. His left wrist was handcuffed to a somewhat scruffy leather briefcase.

Graham returned the salute, although he wasn't in uniform, and he didn't think even the Army exchanged salutes unless both the saluter and the salutee were in uniform.

"Lieutenant Colonel Raymond, sir. From Vint Hill Farms Station." Raymond then looked at Dulles, then back at Graham, making it a question.

"Well, he may look like a Nazi," Graham said, "but actually, Mr. Dulles is the OSS deputy director for Europe and has all the appropriate security clearances. What have you got for me, Colonel?"

"I have a message from Tex for you, sir. I apologize for the delay."

Graham wagged his fingers in a *Let's have it* gesture, then asked, "What caused the delay?"

"It came in last night, sir, but neither the colonel nor I, sir, was immediately available to decrypt it."

"And only you or the colonel is able to do that?"

"Plus, of course, Lieutenant Fischer," Lieutenant Colonel Raymond said. "And he isn't available."

Graham realized his temper was about to flare.

You could have sent the still-encrypted message over here, rather than wait hours until they found you, Colonel. Believe it or not, we could have decrypted it here.

"Well, Fischer's on his way back, Colonel," Graham said, finally and calmly. "The last word I had was that he'll probably be here tomorrow."

"Yes, sir," Lieutenant Colonel Raymond said.

Graham watched as Raymond first freed himself from his handcuff, then unlocked the briefcase, took from it a large manila envelope—stamped TOP SECRET—and then took from that a business-size envelope—also stamped TOP SECRET—and handed that to Graham.

"Thank you," Graham said. "Please have a seat, Colonel. There will probably be a reply. Can I offer you a little something?"

"No, sir. Thank you, sir."

"Coffee, maybe?"

"Yes, sir. If it wouldn't be a problem," Raymond said as he sat in one of the armchairs.

Graham raised his voice. "Alice, it's Maxwell House time in here."

"Coming right up!"

Graham opened the envelope and removed the contents. He read it as far as the first paragraph before he knew he wasn't going to like it.

"Alice," he called. "Belay the coffee in here! The colonel will take it in your office." He looked at Raymond. "This is not quite what I expected. Would you mind . . ."

Raymond was already on his feet.

"Yes, sir," Raymond said. "I understand, sir. I did the decryption myself. That message is a bit unusual, isn't it, sir?"

Again Graham felt his temper flare. This time he had an even harder time keeping it contained.

What Raymond had said he shouldn't have said, although it was true. "A bit unusual" was something of an understatement. But what had ignited Graham's anger was that Raymond acknowledged that he had read the message during the decryption process.

The only way to avoid that was for the individual actually writing the message to encrypt it, and then transmit it, himself, and for the recipient to personally receive and then decrypt it.

Otherwise, any number of people who had no business being familiar with the message at all—secretaries, cryptographers, radio operators, typists—had a valid reason to read the message and thus become familiar with it.

This system made necessary the use of code names for people and places and operations *within* the encrypted message itself. The theory being that if only the author and the recipient knew that "Tex" was Major Cletus Frade and "Aggie" was Colonel A. F. Graham, et cetera, the clerks, et cetera, involved in the transmission and receipt of the message who had read it would not know what they had read.

"Yes, it is," Graham replied, his temper under control. "This shouldn't take long, Colonel. Thank you for your patience."

"Not at all, sir."

Lieutenant Colonel Raymond left the office, closing the door after himself.

Dulles got up and walked to Graham's desk and looked over his shoulder at the message.

URGENT

TOP SECRET LINDBERGH

```
DUPLICATION FORBIDDEN

FROM TEX

MSG NO 404 1915 LOCAL 2015 2 OCTOBER 1943

TO AGGIE

I'M GLAD I'M TOO FAR AWAY FOR YOU TO BE ABLE TO
SHOOT THE MESSENGER AS I HAVE TO REPORT THAT NOT
ONLY ARE JUST ABOUT ALL OF THE COWS PLUS THE
VALKYRIES OUT OF THE BARN BUT ALSO THAT I HAVE NAMED
YOUR NEW KRAUT BUDDY PINOCCHIO. DETAILS FOLLOW IN NO
PARTICULAR ORDER SINCE I DON'T HAVE ANY IDEA WHICH
YOU WILL CONSIDER THE MOST IMPORTANT.

AT THE MOMENT THE TOURISTS ARE UNDER THE PROTECTION
OF POLO AT THE BREWERY. STRUBEL, NOW MOLLER,
HEREINAFTER TEAPOT AND NIEDERMEYER, NOW KORTIG,
HEREAFTER TEACUP, AND ALL FAMILY MEMBERS WILL MOVE
TO BREWERY TOMORROW MORNING.

TEAPOT WANTED ME TO SEND A CODED MESSAGE TO PINOCCHIO.
I REFUSED TO DO SO, AND TOLD HIM I WOULD HAVE HIM
SHOT IF I CAUGHT HIM SENDING ANY MESSAGE TO ANYBODY.
TEAPOT TOLD ME HE CONSIDERS HIMSELF A SERVING OFFICER
AND THAT HE REGARDS AS A TRAITOR ANYONE WHO IS
VIOLATING HIS OATH OF PERSONAL ALLEGIANCE TO HITLER.

BIG-Z ARRIVED BLACK ABOARD A SUB FOUR DAYS AGO AND
IS NOW IN MONTEVIDEO WITH BAGMAN. THE REASON I KNOW
THIS IS THAT SAUSAGE TOLD CAVALRY WHO TOLD ME.
```

Graham knew what all the code names meant, but Dulles had to ask about some of them:

"Pinocchio? Who's that?"

"He said 'new Kraut buddy.' Probably Gehlen."

"Pinocchio because his nose grows when he's lying?"

"What else, Allen?" Graham said.

"Polo?"

"Captain Madison R. Sawyer III, formerly Number Three on the Ramapo Valley polo team."

"The Brewery is where Frade has the Froggers?"

"It's his house in the vineyards of his Estancia Don Guillermo in the foothills of the Andes Mountains near Mendoza. He told me the entire Marine Raider Battalion couldn't get up the mountain to take it."

Dulles chuckled, then asked, "Big-Z?"

"SS-Brigadeführer Manfred von Deitzberg."

"Bagman?"

"Sturmbannführer Werner von Tresmarck, who runs that obscene confidential fund operation; he's light on his feet and does exactly what von Deitzberg tells him because otherwise he goes to Sachsenhausen with a pink triangle on his chest."

"That would tend to make him behave, I suppose. Sausage?"

"Anton von Gradny-Sawz, first secretary of the German Embassy."

"Cavalry?"

"Major Frade has declined to give me his name," Graham said dryly. "But I suspect he's Colonel Alejandro Martín of the BIS. I don't think Frade has turned him, but I think it's safe to say that Martín has decided that the gringos are less of a danger to Argentina than the Nazis. He's been helpful. Very helpful."

> SAUSAGE ALSO TOLD CAVALRY THAT BIG-Z IS UNDER ORDERS
> TO DESTROY MY BIGTOYS, THE TOURISTS, AND ME.

"I presume 'Bigtoys' means the Constellations?" Dulles said.

"What else could it mean? But what's that about von Deitzberg being ordered to destroy them? Ordered by who?"

"The only thing that comes to mind is that Propaganda Minister Joseph Goebbels is unhappy—for his propaganda purposes—with Argentina having better transport aircraft than Lufthansa," Dulles said. "But I rather doubt that he has that much influence over Himmler, who would have to issue that order."

"Maybe it came from Hitler; Goebbels has influence with him."

"I just don't know," Dulles said.

```
AT THIS POINT I DECIDED THERE WAS NO SENSE IN
PLAYING GAMES ANY LONGER WITH CAVALRY AND TOLD HIM
JUST ABOUT EVERYTHING MOST OF WHICH HE ALREADY KNEW.
```

"Now, that's worrisome," Dulles said.

"Yes, it is."

"The question is who turned whom."

"My God, Allen! He's a Marine with the Navy Cross! What I meant was that he told him 'just about everything.'"

Dulles looked as if he was about to reply but then had changed his mind.

```
CAVALRY FURTHER CONFIDED HE KNOWS THAT VALKYRIES
AREN'T ALWAYS LADIES ON HORSEBACK. YOU WILL REMEMBER
I SUGGESTED THAT PRINCETON TRY TO MAKE FRIENDS WITH
CAVALRY'S DIPLOMAT FRIEND.
```

"Well, I can make a good guess who he means by 'Princeton,'" Allen W. Dulles, BA Princeton '14, MA Princeton '16, said, smiling. "But the Valkyrie business is worrisome."

"You did get that message? That Martín has someone in the Argentine Embassy in Berlin?"

"And I have been working on it, so far unsuccessfully."

Graham nodded thoughtfully, then said, "Are you going to pass around that the Argentines know about Valkyrie?"

"I'll have to think, very carefully, about that. All of those involved do not have von Stauffenberg's courage and determination; if they heard this they'd be likely to pull back. I wish there was some way I could get to Argentina and discuss the players with Colonel Frogger, but I don't see how I could arrange that."

"We can ask Frade to ask him, Allen."

"Let's put that on the back burner for the moment."

Graham nodded.

> CAVALRY HAS ANOTHER FRIEND, A POLICEMAN, HEREINAFTER
> RENFREW WHO NOW ALSO KNOWS EVERYTHING.

"Why Renfrew?" Dulles said.

"After the movie."

Renfrew of the Royal Mounted had been a surprisingly successful B movie of 1937 starring James Newill as Sergeant Renfrew, of the Royal Canadian Mounted Police, who pursued the evildoers, assisted by his dog, a German shepherd named Lightning.

"Why not Dick Tracy?" Dulles said. "*Renfrew* must've meant something to Frade."

"Who," Graham replied, "was (a) still not much more than a boy when that movie came out, and (b) was almost certainly fairly well lubricated when he wrote this message."

"Is there an Argentine equivalent of the Royal Canadian Mounted Police?" Dulles pursued.

After a moment, Graham said, "Yeah. The Gendarmería Nacional."

"Would you care to wager a small amount that Renfrew has something to do with the Gendarmería Nacional?"

"If he's a pal of Cavalry, he probably runs the Gendarmería Nacional," Graham said. "Don't let this go to your head, but for a Princetonian you're pretty clever."

"And are you going to reward me with another taste from our Pinch bottle?"

"I thought you would never ask," Graham said, and rose from his desk and went to the coffee table where he poured scotch whisky in glasses for both of them.

Dulles sat in Graham's chair and resumed reading.

Graham returned with their drinks, set them on the desk, and then went to take one of the chairs in front of his desk to move it next to Dulles.

RENFREW AND CAVALRY ARE BEING VERY HELPFUL PRIMARILY
BECAUSE THEY DON'T WANT A CIVIL WAR AND BECAUSE THEY
DISLIKE THE GODLESS COMMUNISTS AS MUCH AS THEY HATE
BIG-Z'S FRIENDS.

"That makes sense," Dulles said. "On both counts. The one thing Argentina doesn't need is a Spanish-type civil war, and all the ingredients for one are there, just waiting for someone to strike a match."

"Yeah. And wouldn't the Chileans and the Brazilians like that?"

EL JEFE FIRST AND THEN RENFREW DECIDED THAT TEAPOT
AND TEACUP WERE NOT TELLING US THE TRUTH AND NOTHING
BUT ABOUT WHO THEY ARE.

WE TOOK TEACUP OUT ON THE PAMPAS AND SHOWED HIM THE
BUZZARDS CIRCLING OVER BEEF CARCASSES. THIS TURNED
HIM INTO A CANARY.

IT TURNS OUT SERGEANT MAJOR TEACUP OF THE SS IS
REALLY OBERSTLEUTNANT TEACUP OF THE WEHRMACHT WHO
WAS—OR STILL IS—PINOCCHIO'S DEPUTY.

HE SAYS PINOCCHIO SENT TEAPOT HERE BECAUSE HE WAS
GETTING TOO CLOSE TO THE LADIES ON HORSES AND THEN
SENT TEACUP TO KEEP AN EYE ON TEAPOT. TEAPOT WAS
TOLD THE SERGEANT MAJOR BUSINESS WAS TO HELP TEACUP
STAY IN THE SHADOWS.

ALL THREE OF US BELIEVE TEACUP. WHAT I'M WONDERING
IS WHETHER PINOCCHIO TOLD YOU ABOUT THIS, AND IF NOT
WHY NOT AND IF SO, WHY YOU DIDN'T TELL ME.

Dulles raised his eyes to Graham's and answered the unspoken question in them:

"I really didn't think Frade would find out," Dulles said.

"But you didn't tell me."

"I planned to."

"He said, lamely."

"Honest to God, Alex, I forgot."

TOMORROW MORNING I AM GOING TO TAKE TEAPOT, TEACUP, AND FAMILIES TO THE BREWERY UNTIL I DECIDE OR YOU TELL ME WHAT TO DO WITH EITHER OR BOTH. RENFREW IS SENDING TWO OF HIS PEOPLE ALONG TO HELP.

I INTEND TO INTRODUCE TEACUP TO THE MAN FROM THE DELTA TO SEE WHAT HAPPENS. WILL ADVISE.

TEX

END

TOP SECRET LINDBERGH

DUPLICATION FORBIDDEN

"'Tomorrow morning,'" Dulles said. "That means this morning, right?"

"Western Union service has been a little slow," Graham said sarcastically. "If he left Buenos Aires—probably, almost certainly, in his Lodestar—at, say, oh nine hundred, he's been there for hours. It's about a four-hour flight."

"*His* Lodestar? A prerogative of being managing director of South American Airways? Very nice."

"No. It is his *personal* Lodestar. His father had a Staggerwing Beechcraft. Our Cletus borrowed it, then got shot down in it dropping flares out of it to illuminate the *Reine de la Mer* so the USS *Devil-Fish* could put a torpedo into her.

"Our commander in chief was so delighted that he made our Cletus a captain, gave him another Distinguished Flying Cross—which he deserved—and then ordered the Air Corps to immediately replace the lost Beechcraft. Not just via some flunky: Roosevelt ordered General Hap Arnold, the Chief of Staff of the Air Corps, to personally see to it.

"The Air Corps didn't happen to have any Staggerwing Beechcrafts in stock—I think they stopped making them in 1940—but they had an order from the President, relayed through General Arnold, to replace the aircraft lost in South America. So they took a Lodestar intended as a VIP transport and sent that to Brazil, where it was painted with the same identification numbers of the Staggerwing—and in Staggerwing Red—and notified me that the 'plane' was ready. I told our Cletus to go get what I thought would be another Staggerwing.

"He did. And when he got to Brazil, he saw the Lodestar as a good way to get the radar and its crew into Argentina. So, with about two hours of instruction in how to fly it, he did just that. Without a copilot.

"And made it. When I heard about it, I caught the next Panagra Clipper and went down there and reamed him a new anal orifice for being so stupidly arrogant as to think he was that good a pilot.

"Frankly, my heart wasn't in that. What I was hoping was that the ass-chewing would make him think twice the next time he wanted to do something so off the wall."

"And did that work?"

"You've met him, Allen, what would you say?"

Dulles looked at Marine Corps Colonel A. F. Graham and with a straight face said, "I would say that Major Frade is a typical Marine officer," then returned his attention to the message.

"Man from the Delta?" Dulles asked.

"Oberstleutnant Frogger," Graham replied. "Frogger's son. We got him out of the VIP POW camp in the Mississippi Delta."

"And he's at the Brewery?"

Graham nodded.

"So what are we going to tell Frade to do?"

"*We* are not going to tell him anything, Allen. You blew your right to tell him anything when you didn't tell him—or me, so that I could tell him—about the phony sergeant major. And, on that subject, is there anything else you think Frade or I should know?"

"No, Alex, there isn't."

"Until about five minutes ago, that would have been good enough. Now I'm not sure."

Dulles's face tightened.

Graham didn't back down. "Goddamn it, we had an agreement—no secrets, nothing that could be misunderstood between us."

"Yes, we did. And I broke it. By oversight, not intention, but I broke it and I said I was sorry."

Graham didn't reply.

"What would you like me to do, Alex? Get on my knees and beg forgiveness? Commit suicide?"

"Good thoughts," Graham said. "How about getting on your knees and committing *hara-kiri* on the White House lawn?"

"As reluctant as I am to correct an always correct military man such as yourself, I have to tell you—presuming you *are* talking about self-disembowelment—the proper term for it is *seppuku*."

"They taught you that at Princeton, did they?"

"Indeed they did."

"In that case, go *seppuku* yourself, Allen."

They smiled at each other.

"So what are *you* going to tell Frade to do?" Dulles asked.

"Watch and listen, Allen. But first get out of my chair."

Dulles got up and Graham sat down.

He pushed the lever on his desk intercom device.

"Alice, would you ask Colonel Raymond to come in, please?"

Graham rummaged in his desk drawer and came up with a book of matches.

Raymond appeared almost instantly at the door. Alice stood behind him.

"Sir?"

"Colonel, can you assure me that there are no copies of this message in some file cabinet—or anywhere else—at Vint Hill Farms Station?"

"Yes, sir, I can."

"There will be a brief reply to this one. Alice, please write this down—not in shorthand—so that Colonel Raymond can take it back to Vint Hill, send it, and then burn it—repeat burn it."

"Yes, sir," Alice said.

" 'Pinocchio did not lie. Princeton didn't think you are as smart as you are. Use your best judgment. Keep me advised. Graham, Colonel, USMCR.' Read it back, please, Alice."

She did so.

"Now give it to Colonel Raymond to make sure he can read your writing."

"Yes, sir."

"I can read it fine, sir," Raymond said a moment later.

"Get that out immediately when you get back to Vint Hill Station, please."

"Yes, sir."

"That will be all, then, Colonel. Thank you."

"Yes, sir," Raymond said, came to attention, and saluted. Graham returned it. Raymond did a crisp about-face and marched out of the office.

When he was gone, Graham said, "Now that it's a done deed, I will listen to your comments."

"I don't think you had any other choice," Dulles said. "At the moment, we have absolutely no control over what Frade will do or won't do, even if we knew what to tell him to do."

"Great minds take similar paths," Graham said. Then he struck a match and, holding Frade's message to him over his wastebasket, set the message on fire.

[FIVE]
Casa Montagna
Estancia Don Guillermo
Km 40.4, Provincial Route 60
Mendoza Province, Argentina
1650 3 October 1943

Mother Superior had made it plain that she regarded Clete Frade's treatment of the mother of his unborn child as the despicable behavior to be expected of someone who had obviously inherited his father's insanity. But, aside from that, Mother Superior had been so cooperative that Clete suspected she had been given her marching orders from whoever in the hierarchy of Holy Mother Church had the authority to order a Mother Superior around.

One of the most important things she had done was to calm Señora Möller and Señora Körtig—and, as important, the children. She spoke fluent German, which made things easier.

"The first thing we have to do," Mother Superior told them, "is get you to speak Spanish, and the best way to do that, of course, is to get you in school. We run a bus up here every morning to take the children who live here to our school. It's inside the convent. And then, of course, it brings them home after school. Is there any reason, Don Cletus, they couldn't do that tomorrow?"

Frade thought, *Translation: Would it be safe to do that?*

Clete had looked at Inspector Peralta and saw that he was looking at

Subinspector Nowicki, who after a thoughtful moment made a subtle thumbs-up gesture, which caused Inspector Peralta to nod in Clete's direction.

Translation: The Gendarmería Nacional can and will protect the bus.

"I can't think of one," Clete said. "It sounds like a very good idea."

"And for the first few days," Mother Superior said, "I suggest that it would be a very good idea if Señora Möller and Señora Körtig came to school, too. Would that be all right?"

As long as I've got their husbands under my thumb here, why not?

"I think that would be a very good idea," Clete said.

"And now, so as to leave you gentlemen to your wine, I suggest that I take the ladies and the children to their apartments. I'll see what things they'll need for school, and answer any questions they might have."

"I think the fathers would like to be in on that," Clete said. "Would that be all right?"

"I think that would be a very good idea," Mother Superior said.

"Would you like to come along, Dorotea?" Mother Superior asked.

"What I think I am going to do is have a little lie-down," Dorotea said. "I'm tired from the flight."

Translation: I am now going to stand behind a partially open door and listen to what the men will say that they probably wouldn't say if I was in the room.

"Well, I can certainly understand why you're tired," Mother Superior said, flashing Clete an icy smile.

A minute later, Clete saw that the bar held men only. Stein was missing.

He's sitting on the SIGABA and waiting—probably in vain—for the graven-on-stone messages from Mount Sinai.

What was it Graham said about the more people knowing about a secret the less chance there is that it will remain a secret?

I trust Nervo and Martín. I trust Inspector Peralta because Nervo trusts him. And I suppose I can trust Subinspector Navarro because he works for Peralta.

That's a hell of a lot of people being told a hell of a lot of secrets.

Not to mention the local Gendarmería boss, Subinspector Nowicki. I don't know him, or where he comes from.

"Don Cletus, did Inspector General Nervo tell you I can read faces?" Inspector Peralta asked.

"Excuse me?"

"I can look at a face and tell what that person is thinking," Peralta said seriously.

What the hell is this?

"Really?"

"Would you like me to tell you what you're thinking?" Peralta said, and then went on without giving Clete a chance to reply. "*Who the hell are all these people? How the hell do I know I can trust them?* Am I close?"

"That thought has run through my mind, now that you mention it," Clete said.

"Don't be embarrassed, Don Cletus. I would have been worried if you were not worried. So let's deal with it: Me, you can trust, because the inspector general said you can, and you trust the inspector general. Subinspector Navarro can be trusted because I tell you he can. That leaves Subinspector Nowicki, whom you keep looking at through the corner of your eye. Despite his shifty eyes, I have learned he is trustworthy. But let him speak for himself. Estanislao?"

Subinspector Nowicki—a burly, totally bald, muscular man in his early forties, who had been sitting slumped in an armchair while sipping steadily at a glass of wine—stood.

"Don Cletus, I am a Pole. I hate Nazis and Communists. I know what they have done to Poland and I don't want either taking over in Argentina. Before I came here, I commanded the Gendarmería squadron in Pila. I was privileged to call your father my friend. When the Nazi bastards murdered him and nearly killed my old friend Enrico, I prayed to God for the chance to avenge el Coronel's murder. I swear before God and on my mother's grave that you can trust me."

He nodded once, then sat down.

"Enrico, why didn't you tell me you were friends?" Clete challenged, more in wonder than anger or even annoyance.

"You didn't ask, Don Cletus," the old soldier said matter-of-factly.

"Well, Don Cletus?" Peralta said. "Now that you're a little less worried about Estanislao . . ."

"I apologize, Inspector," Clete said.

"No need," Nowicki said simply.

". . . where shall we start?" Peralta finished his question.

"The arms cache?" Clete replied. "The perimeter defense of this place?"

"There are more arms, heavier arms, than I expected," Peralta said. "Fifty-caliber machine guns, mortars. And a great deal of ammunition. Which makes me wonder whether el Coronel Schmidt is really after that, rather than using the weapons cache as an excuse to look for the Froggers."

"Why would he want the weapons? He's got a regiment."

"Doesn't the U.S. Corps of Marines teach its officers that guns are like sex? You can never have too much."

"Point taken, Inspector," Clete said.

"But now that we're on the subject of el Coronel Schmidt, let's get that clear between us, Don Cletus. My orders from Inspector General Nervo are to assist you in any way I can, short of helping you start, or involving the Gendarmería in, a civil war."

"I have no intention of starting a civil war," Clete replied. "Is that what Inspector General Nervo thinks?"

"It's not you he's worried about," Nowicki said. "It's that Nazi bastard Schmidt."

"Schmidt wants to start a civil war? What the hell for?"

"To put in the Casa Rosada someone who understands that the Nazis—and until last week, the Italians—were fighting the good fight against godless Communism," Peralta said. "And what makes him especially dangerous is that the bastard really believes he's on God's side."

"Who does he want to put in the Casa Rosada? A colonel named Schmidt?"

"Maybe a colonel named Perón," Peralta said. "But probably Obregón."

"The head of the Bureau of Internal Security?"

"I've known for some time—as have Nervo, Martín, and some others—that el General de División Manuel Frederico Obregón likes to think of himself as the Heinrich Himmler of Argentina," Peralta said. "Not the concentration camp Himmler, of course, but as the patriot rooting out godless Communists and other opponents of National Socialism wherever found. Rawson—and others; el Coronel Wattersly, for example—keep him on a pretty tight leash, which Schmidt would love to remove.

"Rawson is a good man, but not very strong. He could be talked into resigning if he thought the alternative was civil war."

"And Obregón would move into the Casa Rosada?"

"More likely Pepe Ramírez—el General Pedro Pablo Ramírez—with Perón as his vice president. They get along pretty well, and nobody really likes Obregón."

"Jesus Christ!" Clete said bitterly. "So, what do you want to do with the weapons to keep them out of Schmidt's hands?"

"I think the best place for them is probably here. The Gendarmería doesn't have any place to store them more securely than they are here. Inspector General Nervo left the decision to me, based on what I found here. And I can't fault your defense of Casa Montagna. What I have to try—try very hard—to do is keep you from having to defend it."

"How are you going to do that?"

"Well, Schmidt can't get here without using the roads, and the Gendarmería owns the roads. We'll know immediately if—I think I should say when—he starts in this direction. You'll probably have two days'—maybe three or four—warning. And Inspector General Nervo will tell Wattersly and the others.

"In the meantime, today we're going to spread the word that the Gendarmería came here, found a small cache of weapons, and took them off your hands. So there's no reason for Schmidt to come looking for them. Maybe that will stop Schmidt. Maybe it won't."

"And if it doesn't?"

"The only thing I can tell you for sure, Don Cletus, is that if there is a civil war, the first battle will not be between Schmidt's Mountain Troops and the Gendarmería."

"But between Schmidt's Mountain Troops and Don Cletus Frade's ragtag little private army?"

"I don't want that to happen either," Peralta said. "But—and this is not a recommendation or even a suggestion—if you could somehow stall Schmidt outside your gates, perhaps there would be time for Ejército Argentino officers senior to Colonel Schmidt to come here and ask him what the hell he was doing. I think that maybe even hearing that this was about to happen would send Schmidt back to San Martín de los Andes."

"Unless, of course," Nowicki said, "the Nazi bastard has decided—or been told—that now is the time to start the civil war."

"Unless, of course, the Nazi bastard, on orders or on his own, *wants to start* a civil war," Peralta said.

"How am I supposed to stall him at the gates?" Clete said.

When he looked at Peralta, he saw that Stein was standing in the door waiting for permission to enter.

"A mortar round or two, or several bursts from a .50-caliber machine gun, might do the trick," Peralta said. "I did not say that."

Stein's eyebrows rose.

"What have you got, Stein?" Clete asked.

"We have just heard from Moses, Major. A graven message fresh from Mount Sinai."

I suppose late is better than never.

"Let's have it," Frade said.

Stein walked to him and handed him Graham's message.

"Oh, shit!" Clete said when he had read it.

He looked around the room.

Peralta looked at him curiously.

"Let me ask a dumb question," Clete said. "Where is it that dead heroes go in the afterlife?"

"Valhalla," Peralta said. "They are taken there by Valkyries."

Okay, so you know.

Captain Madison R. Sawyer III does not know, nor does Staff Sergeant/Major Sigfried Stein.

What about Subinspector Estanislao Nowicki and Subinspector Navarro?

From the looks on everybody's faces, nobody except Peralta has a clue.

Dead heroes in the afterlife? Valkyries? What the hell?

Who am I fooling?

I'm going to have to tell Sawyer and Stein; I really should have told them before. I promised everybody on Team Turtle there would be no secrets between us.

And Subinspectors Navarro and Nowicki are going to ask Inspector Peralta what the hell is going on, and he's going to tell them.

And what are my detailed orders from Mount Sinai?

"Use your best judgment."

"I would appreciate it if you listen carefully to this," Clete said.

Everyone looked at him.

"Señor Körtig and Señor Möller are German officers," Clete began. "Möller is an SS major who told me he believes any officer who violates his oath of personal allegiance to Adolf Hitler is a traitor—"

"You brought a goddamn Nazi into Argentina?" Nowicki exploded.

"Easy, Estanislao," Peralta said.

Frade was nodding. "For reasons—good reasons—known to Inspector Peralta. He can explain them to you if he wishes later, but let me continue.

"Körtig is a lieutenant colonel. He tells me that he is privy to a very important secret with the code name Valkyrie. He also told me that he was sent on this duty—ostensibly as a suboficial mayor—to keep an eye on Möller, who was sent here because he was getting too close to the Valkyrie secret." He paused, then asked, "Have I succeeded in confusing everybody?"

"I will tell you what I can of this later," Peralta said to the Gendarmería officers, then gestured to Frade. "Go on, please, Don Cletus."

"What we know now is that Möller cannot be trusted."

"If he can't be trusted, kill him," Nowicki said.

"You and Enrico think alike," Clete said. "But right now that wouldn't be smart. There is another German officer here, another lieutenant colonel, who is privy to Valkyrie. I know about this man. If he recognizes Körtig, then Körtig can be trusted."

"That's the South African?" Peralta asked. "The wine expert?"

"Uh-huh."

"I wondered about him."

"How did you hear about him?" Frade said.

"Subinspector Nowicki heard he was here. He asked me what to do. I asked Subinspector Nervo, who asked Colonel Martín, who asked Inspector General Nervo to back off. We backed off."

"I'm glad you did."

"Before I get them in here, I want to make it clear that I don't want Möller to know that the wine expert is anything but a wine expert, or that I put him—he's using the name Fischer; his real name is Frogger—together with Körtig."

"That's presuming your man knows Körtig, right?" Peralta asked.

"What if your man, the one you trust, knows Körtig as a goddamn Nazi?" Nowicki asked.

"That's a possibility," Frade admitted. "If that happens, I'll turn both Möller and Körtig over to you and Rodríguez."

"Clete, you better make sure they understand that was a joke," Madison R. Sawyer III said. It was the first time he'd opened his mouth.

Frade met Sawyer's eyes. "It wasn't a joke, Captain Sawyer."

"But they have their wives and children . . ."

"Nothing will happen to the wives and children."

"Jesus Christ, Clete!"

"Enrico, go get Körtig. And, Stein, you go get Fischer."

"Clete, I can't believe you're serious," Sawyer said.

"I have heard your comments, Captain Sawyer. Don't question any decision I make, or order I give, ever again."

Sawyer looked at him incredulously.

"The answer I anticipate, Captain, is, 'Yes, sir. I understand, sir.'"

After a long moment, Sawyer exhaled audibly, then said, "Yes, sir. I understand, sir."

Fischer came into the bar first.

He looked curious but not concerned.

"Gentlemen, this is Señor Fischer," Clete said, "who came all the way from South Africa to help us improve our grapes."

The handshaking took about a minute.

"A little grape for the grape expert?" Clete asked, holding up a bottle.

"I could use one," Fischer said. "I have had a hard day."

Rodríguez led Körtig into the room a minute later.

Neither German could conceal his surprise.

"Ach, du lieber Gott!" Fischer said softly.

"Willi," Körtig said, "we heard you were captured in North Africa!"

"I gather introductions are not necessary," Clete said.

Both Germans turned to look at Frade.

"Colonel Frogger, I presume you are prepared to vouch for Colonel Niedermeyer?"

"Absolutely! Absolutely!"

"And you would say that Colonel Niedermeyer knows that Valkyrie means more than some oversexed woman on a horse?"

"Major Frade," Niedermeyer said, "Colonel Frogger has been part of Valkyrie from the beginning."

"Sorry, Nowicki," Frade said. "It doesn't look as if you're going to get to shoot him."

Peralta chuckled.

"From this moment, Captain Sawyer," Clete said, "while he has the freedom of the compound, I want someone watching Möller twenty-four hours a day. If he tries to escape, kill him. And tell him if his wife tries to escape, we'll kill both of them."

"Yes, sir," Sawyer said.

XV

When SS-Brigadeführer Ritter Manfred von Deitzberg had telephoned the German Embassy almost immediately after stepping ashore from the motor vessel *Ciudad de Cádiz* in Buenos Aires, he asked for "Commercial Counselor" Cranz.

"One moment, please, Señor."

A moment later, a voice announced somewhat arrogantly: "Herr Cranz is not available."

"With whom have I the pleasure of speaking?"

"This is Assistant Commercial Counselor Raschner."

"He's not available, Raschner, or he can't be troubled talking to ordinary people?" von Deitzberg snapped.

"Who is this?" Raschner had asked. Most of the arrogance was gone from his voice, telling von Deitzberg that Raschner had recognized his voice.

Von Deitzberg hadn't deigned to reply directly.

"I need to talk to you, and Cranz, somewhere where we won't be seen together, without the ambassador knowing, and right now. Do not use my name or rank when you reply."

There was only a moment's delay.

"At the rear of the Colón Opera House, Mein Herr, is the Café Colón. We can be there in thirty minutes, if that is satisfactory, Mein Herr."

"Weren't you listening when I said, 'somewhere where we won't be seen together'?"

"What I respectfully suggest, Mein Herr, is that when you see me come into the Café Colón and then leave, you leave yourself and follow me to a place where no one will see us together."

"Thirty minutes, Raschner," von Deitzberg said, and hung up.

It took nearly that long for von Deitzberg to find a taxi and then be driven to the Café Colón.

He had just been served a *café con crema*—which came with a little cup full of solid lumps of real cream, and a little spoon, which triggered the thoughts that Buenos Aires was really a beautiful city—*indeed "The Paris of South America," as they said—and that the Colón Opera House was larger than the opera houses in Berlin, Paris, and Vienna; and that in 1939 Argentina was said to have the largest gold reserves in the world; and that all things considered—such as that Berlin was already half destroyed and the rest would certainly soon be—Buenos Aires was a pretty nice place in which to live*—when Raschner walked through the door. He looked around the café long enough to spot and be spotted by von Deitzberg and then turned and left.

Von Deitzberg decided that appreciatively drinking his *café con crema* was more important than jumping up to join Raschner, and did so.

When he finally left the Café Colón, he saw Raschner standing near the corner but did not at first see Cranz. His temper flared until he spotted him standing on the corner of the street diagonally across from Raschner.

When he started to walk toward Raschner, Raschner crossed the street, walked toward Cranz and then past him, taking a gravel walk that ran diagonally through a small park.

Von Deitzberg saw that Cranz was now bringing up the rear. Raschner crossed another street and then entered the lobby of a building near the corner. As von Deitzberg approached the door, he saw that the Argentine version of a concierge was holding open an elevator door, obviously waiting for von Deitzberg. When he got on the elevator and turned, he saw that Cranz was about to get on.

Not a word or a look of recognition was exchanged as the elevator rode slowly upward, nor as Raschner opened it and stepped out to put a key into one of the two doors opening on the elevator landing.

Von Deitzberg and Cranz followed Raschner into the apartment.

Raschner popped to attention, his right arm shot out, and he barked "Heil Hitler!" After a moment, Cranz repeated the gesture.

Von Deitzberg returned the greeting casually without the "Heil Hitler!"

"What is this place?" he asked.

"It is the former Frogger apartment, Herr Brigadeführer," Cranz said.

"The name I am using is Jorge Schenck," von Deitzberg said. "Use that only, please."

"*Jawohl, Herr Schenck,*" both Cranz and Raschner said, almost in unison.

"*Señor Schenck,*" von Deitzberg corrected them.

"*Jawohl, Señor Schenck,*" they said, together.

"I want to talk about those swine," von Deitzberg said. "But right now, I want a cup of coffee, with cream. And some sweet rolls. The voyage from Montevideo was tiring; I hardly slept, and my breakfast was inadequate."

"There's a café around the corner," Cranz said. "Actually, there's a café around every corner in Buenos Aires. But this one, the Café Flora, delivers."

"And the telephone is still operable?"

Cranz nodded.

"Then get on it, and have this Café Flora bring us some coffee with cream, real cream; make sure they bring enough, and some sweet rolls. Lots of both— what we have to discuss may take some time."

"Raschner," Cranz ordered, and pointed toward a telephone on the table.

"Herr Obersturmbannführer," von Deitzberg said icily. "I told *you* to get on the phone."

Cranz's face flushed, but he walked quickly toward the telephone.

"The number is on the first page of that little phone book, Herr Obersturmbannführer," Raschner said, helpfully.

"So, Erich," von Deitzberg said. "What can you tell me about the Froggers?"

"So what you are telling me," von Deitzberg said, "is that the Froggers *may be* on Frade's estancia or they *may be* in the foothills of the Andes, on *another* of Frade's estancias—no one knows for sure?"

"Oberst Schmidt is working on an idea to see if they are in Mendoza," Raschner said.

"And how close is Oberst Schmidt to putting his idea into play?" von Deitzberg asked.

As Cranz opened his mouth, von Deitzberg went on: "Well, let me tell you why I am so interested in the Froggers: I am, of course, determined to comply with my orders from Reichsführer-SS Himmler to eradicate them wherever and whenever found.

"But there is more to it than that. One of the things I did in Montevideo was to shut down the confidential fund operation. I can tell you now that the Reichsführer never knew anything about it.

"Both of you know the Reichsführer well enough to guess how he would react to learning that some of his closest subordinates were involved. . . ."

"Jesus Christ!" Raschner blurted. "Himmler didn't know?"

"Do you think he will find out?" Cranz asked.

"One of the ways to make that less likely is to comply with his orders that the Froggers be eliminated," von Deitzberg said. "Wouldn't you agree? Wouldn't you say that should be our highest priority?"

"Von Tresmarck!" Raschner said. "That queer sonofabitch has to go! And that whore of a wife of his! She has to know a lot about the confidential fund."

"If you will do me the courtesy of hearing me out, Erich, I was about to get to the von Tresmarcks."

"Sorry."

"If von Tresmarck were to be eliminated, our colleagues in Germany would wonder why that was necessary under the circumstances. They would also wonder what was going to happen to their share of their assets in the confidential fund. . . ."

The doorbell rang.

"Ah, that must be our *Kaffee mit schlagobers!*" von Deitzberg said. "Be so good as to answer the door, Erich."

"I was thinking just before," von Deitzberg said as he set his coffee cup down, "in the Café Colón, when I had one of these, that it will probably be a very long time before *Kaffee mit schlagobers* is again available in Demel in Vienna. There might not even be a Demel in Vienna after the war. Or, for that matter, a Vienna—or a Berlin—that any of us would recognize."

He picked up and took a healthy bite from a jelly-filled roll sprinkled with confectioners' sugar.

"Or one of these," he said. He paused. "Except, of course, here in Argentina."

He took another bite of the roll, and when he had finished swallowing, said, "Erich, a moment before, you referred to Frau von Tresmarck as a whore."

"Isn't she?" Raschner replied.

"There are some things about her you didn't need to know. Until now. Were either of you aware that she is the widow of a distinguished brother officer of ours?"

He looked between them and, after both had shaken their heads, he said, "Obersturmbannführer Erich Kolbermann, of the Waffen-SS, gave his life for the Fatherland in the east, shortly before von Paulus surrendered the Sixth Army at Stalingrad. You were not aware of this?"

Again, both shook their heads.

Like schoolboys, he thought, *who don't have any idea how to spell "potassium."*

"Well, we didn't take advertisements in the newspapers, for obvious reasons, to remind people of this, but shortly after the death of her husband, the then

Frau Kolbermann came to work for the Sicherheitsdienst. She mined the bars at the Hotel Adlon, the Hotel Am Zoo, and elsewhere, for matters of interest to us. She was quite good at it.

"And then when Obergruppenführer Heydrich—I presume both of you know it was Reinhardt Heydrich's idea that the confidential fund be set up—"

This time Cranz nodded, and Raschner said, "I always thought it was Reichsführer Himmler."

"It was Heydrich," von Deitzberg said. "And he gave me the responsibility of administering the program. We eventually realized we needed someone trustworthy to handle things in Uruguay. The obergruppenführer thought that von Tresmarck was a likely choice; he was intelligent, he spoke Spanish, and he didn't want to go to Sachsenhausen wearing a pink triangle.

"But who was to watch von Tresmarck? The obergruppenführer was familiar with Frau Kolbermann's work for the Sicherheitsdienst and suggested that it might be appropriate duty for her. Von Tresmarck needed a wife—we didn't want his sexual proclivities drawing attention to him—and who could better remind him of that than a 'wife' he knew was working for the Sicherheitsdienst? She could also keep an eye on the ambassador, on Hauptsturmführer Forster, and, frankly, on the people in the embassy here."

He paused, chuckled, and said, "I'm sure you will be delighted to hear that Frau von Tresmarck had only flattering things to tell me about your performance of duty."

He paused again, then went on: "So when I came here this time, I naturally went to Montevideo and looked up Frau von Tresmarck. Before I told her the confidential fund operation was to be shut down, I received her report on how it was going.

"She told me two interesting things: first, that von Tresmarck had a gentleman friend, a Uruguayan, and second, that at the recommendation of this friend, he had begun to invest the confidential fund's money in Paraguay. He—they—were then in fact in Paraguay doing just that. Von Tresmarck was under orders not to leave Uruguay without my specific permission.

"That was, of course, all the justification I needed to eliminate him, and his gentleman friend, and assume responsibility for the fund myself—I'll get into that in a moment.

"But then I realized that once our associates in the Fatherland heard about this, they would be worrying about their share of the fund's assets. And the more people who talked about the fund, especially in my absence, the greater the chance the talk would come to the attention of Reichsführer-SS Himmler.

"But what if, I asked myself, what if von Tresmarck and his gentleman friend disappeared, *à la* the Froggers, taking with them just about all of the fund's assets?

"That would nip in the bud any questions about their share of the fund's assets on the part of our associates. The assets would have disappeared. They would know that I was hot on the trail of von Tresmarck to get them back. That would be the best they could hope for under the circumstances."

"You have taken care of von Tresmarck, Herr Brigadeführer?" Cranz asked.

"If you use my rank again, Cranz, or my name, I will be obliged to decide that you are unreliable and will have to be 'taken care of,'" von Deitzberg said.

"I sincerely apologize, Señor Schenck," Cranz said.

"To answer your question: Von Tresmarck, his gentleman friend, and about two hundred fifty thousand pounds sterling have disappeared. I wouldn't be surprised if they were in Paraguay. When I have time I will look into that. It is highly unlikely that either will ever return to Montevideo—or, frankly, that I will find them when I eventually go looking for them.

"I have assumed control of the former confidential fund and its assets. . . ."

"Excuse me, Señor Schenck," Raschner interrupted. "'Former confidential fund'?"

"It is now 'Operation Adler,'" von Deitzberg said. "The purpose of which is to provide a safe nest for SS officers here in South America should—God forbid!—the Final Victory not come as we all hope it will, and we have to protect our brother officers from the savage revenge of the godless Communists."

"You're going to tell them about this?" Cranz asked.

"I don't think so, Karl," von Deitzberg said. "They're all very busy defending the Fatherland. For example, according to the radio station in Montevideo, the SS was deeply involved in destroying the port and railroad facilities of Naples to deny their use to the American Fifth Army, which moved into the city on second October."

"And we are going to use the assets of Operation Adler for the benefit of our brother officers?" Cranz asked.

"Precisely," von Deitzberg said. "If that becomes necessary, and presuming that they can get out of Germany and make their way here. I've been thinking that it would only be fair if we were paid a compensation—say, twenty-five percent of all assets—for our management services. What we are going to do is essentially a smaller version of Operation Phoenix. Strictly for the SS."

"Twenty-five percent seems reasonable to me," Cranz agreed.

"May I ask questions, Señor Schenck?" Raschner asked.

"Of course, Erich."

"When will you be returning to the Fatherland?"

"Well, I just don't know. The Führer—among other tasks he has assigned to me—wants to be sure that all parts of Operation Phoenix are in place. I can see where that will take a good deal of time.

"As will locating and eliminating the Froggers—which, as I'm sure you will agree, now is even more important, as those swine know much too much about the former confidential fund.

"And then there is the problem of destroying these new aircraft, which is compounded by the fact that I don't know where they are, what they look like, or have even seen a picture of one of them."

"They're actually quite impressive aircraft," Cranz said. "Von Wachtstein managed to arrange a tour through his mother-in-law, and he told me—"

"Ah, yes, Baron von Wachtstein," von Deitzberg interrupted. "The lucky fellow doesn't have to worry about what happens to him after the war, does he? As soon as he gets out of the POW cage, he just comes 'home' to his wife's Argentine estancia."

"That thought has occurred to me," Cranz said.

"You were saying, Karl?"

"The aircraft, which von Wachtstein says are magnificent . . ."

"I wonder if that language falls into the category of defeatism," von Deitzberg asked.

"I'd say it was a professional judgment," Cranz said. "Ambassador von Lutzenberger told him to find out as much as he could about the airplanes."

"Where did you say they are?"

"They're based outside Buenos Aires, on an airfield near Morón that Frade built and then named after the late Oberst Frade. They're under the guard of what I've come to think of as 'Frade's Private Army.' They're all former soldiers of the Oberst's cavalry regiment."

"We have some SS troopers here, don't we?"

"The last time we sent SS troopers to deal with Frade, they vanished from the face of the earth," Raschner said. "Leaving behind only a great deal of their blood in Frade's country house."

"Well, as I said, it may be necessary for me to remain here for some time."

"And what if either Raschner or I am ordered home?" Cranz asked.

"Well, I'll do my best, of course, to see that doesn't happen."

"But if it does?"

"If it does, then I wouldn't be surprised if we had to ask ourselves what was really more important. Returning to God only knows what—the Eastern Front, perhaps—or staying here to prepare Operation Adler. I would tend to think the latter."

"What about Frau von Tresmarck?" Raschner asked.

"She is at the moment in the Alvear Palace Hotel, where she tells me she is going to have a facial, a massage, and a hair-curling. Then she will go shopping—leaving a message to that effect with the hotel telephone operator. And then she will walk out onto Avenida Alvear and vanish from the face of the earth."

"How did she get to the Alvear Palace?"

"Von Gradny-Sawz was kind enough to meet the ship from Montevideo. He put her into a taxi."

"*Von Gradny-Sawz?*" Cranz asked. He was not able to mask his surprise.

Von Deitzberg nodded and said, "Von Gradny-Sawz will meet her somewhere on Avenida Alvear and take her to my flat in Belgrano, where she will become Señora Schenck."

"What's that all about?" Raschner blurted, quickly adding, "If I am permitted to ask."

"Are you curious about von Gradny-Sawz's role in all this, or about my new wife?"

"Both," Cranz answered for him. He tried to temper the immediacy of his answer with a smile.

"Von Gradny-Sawz has been wondering for some time about where he will go should the unthinkable happen. He knows the Russians will seize his estates, either before or after hanging him. Or perhaps skinning him alive; they like aristocrats only a bit less than they like SS officers.

"He managed to get quite a bit of money and jewels out of Austria—excuse me, *Ostmark*—and has, so to speak, set up his own small, personal, Operation Phoenix. This, of course, came to my attention. I decided his knowledge of the culture and geography—and the people he has cultivated—here would be of great value to Operation Adler, and have conferred on him sort of an honorary membership in the SS.

"So far as Frau von Tresmarck is concerned: She knows all about the investments of the former confidential fund, both those von Tresmarck told us about and those that he didn't.

"Since she has nothing to go back to in Germany, family or property, I thought perhaps she might consider helping herself to some of Operation

Adler's assets and disappearing. Obviously, I can't take the risk of that happening. A man and a good-looking blonde traveling around together, buying property, that sort of thing, causes curiosity and talk. A man and his wife doing the same thing causes less.

"God only knows when I can get my wife and children out of Germany, but until I can arrange that—and it might not be until after the war—I will not have the problem of having two wives."

"And when that happens?" Cranz asked. "It's none of my business, I realize . . ."

"No, Karl. It is none of your business. All I can tell you is that Frau von Tresmarck fully understands that this is a temporary charade, and that I am a happily married man and an honorable SS officer not at all interested in her physical charms."

"I didn't mean to suggest—"

Von Deitzberg silenced him with a raised hand.

"Sometime late this afternoon, Hauptsturmführer Forster is going to seek an audience with Ambassador Schulker in Montevideo. He will tell the ambassador he's very afraid something is very wrong: Sturmbannführer Werner von Tresmarck had told him that he and his wife were going to take a week's vacation at someplace called Punta del Este. Forster will report that that is not the case; they are not in the hotel where they said they were going to stay. Frau von Tresmarck booked passage on the overnight steamer last night—

"Actually," von Deitzberg interrupted himself, "that's a rather nice trip. You board, have a very nice dinner, go to bed, and when you waken, the ship is docking in Buenos Aires—"

Von Deitzberg took a sip of his *Kaffee mit schlagobers* and then went on. "Frau von Tresmarck did not tell him she was doing so. Inquiry of their neighbors revealed that von Tresmarck himself has not been seen for a week or more.

"Forster will ask the ambassador for direction. Schulker, being Schulker, will almost certainly decide on patience and calm. Which means it will probably be tomorrow, or even the day after, before he informs the local police and of course our own Ambassador von Lutzenberger.

"Your slow and careful investigation will then begin. You will after some time—two days, perhaps three—learn from von Gradny-Sawz that he received a telephone call from Frau von Tresmarck asking him to make reservations at the Alvear Palace for her—alone—for a week, and to meet her at the pier when the ship arrived. He will tell you he did so, took her by taxi to the hotel, saw her inside, and has not seen or heard from her again. She offered no explanation for her being in Buenos Aires. You will believe him.

"Your investigation will continue, but when you can spare a few minutes from your relentless search for the missing Frau von Tresmarck, I want you to get me maps—detailed maps—of Frade's estancia near here, the airfield where these airplanes are parked, and of his estancia in Mendoza."

"That's not going to be easy," Raschner said.

"I didn't ask for your opinion of the difficulty of the task, Erich, I told you to do it."

"Jawohl, Mein Herr."

"Perhaps von Wachtstein could be of assistance," von Deitzberg said. "Aerial photos of the airfields and the estancias?"

"With respect, *Mein Herr.* The airfield at Morón, certainly. The estancia near here, Estancia San Pedro y San Pablo, is as large as Berlin or Munich. What should I photograph? And at this moment, I don't have any idea where Frade's estancia in Mendoza is."

"You're a good man, Raschner. You'll figure it out."

Von Deitzberg reached for another jelly-filled roll.

[TWO]
Río Hermoso Hotel
San Martín de los Andes
Neuquén Province, Argentina
2035 5 October 1943

SS-Brigadeführer Ritter Manfred von Deitzberg was frankly astonished—pleased but astonished—that he had any energy left for that sort of thing after that incredibly long drive from Buenos Aires, but when he came out of the bathroom, Inge, waiting to have a shower herself, had stripped down to her underwear and one thing had quickly—very quickly—led to another.

They could have come by train. Von Gradny-Sawz had told him that while the Argentine rail system was nothing like the Deutsche Reichsbahn—the prewar Deutsche Reichsbahn—the British-built system here left little to be desired. The trouble was that San Martín de los Andes was literally in the middle of nowhere, and he would have had to change trains and then take a bus.

That ended the pleasing notion of rolling across Argentina in a first-class railway compartment with Inge. He didn't want to get on a bus, and he thought an automobile would probably turn out to be useful.

Von Gradny-Sawz had bought a car for him, paying an outrageous price for a two-year-old American Ford "station wagon"—von Deitzberg had no idea what that meant—with not very many miles on the odometer. The Automobile Club of Argentina had provided excellent road maps free of charge when he went to their headquarters to personally buy the required insurance. Von Gradny-Sawz said that the Automobile Club was a law unto itself, and that they demanded to see in person the individual the Caja Nacional de Ahorro Postal was about to insure.

On the map, San Martín de los Andes did not look to be very far from Buenos Aires until he looked at the scale of the map, then checked the chart of distances on the reverse.

It was about fifteen hundred kilometers from Buenos Aires to San Martín de los Andes. He remembered that a little more than five hundred kilometers was all that separated Berlin and Vienna.

There was no way, he decided, that he was going to be able to drive a distance three times that between Berlin and Vienna in the "fairly easy two days" von Gradny-Sawz estimated it would take.

The silver lining to that dark cloud was the prospect of spending three nights—perhaps even four—in some of the bucolic roadside inns the ACA recommended on their maps. He was in no particular hurry, and after that *gottverdammt* submarine, he was entitled to a little rest and relaxation.

It didn't turn out that way. Once they were fifty kilometers or so from Belgrano, they were into the pampas. The road stretched in a straight line to the horizon. There was very little traffic, and the American Ford V-8 engine propelled the station wagon easily at eighty miles per hour, which translated to about 130 kph.

That first day, they reached an idyllic roadside inn near Santa Rosa in time for cocktails and dinner, during which he checked the map and saw they were halfway to San Martín de los Andes.

The next day, although they came out of the pampas and had to travel winding roads through what he supposed were the foothills of the Andes Mountains, they made just about as good time.

He was pleased that he had decided to bring Inge with him for several reasons, in addition to the carnal. He had decided, telling himself he had to be honest about it, that her enthusiasm was probably because she was both afraid of him and needed him, rather than because of his masculine charm and good looks.

It didn't matter *why* she was willing to do all sorts of things the instant he ordered them—or even suggested them—only that she was.

But aside from that, Inge proved to be a fountain of information regarding the investments of both the Operation Phoenix funds and those of the confidential fund. She had spent a good deal of the trip explaining details to him, often taking the appropriate documents from those he'd liberated from von Tresmarck's safe, as well as the ones he had ordered Cranz to bring him from the embassy in Buenos Aires.

He had learned that Oberst Schmidt had been very useful in locating and dealing with the middlemen necessary to the acquisition process. Until Inge had uncovered this, he had thought Schmidt had been useful only in the military matters, providing security at Samborombón Bay and putting up the SS men Himmler had insisted on sending to guard the special shipments.

Von Deitzberg had come to San Martín de los Andes primarily to avail himself of Schmidt's military assets; eliminating the Froggers had to be accomplished as quickly as possible. But what he had learned driving across the pampas made him think very seriously about the whole operation.

What had been done from the beginning of Operation Phoenix, when Oberst Grüner, the military attaché, had been running things, was first to hide the cash and gemstones and gold in the safety-deposit boxes of reliable ethnic Germans who held Argentine citizenship.

Step two was to systematically turn the gemstones and gold into cash and then, slowly, so as not to attract attention, get the cash out of the safety-deposit boxes and into the bank accounts of the ethnic Germans.

Step three, using the money now in the ethnic Germans' bank accounts, was to purchase the businesses and real estate that were the rock upon which Operation Phoenix would stand. The deeds to all the property were held by the same reliable ethnic Germans.

The ethnic Germans could be trusted for two reasons. First, it was jokingly said that the *Ausländischer Deutsch* tended to be better Nazis than, say, Göring or Goebbels, if not the Führer himself.

Second, perhaps of equal importance, the *Ausländischer Deutsch* knew that Oberst Grüner, in addition to his military attaché duties, had been secretly the highest-ranking member of the Sicherheitsdienst in South America. That meant they knew that anything less than total honesty when dealing with the assets of Operation Phoenix would be rewarded with the painful death of everybody in the family in Argentina, and with the even more painful deaths of any relatives of the *Ausländischer Deutsch* who happened to be fortunate enough to be still living in the Fatherland.

Grüner's death on the beach at Samborombón Bay had of course taken some of the glitter from the notion of German invincibility, and with that the certainty of punishment. Cranz was good, but not nearly as menacing a figure as Grüner had been.

The current situation would prevail, of course, but only until it looked to the *Ausländischer Deutsch* that the Germans were about to lose the war—or, God forbid, had actually lost it—when they would begin to consider that the property and money placed into their care was now theirs.

The honesty of people depends in large part on their judgment of whether or not they will be caught stealing.

The next step in that line of thinking, should the unthinkable happen, would be for them to ask themselves, "How likely is it that Hermann Göring will show up at my door and ask for directions to, and the keys to, the estancia I bought for him? Bought for him in my name."

I have already transferred all of the Operation Adler property in Uruguay to Herr Jorge Schenck—in other words, to me. It doesn't matter that I did so because I frankly didn't know what else to do with it. I had to take it away from von Tresmarck, and obviously I couldn't, even as fond as I am growing of Inge, risk putting it in her name.

What I will do here, right now, is take a look at the various real-estate properties owned by the former confidential fund and transfer one of them—perhaps two, but I don't want to move too quickly and draw attention to Herr Schenck—to me.

Von Deitzberg finished dressing, examined himself admiringly in the mirror, and decided the tailors in Buenos Aires were every bit as good as the ones in Berlin, the main difference being that here the tailors' shops were full of fine woolens and the ones in Berlin had either been destroyed in the bombing or were out of material, even to those with the special SS clothing ration coupons.

His mind turned back to the present: *If I report to Himmler that I am taking the appropriate steps not only to recover the Operation Phoenix assets von*

Tresmarck stole, but to protect our assets in Argentina from disappearing by putting them in my name, he will understand. And that will give me an excuse—"It's not going as quickly as one would wish"—to stay here.

It might also serve as the reason to keep Cranz and Raschner here, so that some of the properties can be transferred to them. I am going to have to give them something, enough to keep them happy. Two birds with one stone.

He walked to the bathroom door and pushed it open. Inge, drying herself, had one foot resting on the water closet.

"Hurry it up," he said. "Schmidt's due any minute."

She smiled and wiggled her buttocks at him.

He turned and went to the window and looked down at the street.

San Martín de los Andes was really nothing more than a small village. There was hardly any vehicular traffic on the street he could see at all.

And then he saw an olive-drab Mercedes touring car coming down the road. The canvas top was down. There was a soldier driving, and two men in the backseat. The younger of them was in civilian clothing; the other was wearing an Argentine army uniform.

That has to be Oberst Schmidt.

"They're almost here," he called. "I'm going to meet them in the lobby. Get rid of your underwear before you come down."

Inge appeared in the bathroom door. Naked.

"You want me to come down without my underwear? Or do you mean get that out of sight?"

She pointed to her underwear on a chair.

"If you came down without your underwear, it would give Oberst Schmidt a heart attack," he said. "And we need him."

Von Deitzberg reached the lobby of the hotel just as el Coronel Erich Franz Schmidt of the 10th Mountain Regiment walked in from the street. The young man in civilian clothing with him, who looked like a recruiting poster for the SS, was SS-Hauptsturmführer Sepp Schäfer of the Leibstandarte Adolf Hitler.

I shall have to be very careful with that young man; not say anything at all that might be construed as defeatism.

Oberst Schmidt did not cut a very military figure. He was portly and rather short.

He looks more like a Bavarian party official—and don't those bureaucrats and clerks love to wear uniforms and boots?—than a soldier.

"El Coronel Schmidt?" von Deitzberg asked, advancing on him.

"At your service, señor," Schmidt said.

Schäfer popped to attention and clicked his heels.

"I don't think clicking your heels in these circumstances is wise, Schäfer," von Deitzberg said coldly.

"I beg pardon."

"We are waiting for one of my agents," von Deitzberg said. "The one thing a distinguished career in the SS-SD has not taught this agent is to be on time, probably because this SS-SD agent is a female."

He got the expected chuckles.

"I don't want to get into anything specific in public, of course, but to clear the air, you may feel free in Señora Schenk's presence to say anything you would say to me."

"Excuse me, sir. 'Señora Schenck'?" Schäfer asked.

"I generally give junior officers one opportunity to ask an inappropriate question of me," von Deitzberg said icily. "That was yours."

"I beg your pardon, Herr Schenck."

"Men traveling with good-looking females to whom they are not married cause gossip. Men traveling with their wives do not. You might try to remember that, Schäfer."

"Yes, sir."

Inge came tripping down the stairs.

From their faces, it was clear that she was not what Schmidt or Schäfer expected to see.

"I apologize, sir, for keeping you waiting," Inge said.

"Don't make a habit of it," von Deitzberg said coldly. "Gentlemen, my wife. She knows your names."

Inge nodded at both of them.

"I thought, Herr Schenck, that if it meets with your approval, we could have dinner at my quarters at the base."

"You are very hospitable, Herr Oberst," von Deitzberg said.

Schmidt waved them toward the door.

[THREE]
Quarters of the Commanding Officer
10th Mountain Regiment
San Martín de los Andes
Neuquén Province, Argentina
2100 5 October 1943

There were five Argentine officers waiting for them in el Coronel Schmidt's dining room. The dining room was much larger than von Deitzberg expected it to be, as the house itself was much smaller than he expected it to be.

It was hardly more than a cottage, sitting in a group of cottages across a road from the barracks, stables, and other buildings of the regiment. Von Deitzberg couldn't see much; nothing was brightly illuminated.

Against one wall of the dining room were three flags: the Argentina colors, a red Nazi flag, and an elaborately embroidered flag, the 10th Mountain Regiment's colors.

As the officers were introduced to Señor and Señora Schenck, young enlisted men in starched white jackets immediately began passing champagne glasses. When everyone held one, Colonel Schmidt said, "Gentlemen, I give you el Presidente Rawson."

Champagne was sipped.

Schmidt toasted again: "Gentlemen, I give you the Führer of the Third Reich, Adolf Hitler, and his Final Victory over the godless Communists."

This time the glasses were drained.

"Well, gentlemen, since my wife and I were never here, I don't suppose it much matters what I say," von Deitzberg said.

He got the expected chuckles and took another sip of the ritual postdinner brandy before going on. It was Argentine, and surprisingly good.

"But let me say it's good to again be with my fellow sailor, Sepp Schäfer— who, come to think of it, is also not here."

That caused applause and laughter.

And reminded everybody that I am important enough, what I'm doing here is important enough, to justify sending us by submarine.

"Let me say something about the current situation," von Deitzberg said. "I'm sure you have all heard that it was necessary for the Wehrmacht to withdraw from Africa, and also that our forces suffered a terrible defeat at Stalingrad. And, of course, that our Italian allies betrayed us, and as a result of that, the Americans are now in Italy.

"Those are facts. Not pleasant facts, but facts. A professional soldier must deal with the facts, not with things as he wishes they were.

"But there is another fact here that applies: The great military philosopher Carl von Clausewitz wrote, *'There is only one decisive victory: the last.'*"

More applause.

"What went wrong? Von Clausewitz also wrote, *'The most insidious enemy of all is time.'*"

Von Clausewitz didn't actually say that, but it sounds like something he would have said if he had thought of it. And I don't think there are any really serious students of von Clausewitz in this room to challenge me.

"Time has been against us," von Deitzberg went on. "The rocket scientists at Peenemunde, while their work has been brilliant, just haven't had the time to develop rockets that not only are more accurate than the ones currently landing in England, but will have the range to strike the United States.

"But it's just a matter of time until they do.

"Luftwaffe engineers have developed a new fighter, the Messerschmitt Me-262, which uses a revolutionary new type of propulsion, the jet engine. It is faster than any other fighter aircraft in the world, and it is armed with 40mm cannon. It can fire at American and British bombers from a distance greater than their .50-caliber machine guns can return fire. Once it goes into action, it will cause unacceptable losses to British and American bombers.

"There is already a squadron of these aircraft flying in Augsburg. But there has been time enough to manufacture only twenty or thirty of them.

"But it's just a matter of time until they do.

"Time has been working for our enemies.

"So now we make it work for us.

"How do we protect our rocket engineers from being killed by the Soviet Communists if they should temporarily overrun our rocket facilities? More important, how do we prevent our rocket scientists from being forced to work for the Soviet Communists?

"The same thing for our aeronautical engineers.

"The same thing for our physicists, who are close to developing a bomb more powerful than the imagination can accept.

"If the Soviets came into possession of German technology, it would mean the end of the Christian world.

"I'm sure the answer has already occurred to many of you.

"We bring them to Argentina, secretly, by submarine. Germany has the largest fleet of submarines in the world.

"And we set them up, with new laboratories, perhaps even manufacturing facilities. If things go even worse for us, with time working against us, *certainly* with manufacturing facilities.

"Where?

"I'm sure that answer has already occurred to many of you, perhaps all of you. I know that it has occurred to el Coronel Schmidt.

"Right here, in this remote corner of Argentina."

There was a burst of applause.

"As you can well understand, this has to be accomplished with the greatest secrecy. The Communists are everywhere. And the Jews. The Antichrist.

"El Coronel Schmidt and others have been working on establishing these refuges for German scientists—and their families—for some time, and will continue to do so.

"But there is another problem, the real reason I am here. This is always distasteful for professional officers, but again, we must deal with things as they are rather than with things as we may wish them to be.

"I am speaking of treason, which von Clausewitz described—I forget the exact quote . . ."

Probably because I just made this one up. But it does sound like something he would say.

". . . but it was to the effect that treason is simply another way of showing cowardice in the face of the enemy. On the battlefield, there is a simple way of dealing with those who throw down their arms and refuse to fight. One conducts a summary court-martial to establish that those are the facts. And if they are, the traitors, the cowards—whatever they are called—are tied to a post, stripped of their military insignia, offered a blindfold, and shot, with as many of their former comrades in arms as can be gathered watching.

"In the First World War, when soldiers of regiments refused to fight, every tenth soldier in the regiment was shot. We Germans believe in honor and justice, and we don't shoot people we don't know for sure have run from the enemy. But we do execute those we *know* have shown their treason, their cowardice.

"I am ashamed to tell you that a trusted officer of the German Embassy in Buenos Aires, Wilhelm Frogger, and his wife—who, like my wife, was an agent of the Sicherheitsdienst, the secret police branch of the SS—have deserted their post and gone over to the enemy.

"They were assisted in running by an American, a slimy Jew by the name of Milton Leibermann, who works for the American FBI. Leibermann thought that—probably with the assistance of the head of the OSS in Argentina, a man named Frade—he could hide the Froggers from us, save them from the execution they so rightly deserve.

"He was wrong. I am almost positive that some excellent detective work on the part of the Sicherheitsdienst agents in the embassy has located them. In Mendoza. Once we are sure of this, SS-Hauptsturmführer Sepp Schäfer and I will carry out the unpleasant duty of executing these swine.

"It gets worse. I have to tell you that an officer of the SS, Sturmbannführer Werner von Tresmarck, has deserted his post in Montevideo, Uruguay. He went—initial investigation indicates this happened within the last week—to Paraguay, taking with him a substantial amount of money he stole from the embassy. There hasn't been time for a summary court-martial, of course—it may have to take place in Germany, as he is entitled to be judged by officers of equal or superior rank and there are not three officers like that available here—but when it takes place, and if it finds this swine guilty, SS-Hauptsturmführer Sepp Schäfer and I will run him down, recover what he stole, and carry out his execution."

I don't think, judging by the looks on the faces of these people, that I would have any trouble at all finding volunteers for a firing squad for either the Froggers or von Tresmarck, or both.

"There is only one thing worse than a traitor," von Deitzberg said solemnly. "And that is someone who encourages—by argument, or by payment—another to betray the duties and obligations which he has sworn an oath to God Almighty to carry out.

"So the silver lining in this despicable black cloud for me will be the opportunity to kill Milton Leibermann of the FBI for doing that to the Froggers, and especially, especially, Don Cletus Frade of the OSS who tried and failed to turn his father into a traitor, and when that distinguished officer refused, murdered his own father—or had him murdered, which is the same thing—so that he could place the Frade assets in the service of Roosevelt and international Jewry."

Von Deitzberg saw the look on el Coronel Schmidt's face.

Didn't know that before, did you, my friend?

Why the hell didn't I think of that until just now?
Goebbels is absolutely right: The bigger the lie, the more people who'll believe it.

[FOUR]
Casa Montagna
Estancia Don Guillermo
Km 40.4, Provincial Route 60
Mendoza Province, Argentina
1300 7 October 1943

Don Cletus Frade, who with his wife was sitting on the verandah of Casa Montagna sipping wine as they watched the fifth chukker of the game between the Ramapo Valley Aces and the Mountain Húsares, did not pay much attention to the dark green 1939 Ford Tudor when it first appeared.

For one thing, the appearance of Gendarmería vehicles—he had come to think of their color as "Gendarmería Green"—was routine, and for another, it was a good match. A dozen new mallets, two dozen new wooden polo balls, and a supply of red-and-blue polo shirts—*real* polo shirts, with the players' position numbers on their chests and backs—had arrived on a training flight of an SAA Lodestar, and there were now four players properly identified on each side.

And everybody on the field knew how to play the game. Captain Sawyer had once told Major Frade, with pride, that he'd been rated as a four-goal player. Captain Sawyer was by no means the best player on the field today.

Frade didn't even pay much attention to the Ford until it drove up to the verandah. There was a sort of motor pool beside one of the outbuildings, and he expected the Ford would go there. And then the driver of the Ford jumped out, ran around the front of the car, and opened the rear door. Two men in civilian clothing got out. One was Inspector General Santiago Nervo of the Gendarmería and the other was el Coronel Alejandro Bernardo Martín of the Bureau of Internal Security.

Both officers walked directly to Doña Dorotea and kissed her, and then—Nervo first—turned to Don Cletus, who stood up and then asked, "What the hell are you doing here?"

"Our duty, Major," Nervo said as he wrapped his arm around Frade's shoulders. "I hope we're not too late for lunch."

"How the hell did you get here?"

El Coronel Martín first embraced Frade, then answered the question.

"With the polo mallets," he said.

"Excuse me?"

"We were on hand to meet the *Ciudad de Buenos Aires* when it returned from Lisbon," Martín said. "I asked your chief pilot, Gonzalo Delgano, if there was any way at all he could think of to get us to San Martín de los Andes in a hurry, and he was kind enough to say he would look into it . . ."

"That was nice of him," Clete said dryly.

". . . and he asked a few questions, and learned that a training flight was scheduled for one of your Lodestars; that, among other things, it was dropping off polo mallets and some other equipment for you at Mendoza; and he could see no reason why it couldn't drop us off at San Martín on the way back."

"Why not?" Clete said. "SAA always tries to cooperate with the BIS."

"So Capitán Delgano . . ."

"I thought he was a major," Clete said.

Nervo chuckled.

"He *was* a major," Martín said. "Now he's retired."

"Oh," Clete said. "I didn't know that."

Nervo, smiling, shook his head.

"So he not only arranged for us to go along with the Polo Mallets Training Flight—until just now, when we drove in, I wondered about those mallets—but flew the plane himself."

"Right after he came back from Lisbon? How obliging of him."

"He said something about there not being much to do but watch the needles on the fuel gauges drop. Anyway, he flew us to San Martín, and now here we are. By a fortunate coincidence, another training flight is scheduled to land here about four, and Major—excuse me, *Capitán*—Delgano has been kind enough to arrange it for us to go back to Buenos Aires on that."

"How nice of him!"

The doorbell at the door behind them sounded loudly.

"Well, that's the chukker," Dorotea announced. "One to go. If my husband will pull me out of this chair, I'll forgo that and see about lunch."

"Subinspector Nowicki may drop by, Doña Dorotea," Nervo said.

"I'll set a place for him," she said, and raised both arms toward Clete.

He gently pulled her out of the chair.

"Thank you," she said. "But don't think I'm ever going to forgive you for putting me into this condition."

Nervo laughed.

Dorotea walked into the house as Wilhelm Fischer came out with a wine-glass. She returned a few minutes later.

"So how were things in San Martín de los Andes?" Clete asked Nervo.

"Why don't we wait until Nowicki and Sawyer are with us?" Martín asked. He pointed at Sawyer.

"I've never met him," Nervo said. "But he's not too bad a polo player—for an American—is he?"

"You were about to tell us, *mi general,*" Clete said, "why your duty took you in such a hurry to San Martín de los Andes." He paused, and raised a bottle. "An-other little sip of our humble Don Guillermo Cabernet Sauvignon, *mi general?*"

"Don't mind if I do," Nervo said. He turned to Fischer. "Before you came here, Señor Fischer, to improve the quality of the grapes, I've been told this stuff was practically undrinkable."

"I'm so glad I've been able to helpful, *mi general,*" Fischer said.

"Then you won't be taking a couple of cases back to Buenos Aires with you?" Frade asked.

"The hell I won't. I accept your gracious offer. But I must say that if I didn't know better, Don Cletus, I might think you're trying to get me to tell you things I shouldn't."

"You bet your ass I am, *mi general,*" Clete said. "What's going on in San Martín de los Andes?"

"Well, among other things, the murderer of your father has finally been identified," Nervo said.

"Really?" Clete asked very softly.

"You did it. Or at least ordered it."

"What?" Dorotea exclaimed.

"Or so Señor Schenck told at dinner to a group of el Coronel Schmidt's officers—one of whom just happens to work for Bernardo."

Clete just looked at him.

"Would you like me to go on, or would you prefer me to start at the beginning?"

"Try the beginning," Clete said.

"If you'd prefer. Well, the first interesting thing that happened was that we now have a beautiful blonde in the picture. Von Gradny-Sawz's friend in the Interior Ministry got her a National Identity booklet identifying her as Señora Griselda Schenck, who you will recall died several years ago in an auto crash that also killed her loving husband, Jorge.

"The second interesting thing that happened was that the Uruguayan authorities asked the Policía Nacional to contact a woman by the name of Inge von Tresmarck. They wanted to know if she could shed any light on the whereabouts of her husband, Sturmbannführer Werner von Tresmarck, the security officer of the German Embassy in Montevideo whom the Germans had reported to be missing. The Uruguayans said they knew Señora von Tresmarck had taken the overnight steamer to Buenos Aires.

"Diligent police work revealed that Señora von Tresmarck had taken a room at the Alvear Palace Hotel. She then went shopping, leaving a message to that effect with the hotel switchboard. She never returned to the Alvear Palace."

"Von Tresmarck is missing?" Clete asked. "What the hell is that all about?"

Nervo did not reply.

"Then we learned that the ever-obliging von Gradny-Sawz purchased a car—a 1941 Ford station wagon—for Señor Schenck. The Automobile Club requires people who want insurance to appear in person. Señor Schenck did so, and while he was there availed himself of the ACA's free travel services. They provided him with road maps, on which the route to San Martín de los Andes was marked, and made a reservation for him and Señora Schenck at the Rio Hermoso Hotel in San Martín."

"Which is where Schmidt is, right?"

Again, Nervo did not reply.

"By the time all these details came to my attention, and Alejandro's—sometimes the Policía Nacional is a little slow—Señor and Señora Schenck were well on their way to San Martín de los Andes.

"By the time we got there, the Schencks had already been entertained at dinner in el Coronel Schmidt's quarters and, the morning following, had departed for San Carlos de Bariloche—"

"That's where Körtig is," Frade interrupted. "Or at least where he's headed."

"Tell me about that," Martín said.

"Welner 'just happened to hear' . . ."

"Father Kurt Welner, S.J.? That Welner?" Nervo asked.

"That Welner."

"And you can't bring yourself to call him 'Father'? Out of simple respect for the cloth?"

"I don't call you 'General' all the time, either, *mi general.*"

"Perhaps you should. A little proper respect goes a long way with me. So tell me, Señor Heathen, what did the Reverend Father Kurt Welner of the Society of Jesus 'just happen to hear'?"

"The other Jesuit, the one who gets National Identity documents . . ."

"The Reverend Father Francisco Silva, S.J.? That Jesuit?"

"That's the one. He showed up here and said that Welner had 'just happened to hear' that a small country hotel in Bariloche was up for sale, and he thought it just might be what we were looking for to put up the Gehlen people."

"Beware of Jesuits bearing gifts," Nervo said.

"And that, since he just happened to be driving that way anyway, he thought I might want to take a look at it."

"Could be one of two things," Nervo said. "Holy Mother Church might want to dump a hotel they own that's not making them enough money—or is termite-infested—on a gringo with money, or our wily Jesuit is being accommodating to this Gehlen fellow, for good reasons of his own that I can't even guess at."

"Well, since real-estate appraisal is not among my many other skills, I gave Körtig a pistol and sent Pablo Alvarez . . ."

"The estancia manager?" Martin asked. "Apparently, he knows what's going on and can be trusted?"

Frade nodded, and picked up the rest: ". . . with him to have a look at the hotel in Bariloche, and at other properties on the way. Pablo has friends all over this part of Argentina."

"Who wouldn't be surprised if he was quietly buying property for a friend of yours?" Martín asked.

"Yeah," Clete said.

"You gave Körtig a pistol?" Nervo asked.

"He asked for one, and I gave him one," Frade replied. "There are people who don't like people who like Valkyries. He wanted to be able to defend himself. That sounded reasonable to me."

"He gave me one, too, General," Fischer said. "For the same reason."

Nervo's eyebrow rose, but he didn't say anything.

"Where's the other German?" Martín asked.

"Well, I didn't give that Nazi sonofabitch a pistol," Frade replied. "If I did, once he finds out—if he doesn't already know—how my grape expert rides around with the Valkyries, he would be duty bound to use it on him. I've got him under sort of house arrest; I don't know what the hell else to do with him."

"Just don't let him get loose," Nervo said.

"I hope he doesn't try to get away. I told him if he or his wife tried, I'd shoot both of them. I don't want him calling my bluff."

Nervo looked as if he was about to reply, then stopped and said: "I was telling you about the dinner party Schmidt gave for some of his officers and the Schencks. According to Martín's guy, they toasted El Presidente, and then the Führer, as Schmidt stood before the Argentine flag and a swastika. . . ."

"What did you say about von Deitzberg accusing me of ordering my father's murder?"

"Señor Schenck gave a little speech, winding it up with saying what great pleasure it was going to give him to do his duty executing not only the Froggers and Sturmbannführer von Tresmarck for treason, but also the even more despicable Milton Leibermann for encouraging the Froggers to desert, and the most despicable of all, the evil Don Cletus Frade, who, when he failed to turn his father into a traitor, ordered his murder and promptly placed all Frade assets in the hands of international Jewry."

"That's absolutely disgusting!" Doña Dorotea exclaimed. "They believed that?"

"Everybody but Martín's guy," Nervo said.

"Are you going to warn Leibermann?" Clete asked.

"For the foreseeable future, Milton is going to be under close BIS surveillance to make sure he does nothing against the interests of the Argentine Republic," Martín said, and chuckled, and added, "And just as soon as I get back to Buenos Aires, I'll explain to him what it's all about."

"Tell him what you told me," Nervo said, and then went on without giving Martín a chance to reply: "He said it would be good training for his agents; that Señor Milton is better at escaping from surveillance than anyone he's ever known."

"You think von Deitzberg will try to assassinate Leibermann?" Clete asked.

"Actually, no. He'd have to do it in Buenos Aires, either himself or using some German from the embassy. I really don't think our assassination professionals would be available. Both Martín and I have gotten the word to them that the season on Americans is closed. And you and Enrico removed three of the best of them from their rolls.

"But is von Deitzberg going to try to assassinate you and the Froggers? Oh, yes. Even if he has to do it himself. When he went to Bariloche, he took with him the SS officer in charge of the SS people who were on the submarine. In private conversation after the dinner, Martín's guy said von Deitzberg was talking about the similarities between 'rescuing' someone from Casa Montagna and the rescue of Mussolini from that mountain in Italy. He said the SS officer—his name is Schäfer, Hauptsturmführer Sepp Schäfer—had gleams of glory in his eyes. He sees a chance for him to become the Otto Skorzeny of South America. What I think Schäfer is going to do is reconnoiter this place."

"If he does, can I shoot him?"

"I'm just a simple . . ."

"Yeah, I know. Señor Simple Policeman. Answer the question."

"They would just send somebody else. If you don't shoot him, then they will think they will have the element of surprise."

"And they won't?"

"It's about fifteen hundred kilometers from San Martín to here," Nervo said. "The rule of thumb for a motor convoy is an average of thirty-five kilometers per hour. That's about forty-three hours. Even pushing—say they try to drive fourteen hours a day—that's three days . . ."

"Gee, I didn't know simple policemen could do that kind of figuring in their heads," Clete said.

Nervo smiled and shook his head. ". . . and what Martín and I have been doing is arranging to stretch that time a little. The convoy is going to have to take detours along primitive roads; they will have to wait while bridge repairs are accomplished. They may even find that twenty-kilo barrels of nails have been spilled onto the roads at various places by careless carpenters, requiring the time-consuming repair of truck tires. . . ."

"Oh, *mi general,* you're evil!" Clete said.

"Thank you. Coming from a patricidal assassin such as yourself, I consider that a great compliment."

"I can't believe you two!" Martín said.

"Neither can I," Doña Dorotea said.

"I estimate," General Nervo said, "that from the time they leave San Martín—and we will learn that the moment they do—you will have at least four days, and possibly five, before they come knocking at your gate.

"At the very least, that should give us time to get el Coronel Wattersly from Buenos Aires to (a) best, Bariloche, or (b) last-ditch defense, here, where he can step into the road and ask el Coronel Schmidt where the hell does he think he's going without the permission of the General Staff of the Ejército."

"Which may get him shot," Clete said.

"Indeed. But that's the best I can do right now. I have to repeat what I told you a while ago, Cletus. If there is to be a civil war, the first battle will not be between the 10th Mountain Regiment and the Gendarmería Nacional."

"Understood," Clete said. "Thank you, Santiago."

General Nervo made a *Don't be silly* gesture.

"What time did you say the plane will be here?" Clete asked.

"It should be here now," Martín said. "Delgano said that the earlier we get on it, the better we'll be."

"Go pack your bags, darling," Clete said to Dorotea.

"I beg pardon?"

"You are going with the nice policeman . . ."

"I am not."

". . . who is going to take you from Aeropuerto Jorge Frade in that Buick of his to the Hospital Británico, where your condition will be evaluated. Depending on that evaluation, you will either stay in what will be the best-guarded room in the Hospital Británico, or go to the house on Libertador, or your mother's house—your choice—which will look like the site of a Gendarmería convention."

"I am not," Dorotea said.

"Doña Dorotea, I am old enough to be your father," Nervo said. "Listen to your husband. Listen to me."

"Dorotea—" Martín began.

"Listen to me," Dorotea interrupted him. "*I'm* the one about to have this child. I don't know exactly when that will happen. But I do know that if I got in a car and rode down the hill on that bumpy road toward the airport, you would have to take me directly to the Convent Hospital instead. And if that didn't happen and I were insane enough to get onto an airplane, I would have this baby at ten thousand feet over the pampas. I don't want to try that, thank you just the same. Thank you all for your kind interest. Discussion closed."

With a great effort, Doña Dorotea hoisted herself out of her chair.

"Have a nice flight," she said. "Give my regards to Capitán Delgano."

Then she walked back into the house.

[FIVE]
Departamento 5B
Arenales 1623
Buenos Aires, Argentina
1835 15 October 1943

El Coronel Juan Domingo Perón crossed the apartment and opened the door to the elevator landing. He was wearing his uniform. But his tie was pulled down and the tunic unbuttoned, revealing worn baggy braces that had seen long service. He obviously had been drinking.

SS-Brigadeführer Ritter Manfred von Deitzberg stood there.

As Perón offered his hand, he said, "A pleasant surprise, Manfred. I wondered why I hadn't heard from you."

"But you knew I was here?"

Perón closed the door to the apartment.

"Cranz told me you were coming, and how," Perón said. "And also that von Gradny-Sawz had told him he'd bought you a car and that you had driven out to San Martín de los Andes to see our friend Schmidt. What was that all about?"

"You're always one step ahead of me, aren't you, Juan Domingo?"

"I try to stay that way."

"Never travel by submarine, Juan Domingo. I am still recovering."

"What was that all about?" Perón asked. "Why didn't you fly on the Condor? Why all the secrecy?"

"So far as the submarine is concerned, the Führer himself wanted to know if that transport system will actually work if needed. . . ."

"Things don't seem to be going very well in the war, do they?"

"As a senior officer, I cannot agree with you. That would constitute defeatist talk. As a friend, in confidence between us, that's an understatement. You heard the Americans are in Naples?"

Perón nodded.

"And things aren't going too well in the east either," von Deitzberg said. "Anyway, I was the guinea pig to check out transportation by submarine. It was a long, long voyage."

"And driving all the way to San Martín de los Andes to see Schmidt?"

"Well, there were two reasons for that. The first was that I wanted to check on our Operation Phoenix properties out there. . . ."

"And the second?"

"Reichsführer-SS Himmler himself told me to do something nice for you, and Schmidt has been working on that for me."

"What would doing something nice for me entail, exactly?" Perón asked suspiciously.

"The Reichsführer wants you to know how much we appreciate all that you have done for us," von Deitzberg said.

"And?"

"How about a nine-room villa on two hundred and fifty hectares on the shore of Lake Nahuel Huapi in Bariloche? Does that sound nice to you?"

"It sounds like something I would have a hard time explaining."

"We'll talk about it. Believe me, Juan Domingo, it can all be handled with the greatest discretion."

"Discretion is very important," Perón said. "And speaking of which, there's someone I want you to meet. And here discretion is really the watchword."

Perón put his index finger below his left eye, closed the right eye, and then pulled down the loose flesh below his left eye.

He pulled the door open and waved von Deitzberg into the apartment.

Von Deitzberg thought: *What's this? I am about to be introduced to his latest conquest from the cradle?*

Perón gestured at a line of liquor bottles.

"A little of that Johnnie Walker would go down nicely, thank you very much," von Deitzberg said.

Perón made the drinks, and as he was handing one to von Deitzberg a not-unattractive blond woman walked into the room and smiled a little uneasily at them.

This one's not thirteen! She has to be at least eighteen.

Eighteen, hell! She's twenty-four, twenty-five, trying to look like she's eighteen. Who the hell is she?

"Evita," Perón said, "say hello to my good friend Manfred."

"It is always a pleasure to meet any acquaintance of el Coronel," the young blonde said.

"I am enchanted, señorita," von Deitzberg said.

"I didn't catch the name, señor," Evita said.

"My name is Jorge Schenck, señorita."

"I thought el Coronel just said your name is Manfred," Evita said.

"What this is, my dear," Perón explained, "is state business. That's not his real name, and you've never seen him."

"Oh!" Evita said. "It's like that, is it?"

Perón repeated the earlier gesture, this time closing his left eye and pulling the skin below the right eye down with his finger.

"Might one guess that you're not a Porteño, Señor Schenck?"

"Only if you call me Jorge," von Deitzberg said. "Actually, I live in Río Negro. Outside Bariloche. I'm what they call an 'ethnic German.' I'm a German who now calls Argentina his home."

"And what, if one may inquire, do you do in Bariloche?"

She talks very strangely, stiltedly formal. What the hell is that all about?

"Well, I have a number of business interests— May I call you Evita, señorita?"

"Of course you may, Jorge."

"I'm glad you raised the question, Evita. Among my interests is real estate. I've come to see Juan Domingo about a property in which I think he will be interested."

"What's that all about?" Evita asked.

"Well, as I'm sure you can appreciate, Evita, a man in Juan Domingo's position here in Buenos Aires is always in the public eye. Sometimes that's bothersome."

"Absolutely," Perón agreed. "Just between us and the wallpaper, just before you came, Manfred, I was explaining to Evita . . . again, I have to say . . . why we have to be careful where we are seen together. I have a number of enemies."

"You also have a lot of friends, including this one, Juan Domingo," von Deitzberg said. "And all of us are sympathetic to your problem."

"You see, Evita?" Perón said. "That's just what I was telling you."

"Sometimes I get the idea you're ashamed of me," she said more than a little petulantly.

"Don't be silly," Perón said. "What you should know, Man . . . *Jorge*, is that Evita herself is in the public eye. She is a radio actress on Radio Belgrano."

"Oh, really?" von Deitzberg said. "I should have guessed. You have a lovely voice, Evita."

"Why, thank you."

"So when we go out to dinner, there is usually someone who sees us and says to their friends, 'Oh, look, there's Evita Duarte, the radio actress, out with some officer.' Or: 'Oh, look at the beautiful blonde with el Coronel Perón.' Or, worst of all: 'Oh, look, there's that beautiful blond radio actress Evita Duarte out with the Secretary of Labor, el Coronel Perón.'"

"It's really not that bad, sweetheart," Evita said. "And it's the price you just have to pay for being prominent."

"Sweetheart"? Suspicion confirmed.

Maybe it's finally occurred to him that there would be objections to a president known to have an affinity for adolescent girls.

This may go easier than I thought it would.

"Well, all I know is that it's a problem even for someone like me," von Deitzberg said. "Who is not in the public eye. Just between us and the wallpaper, I have a lady friend, and we have the same problem."

"You're married, Jorge, is that what you're saying?" Evita asked.

"We haven't lived together for some time," von Deitzberg said. "It just didn't work out, and then it turned nasty. We can't go to dinner anywhere in Buenos Aires. My lady friend and I, I mean. If we do, my wife hears about it by breakfast and— Well, you can imagine."

"I understand," Evita said sympathetically. "So what do you do?"

"We do what I came here to suggest to Juan Domingo—and this was, of course, before I had the pleasure of your acquaintance, Evita—that he seriously consider doing himself."

"Which is?" Perón asked.

"Have a vacation retreat in Bariloche," von Deitzberg said. "And I think I have found just the place for you. For you both."

"Oh, really?" Evita said.

"I left my briefcase by the door," von Deitzberg said. "Let me go get it."

"Well, there it is," von Deitzberg said, pointing to a dozen or more large photographs laid out on Perón's dining room table. "Estancia Puesta de Sol, two hundred and fifty hectares on the shore of Lake Nahuel Huapi. A nine-room villa, plus servants' quarters, with most of the land in forest. Harvestable forest. What do you think, Juan Domingo?"

"I love it," Evita said. "Oh, sweetheart!"

I should have been a real-estate salesman.

"Again between us and the wallpaper, I'm a little strapped for cash," Perón said.

"That's not a problem," Von Deitzberg said. "I took title to this place when it came on the market, and your credit is good enough with me."

Perón obviously was trying to come up with the words to squirm out of it.

"But this is something you would want to consider at your leisure," von Deitzberg said. "Not just jump into."

"Yes, I would agree with that," Perón said. "Haste *does* make waste."

"So what I would suggest you and Evita do is go have a look at it."

"I'd love to," Evita said.

"How would we do that?" Perón quickly objected. "It's three days by train out there. If we only spent a day there, we'd be gone a week. I don't have the time for that."

"And eight hours by air," von Deitzberg said. "I know because I just came back to Buenos Aires by air."

"Really?" Evita asked.

"South American Airways now flies there twice a day, with a stop at San Martín de los Andes," von Deitzberg said. "The morning flight leaves Aeropuerto Jorge Frade at eight-thirty."

"You're not suggesting we do this tomorrow?" Perón asked, incredulous.

"Oh, darling, why not?" Evita said. "I'm so sick of this dreadful little apartment. And I've never flown. Please?"

"I'm not sure we could get seats on such short notice," Perón said.

Evita said what von Deitzberg was thinking: "Of course you can. You're on the board of directors of SAA. They'll find seats for us. Will your lady friend be going, too, Jorge?"

"Yes, of course. I think you'll like each other."

Inge will be a little surprised, and probably not pleased to hear we're going back to Bariloche. She really got airsick on the way here.

Too bad. This is all I could ask for, and more.

We came back to Buenos Aires so that I wouldn't be anywhere near that fool Schmidt when he goes to Mendoza. Better safe than sorry.

Casanova Perón will be out of Buenos Aires and in no position to do anything about stopping what's going to happen to his beloved godson, Don Cletus, in case he should hear about it—and if he was here, that would possibly, even likely, happen.

And once Juan Domingo takes possession of Estancia Puesta de Sol—which he will if Evita has anything to say about it, and she will—I'll have him in my pocket. There's no way he could satisfactorily explain how, on his army pay, he came into possession of an estancia worth half a million pesos from a man who died years ago in a car crash.

"I'll look in the book for the number, darling," Evita said. "And then you can call about the tickets."

"Can I make anybody another drink?" von Deitzberg asked.

"Oh, yes, please," Evita said. "It's a celebration, isn't it?"

XVI

[ONE]
Casa Montagna
Estancia Don Guillermo
Km 40.4, Provincial Route 60
Mendoza Province, Argentina
0430 16 October 1943

After failing to do so with several gentle nudges, Doña Dorotea Mallín de Frade awakened her husband by jabbing her elbow into his side.

Startled, he sat up and looked down at her.

"Why don't you go get Mother Superior?" Dorotea asked.

"Is something wrong?" Clete asked.

"No. I just want to start my catechism lessons a little early today. Right after that, I'm going to have a baby. Go get her, goddamn it, Cletus!"

"Oh, shit!"

He jumped out of bed, hastily pulled on his trousers, and ran out of the room.

"You're not needed in here, Cletus," Mother Superior said. "Go find something useful to do. Perhaps you can come back later."

Don Cletus Frade had been deep in thought as he watched Mother Superior and her crew—Sister Carolina, the huge nun whom Clete thought of as Mother Superior's sergeant major; Sister Mónica; and two others whose names he didn't know—start turning his bedroom into what was obviously going to be the delivery room.

"Excuse me?"

"I said get out. Go find something useful to do."

"Like what?"

"Prayer comes to mind."

He looked at her for a moment, then left the room.

What the hell, why not?

God, if anything bad is going to happen, make it happen to me, not Dorotea or her baby. Our baby.

Thank you.

[TWO]
Aeropuerto Coronel Jorge G. Frade
Morón, Buenos Aires Province, Argentina
0835 16 October 1943

SAA Chief Pilot Gonzalo Delgano stepped outside the passenger terminal and watched SAA Flight 455, one-stop Lodestar service to San Carlos de Bariloche, take off, desperately—and futilely—hoping that a red warning flag would appear on the instrument panel, causing the pilot to return to the field.

When that didn't happen, he went into his office in the passenger terminal, picked up the telephone, and dialed a number he had been dialing at least once every five minutes since seven o'clock.

"Extension 7177," a male voice answered.

"Is he there? Or do you know—"

"He's here, Major," "Suboficial Mayor" José Cortina said. "Hold on."

Delgano heard, faintly: "It's Delgano, Coronel."

El Coronel Alejandro Martín came on the line: "What's so important, Gonzalo?"

"Coronel, von Deitzberg, that blond German woman from Uruguay, el Coronel Juan D. Perón, and some other blond woman by the name of Duarte just took off for Bariloche. I didn't know whether to stop them or not. I tried to—"

"Perón and von Deitzberg—all of them—were traveling together?" Martín interrupted.

"Yes, sir. I heard about Perón going when I came in this morning. He called last night and said he needed four seats even if that meant taking somebody off the plane."

"When's the next flight out there?"

"At half past one."

"Hold four seats on that. Six. Cancel the flight."

"That won't be hard. It may not go anyway."

"What?"

"It's undergoing maintenance. They may not be finished in time. If they can't leave at half past one, they get into San Martín de los Andes too late. The runways there are not lit. We're working on it, but . . ."

"Is there any other way to get there in a hurry?"

"No, sir."

"You're going to be at the airport?"

"Yes, sir."

"Stay there. I'll get back to you."

[THREE]
Círculo Militar
Santa Fé 750
Buenos Aires, Argentina
0915 16 October 1943

"I hope this is important," Capitán Roberto Lauffer said as he walked into the private dining room. "My boss is going to wonder where the hell I am."

"Maybe you'll have the chance to tell him, Bobby," el Coronel Edmundo Wattersly said.

"We have some problems," Martín said.

Inspector General Nervo said, "Schmidt has apparently decided to start the civil war we were talking about—"

"We don't *know* that, Santiago," Martín interrupted.

"—with the assistance of Brigadeführer von Deitzberg," Nervo went on. "And that of el Coronel Juan D. Perón."

"I repeat, we don't *know* that," Martín said.

"What we *do* know," Nervo said firmly, "is that Perón and von Deitzberg are at this moment on their way to Bariloche by air. What we *do* know is that a ten-truck convoy of the 10th Mountain Regiment has departed its barracks in San Martín de los Andes on Route 151 in the direction of General Alvear—which is also in the direction of Mendoza.

"We also know that on the evening of the fifth of this month, el Coronel Schmidt gave a dinner for von Deitzberg, who is now running around as a dead man named Jorge Schenck, and Señora Schenck, who is almost certainly Frau von Tresmarck, the missing woman from the German Embassy in Uruguay. At this dinner, at which the Nazi flag was displayed, Schmidt toasted Adolf

Hitler, and von Deitzberg slash Schenck announced he was going to take plea-sure in killing the two traitors from the German Embassy—what's their name, Señor BIS?"

"Frogger," Martín furnished.

"Right. Thank you. And especially Don Cletus Frade, who, in addition to having the Froggers hidden at his Estancia Don Guillermo in Mendoza, is known to have ordered the murder of his father because el Coronel Frade was unwilling to betray Argentina and become an agent of international Jewry."

"Good God!" Wattersly exclaimed.

"Von Deitzberg actually said that?" Lauffer asked.

"And el Coronel Schmidt seemed to suggest he had suspected something like that all along," Nervo said. "A few days after this dinner party, von Deitzberg and the blond woman flew back here, then turned right around and went back, now with Perón and his lady friend.

"The good news is that Juan Domingo's new lady friend is not thirteen years old—I believe she's twenty-four—and el Coronel Perón's sexual perversions apparently will no longer embarrass you gentlemen of the Ejército Argentino officer corps. She is in fact a, quote, radio actress, unquote, by the name of Eva Duarte, employed by Radio Belgrano."

"My God!" Wattersly said.

"That was very entertaining, Santiago," Martín said. "But I'll repeat again that we don't *know* what Schmidt is actually up to."

"Did I mention the fact that the Edificio Libertador is having trouble com-municating with the 10th Mountain Regiment?" Nervo said. "And that as this little, not-authorized motor march exercise has gone up Route 151—did I mention that's the way to Mendoza?—telephone communication seems to have been lost. My people suspect that's because the wire has not only been cut but has been taken away. Telephone communication will not be restored until the wire is replaced. Not just spliced."

"What exactly is it you think Schmidt plans to do in Mendoza?" Wattersly asked. "Rescue those people Frade has there?"

"I think he plans to lay his hands on the arms cache, which is his excuse for going there in the first place," Martín said.

"And while he's there, since he's come all that way, maybe kill the Froggers," Nervo said. "And the Frades—did I mention that Frade's wife is very, very pregnant? Maybe they'll just let her go."

"You're saying Frade will fight Schmidt?" Wattersly asked.

"Well, Coronel, I'm just a simple policeman. You're the military man. What do you think he'll do?" Nervo said.

"We're going to have to go to the president," Lauffer said.

"You're pretty good, are you, Bobby, swimming with your hands tied behind you?" Wattersly asked softly.

"If it comes to that, sir," Lauffer said, "I guess I'll find out."

Lauffer walked to a telephone on a side table and dialed a number from memory.

"This is Capitán Lauffer," he said a moment later. "Put me through to the president, please."

There was a delay.

"He's not in his office," Lauffer said. "They're looking for him."

"Wattersly, you look as if you think we should have put going to the president to a vote," Nervo said.

"Actually, General, I was thinking that I should have been the one to get on the telephone."

Everyone looked at Lauffer for a very long ninety seconds, until he suddenly stood straight and spoke into the telephone again.

"Lauffer, sir. *Mi general,* something has come up. . . ."

"I'm in the Círculo Militar, sir. . . ."

"Yes, sir. With el General Nervo, el Coronel Wattersly, and . . ."

There was a brief pause, and then Lauffer said, "Yes, sir. We're in the private dining room at the end of the corridor, sir. Yes, sir. Thank you, sir."

He laid the phone in its cradle and turned to the others.

"The president was having breakfast in the main dining room. He saw everybody arrive. He's coming here."

Eyebrows were still being raised when el General de División Arturo Rawson— a good-looking, silver-haired man in his fifties with a precisely trimmed mustache—walked into the room. The president of the Argentine Republic was in uniform.

Everyone stood up and came to attention, everyone more quickly than Inspector General Nervo.

"Relax, gentlemen," Rawson said. "Good morning." He smiled at each man individually. "If I didn't know you all so well, I'd think I'd come upon a meeting of conspirators. What's going on?"

No one replied.

Finally, Nervo broke the silence.

"Mi general," he said, "you have a crazy Nazi coronel who is about to start a civil war."

"And which crazy Nazi coronel would that be, General Nervo?"

Wattersly answered for him.

"Schmidt, Señor Presidente. My cousin, el Coronel Erich Schmidt of the 10th Mountain Division."

"You agree with General Nervo, Edmundo?" Rawson asked.

"Yes, sir, I do."

Rawson looked at Martín.

"And what does General Obregón think about all this? And where, incidentally, is he? Why is he not here? And why are we all not in the Casa Rosada or the Edificio Libertador?"

El General de División Manuel Frederico Obregón was director of the Bureau of Internal Security.

Martín came to attention.

"I haven't told General Obregón, Señor Presidente," Martín said.

"Why not?" Rawson said.

Nervo answered: "He doesn't swim too well with his hands tied, Señor Presidente. None of us do."

Rawson glared at him for a moment before softly asking: "And you think that would have happened?"

"I didn't want to take the chance," Nervo said.

Rawson exhaled, then looked at Martín.

"If you had taken the BIS and the promotion to general that went with it, Martín, when I offered it to you, you wouldn't have this problem now, would you?"

"With respect, sir, that wouldn't have worked," Martín said.

"I shouldn't be talking to any of you," Rawson said. "General Nervo, you should have taken these frankly incredible suspicions of yours to the interior minister. Martín, you know you should have taken these suspicions to General Obregón—"

"At this moment, Señor Presidente," Nervo interrupted him, "Schmidt is leading a ten-truck convoy toward Mendoza."

"Mendoza? What's going on in Mendoza?"

"Well, for one thing," Nervo said, "the arms cache that the late Coronel

Frade established on Estancia Don Guillermo is there. And he wants that. And then I think he wants to watch the execution of Don Cletus Frade."

" 'The execution of Don Cletus Frade'? Did I hear you correctly, General Nervo?"

"Yes, sir, you did."

"That's preposterous! Why would Schmidt want to execute Cletus Frade?"

"Schmidt won't be the executioner, Señor Presidente. That honor has been reserved for SS-Hauptsturmführer Sepp Schäfer. But I think Schmidt would really like to watch."

"What the hell are you talking about, Nervo?" Rawson snapped.

"Well, what SS-Brigadeführer Ritter Manfred von Deitzberg told Schmidt was that Don Cletus had been sentenced to death by a summary court-martial for ordering the execution of his father, who had nobly refused to ally himself with international Jewry."

"I can't believe my ears. The only von Deitzberg I know is that German general who was here—who came here—to offer the condolences of the German officer corps on the death of Jorge Frade."

"Same chap, actually," Wattersly said. "But he's not really a German general, but in the SS. He's Himmler's chief adjutant. And this time when he came back here, he came by U-boat—by submarine."

"By submarine! That's preposterous!"

"I saw him come ashore at Samborombón Bay, Señor Presidente," Martín said.

"Why didn't you arrest him?"

"At the time, I wanted to see what he was up to, sir."

"And I agreed at the time," Nervo said.

"And when I learned of this, I agreed with Martín, Señor Presidente," Wattersly said.

"And so did I, sir," Lauffer said.

Rawson was silent for a long moment.

"When I walked in here just now, I jokingly said something to the effect that if I didn't know you all so well, I'd think you're conspirators. It's a damned good thing for you that I do know you all so well; otherwise I would call for the Policía Militar to haul you off to Campo de Mayo for confinement pending court-martial.

"But what we are going to do now is this: You are going to tell me everything. And I mean everything. I think we'll start with you, Martín, if you please."

"And Perón and von Deitzberg are now in San Martín de los Andes?" Rawson said fifteen minutes later.

"They are en route, sir," Martín said. "They and their lady friends."

"And what are they going to do when they get there?"

"I have no idea, sir," Martín said. "But I don't think they went there for the trout fishing."

"Is there some way you can put them under surveillance from the moment their airplane lands?"

"The Gendarmería Nacional is taking care of that, Señor Presidente," Nervo said. "And it's not only keeping an eye on Schmidt's convoy but doing its best to slow it down."

"The Húsares de Pueyrredón will take care of slowing el Coronel Schmidt down," Rawson said.

"Excuse me, Señor Presidente?" Nervo said.

"Just as soon as I can get to a military phone—" Rawson interrupted himself and turned to Lauffer. "Bobby, call down and have my car ready two minutes ago."

"Yes, sir," Lauffer said, and picked up the telephone.

"I'm going to order the Húsares to saddle up immediately for Mendoza," Rawson finished.

He saw what he correctly interpreted to be something close to contempt on Nervo's face.

"Figuratively speaking, of course, General Nervo. I'm going to order the Húsares to immediately begin to move to Mendoza *by truck*. They have enough trucks to move a troop with their mounts."

Nervo did not respond, and the look of near contempt remained.

"That was one of el Coronel Frade's innovations when he had the Húsares de Pueyrredón," Rawson said. "He called it his Immediate Reaction Force."

When there was no response to that either, Rawson said, "Jorge Frade even got airplanes for his regiment. Piper Cubs. Cletus flew me into Buenos Aires in one of them during Operation Blue, and I was able to prevent two regiments from inadvertently engaging each other as they marched on the Casa Rosada."

Nervo was still silent.

"General, if you have something on your mind, please say it."

"You're sure, Señor Presidente?"

"Consider it an order, General!"

"When I joined the Gendarmería, I was advised by a man I respected that I was never going to get anywhere in the Gendarmería unless I learned to keep my mouth shut and never tell any of my superiors anything they didn't want to hear, or, more importantly, that they were wrong.

"I followed that advice, and it worked. Here I am, inspector general of the Gendarmería Nacional. I don't have to worry about getting promoted anymore. What I have to worry about now is keeping stupid bastards like Schmidt from starting a civil war that will destroy Argentina. And, of course, from keeping General Obregón from sending me swimming with my hands tied behind me. . . ."

"If you have something to say to me, Inspector General, say it!" Rawson said angrily.

"Well, I'm just a simple policeman, Señor Presidente, but I see several things wrong with you sending the Húsares charging down the highway in trucks to Mendoza to roadblock Schmidt and the 10th Mountain Troops."

"Is that so?"

"For one thing, the Húsares wouldn't know where to find the Mountain Troops. The last word I had from my people who are following them is that they plan to halt for the night near General Alvear.

"That means in the morning they can do one of two things. They can turn right in San Rafael and take Highway 146 to San Luis, and then Highway 7 to Mendoza."

"I know the area," General Rawson said thoughtfully.

"Or," Nervo went on, "they can turn left at San Rafael and then about twenty kilometers down 146 get on the secondary roads to Mendoza. They're not paved and some of them are in bad shape, but it's only two-thirds—maybe half as far—going that way.

"We don't know which route Schmidt will take. So you won't know where to order the Húsares to set up their roadblock. And you can't split the Húsares and put half on one route and half on the other. How big is Frade's—el Coronel Frade's—Immediate Reaction Force? A troop? What's that, maybe fifty guys on horses?"

"About sixty-two, I think," Lauffer said.

"Okay. You split that many in half, you have thirty-one guys on horseback, armed with nothing heavier than Thompson submachine guns and Mauser carbines. On Schmidt's trucks are two hundred, give or take, men armed with everything up to .30- and .50-caliber machine guns, mortars, and God only knows what else.

"The Húsares won't stand a chance against the Mountain Troops. All they'll be is a footnote in the history books: 'The first battle in the Argentine Civil War of 1943–53 was between the 10th Mountain Regiment and the Húsares de Pueyrredón, who were wiped out near General Alvear.'"

He paused, then asked, "You want me to go on, Señor Presidente?"

"Please do so, Inspector General."

"'When word reached Buenos Aires that the 10th Mountain Regiment troops—who were now calling themselves the National Socialist 10th Mountain Regiment—had executed Don Cletus Frade, prominent estanciero and son of the former commander of the Húsares de Pueyrredón, for treason, troops of the 3rd Cavalry Regiment rushed from Campo de Mayo to the Casa Rosada to protect el Presidente Rawson, who was known to be a close friend of Don Cletus. They were met by the 2nd Regiment of Grenadiers—now the National Socialist Grenadiers—who wanted to execute Rawson. A battle ensued in the vicinity of the Retiro Railway Station.'"

He paused, met Rawson's eyes, and went on: "It won't matter who wins that battle, Señor Presidente. The civil war will have begun."

There was silence for a full sixty seconds.

Finally, Rawson said, "If you have any suggestions as to how your scenario might be averted, Inspector General, I'd like to hear them."

Nervo nodded. "You prepare three orders, Señor Presidente. The first one orders Schmidt to immediately return to San Martín de los Andes. El Coronel Wattersly and I personally hand this order to el Coronel Schmidt—"

"How are you going to do that? You're here, and he's . . . where exactly?"

"El Coronel Martín has ordered SAA to hold an SAA Lodestar for us, Señor Presidente. We would fly to Mendoza, find out where Schmidt is, and drive there."

Rawson nodded. "And if Colonel Schmidt chooses to ignore the order?"

"Then we hand him the second order, which relieves him of command of the 10th Mountain and orders him to consider himself under arrest pending court-martial for disobedience of a lawful order. The same order appoints Edmundo to assume command of the 10th Mountain, which he then orders to return to San Martín de los Andes."

"And if Schmidt refuses to acknowledge the second order?" Rawson asked.

"Then I will kill him," Nervo said.

"Whereupon el Coronel Schmidt's loyal—loyal to him—officers will kill you. Kill you and Wattersly. Have you considered that?"

"That possibility has run through my mind," Nervo said.

"You said three orders," Rawson said.

"The third order is to el Coronel Perón. It is for him to report to you immediately in person here in Buenos Aires."

"Two questions there, Inspector General," the president replied. "First, how would you get this order to Coronel Perón? And what makes you think he would obey it?"

"My deputy, Subinspector General Nolasco, will be on the Lodestar, Señor Presidente. After it drops Edmundo and me off in Mendoza, it will take him to San Martín de los Andes, where Perón will already be under surveillance. He will give the order to Perón and then offer to fly him to Buenos Aires in the Lodestar, which will leave for Buenos Aires just as soon as Nolasco concludes the business—unspecified—he has in San Martín. If Perón gives him any trouble, or makes any effort to contact Schmidt, he will be arrested."

"And then what?"

"That's as far as I got, Señor Presidente," Nervo said.

"Anyone else have anything to say?" Rawson asked.

"Señor Presidente . . . ," Wattersly began.

"Hold it a second, Edmundo. Let's follow the practice of asking the junior officers first. Bobby? What have you got to say?"

"*Mi general,* I'm your aide-de-camp, a capitán . . ."

"Who is in this mess up to his nostrils. Tell me what you think of the inspector general's proposal."

"The only thing I was thinking, sir, was two things. The first was that if we had the Piper Cubs you say the Húsares de Pueyrredón has sent to Mendoza, they would be useful to find el Coronel Schmidt."

"Good idea!" Rawson said. "And?"

"If the president would give me permission to accompany Inspector General Nervo and el Coronel Wattersly when they go to meet el Coronel Schmidt, I think it would lend weight to their position. If I was there, your aide-de-camp, el Coronel Schmidt . . ."

"If I sent you with these two, Bobby, what would happen would be that all three of you would be shot to death," Rawson said. He turned to Martín. "Okay, Martín, what have you got to say?"

For fifteen seconds Martín almost visibly formed his reply.

"I was thinking—I realize this might be construed the wrong way; that I'm trying not to go out there—I would be of more use staying here in Buenos Aires with you, Señor Presidente. If things go bad when Edmundo and Santiago meet Schmidt, or with el Coronel Perón when Subinspector General Nolasco goes to San Martín to deal with him, I think it would be useful for you, sir, to have at your side at least one man whose loyalty to you is known."

"In other words, you would prefer to be shot against a wall here with me than on some country road with Edmundo and the inspector general. Is that what you're saying?"

Nervo laughed. Rawson gave him a dirty look.

"Well, you'll be with me, Martín, but in Mendoza, not here," Rawson said. "Now, here's what's going to happen: just about everything Nervo proposed, with one major exception. Edmundo is going to stay here at the Edificio Libertador, and I'm going to meet with Schmidt wherever the Húsares de Pueyrredón's Piper Cubs find him.

"I am going from here to the Edificio Libertador, where I am going to get on the military telephone to el Coronel Pereitra of the Húsares de Pueyrredón. I am going to order him to move—immediately, in secrecy—his regiment to Mendoza, in three stages. First the observation aircraft, second the Immediate Reaction Force, and then the balance of the regiment.

"I am then going to dictate and have typed the orders Inspector General Nervo suggested that I issue. Then I am going to Aeropuerto Jorge Frade and get on the airplane Martín ordered them to hold for him and fly to Mendoza."

"Señor Presidente, everyone will know you've left Buenos Aires," Martín protested.

"Possible, even probably," Rawson agreed. "But so what? Bobby, let's go. The car should be at the door by now."

[FOUR]
Aeropuerto Coronel Jorge G. Frade
Morón, Buenos Aires Province, Argentina
1120 16 October 1943

When the president of the Argentine Republic stepped out of the official presidential limousine in front of the passenger terminal, a familiar face was there to greet him.

"Well, Father Kurt," El Presidente said. "What an unexpected pleasure! Whatever are you doing here?"

"I would think I'm here for the same reason you are, Arturo."

"And what would that be?"

"To try to keep some smoldering embers in Mendoza from turning into a conflagration."

"I have no idea what you're talking about, of course."

"Lying to a priest—especially to the priest who is your confessor—is a sin, Arturo. I've told you that before."

Rawson didn't reply.

"I think I might be of some help, Arturo."

Rawson gestured toward the Lodestar sitting on the tarmac.

"Why don't we take a little ride, Father? And, on the way, perhaps you'll be good enough to tell me how you found out about this."

"I'd love to, Arturo, really I would. But that would violate a priestly confidence, and that, too, would be a sin. I'm sure you understand."

[FIVE]
Casa Montagna
Estancia Don Guillermo
Km 40.4, Provincial Route 60
Mendoza Province, Argentina
1210 16 October 1943

Don Cletus Frade opened his eyes and saw Mother Superior's face very close to his.

"Try not to move," she said. "This will sting a little."

He tried to raise his head.

"Hold him," Mother Superior ordered.

A massive hand pushed his head back against the floor.

He saw Mother Superior's hands approaching his head. One hand held a pad of surgical gauze, the other a curved needle laced with a black thread.

He felt his forehead being mopped, then saw the needle getting close.

"Jesus H. Christ!" he exclaimed as the needle penetrated the skin on his forehead.

"Is he all right?" Doña Dorotea asked.

"I told you bringing him in here would be a mistake," Mother Superior replied.

The needle penetrated his skin again.

"What the hell happened?" Clete asked.

Dorotea groaned in pain and took the Lord's name in vain.

Clete tried to rise. The massive hand again pushed him back against the floor.

That has to be the hand of Sister Suboficial Mayor.

What the hell is going on?

The needle struck again.

"That should hold it for the time being," Mother Superior said. "Stay there until I say you can get up." She added, "Don't let him move."

"Yes, Mother Superior," Sister Suboficial Mayor said.

"Oh, God!" Dorotea groaned loudly.

"Push," Mother Superior said. "I can see the head."

Clete tried and failed to raise his head.

"Dorotea? Are you all right, baby?"

"No, goddamn it, I'm not. . . . Oh, God!"

"Stop blaspheming and push, Dorotea," Mother Superior said.

"Well, that's a shame," Mother Superior said.

"What's a shame?" Clete asked in horror from the floor.

"I was sort of hoping for a future postulant for the Order of the Little Sisters of Santa María del Pilar. But what we have here is what looks like a healthy male."

"May I let him up, Mother Superior?" Sister Suboficial Mayor asked.

"Give me a minute to clean up the baby," Mother Superior said.

[SIX]
Casa Montagna
Estancia Don Guillermo
Km 40.4, Provincial Route 60
Mendoza Province, Argentina
1240 16 October 1943

Subinspector Estanislao Nowicki found Don Cletus Frade and Enrico Rodríguez in the bar. Frade was holding a brandy snifter in his hand. There was a bandage on his head, and his shirt was bloody. Nowicki looked at Enrico for an explanation and Enrico shook his head: *Don't ask.*

Frade looked at Nowicki.

"Go ahead, ask," Clete said.

"What happened?"

"Ten minutes ago, my wife was delivered of a healthy baby boy."

"That's wonderful, Don Cletus!"

"I was at the time on the floor. Estanislao, never be present when your wife is having a baby."

"You passed out," Nowicki said. "That happened to me."

"I can't tell you how happy I am to hear that," Clete said. "Maybe that will wipe the smirk off Enrico's face. Enrico doesn't have any children."

"Having a baby, Enrico," Nowicki said, "is something a woman should do alone. Or at least with other women. Or with a doctor. But not with her husband anywhere around. When my wife had her first child, she swore at me with words I didn't even know she knew."

"So what's up, Estanislao?" Clete asked.

"You heard that that Nazi bastard Schmidt and ten 10th Mountain Regiment trucks are moving toward General Alvear?"

Frade nodded. "Segundo Comandante Garcia told me."

"Garcia just told me there's been a message from General Nervo. An important person will arrive at El Plumerillo around two-thirty or three and suggests you be there."

"He say what important person?" Clete asked.

Nowicki shrugged.

"Maybe the general. And/or somebody else."

Clete looked at his watch.

"Well, I guess I better go change my shirt. Never meet an important person at an airport in a bloody shirt. Enrico, I can really change my shirt without help. Go get the Lincoln."

The Lincoln, two Gendarmería Nacional Fords, and a truck were lined up in front of the house when Clete came out ten minutes later. Enrico was standing beside the Lincoln, holding the door open for Clete.

"With your permission, Don Cletus, I will not go. I want to have a look around the perimeter. You will not be alone." He gestured at the gendarmes. "And you will have more room in case there is more than one important person at the airport."

"Try not to fall down the mountain, Enrico," Clete said, and got behind the wheel.

[SEVEN]
Edelweiss Hotel
San Martín 202
San Carlos de Bariloche
1505 16 October 1943

"It is a great honor to have you in our hotel, Coronel Perón," the manager said, "and a pleasure to see you back so soon, Señor Schenck."

"I'm here privately," Perón said.

"We're thinking very seriously of buying a small estancia here," Evita said.

"Now, as I'm sure you can understand, we don't want that getting out," Perón said.

"I understand completely. You may trust my discretion and that of everybody in the Edelweiss."

"Thank you."

"How much trouble will it be to get my car from the garage?" Señor Schenck asked.

"I can have it at the door in five minutes," the manager said.

"Oh, good!" Evita said. "I'm so anxious to see this place!"

"I'd like to clean up a little . . . ," Perón said.

"Me too," Evita said happily. "My back teeth are floating, as they say."

Perón looked as if he wanted to choke her.

And she's not talking in that stilted language anymore. I suppose she figures she doesn't have to impress me with her culture now that we're all such good friends.

When Señor and Señora Schenck got to their room, she beat him into the bathroom and he waited impatiently for her to come out.

"Teeth no longer floating?" he asked sarcastically as he brushed past her.

"What does he see in her?" Inge said, ignoring it.

"I don't know, but I'm glad he sees whatever it is. With a little luck, I'll have his signature on that deed this afternoon—because of her."

When he came out of the bathroom, he went directly to the telephone and, consulting a business card, asked the hotel operator to get him a number.

"Señor Suarez, this is Jorge Schenck," von Deitzberg said. "I managed to convince el Coronel Perón to have a look at the property. I have reason to believe he'll like it. I'd like to strike, so to speak, when the iron is hot, by which I mean later today.

"What do you mean it'll take longer than that?"

Señor Suarez took forever to explain the bothersome details of completing such a transaction, the Argentine bureaucracy being what it was.

"Bribe somebody," von Deitzberg snapped. "Now, this is what I want done. I want you to be having a drink in the Edelweiss Hotel bar from five o'clock—make that half past four—until I get there.

"I will express surprise at seeing you, and I will tell you that I have been showing Perón Estancia Puesta de Sol, and one thing will lead to another and you will ultimately say something to the effect that there's no reason the deed can't be transferred right there in the bar if that's what he wishes to do."

Señor Suarez asked how sure could Señor Schenck be that Perón would want to do that.

"Trust me, he'll want to do that," von Deitzberg said. "You just be in the bar when we walk in."

[EIGHT]
El Plumerillo Airfield
Mendoza, Mendoza Province, Argentina
1505 16 October 1943

The first person to stand in the open door of SAA's *Ciudad de San Miguel* was Inspector General Santiago Nervo of the Gendarmería Nacional. He took a quick look around, which caused the dozen gendarmes from the truck to pop to attention, then got off the airplane.

Next to get off, surprising Clete, was Capitán Roberto Lauffer, and then, surprising Clete even more, the president of the Argentine Republic appeared in the door and got off. He was followed by Subinspector General Nolasco, el Coronel Martín, and the Reverend Kurt Welner, S.J.

What the hell is he doing here?

Finally, two men in the powder blue uniforms of SAA pilots came through the door. One of them was Capitán Gonzalo Delgano. The other—obviously Delgano's copilot—he recognized but could not remember his name.

"Cletus, what did you do to your head?" Rawson asked, even before saying "hello" or embracing him.

"Like President George Washington, Señor Presidente, I cannot tell a lie. I passed out as Dorotea was giving birth to our son, and cracked my head on the floor."

He realized that was the first time he had ever used the term "our son," and the sound of it produced a strong and unexpected reaction: His eyes watered and his throat tightened.

"When did that happen?" Rawson asked. "The baby. Not your head."

"Just after noon, sir," Clete said.

"Well, then, I will be able to say I was among the first to be able to offer my congratulations. How is Dorotea?"

"Very well, sir. Thank you."

"And I will have the happy privilege of baptizing your son," Father Welner said.

First things first, right? Sprinkle my son with water before some heathen Episcopalian can get to him?

"I see the Pipers have yet to arrive," Rawson said.

"Pipers"? What Pipers?

"Excuse me, sir?"

"They should be here by now," Rawson said. "I ordered el Coronel Pereitra to send them immediately."

Rawson saw the confusion on Clete's face and explained to him what had happened, what orders he had issued, and what he hoped would happen.

The Pipers had not arrived when he had finished.

"Well, I don't intend to stand around here waiting for them; they'll arrive sooner or later," Rawson said. "What I think we should do now is send Subinspector General Nolasco to San Martín to deal with el Coronel Perón . . ." He stopped when he saw the look on Nervo's face.

"If, of course," Rawson said, more than a little sarcastically, "this meets with General Nervo's approval. Cletus, you would be surprised at how helpful General Nervo has been. One would think he went to the Military Academy and into the army instead of becoming a simple policeman."

"Actually, *mi general*," Nervo said. "I thought about going to the Military Academy, but I couldn't. My parents were married."

Father Welner, Subinspector General Nolasco, Capitáns Lauffer and Delgano, and the copilot whose name—Garcia—Clete suddenly remembered looked horrified.

There was a hushed silence, broken only when Cletus chuckled and then laughed out loud.

"You think that's funny, Cletus?" Rawson asked, as if torn between indignation and curiosity.

"General, it's what reserve Marine Corps officers, like me, who didn't go to the Naval Academy, say to regular Marine Corps officers, who did."

"*Mi general,*" Nervo said, "I should not have said that. It just slipped out. Apparently, I cannot handle my newfound freedom to say what I'm thinking without considering the consequences."

"General Nervo believes he is about to be thrown into the River Plate with his hands tied behind him," Rawson said. "And if he ever says something like that again to me, I'll throw him into the River Plate myself."

"And I will help, *mi general,*" Capitán Lauffer said.

"Bobby," Frade said. "We call people like you 'ring knockers.'"

"A reference, no doubt, to a wedding ring?" Rawson asked.

"No. Naval Academy graduates wear Naval Academy rings. When someone who is not 'Regular Navy' says something they don't like, they knock their rings on a table, or whatever, to remind us amateurs that we are challenging regulars who went to the Academy and therefore know everything about everything and are never wrong."

"How interesting," Rawson said. "'People like you' would obviously include me. Your father, Cletus, had the odd notion that the Ejército Argentino was making a serious mistake in restricting the officer corps to graduates of the Military Academy."

"Well, I have to agree with that, sir," Cletus said.

"Perhaps we are," Rawson said, his tone suggesting he didn't believe that for a moment. "So tell me, General Nervo, what—as an amateur—it is that you find wrong with my idea of sending Subinspector General Nolasco to San Martin to deal with Perón?"

"Sir, I don't think we should arrest Perón until we know more about his involvement in this," Nervo said. "Send Nolasco to San Martín to locate Perón and keep an eye on him, but not arrest him until he hears from you."

Rawson nodded but did not reply.

"General," Clete said. "We don't know if the Pipers will arrive—"

"I ordered el Coronel Pereitra to send them," Rawson said impatiently, then heard what he had said. "And if they don't?"

Clete said, "Even if the Húsares de Pueyrredón's Pipers do arrive, we won't know if they'll work until I have a look at them. And without the Pipers, we're just pissing in the wind. Which means we're going to have to think of something else, like commandeering a couple of those."

He pointed across the airfield to hangars in which at least four privately owned Piper Cubs were parked.

"And what is your suggestion in that regard, Cletus?" Rawson asked.

"Send the general over there with me to commandeer those airplanes."

"And what would you suggest regarding el Coronel Perón?"

"I agree with the general, sir. Don't arrest my beloved Tío Juan until we know more than we do."

"All right," Rawson said. "Here's what we are going to do: Subinspector General Nolasco, get back on the airplane. Find and keep your eye on el Coronel Perón in San Martín, but take no action until you hear from either General Nervo or me."

"Yes, sir."

"Capitán Lauffer, you, General Nervo, Coronel Martín, and I are going to walk over there with Don Cletus to select which of those airplanes are to be commandeered into the service of the Argentine Republic."

"Yes, sir."

[NINE]
Estancia Don Guillermo
Km 40.4, Provincial Route 60
Mendoza Province, Argentina
1525 16 October 1943

Hauptsturmführer Sepp Schäfer—on detached service from the Leibstandarte Adolf Hitler—had his Schmeisser at the ready as he moved as rapidly and as quietly as he could down the area between long rows of grapevines.

He and the five men following him were wearing brown coveralls over their black SS uniforms. It was Hauptsturmführer Schäfer's intention, should anything go wrong—and it looked at this moment as if that had happened—to shed the coveralls, which would permit him and his men to claim the protection of the Geneva Convention and POW status.

He wasn't sure if that was the case.

How did the Geneva Convention feel about armed soldiers of a belligerent power being discovered—possibly after having taken some lives—roaming around a neutral country?

At the very least, Schäfer had decided, it would buy them some time until SS-Brigadeführer von Deitzberg and the Argentine oberst, Schmidt, found out they had been arrested and could start working on getting them freed.

He could now see the end of the row of grapevines. There was nothing in it. He held up his hand for the men behind him to stop, then gestured for them to move to the left and right, into the spaces between adjacent rows of vines.

A minute later, he heard the soft chirp of a whistle, telling him that one of his men had found something.

Reminding himself that stealth was still of great importance, he moved quietly through two rows to the left.

One of his troopers pointed to the end of that row.

Another of his men was standing there holding what looked like an American Thompson submachine gun. His legs straddled a body on the ground.

Schäfer ran down the path to him.

The man came to attention when Schäfer got close.

"Report!" Schäfer snapped.

"I had no choice, sir. He was coming through the vines toward me. When he came into this one, I shot him."

Something will have to be done with the body. I can't just leave it here.

It will fit in the trunk of one of the cars.

But what if one of the gendarmes at one of their checkpoints doesn't just wave us through in the belief that a sedan belonging to the 10th Mountain Regiment poses no threat to anything?

How the hell would I explain a body?

He pointed to one of his men. "In the back of one of the cars is a shovel," Schäfer ordered. "Go to it, get the shovel, and come back here. The rest of you move the body farther away from the road. Move quickly!"

"That's deep enough," Schäfer announced. "It only has to serve for a short time. Put him in it, and then start spreading the earth around."

"Tamp it down. I don't want anybody looking down the row and wondering why it's not level."

Schäfer handed the Thompson, which he had decided was not nearly as good a submachine gun as the Schmeisser, to one of his men and then stepped gingerly onto the tamped-down dirt on the grave.

"*Hände hoch!*" a voice barked.

This was immediately followed by a very loud burst of automatic weapons fire. The man holding the Thompson fell backward, still holding the Thompson.

Schäfer now saw that a very large man was pointing a Thompson at him.

And then a smaller man who appeared to be wearing an American uniform—there were chevrons on the sleeve of his shirt that looked American—pushed down the barrel of the larger man's submachine gun.

"Enrico," the smaller man flared, "you stupid sonofabitch!"

Then he turned to Schäfer and repeated, "*Hände hoch!*" and then added, in fluent German, "My friend would like nothing better than to shoot all of you."

Schäfer now saw there were half a dozen men, in addition to the big one who had fired the Thompson and the little one, the sergeant obviously in charge, in the passage between the rows of vines, three on each side of the grave.

They were all in civilian clothing. Three of them held Thompsons and the rest had Mauser cavalry carbines.

Schäfer raised his hands over his shoulders.

"I surrender. I am an officer of the Waffen-SS—" Schäfer began, then paused when he saw that the large man had trained the muzzle of the Thompson back at him.

"Enrico, we need to question them," Staff Sergeant Stein said in Spanish.

The big man nodded. "I was wrong," he said.

Schäfer went on: "—under the protection of Oberst Sch—"

"Shut your mouth, you sonofabitch, before *I* shoot you," Stein barked in perfect German. He pointed to one of the SS troopers. "Start digging him out of there."

Then Enrico gave an order of his own. "Rafael, send someone for the horses."

"*Sí, Suboficial Mayor,*" one of the natives said.

[TEN]
El Plumerillo Airfield
Mendoza, Mendoza Province, Argentina
1635 16 October 1943

Clete had just finished his inspection of the fourth Piper Cub in the hangar when he heard the familiar sound that the Continental A-65-8 flathead, four-cylinder, 65-horsepower engine made.

He looked at his hands, which were covered with grease.

"Why am I not surprised?" he asked.

"Is that them, Cletus?" General Rawson asked.

"It's either them," Clete said as he walked to the hangar door, "or somebody else has two Cubs."

A Piper painted in Ejército Argentino olive drab touched down on the runway. A second was a thousand meters behind it.

Clete ran across the tarmac and made the appropriate arm signals, telling the pilot to come to where he was standing. The pilot ignored him and taxied toward the passenger terminal. And so did the pilot of the second Cub when he landed.

The president of the Argentine Republic, the senior officer of the Gendarmería Nacional, the chief of the Ethical Standards Office, and the aide-de-camp to the president followed Don Cletus Frade as he walked across the airfield toward the passenger terminal, trailed by six gendarmes.

By the time they got there, Father Kurt Welner, S.J., who had been left with the cars and trucks, had told the pilots who was who, and the pilots—both young tenientes—were now standing, visibly uncomfortable, waiting for the sword of presidential wrath to fall.

"Good afternoon, gentlemen," Rawson said courteously, returning their salute. "Please stand at ease."

"Where the hell have you been?" General Nervo inquired, far less courteously.

"*Mi general,* we had to stop at Córdoba to refuel," one of the pilots said.

A civilian wearing a bloody bandage on his forehead and in a grease-stained polo shirt and khaki trousers, went to one of the Cubs and with grease-stained hands opened the engine compartment. Neither pilot thought this was the appropriate time to ask questions.

The civilian turned from the engine.

"I don't think I have ever seen such a clean engine," he said.

"Gentlemen, may I introduce Don Cletus Frade, who is an experienced Piper pilot. He is the son of the late Coronel Jorge Frade, whose last active duty command was of the Húsares de Pueyrredón."

Neither lieutenant seemed to know quite how to deal with that revelation. An indelicate sophistry from Major Frade's own military experience popped into his mind: *Those poor bastards don't know whether to shit or go blind.*

He took pity on them.

"Tenientes," he said, "are these aircraft in as good shape as they appear to be?" One of them found his voice.

"Sir, so far as I know, they are in perfect shape."

"May I ask how much experience you have in short-field landing?"

"Sir, we practice that technique regularly."

"In other words, you would have no trouble with putting one of these down on a field a little longer than a polo field?"

After a moment's thought, one of the lieutenants said, "No, sir."

Clete unkindly suspected that their practice had been trying to put a Piper down as close to the end of a runway as they could, then trying to see how short they could make the landing roll.

Well, there's nothing that can be done about that.

"What we're going to do now is: I am going to take one of these and fly it to my house. One of you will take the other one and follow me. All I can tell you is to suggest you make your approach as slowly and carefully as you know how."

"Yes, sir."

Frade turned to Rawson.

"Well, sir, I'll see everybody at Casa Montagna," he said, and then made a little joke. "Unless, of course, you want to ride up there with me and save yourself an hour's drive."

"I'll go with you," Rawson announced. "General Nervo can go in the other airplane."

"Sir, I was kidding."

"I wasn't," President Rawson said. "Father Kurt tells me you have a radio there capable of talking to Buenos Aires."

"To Jorge Frade, sir. The airfield and Estancia San Pedro y San Pablo. Only."

"Whatever its limitations, we'll have more communication than we have now standing around here. How soon can we leave?"

"Just as soon as I top off the fuel tanks," Clete said, and motioned for General Nervo to get into one of the Cubs. "I'm sure you will find this interesting, Simple Policeman. In Texas, they use these airplanes to catch speeders on the highways."

[ELEVEN]
Edelweiss Hotel
San Martín 202
San Carlos de Bariloche
1635 16 October 1943

Although Señor Jorge Schenck and Señor Otto Körtig arrived at the Edelweiss within minutes of each other, they didn't see each other for some time.

When Schenck, his wife, el Coronel Juan D. Perón, and Señorita Evita Duarte returned from their visit to Estancia Puesta de Sol Schenck, they had parked the Ford station wagon in front of the hotel on Calle San Martín. Then they had gone to the bar via the lobby.

As they were being shown to a table, Schenck saw Señor Suarez, the real-estate man, sitting with another man he correctly guessed to be the bureaucrat who was going to be necessary to witness Perón's signature on the deed. Schenck made a simple series of gestures telling Señor Suarez not to recognize him and to stay where he was until summoned.

Then he followed the others to a table, where he announced he needed a drink, a real drink.

Señorita Duarte thought that was a splendid idea, and said so. El Coronel Perón said that he would have a little taste of Johnnie Walker Black himself. When the waiter came, Señor Schenck ordered Johnnie Walker Black, doubles, all around.

Two or three rounds like that and Casanova, if encouraged by Señorita Evita, will happily sign the menu or anything else she puts in front of him.

When Señor Pablo Alvarez, the Reverend Francisco Silva, S.J., and Señor Otto Körtig arrived at the hotel about fifteen minutes later, after a full and exhausting day of examining the Hotel Lago Vista in detail, they parked the 1940 Ford Fordor from Casa Montagna in the parking lot behind the hotel, as they would have no further need for it until the morning.

Then they started to enter the hotel from the parking lot. But as they did, they came to sort of an adjunct of the hotel bar, a glass-roofed area outside the more formal inside bar. It had a dozen or so cast-iron tables with umbrellas, six or seven of which were occupied by people having a drink and munching on cheese and salami.

"Am I the only one who's tempted?" Señor Alvarez asked.

"How's the beer in Argentina?" Señor Körtig inquired. "I haven't had a decent glass of beer in months."

"I think you will be pleased, Otto," Father Silva said.

"Are you a beer drinker, Father?"

"On occasion," the priest confessed.

Three liters of Quilmes lager later, Señor Körtig excused himself to visit the gentlemen's rest facility.

"It's right inside the lobby to the right, Otto," Father Silva said.

"Thank you. Order another liter of the Quilmes while I'm gone, will you?"

"It will be my pleasure," Señor Alvarez said.

In the main bar, Señor Schenck looked up from stuffing his copy of the just executed change-of-owner documentation for Estancia Puesta de Sol into his briefcase.

That Johnnie Walker is getting to me. If I didn't know better, I'd swear I just saw Oberstleutnant Otto Niedermeyer walk past.

Ridiculous!

He works for Canaris in Abwehr Ost. What could he possibly be doing here in the Andes mountains of Argentina?

And if you do something foolish, like chase some strange man into a men's room and . . .

"Excuse me, please," Schenck said, and got up from the table and followed a strange man toward the men's room.

Rather than porcelain urinals mounted to a wall, the urinal in the Hotel Edelweiss lobby men's room was the wall itself. Below waist height, the wall was tiled. A copper pipe just above the tiles fed a never-ending stream of water gently down the white tiles toward a sort of trough at the bottom.

When Señor Schenck entered the men's room, the strange man was facing the wall.

Schenck waited until the man turned, and he had a chance for a good look.

"*Wie geht's*, Otto?" he asked cordially, smiling.

"*Ach, Gott!*" Oberstleutnant Otto Niedermeyer, visibly surprised, said. "What in the world are you doing here?"

Niedermeyer put his index finger before his lips and looked quickly at the water closet stalls—all of which were empty.

He threw out his arm in the Nazi salute.

"Heil Hitler!" he said, and then, "May the oberstleutnant respectfully suggest that the SS-brigadeführer attend to his personal business first?"

Von Deitzberg smiled.

"Good idea," he said.

He stepped to the urinal wall, unzipped his trousers, and started to attend to his personal business.

SS-Brigadeführer Ritter Manfred von Deitzberg turned his head to look at Oberstleutnant Niedermeyer just in time to see the muzzle of the barrel of Niedermeyer's Ballester-Molina Pistola Automatica Calibre .45 before it fired.

Von Deitzberg slumped to the floor, leaving a tracing of brain tissue and blood on the urinal's tiles. The stream of water caused first the blood to start sliding down the tiles, and then the smaller pieces of brain tissue.

Niedermeyer quickly examined his clothing to see if he had been splattered with either. He had not been. He looked down at von Deitzberg, said, "God forgive me," returned the pistol to the small of his back, and calmly walked out of the men's room.

My ears are ringing from the noise of that gun firing in there. My hearing has been impaired.

I will have to remember to speak softly. Deaf people speak loudly.

He walked to the table and sat down.

"I heard what sounded like a shot," Alvarez said.

"Father," Körtig said softly, "if it looks as if I am about to be arrested, I will have to take my own life; otherwise many good men and their families will die."

[TWELVE]
Casa Montagna
Estancia Don Guillermo
Km 40.4, Provincial Route 60
Mendoza Province, Argentina
1705 16 October 1943

Clete set the Cub down with landing roll to spare on the first try. The pilot of the Cub following him decided to go around twice before finally coming in for a landing.

"He's not as skilled as you are," President Rawson said.

"What he is is smarter than I am," Clete replied. "He didn't bring it in until he was sure he could."

Captain Madison R. Sawyer III walked up to them. He was wearing an olive-drab shirt with the silver railroad tracks of his rank and the crossed sabers of cavalry pinned to the collar points. He had a Thompson slung from his shoulder.

"Well, look what you brought home," he said, and only then recognized the president of the Argentine Republic. He saluted.

"General Rawson, this is Captain Sawyer," Clete said.

"How do you do, Capitán?"

"Sir," Sawyer said, then: "Major, may I have a word in private?"

"Anything you have to say to me, Captain, you may say in the presence of the president."

"Yes, sir. Sir, maybe you better come with me."

The body had been laid on and under a blanket outside one of the small outbuildings.

"Please tell me this is not one of ours," Clete said.

"There is one of ours, sir, but he's inside on the bed."

Sawyer pulled off the blanket.

The eyes of the corpse were open. His face showed what could have been surprise. His coveralls had been unbuttoned, exposing the blood-soaked black SS uniform underneath. On his chest were his identity tags and his identity card.

"Close his eyes, for Christ's sake," Clete snapped.

Sawyer looked at him in horror.

Clete leaned and closed the corpse's eyelids, then pulled the blanket over the body.

"Okay, what happened?" Frade asked.

"There were about six of them running around the vineyard. One of them shot one of our guys. Stein and Enrico were running around down there, heard the shot, and went looking.

"Before Stein could stop him, Rodríguez blew this one away with his Thompson. We have the rest of them, including a hauptsturmführer who says he's under the protection of Colonel Schmidt."

"Now, that's interesting," Rawson said. "Where is he? Are they?"

"Over there, sir. In the woodshed," Sawyer said, and pointed.

General Nervo came walking quickly to them.

"What's this?"

Clete said, "It's a dead SS trooper, who killed one of my men. There're six more—"

"Including an officer, General Nervo," Rawson interrupted, "who says he is under the protection of el Coronel Schmidt."

"—over there in the woodshed," Clete finished.

"Who killed this one?"

"Rodríguez," Clete said.

Nervo leaned over the body and pulled down the blanket.

"Why is the ID on his chest?" he asked.

"That was Rodríguez's idea. He said that when they killed the ones at Tandil, they took their pictures with their IDs before they buried them."

"Would you mind going over that again for me, please, Capitán?" the president asked courteously.

"Yes, sir. Well, when Perón and Schmidt and the SS guys tried to kill the Froggers at Don Cletus's house in Tandil—"

"You knew of this, General Nervo?" Rawson interrupted.

"Yes, sir."

"Odd, don't you think, that no one thought I would be interested?" the president asked. "Please continue, Capitán."

"Yes, sir. Well, when Rodríguez and the guys from Estancia San Pedro y San Pablo killed the SS guys in Tandil, Stein took their pictures so we could prove they were there. So we did the same thing with this guy."

"Cletus, I think it would be a very good idea if we had those pictures when we go talk to el Coronel Schmidt. Or el Coronel Perón."

"There's a set in the safe in the house, sir," Clete said.

"And the Froggers are where?"

"They're also in the house, sir. Frau Frogger is out of her mind."

"And you have what? Chained her to a wall?"

"No, sir. She is under the care of the Little Sisters of Pilar, or whatever the hell they're called."

"You'd better get the name of the order straight in your mind before Father Welner gets here. And when will that be?"

"I would estimate twenty minutes to half an hour, sir."

"Before he gets here, I want to hear what this SS officer has to say," the president said.

"From behind a sheet, and Colonel Frogger asks the questions. Right, Don Cletus? I don't think we want to let this SS officer know the president is here."

[THIRTEEN]
1725 16 October 1943

"I wondered," Doña Dorotea said to her husband, "if you were going to be able to find time in your busy schedule one of these days to drop in and say a few words to your wife and son."

He walked to the bed and looked down at his son, who was being nursed.

"A lot has happened, and is going on," Clete said.

"Who was in the airplanes? That was you, right? Who else would be crazy enough to fly in here?"

"How about the president of the Argentine Republic?" Clete asked, then: "Doesn't he hurt you doing that?"

"Yes, as a matter of fact, he does. Mother Superior says it will hurt less over time. What about the president of the Argentine Republic? You're not telling me Arturo Rawson's here? That you *flew* him in here? Up here?"

"Yeah, I am. And just as soon as he finishes talking to some people, he's going to come in the house and watch Father Welner baptize the baby."

"He's here, too?"

"And General Nervo."

"I don't want our son to be a Roman Catholic. Do you?"

"No, but between Father Kurt and Mother Superior, I don't think we have a choice."

"Tell me the truth about you and Arturo Rawson and the airplanes," she said. "And look me in the eye when you tell me."

"Okay. First thing tomorrow morning, we're going to go looking for Colonel Schmidt, who is somewhere around General Alvear and out of contact. . . ."

"I should have known that wouldn't work," Dorotea said ninety seconds later. "But it's useful to know."

"What are you talking about?"

"That you can look right into my eyes and lie through your teeth," she said. "That man Schmidt—who thinks God is on his side, which makes it worse—is not going to tuck his tail between his legs and go back to San Martín, even if Arturo Rawson personally tells him to. And you know it. So then what happens?"

"I just don't know, sweetheart."

"Who's the 'some people' Rawson is talking to?"

"Enrico and Stein caught some SS people in the vineyard. They're being interrogated. Colonel Frogger is telling Stein what questions to ask and when he thinks the lieutenant we caught is lying. They're doing it behind a sheet so the SS guy won't know Rawson is here."

"How many SS people did Enrico and Stein catch in the vineyards?"

"Five."

"That means there were seven, all told, including the two they killed?"

He didn't reply.

"There's a window in here, Cletus. I saw them bring the bodies in on horses."

"They killed one of ours and we killed one of theirs."

"And how many more are still out there?"

"I don't think there are any still out there," he said.

"And when do you think Schmidt and his men are going to get here?"

The door opened and Father Kurt Welner, S.J., trailed by Mother Superior, came into the room.

"Well, you two, are you about ready to have that beautiful baby of yours baptized?"

"Would it matter?" Dorotea asked. "We're outnumbered."

"Dorotea!" Mother Superior said. "You should be ashamed of yourself."

"And when we have that out of the way, Dorotea," Welner said, "Mother Superior and I have been talking about moving you to the hospital. You'd be more comfortable there."

"What is that, what they call a double standard?" Dorotea challenged. "We can't lie to you, but you can lie to us? You don't give a tinker's damn about my comfort. You think I'd be safer in the convent when Schmidt comes here."

"Baby, you would," Clete said.

"Call me Ruth, Cletus."

"What?"

"'Whither thou goest, I will go,' and I'm not going anywhere *without* you. This house is where we live. I'm going to be here when my husband leaves to do what he has to do about this Coronel Schmidt, and I'm going to be right here when my husband comes back."

There was a long silence.

"You don't deserve her, Cletus," Mother Superior then said.

"I know," he said.

[FOURTEEN]
Casa Montagna
Estancia Don Guillermo
Km 40.4, Provincial Route 60
Mendoza Province, Argentina
1905 16 October 1943

Don Cletus Frade, having been run out of his bedroom by Mother Superior, went to the bar, wondering if he should feel guilty that this was going to give him the opportunity to have a stiff drink.

"Gentlemen," the president of the Argentine Republic called, "I give you Don Cletus Frade, proud papa of Jorge Howell Frade."

There was applause.

"Sleepless nights and diaper changing will come later," the president added.

Not knowing how to respond, Clete walked to the bar, reached for a bottle of Jack Daniel's, poured, had a healthy sip, and then turned to face the men in the bar. He raised the glass to them.

The bar was crowded. Everybody but General Nervo seemed to be there, even the two Húsares de Pueyrredón Cub pilots and Siggie Stein.

The president reached over and patted the seat of an armchair next to where he was sitting with el Coronel Martín, Roberto Lauffer, and the Reverend Kurt Welner, S.J.

I'll be damned—they saved a seat for me.

He took it.

"Where's General Nervo?" he asked.

"Right there," Father Kurt said, pointing to the door. Nervo was walking through it.

Nervo started toward them, changed his mind, went to the bar, made himself a drink, and then came to them, taking the last empty armchair.

"Tell me, Don Cletus, what kind of a pistol did you give Señor Körtig when he went real-estate shopping?"

"One of the Ballester-Molinas from the arms cache. Why?"

"And you did remember to give him ammunition?"

"Of course I did. Actually, what I did was give him a couple of my magazines. The 1911 and the Ballester-Molina are almost identical, and I didn't want to have to root around in the arms cache for first magazines and then ammo."

"In other words, you would say that Körtig's pistol was loaded with ammunition from your Springfield Arsenal?"

"Either Springfield or Rock Island Arsenal. Why the curiosity?"

"Because a .45 ACP shell casing marked Springfield Arsenal was found on the floor of the men's room of the Hotel Edelweiss in Barlioche. Also in the men's room was the corpse of a man carrying the National Identity booklet of Jorge Schenck.

"Someone blew his brains all over the wall."

"My God!" Father Welner exclaimed.

"When did you learn this?" President Rawson asked.

"I just talked to Subinspector General Nolasco. He tells me that he was sitting outside the hotel keeping an eye on el Coronel Perón when a shot was heard. He went inside, where patrons pointed him toward the men's room. On his way there, he saw Father Silva, Señor Alvarez, and Señor Körtig sitting at a table in a sort of outside bar. In the men's room, he found Señor Schenck sitting in the urinal, his back against the wall with a small entrance wound—surrounded by powder burns—in his forehead, and a much larger exit hole in the rear of his skull. And the cartridge case I mentioned.

"Now, I'm just a simple policeman, but I'm wondering how many other people besides Señor Körtig and armed with a pistol firing cartridges made in the United States were likely to have also been in the Hotel Edelweiss at the time."

"Nolasco has arrested this man?"

"Your orders, Mr. President, were for Nolasco to keep an eye on Coronel Perón but to take no action unless directed by you or me."

"Did this man know Schenck, Cletus? Von Deitzberg?"

"After hearing this, I'd said they had at least a casual acquaintance," Clete said. "Körtig was trying to protect Valkyrie."

"Körtig is involved in Valkyrie?" the president asked. When he saw the look on Frade's face, he added, "Yes, I know about Valkyrie. Unlike some other senior officials of my government, the foreign minister keeps me abreast of things in which he thinks I might be interested."

Clete nodded.

"What I'm wondering now is whether my Tío Juan knows who blew von Deitzberg away," he said.

"I'm still wondering what Perón is doing in Bariloche," Martín said. "It seems to me that if he knows what Schmidt is up to, he would be in Buenos Aires."

"Yeah," Nervo said thoughtfully. "He told the local police he was on a little holiday."

"Nolasco hasn't spoken to Coronel Perón?" President Rawson asked.

Nervo shook his head.

"Well, what do we do?"

"Arturo, before you make any decision," Father Welner said, "I am compelled to tell you that Señor Körtig is of special interest to the church."

"What the hell does that mean?" Clete asked. "That the Vatican, the Pope, knows about Valkyrie? Are they for it, against it?"

"My orders, Arturo," Welner said, "are to assist Señor Körtig in any way possible. If you feel it necessary, I'm sure the Papal Nuncio will confirm this."

"My God!" Rawson said.

"I'm sure you will make any decision you do only after careful, prayerful thought," Welner said.

"Señor President," Martín said. "If el Coronel Perón is involved with Schmidt—and I think he is—he wouldn't admit it, and it would be very hard to prove."

"Cat got your tongue, Nervo?" the president said. "Usually, you're bubbling over with helpful suggestions."

"First thing in the morning, Mr. President, instead of Cletus taking you flying in one of those little airplanes looking for Schmidt, he flies you to Buenos Aires. You can do that, right, Cletus, in your red airplane?"

Clete nodded. "I can do that."

"And Martín and I go looking for Schmidt in those little airplanes. And stop him."

"Which would see you both lying in a pool of blood on a country road," President Rawson said.

"But you would be in the Casa Rosada, Mr. President," Martín argued.

"Unless I am in a position to look my senior officers—some of whom doubtless know what Schmidt plans—in the eye and tell them I have personally placed el Coronel Schmidt under arrest pending court-martial, my being in the Casa Rosada would be like—what was that phrase Cletus used?— *'pissing into the wind.'*

"What we're going to do is what we originally decided. We will search for Colonel Schmidt and, when we find him, order him to return to San Martín, and when that's done, Cletus can fly me to Buenos Aires."

"And what if shortly after you find Schmidt, you find yourself under arrest?" Nervo challenged. "Or in that pool of blood on a country road that you mentioned?"

"Well, if that happens, General, there won't be anything else we can do to stop this country from having a civil war, will there?"

[FIFTEEN]
The Wansee Suite
Edelweiss Hotel
San Martín 202
San Carlos de Bariloche
19555 16 October 1943

"Sweetheart, I'd really like to go down to the bar," Señorita Evita Duarte said to el Coronel Perón.

"Out of the question," Perón snapped. "And we're going to have dinner and breakfast up here, not in the dining room."

She looked at him with hurt eyes.

"Evita," Inge Schenck said, "going into the lobby or the restaurant is not a very good idea. The press is down there. They already know Juan Domingo is here, which means that Juan Domingo's name is going to be in every newspaper in the country tomorrow."

"Listen to her, Evita," Perón said.

"It would be a lot worse if his picture, with you, was in the newspapers," Inge said.

"What about you, Inge?" Evita asked. "What would happen to you if your picture was all over *La Nación*?"

"I don't intend to let that happen. That's why I'm not going down to the bar."

"But what if it did?" Evita pursued. "How would that affect what happens to you next? And while we're on that subject, what happens to you next?"

"I haven't given that much thought," Inge said.

"Oh, the hell you haven't," Evita said. "You've not had one little itty-bitty thought about who now owns all the property of the late SS-Brigadeführer Ritter Manfred von Deitzberg—excuse me, Jorge Schenck?"

Inge didn't reply.

"How long do you think it's going to take the Gendarmería to find out Señor Schenck was already dead when somebody shot him?" Evita asked.

"I wonder who shot him," Perón said. "Maybe it was just a simple robbery. Manfred resisted and was shot."

"Oh, come on, Juan Domingo, you know better than that," Evita said. She let that sink in for a moment. "And that you are, too, Inge. Dead, I mean."

"Well, I still have my diplomatic passport as Frau von Tresmarck," Inge said.

"You should have thought of that when the gendarmes asked for your papers," Evita said. "You handed them Inge Schenck's Argentine National Identity booklet."

"I didn't even know Manfred had been shot when they came in," Inge protested.

"And did you notice that the gendarmes were in the hotel after the shooting *before* the local police were?" Evita asked. "Maybe they were sitting outside in a car."

"Why would they be doing that?" Perón asked.

Evita shrugged.

"It could be they were protecting the secretary of labor. Or wondering what he was doing in Bariloche," Evita said. "Did they ask you that, what you are doing here?"

"No."

"They will. And what are you going to tell them?"

"I don't know. That I was having a little holiday. People do that—come to Bariloche for a little holiday."

"They're questioning everybody," Evita said. "That real-estate man and the notary are going to tell them you bought Estancia Puesta de Sol from Schenck."

"So that's what I'll tell them. There's nothing illegal about that."

"Well, that brings us back to what happens to the rest of Señor Schenck's properties," Evita said, and turned to Inge. "There's a lot of property, right?"

Inge nodded.

"There's a lot of property. Hundreds of millions of pesos' worth of property. Here and in Uruguay."

"What's that all about?" Evita asked.

"Very briefly, Evita," Inge explained. "The money came from the German Embassy. The real estate is to provide someplace for senior officials of the German Reich to go if they lose the war."

"You knew about this, Juan Domingo?" Evita asked.

After a moment, he nodded.

"You're going to have to learn to trust me. Tell me about things like this."

And, again, after a moment, he nodded.

"What happens to the property of a dead man? It goes to his wife, right?"

"Right."

"That would be fine, but the wife is already dead. Then what?"

Perón thought about that a moment, then said, "They would look for other relatives, who would have the right of inheritance."

"But not back to the German Embassy, right?"

"No, of course not. The Germans don't want anything about this program to come out."

"So what happens to you, Inge," Evita asked, "when the Germans find out their hundreds of millions of pesos' worth of property is now going to the Argentine relatives of a dead man they never heard of?"

"I would either be taken back to Germany and, after they tortured me enough to convince themselves I was telling the truth, executed. I know too much. Or they might just execute me here."

"Which means that the relatives get the properties," Evita said. "What about this? We go back to Buenos Aires. We find some notary we can trust and Inge transfers all the properties to someone else. Tomorrow. As soon as we get back to Buenos Aires. And then Inge Schenck disappears. You've got some cash?"

Inge nodded. "There was a lot of cash in Manfred's briefcase. It's now in my luggage."

"Perhaps it would be wise to let me keep it for you," Perón suggested.

Inge did not reply.

"So the whole thing depends on us getting to Buenos Aires before the Gendarmería finds out Inge is dead. Can we do that, Juan Domingo?"

He took a long moment to consider the question.

"They told me that 'senior officials' will be here in the morning," he replied, "and as soon as they are here, we'll be free to go. I will suggest that Señora Schenck be allowed to fly the body to Buenos Aires for burial; that will serve to avoid the questions of a funeral service and interment here." He paused. "Yes, it can be done. Will be done."

"You know someone who can be trusted to hold this property for us?"

"Oh, yes."

"Inge," Evita asked. "Would you say that sharing half of these properties with us would be a fair price for getting you out of your predicament?"

After a moment, Inge nodded.

[SIXTEEN]
Altitude 500 meters
Above Highway 146
Five Kilometers West of Highway 146/143 Intersection
Mendoza Province, Argentina
17 October 1943

Don Cletus Frade pointed out the front window of the olive-drab Piper Cub.

Two kilometers ahead, and five hundred or so meters above, an identical Piper was flying in wide circles to the right of Highway 146.

Two minutes after that, Clete pointed out the window again, this time downward to a large cloud of dust raised by a vehicular convoy of ten large Ejército Argentino trucks, preceded by a Mercedes sedan and followed by two pickup trucks, the bed of one filled with cans of gasoline and the other with spare tires on wheels.

The president of the Argentine Republic looked where Frade was pointing and then, cupping his hands around his mouth, shouted, "So far, so good."

Clete had taken off shortly after 0500—as soon as he had enough visibility to do so—and flown cross-country toward a guesstimate position eighty kilometers southeast from San Luis on Highway 146.

An hour and thirty minutes later, just about the time he had decided that putting a twenty-liter can of avgas in the lap of the president of the republic just before takeoff had been the right thing to do, dark smoke rising from gas- and oil-filled cans told him that gendarmes from San Luis had come through.

The smoke pots on the highway had the "runway" marked out to Clete's specifications: "No rocks and twice the length of a polo field."

He landed, took the gas can from the lap of General Rawson, and then topped off the Cub's fuel by pouring the avgas the gendarmes had brought from a can through a chamois cloth filter.

Fifteen minutes after landing, he was airborne again.

The second Húsares de Pueyrredón Piper, the one he saw now, had taken off immediately after he had and flown the dirt road from Mendoza, carrying General Nervo, to its refueling point. Then it had taken off and continued down the dirt road until it intersected Highway 146, onto which it had turned to the northeast.

It came upon the convoy first—which wasn't surprising, as it had less a distance to fly—and had then followed orders by flying wide circles to the right of the road.

Clete flew his Cub to intercept the other one, and signaled to the pilot that he was going to fly low over the road to make sure it wasn't full of large rocks and then land. The Húsares de Pueyrredón pilot nodded his understanding.

Clete pushed the nose down and headed for the road. At probably three hundred feet, using the cloud of dust as a wind sock, he decided that he had gotten lucky. By flying into the prevailing wind, which was the way you were supposed to do it, he would end his landing roll right in front of the Mercedes.

He could see nothing on the road that would keep him from landing, and also that the passengers in the Mercedes were looking up at him incredulously.

He went around, came in low and slow—and touched down.

The Mercedes was two hundred meters down the road. General Rawson got out, tugged on the skirt of his tunic, and then, with his back to the Mercedes, checked his pistol.

He had shown it to Clete just before they had taken off. It was a pretty little Colt short-barreled revolver chambered for the .32 Police cartridge. Clete thought it would probably be about as lethal as the Red Ryder Daisy BB gun he had been given for his fifth birthday.

He reached onto the floor of the Cub and picked up his Model 1911A1 .45 semiautomatic pistol and slipped that into the pocket of his JACKET, LEATHER, NAVAL AVIATORS W/FUR COLLAR, and then, to be sure he wasn't going to be outgunned, took a Thompson .45 ACP submachine gun from where he had propped it between the fuselage skin and the instrument panel.

By then the other Cub was down, and General Nervo and the pilot—who looked more than a little nervous—had walked up to them.

Colonel Schmidt and several officers were standing in front of the Mercedes. They were wearing Wehrmacht steel helmets. Clete remembered that the first time he'd ever seen a picture of his father—Colonel Graham had shown it to him in the hotel in Hollywood—his father had been dressed just like this.

"Do we go there, or what?" Nervo asked.

"I'm the president of the Argentine Republic," Rawson said softly. "People come to me."

A very long sixty seconds later, the officers with Colonel Schmidt came to attention and marched toward the people standing by the airplanes.

"Do you think they've spotted the president?" Nervo asked quietly.

"We'll soon find out," Rawson himself answered.

The expression on el Coronel Schmidt's face didn't change even when he was so close to Rawson that it would have been impossible not to recognize him.

Schmidt saluted. Rawson returned it.

"All right, Colonel," Rawson said. "If you have an explanation, I'm ready to hear it."

"Mi general," Schmidt said, "I very much regret that I must ask you to consider yourself under arrest pending court-martial."

Clete saw that one of the officers with Schmidt—there were four of them—had his hand in his overcoat pocket.

That sonofabitch has one of those toy Colt revolvers in there!

"Arrest? Court-martial? I'll remind you, Colonel, that I am the president of the Argentine Republic."

"You are a traitor to the Argentine Republic, Gen—"

He did not get to finish the sentence. Seven 230-grain, solid-point bullets from Don Cletus Frade's Thompson struck him in his midsection, from just above his crotch on his right side to just below his shoulder joint on his left.

Schmidt fell backward.

Clete turned the Thompson on the officer he thought might have a little Colt revolver and, just as the pistol cleared the officer's pocket, put four rounds of .45 in him.

"Cletus! My God!" President Rawson exclaimed. "What have you done?"

"He kept us alive is what he did," Nervo said.

Nervo now had his pistol drawn.

"On the ground, the rest of you, or you're dead!" Cletus ordered, gesturing with the muzzle of the Thompson.

The others dropped to the ground, one of them trying without success to keep away from the blood now leaking from the bodies of el Coronel Schmidt and the man who had tried to use his little Colt revolver.

Clete turned to the pilot of the second Cub, who was ashen-faced.

"What you're going to do, Lieutenant, is first get yourself together, then go halfway to that convoy, put your hands on your hips, and bellow 'Senior noncommissioned officer, front and center,' or words to that effect. And when he presents himself, bring him to me."

The lieutenant didn't move.

"Lieutenant, do what Don Cletus has ordered," President Rawson said.

The lieutenant straightened, then walked around the bodies on the ground and toward the convoy.

Three minutes later, the lieutenant returned, following a large, middle-aged man who had a Thompson hanging from his shoulder.

Next time, Lieutenant, you might think of taking his fucking weapon away from him!

The man saluted. "*Mi general,* Suboficial Mayor Martínez of the 10th Mountain Regiment reporting as ordered."

Rawson returned the salute and then looked at Cletus with an *Okay, now what?* look on his face.

"Sergeant Major," Clete said, "I am Major Cletus—"

"I know who you are, Don Cletus," Suboficial Mayor Martínez said. "Enrico has been my lifelong friend. It was I who called him to warn him that el Coronel Schmidt was coming to your house in Tandil."

"With God as your witness, you are loyal to General Rawson?" Clete asked.

"With God as my witness, *mi general.*"

"Suboficial Mayor," General Rawson said, "if I ordered you to take the regiment back to San Martín de los Andes, with these officers under arrest, what would you do?"

"I would have the regiment turned and moving in five minutes, *mi general.*"

"Do it, Suboficial Mayor," General Rawson ordered.

As they watched Suboficial Mayor Martínez march away, Nervo said, "What do we do about Perón, Mr. President?"

"You go to Bariloche in the other Cub and place him in protective custody. Suggest to him that he return to Buenos Aires as soon as possible. Arrange things so that 'as soon is possible' is tomorrow. Not before. By that time, I should have things straightened out, at least to the point where I can make an intelligent decision about how to deal with el Coronel Perón."

He turned to Cletus. "Let's go, Cletus. Now that you've saved my life, the sooner I can get to Buenos Aires, the better."

Clete looked at Nervo.

"Have a good time in Bariloche, General."

Nervo smiled. "And you in Buenos Aires. Don't think you're going to be able to relax, Don Cletus. I have a feeling we're all going to be very busy very soon."

POSTSCRIPT

In this fictional work, reference was made to the actual Nazi massacre of 335 men and boys in the Ardeatine Caves in Rome during World War II.

The story line dealt with the escape of Nazis from Allied retribution during and after the war, and several scenes were laid in San Carlos de Bariloche, which is today sometimes known as "Argentina's Vail," making reference to the wonderful skiing in Vail, Colorado.

In 1996, the SS officer second in command of the mass murders in the Ardeatine Caves, Erich Priebke—who had escaped to Argentina on a false passport and other documents provided, he said, by Vatican authorities—was put aboard a Falcon DA 90 aircraft sent by the Italian government and extradited to Italy to finally face trial.

He had lived in Bariloche for fifty years, and owned a hotel there.

Argentina's interior minister, Carlos Corach, suspended several Bariloche police officers who had embraced Priebke fondly just before he boarded the airplane.